This book is dedicated to young people who make friends with Joy, Laughter and Kindness.

God Bless,

Leo Zarko

D1570983

Mory is in a bit of trouble today. Our little mouse friend is a very smart character, most days, today is not one of those days. You see, his tail is caught in a mouse trap. This is not the first time it has happened. Mice learn early on to stay clear of cheese out in the middle of the floor, but not Mory, he enjoys the challenge.

Mory is clever. At night he watches the farmer set the traps and by doing so he learns how they work. When he does get trapped he always carries a little pry bar to free himself.

Mory lives on a farm in the country. His family loves the open space and since other animals share the barn, food is plentiful. Mice on the farm find Mory to be so friendly and funny. He is always showing off and playing pranks. He most always gets a good laugh out of his crazy antics.

The thing about him was that he entertained most everyone in the barnyard. He just had a way about him. You would think he'd have even more friends; after all, he is popular. Somehow, the pranks didn't seem as funny to the animals he was playing them on.

4

Mory liked adventure and he also had a nice way of getting others involved in his silly ways. His mother knew her son was very smart and she wished he would put that mind of his to good use.

Mory did have good ideas sometimes. The barnyard cat had never had a chance to rid the barn of mice because Mory protected others from him.

Once, Mory set four mouse traps in place and covered them with hay. Then he lured the cat in by making funny faces and laughing at him. The entire barnyard looked on as the cat stepped in all four traps, one on each paw. The laughter went on for at least five minutes.

Mory had found much success with many of his inventions. After having his tail pinched a few times, he invented fake mice out of hair that he found around the barn. Then he would throw them on the mouse traps to set them off. The free cheese was a bonus and made for a wonderful meal for all his family and friends. Plus, the farmer never even knew the difference.

Taking risk was something Mory enjoyed a lot, but to be honest, he was fearful just like everyone else. He made more mistakes than he would care to mention. He only wanted to appear braver than the others.

Mory's mom kept a close eye on him just in case he went too far. The mice were organized and attended school. The teacher had a hard time with Mory simply because he disrupted her class daily. He would raise his hand often to answer the questions, only to make a joke for attention.

He spent many an hour in the principal's office. As he sat there he dreamt of becoming a movie star or perhaps joining the circus and performing on stage. It seemed he never gave much thought about others.

This time turned out a little different because the principal told him he no longer was welcome at the school. He handed him a note to deliver to his mother. Mory's dreams somehow vanished and all he could think about was the trouble he caused. The principal said he could return if he changed his ways.

Of course, Mory's mom was upset as she read the note. "You've gone too far this time, mister, and I'm sending you to see your grandfather." Mory hadn't seen Gramps much, but he remembered how he was always telling stories that somehow ended in some kind of lesson. That next morning Mory's mom packed him a lunch and sent him on his way.

As Mory made his way down the pathway, it felt kind of odd being alone. He had no one to play pranks on or to make fun of. When he got closer to Gramps' house he noticed two cats walking his way. This time he had no cover to run to. He put his head down as if to show he wasn't looking for trouble. Then it dawned on him how others would do the same when they saw him.

The cats quickly grabbed his sack lunch and ate it right in front of him. He didn't move because he thought these cats just might enjoy a little mouse for dessert. Lucky for Mory a skunk was walking by and as he did he sprayed the cats in the face. Mory laughed so hard but soon realized he had better run.

Mory thanked the skunk and then ran as fast as he could. He arrived and told his Gramps the news. "Close call youngster!" his Gramps said, "I hope you learned something." Mory said, "I sure did. Skunks stink, but I still like them!" They both laughed.

His Gramps said he had heard the news about his behavior. He told Mory that as a young mouse he too enjoyed a prank or two. He said, "I can see a little of me in you and that's why I want you to know that all that energy you have can be put to much better use than getting into trouble and hurting others feelings."

Mory was just thinking about playing a prank on Gramps but figured right now would be bad timing. Mory said, "I like when others laugh at the silly things I do. I don't mean any harm." Just as he said that he noticed his Gramps putting on a clown suit, with makeup and all.

Mory had no idea that his Gramps was a circus performer. Gramps played jokes on him and showed him how to do card tricks and make animal balloons. He showed him how to walk a tightrope and ride a bicycle backwards. Mory was amazed at all the things his Gramps knew. It filled his heart with joy. "Can you teach me to do all those things?" "I sure can," said his Gramps with a big smile.

Mory knew his Gramps liked to make deals and sure enough, Mory thought, "He's going to ask me to change my ways." So Gramps asked that very question and Mory replied "OK, it's a deal."

These tricks took a lot more skill than Mory could imagine. Nevertheless, he learned them fast and his Gramps was pleased. "You got talent, my boy and I would like to see you use it for the good! Now get back home to your mom and behave in school." At that moment Mory thought, "My Gramps sure is one cool mouse."

When he started his walk home, the skunk kept an eye out for him, making sure he got home safe. Mory had a couple of black and white balloons that he quickly twisted into the shape of a skunk and gave it to his new friend.

Mory told him that he was welcome to stop by the barn anytime to visit and maybe have a little fun with the cat. They laughed and smiled, then parted ways.

21

Mory gave his mom a big hug and told her all about his time away from home. He didn't tell her about the deal because he wanted it to be a surprise. First he cleaned his room and then started right in on school work. He also was polite to everyone he had offended.

The animals figured this must be one of his new ideas to play a big joke on them all later. A few days passed and Mory was back in school raising his hand and giving the right answers with no joke afterwards. The funny thing was that as bad as he had been, the others missed all the crazy things he did.

Mory found that hard to believe, but he stayed true to his word to behave. Mory needed a way to get animals to laugh without breaking his word.

Then it dawned on him to use the skills his Gramps taught him. "I will put together a variety show that is sure to bring laughter back and help others see I still got it!" When he arrived home he got right to work on his show. There would be plenty of tricks and acts of daring to entertain all.

He even talked the cat into laying off chasing mice for a while and get up on stage as a partner. The cat agreed simply because he found it amusing to see a bunch of mice clapping for a cat. Soon everything was ready and Mory invited all his friends and family to come out and see his show, even the skunk. He also told everyone about a special surprise at the end of the show.

Mory's teacher told him he would be getting good grades for all his effort and good behavior. That news gave Mory a real boost of energy leading up to the show. As soon as the farmer closed the barn door the curtain opened. Mory came out on the cat's back and then told the cat to chase his tail. Around and around they went. It lasted about eight seconds, just like a rodeo. Mory jumped off and the cat fell off the stage from dizziness. The crowd laughed as the cat recovered and took a bow.

Next was the tight rope walk, and then Mory lined up the rabbits, who had combed their hair as if to look like lions. They even let out little roars as they did tricks and jumped around on stage. The show was a big success and Mory's mom smiled and gave him a big wink.

Mory took center stage and told jokes and made fun of himself mostly. He felt like he could regain a little respect if he picked on himself for a while instead of others. He then said in a small humble voice, "I'd like to share my surprise now." The crowd was amazed to see Gramps dressed in his old magic suit as he got up on stage. Gramps then asked the cat to return and be very still as he covered him in a large sheet. He then said to the crowd, "Would you like this cat to disappear?" As the crowd yelled "Yes!" Gramps pulled the sheet and surprise! The cat was gone.

Mory said, "You still got it Gramps! I love you very much for teaching me that laughter should be used to ease troubles, not cause them."

The End

BRAIN DEVELOPMENT

BRAIN DEVELOPMENT

NORMAL PROCESSES AND THE EFFECTS OF ALCOHOL AND NICOTINE

EDITED BY

Michael W. Miller

UNIVERSITY PRESS

2006

OXFORD

UNIVERSITY PRESS

Oxford University Press, Inc., publishes works that further
Oxford University's objective of excellence
in research, scholarship, and education.

Oxford   New York
Auckland   Cape Town   Dar es Salaam   Hong Kong   Karachi
Kuala Lumpur   Madrid   Melbourne   Mexico City   Nairobi
New Delhi   Shanghai   Taipei   Toronto

With offices in
Argentina   Austria   Brazil   Chile   Czech   Republic   France   Greece
Guatemala   Hungary   Italy   Japan   Poland   Portugal   Singapore
South Korea   Switzerland   Thailand   Turkey   Ukraine   Vietnam

Published by Oxford University Press, Inc.
198 Madison Avenue, New York, New York 10016

www.oup.com

Oxford is a registered trademark of Oxford University Press

Library of Congress Cataloging-in-Publication Data
Brain development : normal processes and the effects of alcohol and nicotine / edited by Michael W. Miller.
p. ; cm.
Includes bibliographical references and index.
ISBN-13 978-0-19-518313-9
ISBN 0-19-518313-4
1. Developmental toxicology.   2. Neurotoxicology.   3. Alcohol–Toxicology.   4. Nicotine—Toxicology.
5. Alcoholism in pregnancy—Pathophysiology.   6. Pregnant women—Tobacco use—Physiological effect.
[DNLM: 1. Brain—drug effects.   2. Brain—growth & development.   3. Ethanol—pharmacology. 4. Fetus—drug effects.
5. Neurons—drug effects.   6. Nicotine—pharmacology. WL 300 B8125 2006]   I. Miller, Michael W.
RA1224.45.B73 2006
616.8'6471—dc22   2005012854

1 3 5 7 9 8 6 4 2
Printed in the United States of America
on acid-free paper

Acknowledgments

As such, the present volume is the product of decades of work by teams of neuroscientists and developmental biologists. I thank the named and nameless of these dedicated researchers who have reached me through both oral and/or written communications. This volume builds on the foundation of research described in a book published 13 years ago, *Development of the Central Nervous System. Effects of Alcohol and Opiates* (Miller, 1992). Since that book was published, our understanding of the mechanisms underlying normal brain development and the effects of ethanol neurotoxicity on neural ontogeny has grown exponentially. Interest in the clinical problem of nicotine exposure has also increased.

Personally, my research has been supported by a host of postdoctoral trainees, graduate and undergraduate students, and technicians. I am greatly indebted to them for working toward our common goal of understanding the intricacies of brain development. Some of my current students (Marla Bruns and Julie Siegenthaler) and collaborators (Sandra Mooney) contributed to the writing of this book. My career has been consistently and substantively supported by the federal government, notably the National Institute of Alcohol Abuse and Alcoholism and the Department of Veterans Affairs. Without the support of these agencies I would not have been able to study normal and abnormal brain development, nor would I have been able to meet the people who wrote chapters for this volume. These people have brought considerable expertise and keen insights to their contributions of outstanding chapters.

The dual sculptors, nature and nurture, have been essential factors in my development as a scientist. My fascination with science—how things work and how they fail—was fostered by my parents and the post-Sputnik American culture. It is my great hope that children of all ages, boys and girls, retain their wonder as to why things are as they are. This sense of marvel should be celebrated and held in awe by society. My candle was stoked by high school and college teachers (including William Harris and William Tully, and

Edward Hodgson and Edward Maly, respectively), research mentors (including Pedro Pasik and Alan Peters), and collaborators (notably Richard Nowakowski and Robert Rhoades). They encouraged me to think broadly and not to be confined by dogma or methods.

Finally, I would like to thank my family, my wife and three children, for their continued support and good humor. They are my sustenance, grounding, and reason for being.

Contents

List of Abbreviations

5-HT   serotonin

8-OH-DPAT   8-hydroxy-2-(di-*n*-propylamino)tetralin

ABCG2   ATP-binding cassette protein

αBgTx   α-bungarotoxin

ACh   acetylcholine

AChE   acetylcholinesterase

ACTH   adrenocorticotropic hormone

ADH   alcohol dehydrogenase

ADHD   attention deficit hyperactivity disorder

ADNF   activity-dependent neurotrophic factor

ADNP   activity-dependent neuroprotective protein

ADP   adenosine diphosphate

ADX   adrenalectomy

AHP   adult hippocampal progenitor

AIDS   acquired immunodeficiency syndrome

AIF   apoptosis inducing factor

ALC   prenatally exposed to alcohol, both with and without dysmorphic features

AMPA   α-amino-3-hydroxy-5-methyl-4-isoxazole-propionic acid

AMPAR   α-amino-3-hydroxy-5-methyl-4-isoxazole propionic acid receptor

AP-1   activating protein-1

APAF   apoptotic protease activating factor

ARIA   acetylcholine receptor-inducing protein

ARND   alcohol-related neurodevelopmental disorder

ASD   atrial septal defect

ASR   acoustic startle reflex

Astn   astrotactin

ATP   adenosine triphosphate

AVP   arginine vasopressin

BDNF   brain-derived neurotrophic factor

BEC   blood ethanol concentration

β-EP   β-endorphin

bFGF   basic fibroblast growth factor (aka fibroblast growth factor 2)

BH   Bcl-2 homology

BMP   bone morphogenic protein

BSID   Bayley Scales of Development

BrdU   bromodeoxyuridine

$[Ca^{2+}]_i$ intracellular concentration of Ca^{2+}

CAM   cell adhesion molecule

cAMP   cyclic adenosine monophosphate

CAP   cell adhesion protein

CBG   corticosterone binding globulin

CC   corpus callosum

CCK   cholecystokinin

CD133   cell determinant 133 (hematopoietic stem cell marker, aka prominin cdk cyclin-dependent kinase

Cdk   cyclin-dependent kinase

cGMP   cyclic guanosine monophosphate

ChAT   choline acetyltransferase

CKI   cyclin-dependent kinase inhibitor

CNS   central nervous system

CON A   concanavalin A

CORT   corticosterone

CP   cortical plate

CREB   cyclic AMP response element binding protein

CRH   corticotropin releasing hormone

CRH-R_1 corticotropin releasing hormone type 1 receptor

CRMP   collapsin response mediator protein

CT   computer tomography

CVLT-C   California Verbal Learning Test- children's version

CYP2E1   cytochrome P450 2E1

CytOx   cytochrome C oxidase

DA   dopamine

Dab   disabled

DCC   deleted in colorectal cancer

DHβE   dihydro-β-erythroidine

DIABLO   direct IAP binding protein

DIV   days in vitro

DNA-PKcs   DNA-dependent protein kinase catalytic subunit

DOI   1-(2,5-dimethoxy-4-iodophenyl)-2-aminopropane hydrochloride

DOR   δ-opioid receptors

DRG   dorsal root ganglia

DTI   diffusion tensor imaging

EC_{50} concentration effecting a half maximal response

ECM   extracellular matrix

EGF   epidermal growth factor

EGFr   epidermal growth factor receptor

EGL   external granular layer of the cerebellum

EM   electron microscopy

ERK   extracellular signal regulated kinase

ES   embryonic stem

ETS   environmental tobacco smoke

FADD   Fas-associated death domain

FAS   fetal alcohol syndrome

FASD   fetal alcohol spectrum disorders

FasL   Fas ligand

FCMD   Fukuyama-type congenital muscular dystrophy

FEE   fetal ethanol-exposed

FGF   fibroblast growth factor

FILIP   filamin A–interacting protein

fMRI   functional magnetic resonance imaging

G   gestational day

GABA   γ-aminobutyric acid

Gadd45γ   growth arrest and DNA damage-inducible

GDF   growth differentiation factor

GDX   gonadectomy

GE   ganglionic eminence

GF   growth fraction

GFAP   glial fibrillary acidic protein

GMC   ganglion mother cell

GnRH   gonadotropin-releasing hormone

GR   glucocorticoid receptor

GRP   glial-restricted precursor

GSH   glutathione

GTPase   guanosine 5′-triphosphatase

HGF   hepatocyte growth factor

hn   heteronuclear

HNE   4-hydroxynonenal

hNSC   human neural stem cell

HPA   hypothalamic-pituitary-adrenal

HPG   hypothalamic-pituitary-gonadal

IAP   inhibitory apoptotic protein

Ig   immunoglobulin

IGF   insulin-like growth factor

IGF-1r   insulin-like growth factor-1 receptor

IGF-BP   insulin-like growth factor binding protein

IHZ   intrahilar zone; or hippocampal field CA4 or the subgranular zone

IL   interleukin

IP   intraperitoneal

IP3   inositol 1,4,5-triphosphate

IQ   intelligence quotient

ISEL   in situ end-labeling

IZ   intermediate zone

KCl   potassium chloride

Ki67   proliferation-associated nuclear antigen

KOR   κ-opioid receptors

Large   like-acetylglucosaminyltransferase

LBW   low birth weight

LC   locus coeruleus

LC-NE   locus coeruleus-noradrenergic (sympathetic adrenal medullary)

LCN   local circuit neuron

LF   leaving fraction

LHRH   luteinizing hormone releasing hormone

Lig IV   ligase IV

LPA   lysophosphatidic acid

LPS   lipopolysaccharide

LTP   long-term potentiation

LV   latent variable

mAChR   muscarinic acetylcholine receptor

MAP   microtubule-associated protein

MAPK   mitogen-activated protein kinase

MDA   malondialdehyde

MEB   muscle-eye-brain disease

MHC   major histocompatibility complex

MHPCD   Maternal Health Practices and Child Development

MNTB   medial nucleus of the trapezoid body

MOR   μ-opioid receptors

MR   mineralocorticoid receptor

MRI   magnetic resonance imaging

MZ   marginal zone

NAc   nucleus accumbens

nAChR   nicotinic acetylcholine receptor

NAD   nicotinamide-adenine dinucleotide

NAP   asn-ala-pro-val-ser-ile-pro-gln

NBL   neuroblastic layer

nCAM   neural cell adhesion molecule

NE   norepinephrine

NGF   nerve growth factor

NgCAM   neuron-glia cell adhesion molecule

NHEJ   non-homologous end-joining

NMD   neuronal migration disorder

NMDA   N-methyl-D-aspartate

NMDAR   N-methyl-D-aspartate receptor

NMJ   neuromuscular junction

NO   nitric oxide

NOND   naturally occurring neuronal death

NPC   neural progenitor cell

Nr-CAM   NgCAM-related cell adhesion molecule

NRT   nicotine replacement therapy

NSC   neural stem cell

NT   neurotrophin

NTS   *nucleus tractus solitarius*

NT-4   neurotrophin 4

OD   ocular dominance

ODC   ornithine decarboxylase

OPPS   Ottawa Prospective Prenatal Study

P   postnatal day

PA   phosphatidic acid

PACAP   pituitary adenylyl cyclase activating polypeptide

PAFAHIb   platelet-activating factor acetylhydrolase isoform Ib, aka LIS1

PARP   poly-adenosine diphosphate ribose polymerase

PCD   programmed cell death

PDGF   platelet-derived growth factor

PEE   prenatal ethanol exposure

PET   positron emission tomography

PEt   phosphatidyl ethanol

PFC   prefrontal cortex

PI3K   phosphatidylinositol 3'-phosphokinase

PKA   protein kinase A

PKC   protein kinase C

PLD   phospholipase

PLS   partial least squares analysis

PM   pial membrane

PN   projection neuron

PNS   peripheral nervous system

POMGnT1   UDP-N-acetylglucosamine protein-O-mannose β1,2-N-acetylglucosaminyl-transferase

POMC   pro-opiomelanocortin

POMT1   protein-O-mannose β1,2-N-acetylglucosaminyltransferase

PPI   prepulse inhibition

PSD   post-synaptic density

PSN   principal sensory nucleus of the trigeminal nerve

PSR   phosphatidylserine receptor

PTE   prenatal tobacco exposure

PTV   Piccolo-Bassoon transport vesicle

PVE   pseudostratified ventricular epithelium

PVN   paraventricular nucleus

PWM   pokeweed mitogen

Q   probability of cell cycle exit

RA   retinoic acid

RAR   retinoic acid receptor

Rb   retinoblastoma protein

RG   radial glia

ROS   reactive oxygen species

SC   subcutaneous

SES   socioeconomic status

Shh   sonic hedgehog

SHRP   stress hyporesponsive period

SKY   spectral karyotyping

SIDS   sudden infant death syndrome

SIN-1   3-morpholinosydnonimine

Smac   second mitochondria-derived activator of caspase

SMase   sphingomyelinase

Smo   Smoothened

sMRI   structural magnetic resonance imaging

SN   substantial nigra

SNARES   soluble n-ethylmaleimide–sensitive fusion protein-attachment protein receptors

SNAP-25   synaptosome associated protein-25

SNRP   stress nonresponsive period

SOD   superoxide dismutase

SPECT   single photon emission computed tomography

SPP   secondary proliferative population

SV   synaptic vesicle

SynCAM   synaptic cell adhesion molecule

SZ   subventricular zone

SZa   anterior subventricular zone

T_C total length of the cell cycle

TCR   T cell receptors

TERT   telomerase reverse transcriptase

TGF   transforming growth factor

TGFβIr   transforming growth factor βI receptor

TGFβIIr   transforming growth factor βII receptor

TH   tyrosine hydroxylase

TNF   tumor necrosis factor

TRF   telomerase-repeat-binding factor

Trk   tyrosine kinase receptor

TUNEL   terminal deoxynucleotidyl transferase mediated deoxyuridine nick end labeling

UCS   unconditioned stimulus

VB   ventrobasal nucleus of the thalamus

VBM   voxel-based morphometry

VDCC   voltage-dependent Ca^{2+} channel

VIP   vasoactive intestinal polypeptide

VLM   ventrolateral medulla

VSD   ventral septic defect

VTA   ventral tegmental area

VZ   ventricular zone

VLDLr   very low density lipoprotein receptor

WCST   Wisconsin Card Sort Task

WRAML   Wide Range Assessment of Memory and Learning

WWS   Walker-Warburg syndrome

Contributors

TONYA R. ANDERSON
Mount Sinai School of Medicine
New York NY

LAYLA AZAM
University of California College of Medicine
Irvine CA

HENRIETTA S. BADA
University of Kentucky College of Medicine
Lexington KY

GREGORY N. BARNES
University of Kentucky College of Medicine
Lexington KY

IDDIL H. BEKIROV
Mount Sinai School of Medicine
New York NY

DEANNA L. BENSON
Mount Sinai School of Medicine
New York NY

PRADEEP G. BHIDE
Massachusetts General Hospital
Harvard Medical School
Boston MA

MARLA B. BRUNS
SUNY- Upstate Medical University
Syracuse NY

SHREYA BUCH
University of Kentucky College of Medicine
Lexington KY

DESMOND T. CHEUNG
Cornell University
Ithaca NY

JEROLD J.M. CHUN
Scripps Research Institute
La Jolla CA

CLAIRE D. COLES
Emory University School of Medicine
Atlanta GA

Marie D. Cornelius
University of Pittsburgh School of Medicine
Pittsburgh PA

Mita Das
University of Colorado Health Sciences Center
Denver CO

Nancy L. Day
University of Pittsburgh School of Medicine
Pittsburgh PA

Katherine A. Debelak-Kragtorp
University of Wisconsin School of Medicine
Madison WI

Nazira El-Hage
University of Kentucky College of Medicine
Lexington KY

Brenda M. Elliott
Uniformed Services University of the Health Sciences
Bethesda MD

Barbara L. Finlay
Cornell University
Ithaca NY

Ryan Franke
University of California College of Medicine
Irvine CA

Susanna L. Fryer
San Diego State University
San Diego CA

Kathy Gallardo
University of California College of Medicine
Irvine CA

Consuelo Guerri
Centro de investigacion Principe Felipe
Valencia, Spain

Neil E. Grunberg
Uniformed Services University of the Health Sciences
Bethesda MD

Kurt F. Hauser
University of Kentucky College of Medicine
Lexington KY

George I. Henderson
University of Texas Health Science Center
San Antonio TX

Paula L. Hoffman
University of Colorado Health Sciences Center
Denver CO

Huaiyu Hu
SUNY-Upstate Medical University
Syracuse NY

Frances M. Leslie
University of California College of Medicine
Irvine CA

Tara A. Lindsley
Albany Medical School
Albany NY

Shahrdad Lotfipour
University of California College of Medicine
Irvine CA

Huibert D. Mansvelder
Vrije Universitat,
Amsterdam, The Netherlands

Christie L. McGee
San Diego State University
San Diego CA

Michael W. Miller
Department of Neuroscience and Physiology and
Developmental Exposure Alcohol Research Center
SUNY-Upstate Medical University
Research Service
Syracuse Veterans Affairs Medical Center
Syracuse NY

C. David Mintz
Mount Sinai School of Medicine
New York NY

Sandra M. Mooney
SUNY- Upstate Medical University
Syracuse NY

Kathryn O'Leary
University of California College of Medicine
Irvine CA

Maria Pascual
Centro de investigacion Principe Felipe
Valencia, Spain

James R. Pauly
University of Kentucky College of Medicine
Lexington KY

STEVENS K. REHEN
Scripps Research Institute
La Jolla CA

EDWARD P. RILEY
San Diego State University
San Diego CA

LORNA W. ROLE
Columbia University
New York NY

GEMMA RUBERT
Centro de investigacion Principe Felipe
Valencia, Spain

JULIE A. SIEGENTHALER
SUNY- Upstate Medical University
Syracuse NY

JOANNA H. SLIWOWSKA
University of British Columbia
Vancouver BC

SUSAN M. SMITH
University of Wisconsin School of Medicine
Madison WI

ANDREA D. SPADONI
San Diego State University
San Diego CA

BERNHARD SUTER
Massachusetts General Hospital
Harvard Medical School
Boston MA

JOANNE WEINBERG
University of British Columbia
Vancouver BC

JENNIFER A. WILLFORD
University of Pittsburgh School of Medicine
Pittsburgh PA

JEREMY C. YOST
Cornell University
Ithaca NY

XINGQI ZHANG
University of British Columbia
Vancouver BC

W. MICHAEL ZAWADA
University of Colorado Health Sciences Center
Denver CO

BRAIN DEVELOPMENT

1

Models of Neurotoxicity Provide Unique Insight into Normal Development

Michael W. Miller

Happy families are all alike; every unhappy family is unhappy in its own way.
Anna Karenina, Leo Tolstoy

The developing nervous system is comprised of complex sets of elements that assemble into a dynamic,
interactive physical, chemical, and electrical mesh.
In the normal animal, this assembly proceeds in an
orderly progression amounting to the sum of additive
(cell proliferation, migration, and neurite outgrowth)
and subtractive processes (pruning of axons and dendrites and neuronal death). Each of these ontogenetic
processes involves the timely, intricate choreography
of molecular and cellular players. That said, development does not follow a rigid sequence.

The developing brain has considerable flexibility
and adaptability. This adaptability can be overcome
by a multitude of challenges, and the variety of responses can be as diverse as the challenges. The challenges can be internal or external. Internal alterations
include changes cascading from a spontaneous mutation in the genome. External challenges can be subtle (response to a stress) or profound (changes caused
by exposure to a toxin or drug). Alterations induced
by internal and external challenges can be superim-
posed and changes may be additive or synergistic. In
any case, an understanding of the responses of the
nervous system provides unique insight into its normal development and its plasticity. Does the challenged nervous system consistently respond in the
same fashion, or does it respond using a variety of
strategies?

Tolstoy's comment on his own work was that *Anna
Karenina* did not solve a single problem; rather, it presented them all, beautifully. Environmental exposure
to substances such as ethanol and nicotine presents
situations of compelling clinical interest. Ethanol is
arguably the most fully studied teratogen. Unlike Tolstoy's self-critique, studies of ethanol toxicity have
not been restricted to phenomenological studies;
many mechanisms of ethanol neurotoxicity have

3

been pursued. Indeed, work on ethanol provides a model of how to study the negative effects of other substances. Moreover, study of the effects of ethanol provides a unique insight into normal development. The approach of this book is to look at three contrasting situations: normal development, and the effects of two different types of challenges. Examination of the normal and abnormal situations informs each of these situations. Thus, it is only through genetic and environmental challenges that a full appreciation of the complexity of brain development can be achieved.

NORMAL DEVELOPMENT

Our understanding of normal neural development has progressed by quanta during the last dozen years. Not only have we begun to understand the myriad genes that are expressed in the developing central nervous system (CNS), but functions for the transcripts and the proteins have been ascribed. Two examples are *rln* and *dlx*, genes that code for proteins important in stopping neuronal migration and in promoting the migration of neocortical local circuit neurons from the ganglion eminence.

The compelling abnormal organization of the brain and the associated dysfunction of the *reeler* mouse have fascinated developmental neurobiologists for more than five decades (e.g., Falconer, 1951; Alter et al., 1968; Bruck and Williams, 1970; Lambert de Rouvroit and Goffinet, 1998). The inverse organization of the reeler mouse has provided unique insights into mechanisms of normal neurogenesis and the formation of neural networks. Yet it is only since 1995 that the genetic basis for this murine mutant has been discovered, the knockout of the gene *rln* (D'Arcangelo et al., 1995; Hirotsune et al., 1995; Ogawa et al., 1995). The function of the gene product, reelin, continues to be debated.

The gene *dlx* is a key player in cortical development (Marin and Rubenstein, 2003). It is critical for the generation of local circuit neurons in the ganglionic eminence. A dearth of local circuit neurons is evident in *dlx* knockout mice. Thus, a new door to understanding the complexity of cortical neuronogenesis and tangential pathways of neuronal migration has been opened.

The section on normal development describes our current understanding of cellular and molecular events that define developmental phenomena. For convenience, neural development has been divided into four phases: cell proliferation, migration, differentiation, and death (Chapters 2, 3, 4, and 5 and 6, respectively). Although these are discrete phases, they are highly integrated. That is, the number of cycling cells has a direct effect on the way in which cells differentiate and on the incidence of cell death. Thus, these chapters address a single developmental phase while placing ontogenetic events in the context of the continuum of neural development. In a provocative essay (Chapter 7) at the end of this section, basic information on ontogenetic events is discussed in terms of mammalian evolution, and their ramifications on the response of the nervous system are addressed.

ETHANOL-AFFECTED DEVELOPMENT

The concept that ethanol affects the development of the mammalian (human) brain came to the fore in 1973 with the publication of papers by Jones and Smith (Jones and Smith, 1973; Jones et al., 1973). These were not the first papers to identify fetal alcohol effects. Though less celebrated, reports by Lemoine and colleagues (1968) and Ulleland (1972) had already described features of fetal alcohol syndrome (FAS). Although it has been suggested that the first evidence linking alcohol consumption during pregnancy and deleterious effects on offspring comes from Greek and Roman mythology and from the Bible, this notion was debunked by Abel (1984).

To the best of my knowledge, the first documentation of someone with FAS can be attributed to the artists Harvey Kurtzman in 1954 and Norman Mingo in 1956. They drew a person originally known as Melvin Coznowski or Mel Haney, later known as Alfred E. Neuman (also spelled Newman).[1] Mr. Neuman has all of the classic pathomnemonic craniofacial malformations of FAS (thin upper lip, deficient, philtrum, narrow palpebral fissures, flattened bridge of the nose, and low set ears), along with acknowledged mental dysfunction and probable intrauterine growth retardation (as evidenced by microencephaly). Although verification of prenatal exposure is unknown, such evidence is not obligatory for a diagnosis of FAS (Stratton et al., 1996). As is typical of accomplished artists, Kurtzman and Mingo were perceptive observers and made associations that were as insightful as those of the experienced pediatricians who described FAS more than a dozen years later. Kurtzman and Mingo did not associate the craniofacial malformations and brain dysfunction with prenatal exposure to alcohol, but they did link the diagnostic features that characterize FAS.

Ethanol can act through a number of mechanisms. This is not to say that ethanol is a "dirty drug". Indeed, evidence shows that it affects the nervous system in very specific ways. Moreover, the manner in which ethanol alters development instructs us about the adaptability and resiliency of the developing nervous system. From a clinical perspective, an understanding of the consequences of early exposure to ethanol is of paramount importance. Prenatal exposure to alcohol affects upwards of 1% of all live births and it is the prime cause of mental retardation in the United States (Sokol et al., 2003). Furthermore, our appreciation of ethanol-induced changes provides a model of and insights into the etiology of numerous neurodevelopmental disorders, such as autism and schizophrenia.

The first set of chapters in Part II addresses global effects of prenatal exposure to ethanol. These include the prevalence of alcohol-induced deficits among humans (Chapter 8), the structural malformations caused by prenatal exposure to ethanol (Chapter 9), and the effects of ethanol on nervous system–endocrine system interactions (Chapter 10). Following this discussion is a series of chapters that focus on the four ontogenetic phases: cell proliferation (Chapters 11 and 12), migration (Chapter 13), differentiation (Chapter 14), and death (Chapters 15 and 16). The last two chapters of this section examine the effects of ethanol on two populations of neural-related cells: neural crest cells (Chapter 17) and glia (Chapter 18).

NICOTINE-AFFECTED DEVELOPMENT

The final section of the book examines the response of the nervous system to a nicotine challenge. Whereas ethanol is acted upon by endogenous enzymes—for example, catalase and alcohol dehydrogenase—it does not act at a specific receptor. In contrast, nicotine allegedly acts though a focused endogenous mechanism at receptors for cholinergic neurotransmission. An understanding of the effects of nicotine is not only important for appreciation of a basic science issue, it is of critical clinical importance. A fetus is exposed to nicotine though increased blood concentrations in the pregnant woman as nicotine freely crosses the placental "barrier," and infants are exposed to nicotine through secondhand smoke.

The clinical problem of fetal nicotine exposure is discussed in Chapter 19. Nicotine is a rather ubiquitous substance—for those who smoke and for those who are exposed to secondhand smoke. Nicotine exposure is often accompanied by exposure to other substances such as alcohol. Thus, clinical studies have fostered the need to conduct well-controlled animal studies to understand the behavioral consequences of exposure to nicotine per se (Chapter 20). Although nicotine is thought to act through specific cholinergic receptors, it has broader effects through catecholaminergic and other systems. These issues are examined in Chapters 21 and 22, respectively. Chapter 23 explores the effects of nicotine on specific ontogenetic events.

Separate studies of normal development and of development altered by ethanol or nicotine provide unique, though limited, insight into brain development. Each line of inquiry opens windows of understanding that otherwise might be inaccessible from other vantage points. By consolidating the information gathered from the three approaches, however, we can gain a fuller appreciation (a) of the complexity of neural development, and (b) of how it can go wrong during a disease process.

Abbreviations

CNS   central nervous system

FAS   fetal alcohol syndrome

Note

1. It was alleged that Harvey Kurtzman and Norman Mingo were not the first to draw a face resembling Alfred E. Neuman. Indeed, two lawsuits (based on copyrights filed in 1914 and 1936) attested that Kurtzman and Mingo were not the originators of the caricature now referred to as Alfred E. Neuman. It was used in advertisements for dental practices (see a copy of the Manitoba Free Press in 1928 [http://www.imagehosting.us/index.php?action = show&ident = 728813]) and an image was even used by the Nazis as part of their anti-Semitic campaign in the 1930s (Djerassi, 1988; see http://garfield.library.upenn.edu/essays/v12p161y1989.pdf). [n.b. The name Alfred E. Neuman and the image of the gap-toothed person were first joined in 1956.] The principal (winning) defense was that earlier artists had themselves copied

a likeness produced before 1914, notably "Mickey Dugan, The Yellow Kid" drawn by Richard Felton Outcault in the late nineteenth century, and various other cartoons and advertisements (see a copy of the Winnipeg Tribune in 1909 [http://www.imagehosting.us/index.php?action = show&ident = 728816]). Interestingly, most of the earlier versions depict a normal upper lip, a distinct philtrum, and normal-appearing eyes. Therefore, it does appear that Kurtzman and Mingo were the first to associate the three characteristic features of FAS: facial dysmorphology, mental dysfunction, and microencephaly.

References

Abel EL (1984) *Fetal Alcohol Syndrome and Fetal Alcohol Effects*. Plenum, New York.

—— (1995) An update on incidence of FAS: FAS is not an equal opportunity birth defect. Neurotoxicol Teratol 17:437–443.

Alter M, Liebo J, Desnick SO, Strommer B (1968) The behavior of the reeler neurological mutant mouse. Neurology 18:289.

Bruck RM, Williams TH (1970) Light and electron microscopic study of the hippocampal region of normal and reeler mice. J Anat 106:170–171.

D'Arcangelo G, Miao GG, Chen SC, Soares HD, Morgan JI, Curran T (1995) A protein related to extracellular matrix proteins deleted in the mouse mutant reeler. Nature 374:719–723.

Djerassi C (1988) The quest for Alfred E. Neuman. Grand Street 8:167–174.

Falconer DS (1951) Two new mutations, *trembler* and *reeler* with neurological action in the house mouse. J Genet 50:192–201.

Hirotsune S, Takahara T, Sasaki N, Hirose K, Yoshiki A, Ohashi T, Kusakabe M, Murakami Y, Muramatsu M, Watanabe S, Nakao K, Katsuki M, Hayashizakiy (1995) The *reeler* gene encodes a protein with an EGF-like motif expressed by pioneer neurons. Nat Genet 10:77–83.

Jones KL, Smith DW (1973) Recognition of the fetal alcohol syndrome in early infancy. Lancet 2:999–1001.

Jones KL, Smith DW, Ulleland CN, Streissguth AP (1973) Pattern of malformation in offspring of chronic alcoholic mothers. Lancet 1:1267–1271.

Lambert de Rouvroit C, Goffinet AM (1998) The reeler mouse as a model of brain development. Adv Anat Embryol Cell Biol 150:1–106.

Lemoine P, Harousseau H, Borteyru J-P, Menuet J-C (1968) Les enfants de parents alcooliques: anomalies observées à propos de 127 cas. Ouest Med 21:476–482.

Marin O, Rubenstein JL (2003) Cell migration in the forebrain. Annu Rev Neurosci 26:441–483.

Ogawa M, Miyata T, Nakajima K, Yagyu K, Seike M, Ikenaka K, Yamamoto H, Mikoshiba K (1995) The *reeler* gene–associated antigen on Cajal-Retzius neurons is a crucial molecule for laminar organization of cortical neurons. Neuron 14:899–912.

Sokol RJ, Delaney-Black V, Nordstrom B (2003) Fetal alcohol spectrum disorder. JAMA 290:2996–2999.

Stratton K, Howe C, Battaglia F (1996) *Fetal Alcohol Syndrome: Diagnosis, Epidemiology, Prevention and Treatment*. National Academy Science Press, Washington, DC.

Ulleland CN (1972) The offspring of alcoholic mothers. Ann NY Acad Sci 197:167–169.

I

NORMAL DEVELOPMENT

2

Cell Proliferation

Bernhard Suter
Pradeep G. Bhide

Cell proliferation is the earliest step in the protracted process of development of the mammalian brain, and the pace of cell proliferation and the number and types of cells produced can be modulated by a variety of genetic and environmental factors. The dynamics of the proliferation of precursor cells in the developing mammalian brain are shaped by various factors. This chapter describes the spatiotemporal features of cell proliferation and effects of neurotransmitters, major constituents of the chemical environment of the developing brain that modulate the process of precursor cell proliferation. It focuses on three neurotransmitters that are among the most abundant ones in the developing brain: dopamine, γ-aminobutyric acid (GABA), and glutamate. The goal is to present an overview of the organization and activity of precursor cell populations and discuss the potential for modulation of precursor cell activity by neurotransmitters. The discussion is limited to cell proliferation in two exemplary structures in the central nervous system (CNS): the cerebral cortex and neostriatum.

ORGANIZATION OF PRECURSOR CELL POPULATIONS IN THE EMBRYONIC TELENCEPHALON

Cells of the nervous system arise from precursor cells lining the inner or ventricular surface of the neural tube. The precursor cells are organized as a pseudostratified columnar epithelium. The epithelium is commonly referred to as the *pseudostratified ventricular epithelium* (PVE), as it borders the ventricular cavities of the embryonic nervous system (Boulder Committee, 1970; Takahashi et al., 1993). The region of the neural tube of the fetal nervous system that contains the PVE is called the *ventricular zone* (VZ), a histologically defined region surrounding the ventricles. Most cells in the PVE are bipolar and span virtually the entire distance between the pial (outer) and the ventricular (inner) surfaces (Fig. 2–1A), especially during early neural tube stages. A small number of cells are round and contact only the ventricular surface; most of these cells are mitotically active.

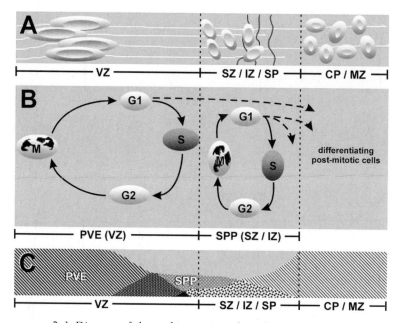

FIGURE 2–1 Diagram of the architectonic and cytokinetic compartments in the developing mammalian brain. The ventricular surface is to the left and the pial surface to the right. **A.** Four cytoarchitectonic compartments can be recognized on the basis of cytological criteria (Boulder Committee, 1970; Smart, 1976): the ventricular zone (VZ, or the ependymal layer), subventricular zone (SZ, or the subependymal layer), the intermediate zone (IZ, or the external sagittal stratum), and three differentiating fields—a subplate (SP), cortical plate (CP), and marginal zone (MZ). Cells in the VZ are organized as a pseudostratified columnar epithelium, whereas the SZ and SP/CP/MZ contain randomly oriented, nonepithelial cells. The IZ consists predominantly of columnar arrays of bipolar cells and growing axons (black lines). The borders of the SZ and IZ are ambiguous. The dashed lines indicate the approximate borders between the different compartments. **B.** Precursor cells can be classified into two groups on the basis of their interkinetic nuclear migratory pattern: a pseudostratified ventricular epithelium (PVE) and a secondary proliferative population (SPP). PVE cells undergo interkinetic nuclear migration (black arrows) such that nuclei of cells in M phase of the cell cycle are located at the ventricular surface and the nuclei of cells in S phase are farthest from the ventricular surface. Nuclei of cells in G1 and G2 phases are at intermediate distances. SPP cells do not undergo interkinetic nuclear migration, and the nuclei of cells in the different cell cycle phases are scattered throughout the VZ and IZ (solid black arrows). PVE cells that leave the cell cycle exit the VZ, migrate through the SZ and IZ (broken, curved arrows), and settle in the CP/MZ. SPP cells that exit the cell cycle also migrate to the CP/MZ. **C.** The spatial distribution of PVE, SPP, and CP/MZ cells is illustrated to show the overlap among the proliferative and postmitotic populations. The PVE near the ventricular surface is a "pure" population; however, the S-phase zone (where nuclei of cells undergoing S phase are located) of the PVE overlaps with the SPP. The CP/MZ is a population of predominantly postmitotic cells near the pial surface (right-hand side of the figure); however, in the SZ/IZ area, some postmitotic cells mix with precursor cells of the SPP. Thus, the architectonic and cytokinetic compartments show considerable overlap in the developing nervous system. (*Source:* Modified from Bhide, 1996).

At later stages of fetal development, various regions interpose between the VZ and the pial surface. Thus, additional architectonic subdivisions and an additional precursor population emerge. An early population of precursor cells that emerges is called the *secondary proliferative population* (SPP). The architectonic subdivision in which the SPP comes to lie is called the *subventricular zone* (SZ) (Boulder Committee, 1970). Around the same time, a preplate appears between the SZ and the pial surface (Boulder Committee, 1970; Marin-Padilla, 1983). Shortly thereafter, the preplate is split into a marginal zone (MZ) and subplate by the cortical plate (CP). These three zones (the subplate, CP, and MZ) are fields that consist largely of postmitotic or differentiating cells produced by the PVE and SPP precursors. In some parts of the nervous system such as the cerebral cortex, another architectonic subdivision called the *intermediate zone* (IZ) develops. The IZ lies between the SZ and the MZ and contains growing axons, migrating postmitotic neurons, and cells in glial lineages. Note that the VZ, SZ, CP, and MZ are architectonic subdivisions of the nervous system whereas the PVE and SPP are cytokinetic subdivisions of the precursor populations. The architectonic and cytokinetic subdivisions overlap extensively, as shown in Figure 2–1C.

The PVE is an interactive community of cells, coupled to one another via intercellular junctions such as gap junctions (LoTurco and Kriegstein, 1991; Bittman et al., 1997). PVE cells share biochemical characteristics with radial glia (Hockfield and McKay, 1985; Miller and Robertson, 1993; Malatesta et al., 2000, 2003; Noctor et al., 2001; Weissman et al., 2003). Until recently, radial glia were considered only to serve the dual functions of guiding newly generated neurons to their final destinations and acting as a transitional stage in astrocytic ontogeny (Rakic, 1972; Voigt, 1989; Takahashi et al., 1990; Misson et al., 1991; Miller and Robertson, 1993).

The PVE cells undergo interkinetic nuclear migration, a hallmark of pseudostratified epithelia in general (Sidman et al., 1959; Fujita, 1960). Thus, nuclei of the PVE cells are distributed within the VZ in accordance with the cell cycle phase (Fig. 2–1B). Nuclei undergoing mitoses are located at the ventricular border, whereas the nuclei in the DNA synthesis or S-phase are in abventricular locations. Nuclei of cells passing through G1 and G2 are located at intermediate distances between the two poles. The interkinetic nuclear migratory pattern distinguishes the PVE from the SPP (His, 1887; Sauer, 1936; Boulder Committee, 1970; Takahashi et al., 1993). SPP cells are not organized into an epithelium and do not display interkinetic nuclear migration (Rakic et al., 1974). The SPP is a major component of the precursor cell pool in some parts of the nervous system, such as the neostriatum and the cerebral cortex, and not in other parts, such as the hippocampus or the hypothalamus.

The PVE is a "pure" population of precursor cells in the sense that daughter cells produced by it and that embark upon the path of differentiation into neurons or glia exit the PVE rapidly (Miller, 1999). In other words, a snapshot of the VZ, which houses the PVE, reveals proliferating precursor cells and virtually no differentiating neurons or glia (Fig. 2–1C). The SZ, by contrast, which includes the SPP, is a mixture of proliferating SPP cells and differentiating daughter cells generated from both the PVE and the SPP. These differences in the cellular environments may bestow unique physiological features on the PVE and SPP precursors and their differential responses to environmental substances such as ethanol (see Chapter 11). The intimate cell–cell contact among precursor cells in the VZ may facilitate contact-mediated signaling between proliferating cells, which is less likely to occur in the SZ, although contact among precursor cells and postmitotic cells may be more likely in the SZ. Close proximity of the SPP to growing axons in the IZ (Fig. 2–1A), in some parts of the nervous system such as the cerebral wall, increases the molecular diversity of the environment further.

Neurons and glia arise from both the PVE and the SPP. Contributions of the PVE and the SPP to the total numbers of cells in different parts of the brain vary significantly. For example, it has been suggested that the PVE and SPP generate neurons primarily in the deep and superficial laminae of neocortex, respectively (Miller, 1989; Miller and Nowakowski, 1991) (Chapter 11). In the neostriatum, the SPP appears to be the major contributor of neurons and glia, whereas in the hippocampus proper, the PVE generates all cell types. The PVE in the hippocampal formation is the source of pyramidal neurons of the hippocampus and granule neurons of the dentate gyrus, early in the fetal period (Angevine, 1965; Stanfield and Cowan, 1979; Altman and Bayer, 1990). In the dentate gyrus cells derived from the PVE early in the embryonic period settle at the border between the granule cell layer and the hilar region and continue to proliferate, forming a second and apparently permanent precursor pool called the subgranular, or *intrahilar zone* (IHZ) (Angevine, 1965; Stanfield and Cowan, 1979; Altman and Bayer, 1990). The IHZ is the source of the majority of granule neurons of the dentate gyrus later in development, including adult life (Angevine, 1965; Bayer, 1982; Cameron et al., 1993; Gage et al., 1998; van Praag et al., 2002; Kempermann et al., 2004).

Although the architectonic and cytokinetic subdivisions mentioned above appear in nearly all parts of the developing telencephalon, considerable regional variation occurs in terms of the size of the different

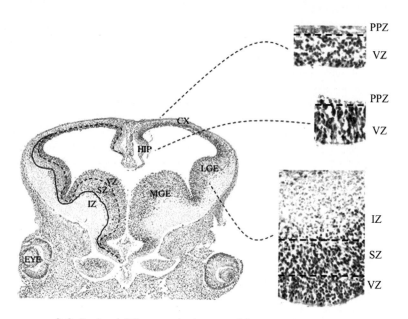

FIGURE 2–2 Regional differences in the size of the cytoarchitectonic compartments in the developing brain. A histological section in the coronal plane though the head of an 11-day-old mouse fetus is shown. The fetus was exposed to the S-phase marker bromodeoxyuridine (BrdU) for 6 hours; BrdU was injected into the pregnant dam and the fetus was harvested 6 hours later. The section was processed immunohistochemically to reveal the distribution of BrdU in proliferating cells. BrdU-labeled cells appear dark and surround the ventricular cavities of the brain (empty space at the center of the micrograph). The compartments of the telencephalon visible at this coronal level are the hippocampus (HIP), cerebral neocortical wall (CX), lateral ganglionic eminence (LGE), and medial ganglionic eminence (MGE). On the left-hand side, the broken line marks the approximate boundary between the ventricular zone (VZ) and the subventricular zone (SZ), and the solid line marks the boundary between the SZ and the intermediate zone (IZ). The broken line is drawn on the basis of differences in the packing density and disposition of the BrdU-labeled cells (higher density in the VZ, aligned in comparison to the SZ, which has a lower density of BrdU-labeled cells that are randomly distributed). The solid line is at the boundary between BrdU-labeled (precursor) and unlabeled (nonproliferating or differentiating) cells. A relatively large VZ, SZ, and IZ area is in the ganglionic region (LGE and MGE) compared to that in the dorsal CX and hippocampal anlage (HIP), even at this early stage of brain development. The higher-magnification images (right) show the histological divisions of VZ, SZ, and PPZ in the different telencepahlic compartments. The primordia of eyes (EYE) are also visible in this section. (*Source*: Modified from Sheth and Bhide, 1997)

subdivisions and the time of emergence of each sub-division in the course of embryonic development. In fact, these regional differences distinguish the precur-sors of the different telencephalic compartments. In the telencephalon of the developing mouse brain, re-gional variation is evident as early as gestational day (G) 11 (the day of conception is designated as G0). In coronal sections of 11-day-old fetal mouse brain, a sizeable SZ can be seen in the lateral ganglionic emi-nence (GE) and medial GE. These specialized seg-ments of the SZ contain precursors of neurons in the basal ganglia and a source of neocortical GABA neu-rons (Fig. 2–2). The murine cerebral cortex, hip-pocampus, and hypothalamic regions do not have a SZ at G11. In fact, an SZ does not develop in the hip-pocampal and hypothalamic regions, although it does develop in the cerebral cortex about 2–3 days later (Miller, 1999).

The VZ is the earliest structure in the developing nervous system, thus it contains the earliest forming precursor cell population (i.e., the PVE). The VZ is present in all parts of the G11 telencephalon (Fig. 2–2). A distinct and sizeable MZ, consisting of newly generated differentiating cells, is evident in the lateral and medial GEs by G11, whereas the other regions of the telencephalon have a relatively smaller MZ at this age. Thus, the size and distribution of both prolifera-tive and postmitotic subdivisions of the telencephalon show considerable variation in the fetal forebrain. The emergence of heterogeneity within the telen-cepahlic anlage reflects influences of transcription fac-tors (Puelles and Rubenstein, 1993; Rubenstein et al., 1998) and/or neurotransmitters (Ohtani et al., 2003) that distribute in a regionally specific manner. The re-gional variation also foreshadows the structural differ-ences that emerge in these regions as development proceeds.

MOLECULAR REGULATION OF
CELL PROLIFERATION

Cell proliferation in the nervous system is an intri-cately regulated process. The regulation occurs by the concerted actions of a variety of genetic and environ-mental factors at the level of the cycling cells in the PVE and SPP. There are at least three interrelated tiers of regulation: (1) the total number of cells pro-duced by the PVE and SPP, (2) the emergence of spe-cific phenotypes among the daughter cells, and (3)

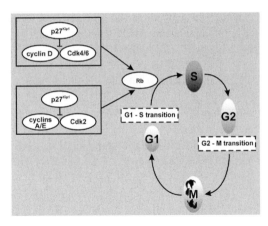

FIGURE 2–3 Role played by the cyclin-dependent ki-nase (Cdk) inhibitor p27^{Kip1} in the regulation of cell cycle at the G1-to-S–phase transition. The progres-sion of the cell cycle can be regulated at the transition from the G2 to M phase or from the G1 to S phase. Genetic and environmental factors that modulate progression of cell cycle in the developing brain ap-pear to influence the G1-to-S–phase transition. This transition is regulated by Cdks (Cdk2, Cdk4, and Cdk6) and their cyclin partners (cyclins A, E, and D). Association of Cdks and their cyclin partners inacti-vates the retinoblastoma protein (Rb) by phosphoryla-tion, which in turn promotes the transition from G1 to S phase by releasing the transcription factor E2F. p27^{Kip1} inhibits the activity of the Cdk–cyclin com-plexes and therefore inhibits the transition from G1 to S phase. Thus, genetic and environmental factors that alter the expression and activity of p27^{Kip1} can modulate cell proliferation in the developing brain.

the temporal sequence of cell production and specifi-cation that is unique to each region of the brain. An understanding of the molecular mechanisms that reg-ulate these processes is important not only for appre-ciating cytogenesis during normal development but also for understanding (a) the way in which cell pro-duction can be induced in specific regions of the adult brain to repair injury by trauma or disease and (b) the mechanisms by which neoplasms in the CNS originate.

Genetic and environmental factors regulate cell proliferation by acting upon the molecular machin-ery that regulates the cell cycle. This machinery con-sists of protein kinases and their regulatory subunits, known as cyclin-dependent kinases (Cdks) and cy-clins, respectively (Fig. 2–3). Essentially, Cdk activity depends on the synthesis and destruction of cyclins as well as on the function of Cdk-activating kinases and Cdk inhibitors (LaBaer et al., 1997; Morgan, 1997; Cheng et al., 1999; Sherr and Roberts, 1999; Murray, 2004). Each Cdk has a preferred cyclin partner(s). For example, Cdk2 associates with cyclins A and E, whereas Cdk4 and Cdk6 associate with D-type cyclins. Association of Cdks with cyclins results in the regulation of the cell cycle at two principal transition points: the transitions from the G1 to S phase, and from G2 to M (Murray and Hunt, 1993) (Fig. 2–3). Cdk2, Cdk4, and Cdk6 are principally involved in the regulation of the transition from G1 to S, whereas Cdk1 regulates the G2–M transition. The transition from G1 to S phase is associated with additional mechanisms of regulation involving the retinoblastoma protein (Rb) and the transcription factor E2F. Association of Cdks with cyclins inactivates Rb by phosphorylation, which in turn results in the release of E2F. E2F promotes the transition from G1 to S and DNA synthesis (Dyson, 1998; Frolov et al., 2001).

Control over cell cycle progression at the G1-to-S-phase transition is exercised by Cdk inhibitors, which inhibit the activity of the Cdk–cyclin complexes (Ferguson et al., 2000). Inhibition of Cdk activity by specific Cdk inhibitors such as p27^{Kip1} or p21^{Waf1} suppresses the entry into the S phase (Zindy et al., 1997, 1999; Delalle et al., 1999; Siegenthaler and Miller, 2005) (Fig. 2–3). Much of the regulation of cytogenesis in the developing brain is thought to occur at the G1/S transition (Caviness et al., 1996; Ross, 1996). Transcription factors, growth factors, hormones, and neurotransmitters are among the most common regulators of cell proliferation in the developing brain. They are believed to act upon the G1/S transition point to increase or decrease the output of neurons or glia (Caviness et al., 1996; Ross, 1996).

Much of our understanding of cell cycle regulation derives from in vitro studies. That said, the PVE and SPP cells in the intact mammalian brain differ from the precursor cells maintained in a Petri dish in one important aspect. PVE and SPP cells in the intact brain serve a histogenetic agenda, which warrants generation of a specific number of specific cell types in a spatiotemporal gradient over a restricted period of time. Therefore, to understand mechanisms that regulate CNS histogenesis we need to analyze cell proliferation in populations of PVE or SPP cells in the intact brain. A challenge faced by developmental

neurobiologists is to assimilate mechanistic insights, gained by analysis of cell cycle regulatory machinery from studies of dissociated cells, into analyses of cell cycle kinetics and cell output from populations of PVE or SPP cells in the intact brain. The following section describes recent progress in efforts along those lines. Complementary insight into these issues is provided by studying the proliferative response in the developing brain following ethanol exposure (see Chapters 11 and 12). Much of our knowledge of the kinetics of PVE and SPP cell cycle in the intact brain is derived from analyses of neocortical PVE cells. Therefore, the following section focuses mainly on cell cycle kinetics of neocortical PVE.

CELL CYCLE KINETICS AND DYNAMICS OF CELL PROLIFERATION IN THE NEOCORTEX

In any tissue or organ system, the precursor cell population initially expands by producing large numbers of new precursor cells. The precursor cell population subsequently depletes itself through (a) the production of large numbers of daughter cells, which exit the cell cycle, differentiate, and acquire mature phenotypes, and (b) the death of cycling cells (see Chapter 5). This type of biphasic growth pattern ensures the production of a large number of cells within a specified time interval. The neocortical PVE follows this growth pattern. It undergoes two phases of growth: an initial phase of expansion during which most daughter cells return to the precursor pool, and a later phase of depletion when most of the daughter cells differentiate into neurons or glia (Smart, 1976; Caviness et al., 1995; Miller and Kuhn, 1995; Takahashi et al., 1996, 1997). Interestingly, during the phase of expansion, the PVE grows in the tangential dimension, and this growth results in expansion of the PVE such that it covers the underlying subcortical structures. There is little expansion of the PVE in the radial dimension; growth in the radial dimension is seemingly reserved for later developmental periods when newborn neurons and glia are released from a depleting PVE (Miller, 1989).

The use of the S-phase marker [^{3}H]thymidine ([^{3}H]dT) revolutionized the analysis of neuroepithelial cell cycle kinetics by permitting identification of nuclei in S phase and tracking the nuclei labeled in S phase as they passed through G2, M, and G1 phases of the cell cycle (Sidman et al., 1959; Angevine and Sidman, 1961; Fujita and Miyake, 1962; Sidman, 1970). It became possible to estimate cell cycle parameters and the time of generation of different cell types through cumulative or pulse labeling with [³H]dT. Recent development of nonradioactive S-phase markers bromodeoxyuridine (BrdU) and iododeoxyuridine further enhanced the versatility of these methods (Miller and Nowakowski, 1988, 1991; Takahashi et al., 1992; Hayes and Nowakowski, 2000; Tarui et al., 2005).

S-phase labeling methods have been exploited, often combining the radioactive and nonradioactive markers to perform sophisticated analyses of cell cycle kinetics and cell output functions of PVE and SPP cells in the embryonic murine neocortex (Miller and Nowakowski, 1991; Caviness et al., 1995; Hayes and Nowakowski, 2000; Takahashi et al., 2002; Siegenthaler and Miller, 2005; inter alia). This work shows that the neocortical PVE cells in fetal mice executed 11 cell cycles throughout the course of generation of neocortical neurons over the week from G11 to G17. During the 11 cell cycles, the length of the cell cycle increases (from about 8 to 18 hours) (Fig. 2–4), the increase being due to the lengthening of G1 (from about 3 to 12 hours). This pattern is also detected in rat neocortical proliferative zones (Miller and Kuhn, 1995).

The probability that a new daughter cell exits the cell cycle (called Q) increased during the period of cortical neuronogenesis (Miller, 1993, 1999; Miller and Kuhn, 1995; Takahashi et al., 1999). It was near zero for cell cycle 1 (on G11 for the mouse) and nearly 100% for cell cycle 11 (G16-17). Each cell cycle is associated with specific values of Q and cell cycle length (i.e., the length of the G1-phase), the two parameters that change (increase) systematically over the course of the 11 cell cycles (Fig. 2–4). The Q value reaches the halfway mark during the seventh and eighth cell cycles, on approximately G14 (Fig. 2–4). This probability value marks a significant milestone in the life history of neocortical PVE, as it indicates the switch from the expansive to the depletive phase of growth and from tangential to radial expansion of the neocortex. Furthermore, it marks a significant milestone in neocortical neuronogenesis: generation of neurons for the infragranular layers (layers V and VI) ceases and that for the granular layer (layer IV) and supragranular layers (layers II and III)

begins (Fig. 2–4). Thus, quantitative estimates of the values of Q at each integer cell cycle have enabled the linkage of Q to laminar destination of the daughter cells. In other words, a novel concept emerges, in which the mechanisms regulating Q are linked to mechanisms regulating cell fate or cell class (Tarui et al., 2005).

Neuronogenesis across the cortical mantle does not proceed simultaneously; it abides by various spatiotemporal gradients (Smart, 1961; Smart and McSherry, 1982; Miller, 1988a; Bayer and Altman, 1991). The transverse gradients reflect the gradients in cell cycle kinetics, especially the value of Q, in the PVE (Caviness et al., 2000, 2003; Tarui et al., 2005). Thus, PVE cells are distributed along a spatial continuum of cell cycle parameters and Q. PVE cells located at the rostrolateral location are more advanced than those at the caudomedial location with respect to cell cycle length and values of Q. That is, rostrolateral precursor cells have longer cell cycle times and higher values of Q than those of caudomedial precursor cells on any given day during the interval G11 to G17. For example, a given location in the neocortical PVE contains precursor cells passing through the entire range of cell cycle times and Q values over the interval G11 to G17. At any given time, the neuroepithelium contains a range of cell cycle times and Q values. Cells destined to multiple layers in multiple neocortical areas arise contemporaneously at multiple locations within the neuroepithelium.

Apart from the tangential neurogenetic gradient discussed above, neocortical neuronogenesis proceeds along a radial dimension, a characteristic common to laminar structures throughout the nervous system. At any given location of the neocortical anlagen, neurons are generated in an inside-out pattern (Angevine and Sidman, 1961; Berry et al., 1964; Berry and Rogers, 1965; Caviness, 1982; Miller, 1985). Deep-layer neurons are generated earlier than the superficial layer neurons. Using a double S-phase labeling method, Takahashi and colleagues (1999) correlated the laminar position of a neocortical neuron with its "birth hour." Through the use of this method, they were able to correlate the time of generation and laminar destination of neocortical neurons with considerably higher spatiotemporal resolution than had been possible previously.

A model correlating the probability of cell cycle exit (which is equivalent to Q) with the probability of the destination of a neuron in a specific neocortical

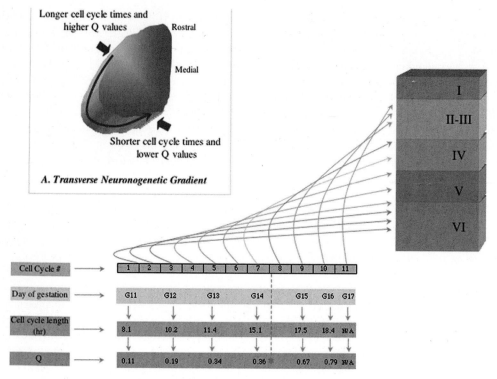

FIGURE 2–4 Spatiotemporal gradients of cell proliferation and neurogenesis in the cerebral cortex. Neurogenesis in the cerebral cortex progresses along tangential (A) and radial (B) gradients. **A.** Neocortical neurogenesis begins at the rostroventrolateral region on gestational day (G) 11 in mice and proceeds toward the caudodorsomedial region in a systematic gradient (curved arrow). This transverse neurogenetic gradient translates into a corresponding gradient in cell cycle length of the precursor population and the probability of cell cycle exit (Q) for the daughter cells. Thus, precursor cells in the pseudostratified ventricular epithelium (PVE) in the rostroventrolateral region have longer cell cycle time and higher values of Q compared to their counterparts in the caudodorsomedial region. **B.** Neurogenesis also proceeds along a radial gradient. Neurons of the deep layers are produced earlier than those in the superficial layers. Each neocortical PVE cell in mice, on average, undergoes 11 cell cycles over a 7-day period from G11 to G17. Cell cycle length increases with each cell cycle and each cycle is associated with a unique value of Q. Thus, the cell cycle length increases from about 8 to 18 hours over the course of 11 cell cycles. The value of Q increases from about 0.1 to 0.8, approaching the maximal value of 1.0, during this interval and reaches the halfway mark (0.5) between cell cycles 7 and 8 on G14 (broken line and asterisk). Each cell cycle produces cells destined for specific neocortical layer(s). Thus, cell cycle number, cell cycle length, Q, and layer destination are linked to one another during normal development. (*Source*: Based on data of Takahashi et al., 1999; Tarui et al., 2005)

layer was then developed by Takahashi and colleagues (1999). Theoretically, neurons produced at any time point during the neurogenetic sequence can have some probability of occupying any neocortical layer. In reality, however, during normal development neurons generated during cell cycle 1 have nearly a 100% probability of occupying layer VI and 0% probability of occupying layer II–III, and neurons generated during cell cycle 11 (the final cell cycle) have a near 100% probability of occupying layer II–III and 0% probability of occupying layer VI. Since a given cell cycle number is associated with given values of Q, another way of interpreting these findings is that the probability that a cell arising from a given cell cycle will occupy a specific layer is tightly linked to the values of Q. Lower Q values predict destination to deeper layers and higher values predict destination to more superficial layers. What factors set the probability values?

Overexpression of the cdk inhibitor p27[kip1] in the PVE increases Q, and that the neurons produced during the cell cycles with the experimentally elevated Q values assume superficial laminar positions that would be appropriate for the higher value of Q (Tarui et al., 2005). Therefore, Q and laminar destination appear to be highly correlated. Also, these findings suggest that p27[kip1] expression and activity play a role in setting the values of Q. Recent data show that another cdk inhibitor, p21, is also involved in cell cycle exit (Siegenthaler and Miller, 2005). Furthermore, a variety of genetic and environmental factors, such as transcription factors, growth factors, and neurotransmitters, influence intracellular p27[kip1] and p21[wof1] content. The combined actions of these factors may regulate Q and, therefore, neocortical neuronal fate during normal development.

The discussion above pertains directly to the regulation of cell proliferation in the neocortical PVE. Neocortical neurons arise not only from the neocortical PVE but also from the proliferative cells in the GE. Neocortical PVE is the source of neocortical (glutamatergic) projection neurons (PNs), which constitute 70%–90% of all neocortical neurons (Peters et al., 1985; Ren et al., 1992; Beaulieu, 1993). In rodents, the majority of GABAergic local circuit neurons (LCNs) of the cerebral cortex, which constitute 10%–30% of all neocortical neurons, is produced in the medial and caudal GEs of the basal forebrain (Anderson et al., 1997a; Tamamaki et al., 1997; Lavdas et al., 1999; Powell et al., 2001; Nery et al., 2002; Ang et al., 2003). These LCNs arrive in the cerebral cortex via tangential migratory pathways. In primates, however, it appears that most GABAergic LCNs of the cerebral cortex derive from the neocortical PVE and only a minority come from the GE (Letinic et al., 2002). Although neocortical PNs and LCNs are produced in different locations, both types of neurons located in the same neocortical layer appear to be produced on the same day, at least in rodents (Miller, 1985, 1988b; 1999; Fairén et al., 1986; Cobas and Fairén 1988; Valcanis and Tan, 2003).

Neocortical glia are generated in the SPP (Smart, 1961; Smart and LeBlond, 1961; LeVine

and Goldman, 1988a, 1988b; Levison and Goldman, 1993). One notable exception to this pattern is that of radial glia, which commonly have cell bodies in the PVE, and may undergo transformation into astrocytes near the end of the neuronogenetic epoch (Voigt, 1989; Takahashi et al., 1990; Misson et al., 1991; Miller and Robertson, 1993). A distinguishable SPP (SZ) appears in the neocortical proliferative region soon after the first cortical neurons are generated, by G13 in the mouse (Miller, 1989; Takahashi et al., 1995). At this time, the size of the SPP is <10% of the total neocortical precursor pool (the PVE being the dominant population), but the SPP size increases to nearly 50% until about G16. Thus, at later stages of gestation, as the PVE wanes the SPP becomes the dominant population. The cell cycle length of the SPP does not appear to change systematically with age and remains relatively constant at around 15 hours, during the interval G13 to G16 (Takahashi et al., 1995). The SPP may also contain a population of precursor cells that arise from the PVE and "wait" in the SZ for varying lengths of time (up to 48 hours) prior to producing daughter cells that differentiate into neurons (Bayer and Altman, 1991; Miller, 1999; Noctor et al., 2004).

CELL CYCLE KINETICS AND NEUROGENESIS IN THE NEOSTRIATUM

Unlike the cerebral cortex, the neostriatum is a non-laminar structure. It consists of the caudate nucleus and the putamen and it is the input center of the basal ganglia. In histological sections of the rodent brain it is difficult to distinguish the boundary between the caudate nucleus and the putamen, making the term *neostriatum* or *caudoputamen* particularly useful. Nearly 90% of neostriatal neurons are GABAergic projection neurons and the remaining cells are cholinergic LCNs (Gerfen and Wilson, 1996). Neostriatal projection neurons are generated in the lateral GE (Hewitt, 1958; Smart, 1976; Smart and Sturrock, 1979; Lammers et al., 1980; Fentress et al., 1981), and the LCNs are generated in the medial GE or the preoptic/anterior entopeduncular areas (Marin et al., 2000). The lateral GE consists of a larger SPP than that of the neocortical neuroepithelium. The SPP in the lateral GE is established as early as G11 in the mouse (Bhide, 1996; Sheth and

Bhide, 1997) (Fig. 2–2). Therefore, the SPP is likely to be a major source of neurons of the neostriatum. This finding concurs with that in the neocortex (see Chapter 11). Studies on the Distalless-related transcription factors *dlx1*, *dlx2*, and *dlx5*, which regulate cell proliferation and migration in the GE, confirm the origin of striatal projection neurons from the SPP of the GE (Anderson et al., 1997b; Stenman et al., 2003). Furthermore, analyses of transgenic mice show that the radial glia in the PVE of the lateral and medial GEs give rise to nearly all of the glia in the neostriatum and only to a subset of LCNs (parvalbumin and Er81-positive LCNs).

Two studies using S-phase labeling methods comparable to those used for the neocortical PVE estimated the cell cycle parameters and cell output from the PVE of the lateral GE (Bhide, 1996; Sheth and Bhide, 1997). The cell cycle was longer and the values of Q were greater in the lateral GE of mice on G11 and G12 compared to the corresponding parameters in the neocortical PVE. Estimation of cell cycle kinetics of the PVE of the lateral GE at later stages of development is complicated by the fact that during the later developmental stages this region acquires migrating cells produced in the adjacent medial GE (Anderson et al., 2001).

The striking structural and functional complexity of the neostriatum (Graybiel, 1990; Gerfen, 1992) has led to a number of investigations of the time of generation of neostriatal neurons. Early studies focused on the time of generation of neurons destined for the patch (striosome) and matrix compartments. These can be identified on the basis of distribution of opioid receptors or neuropeptide content of the neurons. Neurons destined for the patch compartment are generated earlier than those destined for the matrix in rodents, carnivores, and primates (Brand and Rakic, 1979; Graybiel and Hickey, 1982; Fishell and van der Kooy, 1987; Fishell et al., 1990; Song and Harlan, 1994). Other studies, which examined the time of generation of neostriatal neurons regardless of location of a neuron within the patch or matrix compartments, found some overlap in the time of generation of PNs and LCNs (Brand and Rakic, 1979; Fernandez et al., 1979; Bayer, 1984). In rodents, striatal neurons containing different types of neurotransmitters or neuropeptides are generated at distinct periods of neurogenesis (Semba et al., 1988; Sadikot and Sasseville, 1997). Neostriatal neurogenesis also follows spatiotemporal gradients (Fernandez et al., 1979;

Marchand and Lajoie, 1986; Bayer and Altman, 1987) that are less systematic than the transverse and radial gradients defining neocortical neuronogenesis. In fact, gradients of neuronogenesis are difficult to define in nonlaminar structures such as the neostriatum (Bayer and Altman, 1987).

NEUROTRANSMITTERS AND CELL PROLIFERATION

Cell proliferation is shaped by a variety of environmental factors such as growth factors and neurotransmitters. Growth factors, as the name indicates, tend to be growth-promoting agents and their influences on cell proliferation are not unexpected. Some growth factors, such as transforming growth factor β, however, have a negative effect on cell proliferation (see Chapter 11). Neurotransmitters have well-characterized functions at the synapse in the mature brain. Neurotransmitters and their receptors appear in the nervous system early in the fetal period, before synaptic contacts develop. Thus, it can be inferred that neurotransmitters influence developmental processes. Nonvesicular transport and release of neurotransmitters (Demarque et al., 2002) and paracrine mechanisms for neurotransmitter receptor activation (Owens et al., 1999) have been proposed in the fetal brain. Such mechanisms are distinct from those used by neurotransmitters in the mature brain, as are the composition and activity of neurotransmitter receptors. For example, GABA receptors in the fetal brain differ in their subunit composition, affinity, sensitivity, and signal transduction mechanisms relative to their counterparts in the mature brain (Owens and Kriegstein, 2002). Thus, a role for neurotransmitters in the fetal brain that may be separate from their role at the synapse in the mature brain appears likely (Lauder, 1988; Levitt et al., 1997; Nguyen et al., 2001; Owens and Kriegstein, 2002; Ohtani et al., 2003). The influence of dopamine, GABA, and glutamate on cell proliferation and neurogenesis in the neocortex and the neostriatum is discussed below.

Dopamine

Dopamine appears in the developing mouse brain as early as G13 (Ohtani et al., 2003). The cerebral cortex and the neostriatum express among the highest amounts of dopamine receptors in the fetal brain

(Sales et al., 1989; Guennoun and Bloch, 1993; Schambra et al., 1994; Bakowska and Morrell, 1995; Jung and Bennett, 1996; Diaz et al., 1997; Shearman et al., 1997; Ohtani et al., 2003). Dopaminergic axons originating in the midbrain penetrate the VZ and SZ of the prefrontal cortex and lateral GE (precursor of the neostriatum) of the mouse brain as early as G13, and growth cones of these axons are in close proximity to PVE and SPP cells in these regions (Ohtani et al., 2003; Popolo et al., 2004).

Dopamine receptor activation influences cell proliferation in the lateral GE and the dorsomedial prefrontal cortex (PFC). In the lateral GE, D1-like receptor activation reduces entry into S (i.e., an antimitogenic effect) and D2-like receptor activation increases the G1/S transition (i.e., a mitogenic effect) (Zhang and Lidow, 2002; Ohtani et al., 2003; Popolo et al., 2004; Zhang et al., 2005). Dopamine itself produces D1-like effects, presumably because of the preponderance of D1-like binding sites in the fetal brain (Ohtani et al., 2003). Dopamine receptor activation influences cell proliferation in the neuroepithelium of the PFC in a manner comparable to that in the lateral GE.

Activating dopamine receptors differentially affects precursor populations in the VZ and SZ (Fig. 2–5). Precursor cells in the VZ respond predominantly to D1-like receptor activation, whereas the precursors in the SZ respond to D2-like receptor activation (Ohtani et al., 2003; Popolo et al., 2004). VZ cells in the lateral ganglionic region are more responsive to D1-like receptor activation than their counterparts in the PFC; a larger dose of the D1-like receptor agonist SKF 81297 is required to elicit a significant response from the PFC (Popolo et al., 2004). Furthermore, D2-like receptor activation did not produce changes in the proliferation of precursor cell in the neocortical VZ, although it produced effects in the VZ of the

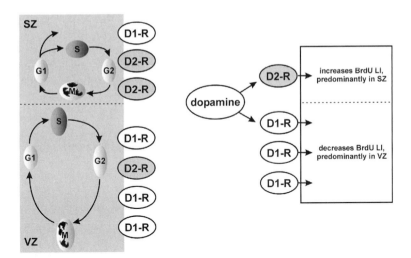

FIGURE 2–5 Schematic representation of distribution of D1-like and D2-like receptors (R). D1-R and D2-R in the ventricular and subventricular zones (VZ and SZ, respectively) of the telencepahlic neuroepithelium (A) and the effects of dopamine receptor activation on cell proliferation (B) are shown. **A.** On the basis of data on incorporation of the S-phase marker bromodeoxyuridine (BrdU), precursor cells in the VZ appear to respond to D1-R activation to a greater extent than D2-R activation, whereas the precursor cells in the SZ have an opposite response (Ohtani et al., 2003; Popolo et al., 2004). **B.** Activation of D1-R decreases the BrdU labeling index, which is a reflection of a decrease in the relative proportions of proliferating cells entering S phase. Activation of D2-R produces the opposite effect (i.e., increases BrdU labeling index). Dopamine produces effects similar to those produced by D1-R activation. (*Source:* Modified from work by Popolo et al., 2004).

lateral ganglionic region. Thus, significant regional variation exists in the responsiveness of progenitors in the neuroepithelial domains of the dorsal and ventral forebrain of the mouse fetus. This pattern likely reflects variation in the relative abundance of dopamine receptor binding sites or differences in signal transduction mechanisms.

The D1-like family of dopamine receptors is coupled to G proteins, which activate adenylate cyclase and increase intracellular cyclic adenylate monophosphate (cAMP) concentrations (Monsma et al., 1990). Increased intracellular cAMP content leads to increases in the amounts of the Cdk inhibitor $p27^{Kip1}$, which in turn inhibits entry into S (Kato et al., 1994; Lu and DiCicco-Bloom, 1997). Thus, the antimitogenic effects of D1-like receptor activation may be mediated via the cAMP–$p27^{Kip1}$ pathway. Other reports suggest that the effects of D1-like receptor activation on neocortical cell proliferation is mediated via a cAMP-independent pathway involving Raf-1, a component of the receptor tyrosine kinase–mitogen-activated kinase pathway (Zhang et al., 2005). Therefore, dopamine receptor activation may activate multiple second messenger systems in neuroepithelial cells.

GABA

GABA receptors appear early in the neuroepithelium and MZ of the fetal brain (Huntley et al., 1988; LoTurco and Kriegstein, 1991; LoTurco et al., 1995; Behar et al., 1998; Haydar et al., 2000). GABA receptors in the fetal brain are excitatory and influence cell proliferation in the VZ and SZ. Early studies indicate that $GABA_A$ receptor activation decreased entry into S (antiproliferative) in neocortical precursor cells (LoTurco et al., 1995). These effects appear to be mediated by endogenously released GABA, as inhibition of the $GABA_A$ receptors increased G1- to S entry in explants of neocortical tissue taken from rat fetuses (LoTurco et al., 1995). The effects of $GABA_A$ receptor inhibition were developmentally regulated in that the effects were pronounced at G19, but not at G14–G16 (LoTurco et al., 1995). Presumably, this finding reflects maturational changes in the activity of the receptors. The effects of $GABA_A$ receptor activation, like the effects of dopamine receptor activation, differ between the VZ and the SZ. $GABA_A$ receptor activation increases G1- to S entry in the VZ and decreases it in the SZ (Haydar et al., 2000). The

intracellular signaling cascade that mediates the effects of GABA receptor activation on the cell cycle machinery is not fully understood. The effects may be secondary to suppression of the action of mitogenic factors such as basic fibroblast growth factor (Antonopoulos et al., 1997).

Glutamate

Glutamate receptor activation influences the proliferation of precursor cells in the cerebral cortex and the neostriatum. Activation of both N-methyl-D-aspartate (NMDA) and α-amino-3-hydroxy-5-methyl-4-isoxazole propionate (AMPA)/kainate receptors influences G1-to-S entry in the precursor cells. Early studies indicated that activation of AMPA/kainate receptors by endogenous glutamate decreased entry into S in the neocortical VZ (LoTurco et al., 1995; Haydar et al., 2000). Activation of AMPA/kainite receptors, however, produced the opposite effects in the SZ by increasing entry into S (Haydar et al., 2000). Although glutamate receptor activation also influenced proliferation of neostriatal precursors, the effects were mediated via the NMDA receptor family rather than through the AMPA/kainate receptors (Luk et al., 2003; Luk and Sadikot, 2004). NMDA receptor activation promoted entry into S among neostriatal precursor cells (Sadikot et al., 1998; Luk et al., 2003; Luk and Sadikot, 2004).

CONCLUSIONS

The discussion above presents an overview of the effects of neurotransmitters on the process of cell proliferation. A summary of the effects of dopamine, GABA, and glutamate on cell proliferation in the neocortex and neostriatum of the developing brain is presented in Table 2–1. These data show that imbalance in the neurochemical environment of the developing brain can alter the process of generation of neurons and glia. Although the direction of the effects may vary depending on the receptor type activated and the precursor population involved (i.e., increase or decrease in proliferation), it is reasonable to assume that exposure of proliferating precursor cells to therapeutic or illicit drugs that target and produce imbalances in the neurotransmitter systems can produce significant changes in the number and phenotype of cells generated.

TABLE 2–1 Summary of effects of dopamine, GABA, and glutamate receptor activation on S-phase labeling indices in neocortical and neostriatal precursor populations of the fetal brain

	Precursor Population	Dopamine		GABA	Glutamate	
		Receptor Subtype				
		D1	D2	GABA_A	NMDA	AMPA/Kainate
Neocortex	VZ	Decrease[*]	No effect[†]	Increase[**] Decrease[††]	No effect[‡‡]	Increase[**] Decrease[**,††,‡‡]
	SZ	Decrease[†]	Increase[†]	Decrease[**]	No effect[‡‡]	Decrease[**] No effect[‡‡]
Neostriatum	VZ	Decrease[††]	Increase[†‡]	Not known	Increase[††]	No effect[‡‡]
	SZ	Decrease[††]	Increase[†‡]	Not known	No effect	No effect[‡‡]

[*]Zhang and Lidow (2002); Popolo et al. (2004).

[†]Popolo et al. (2004).

[‡]Ohtani et al. (2003).

[**]Haydar et al. (2000); Owens and Kriegstein (2002).

[††]LoTurco et al. (1995).

[‡‡]Sadikot et al. (1998); Luk et al. (2003); Luk and Sadikot (2004).

Abbreviations

AMPA   α-amino-3-hydroxy-5-methyl-4-isoxazole propionate

BrdU   Bromodeoxyuridine

cAMP   cyclic adenylate monophosphate

Cdk   cyclin-dependent kinase

CNS   central nervous system

CP   cortical plate

G   gestational day

GABA   γ-aminobutyric acid

GE   ganglionic eminence

[^{3}H]thymidine   [^{3}H]dT

IHZ   intrahilar zone

IZ   intermediate zone

LCN   local circuit neuron

MZ   marginal zone

NMDA   N-methyl-D-aspartate

PFC   prefrontal cortex

PN   projection neuron

PVE   pseudostratified ventricular epithelium

Q   probability of cell cycle exit

Rb   retinoblastoma protein

SPP   secondary proliferative population

SZ   subventricular zone

VZ   ventricular zone

References

Altman J, Bayer SA (1990) Migration and distribution of two populations of hippocampal granule cell precursors during the perinatal and postnatal periods. J Comp Neurol 301:365–381.

Anderson SA, Eisenstat DD, Shi L, Rubenstein JLR (1997a) Interneuron migration from basal forebrain to neocortex: dependence on *dlx* genes. Science 278:474–476.

Anderson SA, Marin O, Horn C, Jennings K, Rubenstein JL (2001) Distinct cortical migrations from the medial and lateral ganglionic eminences. Development 128:353–363.

Anderson SA, Qiu MS, Bulfone A, Eisenstat DD, Meneses J, Pedersen R, Rubenstein JLR (1997b) Mutations of the homeobox genes *dlx-1* and *dlx-2* disrupt the striatal subventricular zone and differentiation of late born striatal neurons. Neuron 19:27–37.

Ang ES Jr, Haydar TF, Gluncic V, Rakic P (2003) Four-dimensional migratory coordinates of GABAergic interneurons in the developing mouse cortex. J Neurosci 23:5805–5815.

Angevine JB, Sidman RL (1961) Autoradiographic study of cell migration during histogenesis of the cerebral cortex in the mouse. Nature 192:766–768.

Angevine JB Jr (1965) Time of neuron origin in the hippocampal region. An autoradiographic study in the mouse. Exp Neurol Suppl 2:1–70.

Antonopoulos J, Pappas IS, Parnavelas JG (1997) Activation of the GABA$_A$ receptor inhibits the proliferative effects of bFGF in cortical progenitor cells. Eur J Neurosci 9:291–298.

Bakowska JC, Morrell JI (1995) Quantitative autoradiographic analysis of D$_1$ and D$_2$ dopamine receptors in rat brain in early and late pregnancy. Brain Res 703:191–200.

Bayer SA (1982) Changes in the total number of dentate granule cells in juvenile and adult rats: a correlated volumetric and ^{3}H-thymidine autoradiographic study. Exp Brain Res 46:315–323.

—— (1984) Neurogenesis in the rat neostriatum. Intl J Dev Neurosci 2:163–175.

Bayer SA, Altman J (1987) Directions in neurogenetic gradients and patterns of anatomical connections in the telencephalon. Prog Neurobiol 29:57–106.

—— (1991) Neocortical Development. Raven Press, New York.

Beaulieu C (1993) Numerical data on neocortical neurons in adult rat, with special reference to the GABA population. Brain Res 609:284–292.

Behar TN, Schaffner AE, Scott CA, O'Connell C, Barker JL (1998) Differential response of cortical plate and ventricular zone cells to GABA as a migration stimulus. J Neurosci 18:6378–6387.

Berry M, Rogers AW (1965) The migration of neuroblasts in the developing cerebral cortex. J Anat 99:691–709.

Berry M, Rogers AW, Eayres JT (1964) Pattern of cell migration during cortical histogenesis. Nature 203:591–593.

Bhide PG (1996) Cell cycle kinetics in the embryonic mouse corpus striatum. J Comp Neurol 374:506–522.

Bittman K, Owens DF, Kriegstein AR, LoTurco JJ (1997) Cell coupling and uncoupling in the ventricular zone of developing neocortex. J Neurosci 17:7037–7044.

Boulder Committee (1970) Embryonic vertebrate nervous system: revised terminology. Anat Rec 166:257–262.

Brand S, Rakic P (1979) Genesis of the primate neostriatum: [^{3}H]thymidine autoradiographic analysis of the time of neuron origin in the rhesus monkey. Neuroscience 4:767–778.

Cai L, Hayes NL, Nowakowski RS (1997a) Local homogeneity of cell cycle length in developing mouse cortex. J Neurosci 17:2079–2087.

—— (1997b) Synchrony of clonal cell proliferation and contiguity of clonally related cells: production of mosaicism in the ventricular zone of developing mouse neocortex. J Neurosci 17:2088–2100.

Cameron HA, Woolley CS, McEwen BS, Gould E (1993) Differentiation of newly born neurons and glia in the dentate gyrus of the adult rat. Neuroscience 56:337–344.

Caviness VS Jr (1982) Neocortical histogenesis in normal and reeler mice: a developmental study based upon (3H) thymidine autoradiography. Dev Brain Res 4:293–302.

Caviness VS Jr, Goto T, Tarui T, Takahashi T, Bhide PG, Nowakowski RS (2003) Cell output, cell cycle duration and neuronal specification: a model of integrated mechanisms of the neocortical proliferative process. Cereb Cortex 13:592–598.

Caviness VS Jr, Sidman RL (1973) Time of origin of corresponding cell classes in the cerebral cortex of normal and reeler mutant mice: an autoradiographic analysis. J Comp Neurol 148:141–152.

Caviness VS Jr, Takahashi T, Miyama S, Nowakowski RS, Delalle I (1996) Regulation of normal proliferation in the developing cerebrum potential actions of trophic factors. Exp Neurol 137:357–366.

Caviness VS Jr, Takahashi T, Nowakowski RS (1995) Numbers, time and neocortical neuronogenesis: a general developmental and evolutionary model. Trends Neurosci 18:379–383.

—— (2000) Neuronogenesis and the early events of neocortical histogenesis. Results Prob Cell Differ 30:107–143.

Cheng M, Olivier P, Diehl JA, Fero M, Roussel MF, Roberts JM, Sherr CJ (1999) The p21(Cip1) and p27(Kip1) CDK 'inhibitors' are essential activators of cyclin D–dependent kinases in murine fibroblasts. EMBO J 18:1571–1583.

Cobas A, Fairén A (1988) GABAergic neurons of different morphological classes are cogenerated in the mouse barrel cortex. J Neurocytol 17:511–519.

Delalle I, Takahashi T, Nowakowski RS, Tsai LH, Caviness VS Jr (1999) Cyclin E-p27 opposition and regulation of the G1 phase of the cell cycle in the murine neocortical PVE: a quantitative analysis of mRNA in situ hybridization. Cereb Cortex 9:824–832.

Demarque M, Represa A, Becq H, Khalilov I, Ben-Ari Y, Aniksztejn L (2002) Paracrine intercellular communication by a Ca^{2+}- and SNARE-independent release of GABA and glutamate prior to synapse formation. Neuron 36:1051–1061.

Diaz J, Ridray S, Mignon V, Griffon N, Schwartz JC, Sokoloff P (1997) Selective expression of dopamine D$_3$ receptor mRNA in proliferative zones during embryonic development of the rat brain. J Neurosci 17:4282–4292.

Dyson N (1998) The regulation of E2F by pRB-family proteins. Genes Dev 12:2245–2262.

Fairén A, Cobas A, Fonseca M (1986) Times of generation of glutamic acid decarboxylase immunoreactive neurons in mouse somatosensory cortex. J Comp Neurol 251:67–83.

Fentress JC, Stanfield BB, Cowan WM (1981) Observations on the development of the striatum in mice and rats. Anat Embryol 163:275–298.

Ferguson KL, Callaghan SM, O'Hare MJ, Park DS, Slack RS (2000) The Rb-CDK4/6 signaling pathway is critical in neural precursor cell cycle regulation. J Biol Chem 275:33593–33600.

Fernandez V, Bravo H, Kuljis R, Fuentes I (1979) Autoradiographic study of the development of the neostriatum in the rabbit. Brain Behav Evol 16:113–128.

Fishell G, Rossant J, van der Kooy D (1990) Neuronal lineage in chimeric mouse forebrain are segregated between compartments and in the rostrocaudal and radial planes. Dev Biol 141:70–83.

Fishell G, van der Kooy D (1987) Pattern formation in the striatum: developmental changes in the distribution of striatonigral neurons. J Neurosci 7:1969–1978.

Frolov MV, Huen DS, Stevaux O, Dimova D, Balczarek-Strang K, Elsdon M, Dyson NJ (2001) Functional antagonism between E2F family members. Genes Dev 15:2146–2160.

Fujita S (1960) Mitotic pattern and histogenesis of the central nervous system. Nature 185:702–703.

Fujita S, Miyake S (1962) Selective labeling of cell groups and its application to cell identification. Exp Cell Res 28:158–161.

Gage FH, Kempermann G, Palmer TD, Peterson DA, Ray J (1998) Multipotent progenitor cells in the adult dentate gyrus. J Neurobiol 36:249–266.

Gerfen CR (1992) The neostriatal mosaic: multiple levels of compartmental organization. Trends Neurosci 15:133–139.

Gerfen CR, Wilson CJ (1996) The basal ganglia. In: Swanson L, Björklund A, Hökfelt T (eds). *Handbook of Chemical Neuroanatomy, Vol. 12, Integrated Systems in the CNS, Part III*. Elsevier. Amsterdam, pp 371–468.

Graybiel AM (1990) Neurotransmitters and neuromodulators in the basal ganglia. Trends Neurosci 13: 244–254.

Graybiel AM, Hickey TL (1982) Chemospecificity of ontogenetic units in the striatum: demonstration by combining [^{3}H]thymidine neuronography and histochemical staining. Proc Natl Acad Sci USA 79: 196–202.

Guennoun R, Bloch B (1993) D_2 dopamine receptor gene expression in the rat striatum during ontogeny: an in situ hybridization study. Dev Brain Res 60:79–87.

Haydar TF, Wang F, Schwartz ML, Rakic P (2000) Differential modulation of proliferation in the neocortical ventricular and subventricular zones. J Neurosci 20:5764–5774.

Hayes NL, Nowakowski RS (2000) Exploiting the dynamics of S-phase tracers in developing brain: interkinetic nuclear migration for cells entering versus leaving the S phase. Dev Neurosci 22:44–55.

Hewitt W (1958) The development of the human caudate and amygdaloid nuclei. J Anat 92:377.

His W (1887) Zur Geschichte des menschlichen Rueckenmarks und der Nervenwurzeln. Abh and lg Saechs Ges Wissensch Math Phys Kl 13:479–513.

Hockfield S, McKay RD (1985) Identification of major cell classes in the developing mammalian nervous system. J Neurosci 5:3310–3328.

Huntley GW, Hendry SH, Killackey HP, Chalupa LM, Jones EG (1988) Temporal sequence of neurotransmitter expression by developing neurons of fetal monkey visual cortex. Brain Res 471:69–96.

Jung AB, Bennett JP Jr (1996) Development of striatal dopaminergic function. 1. Pre- and postnatal development of mRNAs and binding sites for striatal D1 (D1a) and D2 (D2a) receptors. Dev Brain Res 94: 109–120.

Kato J-Y, Matsuoka M, Polyak K, Massagué J, Sherr CJ (1994) Cyclic AMP–induced G1 phase arrest mediated by an inhibitor (p27kip1) of cyclin-dependent kinase 4 activation. Cell 79:487–496.

Kempermann G, Jessberger S, Steiner B, Kronenberg G (2004) Milestones of neuronal development in the adult hippocampus. Trends Neurosci 27:447–452.

LaBaer J, Garrett M, Stevenson L, Slingerland J, Sandhu C, Chou H, Harlow E (1997) New functional activities for the p21 family of CDK inhibitors. Genes Dev 11:847–862.

Lammers GJ, Gribnau AAM, Ten Donkelaar HJ (1980) Neurogenesis in the basal forebrain in the Chinese hamster (*Cricetululus griseus*). II. Site of neuron origin: morphogenesis of ventricular ridges. Anat Embryol 158:193–211.

Lauder JM (1988) Neurotransmitters as morphogens. Prog Brain Res 73:365–387.

Lavdas AA, Grigoriou M, Pachnis V, Parnavelas JG (1999) The medial ganglionic eminence gives rise to a population of early neurons in the developing cerebral cortex. J Neurosci 99:7881–7888.

Letinic K, Zoncu R, Rakic P (2002) Origin of GABAergic neurons in the human neocortex. Nature 417: 645–649.

LeVine SM, Goldman JE (1988a) Embryonic divergence of oligodendrocyte and astrocyte lineages in developing rat cerebrum. J Neurosci 8:3992–4006.

—— (1988b) Spatial and temporal patterns of oligodendrocyte differentiation in rat cerebrum and cerebellum. J Comp Neurol 277:441–455.

Levison SW, Goldman JE (1993) Both oligodendrocytes and astrocytes develop from progenitors in the subventricular zone of postnatal rat forebrain. Neuron 10:201–212.

Levitt P, Harvey JA, Friedman E, Simansky K, Murphy EH (1997) New evidence for neurotransmitter influences on brain development. Trends Neurosci 20:269–274.

LoTurco JJ, Kriegstein AR (1991) Clusters of coupled neuroblasts in embryonic neocortex. Science 252: 563–566.

LoTurco JJ, Owens DF, Heath MJS, Davis MBE, Kriegstein AR (1995) GABA and glutamate depolarize cortical progenitor cells and inhibit DNA synthesis. Neuron 15:1287–1298.

Lu NR, DiCicco-Bloom E (1997) Pituitary adenylate cyclase–activating polypeptide is an autocrine inhibitor of mitosis in cultured cortical precursor cells. Proc Natl Acad Sci USA 94:3357–3362.

Luk KC, Kennedy TE, Sadikot AF (2003) Glutamate promotes proliferation of striatal neuronal progenitors by an NMDA receptor–mediated mechanism. J Neurosci 23:2239–2250.

Luk KC, Sadikot AF (2004) Glutamate and regulation of proliferation in the developing mammalian telencephalon. Dev Neurosci 26:218–228.

Malatesta P, Hack MA, Hartfuss E, Kettenmann H, Klinkert W, Kirchhoff F, Gotz M (2003) Neuronal or glial progeny: regional differences in radial glia fate. Neuron 37:751–764.

Malatesta P, Hartfuss E, Gotz M (2000) Isolation of radial glial cells by fluorescent-activated cell sorting reveals a neuronal lineage. Development 127:5253–5263.

Marchand R, Lajoie L (1986) Histogenesis of the striopallidal system in the rat. Neurogenesis of its neurons. Neuroscience 17:573–590.

Marin O, Anderson SA, Rubenstein JL (2000) Origin and molecular specification of striatal interneurons. J Neurosci 20:6063–6076.

Marin-Padilla M (1983) Structural organization of the human cerebral cortex prior to the appearance of the cortical plate. Anat Embryol 168:21–40.

Miller MW (1985) Cogeneration of retrogradely labeled corticocortical projection and GABA-immunoreactive local circuit neurons in cerebral cortex. Brain Res 355:187–192.

—— (1988a) Effect of prenatal exposure to ethanol on the development of cerebral cortex: I. Neuronal generation. Alcohol Clin Exp Res 12:440–449.

—— (1988b) Maturation of rat visual cortex. IV. Generation, migration, morphogenesis and connectivity of a typically oriented pyramidal neurons. J Comp Neurol 274:387–405.

—— (1989) Effects of prenatal exposure to ethanol on neocortical development: II. Cell proliferation in the ventricular and subventricular zones of the rat. J Comp Neurol 287:326–338.

—— (1993) Migration of cortical neurons is altered by gestational exposure to ethanol. Alcohol Clin Exp Res 17:304–314.

—— (1999) Kinetics of the migration of neurons to rat somatosensory cortex. Dev Brain Res 115:111–122.

Miller MW, Kuhn PE (1995) Cell cycle kinetics in fetal rat cerebral cortex: effects of prenatal treatment with ethanol assessed by a cumulative labeling technique with flow cytometry. Alcohol Clin Exp Res 19: 233–237.

Miller MW, Nowakowski RS (1988) Use of bromodeoxyuridine-immunohistochemistry to examine the proliferation, migration and time of origin of cells in the central nervous system. Brain Res 457:44–52.

—— (1991) Effect of prenatal exposure to ethanol on the cell cycle kinetics and growth fraction in the proliferative zones of fetal rat cerebral cortex. Alcohol Clin Exp Res 15:229–232.

Miller MW, Robertson S (1993) Prenatal exposure to ethanol alters the postnatal development and transformation of radial glia to astrocytes in the cortex. J Comp Neurol 337:253–266.

Misson J-P, Austin CP, Takahashi T, Cepko CL, Caviness VS Jr (1991) The alignment of migrating neural cells in relation to the murine neopallial radial glial fiber system. Cereb Cortex 1:221–229.

Miyama S, Takahashi T, Goto T, Bhide PG, Caviness VS Jr (2001) Continuity with ganglionic eminence modulates interkinetic nuclear migration in the neocortical pseudostratified ventricular epithelium. Exp Neurol 169:486–495.

Monsma FJ, Mahan LC, McVittie LD, Gerfen CR, Sibley DR (1990) Molecular cloning and expression of a D1 dopamine receptor linked to adenylyl cyclase activation. Proc Natl Acad Sci USA 87:6723–6727.

Morgan DO (1997) Cyclin-dependent kinases: engines, clocks, and microprocessors. Annu Rev Cell Dev Biol 13:261–291.

Murray A, Hunt T (1993) The Cell Cycle. WH Freeman, New York.

Murray AW (2004) Recycling the cell cycle: cyclins revisited. Cell 116:221–234.

Nery S, Fishell G, Corbin JG (2002) The caudal ganglionic eminence is a source of distinct cortical and subcortical cell populations. Nat Neurosci 5:1279–1287.

Nguyen L, Rigo JM, Rocher V, Belachew S, Malgrange B, Rogister B, Leprince P, Moonen G (2001) Neurotransmitters as early signals for central nervous system development. Cell Tissue Res 305:187–202.

Noctor SC, Flint AC, Weissman TA, Dammerman RS, Kriegstein AR (2001) Neurons derived from radial glial cells establish radial units in neocortex. Nature 409:714–720.

Noctor SC, Martinez-Cerdeno V, Ivic L, Kriegstein AR (2004) Cortical neurons arise in symmetric and asymmetric division zones and migrate through specific phases. Nat Neurosci 7:136–144.

Ohtani N, Goto T, Waeber C, Bhide PG (2003) Dopamine modulates cell cycle in the lateral ganglionic eminence. J Neurosci 23:2840–2850.

Owens DF, Kriegstein AR (2002) Is there more to GABA than synaptic inhibition? Nat Rev Neurosci 3: 715–727.

Owens DF, Liu X, Kriegstein AR (1999) Changing properties of GABA(A) receptor–mediated signaling during early neocortical development. J Neurophysiol 82:570–583.

Peters A, Kara DA, Harriman KM (1985) The neuronal composition of area 17 of rat visual cortex. III. Numerical considerations. J Comp Neurol 238: 263–274.

Popolo M, McCarthy DM, Bhide PG (2004) Influence of dopamine on precursor cell proliferation and differentiation in the embryonic mouse telencephalon. Dev Neurosci 26:229–244.

Powell EM, Mars WM, Levitt P (2001) Hepatocyte growth factor/scatter factor is a motogen for interneurons migrating from the ventral to dorsal telencephalon. Neuron 30:79–89.

Puelles L, Rubenstein JLR (1993) Expression patterns of homeobox and other putative regulatory genes in the embryonic mouse forebrain suggests a neuromeric organization. Trends Neurosci 16: 472–479.

Rakic P (1972) Mode of cell migration to the superficial layers of fetal monkey neocortex J Comp Neurol 145:61–84.

Rakic P, Stensas LJ, Sayre E, Sidman RL (1974) Computer-aided three-dimensional reconstruction and quantitative analysis of cells from serial electron microscopic montages of foetal monkey brain. Nature 250:31–34.

Ren JQ, Aika Y, Heizmann CW, Kosaka T (1992) Quantitative analysis of neurons and glial cells in the rat somatosensory cortex, with special reference to GABAergic neurons and parvalbumin-containing neurons. Exp Brain Res 92:1–14.

Ross ME (1996) Cell division and the nervous system: regulating the cycle from neural differentiaition to death. Trends Neurosci 19:62–68.

Rubenstein JL, Shimamura K, Martinez S, Puelles L (1998) Regionalization of the prosencephalic neural plate. Annu Rev Neurosci 21:445–477.

Sadikot AF, Burhan AM, Belanger MC, Sasseville R (1998) NMDA receptor antagonists influence early development of GABAergic interneurons in the mammalian striatum. Dev Brain Res 105:35–42.

Sadikot AF, Sasseville R (1997) Neurogenesis in the mammalian neostriatum and nucleus accumbens: parvalbumin-immunoreactive GABAergic interneurons. J Comp Neurol 389:193–211.

Sales N, Martres MP, Bouthenet ML, Schwartz JC (1989) Ontogeny of dopaminergic D2 receptors in the rat nervous system: characterization and detailed autoradiographic mapping with [^{125}I]iodosulpiride. Neuroscience 28:673–700.

Sauer FC (1936) The interkinetic migration of embryonic epithelial nuclei. J Morphol 60:1–11.

Schambra UB, Duncan GE, Breese GR, Fornaretto MG, Caron MG, Fremeau RT Jr (1994) Ontogeny of D1A and D2 dopamine receptor subtypes in rat brain using in situ hybridization and receptor binding. Neuroscience 62:65–85.

Semba K, Vincent SR, Fibiger HC (1988) Different times of origin of choline acetyltransferase- and somatostatin-immunoreactive neurons in the rat striatum. J Neurosci 8:3937–3944.

Shearman LP, Zeitzer J, Weaver DR (1997) Widespread expression of functional D1-dopamine receptors in fetal rat brain. Dev Brain Res 102:105–115.

Sherr CJ, Roberts JM (1999) CDK inhibitors: positive and negative regulators of G1-phase progression. Genes Dev 13:1501–1512.

Sheth AN, Bhide PG (1997) Concurrent cellular output from two proliferative populations in the early embryonic mouse corpus striatum. J Comp Neurol 383:220–230.

Sidman RL (1970) Autoradiographic methods and principles for study of the nervous system with thymidine-H^3. In: Nauta WJH, Ebbesson SOE (eds). *Contemporary Research Methods in Neuroanatomy.* Springer, New York, pp 252–274.

Sidman RL, Miale IL, Feder N (1959) Cell proliferation and migration in the primitive ependymal zone: an autoradiographic study of histogenesis in the nervous system. Exp Neurol 1:322–333.

Siegenthaler JA, Miller MW (2005) Transforming growth factor β1 promoter cell cycle exit through the cyclin-dependent kinose inhibitor p21 in the developing cerebral cortex. J Neurosci 25:8627–8636.

Smart IH (1961) The subependymal layer of the mouse brain and its cell production as shown by radioautography after thymidine-H^3 injection. J Comp Neurol 116:325–347.

Smart IH, LeBlond CP (1961) Evidence for division and transformations of neuroglia cells in the mouse brain, as derived from radioautography after injection of thymidine-H^3. J Comp Neurol 116:349–367.

Smart IHM (1976) A pilot study of cell production by the ganglionic eminences of the developing mouse brain. J Anat 121:71–84.

Smart IHM, McSherry GM (1982) Growth patterns in the lateral wall of the mouse telencephalon. II. Histological changes during and subsequent to the period of isocortical neuron production. J Anat 134:415–442.

Smart IHM, Sturrock RR (1979) Ontogeny of the neostriatum. In: Divac I, Oberg R (eds). *The Neostriatum*. Plenum Press, Oxford, pp 127–146.

Song DD, Harlan RE (1994) Genesis and migration patterns of neurons forming the patch and matrix compartments of the rat striatum. Dev Brain Res 83: 233–245.

Stanfield BB, Cowan WM (1979) The development of the hippocampus and dentate gyrus in normal and reeler mice. J Comp Neurol 185:423–459.

Stenman J, Toresson H, Campbell K (2003) Identification of two distinct progenitor populations in the lateral ganglionic eminence: implications for striatal and olfactory bulb neurogenesis. J Neurosci 23:167–174.

Takahashi T, Caviness VS Jr, Bhide PG (2002) Analysis of cell generation in the telencephalic neuroepithelium. Methods Mol Biol 198:101–113.

Takahashi T, Goto T, Miyama S, Nowakowski RS, Caviness VS Jr (1999) Sequence of neuron origin and neocortical laminar fate: relation to cell cycle of origin in the developing murine cerebral wall. J Neurosci 19:10357–10371.

Takahashi T, Misson J-P, Caviness VS Jr. (1990) Glial process elongation and branching in the developing murine neocortex: a qualitative and quantitative immunohistochemical analysis. J Comp Neurol 302:15–28.

Takahashi T, Nowakowski RS, Caviness VS Jr (1992) BUdR as an S-phase marker for quantitative studies of cytokinetic behaviour in the murine cerebral ventricular zone. J Neurocytol 21:185–197.

—— (1993) Cell cycle parameters and patterns of nuclear movement in the neocortical proliferative zone of the fetal mouse. J Neurosci 13:820–833.

—— (1995) Early ontogeny of the secondary proliferative population of the embryonic murine cerebral wall. J Neurosci 15:6058–6068.

—— (1996) The leaving or Q fraction of the murine cerebral proliferative epithelium: a general model of neocortical neueonogenesis. J Neurosci 16:6183–6196.

—— (1997) The mathematics of neocortical neuronogenesis. Dev Neurosci 19:17–22.

Tamamaki N, Fujimori KE, Takauji R (1997) Origin and route of tangentially migrating neurons in the developing neocortical intermediate zone. J Neurosci 17:8313–8323.

Tarui T, Takahashi T, Nowakowski RS, Hayes NL, Bhide PG, Caviness VS (2005) Overexpression of p27Kip1, probability of cell cycle exit, and laminar destination of neocortical neurons. Cereb Cortex 15: 1345–1355.

Valcanis H, Tan SS (2003) Layer specification of transplanted interneurons in developing mouse neocortex. J Neurosci 23:5113–5122.

van Praag H, Schinder AF, Christie BR, Toni N, Palmer TD, Gage FH (2002) Functional neurogenesis in the adult hippocampus. Nature 415:1030–1034.

Voigt T (1989) Development of glial cells in the cerebral wall of ferrets: direct tracing of their transformation from radial glia into astrocytes. J Comp Neurol 289:74–88.

Weissman T, Noctor SC, Clinton BK, Honig LS, Kriegstein AR (2003) Neurogenic radial glial cells in reptile, rodent and human: from mitosis to migration. Cereb Cortex 13:550–559.

Zhang L, Bai J, Undie AS, Bergson C, Lidow MS (2005) D1 dopamine receptor regulation of the levels of the cell-cycle-controlling proteins, cyclin D, p27 and Raf-1, in cerebral cortical precursor cells is mediated through cAMP-independent pathways. Cereb Cortex 15:74–84.

Zhang L, Lidow MS (2002) D1 dopamine receptor regulation of cell cycle in FGF- and EGF-supported primary cultures of embryonic cerebral cortical precursor cells. Intl J Dev Neurosci 20:593–606.

Zindy F, Cunningham JJ, Sherr CJ, Jogal S, Smeyne RJ, Roussel MF (1999) Postnatal neuronal proliferation in mice lacking Ink4d and Kip1 inhibitors of cyclin-dependent kinases. Proc Natl Acad Sci USA 96:13462–13467.

Zindy F, Soares H, Herzog KH, Morgan J, Sherr CJ, Roussel MF (1997) Expression of INK4 inhibitors of cyclin D-dependent kinases during mouse brain development. Cell Growth Differ 8:1139–1150.

3

Neuronal Migration

Huaiyu Hu

During development of the mammalian central nervous system (CNS), neurons are commonly generated at sites far from their final location (see Chapters 2, 11, and 12). They migrate to an anlage before differentiating into their final morphology and making synaptic connections (see Chapter 4). Disturbances of neuronal migration underlie brain disorders such as mental retardation and epilepsy (Dobyns and Truwit, 1995; Raymond et al., 1995; Dobyns et al., 1996).

Neuronal migration is widespread throughout the developing peripheral nervous system. For example, neurons using luteinizing hormone releasing hormone (LHRH) are generated in the developing olfactory placode, a transient structure outside the brain. They migrate long distances to their final locations in the medial basal forebrain and hypothalamus. In contrast, some neurons migrate from the CNS. A prime example is neural crest cells. These cells are derived from the dorsal neural tube and give rise to

the neurons and glia of the peripheral nervous system as well as non-neural cells, for example, facial skeleton, segments of the heart and great arteries, and pigment cells in the skin (see Chapter 17).

Most studies of neuronal migration have focused on neocortex. This is (a) because defects in neuronal migration causing clinical disorders are commonly associated with cortex and (b) because cortex has a highly defined structural and functional organization that derives chiefly from an orderly neuronal migration. Cortical neurons are generated in the neuroepithelium surrounding the lateral ventricles (Chapters 2, 11, and 12). The rules defining neuronal migration appear to be similar among mammalian species. This present chapter focuses on rodents.

Neuronal migration involves four coordinated steps outlined below.

1. The process begins as cells pass through mitosis and permanently exit from the cell cycle (see

Chapters 2 and 11). In the rodent, this occurs during the second half of gestation (Angevine and Sidman, 1961; Lund and Mustari, 1977; Gardette et al., 1982; Miller, 1985).

2. Postmitotic neurons prepare to migrate. They remain in the proliferative zones for up to 18–26 hours, the amount of time increasing with the age of the fetus (Miller, 1999). During this time young neurons extend their leading processes which boast pioneering filopodia and lamellipodia that explore the environment and define the direction of movement (Rakic, 1972). They may move laterally within the proliferative zones (Noctor et al., 2004).

3. The neurons actively move from the proliferative zones through the intermediate zone and enter the immature gray matter. This step involves the choreographed movement of the nucleus toward the leading process and the retraction of the trailing process (Hatten and Mason, 1990; Rakic et al., 1996). Neuronal migration in the neocortex of mice and rats is completed by the end of the first postnatal week (Berry and Rogers, 1965; Miller, 1999).

4. When a neuron reaches its final destination, its nucleus ceases the forward movement. At this site, the neuron differentiates and elaborates a characteristic morphology (Miller, 1981, 1986).

The migration of neocortical neurons can follow a radial or tangential path (Rakic, 1990; Miller, 1992; Nadarajah and Parnavelas, 2002) (Fig. 3–1). The former describes a process whereby neurons migrate in a direction perpendicular to the surface of the lateral

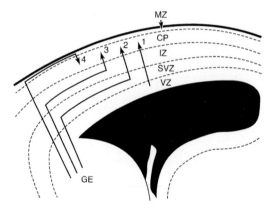

FIGURE 3–1 Multiple migration routes of cerebral cortical neurons. Cerebral cortical projection neurons are generated in the ventricular zone (VZ) and subventricular zone (SZ) of the developing cerebral wall. The migration route of these neurons is radial (1). Local circuit neurons are generated in the medial ganglionic eminence (GE). They undertake several migration routes (2, 3, and 4) that involve tangential migration and radial migration. CP, cortical plate; IZ, intermediate zone; MZ, marginal zone.

ventricles (pathway 1), whereas the latter refers to neurons as they migrate along a pathway that parallels the surface of the lateral ventricle (pathways 2–4). This chapter reviews the basic principles of radial and tangential migration, molecular events underlying normal neuronal migration, and some molecular defects that disturb neuronal migration to cause neurological disorders (Table 3–1).

TABLE 3–1 Genetics of neuronal migration disorders in humans

Protein and Function	Gene	Structural Phenotype
Filamin A, actin binding protein	FLNA	Periventricular heterotopia
Doublecortin, microtubule-associated protein	Dcx	Double cortcortex syndromes Subcortical band heterotopia
LIS1/PAFAHIb, interacts with tubulin, dynein, NUDEL, mNUDE	PAFAHIB	Type I lissencephaly
Reelin, ECM protein	Reln	Lissencephaly
POMT1, presumed glycosyltransferase	POMT1	Walker-Warburg syndrome Polymicrogyria
POMT2, presumed glycosyltransferase	POMT2	Walker-Warburg syndrome Polymicrogyria
POMGnT1, glycosyltransferase	POMGnT1	Muscle–eye–brain disease Polymicrogyria
Fukutin, presumed glycosyltransferase	FCMD	Fukuyama congenital muscular dystrophy Polymicrogyria
Large, presumed glycosyltransferase	Large	MDC1D, Polymicrogyria

PATHWAYS OF MIGRATION

Radial Migration

Most cortical neurons, notably projection neurons, are derived from progenitors in the ventricular zone (VZ) and subventricular zone (SZ). These zones are located along the internal aspect of the cerebral wall. Most VZ and SZ cells migrate to cortex via a radial pathway. Radial migration appears to involve at least two mechanisms.

The first cohort of neurons that moves out of the germinal area forms the preplate (Marin-Padilla, 1978; Allendorfer and Shatz, 1994). During the earliest stages of cortical development, neurons take positions in the preplate via somatic translocation (Brittis et al., 1995; Miyata et al., 2001; Nadarajah et al., 2001; Nadarajah and Parnavelas, 2002). Each of these neurons sends a long process toward the pial surface as it leaves the VZ. Subsequently, a migrating neuron releases its ventricular attachments, but maintains its pial contacts.

The second, and larger cohort of migrating neurons splits the preplate into two layers: the marginal zone (MZ) and the subplate (SP), the anlage of layers I and VIb, respectively. These newly arrived neurons take a position between the MZ and SP and form the cortical plate (CP). The CP is laid down by an inside-out sequence in which early-generated neurons take a position in the deeper CP and waves of later-generated neurons migrate to position in succeedingly superficial positions (Angevine and Sidman, 1961; Rakic, 1974; Miller, 1985; McConnell, 1995). The CP differentiates into layers II–VIa.

Neurons move into the CP migrate radially via a different mode of migration than that used by neurons forming the preplate. The CP-destined neurons use radial glia as a physical substrate for their migration (Rakic, 1972, 1990; Hatten, 1999) (Fig. 3–2). During migration, each neuron has a short leading process that is not attached to the pial surface and a trailing process that eventually loses its contact with the ventricular surface. Radial glial guidance provides a mechanism for later-generated neurons to find positions beyond the postmigratory neurons, hence establishing the inside-out pattern characteristic of the CP. This migration is relatively fast. Apparently, regardless of when the neurons are generated, they migrate at a rate of ~120 μm per day (Miller, 1999). Similar rates are evident in the radial migration of hippocampal neurons from the VZ (Nowakowski and Rakic, 1981).

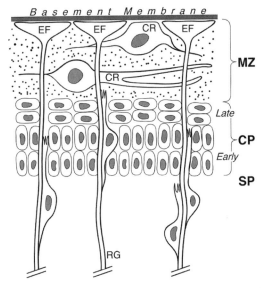

FIGURE 3–2 Radial migration during development of the cerebral cortex. Neurons migrate along the radial glia (RG) to the cortical plate (CP) where later-born neurons migrate past the early-born neurons. Reelin (illustrated as dots) secreted by Cajal-Retzius neurons (CR) in the marginal zone (MZ) is required for the inside-out pattern of lamination. Within the MZ, radial glial endfeet (EF) form the so-called glial-limiting membrane. Together with some Cajal-Retzius cells, these endfeet appose the brain surface basement membrane. SP, subplate.

Radial glia span the full depth of the developing cerebral wall. In the intermediate zone (IZ), the radial glial fibers are grouped in fascicles (Gressens and Evrard, 1993). In the mouse, these cells are evident during the period of neurogenesis and beyond the cessation of neuronal migration in neocortex (Miller and Robertson, 1993). After neuronal migration is complete, radial glia appear to transform to astrocytes (Schmechel and Rakic, 1979; Misson et al., 1988; Voigt, 1989; Miller and Robertson, 1993). For many years, the identity of radial glia has been considered part of the astrocyte lineage. On the basis of recent data, however, it appears that radial glia are not glia—rather, they are neural stem cells (Malatesta et al., 2000; Miyata et al., 2001; Noctor et al., 2001). They express markers for cytoskeletal proteins for immature (stem) cells, for example, nestin and RC-2, and they can generate neurons and glia.

Tangential Migration

Analyses of forebrain neurons with retroviral markers show that a neuronal clone derived from a single founder is dispersed far wider than would have been predicted if neurons only migrated radially (Luskin et al., 1988; Walsh and Cepko, 1988). Although most neurons are tightly distributed in radial columns of ~200 µm, a notable number are located as much as 2 mm from this column. In these clones, cells tend to be projection neurons or local circuit neurons (LCNs) (Luskin et al., 1988, 1993; Parnavelas et al., 1991). The distribution of the retrovirally labeled cells is equally broad for clones of projection and local circuit neurons. This dispersion principally results from the tangential movement of cells within the proliferative zones before they ascend radially.

On the basis of findings from tract tracing studies, it appears that neurons generated in the ganglionic eminence (GE) migrate to neocortex (de Carlos et al., 1996). Molecular and anatomical studies show that these neurons are LCNs (e.g., Anderson et al., 1997; Powell et al., 2001; Marin and Rubenstein, 2003). These LCNs migrate through the SZ, IZ, or MZ (Fig. 3–1) (Tamanaki et al., 1997; Lavdas et al., 1999; Anderson et al., 2001; Ang et al., 2003). Accordingly, the neurons loop around the lateral GE and course along the VZ–SZ interface, in the IZ external to the SZ, or through the MZ. After finding their tangential position, the neurons associate with a radial glia and migrate radially to their appropriate laminar residence. This is supported by data showing that LCNs migrate to cortex via an inside-out pattern (Miller, 1985, 1986, 1992; Fairén et al., 1986; Cobas and Fairén, 1988). An exception is a subpopulation of LCNs that express vasoactive intestinal polypeptide (Miller, 1992). For these neurons, there is no birthdate- or lamina-specific pattern of the migration.

The tangential pathways are important because many neocortical LCNs migrate via one of these pathways; dlx knockout mice (mice in which no neurons are generated in the GE) have less than one-quarter of the LCNs evident in wild-type mice (Anderson et al., 1997). This finding concurs with those from retroviral tracing studies showing that clones commonly consist of either projection neurons or LCNs (Luskin et al., 1988, 1993; Parnavelas et al., 1991). Recent evidence (Ang et al., 2003; Noctor et al., 2004) shows that LCNs derived from the GE that migrate at the VZ–SZ interface can dip into the VZ and re-enter the cell cycle before they begin their radial migration. This observation contributes to the finding that cells remain in the proliferative zones before they commence their radial migration (Miller, 1999). Nevertheless, the tangential migration is sufficiently fast that LCNs generated in the GE and cohort projection neurons generated concurrently in the VZ and SZ migrate to cortex in tandem (Miller, 1985, 1986, 1988, 1997).

Neurons migrating tangentially rely on diverse substrates. LHRH expressing neurons migrate on axons as they move to their target (Schwanzel-Fukuda and Pfaff, 1990). Other migrating neurons migrate over "resident" cells. These include olfactory LCNs migrating through the anterior subventricular zone (SZa) on their way to the olfactory bulb (Luskin, 1993; Lois et al.,1996). The substrate for the tangential migration of neurons from the medial GE to neocortex is unknown; there is no axonal or glial system for guidance. Thus, these neurons presumably migrate over cells in the various compartments of the developing cerebral wall (Anderson et al., 1997).

FACTORS REGULATING NEURONAL MIGRATION

Soluble Stimulating Factors

Soluble factors can modulate radial migration. Migrating cortical neurons express TrkB, the high-affinity receptor for brain-derived neurotrophic factor (BDNF) and neurotrophin-4 (NT-4) (Behar et al., 1997). This suggests a role of BDNF and NT-4 in their migration. Indeed, BDNF and NT-4 promote the migration of cortical neurons in vitro. Consistent with culture studies, BDNF or NT-4 infusion into the lateral ventricle or application in culture slices induces heterotopias, which result from the overmigration of neurons (Brunstrom et al., 1997). Epidermal growth factor receptor (EGFr) and its ligands, including epidermal growth factor and transforming growth factor (TGF) α, are expressed in the developing cortex (Kornblum et al., 1997). Mice lacking EGFr exhibit more cells in the proliferative zones, a finding suggesting inhibited migration, whereas high concentrations of EGFr in the embryonic cortex enhance radial migration (Threadgill et al., 1995, Caric et al., 2001).

Tangential migration is stimulated by growth factors. One such ligand is hepatocyte growth factor (HGF). It is expressed in the telencephalon during LCN migration from the medial GE to the pallium (Powell et al., 2001). HGF increases the number of cells migrating away from the subpallium, and neutralization of HGF by blocking antibodies inhibits this migration. In addition, BDNF and NT-4 strongly stimulate the migration of LCNs that use γ-aminobutyric acid (GABA) as a neurotransmitter (Polleux et al., 2002).

TGFβ promotes neuronal migration. TGFβ1 and 2 are expressed by cells in the developing cortex; TGFβ1, by neurons; and TGFβ2, by radial glia, particularly their inner segments (Miller, 2003). Elements in developing cortex also express TGFβ receptors—TGFβIr predominantly by radial glia and TGFβIIr by neurons. Thus, developing cortex contains the components needed for TGFβ to mediate neuron–glia interactions through bidirectional paracrine mechanism. Also, it appears that TGFβ is involved in early stages of neuronal migration (stages 1, 2, and 3). These conclusions are supported by findings from complementary *in vitro* studies. TGFβ1 inhibits the proliferation of B104 neuroblastoma cells (Luo and Miller, 1999) and cultured cortical neurons (Miller and Luo, 2002a). In addition, TGFβ1 moves VZ cells in slices of cerebral cortex out of the cycling population and accelerates the rate of neuronal migration by 70% (Siegenthaler and Miller, 2005). The latter effect is concentration-dependent. Migration is maximally potentiated by exposure to TGFβ1 at a concentration of 10 ng/ml. In contrast, exposure to a higher or lower concentration has little effect or it can even retard neuronal migration.

Besides growth factors, neurotransmitters are involved in modulating neuronal migration. GABA is present in the developing cortex (Rickmann et al., 1977; Miller, 1986). It promotes cortical neurons to migrate through GABA receptors (Behar et al., 1996, 2001). It appears that $GABA_{A/C}$ receptors are involved in migration from the proliferative zones to the IZ whereas $GABA_B$ receptors are involved in migration from the IZ to the CP. Another neurotransmitter, N-methyl-D-aspartate (NMDA), is also shown to modulate radial migration (Behar et al., 1999). Pharmacological blockade of NMDA receptor activity decreases migration whereas enhancement of NMDA receptor activity increases the rate of cell movement.

Cell Adhesion Molecules

Interactions between migrating neurons and their substrates are mediated by cell adhesion molecules.

Astrotactin (Astn) 1 is a glycoprotein expressed by the migrating neurons (Fishell and Hatten, 1991; Zheng et al., 1996). Antibodies that block the functions of astrotactin abolish the adhesion between neurons and glia, thus reducing the rate of migration (Stitt and Hatten, 1990). In vivo, mice deficient in astrotactin display slowed radial migration (Adams et al., 2002).

Integrins are cell surface receptors that have been shown to regulate the migration of many cell types including neurons. They mediate essential cell–cell and cell–extracellular matrix interactions required for cell migration. Blocking of integrin α_3 by specific antibodies reduces the rate of migration and results in detachment of neurons from radial glial fibers (Anton et al., 1999; Dulabon et al., 2000). In mice deficient in integrin α_3, some neurons appear to stop migrating prematurely and fail to migrate to their appropriate layer. Similarly, antibodies against α_v integrin also perturb neuron–glia interactions and may affect neuronal migration as well.

The *neural cell adhesion molecule* (nCAM) is a member of the immunoglobulin superfamily of cell adhesion molecules thought to play a role in chain migration. It has an unusual carbohydrate modification called *polysialic acid*, a linear polymer of sialic acid (Finne et al., 1983; Rutishauser, 1996). In nCAM knockout mice, many olfactory LCN precursors are retarded in the SZa and fail to migrate to the olfactory bulb (Tomasiewicz et al., 1993; Cremer et al., 1994). Interestingly, removal of the polysialic acid moiety of nCAM by a specific enzyme in wild-type animals completely mimicked this knockout phenotype (Ono et al., 1994). Cell migration in vitro is severely abolished in collagen cultures in which polysialic acid is removed (Hu et al., 1996). Thus, the carbohydrate modification of nCAM, polysialic acid, plays an important role in the migration of olfactory LCNs.

TGFβ1 induces nCAM and integrin expression. Studies of cortical slices show that these effects are concentration-dependent; nCAM and integrin expression increase with increased TGFβ1 concentration (Siegenthaler and Miller, 2004). Likewise, TGFβ1 potentiates nCAM expression by cultured cortical astrocytes (Luo and Miller, 1999), neurons, and neuroblastoma cells (Miller and Luo, 2002b). In light of the effect of TGFβ1 on the rate of neuronal migration (see above), it appears that increased nCAM and integrin expression is facilitatory, but only to a certain point. If the extracellular space becomes too rich in cell adhesion proteins, neuronal migration is impeded, possibly because the microenvironment becomes too sticky.

Extracellular Matrix Molecule Reelin

Modern mouse genetics have provided some mutations with neuronal migration disorders (Table 3–2). The *reeler* mouse has received greater attention from developmental neurobiologists than has any other mouse mutants. This mouse exhibits characteristic lamination defects of cerebral cortex, the hippocampus, and the cerebellum (Rakic and Caviness, 1995; Lambert de Rouvroit and Goffinet, 1998). In the mutants, neocortical neurons are generated in the VZ and SZ as in the wild-type animals and initially their migration seems normal. A major difference is that the preplate is never split into the MZ and the SP; therefore, the CP forms under the so-called superplate. As the migrating neurons approach the CP, neurons in the *reeler* mice fail to form normal architectonic organizations. Instead of forming by an inside-out pattern of neuronogenesis, the birthdate of neurons in the mutant cortex is reversed. Early-generated neurons are located superficially and late-generated neurons are distributed in deep cortex. Remarkably, despite the positioning defects, neurons do make correct connections, although the axonal pathways are distorted.

The cloning of the defective gene *relin* has increased interest in this mutation (D'Arcangelo et al., 1995). Reelin is expressed by Cajal-Retzius neurons in the MZ of the developing cerebral wall (D'Arcangelo et al., 1997). How reelin functions in neuronal migration is an area of intense research; no consensus has been reached. Most results support the idea that reelin controls lamination by acting as a stop signal for migrating neurons (Dulabon et al., 2000). Accordingly, neurons migrate past the previously deposited neurons in the lower CP where reelin is not expressed. The migrating neurons proceed to the superficial edge of the CP bordering the MZ where reelin is expressed (Curran and D'Arcangelo, 1998). This finding implies that reelin tells the neurons to stop migrating. Some of the migration defects characteristic of the *reeler* mice, such as the lack of splitting of the preplate, is rescued in transgenic mice in which reelin expression is targeted in the VZ and SZ. Thus, the role of reelin in developing cortex is more complicated than simply providing a migratory stop signal (Magdaleno et al., 2002).

Reelin binds to two receptors expressed by migrating neurons, ApoE receptor 2 and very low–density lipoprotein receptor (VLDLr) (D'Arcangelo et al.,

TABLE 3–2 Mouse mutations that affect neuronal migration

Protein and Function	Gene	Structural Phenotype
Reelin, ECM protein	reln	reeler mouse, inverted cortical layering, absence of preplate split
Astrotactin 1, neuron–glia cell adhesion molecule	astn	Slowed radial migration
Integrin α_3 subunit, cell surface receptor binds to reelin	itga3	Abnormal laminar positioning of projection neurons
Integrin α_6 subunit, cell surface receptor binds to laminin	itga6	Basement membrane breach Cortical layering perturbation
Integrin β_1, cell surface receptor interacts with reelin, laminin	itgb1	Basement membrane breach Cortical layering perturbation
Laminin γ_1 subunit, ECM protein	lamc1	Basement membrane breach Cortical layering perturbation
Very low–density lipoprotein receptor, reelin receptor	vldlr	Reeler phenotype in Vldlr/Lrp8 double knockout
Low-density lipoprotein receptor–related protein, reelin receptor also known as ApoE receptor 2	lrp8	Reeler phenotype in Vldlr/Lrp8 double knockout
Disabled homolog 1, interacts with VLDLr/Lrp8	dab1	Reeler phenotype, mutated in yotari and scrambler
Cyclin-dependent kinase 5, phosphorylates Dab1 and NUDEL	cdk5	Inverted cortical layering
LIS1/PAFAHIb, binds to dynein, microtubule	PAFAHIb	Null is lethal, hypomorphic mutations cause migration defect
Doublecortin, microtubule-associated protein	dcx	No migration phenotype

1999; Hiesberger et al., 1999). Mice deficient in both of these receptors exhibit phenotypes identical to that of the *reeler* mouse (Trommsdorff et al., 1999). There may be other receptors involved in transducing the reelin signal. Reelin also binds to integrin $\alpha_3\beta_1$ and cadherin-related neuronal receptors (Senzaki et al., 1999; Dulabon et al., 2000). Apparently, reelin–integrin binding is not required for reelin function because integrin β_1 knockout mouse does not exhibit a *reeler*-like phenotype.

Downstream reelin-induced signaling involves the phosphorylation of *Drosophila* disabled homologue (Dab) 1 (Howell et al., 1999). Mice with mutations in the genes *dab1*, *scrambler*, and *yotari* exhibit phenotypes similar to that of *reeler* mice. Dab1 binds to the intracellular domains of lipoprotein receptors and is tyrosine phosphorylated upon ligand-receptor binding (Trommsdorff et al., 1998; Keshvara et al., 2001). Surprisingly, reelin has been shown to possess a serine protease activity and can digest extracellular matrix molecules (Quattrocchi et al., 2002). Whether its enzymatic activity regulates neuronal migration remains to be evaluated.

The mouse knockout of cyclin-dependent kinase (Cdk) 5 (a serine/threonine kinase) or of its activator protein, p35, exhibits a *reeler*-like cortical migration phenotype (Gilmore et al., 1998; Kwon and Tsai, 1998). A major difference is that the preplate is split into the MZ and the SP in these mutant mice. Thus, Cdk5 and p35 may function in a different pathway to control neuronal migration from reelin. Cdk5 can phosphorylate Dab1 independent of reelin binding to its receptors (Keshvara et al., 2002). There may be crosstalk between the reelin signaling pathway and the Cdk5 pathway.

MIGRATION DEFECTS

X-linked Periventricular Heterotopias: Failure to Initiate Migration

X-linked periventricular heterotopias are nodules of neurons lining the VZ or SZ. Presumably there is a failure of neurons to migrate out of proliferative zones. The genetic defect in X-linked periventricular heterotopia is mutations in *FLNA*, an X-linked gene encoding filamin A (Fox et al., 1998). Filamin A is a large actin-binding phosphoprotein with a molecular weight of 280 kDa. It is necessary for the locomotion of several cell types and is expressed by cells in all layers of the developing cerebral cortex. Hemizygous males with null mutations die during the embryonic period. Heterozygous females have epilepsy that can be accompanied by other manifestations such as patent *ductus arteriosus*. It is believed that random X-chromosome inactivation results in inactivation of *FLNA* expression in stranded neurons. Recently, affected males with likely partial loss-of-function mutations in *FLNA* (e.g., amino acid 656 Leu to Phe and amino acid 2305 Tyr to stop codon) have been reported (Sheen et al., 2001; Moro et al., 2002). Interestingly, males with these mutations have neurons that either migrate normally or exhibit complete migratory arrest. This dichotomy suggests that other functionally related genes can compensate for filamin A deficiency. Indeed, a structurally related gene, *FLNB*, is also expressed in the developing cerebral cortical wall, and both proteins can form heterodimers (Sheen et al., 2002).

The mechanism through which filamin A regulates the initiation of migration is unclear. Likely it involves the ability of filamin A to cross-link F-actin into isotropic, orthogonal arrays (Stossel et al., 2001). Cross-linking of F-actin increases the viscosity and stiffness of actin and may be involved in the initiation of migration. In the VZ and SZ, *FLNA* is expressed by all cells — mitotic and postmitotic cells. If filamin A regulates the initiation of neuronal migration, why do only postmitotic neurons migrate out of the VZ and SZ when all cells express *FLNA*? A potential mechanism involves filamin A–interacting protein (FILIP). FILIP is expressed in the VZ and SZ, but not in postmitotic migrating neurons (Nagano et al., 2002). FILIP–filamin A binding induces the degradation of filamin A. Thus, the loss of FILIP expression in postmitotic neurons may enable filamin A to control the start of migration.

Double Cortex Syndrome and Type I Lissencephaly: Premature Cessation of Neuronal Migration

Double cortex describes a condition in which a subcortical-band heterotopia forms in the subcortical IZ, the anlage of the white matter. Mutations in an X-linked gene, *doublecortin* (*dcx*), are a genetic cause of the disorder (des Portes et al., 1998; Gleeson et al., 1998). Doublecortin is a 40 kDa protein, expressed by migrating and many differentiating neurons. It is a microtubule-associated protein with no known homology with other microtubule-associated proteins (Francis et al., 1999; Gleeson et al., 1999; Horesh et al., 1999). Doublecortin stimulates microtubule polymerization by binding to 13 protofilament microtubules (Moores et al., 2004). It is principally localized in the leading processes of migrating neurons (Friocourt et al., 2003). Thus, doublecortin may promote movement by inducing microtubule polymerization in the leading processes of migrating neurons.

Classical lissencephaly (type I) is a brain malformation characterized by absent or reduced gyration and a cortex that is thicker and has a rudimentary four layers. It is associated with severe mental retardation, epilepsy, and cerebral palsy. Most cases are due to mutations of *lis1*, encoding LIS1 or platelet-activating factor acetylhydrolase isoform Ib (PAFAHIb, a non-catalytic subunit of the enzyme) (Reiner et al., 1993; Hattori et al., 1994). Besides being part of an enzyme, LIS1/PAFAHIb has a nonenzymatic function. The homolog in fungus *Aspergillus* is NudF, an essential part of a signaling pathway that regulates nuclear migration (Wynshaw-Boris and Gambello, 2001). Evidence indicates that LIS1/PAFAHIb regulates nuclear movement by an evolutionary-conserved mechanism similar to that of the fungus. It binds to and regulates the function and distribution of dynein (mammalian NudA homolog), which functions as a minus end-directed microtubule-associated motor protein. Thus, LIS1/PAFAHIb may be part of the protein complex that exerts forces on the microtubules surrounding the nucleus in migrating neurons and pulling the nucleus into the leading process (Tanaka et al., 2004). A role for LIS1/PAFAHIb in nuclear translocation is also supported by its binding to two other dynein interacting proteins, NUDEL and mNUDE (mammalian NudE homologs) (Feng et al., 2000; Liang et al., 2004). NUDEL and mNUDE colocalize at the centromere that migrates ahead of the nucleus. The distance between the centromere and the nucleus is enlarged in LIS1/PAFAHIb-deficient neurons (Tanaka et al., 2004). Thus, LIS1/PAFAHIb plays an important role in nuclear translocation during neuronal migration.

Type II Lissencephaly: Overmigration

Several forms of congenital muscular dystrophies—Walker-Warburg syndrome (WWS), muscle–eye–brain disease (MEB), and Fukuyama-type congenital muscular dystrophy (FCMD)—are associated with cortical dysplasia. These are autosomal recessive disorders characterized by congenital muscular dystrophy, ocular abnormalities, and cortical dysplasia (Santavuori et al., 1989). Magnetic resonance imaging of MEB patients reveals hydrocephalus associated with polymicrogyra or pachygyra caused by ectopic location of neural tissues in the leptomeninges, also known as cobblestone complexes or type II lissencephaly (Valanne et al., 1994; Cormand et al., 2001). Presumably, these abnormalities result when the neurons migrate too far, passing through the MZ, the glial-limiting membrane, the pial basement membrane (PM), and the pia (Ross and Walsh, 2001).

Each of the congenital muscular dystrophies has been associated with mutation of a specific gene. In WWS, mutations are in the genes coding for protein-O-mannosyl transferases (POMT1 and POMT2) (Beltran-Valero et al., 2002; van Reeuwijk et al., 2005). The defective gene for MEB maps to chromosome 1p32–34 (Cormand et al., 1999), and the mutated gene is POMGnT1. People with FCMD have a retrotransposon insertion into the 3' untranslated region of FCMD. This insertion results in a dramatic reduction in FCMD expression.

The myodystrophy (*myd*) mouse has muscle, eye, and neuronal migration defects in the brain similar to those in humans with congenital muscular dystrophies (Holzfeind et al., 2002). This *myd* mouse has muscle, eye, and brain defects associated with overmigration (Holzfeind et al., 2002). In the *myd* mouse, the genetic defect is a functional deletion in the *Large* gene (like-acetylglucosaminyltransferase) (Grewal et al., 2001). The *myd* mutation is now designated *Large^myd*. In humans, mutations in Large gene cause congenital muscular dystrophy MDC1D (Longman. et al., 2003) Thus, four new genes, POMT1, POMGnT1, FCMD, and *Large*, have been associated with congenital muscular dystrophies, and each causes similar overmigration defects when mutated.

The function of POMGnT1 has been described in vitro. POMGnT1 encodes an enzyme involved in O-mannosyl glycosylation of proteins called UDP-N-acetylglucosamine: protein-O-mannose β-1,2-N-acetylglucosaminyl transferase (POMGnT1). The enzyme catalyzes the following reaction:

$$UDP\text{-}GlcNAc + Man\text{-}R$$
$$\rightarrow GlcNAc\beta1\text{-}2Man\text{-}R + UDP$$

where R is a protein and Man is anchored to Ser/Thr residues (Takahashi et al., 2001; Yoshida et al., 2001). The functions of POMT1, fukutin, and Large, gene products of *POMT1*, *FCMD*, and *Large*, have not been determined. Bioinformatics studies, however, show that each protein has a glycosyltransferase-like domain (Aravind and Koonin, 1999; Jurado et al., 1999; Peyrard et al., 1999; Beltran-Valero et al., 2002). The implication is that the dystrophies and migration defects result from abnormal protein glycosylation. How can protein glycosylation enzymes regulate neuronal migration?

Conceivably, migration involves glycosylation substrate proteins. A candidate substrate is α-dystroglycan, a heavily glycosylated membrane protein. The mucin-like domain of α-dystroglycan is heavily substituted by O-linked mannosyl glycans that contain the linkage catalyzed by POMGnT1 (Chiba et al., 1997). The O-mannosyl glycans may play important roles in mediating α-dystroglycan interactions with laminin (Ervasti and Campbell, 1993; Smalheiser, 1993), a major component of the basement membrane. Further, α-dystroglycan in some of these diseases is underglycosylated and binding to laminin is reduced (Hayashi et al., 2001; Holzfeind et al., 2002; Kano et al., 2002; Michele et al., 2002). These results suggest a connection between hypoglycosylation of α-dystroglycan and neuronal migration defects in the brain. An important role for α-dystroglycan in this process is also supported by findings of neuronal migration defects in the brains of mice in which dystroglycan is conditionally knocked out (Michele et al., 2002; Moore et al., 2002).

Mechanisms of overmigration may involve abrogation of the PM. The PM is composed mainly of laminin, collagen IV, nidogen, and perlecan, all of which regulate cell proliferation, migration, and differentiation by interacting with mainly two cell surface receptors: integrins and α-dystroglycan. The PM, to which radial glial endfeet are attached, is located between the pia mater and the MZ. Electron microscopic analyses show breaches in the PM at sites of ectopic neural clusters of patients with FCMD (Nakano et al., 1996; Ishii et al., 1997; Saito et al., 1999). Laminin is reduced or abnormally distributed in the brain surface PM of several mutant mice with overmigration, including Lmx1a (*Dreher*) mice (Sekiguchi et al., 1994; Costa et al., 2001) and mice lacking myristolated alanine-rich C kinase substrate (Blackshear et al., 1997), integrin α₆ (Georges-

Labouesse et al., 1998), and integrin β₁ (Graus-Porta et al., 2001). Interestingly, integrin β₁ null neurons migrate to appropriate positions in the cerebral cortex in chimeric mice (Fassler and Meyer, 1995), implying that overmigration is not caused by an intrinsic defect of the migrating neurons but by a defective environment in this mutant. Whether breaches in the PM are the cause or the result of overmigration remains to be clarified.

DIRECTIONAL GUIDANCE OF NEURONAL MIGRATION BY DIFFUSABLE FACTORS

LCNs of the olfactory bulb (granule cells and periglomerular cells) are mainly generated postnatally, during the first 2 to 3 weeks after birth (Altman and Das, 1966; Hinds, 1968), although some neuronogenesis continues in the adult (Corotto et al., 1993; Lois and Alvarey-Buylla, 1994). Retroviral-labeling studies demonstrate that most of the LCNs are generated in the SZ near the anterior forebrain (SZa) and migrate to the olfactory bulb through an SZ pathway (Fig. 3–3) (Luskin, 1993; Zigova et al., 1996). Apparently, olfactory LCNs do not migrate on radially oriented glial processes, as the orientation of the radial glial fibers is orthogonal to the migration trajectory (Kishi et al., 1990). Further, the migration pathway in the SZ is also devoid of axon projections (Kishi, 1987).

How do olfactory LCN migrate? Immunohistochemical studies of polysialic acid and TuJ1 expression in the adult SZ pathway show that migrating cells tend to travel in chains or streams of cells (Rousselot et al., 1995; Doetsch and Alvarez-Buylla, 1996; Jankovski and Sotelo, 1996; Lois et al., 1996; Doetsch et al., 1997; Garcia-Verdugo et al., 1998). Although these chains of migrating cells cannot be observed in newborn animals because many cells are migrating at the same time, such chains are often observed in cultures of SZ cells plated on collagen gels (Hu et al., 1996) or Matrigel (Wichterle et al., 1997). Therefore, chain migration of olfactory LCN precursors seems to be mechanistically distinct from radial migration relying on radial glia.

In vivo studies show that olfactory LCN precursors migrate from the SZa to the olfactory bulb in a unidirectional manner (Luskin, 1993; Hu and Rutishauser, 1996). This finding implies an active guidance

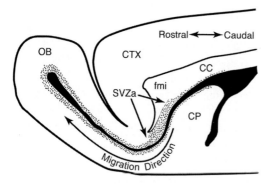

FIGURE 3–3 Tangential migration of olfactory local circuit neurons (LCNs). A parasagittal section through the middle of the olfactory bulb (OB) of the forebrain of the mouse is shown. Olfactory LCNs are generated in the anterior subventricular zone (SVZa; shown between arrows). They migrate to the OB within the SVZa (shown in dotted areas). After arriving in the bulb, they migrate in a radial fashion to reach their final locations in the granule cell layer and glomerular layer. The septum is located medial to this section. CC, corpus callosum; CP, caudoputamen; CTX, cerebral cortex; fmi, forceps minor corpus callosum.

mechanism. The olfactory bulb may secrete a chemoattractant(s) (Liu and Rao, 2003). Furthermore, the caudal parts of the septum and the choroid plexus, which lie behind the migration pathway, secrete a chemorepulsive factor(s) (Hu and Rutishauser, 1996). The chemorepulsive activity secreted from the septum is a member of the Slit family of proteins (Slit1, Slit2, and Slit3) (Hu, 1999; Wu et al., 1999). Slit, first discovered in *Drosophila*, and also found in mammals, regulates the growth of axons crossing at the midline (Ba-Charvet et al., 1999; Li et al., 1999) by interacting with roundabout (Robo) receptors (Kidd et al., 1998). Robo receptors are members of the immunoglobulin superfamily of transmembrane molecules (Zallen et al., 1998; Kidd et al., 1999). The Slit/Robo repulsive signal is mediated in part by the proteins enabled and abelson, Rho family guanidine triphosphotases (GTPases), and Slit-Robo GTPase activating proteins (srGAPs) (Bashaw et al., 2000; Wong et al., 2001).

Soluble factors may also be involved in active guidance in the migration of cortical neurons. This conclusion is supported by studies of LCN migration from the GE to the cerebral cortex. In vitro, these migrating neurons are repelled by the Slit proteins that

are expressed by the GE (Zhu et al., 1999) and attracted by substances released by the developing cortex (Marin et al., 2003; Wichterle et al., 2003). *Neuropilins* are transmembrane receptors that mediate the repulsive guidance activities of class 3 semaphorins. Neuropilin 1 and 2 are expressed by the LCNs that migrate from the GE to cerebral cortex (Marin et al., 2001). Neuropilin knockout mice have decreased numbers of LCNs in neocortex.

Successful navigation of neurons involves more than attraction and repulsion. While en route within the SZa pathway, olfactory LCNs do not deviate from their route into surrounding regions (Luskin, 1993). What confines the cells to the SZa pathway? The SZ migration pathway in adult mice is rich in astrocytes, tenascin, and chondroitin sulfate proteoglycan (Thomas et al., 1996). Thus, it is possible that the migrating cells might have stronger affinity for the SZ, because the SZ contains different extracellular matrix molecules and cell types from those in surrounding regions.

SUMMARY AND CONCLUSIONS

Neuronal migration is a complex phenomenon regulated by many factors. In vitro perturbation studies and molecular studies in both the mouse and humans identify some key molecules that are involved. Examples include factors extrinsic and intrinsic to a migrating neuron. These extrinsic factors, such as soluble and extracellular matrix molecules (neurotrophins, reelin, and Slit), and intrinsic factors, such as cytoskeletal proteins (filamin, doublecortin, and PAFAHIb), work in concert. They likely interact with cell surface receptors and signaling pathways. Some of the mechanisms are just beginning to emerge. In addition, there are critical interactions between genetic and environmental or epigenetic factors.

Abbreviations

Astn   astrotactin

BDNF   brain-derived neurotrophic factor

Cdk   cyclin-dependent kinase

CP   cortical plate

Dab   disabled

EGFr   epidermal growth factor receptor

FCMD   Fukuyama-type congenital muscular dystrophy

FILIP   filamin A–interacting protein

GABA   γ-aminobutyric acid

GE   ganglionic eminence

GTPase   guanidine triphosphotase

HGF   hepatocyte growth factor

IZ   intermediate zone

Large   like-acetylglucosaminyltransferase

LCN   local circuit neuron

LHRH   luteinizing hormone releasing hormone

MEB   muscle-eye-brain disease

MZ   marginal zone

nCAM   neural cell adhesion molecule

NMDA   N-methyl-D-aspartate

NT-4   neurotrophin-4

PAFAHIb   platelet-activating factor acetylhydrolase isoform Ib, a.k.a. LIS1

PM   pial basement membrane

POMGnT1   UDP-N-acetylglucosamine protein-O-mannose β1,2-N-acetylglucosaminyltransferase

POMT1   protein-O-mannosyl transferase

SZ   subventricular zone

SZa   anterior subventricular zone

TGF   transforming growth factor

VZ   ventricular zone

VLDLr   very low–density lipoprotein receptor

WWS   Walker-Warburg syndrome

ACKNOWLEDGMENTS The author thanks Dr. Eric Olson for critical reading of the manuscript. Results from the author's laboratory were supported by grants NS038877 and HD044011 from the National Institutes of Health.

References

Adams NC, Tomoda T, Cooper M, Dietz G, Hatten ME (2002) Mice that lack astrotactin have slowed neuronal migration. Development 129:965–972.

Allendoerfer KL, Shatz CJ (1994) The subplate, a transient neocortical structure: its role in the development of connections between thalamus and cortex. Annu Rev Neurosci 17:185–218.

Altman J, Das GD (1966) Autoradiographic and histological studies of postnatal neurogenesis. I. A longitudinal investigation of the kinetics, migration and transformation of cells incorporating tritiated thymidine in neonate rats, with special reference to postnatal neurogenesis in some brain regions. J Comp Neurol 126:337–389.

Anderson SA, Eisenstat DD, Shi L, Rubenstein JL (1997) Interneuron migration from basal forebrain to neocortex: dependence on dlx genes. Science 278: 474–476.

Anderson SA, Marin O, Horn C, Jennings K, Rubenstein JL (2001) Distinct cortical migrations from the medial and lateral ganglionic eminences. Development 128:353–363.

Ang ES Jr, Haydar TF, Gluncic V, Rakic P (2003) Four-dimensional migratory coordinates of GABAergic interneurons in the developing mouse cortex. J Neurosci 23:5805–5815.

Angevine JB Jr, Sidman RL (1961) Autoradiographic study of cell migration during histogenesis of cerebral cortex in the mouse. Nature 192:766–768.

Anton ES, Kreidberg JA, Rakic P (1999) Distinct functions of α_3 and α_v integrin receptors in neuronal migration and laminar organization of the cerebral cortex. Neuron 22:277–289.

Aravind L, Koonin EV (1999) The fukutin protein family—predicted enzymes modifying cell-surface molecules. Curr Biol 9:R836–R837.

Ba-Charvet KTN, Brose K, Marillat V, Kidd T, Goodman CS, Tessier-Lavigne M, Sotelo C, Chedotal A (1999) Slit2-mediated chemorepulsion and collapse of developing forebrain axons. Neuron 22:463–473.

Bashaw GJ, Kidd T, Murray D, Pawson T, Goodman CS (2000) Repulsive axon guidance: abelson and enabled play opposing roles downstream of the roundabout receptor. Cell 101:703–715.

Bayer SA (1983) ^{3}H-thymidine-radiographic studies of neurogenesis in the rat olfactory bulb. Exp Brain Res 50:329–340.

Behar TN, Dugich-Djordjevic MM, Li YX, Ma W, Somogyi R, Wen X, Brown E, Scott C, McKay RD, Barker JL (1997) Neurotrophins stimulate chemotaxis of embryonic cortical neurons. Eur J Neurosci 9:2561–2570.

Behar TN, Li YX, Tran HT, Ma W, Dunlap V, Scott C, Barker JL (1996) GABA stimulates chemotaxis and chemokinesis of embryonic cortical neurons via calcium-dependent mechanisms. J Neurosci 16: 1808–1818.

Behar TN, Scott CA, Greene CL, Wen X, Smith SV, Maric D, Liu QY, Colton CA, Barker JL (1999) Glutamate acting at NMDA receptors stimulates embryonic cortical neuronal migration. J Neurosci 19:4449–4461.

Behar TN, Smith SV, Kennedy RT, McKenzie JM, Maric I, Barker JL (2001) GABA(B) receptors mediate motility signals for migrating embryonic cortical cells. Cereb Cortex 11:744–753.

Beltran-Valero DB, Currier S, Steinbrecher A, Celli J, Van Beusekom E, Van Der ZB, Kayserili H, Merlini L, Chitayat D, Dobyns WB, Cormand B, Lehesjoki AE, Cruces J, Voit T, Walsh CA, van Bokhoven H, Brunner HG (2002) Mutations in the Omannosyl-transferase gene POMT1 give rise to the severe neuronal migration disorder Walker-Warburg Syndrome. Am J Hum Genet 71:1033–1043.

Berry M, Rogers AW (1965) The migration of neuroblasts in the developing cerebral cortex. J. Anat 99:691–709.

Blackshear PJ, Silver J, Nairn AC, Sulik KK, Squier MV, Stumpo DJ, Tuttle JS (1997) Widespread neuronal ectopia associated with secondary defects in cerebrocortical chondroitin sulfate proteoglycans and basal lamina in MARCKS-deficient mice. Exp Neurol 145:46–61.

Brittis PA, Meiri K, Dent E, Silver J (1995) The earliest patterns of neuronal differentiation and migration in the mammalian central nervous system. Exp Neurol 134:1–12.

Brunstrom JE, Gray-Swain MR, Osborne PA, Pearlman AL (1997) Neuronal heterotopias in the developing cerebral cortex produced by neurotrophin-4. Neuron 18:505–517.

Caric D, Raphael H, Viti J, Feathers A, Wancio D, Lillien L (2001) EGFRs mediate chemotactic migration in the developing telencephalon. Development 128: 4203–4216.

Chiba A, Matsumura K, Yamada H, Inazu T, Shimizu T, Kusunoki S, Kanazawa I, Kobata A, Endo T (1997) Structures of sialylated O-linked oligosaccharides of bovine peripheral nerve α-dystroglycan. The role of a novel O-mannosyl-type oligosaccharide in the binding of α-dystroglycan with laminin. J Biol Chem 272:2156–2162.

Cobas A, Fairén A (1988) GABAergic neurons of different morphological classes are cogenerated in the mouse barrel cortex. J Neurocytol 17:511–519.

Cormand B, Avela K, Pihko H, Santavuori P, Talim B, Topaloglu H, de la Chapelle A, Lehesjoki AE (1999) Assignment of the muscle-eye-brain disease gene to 1p32–p34 by linkage analysis and homozygosity mapping. Am J Hum Genet 64:126–135.

Cormand B, Pihko H, Bayes M, Valanne L, Santavuori P, Talim B, Gershoni-Baruch R, Ahmad A, van Bokhoven H, Brunner HG, Voit T, Topaloglu H, Dobyns WB, Lehesjoki AE (2001) Clinical and genetic distinction between Walker-Warburg syndrome and muscle-eye-brain disease. Neurology 56:1059–1069.

Corotto FS, Henegar JA, Maruniak JA (1993) Neurogenesis persists in the subependymal layer of the adult mouse brain. Neurosci Lett 149:111–114.

Costa C, Harding B, Copp AJ (2001) Neuronal migration defects in the Dreher (Lmx1a) mutant mouse: role of disorders of the glial limiting membrane. Cereb Cortex 11:498–505.

Crandall JE, Hackett HE, Tobet SA, Kosofsky BE, Bhide PG (2004) Cocaine exposure decreases GABA neuron migration from the ganglionic eminence to the cerebral cortex in embryonic mice. Cereb Cortex 14:665–675.

Cremer H, Lange R, Christoph A, Plomann M, Vopper G, Roes J, Brown R, Baldwin S, Kraemer P, Scheff S (1994) Inactivation of the N-CAM gene in mice results in size reduction of the olfactory bulb and deficits in spatial learning. Nature 367:455–459.

Curran T, D'Arcangelo G (1998) Role of reelin in the control of brain development. Brain Res Rev 26: 285–294.

D'Arcangelo G, Homayouni R, Keshvara L, Rice DS, Sheldon M, Curran T (1999) Reelin is a ligand for lipoprotein receptors. Neuron 24:471–479.

D'Arcangelo G, Miao GG, Chen SC, Soares HD, Morgan JI, Curran T (1995) A protein related to extracellular matrix proteins deleted in the mouse mutant reeler. Nature 374:719–723.

D'Arcangelo G, Nakajima K, Miyata T, Ogawa M, Mikoshiba K, Curran T (1997) Reelin is a secreted glycoprotein recognized by the CR-50 monoclonal antibody. J Neurosci 17:23–31.

de Carlos JA, Lopez-Mascaraque L, Valverde F (1996) Dynamics of cell migration from the lateral ganglionic eminence in the rat. J Neurosci 16:6146–6156.

des Portes V, Pinard JM, Billuart P, Vinet MC, Koulakoff A, Carrie A, Gelot A, Dupuis E, Motte J, Berwald-Netter Y, Catala M, Kahn A, Beldjord C, Chelly J (1998) A novel CNS gene required for neuronal migration and involved in X-linked subcortical laminar heterotopia and lissencephaly syndrome. Cell 92: 51–61.

Dobyns WB, Andermann E, Andermann F, Czapansky-Beilman D, Dubeau F, Dulac O, Guerrini R, Hirsch B, Ledbetter DH, Lee NS, Motte J, Pinard JM, Radtke RA, Ross ME, Tampieri D, Walsh CA, Truwit CL (1996) X-linked malformations of neuronal migration. Neurology 47:331–339.

Dobyns WB, Truwit CL (1995) Lissencephaly and other malformations of cortical development: 1995 update. Neuropediatrics 26:132–147.

Doetsch F, Alvarez-Buylla A (1996) Network of tangential pathways for neuronal migration in adult mammalian brain. Proc Natl Acad Sci USA 93:14895–14900.

Doetsch F, Garcia-Verdugo JM, Alvarez-Buylla A (1997) Cellular composition and three-dimensional organization of the subventricular germinal zone in the adult mammalian brain. J Neurosci 17:5046–5061.

Dulabon L, Olson EC, Taglienti MG, Eisenhuth S, McGrath B, Walsh CA, Kreidberg JA, Anton ES (2000) Reelin binds $\alpha_3\beta_1$ integrin and inhibits neuronal migration. Neuron 27:33–44.

Ervasti JM, Campbell KP (1993) A role for the dystrophin–glycoprotein complex as a transmembrane linker between laminin and actin. J Cell Biol 122:809–823.

Fairén A, Cobas A, Fonseca M (1986) Times of origin of glutamic acid decarboxylase immunoreactive neurons in mouse somatosensory cortex. J Comp Neurol 251:67–83.

Fassler R, Meyer M (1995) Consequences of lack of β_1 integrin gene expression in mice. Genes Dev 9:1896–1908.

Feng Y, Olson EC, Stukenberg PT, Flanagan LA, Kirschner MW, Walsh CA (2000) LIS1 regulates CNS lamination by interacting with mNudE, a central component of the centrosome. Neuron 28:665–679.

Finne J, Finne U, Deagostini-Bazin H, Goridis C (1983) Occurrence of α 2-8 linked polysialosyl units in a neural cell adhesion molecule. Biochem Biophys Res Commun 112:482–487.

Fishell G, Hatten ME (1991) Astrotactin provides a receptor system for CNS neuronal migration. Development 113:755–765.

Fox JW, Lamperti ED, Eksioglu YZ, Hong SE, Feng Y, Graham DA, Scheffer IE, Dobyns WB, Hirsch BA, Radtke RA, Berkovic SF, Huttenlocher PR, Walsh CA (1998) Mutations in filamin 1 prevent migration of cerebral cortical neurons in human periventricular heterotopia. Neuron 21:1315–1325.

Francis F, Koulakoff A, Boucher D, Chafey P, Schaar B, Vinet MC, Friocourt G, McDonnell N, Reiner O, Kahn A, McConnell SK, Berwald-Netter Y, Denoulet P, Chelly J (1999) Doublecortin is a developmentally regulated, microtubule-associated protein expressed in migrating and differentiating neurons. Neuron 23:247–256.

Friocourt G, Koulakoff A, Chafey P, Boucher D, Fauchereau F, Chelly J, Francis F (2003) Doublecortin functions at the extremities of growing neuronal processes. Cereb Cortex 13:620–626.

Garcia-Verdugo JM, Doetsch F, Wichterle H, Lim DA, Alvarez-Buylla A (1998) Architecture and cell types of the adult subventricular zone: in search of the stem cells. J Neurobiol 36:234–248.

Gardette R, Courtois M, Bisconte JC (1982) Prenatal development of mouse central nervous structures: time of origin and gradients of neuronal production. A radioautographic study. J Hirnforsch 23:415–431.

Georges-Labouesse E, Mark M, Messaddeq N, Gansmuller A (1998) Essential role of alpha 6 integrins in cortical and retinal lamination. Curr Biol 8:983–986.

Gilmore EC, Ohshima T, Goffinet AM, Kulkarni AB, Herrup K (1998) Cyclin-dependent kinase 5–deficient mice demonstrate novel developmental arrest in cerebral cortex. J Neurosci 18:6370–6377.

Gleeson JG, Allen KM, Fox JW, Lamperti ED, Berkovic S, Scheffer I, Cooper EC, Dobyns WB, Minnerath SR, Ross ME, Walsh CA (1998) Doublecortin, a brain-specific gene mutated in human X-linked lissencephaly and double cortex syndrome, encodes a putative signaling protein. Cell 92:63–72.

Gleeson JG, Lin PT, Flanagan LA, Walsh CA (1999) Doublecortin is a microtubule-associated protein and is expressed widely by migrating neurons. Neuron 23:257–271.

Graus-Porta D, Blaess S, Senften M, Littlewood-Evans A, Damsky C, Huang Z, Orban P, Klein R, Schittny JC, Muller U (2001) β_1-class integrins regulate the development of laminae and folia in the cerebral and cerebellar cortex. Neuron 31:367–379.

Gressens P, Evrard P (1993) The glial fascicle: an ontogenic and phylogenic unit guiding, supplying and distributing mammalian cortical neurons. Dev Brain Res 76:272–277.

Grewal PK, Holzfeind PJ, Bittner RE, Hewitt JE (2001) Mutant glycosyltransferase and altered glycosylation of α-dystroglycan in the myodystrophy mouse. Nat Genet 28:151–154.

Hatten ME (1999) Central nervous system neuronal migration. Annu Rev Neurosci 22:511–539.

Hatten ME, Mason CA (1990) Mechanisms of glial-guided neuronal migration in vitro and in vivo. Experientia 46:907–916.

Hattori M, Adachi H, Tsujimoto M, Arai H, Inoue K (1994) Miller-Dieker lissencephaly gene encodes a subunit of brain platelet–activating factor acetylhydrolase. Nature 370:216–218.

Hayashi YK, Ogawa M, Tagawa K, Noguchi S, Ishihara T, Nonaka I, Arahata K (2001) Selective deficiency of α-dystroglycan in Fukuyama-type congenital muscular dystrophy. Neurology 57:115–121.

Hiesberger T, Trommsdorff M, Howell BW, Goffinet A, Mumby MC, Cooper JA, Herz J (1999) Direct binding of Reelin to VLDL receptor and ApoE receptor 2 induces tyrosine phosphorylation of disabled-1 and modulates tau phosphorylation. Neuron 24:481–489.

Hinds JW (1968) Autoradiographic study of histogenesis in the mouse olfactory bulb. I. Time of origin of neurons and neuroglia. J Comp Neurol 134: 287–304.

Holzfeind PJ, Grewal PK, Reitsamer HA, Kechvar J, Lassmann H, Hoeger H, Hewitt JE, Bittner RE (2002) Skeletal, cardiac and tongue muscle pathology, defective retinal transmission, and neuronal migration defects in the Large(myd) mouse defines a natural model for glycosylation-deficient muscle-eye-brain disorders. Hum Mol Genet 11:2673–2687.

Horesh D, Sapir T, Francis F, Wolf SG, Caspi M, Elbaum M, Chelly J, Reiner O (1999) Doublecortin, a stabilizer of microtubules. Hum Mol Genet 8: 1599–1610.

Howell BW, Herrick TM, Cooper JA (1999) Reelin-induced tryosine phosphorylation of disabled 1 during neuronal positioning. Genes Dev 13:643–648.

Hu H (1999) Chemorepulsion of neuronal migration by Slit2 in the developing mammalian forebrain. Neuron 23:703–711.

—— (2000) Polysialic acid regulates chain formation by migrating olfactory interneuron precursors. J Neurosci Res 61:480–492.

Hu H, Rutishauser U (1996) A septum-derived chemorepulsive factor for migrating olfactory interneuron precursors. Neuron 16:933–940.

Hu H, Tomasiewicz H, Magnuson T, Rutishauser U (1996) The role of polysialic acid in migration of olfactory bulb interneuron precursors in the subventricular zone. Neuron 16:735–743.

Ishii H, Hayashi YK, Nonaka I, Arahata K (1997) Electron microscopic examination of basal lamina in Fukuyama congenital muscular dystrophy. Neuromuscul Disord 7:191–197.

Jankovski A, Sotelo C (1996) Subventricular zone-olfactory bulb migratory pathway in the adult mouse: cellular composition and specificity as determined by heterochronic and heterotopic transplantation. J Comp Neurol 371:376–396.

Jurado LA, Coloma A, Cruces J (1999) Identification of a human homolog of the Drosophila rotated abdomen gene (POMT1) encoding a putative protein O-mannosyl-transferase, and assignment to human chromosome 9q34.1. Genomics 58:171–180.

Kano H, Kobayashi K, Herrmann R, Tachikawa M, Manya H, Nishino I, Nonaka I, Straub V, Talim B, Voit T, Topaloglu H, Endo T, Yoshikawa H, Toda T (2002) Deficiency of α-dystroglycan in muscle-eye-brain disease. Biochem Biophys Res Commun 291:1283–1286.

Keshvara L, Benhayon D, Magdaleno S, Curran T (2001) Identification of reelin-induced sites of tyrosyl phosphorylation on disabled 1. J Biol Chem 276:16008–16014.

Keshvara L, Magdaleno S, Benhayon D, Curran T (2002) Cyclin-dependent kinase 5 phosphorylates disabled 1 independently of reelin signaling. J Neurosci 22:4869–4877.

Kidd T, Bland KS, Goodman CS (1999) Slit is the midline repellent for the robo receptor in Drosophila. Cell 96:785–794.

Kidd T, Brose K, Mitchell KJ, Fetter RD, Tessier-Lavigne M, Goodman CS, Tear G (1998) Roundabout controls axon crossing of the CNS midline and defines a novel subfamily of evolutionarily conserved guidance receptors. Cell 92:205–215.

Kishi K (1987) Golgi studies on the development of granule cells of the rat olfactory bulb with reference to migration in the subependymal layer. J Comp Neurol 258:112–124.

Kishi K, Peng JY, Kakuta S, Murakami K, Kuroda M, Yokota S, Hayakawa S, Kuge T, Asayama T (1990) Migration of bipolar subependymal cells, precursors of the granule cells of the rat olfactory bulb, with reference to the arrangement of the radial glial fibers. Arch Histol Cytol 53:219–226.

Kobayashi K, Nakahori Y, Miyake M, Matsumura K, Kondo-Iida E, Nomura Y, Segawa M, Yoshioka M, Saito K, Osawa M, Hamano K, Sakakihara Y, Nonaka I, Nakagome Y, Kanazawa I, Nakamura Y, Tokunaga K, Toda T (1998) An ancient retrotransposal insertion causes Fukuyama-type congenital muscular dystrophy. Nature 394:388–392.

Kornblum HI, Hussain RJ, Bronstein JM, Gall CM, Lee DC, Seroogy KB (1997) Prenatal ontogeny of the epidermal growth factor receptor and its ligand, transforming growth factor alpha, in the rat brain. J Comp Neurol 380:243–261.

Kwon YT, Tsai LH (1998) A novel disruption of cortical development in p35−/− mice distinct from reeler. J Comp Neurol 395:510–522.

Lambert de Rouvroit C, Goffinet AM (1998) The reeler mouse as a model of brain development. Adv Anat Embryol Cell Biol 150:1–106.

Lavdas AA, Grigoriou M, Pachnis V, Parnavelas JG (1999) The medial ganglionic eminence gives rise to a population of early neurons in the developing cerebral cortex. J Neurosci 19:7881–7888.

Li HS, Chen JH, Wu W, Fagaly T, Zhou L, Yuan W, Dupuis S, Jiang ZH, Nash W, Gick C, Ornitz DM, Wu JY, Rao Y (1999) Vertebrate slit, a secreted ligand for the transmembrane protein roundabout, is a repellent for olfactory bulb axons. Cell 96: 807–818.

Liang Y, Yu W, Li Y, Yang Z, Yan X, Huang Q, Zhu X (2004) Nudel functions in membrane traffic mainly through association with Lis1 and cytoplasmic dynein. J Cell Biol 164:557–566.

Liu G, Rao Y (2003) Neuronal migration from the forebrain to the olfactory bulb requires a new attractant persistent in the olfactory bulb. J Neurosci 23: 6651–6659.

Lois C, Alvarez-Buylla A (1994) Long-distance neuronal migration in the adult mammalian brain. Science 264:1145–1148.

Lois C, Garcia-Verdugo JM, Alvarez-Buylla A (1996) Chain migration of neuronal precursors. Science 271:978–981.

Longman C, Brockington M, Torelli S, Jimenez-Mallebrera C, Kennedy C, Khalil N, Feng L, Saran RK, Voit T, Merlini L, Sewry CA, Brown SC, Muntoni F (2003) Mutations in the human LARGE gene cause MDC1D, a novel form of congenital muscular dystrophy with serve mental retardation and abnormal glycosylation of alpha-dystroglycan. Hum Mol Genet 12:2853–2861.

Lund RD, Mustari MJ (1977) Development of the geniculocortical pathway in rats. J Comp Neurol 173:289–306.

Luo J, Miller MW (1999) Transforming growth factor β1-regulated cell proliferation and expression of neural cell adhesion molecule in B104 neuroblastoma cells: differential effects of ethanol. J Neurochem 72:2286–2293.

Luskin MB (1993) Restricted proliferation and migration of postnatally generated neurons derived from the forebrain subventricular zone. Neuron 11:173–189.

Luskin MB, Parnavelas JG, Barfield JA (1993) Neurons, astrocytes, and oligodendrocytes of the rat cerebral cortex originate from separate progenitor cells: an ultrastructural analysis of clonally related cells. J Neurosci 13:1730–1750.

Luskin MB, Pearlman AL, Sanes JR (1988) Cell lineage in the cerebral cortex of the mouse studied in vivo and in vitro with a recombinant retrovirus. Neuron 1:635–647.

Magdaleno S, Keshvara L, Curran T (2002) Rescue of ataxia and preplate splitting by ectopic expression of reelin in reeler mice. Neuron 33:573–586.

Malatesta P, Hartfuss E, Gotz M (2000) Isolation of radial glial cells by fluorescent-activated cell sorting reveals a neuronal lineage. Development 127:5253–5263.

Marin O, Plump AS, Flames N, Sanchez-Camacho C, Tessier-Lavigne M, Rubenstein JL (2003) Directional guidance of interneuron migration to the cerebral cortex relies on subcortical Slit1/2-independent repulsion and cortical attraction. Development 130:1889–1901.

Marin O, Rubenstein JL (2003) Cell migration in the forebrain. Annu Rev Neurosci 26:441–483.

Marin O, Yaron A, Bagri A, Tessier-Lavigne M, Rubenstein JL (2001) Sorting of striatal and cortical interneurons regulated by semaphorin–neuropilin interactions. Science 293:872–875.

Marin-Padilla M (1978) Dual origin of the mammalian neocortex and evolution of the cortical plate. Anat Embryol 152:109–126.

McConnell SK (1995) Constructing the cerebral cortex: neurogenesis and fate determination. Neuron 15: 761–768.

Michele DE, Barresi R, Kanagawa M, Saito F, Cohn RD, Satz JS, Dollar J, Nishino I, Kelley RI, Somer H, Straub V, Mathews KD, Moore SA, Campbell KP (2002) Post-translational disruption of dystroglycan ligand interactions in congenital muscular dystrophies. Nature 418:417–421.

Miller MW (1981) Maturation of rat visual cortex. I. A quantitative study of Golgi-impregnated pyramidal neurons. J. Neurocytol 10:859–878.

—— (1985) Co-generation of projection and local circuit neurons in neocortex. Dev Brain Res 23: 187–192.

—— (1986) The migration and neurochemical differentiation of γ-aminobutyric acid (GABA) immunoreactive neurons in rat visual cortex as demonstrated by a combined immunocytochemical-autoradiographic technique. Dev Brain Res 28:41–46.

—— (1987) Effect of prenatal exposure to alcohol on the distribution and time of origin of corticospinal neurons in the rat. J Comp Neurol 257:372–382.

—— (1988) Maturation of rat visual cortex: IV. The generation, migration, morphogenesis, and connectivity of atypically oriented pyramidal neurons. J Comp Neurol 274:387–405.

—— (1992) Migration of peptide-immunoreactive local circuit neurons to rat cingulate cortex. Cereb Cortex 2:444–455.

—— (1997) Effects of prenatal exposure to ethanol on callosal projection neurons in rat somatosensory cortex. Brain Res 766:121–128.

—— (1999) Kinetics of the migration of neurons to rat somatosensory cortex. Dev Brain Res 115:111–122.

—— (2003) Expression of transforming growth factor-beta in developing rat cerebral cortex: effects of prenatal exposure to ethanol. J Comp Neurol 460: 410–424.

Miller MW, Luo J (2002a) Effects of ethanol and transforming growth factor (TGFβ) on neuronal proliferation and nCAM expression. Alcohol Clin Exp Res 26:1281–1285.

—— (2002b) Effects of ethanol and basic fibroblast growth factor on the transforming growth factor-β1 regulated proliferation of cortical astrocytes and C6 astrocytoma cells. Alcohol Clin Exp Res 26: 671–676.

Miller MW, Robertson S (1993) Prenatal exposure to ethanol alters the postnatal development and transformation of radial glia to astrocytes in the cortex. J Comp Neurol 337:253–266.

Misson JP, Edwards MA, Yamamoto M, Caviness VS Jr (1988) Mitotic cycling of radial glial cells of the fetal murine cerebral wall: a combined autoradiographic and immunohistochemical study. Brain Res 466:183–190.

Miyata T, Kawaguchi A, Okano H, Ogawa M (2001) Asymmetric inheritance of radial glial fibers by cortical neurons. Neuron 31:727–741.

Moore SA, Saito F, Chen J, Michele DE, Henry MD, Messing A, Cohn RD, Ross-Barta SE, Westra S, Williamson RA, Hoshi T, Campbell KP (2002) Deletion of brain dystroglycan recapitulates aspects of congenital muscular dystrophy. Nature 418: 422–425.

Moores CA, Perderiset M, Francis F, Chelly J, Houdusse A, Milligan RA (2004) Mechanism of microtubule stabilization by doublecortin. Mol Cell 14:833–839.

Moro F, Carrozzo R, Veggiotti P, Tortorella G, Toniolo D, Volzone A, Guerrini R (2002) Familial periventricular heterotopia: missense and distal truncating mutations of the FLN1 gene. Neurology 58: 916–921.

Nadarajah B, Brunstrom JE, Grutzendler J, Wong RO, Pearlman AL (2001) Two modes of radial migration in early development of the cerebral cortex. Nat Neurosci 4:143–150.

Nadarajah B, Parnavelas JG (2002) Modes of neuronal migration in the developing cerebral cortex. Nat Rev Neurosci 3:423–432.

Nagano T, Yoneda T, Hatanaka Y, Kubota C, Murakami F, Sato M (2002) Filamin A–interacting protein (FILIP) regulates cortical cell migration out of the ventricular zone. Nat Cell Biol 4:495–501.

Nakano I, Funahashi M, Takada K, Toda T (1996) Are breaches in the glia limitans the primary cause of the micropolygyria in Fukuyama-type congenital muscular dystrophy (FCMD)? Pathological study of the cerebral cortex of an FCMD fetus. Acta Neuropathol 91:313–321.

Noctor SC, Flint AC, Weissman TA, Dammerman RS, Kriegstein AR (2001) Neurons derived from radial glial cells establish radial units in neocortex. Nature 409:714–720.

Noctor SC, Martinez-Cerdeno V, Ivic L, Kriegstein AR (2004) Cortical neurons arise in symmetric and asymmetric division zones and migrate through specific phases. Nat Neurosci 7:136–144.

Nowakowski RS, Rakic P (1981) The site of origin and route and rate of migration of neurons to the hippocampal region of the rhesus monkey. J Comp Neurol 196:129–154.

Ono K, Tomasiewicz H, Magnuson T, Rutishauser U (1994) N-CAM mutation inhibits tangential neuronal migration and is phenocopied by enzymatic removal of polysialic acid. Neuron 13:595–609.

Parnavelas JG, Barfield JA, Franke E, Luskin MB (1991) Separate progenitor cells give rise to pyramidal and nonpyramidal neurons in the rat telencephalon. Cerebr Cortex 1:463–468.

Peyrard M, Seroussi E, Sandberg-Nordqvist AC, Xie YG, Han FY, Fransson I, Collins J, Dunham I, Kost-Alimova M, Imreh S, Dumanski JP (1999) The human LARGE gene from 22q12.3–q13.1 is a new, distinct member of the glycosyltransferase gene family. Proc Natl Acad Sci USA 96:598–603.

Polleux F, Whitford KL, Dijkhuizen PA, Vitalis T, Ghosh A (2002) Control of cortical interneuron migration by neurotrophins and PI3-kinase signaling. Development 129:3147–3160.

Powell EM, Mars WM, Levitt P (2001) Hepatocyte growth factor/scatter factor is a motogen for interneurons migrating from the ventral to dorsal telencephalon. Neuron 30:79–89.

Quattrocchi CC, Wannenes F, Persico AM, Ciafre SA, D'Arcangelo G, Farace MG, Keller F (2002) Reelin is a serine protease of the extracellular matrix. J Biol Chem 277:303–309.

Rakic P (1972) Mode of cell migration to the superficial layers of fetal monkey neocortex. J Comp Neurol 145:61–83.

—— (1974) Neurons in rhesus monkey visual cortex: systematic relation between time of origin and eventual disposition. Science 183:425–427.

—— (1990) Principles of neural cell migration. Experientia 46:882–891.

Rakic P, Caviness VS Jr (1995) Cortical development: view from neurological mutants two decades later. Neuron 14:1101–1104.

Rakic P, Knyihar-Csillik E, Csillik B (1996) Polarity of microtubule assemblies during neuronal cell migration. Proc Natl Acad Sci USA 93:9218–9222.

Raymond AA, Fish DR, Sisodiya SM, Alsanjari N, Stevens JM, Shorvon SD (1995) Abnormalities of gyration, heterotopias, tuberous sclerosis, focal cortical dysplasia, microdysgenesis, dysembryoplastic neuroepithelial tumour and dysgenesis of the archicortex in epilepsy. Clinical, EEG and neuroimaging features in 100 adult patients. Brain 118: 629–660.

Reiner O, Carrozzo R, Shen Y, Wehnert M, Faustinella F, Dobyns WB, Caskey CT, Ledbetter DH (1993) Isolation of a Miller-Dieker lissencephaly gene containing

G protein beta-subunit-like repeats. Nature 364: 717–721.

Rickmann M, Chronwall BM, Wolff JR (1977) On the development of non-pyramidal neurons and axons outside the cortical plate: the early marginal zone as a pallial anlage. Anat Embryol 151:285–307.

Ross ME, Walsh CA (2001) Human brain malformations and their lessons for neuronal migration. Ann Rev Neurosci 24:1041–1070.

Rousselot P, Lois C, Alvarez-Buylla A (1995) Embryonic (PSA) N-CAM reveals chains of migrating neuroblasts between the lateral ventricle and the olfactory bulb of adult mice. J Comp Neurol 351: 51–61.

Rutishauser U (1996) Polysialic acid and the regulation of cell interactions. Curr Opin Cell Biol 8:679–684.

Saito Y, Murayama S, Kawai M, Nakano I (1999) Breached cerebral glia limitans-basal lamina complex in Fukuyama-type congenital muscular dystrophy. Acta Neuropathol 98:330–336.

Sanes JR (1989) Analysing cell lineage with a recombinant retrovirus. Trends Neurosci 12:21–28.

Santavuori P, Somer H, Sainio K, Rapola J, Kruus S, Nikitin T, Ketonen L, Leisti J (1989) Muscle-eye-brain disease (MEB). Brain Dev 11:147–153.

Schmechel DE, Rakic P (1979) A Golgi study of radial glial cells in developing monkey telencephalon: morphogenesis and transformation into astrocytes. Anat Embryol 156:115–152.

Schwanzel-Fukuda M, Pfaff DW (1990) The migration of luteinizing hormone–releasing hormone (LHRH) neurons from the medial olfactory placode into the medial basal forebrain. Experientia 46: 956–962.

Sekiguchi M, Abe H, Shimai K, Huang G, Inoue T, Nowakowski RS (1994) Disruption of neuronal migration in the neocortex of the *Dreher* mutant mouse. Dev Brain Res 77:37–43.

Senzaki K, Ogawa M, Yagi T (1999) Proteins of the CNR family are multiple receptors for reelin. Cell 99: 635–647.

Sheen VL, Dixon PH, Fox JW, Hong SE, Kinton L, Sisodiya SM, Duncan JS, Dubeau F, Scheffer IE, Schachter SC, Wilner A, Henchy R, Crino P, Kamuro K, DiMario F, Berg M, Kuzniecky R, Cole AJ, Bromfield E, Biber M, Schomer D, Wheless J, Silver K, Mochida GH, Berkovic SF, Andermann F, Andermann E, Dobyns WB, Wood NW, Walsh CA (2001) Mutations in the X-linked filamin 1 gene cause periventricular nodular heterotopia in males as well as in females. Hum Mol Genet 10:1775–1783.

Sheen VL, Feng Y, Graham D, Takafuta T, Shapiro SS, Walsh CA (2002) Filamin A and filamin B are co-expressed within neurons during periods of neuronal migration and can physically interact. Hum Mol Genet 11:2845–2854.

Siegenthaler JA, Miller MW (2004) Transforming growth factor β1 modulates cell migration in rat cortex: effects of ethanol. Cereb Cortex 14:791–802.

—— (2005) TGFβ1 potentiates cell cycle exit in developing cerebral cortex. J Neurosci 25:8627–8636.

Smalheiser NR (1993) Cranin interacts specifically with the sulfatide-binding domain of laminin. J Neurosci Res 36:528–538.

Stitt TN, Hatten ME (1990) Antibodies that recognize astrotactin block granule neuron binding to astroglia. Neuron 5:639–649.

Stossel TP, Condeelis J, Cooley L, Hartwig JH, Noegel A, Schleicher M, Shapiro SS (2001) Filamins as integrators of cell mechanics and signalling. Nat Rev Mol Cell Biol 2:138–145.

Takahashi S, Sasaki T, Manya H, Chiba Y, Yoshida A, Mizuno M, Ishida H, Ito F, Inazu T, Kotani N, Takasaki S, Takeuchi M, Endo T (2001) A new β-1,2-N-acetylglucosaminyltransferase that may play a role in the biosynthesis of mammalian O-mannosyl glycans. Glycobiology 11:37–45.

Tamamaki N, Fujimori KE, Takauji R (1997) Origin and route of tangentially migrating neurons in the developing neocortical intermediate zone. J Neurosci 17:8313–8323.

Tanaka T, Serneo FF, Higgins C, Gambello MJ, Wynshaw-Boris A, Gleeson JG (2004) Lis1 and doublecortin function with dynein to mediate coupling of the nucleus to the centrosome in neuronal migration. J Cell Biol 165:709–721.

Thomas LB, Gates MA, Steindler DA (1996) Young neurons from the adult subependymal zone proliferate and migrate along an astrocyte, extracellular matrix–rich pathway. Glia 17:1–14.

Threadgill DW, Dlugosz AA, Hansen LA, Tennenbaum T, Lichti U, Yee D, LaMantia C, Mourton T, Herrup K, Harris RC (1995) Targeted disruption of mouse EGF receptor: effect of genetic background on mutant phenotype. Science 269:230–234.

Tomasiewicz H, Ono K, Yee D, Thompson C, Goridis C, Rutishauser U, Magnuson T (1993) Genetic deletion of a neural cell adhesion molecule variant (N-CAM-180) produces distinct defects in the central nervous system. Neuron 11:1163–1174.

Trommsdorff M, Borg JP, Margolis B, Herz J (1998) Interaction of cytosolic adaptor proteins with neuronal apolipoprotein E receptors and the amyloid precursor protein. J Biol Chem 273:33556–33560.

Trommsdorff M, Gotthardt M, Hiesberger T, Shelton J, Stockinger W, Nimpf J, Hammer RE, Richardson JA, Herz J (1999) Reeler/Disabled-like disruption of neuronal migration in knockout mice lacking the VLDL receptor and ApoE receptor 2. Cell 97: 689–701.

Valanne L, Pihko H, Katevuo K, Karttunen P, Somer H, Santavuori P (1994) MRI of the brain in muscle-eye-brain (MEB) disease. Neuroradiology 36: 473–476.

Van Reeuwijk J, Janssen M, van den Elzen C, Beltran-Valero de Bernabe D, Sabatelli P, Merlini L, Boon M, Scheffer H, Brockington M, Muntoni F, Huynen M, Verrips A, Walsh C, Barth P, Brunner H, van Bokhoven H (2005) POMT2 mutations cause alphadystroglycan hypoglycosylation and Walker-Warburg syndrome. J Med Genet. In press.

Voigt T (1989) Development of glial cells in the cerebral wall of ferrets: direct tracing of their transformation from radial glia into astrocytes. J Comp Neurol 289:74–88.

Walsh C, Cepko CL (1988) Clonally related cortical cells show several migration patterns. Science 241:1342–1345.

Wichterle H, Garcia-Verdugo JM, Alvarez-Buylla A (1997) Direct evidence for homotypic, glia-independent neuronal migration. Neuron 18:779–791.

Wichterle H, Varez-Dolado M, Erskine L, Alvarez-Buylla A (2003) Permissive corridor and diffusible gradients direct medial ganglionic eminence cell migration to the neocortex. Proc Natl Acad Sci USA 100:727–732.

Wong K, Ren XR, Huang YZ, Xie Y, Liu G, Saito H, Tang H, Wen L, Brady-Kalnay SM, Mei L, Wu JY, Xiong WC, Rao Y (2001) Signal transduction in neuronal migration: roles of GTPase activating proteins and the small GTPase Cdc42 in the Slit-Robo pathway. Cell 107:209–221.

Wu W, Wong K, Chen J, Jiang Z, Dupuis S, Wu JY, Rao Y (1999) Directional guidance of neuronal migration in the olfactory system by the protein Slit. Nature 400:331–336.

Wynshaw-Boris A, Gambello MJ (2001) LIS1 and dynein motor function in neuronal migration and development. Genes Dev 15:639–651.

Yoshida A, Kobayashi K, Manya H, Taniguchi K, Kano H, Mizuno M, Inazu T, Mitsuhashi H, Takahashi S, Takeuchi M, Herrmann R, Straub V, Talim B, Voit T, Topaloglu H, Toda T, Endo T (2001) Muscular dystrophy and neuronal migration disorder caused by mutations in a glycosyltransferase, POMGnT1. Dev Cell 1:717–724.

Zallen JA, Yi BA, Bargmann CI (1998) The conserved immunoglobulin superfamily member SAX-3/Robo directs multiple aspects of axon guidance in C. elegans. Cell 92:217–227.

Zheng C, Heintz N, Hatten ME (1996) CNS gene encoding astrotactin, which supports neuronal migration along glial fibers. Science 272:417–419.

Zhu Y, Li H, Zhou L, Wu JY, Rao Y (1999) Cellular and molecular guidance of GABAergic neuronal migration from an extracortical origin to the neocortex. Neuron 23:473–485.

Zigova T, Betarbet R, Soteres BJ, Brock S, Bakay RA, Luskin MB (1996) A comparison of the patterns of migration and the destinations of homotopically transplanted neonatal subventricular zone cells and heterotopically transplanted telencephalic ventricular zone cells. Dev Biol 173:459–474.

4

Neuronal Differentiation: From Axons to Synapses

C. David Mintz

Iddil H. Bekirov

Tonya R. Anderson

Deanna L. Benson

A newly born neuron generates a single axon and a somatodendritic domain. As it matures, it engages, by way of synapses, a select population of the 20 billion other differentiating neurons in the human central nervous system (CNS). Amazingly, the connections that ultimately form are stereotyped and, for the most part, faithfully recapitulated across individuals. This chapter outlines major events in differentiation, highlighting the key cellular events and molecular mechanisms governing the process.

ACQUISITION OF NEURONAL POLARITY

The neuroanatomist Jan Purkinje was the first to note that there are two morphologically distinct types of nerve fibers in the adult nervous system, axons and dendrites (Shepherd, 1991). Axons traverse long distances, maintain a constant caliber, and commonly branch at right angles. In contrast, dendrites, which are usually shorter, taper with distance from the soma and generally branch at acute angles. Early in development, neurites are morphologically indistinguishable from one another. Over the course of maturation they assume the characteristics of axons and dendrites in a process known as polarization.

Stages of Neurite Maturation

Time-lapse imaging of individual neurons growing in dissociated cultures reveals a stereotyped sequence of stages in neurite development, diagrammed in Figure 4–1 (Dotti et al., 1988). In Stage 1, the neuron exists as a round soma with lamellipodia and filopodia, but without neurites. Immature neurites, which cannot be identified as either axons or dendrites, emerge during Stage 2. In Stage 3, a single process undergoes rapid growth and becomes the axon. The shorter processes develop into dendrites in Stage 4. During Stage 5, there is further elaboration and maturation of dendrites and axons as synapses form. Though it is not yet

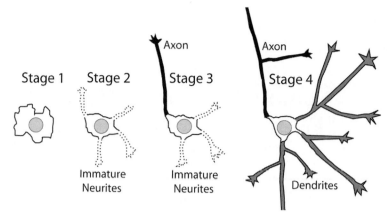

FIGURE 4–1 Stages of neurite development. The Stage 1 neuron lacks neurites entirely. In Stage 2, immature neurites emerge that are capable of becoming either axons or dendrites. When one of the immature neurites outgrows the others it becomes the axon and the neuron reaches Stage 3. The remaining immature processes become dendrites and elaborate and branch in Stage 4. Synaptogenesis and spinogensis occur in Stage 5, which is not shown in this diagram.

proven definitively, it is generally believed that the stages of neurite development observed in culture also occur in situ. Nearly all data that address questions about neuronal polarity are derived from experiments in which neurons are grown in dissociated cultures where individual processes can be identified and followed over time.

Polarization is Initiated by Axon Specification

All early neurites on a particular neuron are capable of becoming axons or dendrites. One ultimately acquires axonal characteristics and the remainder assume a dendritic fate. In a Stage 2 neuron, each process undergoes cycles of extension and retraction until one neurite outgrows the others by a critical length—10 μm in hippocampal neurons—and becomes the axon (Goslin and Banker, 1989). If a recently formed axon is transected to a length comparable to that of the other neurites, one of the other minor processes typically becomes the axon and the stump of the original axon adopts dendritic characteristics (Dotti and Banker, 1987). Thus, every Stage 2 process has the potential to become the axon, but the presence of a specified axon actively promotes a

dendritic fate for the remaining neurites. This model is supported by data showing that dendritic maturation can occur only after axon specification (Caceres et al., 1991).

As one neurite outgrows the others by virtue of interactions with local environmental factors, it gives rise to a positive feedback loop that creates two distinct compartments (Craig and Banker, 1994). As development continues, some proteins and organelles become segregated into one of the two compartments, and the different complements of proteins in mature axons and dendrites underlie the functional and morphological differences between the two types of neurites. In recent years, some progress has been made in elucidating the molecular basis of axon specification and subsequent maturation events, but a complete model has not yet been formulated.

Role of the Cytoskeleton in the Establishment of Polarity

A considerable body of evidence supports the hypothesis that microtubules are involved in axon specification. Quantitative analyses of serial electron microscopy (EM) reconstructions of minor processes and axons in Stage 2 and Stage 3 neurons reveal that axon specification coincides with a dramatic increase in microtubule number (Yu and Baas, 1994). This increase raises the possibility that selective transport of microtubules to a single neurite produces rapid growth and subsequent acquisition of axonal characteristics (Baas, 1999).

The efficiency of microtubule assembly and the stability of microtubules once formed are inextricably linked to the local composition of microtubule-associated proteins (MAPs). Data from cultured neurons indicate that MAPs such as Tau and MAP1b, which are enriched in axons, may also play a role in axon specification (Caceres and Kosik, 1990; DiTella et al., 1996). Mice deficient in both Tau and MAP1b, however, have only modest defects in axon development (Takei et al., 2000), a finding suggesting that the dependence on MAPs is exaggerated in culture or compensated for over the long term *in situ*. At the very least, MAPs stabilize microtubules, and this stabilization contributes to rapid microtubule-dependent neurite outgrowth. Other proteins that regulate microtubules may play a more crucial role in axon specification. For example, collapsin response mediator protein (CRMP) 2 is enriched in the distal region of Stage 3 axons where it apparently facilitates microtubule assembly (Fukata et al., 2002a). Supporting this possibility, a dominant negative CRMP-2 lacking the tubulin binding site prevents axon specification in cultured neurons (Inagaki et al., 2001). Also, recent studies have demonstrated that glycogen synthase kinase 3β and other signaling molecules directly upstream from CRMP-2 can influence axon formation (Jiang et al., 2005; Yoshimura et al., 2005). It must be noted, however, that CRMP-2 and the axonal MAPs are multifunctional proteins, making the precise significance of microtubules in the establishment of neuronal polarity unclear.

The actin cytoskeleton has been implicated in axon specification. Local application of cytochalasin D, an actin-depolymerizing agent, to the growth cone of a single neurite of a Stage 2 neuron increases the likelihood that this neurite will become the axon. Bath application of the same reagent results in an increase in neurons bearing multiple axons (Bradke and Dotti, 1999). It should be noted, however, that a subsequent study argues that this effect is actually the result of faster growth of all neurites, rather than aberrant polarization (Ruthel and Hollenbeck, 2000). In *Aplysia* growth cones, actin depolymerization can trigger increased microtubule elongation (Forscher

and Smith, 1988). Hence, it is likely that axon specification depends on the coordinated regulation of both actin depolymerization and microtubule assembly.

Signaling Pathways That Control Polarization

The emergence of polarity requires coordination between Stage 2 neurites, suggesting the existence of intracellular signaling pathways. The Rho family of small GTPases, which includes Rho, Rac, and Cdc42, are candidates to control polarization, as they can regulate both actin and microtubules (Burridge and Wennerberg, 2004; Gundersen et al., 2004). Broad-based inhibition of the entire Rho family in Stage 2 neurons results in the emergence of multiple axons (Bradke and Dotti, 1999). Additional work supports the notion that Rho, Rac, and Cdc42 can each play distinct roles. Expression of a Rac dominant-negative mutant in *Drosophila* reduces axon outgrowth (Luo et al., 1994), whereas expression of a constitutively active Cdc42 mutant in cultured hippocampal neurons induces multiple axons (Schwamborn and Puschel, 2004). In contrast, Rho can induce the collapse of the distal ends of neurites via phosphyorlyation of CRMP-2 (Arimura et al., 2000). According to one model, the speed of outgrowth of any given neurite is determined by a balance between retraction and collapse promoted by Rho and outgrowth promoted by Rac and Cdc42 (Fukata et al., 2002b). This hypothesis, which has not been fully validated in mammalian neurons, has the potential to explain differential growth of axons and dendrites in terms of local Rho family activity.

There are many parallels between neuronal and non-neuronal cell polarization (Rodriguez-Boulan and Powell, 1992), and there is evidence that some signaling pathways related to polarization are conserved among different cell types. The Par complex, which consists of Par3, Par6, and atypical phosphokinase C, controls the establishment of polarity in a broad range of species and cell types via regulation of actin and microtubules (Wodarz, 2002). Recent data suggest that the Par complex may control axon specification upstream from the Rho family. Par3 and Par6 are polarized to the axons of hippocampal neurons, and overexpression of ectopic Par prevents polarization (Shi et al., 2004). Segregation of Par complex members to a single neurite, which can occur as early as Stage 2, is preceded by polarization of Rap1B, a small GTPase that is a Ras family member (Schwamborn and Puschel, 2004). The data indicate that Rap1B is upstream of both the Par complex and Cdc42 with respect to axon specification (Schwamborn and Puschel, 2004). It is thought that extracellular factors, as yet unidentified, might mediate the effects of the local environment on polarization by acting upstream from intracellular signaling molecules such as Rho, Par, and Rap1B.

Polarized Distribution of Proteins and Organelles

The differences in morphology and function that distinguish axons and dendrites reflect different complements of proteins and organelles in each type of neurite. In the adult brain, certain proteins have a polarized distribution, meaning that they are concentrated or even exclusively present in either dendrites or axons. This asymmetry must be created during development by compartment-specific trafficking and retention of these proteins. The Stage 2 neurite that becomes the axon in Stage 3 typically receives more organelles, cytosolic proteins, and Golgi-derived vesicles than the processes that become dendrites (Bradke and Dotti, 1997). Intact trafficking is required for polarization, as it is possible to prevent axon specification by blocking the trafficking of Golgi-derived vesicles with brefeldin A (Jareb and Banker, 1997). The polarized distribution of some proteins may either promote the emerging differences between developing axons and dendrites or simply reflect those differences. The details of how each polarized protein reaches its appropriate destination in one compartment but not the other remain largely speculative.

The polarization of proteins may result from retention specific to the appropriate compartment. Experiments with optical tweezers, which allow traction force to be applied to specific proteins, show that a barrier to the diffusion of some axon-specific membrane proteins exists at the axon initial segment (Winckler et al., 1999; Fache et al., 2004). The barrier appears to be an accumulation of actin-tethered membrane proteins. Analysis of phospholipid diffusion in the membrane suggests that the diffusion barrier does not exist prior to axon specification (Nakada et al., 2003), but it may play an important role in subsequent maturation. The extent to which the diffusion barrier is a cause or consequent of the establishment of neuronal polarity remains unknown.

NEURITE MOTILITY

The neuroanatomist Santiago Ramon y Cajal (1894) observed that the distal extent of a growing neurite "end[s] in a spherical conical swelling . . . with a large number of thick protrusions and lamellar processes," which he speculated were like "an amoebic mass that acts as a battering ram to spread the elements along its path." He named this morphological specialization the *growth cone*, and decades of subsequent research have supported his inference that growth cones are highly motile structures required for the elongation of both axons and dendrites. Much is known about the structure and function of growth cones. The motility of growth cones depends on actin and microtubules and the proteins that regulate them. Additionally, growth cones are the sensory organs for extracellular cues that guide axons to engage in the directed growth required for the establishment of correct connectivity. Though much work remains to be done, an understanding of how growth cones function in neurite growth is emerging.

Growth Cone Structure

Although neuronal growth cones vary considerably in shape and size, they generally share some common structural features. Most investigators recognize three morphological zones known as the central, transitional, and peripheral domains, which are indicated in Figure 4–2 (Forscher and Smith, 1988; Bridgman and Dailey, 1989). The relatively thick central domain abuts the neurite and is enriched with microtubules. The transitional domain, which lies between the central and peripheral domains, contains meshwork, arcs, and radial ridges of F-actin. The peripheral domain consists of the lamellipodium, a wide, flat region, and filopodia, which are fine membrane protrusions that extend distally from the lamellipodium. The peripheral domain is greatly enriched with F-actin, organized as meshwork and arcs in the lamellipodia. Filopodia contain bundles of filaments with the barbed ends pointing distally. Compared to the central domain, the peripheral domain has a lower density of microtubules and they are notably more dynamic (Schaefer et al., 2002). The leading edge of migrating fibroblasts was thought to have a structure similar to that of the neuronal growth cone. Recent findings, however, show that the cytoskeletal configuration and mechanics of motility in these two

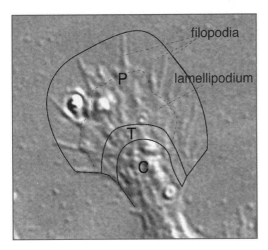

FIGURE 4–2 Structure of the growth cone. The morphological zones of a growth cone are shown using a differential interference contrast micrograph of a dendritic growth cone from a cultured rat neocortical neuron. Note the thick central zone (C), separated from the flat peripheral zone (P) by the transitional zone (T). Also, in the peripheral zone, the lamellipodium and several filopodia are indicated by dashed lines.

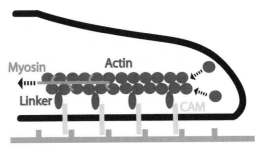

FIGURE 4–3 The actin treadmill model of motility. The two principle features of the treadmill model are the retrograde flow of actin, which is due to myosin motors, and the polymerization of actin at the leading edge of the filopodia (on right). If polymerization is faster that retrograde flow, there is forward movement; if it is slower, there is retraction. Note that actin is coupled to the substrate by linker proteins that bind transmembrane CAMs.

structures differ considerably (Strasser et al., 2004). Thus, the present discussion of growth cone motility is confined to models from experiments done on neuronal growth cones.

Growth Cone Motility

The exact relationship between filopodial, lamellipodial, and neurite motility is not completely understood. Filopodia sample the environment for cues to determine the direction of growth (O'Connor et al., 1990), and thus filopodial motility tends to reflect this scanning pattern rather than demonstrating a tight link with neurite growth. The movements of lamellipodia are better correlated with neurite growth than those of filopodia, but lamellipodia commonly engage in extension and retraction that do not directly correlate with alterations in the trajectory of the growing neurite.

Growth cone motility requires dynamic regulation of the cytoskeleton. The treadmill model, which is based on observations in filopodia, focuses on the role of actin (Fig. 4–3) (Lin et al., 1994). Filaments of actin are simultaneously polymerized at the distal tips of filopodia and retracted proximally by myosin

motors (Lin et al., 1996). If the rate of actin polymerization at the leading edge is greater than the rate of actin retrograde flow, the filopodia advances. If polymerization is slower than retrograde flow, the filopodia retracts. If polymerization and retrograde flow are balanced, there is no net change in the position of the filopodia. The substrate on which a neurite grows can interact with transmembrane adhesion molecules, which are attached to actin indirectly via linker proteins. The coupling of the substrate to the actin cytoskeleton (a) allows for the generation of tension when forces are applied to actin and (b) accounts for the influence of substrate on growth cone motility (Suter and Forscher, 1998). This model is not complete, as axons treated with actin depolymerizing agents still demonstrate net growth (Bentley and Toroian-Raymond, 1986), and application of microtubule destabilizing reagents can prevent neurite outgrowth (Bamburg et al., 1986). It should be noted that current models of growth cone motility are largely based on experiments in unpolarized *Aplysia* neurons or in spinal or sensory neurons isolated from frogs and chicks. Some mechanisms of growth cone motility may differ among species, cell types, and neurite type, but the regulatory molecules are likely to be conserved.

A large and diverse group of proteins that modulate cytoskeletal dynamics through intracellular signaling or direct action is involved in regulating growth cone motility. The Rho family of proteins, which can influence both the actin and microtubule cytoskeleton, plays an important role in regulating growth cone motility. The control of actin polymerization at the leading edge of growth cones is an area of active study. Members of the Ena/Vasp family, which prevent barbed actin capping, can regulate the behavior of filopodia (Lebrand et al., 2004). Other molecules that may play roles in actin dynamics at the leading edge include profilin, fascin, and actin depolymerizing factor/cofilin (Wills et al., 1999; Meberg and Bamburg, 2000; Cohan et al., 2001). Further work is required to construct a cohesive model of how these and other proteins regulate cytoskeletal dynamics at the leading edge of the growth cone.

Directed Growth

Growth cones are generally considered to mediate the response of growing axons and dendrites to the myriad of guidance cues that direct the establishment of appropriate connectivity. It is possible to alter the trajectory of neurite growth by applying a gradient of a chemotropic molecule to a growth cone in vitro (Zheng et al., 1994). In fact, this assay is now commonly used to test whether a protein can serve as a guidance cue. Furthermore, many receptors for known guidance cues are expressed in the plasma membrane of growth cones. It is believed that gradients of guidance cues across the surface of the growth cone produce asymmetric effects on receptors that mediate growth cone steering (Goodman, 1996).

The response of growth cones to guidance cues depends on both the actin and microtubule components of the cytoskeleton and the effectors that regulate them downstream from guidance receptors. It has been proposed that growth cone turning occurs when actin is polymerized asymmetrically within the growth cone and when there is a subsequent increase in microtubule entry into and polymerization in the actin rich zone (Dent and Gertler, 2003). Consistent with this model, disruptions of regulators of either the actin or the microtubule cytoskeleton can result in defective axon guidance. Examples include the actin interactors Arp2/3 and Ena/Vasp (Lanier et al., 1999; Lee et al., 2004; Strasser et al., 2004) as well as the microtubule interactors, plus end-tracking proteins (Lanier et al., 1999; Lee et al., 2004). The precise significance of these molecules in directed growth, however, remains a subject of active investigation.

Several molecules that can signal between guidance receptors and the cytoskeleton in growth cones have been identified. Rho family members, which can regulate both actin and microtubules, have been implicated in signaling downstream from guidance receptors (Guan and Rao, 2003). Also, relative concentrations of cyclic nucleotides (cyclic adenosine monophosphate [cAMP] and cyclic guanosine monophosphate [cGMP]) can modulate the response of growth cones to guidance cues. For instance, a gradient of brain-derived neurotrophic factor (BDNF), a factor that is usually attractive for *Xenopus* growth cones, becomes repulsive if the growth cone is treated with a cAMP inhibitor (Song et al., 1997). Another potential signal downstream from guidance receptors is Ca^{2+}. Live imaging of growth cones in culture shows that transient increases in Ca^{2+} on one side of the growth cone correlate with turning toward the contralateral side (Gomez et al., 2001). Interestingly, larger Ca^{2+} transients can result in ipsilateral turning. This paradox is explained by data indicating that low concentrations of Ca^{2+} act primarily through calcineurin phosphatase, whereas higher concentrations act via calcium-calmodulin–dependent protein kinase II (Wen et al., 2004). The recent finding that Ca^{2+} concentrations in the growth cone can be modulated by cAMP and cGMP control of calcium channels suggests that Ca^{2+} acts on growth cone guidance downstream from the cyclic nucleotides (Nishiyama et al., 2003). Though data on interactions between receptors, signals, effectors, and the cytoskeleton are emerging, much remains to be done before a complete model of how a specific guidance cue results in a change in growth cone motility can be constructed.

AXON GUIDANCE

In the late nineteenth century, Ramon y Cajal proposed that axons could be guided chemotropically, but the idea fell out of fashion and was untested until it was revisited by Roger Sperry in the 1940s (Sperry, 1963). In a series of classic experiments, Sperry severed a frog optic nerve, rotated the eye 180°, and then allowed connections to form again. These frogs made 180° errors in their attempts to catch flies. In contradiction to the popular view, including that of his thesis advisor, Sperry concluded that the regenerated axons did not innervate new target regions to compensate for the eye rotation, but projected to their original sites in the tectum. The outcomes of this and other related experiments led Sperry to propose that extending axons are guided by "cytochemical tags." He further proposed that neural connectivity is specified with only a few such tags or cues distributed in orthogonal gradients (Sperry, 1963). Several of these cues have now been identified, validating these principles and indicating that axon guidance is best considered in their context.

Guidance cues can be secreted from a restricted source to form long-range, diffusible gradients that act as molecular beacons, whereas membrane-attached cues can form short-range, standing gradients (see Directed Growth, above). Concurrently, adhesion molecules expressed along the surface of axons can interact with other axons or particular substrates to promote axon fasciculation, extension, turning, or stopping. Most cues have different functions at different stages of development or in different pathways, and many have multiple receptors and co-receptors that can mediate different responses. This high degree of complexity makes it difficult to sort out which interactions are important for the generation of particular connections, but it supports Sperry's idea that a small number of guidance cues can generate the diverse responses required for high-fidelity network development. In light of this diversity, exemplary cases of axon guidance have been selected to illustrate how the challenges of directed growth and specificity are met.

Many individual growth cones appear to express all of the receptors required at the appropriate time and place to respond to the cues necessary for their final targeting. Some pathways capitalize on the efforts of a few pioneer neurons. Pioneers are best understood in invertebrates, where it is well established that they differentiate and make connections early in development when distances are small. The connections provide a path for axons extending from later-born neurons. In mammalian cerebral cortex, the developing cortical plate is sandwiched between transient layers called the *marginal zone* and *subplate* that contain the earliest born neurons (Marin-Padilla, 1971). Populations of subplate neurons send axons to the thalamus before the layer V and VI neurons that form the adult projections are even born (McConnell et al., 1989). In a very different way, Cajal-Retzius neurons in the marginal zone pioneer local intracortical connections and may be important for generating a columnar organization of cortical networks (Sarnat and Flores-Sarnat,

2002). In this way, pioneer neurons produce frameworks that, for particular networks, are critical for specifying pathways.

Midline Crossing in Vertebrate Ventral Spinal Cord

After closely examining the appearance and trajectories of Golgi-impregnated neurons in the spinal cord, Ramon y Cajal hypothesized that groups of dorsally disposed neurons give rise to axons that are attracted to the ventral midline. The proof came nearly 100 years later, when dissected midline explants were demonstrated to be attractive to commissurally projecting axons (Tessier-Lavigne et al., 1988) (Fig. 4–4). This system was used as a bioassay to isolate netrin-1 and -2, which are soluble cues that act as attractive proteins for commissural axons. Subsequent work has demonstrated that netrin's attractive action is mediated by binding to its receptor, deleted in colorectal cancer (DCC) (Kennedy et al., 1994; Serafini et al., 1994; Keino-Masu et al., 1996; Fazeli et al., 1997). Interestingly, mutant mice hypomorphic for the netrin-1 allele or lacking DCC still show some commissural axon crossing (Serafini et al., 1996; Fazeli et al., 1997). This finding indicates that netrin does not act alone. Sonic hedgehog (Shh), a morphogen secreted by the floor plate, is better known for its role in neural progenitor specification (Charron et al., 2003; Yoshikawa and Thomas, 2004). Shh can also attract or influence the direction of polarization of commissural axons through its receptor smoothened (Smo). Assisting the actions of both Shh and netrin, heterodimers of bone morphogenic protein 7 (BMP7) and growth differentiation factor 7 (GDF7) secreted from dorsal roof plate cells repel the incipient commissural axons away from the dorsal midline (Augsburger et al., 1999; Butler and Dodd, 2003).

Once attracted to the floor plate, commissural axons cross the midline (Seeger et al., 1993). Other axons turn back and form ipsilateral longitudinal tracts. Crossing is regulated in part by the signaling of chemorepellants of the Slit family which are secreted by midline glia and bind Robo family receptors on commissurally projecting growth cones (Rothberg et al., 1988, 1990; Brose et al., 1999; Long et al., 2004). Unlike other Robo family members, the receptor Rig-1 appears to attenuate Slit sensitivity, since commissural axons never cross the midline in Rig-1-deficient mice (Sabatier et al., 2004). In wild-type

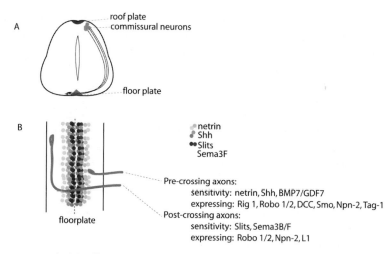

FIGURE 4–4 Midline guidance. Schematic diagrams of developing mammalian spinal cord depict the trajectories of commissurally projecting neurons relative to the roof plate and floor plate in cross-section (**A**) or molecular gradients in longitudinal preparation through the ventral midline (**B**). Pre-crossing axons are repelled from dorsal midline by BMP7 in the roof plate (not shown) and attracted ventrally by netrin and Shh gradients emanating from the floor plate (shaded circles). Post-crossing axons become sensitive to Slit- and Semaphorin 3B and F-mediated repulsion and do not return to the floor plate. (*Source*: Modified from Williams et al., 2004)

animals, Rig-1 concentrations decrease and Robo-1 and -2 amounts increase soon after crossing, which may serve to expel axons from the midline (Sabatier et al., 2004). This expulsion is probably aided by Robo-1's ability to silence DCC-mediated attraction to netrin by binding directly to DCC in the presence of Slit (Stein and Tessier-Lavigne, 2001) or by growth cone desensitization to the high concentrations of netrin at the midline (Piper et al., 2005). Sema-3B, an additional soluble repellant secreted by the floor plate, prevents axons from returning to the midline via interactions with its receptor neuropilin-2 (Zou et al., 2000). After crossing, the position of longitudinally running tracts appears to be regulated by the midline Slit gradient interacting with Robo-1 or -2 (Rajagopalan et al., 2000; Simpson et al., 2000). Concurrently, Wnt-4, acting through its receptor frizzled3, and Shh, acting through hedgehog interacting protein, help orient axons anteriorly in the longitudinal axis (Lyuksyutova et al., 2003; Bourikas er al., 2005), but the interaction between these cues has yet to be investigated. Collectively, these data support the ideas that certain guidance cues can

trump the others and suggest that cues are processed hierarchically rather than being integrated.

Generating Retinotectal Maps

Once axons reach their target region, they terminate in highly organized patterns that reflect their points of origin. The projections extending from retinal ganglion cells to the tectum in fish and frogs and to the superior colliculus in rodents has served as the canonical system for studying the development of patterning. In most mammals, a light shown in the far left visual field projects on the ventronasal part of the left retina, which in turn projects contralaterally to the caudomedial region of the superior colliculus (Fig. 4–5). If an experimenter systematically moves a recording electrode rostrally through the superior colliculus, the stimulating light source needs to be moved in an orderly progression from left to right to activate the neurons. Thus, the superior colliculus contains topographic maps of the visual field.

A large body of data support the correlation of ephrin gradients in the retina and superior colliculus interactions (McLaughlin et al., 2003; van Horck et al., 2004). EphA receptor protein kinases are expressed in high in temporal and low in nasal retina. EphrinA ligands are expressed mostly in high caudal to low rostral gradients in the superior colliculus. The ligands guide the formation of retinotopic maps oriented in a rostral-to-caudal progression by repulsive eyes. Mice having targeted disruptions in both ephrinA2 and A5 genes show a near complete loss of rostral-to-caudal patterning in the superior colliculus (Feldheim et al., 2000). Introducing new gradients by overexpressing additional EphA receptors in subpopulations of retinal ganglion cells results in the creation of two maps along the rostral-to-caudal axis (Brown et al., 2000). Orthogonal gradients of EphB2 in the retina and ephrin-B1 and 2 in the tectum label the dorsoventral axis (Braisted et al., 1997). Members of the ephrinB subfamily appear to operate principally via attractive rather than repulsive interactions (Hindges et al.,

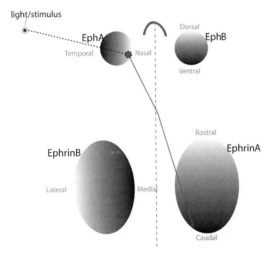

FIGURE 4–5 The retinocollicular map. Schematic diagram depicts orthogonal gradients of Ephs and ephrins that mediate retinotopic mapping together with the trajectory of a single projection in the rodent projection from retina to superior colliculus. Light from a point in the far left visual field strikes the nasal retina of the left eye (circle) in its monocular region. Ganglion cells in this zone project (dark axon) to caudal–medial points on the right superior colliculus (oval). EphA tyrosine kinases bind and are repelled from high concentrations of ephrinA ligands, whereas EphB tyrosine kinases bind and are attracted to high concentrations of EphB ligand.

2002; Mann et al., 2002). The mechanisms guiding retinal ganglion cell axons appear to follow Sperry's chemoaffinity model of targeting by orthogonal standing gradients (Sperry, 1963). In an important extension on this model, recent work indicates that at low concentrations, EphA–ephrinA interactions are attractive for axon extension, whereas high concentrations elicit a repulsive response. Thus axons will readily extend into the superior colliculus until they reach a point where positive and negative influences are balanced (Hansen et al., 2004).

It is noteworthy that in mice lacking ephrinA2 and A5, retinal ganglion cell axons still target the superior colliculus, and their axonal arbors are evenly distributed within the entire space allotted (Feldheim et al., 2000). The mechanism determining this interaxonal spacing remains unknown. Furthermore, in the same mice, there is evidence in the clustering of optic nerve terminals that some nearest-neighbor relationships, and thus some topographic ordering, is maintained over small distances. Such clustering has been proposed to be the result of correlated activity (Feldheim et al., 2000) and supports the idea that activity plays a major role in the pruning and shaping of the final maps that are generated by standing Eph and ephrin gradients.

Cues Are Bifunctional

Netrins are generally attractive and EphA–ephrinA interactions, repulsive, but nearly all guidance cues can generate diametrically opposed responses in particular circumstances (Fig. 4–6). Different responses are sometimes the function of different cell types. For example, netrin-1, secreted by the ventral floor plate, repels motor axons extending from the trochlear nucleus such that they exit the dorsal aspect of the brain at the midbrain–hindbrain border. This stands in stark contrast to its attraction for spinal commissural axons (Colamarino and Tessier-Lavigne, 1995). More commonly, changes between attraction and repulsion occur at different stages of outgrowth and appear to be employed within individual growth cones. Such dynamic signaling appears to be required for steady axon extension through transition zones, such as the ventral midline, and to titrate growth cone responsiveness within a target to achieve a smooth representational map.

Bifunctional responses result from differential activation of downstream signaling pathways that

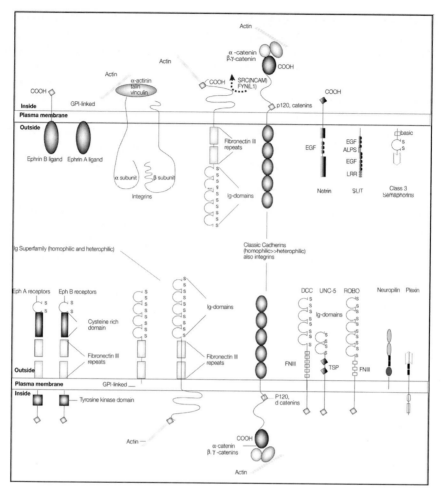

FIGURE 4–6 Guidance cues. Examples of long- and short-range axon guidance proteins used in vertebrates. Molecules are depicted across from one another as they would be in situ. Members of the ephrin family generate topographic maps, such as that found in the retinotectal projection. Integrins, and immunoglobulin (Ig) superfamily members of the calcium-dependent (classic cadherins) and calcium-independent classes (e.g., Ng-CAM) mediate short-range guidance through contact-dependent mechanisms. Three major families of long-range axon guidance are indicated here: netrin and its receptor, DCC; Slit and its receptor, Robo; and class 3 Semaphorins and its co-receptor complex, neuropilins and plexins. (*Source:* Modified from Benson et al., 2001, and Yu and Bargmann, 2001)

ultimately regulate actin dynamics (for review, see Pasterkamp and Kolodkin, 2003). For instance, attractive growth cone turning of *Xenopus* spinal motor growth cones to gradients of netrin-1 can be converted to repulsion upon association of the cytoplasmic domains of the netrin DCC receptor with a co-receptor, UNC5 (Hong et al., 1999). Additionally, changing amounts of cyclic nucleotides can change growth cone responses to BDNF, netrin-1, and Sema3D (Ming et al., 1997; Song et al., 1998), results suggesting that previous experience or environment can alter responsiveness. In support of this possibilty, *Xenopus* retinal ganglion cell axons grown on laminin have decreased ratios of cAMP/cGMP relative to those grown on fibronectin, and are repulsed rather than attracted by netrin (Hopker et al., 1999). These examples

(a) suggest that the response to a cue can be modified by both outside-in (receptor to signaling pathway) and inside-out (signaling molecule to altered state of receptor responsiveness) mechanisms and (b) support the idea that growth cones have multiple means by which to finely tune their responses.

Adhesion and Guidance

Growth cones explore their environment by regulating their attachment to other neurons, glia, or components of the extracellular matrix (ECM). Contact-dependent interactions between cell adhesion molecules (CAMs) of the immunoglobulin superfamily, cadherin superfamily, integrins, and the ECM generate traction sufficient for growth cone extension. Interactions between CAMs and ECMs that are inhibitory to growth create boundaries (Snow and Letourneau, 1992). It has long been suspected that standing gradients of ECMs may also be able to orient or steer growth cones, but the data directly supporting this role as a guidance cue are quite recent because of the difficulty of generating continuous, substrate-bound gradients (Adams et al., 2005). Cell–cell and cell–substrate interactions can promote axon bundling (fasciculation) and defasciculation, thereby making the process of guidance more efficient. On the other hand, there is little evidence indicating that selective fasciculation serves as a critical guidance cue (Benson et al., 2001).

Contact-dependent interactions can stop axon extension when it has reached its final target region, preceding the formation of terminal branches and synapses. Axons usually terminate within small neural groups or a restricted number of layers, greatly reducing the number of potential individual neural targets. Homophilic N-cadherin adhesion appears to prevent thalamocortical and retinocollicular axons from extending past their target layers (Inoue and Sanes, 1997; Poskanzer et al., 2003) and can apically restrict mossy-fiber terminal fields in hippocampus (Bekirov et al., 2002). Similarly, attractive interactions between axonin-1/transient axonal glycoprotein 1 and neuron–glia CAM (Ng-CAM), and between F11/contactin and Ng-CAM-related CAM (Nr-CAM) contribute to lamina-specific terminations of nociceptive and proprioceptive fibers, respectively, in chick spinal cord (Perrin et al., 2001). Thus, CAMs appear to encode laminar recognition cues, but they may also provide a stop signal, preventing axons from extending further. Whether recognition and stopping are mediated concomitantly by a particular cue or combination of cues has yet to be investigated.

Few experiments have addressed directly how adhesive cues become integrated with other guidance cues. The emerging picture promises a complicated answer. The CAM L1 can support rapid axon extension, but in a *cis* complex with the receptor neuropilin-1, it also appears to be required for repulsion of cortical axons by the soluble ligand Sema3A (Castellani et al., 2000). Additionally, soluble L1 (which can be generated by metalloprotease cleavage) can convert a repulsive Sema3A response to attraction (Castellani et al., 2000) in a manner reminiscent of laminin's ability to convert an attractive netrin response to one of repulsion (see Cues Are Bifunctional, above) (Hopker et al., 1999).

Interactions between substrate and soluble cues may underlie how commissural axons can traverse the neutral midline and extend laterally toward longitudinal tracts. Robo activation by Slit can eliminate N-cadherin-based adhesion that normally promotes rapid extension (Rhee et al., 2002). This activation correlates with the formation of a complex between Robo, N-cadherin, and Abelson kinase and is accompanied by phosphorylation of β-catenin, a necessary cadherin binding partner. Participation in this complex, in turn, occludes interaction of N-cadherin with the actin cytoskeleton. One can imagine that rapid N-cadherin-mediated outgrowth concurrent with high Rig-1 expression would suffice to permit progression through an otherwise neutral midline to the point at which Robo concentrations increase, where axons would disengage from N-cadherin, turn, and grow longitudinally by a different mechanism.

Thus, several attractive and repulsive, short- and long-ranged cues act hierarchically and occasionally collaborate to generate a final stereotyped targeting outcome. Some cues act similarly throughout the rostral–caudal extent of the developing nervous system, but the actions of others appear to differ across CNS regions. Additionally, certain molecules are co-opted during multiple epochs of development for slightly different purposes. The temporal sensitivities of such cues are just beginning to be appreciated with the advent of conditional genetic tools and improved methods for transient transfections. These techniques are useful for determining the virtually unknown mechanisms that stop axon extension or stimulate the generation of terminal arbors for synapse formation.

SYNAPTOGENESIS

Sherrington coined the term *synapse* in 1897 to describe the sites where axons contact the dendrites or soma of other neurons, in keeping with the neuron doctrine that nervous tissue comprises separate cells. Although this doctrine also was espoused by Ramon y Cajal, Kölliker, His, Forél, and several other contemporaries, Golgi and others fervently supported an opposing reticular theory that the nervous system was an anastomosing network (Shepherd, 1991). Since arguments from both sides were based mostly on Golgi-impregnated samples viewed by light microscopy, unequivocal evidence supporting the former doctrine did not come until half a century later from a series of electrophysiological and EM studies. Kuffler (1942) and Fatt and Katz (1951) demonstrated at the frog neuromuscular junction that the current underlying changes in membrane potential at the postsynaptic muscle endplate could not derive directly from the presynaptic motor axon, as the reticular theory would have predicted. Then studies by Palade and Palay (1954) and De Robertis and Bennett (1955) in the mid-1950s provided clear, high-resolution EM images of a cleft separating pre- and postsynaptic membranes at chemical synapses. Ironically, solid evidence supporting the existence of an electrotonic synapse came shortly thereafter, with the identification of gap junctions, where Bennett (1963) and others demonstrated that ionic current can flow directly from one neuron to another (Peters et al., 1991; Shepherd, 1991).

Subsequent electrophysiological, anatomical, and biochemical findings continue to challenge our collective notion of the synapse beyond Sherrington's general conceptualization. Though characterizing the mature synapse in differentiated neural networks has occupied neurobiologists for more than a century, more recent work indicates that earlier stages of assembly and differentiation are crucial for generating a normal network. In this vein, the last sections of this chapter describe how axonal and dendritic morphologies and composition are modified to assemble synapses in the vertebrate CNS. Since maturation is generally assessed by the extent to which adult features are present, the following discussion of chemical

and electrical synapses begins with descriptions of their mature form and composition.

Structure and Composition of Mature Chemical Synapses

Ultrastructural Features

The mature chemical synapse is a polarized, adhesive junction formed most commonly between axons and dendrites. In electron micrographs this synapse (sometimes called a *zonula adherens*) is characterized by rigidly parallel pre- and postsynaptic membranes, separated by a cleft of 12 to 20 nm, electron-dense material within the cleft and, in most cases, thick, electron-dense material in the cytosol subjacent to the postsynaptic membrane (Fig. 4–7). This synapse resembles other adhesive junctions, but can be distinguished by the presence of synaptic vesicles (SVs) close to the junction in the presynaptic cytosol (Gray, 1963). In aldehyde-fixed EM specimens, SVs are roughly 40–50 nm in width, can appear spherical or oblong (pleomorphic), and can have agranular or electron-dense cores (Grillo and Palay, 1963; Valdivia, 1971). At most synapses they are found in a readily releasable pool near the plasma membrane or in a more removed reserve pool. Vesicles within this pool can be found docked within a gridded array of presynaptic cytomatrix components or, in photoreceptors, along a presynaptic ribbon that runs orthogonal to the junction (Sjostrand, 1958; Gray, 1959a; Bloom and Aghajanian, 1966, 1968). Mitochondria are often found both pre- and postsynaptically (Ibata and Otsuka, 1968; Bodian, 1971), and a postsynaptic web of filaments is often subjacent to the postsynaptic density (PSD) (De Robertis et al., 1961; Gray, 1963; Peters and Kaiserman-Abramof, 1969; Steward and Levy, 1982; Spacek and Harris, 1997).

Although dendrodendritic, dendrosomatic, and all other conceiveable pairings do occur in the vertebrate CNS, the large majority of chemical synapses encountered are axosomatic or axodendritic (Peters et al., 1991). Axodendritic synapses occur on either smooth dendritic shafts or mushroom-shaped protrusions called *spines* that stud the dendritic arbors of most glutamatergic neurons (Nimchinsky et al., 2002). Spine synapses are typified by a pronounced PSD, a relatively wide cleft (near 20 nm), polyribosomes in close proximity to smooth endoplasmic reticulum, and rounded presynaptic vesicles in

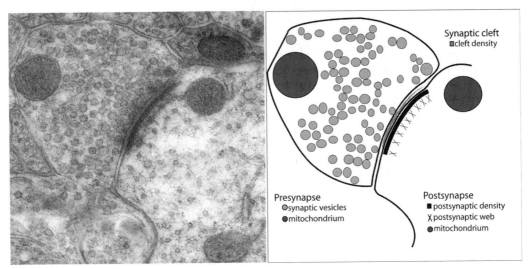

FIGURE 4–7 Chemical synapse. This electron micrograph (left) and schematic diagram (right) of unstained tissue sections taken from adult rat spinal cord depict several ultrastructural features typical of mature type I, asymmetric synapses. Among these features, abundant presynaptic vesicles and a pronounced postsynaptic density (PSD) are the most reliable and conspicuous. Also visible are the electron-dense collection of transmembrane and matrix molecules in the synaptic cleft and the filamentous web subjacent to the PSD. Mitochondria are present in both the presynaptic terminal and the dendritic spine.

aldehyde-fixed tissues. By comparison, some shaft and nearly all somal synapses have a much less pronounced or absent PSD, a narrower cleft (near 12 nm), and contain both rounded and oblong (pleomorphic) vesicles. In Gray's studies of cerebral cortex, he termed these synapses types I and II, respectively, although Colonnier's distinction of asymmetrical and symmetrical synapses based on the appearance of the PSD is more widely used (Gray, 1959b; Colonnier, 1968).

Molecular Constituents

Morphological distinctions between synapses reflect functional differences: round SVs at asymmetric synapses usually release glutamate, and pleomorphic SVs at symmetric sites commonly carry inhibitory neurotransmitters (Eccles et al., 1961; Uchizono, 1965). Small dense-core SVs, in contrast, generally carry catecholaminergic neuromodulators, and large dense-core vesicles (~100–200 nm) carry neuropeptides (De Robertis and Pelligrino de Iraldi, 1961; Wolfe et al., 1962). As with most classification schemes, these correlations have notable exceptions. For instance, some small, clear SVs contain neuropeptides such as oxytocin or a combination of neurotransmitter and neuropeptide (Meister et al., 1986), and some 80 nm dense-core vesicles can carry catecholamines. Additionally, another type of 80 nm dense-core vesicle is thought to deliver proteins required at nascent synapses (Ahmari et al., 2000; Bresler et al., 2001; Shapira et al., 2003). The latter also has been called a *Piccolo-Bassoon transport vesicle* (PTV) for the proteins used to identify it during purification (Zhai, 2001).

Converging technical approaches have been used to identify and characterize a bevy of synaptic constituents, such as those involved in vesicle trafficking (Sudhof, 2004). Synapsins in the vesicle membrane tether SVs to an actin framework until they are phosphorylated by calcium-dependent kinases following Ca^{2+} influx (Bahler and Greengard, 1987; Petrucci and Morrow, 1987). Membrane-bound Rab3 appears to modulate transport of these liberated vesicles to active zones (Leenders et al., 2001). SVs dock at these sites through the binding of soluble N-ethylmaleimide-sensitive fusion protein attachment protein receptors (SNARES) in the vesicle membrane to targets at the plasma membrane. Among these interactions, the complex formed by the vesicular SNARES synaptobrevin/vesicle–associated membrane protein with its target SNARES, synapto-somal associated protein (SNAP) 25 and syntaxin, was the first identified and is the most widely known (Soll-ner et al., 1993; Pevsner et al., 1994). Syntaxins, in turn, can bind to either Munc18 or Munc13 in the presynaptic grid to modulate the priming events for vesicle fusion (Hata et al., 1993; Ashery et al., 2000; Misura et al., 2000). SNAP-25 binding by synaptotag-min in the vesicle membrane appears to regulate subsequent fusion pore opening during calcium-dependent exocytosis (Jorgensen et al., 1995; Sugita and Sudhof, 2000; Littleton et al., 2001).

ECM proteins such as laminins, collagens, and pro-teoglycans are found in and around the synaptic cleft (Dityatev and Schachner, 2003). As with other adhe-sive junctions, the density within the synaptic cleft con-tains CAMs such as Ng-CAM and N-cadherin (Chavis and Westbrook, 2001; Phillips et al., 2001; Schuster et al., 2001; Guan and Rao, 2003). Members of receptor-ligand families such as Eph-ephrins and the neurexin-neuroligins are also present (Scheiffele et al., 2000; Henderson et al., 2001; Dean et al., 2003; Grunwald et al., 2004). Transmembrane proteases such as metalloprotease-disintegrins cleave the ectodomains of these transynaptic molecules to attenuate signaling (Tanaka et al., 2000; Matsumoto-Miyai et al., 2003). Other extracellular proteases such as plasminogen acti-vators can degrade components of the ECM in a man-ner suspected to permit morphological changes at the synapse during development and plasticity (reviewed in Dityatev and Schachner, 2003; Berardi et al., 2004).

In the postsynapse, the PSD comprises a number of signaling and scaffolding molecules for receptors in the plasma membrane (Walsh and Kuruc, 1992; Wa-likonis et al., 2000; Kim and Sheng, 2004; Peng et al., 2004; Phillips et al., 2004; Collins et al., 2005). One quintessential component is PSD-95, a member of the PSD/synapse–associated protein/membrane–associated guanylate kinase family of scaffolding mol-ecules. It is typically found at excitatory synapses and directly binds transmembrane components such as the N-methyl-D-aspartate receptor (NMDAR) neuroli-gin, as well as molecules involved in secondary signal-ing such as neuronal nitric oxide synthetase and regulatory proteins such as synaptic guanidine triphos-photase activating protein for Ras (Irie et al., 1997; Kim and Sheng, 2004). Similarly, glutamate receptor–interacting protein interacts with the α-amino-3-hydroxy-5-methyl-4-isoxazole propionate receptor (AMPAR) and gephyrin with the glycine receptor

(Meyer et al., 1995; Dong et al., 1997; Levi et al., 2004). The cytoskeletal proteins actin and spectrin concentrate at both the pre- and postsynapse. These proteins, along with tubulin, are thought to under-lie the characteristic filamentous appearance of the postsynaptic web and may contribute to changes in postsynaptic receptor composition during develop-ment and plasticity (Matus et al., 1980; Fischer et al., 2000; Kim and Lisman, 2001; Wu et al., 2002; re-viewed in Moss and Smart, 2001; Luscher and Keller, 2004; van Zundert et al., 2004).

Structural Correlates of Synapse Assembly and Maturation

The pre- and postsynaptic elements of developing cir-cuits arise principally from interactions between ax-onal and somatodendritic filopodia. Axonal growth cones may form terminal boutons as they do at the neuromuscular junction (NMJ), but predominantly form en passant ("in passing") along the length of an axon (Bodian, 1968; Hinds and Hinds, 1972; Skoff and Hamburger, 1974; Vaughn et al., 1977; Vaughn and Sims, 1978; Mason, 1982). Coated vesicles and smooth endoplasmic reticulum in branching axons and coated pits near the postsynaptic densities of nas-cent contacts may participate in trafficking of synap-tic components or membrane recycling during early periods of synaptogenesis (reviewed in Vaughn, 1989). Eighty-nanometer granulated PTVs also have been found in the vicinity of nascent synapses (May and Biscoe, 1973; Ahmari et al., 2000). Another char-acteristic feature of many immature synapses is a reversed asymmetry, from the early presence of presy-naptic vesicles in the absence of a pronounced PSD (Hayes and Roberts, 1973; Vaughn et al., 1977; Newman-Gage and Westrum, 1984). As the synapse differentiates, the PSD thickens, at least at type I sites, and presynaptic vesicles steadily increase in number (Bloom and Aghajanian, 1966, 1968; Jones, 1983; Steward and Falk, 1986; Vaughn, 1989).

Mechanisms of Synapse Initiation

Spinal motor neuron dendrites arborize extensively as they enter the marginal layer, a zone occupied pro-fusely by axonal terminals (Vaughn et al., 1988). Ob-servations such as this one and the branching of dendritic filopodia at sites of PSD-95 clustering suggest a "synaptotropic" branching of dendritic arbors in response to presynaptic signals (Vaughn et al., 1988; Niell et al., 2004). Axon collaterals similarly form at sites of synaptobrevin II clustering during initial contact, consistent with a role for retrograde signaling in presynaptic differentiation. Signals promoting early stages of synapse formation derive from both pre- and postsynaptic sources, but the source and identity of the signal initiating this cascade of events are still the subject of intense investigation. Some initial clues have come from a series of biochemical and genetic studies at the NMJ, which demonstrate that motor neuron–derived agrin promotes clustering of acetylcholine receptors at sites of innervation, whereas an unidentified retrograde myotube-derived signal is required in turn for normal differentiation of the presynapse (DeChiara et al., 1996; Gautam et al., 1996).

This bidirectional signaling during NMJ differentiation is recapitulated at central synapses. Analogous to agrin at the NMJ, the secreted lectin Narp can cluster AMPAR and promote AMPAR-dependent NMDAR clustering at synapses in cultures of dissociated hippocampal or spinal neurons (O'Brien et al., 1999; Mi et al., 2004). Vesicles can be recruited to the presynapse either through the binding of postsynaptic neuroligins to presynaptic β-neurexin receptors or the presumably homophilic binding of SynCAM (Scheiffele et al., 2000; Biederer et al., 2002; Dean et al., 2003; Graf et al., 2004). SynCAM signaling also can promote glutamatergic transmission in non-neuronal cells partnered with neurons in culture (Biederer et al., 2002). Whether the loss of SynCAM blocks or attenuates synapse induction remains to be demonstrated; down-regulation or blockade of neuroligin isoforms attenuates synapse induction (Chih et al., 2005). Additionally, blockade of cadherin function or ECM–integrin signaling soon after synapse assembly compromises nascent or mature synapse structure, respectively (Togashi et al., 2002; Bozdagi et al., 2004). Blocking of ECM–integrin signaling similarly compromises mature synapse structure (Chavis and Westbrook, 2001; Schuster et al., 2001; Chan et al., 2003). Together these findings support the idea that several recognition and adhesion factors initiate and maintain synapses coordinately.

Maturation of Synapse Composition

Naive sites of contact become competent for neurotransmission through the progressive transport and stable recruitment of synaptic components. N-cadherin and the presynaptic grid components Bassoon, Piccolo, and Rab3-interacting molecule appear to be transported to presynaptic sites by PTVs (Wang et al., 1997; Richter et al., 1999; Ahmari et al., 2000; Bresler et al., 2001; Phillips et al., 2001; Altrock et al., 2003; Shapira et al., 2003; Jontes et al., 2004). Postsynaptically, PSD-95, NMDAR, and AMPAR in the dendrite accumulate at the synapse over a more protracted time period covering a couple of hours. Time-lapse imaging of dissociated hippocampal neurons grown for 8–12 days in culture shows that PSD-95 and NMDAR accumulate at synapses gradually, implying that these components are added piecewise rather than in larger increments by a fusion particle (Friedman et al., 2000; Bresler et al., 2001, 2004). Similar work in dissociated cortical neurons grown for 2–4 days suggests that NMDAR and AMPAR can be delivered in packets akin to presynaptic transport vesicles, potentially implicating distinct mechanisms for receptor delivery at different stages of development or in different neuron types (Washbourne et al., 2002).

Young synapses exhibit heterogeneity in receptor composition. For instance, many immature glutamatergic sites contain NMDAR clusters but are thought to lack functional AMPAR. Over time, the occurrence of these "silent" synapses diminishes with the insertion of AMPAR at these sites (Isaac, 2003). The NMDAR subunit composition also is developmentally regulated, as the NR2A subunit replaces NR2B at synaptic sites (Sheng et al., 1994). Maturation of synapse receptor content and receptor subunit composition in these cases is thought to be activity-dependent (Rao et al., 1998; Tovar and Westbrook, 1999; Moss and Smart, 2001; Christie et al., 2002; Anderson et al., 2004; Luscher and Keller, 2004; van Zundert et al., 2004).

Dale originally postulated that individual neurons release only one type of neurotransmitter to account for differential muscle responses to preganglionic and postganglionic sympathetic fiber stimulation. This principle has been reinterpreted as counterexamples, primarily in developing systems, have come to light.[1] Analogous to the aforementioned combination of neuropeptide- and neurotransmitter-carrying vesicle populations in some adult terminals (De Robertis and Pellegrini de Iraldi, 1961), the vesicular glutamate transporter-3 co-distributes with vesicular transporters for glycine, γ-aminobutyric acid (GABA), acetylcholine, and monoamine neurotransmitters during early brain development (McIntire et al., 1997; Chaudhry et al., 1998; Takamori et al., 2000; Boulland et al., 2004). In a similar vein, glycine and GABA are co-released in individual vesicles by afferents of the medial nucleus of the trapezoid body (MNTB) onto the lateral superior olivary nucleus during a developmentally regulated switch in neurotransmitter (Nabekura et al., 2004). Most of these afferents are concurrently glutamatergic during the first postnatal week, but over time the incidence of this glutamatergic phenotype among MNTB neurons diminishes (Gillespie et al., 2005). Likewise, several lines of evidence suggest that glutamatergic dentate gyrus granule cells can synthesize and release GABA and that the appearance of this GABAergic phenotype is developmentally regulated (Gutierrez, 2003).

Mechanisms of Synapse Maintenance and Disassembly

A *Munc18-1* null mutation abrogates vesicular neurotransmitter release (Verhage et al., 2000; Voets et al., 2001). Despite the apparent role for presynaptically derived signals in early synaptogenesis, prenatal cytoarchitecture and synapse ultrastructure in *Munc18-1* mice appear surprisingly normal. But by birth, massive neurodegeneration has ensued (Verhage et al., 2000), which suggests that presynaptic release is not required for synapse formation but is important for maintenance. Thyroid hormone deficiencies similarly reduce dendritic spine number (Bicknell, 1998; Thompson and Potter, 2000). The augmentation of spine number by estradiol and terminal number by BDNF and glial-derived factors is consistent with the proposed roles for these factors in synapse maintenance as well (McEwen, 1999; Mauch et al., 2001; Ullian et al., 2001, 2004).

An exuberance of initial contacts is thought to be pruned several-fold over the course of normal development (Knyihar et al., 1978; Huttenlocher, 1979; Rakic et al., 1986), implicating mechanisms for selective synapse maintenance and elimination. The early F-actin dependence of postsynaptic composition suggests that synapse-specific factors interacting with the actin cytoskeleton can promote the maintenance of a subset of sites in the vertebrate CNS (Allison et al., 1998; Zhang and Benson, 2001). Additional studies suggest that stabilization of particular postsynaptic sites depends on transmitter-evoked receptor activation, Ca^{2+} release, or local protein synthesis (Frey and

Morris, 1997; Martin et al., 1997; Engert and Bonhoeffer, 1999; Lohmann et al., 2002; Hashimoto and Kano, 2003; Tashiro et al., 2003; Nagerl et al., 2004). Conversely, depressed or blocked activity leads to the elimination of affected spines in developing hippocampal slices (Nagerl et al., 2004; Zhou et al., 2004).

Notably, the effects of activity on synapse number in the brain appear to be developmentally restricted (Fiala et al., 2002; Grutzendler et al., 2002; Nagerl et al., 2004). This window for activity-dependent changes in synapse number, and pruning in general, has been proposed to underlie critical periods of experience-dependent plasticity in the neocortex and cerebellum. Consistent with this possibility, the effects of monocular deprivation on ocular dominance (OD) in cortex are attenuated when protein synthesis is blocked during the critical period. Furthermore, degradation of chondroitin sulfate proteoglycans in the perisynaptic ECM, which are thought to inhibit axonal sprouting, reactivates this OD plasticity in adult mice (Berardi et al., 2004). Additionally, blocking of NMDAR activation during a critical period increases climbing fiber innervation in the cerebellum that correlates with impaired motor coordination (Kakizawa et al., 2000).

Cellular and Subcellular Target Specificity

An axon guided to its target lamina must be able to identify its appropriate target cell type (e.g., GABAergic interneuron vs. glutamatergic projection neuron) and subcellular domain (e.g., distal vs. proximal dendrite). This final stage of axon guidance is thought to be mediated by the cell- and domain-specific expression of CAMs or receptor-ligand combinations with singular affinities. For instance, GABAergic basket-cell axons are guided along cerebellar Purkinje axons by an ankyrinG-based gradient of neurofascin (also called neurofilament 168) to form axo-axonal synapses at the axon initial segment (Jenkins and Bennett, 2001; Ango et al., 2004). This hypothesis of subcellular targeting, though widely accepted, is otherwise untested except with N-cadherin, which appears not to function in this capacity (Bozdagi et al., 2004).

A challenge for the developing network is how to recruit or selectively retain synaptic components at specific sites of innervation. GluR6-containing kainate receptors are recruited to sites of N-cadherin activation (Coussen et al., 2002). Similarly, the EphB2 receptor directly clusters NMDAR when activated by its cognate ephrinB2 ligand in young hippocampal neurons (Dalva et al., 2000). Neurexin can induce independent postsynaptic clustering of GABA receptor, NMDAR, gephyrin, and PSD-95, as well as neuroligins-1 and -2. In turn, neuroligin-2 can cluster vesicles expressing vesicular transporters for glutamate, vesicular GABA transporter, or the GABA-synthesizing enzyme glutamic acid decarboxylase 65 (Graf et al., 2004; Chih et al., 2005). The abundance of synaptic factors with distinct binding specificities and clustering activities suggests that, in combination, these factors not only specify synapse placement but also encode synapse composition during maturation and plasticity.

Electrotonic Synapses

Whereas most of the literature on synapses focuses on the nature, modulation, and assembly of chemical synapses, there is growing appreciation for the functional contributions of electrical synapses (also called *gap junctions*). Electrotonic synapses are formed by the abutment of molecular hemichannels called *connexons* (Fig. 4–8). The coupled connexons, which are integral membrane proteins, produce a hermetic

channel and a synaptic gap just 2 nm wide (Goodenough, 1976). Gap junctions often form between the same subcellular domains, such as two dendrites or two somata (Peinado et al., 1993). These synapses are commonly found in lower vertebrates like the frog or chicken between axons and dendrites within the spinal cord and some brain nuclei. In mammals, these synapses are widespread in the retina and also are found in the brain and spinal cord (Paternostro et al., 1995; Rash et al., 1998; Venance et al., 2000). Gap junctions are found with greater frequency at earlier developmental stages, and it has been hypothesized that strong electrical coupling synchronizes activity and stabilizes synaptic interactions during development (Connors et al., 1983; Peinado et al., 1993). "Mixed" synapses, which contain both electrotonic and chemical elements, may serve this stabilizing role in lower vertebrates and the rat spinal cord (Rash et al., 1998, 2000).

Vertebrate connexons are hexamers of connexin isoforms (Goodenough, 1976; Segretain and Falk, 2004). Connexin composition determines channel gating properties and confers gap junctions with selective permeabilities for distinct ions and second messengers. Connexon composition in the nervous system, as in other tissues, is cell-type specific and developmentally

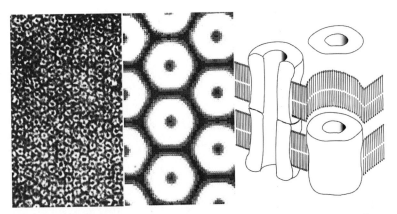

FIGURE 4–8 Gap junction. Gap junction connexons purified from mouse liver and visualized by transmission electron microscopy (left) and X-ray diffraction (middle) form orderly lattices, indicative of their sixfold symmetry and composition. A schematic representation of gap junctions in the plasma membrane (right) depicts how the abutment of connexon hemichannels in the lipid bilayer of each synaptic membrane produces a hermetic channel and a narrow synaptic gap. (*Source*: Images modified from Caspar and colleagues, 1977, and reprinted with permission from the publisher.)

regulated (Bevans et al., 1998; Suchyna et al., 1999; Bukauskas and Verselis, 2004). This spatiotemporal control of gap junction gating and permeability is likely to have consequences for nervous system assembly; however, the effect of connexin or gap junction deficiencies on synapse formation, targeting, or stability have yet to be examined.

The mechanisms guiding spatial targeting of connexins or cell type–coupling specificity in the nervous system also have yet to be examined. Work in non-neural tissues, however, suggests that molecules typically associated with other types of junctions facilitate connexin targeting to sites in the plasma membrane. For example, E-cadherin overexpression can promote normal concentrations of connexin targeting to the plasma membrane in skin papilloma cells and alter coupling preferences in transfected melanomas (Prowse et al., 1997; Hsu et al., 2000; Hernandez-Blazquez et al., 2001). Additionally, normal gap junction formation between lens cells is disturbed in Nr-CAM-deficient mice and by antibodies against N-cadherin (Frenzel and Johnson, 1996; Lustig et al., 2001). The tight junction components *zonula occludens* 1 and some claudins also associate with gap junctions with as yet undetermined functional consequences (Duffy et al., 2002).

CONCLUSIONS

Neuroscientists have defined a series of significant events or stages essential for normal differentiation and integration of neurons into a functional network. Recent work links particular stages of differentiation with the function of particular molecules or molecular families, and this work has provided the necessary tools with which mechanisms can be pursued. One challenge for future experimenters is to determine how molecular pathways of apparent overlapping or converging function are parsed into specific and meaningful outcomes.

Abbreviations

AMPAR α-amino-3-hydroxy-5-methyl-4-isoxazole propionate receptor

BDNF brain-derived neurotrophic factor

BMP bone morphogenic protein

CAM cell adhesion molecule

cAMP cyclic adenosine monophosphate

cGMP cyclic guanosine monophosphate

CNS central nervous system

CRMP collapsin response mediator protein

DCC deleted in colorectal cancer

ECM extracellular matrix

EM electron microscopy

GABA γ-aminobutyric acid

GDF growth differentiation factor

MAP microtubule-associated protein

MNTB medial nucleus of the trapezoid body

Ng-CAM neuron–glia cell adhesion molecule

NMDAR N-methyl-D-aspartate receptor

NMJ neuromuscular junction

Nr-CAM NgCAM-related cell adhesion molecule

OD ocular dominance

PSD postsynaptic density

PTV Piccolo-Bassoon transport vesicle

Shh sonic hedgehog

Smo smoothened

SNARES soluble *n*-ethylmaleimide–sensitive fusion protein-attachment protein receptors

SNAP-25 synaptosome associated protein-25

SV synaptic vesicle

SynCAM synaptic cell adhesion molecule

ACKNOWLEDGMENTS The authors thank Ioana Carcea, Elizabeth Kichula, and Cynthia Kwong for their careful reading and critical comments on this chapter and Alice Elste for her image of a chemical synapse. The authors are supported by the National Institutes of Health (CDM, IHB, and DLB), Society for Neuroscience (TRA), and an Irma T. Hirschl Award (DLB).

Equal contributions for the writing of this chapter from Mintz (polarity and motility), Bekirov (guidance), and Anderson (synaptogenesis).

Notes

1. "Dale's principle," based on arguments that transmitter function of a neuron is distinctive and "unchangeable" (Dale, 1935), actually was first defined by Eccles (1957) to state "that the same chemical transmitter is released from all the synaptic terminals

of a neurone." During the period of Dale's Nobel prize–winning research, only two neurotransmitters (acetylcholine and adrenaline) had been identified. A restatement of the principle by Eccles (1982), that "at all the axonal branches of a neuron the same transmitter substance or substances are liberated," is consistent with the later finding that neurotransmitter and neuropeptide can be released from the same nerve terminal (De Robertis and Pelligrini de Iraldi, 1961) and also encompasses the more recent findings described in this chapter's discussion.

References

Adams DN, Kao EY, Hypolite CL, Distefano MD, Hu WS, Letourneau PC (2005) Growth cones turn and migrate up an immobilized gradient of the laminin IKVAV peptide. J Neurobiol 62:134–147.

Ahmari SE, Buchanan J, Smith SJ (2000) Assembly of presynaptic active zones from cytoplasmic transport packets. Nat Neurosci 3:445–451.

Allison DW, Gelfand VI, Spector I, Craig AM (1998) Role of actin in anchoring postsynaptic receptors in cultured hippocampal neurons: differential attachment of NMDA versus AMPA receptors. J Neurosci 18:2423–2436.

Altrock WD, tom Dieck S, Sokolov M, Meyer AC, Sigler A, Brakebusch C, Fassler R, Richter K, Boeckers TM, Potschka H, Brandt C, Loscher W, Grimberg D, Dresbach T, Hempelmann A, Hassan H, Balschun D, Frey JU, Brandstatter JH, Garner CC, Rosenmund C, Gundelfinger ED (2003) Functional inactivation of a fraction of excitatory synapses in mice deficient for the active zone protein bassoon. Neuron 37:787–800.

Anderson TR, Shah PA, Benson DL (2004) Maturation of glutamatergic and GABAergic synapse composition in hippocampal neurons. Neuropharmacology 47:694–705.

Ango F, di Cristo G, Higashiyama H, Bennett V, Wu P, Huang ZJ (2004) Ankyrin-based subcellular gradient of neurofascin, an immunoglobulin family protein, directs GABAergic innervation at purkinje axon initial segment. Cell 119:257–272.

Arimura N, Inagaki N, Chihara K, Menager C, Nakamura N, Amano M, Iwamatsu A, Goshima Y, Kaibuchi K (2000) Phosphorylation of collapsin response mediator protein-2 by Rho-kinase. Evidence for two separate signaling pathways for growth cone collapse. J Biol Chem 275:23973–23980.

Ashery U, Varoqueaux F, Voets T, Betz A, Thakur P, Koch H, Neher E, Brose N, Rettig J (2000) Munc13-1 acts as a priming factor for large dense-core vesicles in bovine chromaffin cells. EMBO J 19:3586–3596.

Augsburger A, Schuchardt A, Hoskins S, Dodd J, Butler S (1999) BMPs as mediators of roof plate repulsion of commissural neurons. Neuron 24:127–141.

Baas PW (1999) Microtubules and neuronal polarity: lessons from mitosis. Neuron 22:23–31.

Bahler M, Greengard P (1987) Synapsin I bundles F-actin in a phosphorylation-dependent manner. Nature 326:704–707.

Bamburg JR, Bray D, Chapman K (1986) Assembly of microtubules at the tip of growing axons. Nature 321:788–790.

Bekirov IH, Needleman LA, Zhang W, Benson DL (2002) Identification and localization of multiple classic cadherins in developing rat limbic system. Neuroscience 115:213–227.

Benson DL, Colman DR, Huntley GW (2001) Molecules, maps and synapse specificity. Nat Rev Neurosci 2:899–909.

Bentley D, Toroian-Raymond A (1986) Disoriented pathfinding by pioneer neurone growth cones deprived of filopodia by cytochalasin treatment. Nature 323:712–715.

Berardi N, Pizzorusso T, Maffei L (2004) Extracellular matrix and visual cortical plasticity; freeing the synapse. Neuron 44:905–908.

Bevans CG, Kordel M, Rhee SK, Harris AL (1998) Isoform composition of connexin channels determines selectivity among second messengers and uncharged molecules. J Biol Chem 273:2808–2816.

Bicknell RJ (1998) Sex-steroid actions on neurotransmission. Curr Opin Neurol 11:667–671.

Biederer T, Sara Y, Mozhayeva M, Atasoy D, Liu X, Kavalali ET, Sudhof TC (2002) SynCAM, a synaptic adhesion molecule that drives synapse assembly. Science 297:1525–1531.

Bloom FE, Aghajanian GK (1966) Cytochemistry of synapses: selective staining for electron microscopy. Science 154:1575–1577.

—— (1968) Fine structural and cytochemical analysis of the staining of synaptic junctions with phosphotungstic acid. J Ultrastruct Res 22:361–375.

Bodian D (1968) Development of fine structure of spinal cord in monkey fetuses. II. Pre-reflex period to period of long intersegmental reflexes. J Comp Neurol 133:113–166.

—— (1971) Presynaptic organelles and junctional integrity. J Cell Biol 48:707–711.

Boulland JL, Qureshi T, Seal RP, Rafiki A, Gundersen V, Bergersen LH, Fremeau RT Jr, Edwards RH, Storm-Mathisen J, Chaudhry FA (2004) Expression of the vesicular glutamate transporters during development indicates the widespread corelease of multiple neurotransmitters. J Comp Neurol 480:264–280.

Bourikas D, Pekarik V, Baeriswyl T, Grunditz Å, Sadhu R, Nardó M, Stoeckli ET (2004) Sonic hedgehog guides commissural axons along the longitudinal axis of the spinal cord. Nat Neurosci 8:297–304.

Bozdagi O, Valcin M, Poskanzer K, Tanaka H, Benson DL (2004) Temporally distinct demands for classic cadherins in synapse formation and maturation. Mol Cell Neurosci 27:509–521.

Bradke F, Dotti CG (1997) Neuronal polarity: vectorial cytoplasmic flow precedes axon formation. Neuron 19:1175–1186.

—— (1999) The role of local actin instability in axon formation. Science 283:1931–1934.

Braisted JE, McLaughlin T, Wang HU, Friedman GC, Anderson DJ, O'Leary DD (1997) Graded and lamina-specific distributions of ligands of EphB receptor tyrosine kinases in the developing retinotectal system. Dev Biol 191:14–28.

Bresler T, Ramati Y, Zamorano PL, Zhai R, Garner CC, Ziv NE (2001) The dynamics of SAP90/PSD-95 recruitment to new synaptic junctions. Mol Cell Neurosci 18:149–167.

Bresler T, Shapira M, Boeckers T, Dresbach T, Futter M, Garner CC, Rosenblum K, Gundelfinger ED, Ziv NE (2004) Postsynaptic density assembly is fundamentally different from presynaptic active zone assembly. J Neurosci 24:1507–1520.

Bridgman PC, Dailey ME (1989) The organization of myosin and actin in rapid frozen nerve growth cones. J Cell Biol 108:95–109.

Brose K, Bland KS, Wang KH, Arnott D, Henzel W, Goodman CS, Tessier-Lavigne M, Kidd T (1999) Slit proteins bind Robo receptors and have an evolutionarily conserved role in repulsive axon guidance. Cell 96:795–806.

Brown A, Yates PA, Burrola P, Ortuno D, Vaidya A, Jessell TM, Pfaff SL, O'Leary DD, Lemke G (2000) Topographic mapping from the retina to the midbrain is controlled by relative but not absolute levels of EphA receptor signaling. Cell 102:77–88.

Bukauskas FF, Verselis VK (2004) Gap junction channel gating. Biochim Biophys Acta 1662:42–60.

Burridge K, Wennerberg K (2004) Rho and Rac take center stage. Cell 116:167–179.

Butler SJ, Dodd J (2003) A role for BMP heterodimers in roof plate-mediated repulsion of commissural axons. Neuron 38:389–401.

Caceres A, Kosik KS (1990) Inhibition of neurite polarity by tau antisense oligonucleotides in primary cerebellar neurons. Nature 343:461–463.

Caceres A, Potrebic S, Kosik KS (1991) The effect of tau antisense oligonucleotides on neurite formation of cultured cerebellar macroneurons. J Neurosci 11:1515–1523.

Caspar DL, Goodenough DA, Makowski L, Phillips WC (1977) Gap junction structures. I. Correlated electron microscopy and X-ray diffraction. J Cell Biol 74:605–628.

Castellani V, Chedotal A, Schachner M, Faivre-Sarrailh C, Rougon G (2000) Analysis of the L1-deficient mouse phenotype reveals cross-talk between Sema3A and L1 signaling pathways in axonal guidance. Neuron 27:237–249.

Chan CS, Weeber EJ, Kurup S, Sweatt JD, Davis RL (2003) Integrin requirement for hippocampal synaptic plasticity and spatial memory. J Neurosci 23:7107–7116.

Charron F, Stein E, Jeong J, McMahon AP, Tessier-Lavigne M (2003) The morphogen sonic hedgehog is an axonal chemoattractant that collaborates with netrin-1 in midline axon guidance. Cell 113:11–23.

Chaudhry FA, Reimer RJ, Bellocchio EE, Danbolt NC, Osen KK, Edwards RH, Storm-Mathisen J (1998) The vesicular GABA transporter, VGAT, localizes to synaptic vesicles in sets of glycinergic as well as GABAergic neurons. J Neurosci 18:9733–9750.

Chavis P, Westbrook G (2001) Integrins mediate functional pre- and postsynaptic maturation at a hippocampal synapse. Nature 411:317–321.

Chih B, Engelman H, Scheiffele P (2005) Control of excitatory and inhibitory synapse formation by neuroligins. Science 307:1324–1328.

Christie SB, Miralles CP, De Blas AL (2002) GABAergic innervation organizes synaptic and extrasynaptic GABAA receptor clustering in cultured hippocampal neurons. J Neurosci 22:684–697.

Cohan CS, Welnhofer EA, Zhao L, Matsumura F, Yamashiro S (2001) Role of the actin bundling protein fascin in growth cone morphogenesis: localization in filopodia and lamellipodia. Cell Motil Cytoskeleton 48:109–120.

Colamarino SA, Tessier-Lavigne M (1995) The axonal chemoattractant netrin-1 is also a chemorepellent for trochlear motor axons. Cell 81:621–629.

Collins MO, Yu L, Coba MP, Husi H, Campuzano I, Blackstock WP, Choudhary JS, Grant SG (2005) Proteomic analysis of in vivo phosphorylated synaptic proteins. J Biol Chem 280:5972–5982.

Colonnier M (1968) Synaptic patterns on different cell types in the different laminae of the cat visual cortex. An electron microscope study. Brain Res 9:268–287.

Connors BW, Benardo LS, Prince DA (1983) Coupling between neurons of the developing rat neocortex. J Neurosci 3:773–782.

Coussen F, Normand E, Marchal C, Costet P, Choquet D, Lambert M, Mege RM, Mulle C (2002) Recruitment of the kainate receptor subunit glutamate receptor 6 by cadherin/catenin complexes. J Neurosci 22: 6426–6436.

Craig AM, Banker G (1994) Neuronal polarity. Annu Rev Neurosci 17:267–310.

Dale H (1935) Pharmacology and nerve-endings. Proc R Soc Med 28:319–332.

Dalva MB, Takasu MA, Lin MZ, Shamah SM, Hu L, Gale NW, Greenberg ME (2000) EphB receptors interact with NMDA receptors and regulate excitatory synapse formation. Cell 103:945–956.

Dean C, Scholl FG, Choih J, DeMaria S, Berger J, Isacoff E, Scheiffele P (2003) Neurexin mediates the assembly of presynaptic terminals. Nat Neurosci 6:708–716.

DeChiara TM, Bowen DC, Valenzuela DM, Simmons MV, Poueymirou WT, Thomas S, Kinetz E, Compton DL, Rojas E, Park JS, Smith C, DiStefano PS, Glass DJ, Burden SJ, Yancopoulos GD (1996) The receptor tyrosine kinase MuSK is required for neuromuscular junction formation in vivo. Cell 85: 501–512.

Dent EW, Gertler FB (2003) Cytoskeletal dynamics and transport in growth cone motility and axon guidance. Neuron 40:209–227.

De Robertis ED, Bennett HS (1955) Some features of the submicroscopic morphology of synapses in frog and earthworm. J Biophys Biochem Cytol 1: 47–58.

De Robertis E, Pelligrino de Iraldi A (1961) Plurivesicular secretory processes and nerve endings in the pineal gland of the rat. J Biophys Biochem Cytol 10:361–372.

De Robertis E, Pelligrino de Iraldi A, Rodriguez de Lores Arnaiz G, Salganicoff L (1961) Electron microscope obervations in nerve endings isolated from rat brain. Anat Rec 139:220–221.

DiTella MC, Feiguin F, Carri N, Kosik KS, Caceres A (1996) MAP-1B/TAU functional redundancy during laminin-enhanced axonal growth. J Cell Sci 109(Pt 2):467–477.

Dityatev A, Schachner M (2003) Extracellular matrix molecules and synaptic plasticity. Nat Rev Neurosci 4:456–468.

Dong H, O'Brien RJ, Fung ET, Lanahan AA, Worley PF, Huganir RL (1997) GRIP: a synaptic PDZ domain–containing protein that interacts with AMPA receptors. Nature 386:279–284.

Dotti CG, Banker GA (1987) Experimentally induced alteration in the polarity of developing neurons. Nature 330:254–256.

Dotti CG, Sullivan CA, Banker GA (1988) The establishment of polarity by hippocampal neurons in culture. J Neurosci 8:1454–1468.

Duffy HS, Delmar M, Spray DC (2002) Formation of the gap junction nexus: binding partners for connexins. J Physiol Paris 96:243–249.

Eccles JC (1957) *The Physiology of Nerve Cells.* Johns Hopkins Press, Baltimore.

Eccles JC (1982) The synapse: from electrical to chemical transmission. Annu Rev Neurosci 5:325–339.

Eccles JC, Oscarsson O, Willis WD (1961) Synaptic action of group I and II afferent fibres of muscle on the cells of the dorsal spinocerebellar tract. J Physiol 158:517–543.

Engert F, Bonhoeffer T (1999) Dendritic spine changes associated with hippocampal long-term synaptic plasticity. Nature 399:66–70.

Fache MP, Moussif A, Fernandes F, Giraud P, Garrido JJ, Dargent B (2004) Endocytotic elimination and domain-selective tethering constitute a potential mechanism of protein segregation at the axonal initial segment. J Cell Biol 166:571–578.

Fatt P, Katz B (1951) An analysis of the end-plate potential recorded with an intracellular electrode. J Physiol 115:320–370.

Fazeli A, Dickinson SL, Hermiston ML, Tighe RV, Steen RG, Small CG, Stoeckli ET, Keino-Masu K, Masu M, Rayburn H, Simons J, Bronson RT, Gordon JI, Tessier-Lavigne M, Weinberg RA (1997) Phenotype of mice lacking functional deleted in colorectal cancer (*Dcc*) gene. Nature 386:796–804.

Feldheim DA, Kim YI, Bergemann AD, Frisen J, Barbacid M, Flanagan JG (2000) Genetic analysis of ephrin-A2 and ephrin-A5 shows their requirement in multiple aspects of retinocollicular mapping. Neuron 25:563–574.

Fiala JC, Allwardt B, Harris KM (2002) Dendritic spines do not split during hippocampal LTP or maturation. Nat Neurosci 5:297–298.

Fischer M, Kaech S, Wagner U, Brinkhaus H, Matus A (2000) Glutamate receptors regulate actin-based plasticity in dendritic spines. Nat Neurosci 3: 887–894.

Forscher P, Smith SJ (1988) Actions of cytochalasins on the organization of actin filaments and microtubules in a neuronal growth cone. J Cell Biol 107: 1505–1516.

Frenzel EM, Johnson RG (1996) Gap junction formation between cultured embryonic lens cells is inhibited by antibody to N-cadherin. Dev Biol 179: 1–16.

Frey U, Morris RG (1997) Synaptic tagging and long-term potentiation. Nature 385:533–536.

Friedman HV, Bresler T, Garner CC, Ziv NE (2000) Assembly of new individual excitatory synapses: time course and temporal order of synaptic molecule recruitment. Neuron 27:57–69.

Fukata Y, Itoh TJ, Kimura T, Menager C, Nishimura T, Shiromizu T, Watanabe H, Inagaki N, Iwamatsu A, Hotani H, Kaibuchi K (2002a) CRMP-2 binds to tubulin heterodimers to promote microtubule assembly. Nat Cell Biol 4:583–591.

Fukata Y, Kimura T, Kaibuchi K (2002b) Axon specification in hippocampal neurons. Neurosci Res 43: 305–315.

Gautam M, Noakes PG, Moscoso L, Rupp F, Scheller RH, Merlie JP, Sanes JR (1996) Defective neuromuscular synaptogenesis in agrin-deficient mutant mice. Cell 85:525–535.

Gillespie DC, Kim G, Kandler K (2005) Inhibitory synapses in the developing auditory system are glutamatergic. Nat Neurosci 8:332–338.

Gomez TM, Robles E, Poo M, Spitzer NC (2001) Filopodial calcium transients promote substrate-dependent growth cone turning. Science 291:1983–1987.

Goodenough DA (1976) The structure and permeability of isolated hepatocyte gap junctions. Cold Spring Harb Symp Quant Biol 40:37–43.

Goodman CS (1996) Mechanisms and molecules that control growth cone guidance. Annu Rev Neurosci 19:341–377.

Goslin K, Banker G (1989) Experimental observations on the development of polarity by hippocampal neurons in culture. J Cell Biol 108:1507–1516.

Graf ER, Zhang X, Jin SX, Linhoff MW, Craig AM (2004) Neurexins induce differentiation of GABA and glutamate postsynaptic specializations via neuroligins. Cell 119:1013–1026.

Gray EG (1959a) Electron microscopy of synaptic contacts on dendrite spines of the cerebral cortex. Nature 183:1592–1593.

—— (1959b) Axo-somatic and axo-dendritic synapses of the cerebral cortex: an electron microscope study. J Anat 93:420–433.

—— (1963) Electron microscopy of presynaptic organelles of the spinal cord. J Anat 97:101–106.

Grillo MA, Palay SL (1963) Granule-containing vesicles in the autonomic nervous system. In: Breese J (ed). *Fifth International Congress on Electron Microscopy, Philadelphia, Vol. 2* New York, Academic Press, p. U-1.

Grunwald IC, Korte M, Adelmann G, Plueck A, Kullander K, Adams RH, Frotscher M, Bonhoeffer T, Klein R (2004) Hippocampal plasticity requires postsynaptic ephrinBs. Nat Neurosci 7:33–40.

Grutzendler J, Kasthuri N, Gan WB (2002) Long-term dendritic spine stability in the adult cortex. Nature 420:812–816.

Guan KL, Rao Y (2003) Signalling mechanisms mediating neuronal responses to guidance cues. Nat Rev Neurosci 4:941–956.

Gundersen GG, Gomes ER, Wen Y (2004) Cortical control of microtubule stability and polarization. Curr Opin Cell Biol 16:106–112.

Gutierrez R (2003) The GABAergic phenotype of the "glutamatergic" granule cells of the dentate gyrus. Prog Neurobiol 71:337–358.

Hansen MJ, Dallal GE, Flanagan JG (2004) Retinal axon response to ephrin-as shows a graded, concentration-dependent transition from growth promotion to inhibition. Neuron 42:717–730.

Hashimoto K, Kano M (2003) Functional differentiation of multiple climbing fiber inputs during synapse elimination in the developing cerebellum. Neuron 38:785–796.

Hata Y, Slaughter CA, Sudhof TC (1993) Synaptic vesicle fusion complex contains unc-18 homologue bound to syntaxin. Nature 366:347–351.

Hayes BP, Roberts A (1973) Synaptic junction development in the spinal cord of an amphibian embryo: an electron microscope study. Z Zellforsch Mikrosk Anat 137:251–269.

Henderson JT, Georgiou J, Jia Z, Robertson J, Elowe S, Roder JC, Pawson T (2001) The receptor tyrosine kinase EphB2 regulates NMDA-dependent synaptic function. Neuron 32:1041–1056.

Hernandez-Blazquez FJ, Joazeiro PP, Omori Y, Yamasaki H (2001) Control of intracellular movement of connexins by E-cadherin in murine skin papilloma cells. Exp Cell Res 270:235–247.

Hindges R, McLaughlin T, Genoud N, Henkemeyer M, O'Leary DD (2002) EphB forward signaling controls directional branch extension and arborization required for dorsal–ventral retinotopic mapping. Neuron 35:475–487.

Hinds JW, Hinds PL (1972) Reconstruction of dendritic growth cones in neonatal mouse olfactory bulb. J Neurocytol 1:169–187.

Hong K, Hinck L, Nishiyama M, Poo MM, Tessier-Lavigne M, Stein E (1999) A ligand-gated association between cytoplasmic domains of UNC5 and DCC family receptors converts netrin-induced growth cone attraction to repulsion. Cell 97: 927–941.

Hopker VH, Shewan D, Tessier-Lavigne M, Poo M, Holt C (1999) Growth-cone attraction to netrin-1 is converted to repulsion by laminin-1. Nature 401: 69–73.

Hsu M, Andl T, Li G, Meinkoth JL, Herlyn M (2000) Cadherin repertoire determines partner-specific gap junctional communication during melanoma progression. J Cell Sci 113(Pt 9):1535–1542.

Huttenlocher PR (1979) Synaptic density in human frontal cortex—developmental changes and effects of aging. Brain Res 163:195–205.

Ibata Y, Otsuka N (1968) Fine structure of synapses in the hippocampus of the rabbit with special reference to dark presynaptic endings. Z Zellforsch Mikrosk Anat 91:547–553.

Inagaki N, Chihara K, Arimura N, Menager C, Kawano Y, Matsuo N, Nishimura T, Amano M, Kaibuchi K (2001) CRMP-2 induces axons in cultured hippocampal neurons. Nat Neurosci 4:781–782.

Inoue A, Sanes JR (1997) Lamina-specific connectivity in the brain: regulation by N-cadherin, neurotrophins, and glycoconjugates. Science 276:1428–1431.

Irie M, Hata Y, Takeuchi M, Ichtchenko K, Toyoda A, Hirao K, Takai Y, Rosahl TW, Sudhof TC (1997) Binding of neuroligins to PSD-95. Science 277: 1511–1515.

Isaac JT (2003) Postsynaptic silent synapses: evidence and mechanisms. Neuropharmacology 45:450–460.

Jareb M, Banker G (1997) Inhibition of axonal growth by brefeldin A in hippocampal neurons in culture. J Neurosci 17:8955–8963.

Jenkins SM, Bennett V (2001) Ankyrin-G coordinates assembly of the spectrin-based membrane skeleton, voltage-gated sodium channels, and L1 CAMs at Purkinje neuron initial segments. J Cell Biol 155: 739–746.

Jiang H, Guo W, Liang X, Rao Y (2005) Both the establishment and the maintenance of neuronal polarity require active mechanisms: critical roles of GSK-3β and its upstream regulators. Cell 120:123–135.

Jones DG (1983) Recent perspectives on the organization of central synapses. Anesth Analg 62:1100–1112.

Jontes JD, Emond MR, Smith SJ (2004) In vivo trafficking and targeting of N-cadherin to nascent presynaptic terminals. J Neurosci 24:9027–9034.

Jorgensen EM, Hartwieg E, Schuske K, Nonet ML, Jin Y, Horvitz HR (1995) Defective recycling of synaptic vesicles in synaptotagmin mutants of Caenorhabditis elegans. Nature 378:196–199.

Kakizawa S, Yamasaki M, Watanabe M, Kano M (2000) Critical period for activity-dependent synapse elimination in developing cerebellum. J Neurosci 20: 4954–4961.

Keino-Masu K, Masu M, Hinck L, Leonardo ED, Chan SS, Culotti JG, Tessier-Lavigne M (1996) Deleted in colorectal cancer (DCC) encodes a netrin receptor. Cell 87:175–185.

Kennedy TE, Serafini T, de la Torre JR, Tessier-Lavigne M (1994) Netrins are diffusible chemotropic factors for commissural axons in the embryonic spinal cord. Cell 78:425–435.

Kim CH, Lisman JE (2001) A labile component of AMPA receptor–mediated synaptic transmission is dependent on microtubule motors, actin, and nethylmaleimide–sensitive factor. J Neurosci 21:4188–4194.

Kim E, Sheng M (2004) PDZ domain proteins of synapses. Nat Rev Neurosci 5:771–781.

Knyihar E, Csillik B, Rakic P (1978) Transient synapses in the embryonic primate spinal cord. Science 202:1206–1209.

Kuffler SW (1942) Responses during refractory period at myoneural junction in isolated nerve-muscle fibre preparation. J Neurophysiol 5:199–209.

Lanier LM, Gates MA, Witke W, Menzies AS, Wehman AM, Macklis JD, Kwiatkowski D, Soriano P, Gertler FB (1999) Mena is required for neurulation and commissure formation. Neuron 22:313–325.

Lebrand C, Dent EW, Strasser GA, Lanier LM, Krause M, Svitkina TM, Borisy GG, Gertler FB (2004) Critical role of Ena/VASP proteins for filopodia formation in neurons and in function downstream of netrin-1. Neuron 42:37–49.

Lee H, Engel U, Rusch J, Scherrer S, Sheard K, Van Vactor D (2004) The microtubule plus end tracking protein Orbit/MAST/CLASP acts downstream of the tyrosine kinase Abl in mediating axon guidance. Neuron 42:913–926.

Leenders AG, Lopes da Silva FH, Ghijsen WE, Verhage M (2001) Rab3a is involved in transport of synaptic vesicles to the active zone in mouse brain nerve terminals. Mol Biol Cell 12:3095–3102.

Levi S, Logan SM, Tovar KR, Craig AM (2004) Gephyrin is critical for glycine receptor clustering but not for the formation of functional GABAergic synapses in hippocampal neurons. J Neurosci 24:207–217.

Lin CH, Espreafico EM, Mooseker MS, Forscher P (1996) Myosin drives retrograde F-actin flow in neuronal growth cones. Neuron 16:769–782.

Lin CH, Thompson CA, Forscher P (1994) Cytoskeletal reorganization underlying growth cone motility. Curr Opin Neurobiol 4:640–647.

Littleton JT, Bai J, Vyas B, Desai R, Baltus AE, Garment MB, Carlson SD, Ganetzky B, Chapman ER (2001) Synaptotagmin mutants reveal essential functions for the C2B domain in Ca^{2+}-triggered fusion and recycling of synaptic vesicles in vivo. J Neurosci 21:1421–1433.

Lohmann C, Myhr KL, Wong RO (2002) Transmitter-evoked local calcium release stabilizes developing dendrites. Nature 418:177–181.

Long H, Sabatier C, Ma L, Plump A, Yuan W, Ornitz DM, Tamada A, Murakami F, Goodman CS, Tessier-Lavigne M (2004) Conserved roles for Slit and Robo proteins in midline commissural axon guidance. Neuron 42:213–223.

Luo L, Liao YJ, Jan LY, Jan YN (1994) Distinct morphogenetic functions of similar small GTPases:

Drosophila Drac1 is involved in axonal outgrowth and myoblast fusion. Genes Dev 8:1787–1802.

Luscher B, Keller CA (2004) Regulation of GABA$_A$ receptor trafficking, channel activity, and functional plasticity of inhibitory synapses. Pharmacol Ther 102:195–221.

Lustig M, Erskine L, Mason CA, Grumet M, Sakurai T (2001) Nr-CAM expression in the developing mouse nervous system: ventral midline structures, specific fiber tracts, and neuropilar regions. J Comp Neurol 434:13–28.

Lyuksyutova AI, Lu CC, Milanesio N, King LA, Guo N, Wang Y, Nathans J, Tessier-Lavigne M, Zou Y (2003) Anterior–posterior guidance of commissural axons by Wnt-frizzled signaling. Science 302:1984–1988.

Mann F, Ray S, Harris W, Holt C (2002) Topographic mapping in dorsoventral axis of the *Xenopus* retinotectal system depends on signaling through ephrin-B ligands. Neuron 35:461–473.

Marin-Padilla M (1971) Early prenatal ontogenesis of the cerebral cortex (neocortex) of the cat (*Felis domestica*). A Golgi study. I. The primordial neocortical organization. Z Anat Entwicklungsgesch 134:117–145.

Martin KC, Casadio A, Zhu H, Yaping E, Rose JC, Chen M, Bailey CH, Kandel ER (1997) Synapse-specific, long-term facilitation of aplysia sensory to motor synapses: a function for local protein synthesis in memory storage. Cell 91:927–938.

Mason CA (1982) Development of terminal arbors of retino-geniculate axons in the kitten—II. Electron microscopical observations. Neuroscience 7:561–582.

Matsumoto-Miyai K, Ninomiya A, Yamasaki H, Tamura H, Nakamura Y, Shiosaka S (2003) NMDA-dependent proteolysis of presynaptic adhesion molecule L1 in the hippocampus by neuropsin. J Neurosci 23:7727–7736.

Matus A, Pehling G, Ackermann M, Maeder J (1980) Brain postsynaptic densities: the relationship to glial and neuronal filaments. J Cell Biol 87:346–359.

Mauch DH, Nagler K, Schumacher S, Goritz C, Muller EC, Otto A, Pfrieger FW (2001) CNS synaptogenesis promoted by glia-derived cholesterol. Science 294:1354–1357.

May MK, Biscoe TJ (1973) Preliminary observations on synaptic development in the foetal rat spinal cord. Brain Res 53:181–186.

McConnell SK, Ghosh A, Shatz CJ (1989) Subplate neurons pioneer the first axon pathway from the cerebral cortex. Science 245:978–982.

McEwen BS (1999) Stress and hippocampal plasticity. Annu Rev Neurosci 22:105–122.

McIntire SL, Reimer RJ, Schuske K, Edwards RH, Jorgensen EM (1997) Identification and characterization of the vesicular GABA transporter. Nature 389:870–876.

McLaughlin T, Hindges R, O'Leary DD (2003) Regulation of axial patterning of the retina and its topographic mapping in the brain. Curr Opin Neurobiol 13:57–69.

Meberg PJ, Bamburg JR (2000) Increase in neurite outgrowth mediated by overexpression of actin depolymerizing factor. J Neurosci 20:2459–2469.

Mcister B, Hokfelt T, Vale WW, Sawchenko PE, Swanson L, Goldstein M (1986) Coexistence of tyrosine hydroxylase and growth hormone–releasing factor in a subpopulation of tubero-infundibular neurons of the rat. Neuroendocrinology 42:237–247.

Meyer G, Kirsch J, Betz H, Langosch D (1995) Identification of a gephyrin binding motif on the glycine receptor β subunit. Neuron 15:563–572.

Mi R, Sia GM, Rosen K, Tang X, Moghekar A, Black JL, McEnery M, Huganir RL, O'Brien RJ (2004) AMPA receptor–dependent clustering of synaptic NMDA receptors is mediated by Stargazin and NR2A/B in spinal neurons and hippocampal interneurons. Neuron 44:335–349.

Ming GL, Song HJ, Berninger B, Holt CE, Tessier-Lavigne M, Poo MM (1997) cAMP-dependent growth cone guidance by netrin-1. Neuron 19:1225–1235.

Misura KM, Scheller RH, Weis WI (2000) Three-dimensional structure of the neuronal-Sec1-syntaxin 1a complex. Nature 404:355–362.

Moss SJ, Smart TG (2001) Constructing inhibitory synapses. Nat Rev Neurosci 2:240–250.

Nabekura J, Katsurabayashi S, Kakazu Y, Shibata S, Matsubara A, Jinno S, Mizoguchi Y, Sasaki A, Ishibashi H (2004) Developmental switch from GABA to glycine release in single central synaptic terminals. Nat Neurosci 7:17–23.

Nagerl UV, Eberhorn N, Cambridge SB, Bonhoeffer T (2004) Bidirectional activity-dependent morphological plasticity in hippocampal neurons. Neuron 44:759–767.

Nakada C, Ritchie K, Oba Y, Nakamura M, Hotta Y, Iino R, Kasai RS, Yamaguchi K, Fujiwara T, Kusumi A (2003) Accumulation of anchored proteins forms membrane diffusion barriers during neuronal polarization. Nat Cell Biol 5:626–632.

Newman-Gage H, Westrum LE (1984) Independent development of presynaptic specializations in olfactory cortex of the fetal rat. Cell Tissue Res 237:103–109.

Niell CM, Meyer MP, Smith SJ (2004) In vivo imaging of synapse formation on a growing dendritic arbor. Nat Neurosci 7:254–260.

Nimchinsky EA, Sabatini BL, Svoboda K (2002) Structure and function of dendritic spines. Annu Rev Physiol 64:313–353.

Nishiyama M, Hoshino A, Tsai L, Henley JR, Goshima Y, Tessier-Lavigne M, Poo MM, Hong K (2003) Cyclic AMP/GMP-dependent modulation of Ca^{2+} channels sets the polarity of nerve growth-cone turning. Nature 423:990–995.

O'Brien RJ, Xu D, Petralia RS, Steward O, Huganir RL, Worley P (1999) Synaptic clustering of AMPA receptors by the extracellular immediate–early gene product Narp. Neuron 23:309–323.

O'Connor TP, Duerr JS, Bentley D (1990) Pioneer growth cone steering decisions mediated by single filopodial contacts in situ. J Neurosci 10:3935–3946.

Palade GE, Palay SL (1954) Electron microscope observations of interneuronal and neuromuscular synapses. Anat Reo 118:335–336.

Pasterkamp RJ, Kolodkin AL (2003) Semaphorin junction: making tracks toward neural connectivity. Curr Opin Neurobiol 13:79–89.

Paternostro MA, Reyher CK, Brunjes PC (1995) Intracellular injections of Lucifer yellow into lightly fixed mitral cells reveal neuronal dye-coupling in the developing rat olfactory bulb. Brain Res Dev Brain Res 84:1–10.

Peinado A, Yuste R, Katz LC (1993) Gap junctional communication and the development of local circuits in neocortex. Cereb Cortex 3:488–498.

Peng J, Kim MJ, Cheng D, Duong DM, Gygi SP, Sheng M (2004) Semiquantitative proteomic analysis of rat forebrain postsynaptic density fractions by mass spectrometry. J Biol Chem 279:21003–21011.

Perrin FE, Rathjen FG, Stoeckli ET (2001) Distinct subpopulations of sensory afferents require F11 or axonin-1 for growth to their target layers within the spinal cord of the chick. Neuron 30:707–723.

Peters A, Kaiserman-Abramof IR (1969) The small pyramidal neuron of the rat cerebral cortex. The synapses upon dendritic spines. Z Zellforsch Mikrosk Anat 100:487–506.

Peters A, Palay SL, Webster HD (1991) The Fine Structure of the Nervous System. Oxford University Press, New York.

Petrucci TC, Morrow JS (1987) Synapsin I: an actin-bundling protein under phosphorylation control. J Cell Biol 105:1355–1363.

Pevsner J, Hsu SC, Braun JE, Calakos N, Ting AE, Bennett MK, Scheller RH (1994) Specificity and regulation of a synaptic vesicle docking complex. Neuron 13:353–361.

Phillips GR, Anderson TR, Florens L, Gudas C, Magda G, Yates JR 3rd, Colman DR (2004) Actin-binding proteins in a postsynaptic preparation: lasp-1 is a component of central nervous system synapses and dendritic spines. J Neurosci Res 78:38–48.

Phillips GR, Huang JK, Wang Y, Tanaka H, Shapiro L, Zhang W, Shan WS, Arndt K, Frank M, Gordon RE, Gawinowicz MA, Zhao Y, Colman DR (2001) The presynaptic particle web: ultrastructure, composition, dissolution, and reconstitution. Neuron 32:63–77.

Piper M, Salih S, Weinl C, Holt CE, Harris WA (2005) Endocytosis-dependent desensitization and protein synthesis–dependent resensitization in retinal growth cone adaptation. Nat Neurosci 8:179–186.

Poskanzer K, Needleman LA, Bozdagi O, Huntley GW (2003) N-cadherin regulates ingrowth and laminar targeting of thalamocortical axons. J Neurosci 23:2294–2305.

Prowse DM, Cadwallader GP, Pitts JD (1997) E-cadherin expression can alter the specificity of gap junction formation. Cell Biol Int 21:833–843.

Rajagopalan S, Vivancos V, Nicolas E, Dickson BJ (2000) Selecting a longitudinal pathway: Robo receptors specify the lateral position of axons in the Drosophila CNS. Cell 103:1033–1045.

Rakic P, Bourgeois JP, Eckenhoff MF, Zecevic N, Goldman-Rakic PS (1986) Concurrent overproduction of synapses in diverse regions of the primate cerebral cortex. Science 232:232–235.

Ramon y Cajal S (1894) New Ideas on the Structure of the Nervous System in Man and Vertebrates. MIT Press, Cambridge MA, p 149.

Rao A, Kim E, Sheng M, Craig AM (1998) Heterogeneity in the molecular composition of excitatory postsynaptic sites during development of hippocampal neurons in culture. J Neurosci 18:1217–1229.

Rash JE, Staines WA, Yasumura T, Patel D, Furman CS, Stelmack GL, Nagy JI (2000) Immunogold evidence that neuronal gap junctions in adult rat brain and spinal cord contain connexin-36 but not connexin-32 or connexin-43. Proc Natl Acad Sci USA 97:7573–7578.

Rash JE, Yasumura T, Dudek FE (1998) Ultrastructure, histological distribution, and freeze-fracture immunocytochemistry of gap junctions in rat brain and spinal cord. Cell Biol Int 22:731–749.

Rhee J, Mahfooz NS, Arregui C, Lilien J, Balsamo J, VanBerkum MF (2002) Activation of the repulsive receptor Roundabout inhibits N-cadherin–mediated cell adhesion. Nat Cell Biol 4:798–805.

Richter K, Langnaese K, Kreutz MR, Olias G, Zhai R, Scheich H, Garner CC, Gundelfinger ED (1999) Presynaptic cytomatrix protein bassoon is localized at both excitatory and inhibitory synapses of rat brain. J Comp Neurol 408:437–448.

Rodriguez-Boulan E, Powell SK (1992) Polarity of epithelial and neuronal cells. Annu Rev Cell Biol 8: 395–427.

Rothberg JM, Hartley DA, Walther Z, Artavanis-Tsakonas S (1988) Slit: an EGF-homologous locus of D. melanogaster involved in the development of the embryonic central nervous system. Cell 55: 1047–1059.

Rothberg JM, Jacobs JR, Goodman CS, Artavanis-Tsakonas S (1990) Slit: an extracellular protein necessary for development of midline glia and commissural axon pathways contains both EGF and LRR domains. Genes Dev 4:2169–2187.

Ruthel G, Hollenbeck PJ (2000) Growth cones are not required for initial establishment of polarity or differential axon branch growth in cultured hippocampal neurons. J Neurosci 20:2266–2274.

Sabatier C, Plump AS, Le M, Brose K, Tamada A, Murakami F, Lee EY, Tessier-Lavigne M (2004) The divergent Robo family protein rig-1/Robo3 is a negative regulator of slit responsiveness required for midline crossing by commissural axons. Cell 117:157–169.

Sarnat HB, Flores-Sarnat L (2002) Role of Cajal-Retzius and subplate neurons in cerebral cortical development. Semin Pediatr Neurol 9:302–308.

Schaefer AW, Kabir N, Forscher P (2002) Filopodia and actin arcs guide the assembly and transport of two populations of microtubules with unique dynamic parameters in neuronal growth cones. J Cell Biol 158:139–152.

Scheiffele P, Fan J, Choih J, Fetter R, Serafini T (2000) Neuroligin expressed in nonneuronal cells triggers presynaptic development in contacting axons. Cell 101:657–669.

Schuster T, Krug M, Stalder M, Hackel N, Gerardy-Schahn R, Schachner M (2001) Immunoelectron microscopic localization of the neural recognition molecules L1, NCAM, and its isoform NCAM180, the NCAM-associated polysialic acid, β_1 integrin and the extracellular matrix molecule tenascin-R in synapses of the adult rat hippocampus. J Neurobiol 49:142–158.

Schwamborn JC, Puschel AW (2004) The sequential activity of the GTPases Rap1B and Cdc42 determines neuronal polarity. Nat Neurosci 7:923–929.

Seeger M, Tear G, Ferres-Marco D, Goodman CS (1993) Mutations affecting growth cone guidance in Drosophila: genes necessary for guidance toward or away from the midline. Neuron 10:409–426.

Segretain D, Falk MM (2004) Regulation of connexin biosynthesis, assembly, gap junction formation, and removal. Biochim Biophys Acta 1662:3–21.

Serafini T, Colamarino SA, Leonardo ED, Wang H, Beddington R, Skarnes WC, Tessier-Lavigne M (1996) Netrin-1 is required for commissural axon guidance in the developing vertebrate nervous system. Cell 87:1001–1014.

Serafini T, Kennedy TE, Galko MJ, Mirzayan C, Jessell TM, Tessier-Lavigne M (1994) The netrins define a family of axon outgrowth-promoting proteins homologous to C. elegans UNC-6. Cell 78:409–424.

Shapira M, Zhai RG, Dresbach T, Bresler T, Torres VI, Gundelfinger ED, Ziv NE, Garner CC (2003) Unitary assembly of presynaptic active zones from Piccolo-Bassoon transport vesicles. Neuron 38: 237–252.

Sheng M, Cummings J, Roldan LA, Jan YN, Jan LY (1994) Changing subunit composition of heteromeric NMDA receptors during development of rat cortex. Nature 368:144–147.

Shepherd GM (1991) Foundations of the Neuron Doctrine. Oxford University Press, New York.

Shi SH, Cheng T, Jan LY, Jan YN (2004) APC and GSK-3β are involved in mPar3 targeting to the nascent axon and establishment of neuronal polarity. Curr Biol 14:2025–2032.

Simpson JH, Kidd T, Bland KS, Goodman CS (2000) Short-range and long-range guidance by slit and its Robo receptors. Robo and Robo2 play distinct roles in midline guidance. Neuron 28:753–766.

Sjostrand FS (1958) Ultrastructure of retinal rod synapses of the guinea pig eye as revealed by three-dimensional reconstructions from serial sections. J Ultrastruct Res 2:122–170.

Skoff RP, Hamburger V (1974) Fine structure of dendritic and axonal growth cones in embryonic chick spinal cord. J Comp Neurol 153:107–147.

Snow DM, Letourneau PC (1992) Neurite outgrowth on a step gradient of chondroitin sulfate proteoglycan (CS-PG). J Neurobiol 23:322–336.

Sollner T, Bennett MK, Whiteheart SW, Scheller RH, Rothman JE (1993) A protein assembly–disassembly pathway in vitro that may correspond to sequential steps of synaptic vesicle docking, activation, and fusion. Cell 75:409–418.

Song H, Ming G, He Z, Lehmann M, McKerracher L, Tessier-Lavigne M, Poo M (1998) Conversion of neuronal growth cone responses from repulsion to attraction by cyclic nucleotides. Science 281: 1515–1518.

Song HJ, Ming GL, Poo MM (1997) cAMP-induced switching in turning direction of nerve growth cones. Nature 388:275–279.

Spacek J, Harris KM (1997) Three-dimensional organization of smooth endoplasmic reticulum in hippocampal CA1 dendrites and dendritic spines of the immature and mature rat. J Neurosci 17: 190–203.

Sperry RW (1963) Chemoaffinity in the orderly growth of nerve fiber patterns and connections. Proc Natl Acad Sci USA 50:703–710.

Stein E, Tessier-Lavigne M (2001) Hierarchical organization of guidance receptors: silencing of netrin attraction by slit through a Robo/DCC receptor complex. Science 291:1928–1938.

Steward O, Falk PM (1986) Protein-synthetic machinery at postsynaptic sites during synaptogenesis: a quantitative study of the association between polyribosomes and developing synapses. J Neurosci 6: 412–423.

Steward O, Levy WB (1982) Preferential localization of polyribosomes under the base of dendritic spines in granule cells of the dentate gyrus. J Neurosci 2: 284–291.

Strasser GA, Rahim NA, VanderWaal KE, Gertler FB, Lanier LM (2004) Arp2/3 is a negative regulator of growth cone translocation. Neuron 43:81–94.

Suchyna TM, Nitsche JM, Chilton M, Harris AL, Veenstra RD, Nicholson BJ (1999) Different ionic selectivities for connexins 26 and 32 produce rectifying gap junction channels. Biophys J 77:2968–2987.

Sudhof TC (2004) The synaptic vesicle cycle. Annu Rev Neurosci 27:509–547.

Sugita S, Sudhof TC (2000) Specificity of Ca^{2+}-dependent protein interactions mediated by the C2A domains of synaptotagmins. Biochemistry 39: 2940–2949.

Suter DM, Forscher P (1998) An emerging link between cytoskeletal dynamics and cell adhesion molecules in growth cone guidance. Curr Opin Neurobiol 8:106–116.

Takamori S, Rhee JS, Rosenmund C, Jahn R (2000) Identification of a vesicular glutamate transporter that defines a glutamatergic phenotype in neurons. Nature 407:189–194.

Takei Y, Teng J, Harada A, Hirokawa N (2000) Defects in axonal elongation and neuronal migration in mice with disrupted tau and MAP1b genes. J Cell Biol 150:989–1000.

Tanaka H, Shan W, Phillips GR, Arndt K, Bozdagi O, Shapiro L, Huntley GW, Benson DL, Colman DR (2000) Molecular modification of N-cadherin in response to synaptic activity. Neuron 25:93–107.

Tashiro A, Dunaevsky A, Blazeski R, Mason CA, Yuste R (2003) Bidirectional regulation of hippocampal mossy fiber filopodial motility by kainate receptors: a two-step model of synaptogenesis. Neuron 38: 773–784.

Tessier-Lavigne M, Placzek M, Lumsden AGS, Dodd J, Jessell TM (1988) Chemotropic guidance of developing axons in the mammalian central nervous system. Nature 336:775–778.

Thompson CC, Potter GB (2000) Thyroid hormone action in neural development. Cereb Cortex 10:939–945.

Togashi H, Abe K, Mizoguchi A, Takaoka K, Chisaka O, Takeichi M (2002) Cadherin regulates dendritic spine morphogenesis. Neuron 35:77–89.

Tovar KR, Westbrook GL (1999) The incorporation of NMDA receptors with a distinct subunit composition at nascent hippocampal synapses in vitro. J Neurosci 19:4180–4188.

Uchizono K (1965) Characteristics of excitatory and inhibitory synapses in the central nervous system of the cat. Nature 207:642–643.

Ullian EM, Christopherson KS, Barres BA (2004) Role for glia in synaptogenesis. Glia 47:209–216.

Ullian EM, Sapperstein SK, Christopherson KS, Barres BA (2001) Control of synapse number by glia. Science 291:657–661.

Valdivia O (1971) Methods of fixation and the morphology of synaptic vesicles. J Comp Neurol 142:257–273.

van Horck FP, Weinl C, Holt CE (2004) Retinal axon guidance: novel mechanisms for steering. Curr Opin Neurobiol 14:61–66.

van Zundert B, Yoshii A, Constantine-Paton M (2004) Receptor compartmentalization and trafficking at glutamate synapses: a developmental proposal. Trends Neurosci 27:428–437.

Vaughn JE (1989) Fine structure of synaptogenesis in the vertebrate central nervous system. Synapse 3: 255–285.

Vaughn JE, Barber RP, Sims TJ (1988) Dendritic development and preferential growth into synaptogenic fields: a quantitative study of Golgi-impregnated spinal motor neurons. Synapse 2:69–78.

Vaughn JE, Sims TJ (1978) Axonal growth cones and developing axonal collaterals form synaptic junctions in embryonic mouse spinal cord. J Neurocytol 7: 337–363.

Vaughn JE, Sims T, Nakashima M (1977) A comparison of the early development of axodendritic and axosomatic synapses upon embryonic mouse spinal motor neurons. J Comp Neurol 175:79–100.

Venance L, Rozov A, Blatow M, Burnashev N, Feldmeyer D, Monyer H (2000) Connexin expression in electrically coupled postnatal rat brain neurons. Proc Natl Acad Sci USA 97:10260–10265.

Verhage M, Maia AS, Plomp JJ, Brussaard AB, Heeroma JH, Vermeer H, Toonen RF, Hammer RE, van den Berg TK, Missler M, Geuze HJ, Sudhof TC (2000) Synaptic assembly of the brain in the absence of neurotransmitter secretion. Science 287:864–869.

Voets T, Toonen RF, Brian EC, de Wit H, Moser T, Rettig J, Sudhof TC, Neher E, Verhage M (2001) Munc18-1 promotes large dense-core vesicle docking. Neuron 31:581–591.

Walikonis RS, Jensen ON, Mann M, Provance DW Jr, Mercer JA, Kennedy MB (2000) Identification of proteins in the postsynaptic density fraction by mass spectrometry. J Neurosci 20:4069–4080.

Walsh MJ, Kuruc N (1992) The postsynaptic density: constituent and associated proteins characterized by electrophoresis, immunoblotting, and peptide sequencing. J Neurochem 59:667–678.

Wang Y, Okamoto M, Schmitz F, Hofmann K, Sudhof TC (1997) Rim is a putative Rab3 effector in regulating synaptic-vesicle fusion. Nature 388:593–598.

Washbourne P, Bennett JE, McAllister AK (2002) Rapid recruitment of NMDA receptor transport packets to nascent synapses. Nat Neurosci 5:751–759.

Wen Z, Guirland C, Ming GL, Zheng JQ (2004) A CaMKII/calcineurin switch controls the direction of Ca(2+)-dependent growth cone guidance. Neuron 43:835–846.

Williams SE, Mason CA, Herrera E (2004) The optic chiasm as a midline choice point. Curr Opin Neurobiol 14:51–60.

Wills Z, Marr L, Zinn K, Goodman CS, Van Vactor D (1999) Profilin and the Abl tyrosine kinase are required for motor axon outgrowth in the *Drosophila* embryo. Neuron 22:291–299.

Winckler B, Forscher P, Mellman I (1999) A diffusion barrier maintains distribution of membrane proteins in polarized neurons. Nature 397:698–701.

Wodarz A (2002) Establishing cell polarity in development. Nat Cell Biol 4:E39–44.

Wolfe DE, Potter LT, Richardson KC, Axelrod J (1962) Localizing tritiated norepinephrine in sympathetic axons by electron microscopic autoradiography. Science 138:440–442.

Wu H, Nash JE, Zamorano P, Garner CC (2002) Interaction of SAP97 with minus-end-directed actin motor myosin VI. Implications for AMPA receptor trafficking. J Biol Chem 277:30928–30934.

Yoshikawa S, Thomas JB (2004) Secreted cell signaling molecules in axon guidance. Curr Opin Neurobiol 14:45–50.

Yoshimura T, Kawano Y, Arimura Y, Kawabata S, Kikuchi A, Kaibuchi K (2005) GSK-3small β regulates phosphorylation of CRMP-2 and neuronal polarity. Cell 120:137–149.

Yu TW, Bargmann CI (2001) Dynamic regulation of axon guidance. Nat Neurosci 4 (Suppl):1169–1176.

Yu W, Baas PW (1994) Changes in microtubule number and length during axon differentiation. J Neurosci 14:2818–2829.

Zhai RG, Vardinon-Friedman H, Cases-Langhoff C, Becker B, Gundelfinger ED, Ziv NE, Garner CC (2001) Assembling the presynaptic active zone: a characterization of an active one precursor vesicle. Neuron 29:131–143

Zhang W, Benson DL (2001) Stages of synapse development defined by dependence on F-actin. J Neurosci 21:5169–5181.

Zheng JQ, Felder M, Connor JA, Poo MM (1994) Turning of nerve growth cones induced by neurotransmitters. Nature 368:140–144.

Zhou Q, Homma KJ, Poo MM (2004) Shrinkage of dendritic spines associated with long-term depression of hippocampal synapses. Neuron 44:749–757.

Zou Y, Stoeckli E, Chen H, Tessier-Lavigne M (2000) Squeezing axons out of the gray matter: a role for slit and semaphorin proteins from midline and ventral spinal cord. Cell 102:363–375.

5

Cell Death

Stevens K. Rehen

Jerold J.M. Chun

Over the past several decades, the importance of cell death in the formation of the nervous system has become well established. Indeed, understanding cell death in the developing brain has been one of the most exciting areas of research in neuroscience. The present chapter focuses on the mammalian fetal cerebral cortex as a paradigm of study.

HISTORICAL RECOGNITION OF PROGRAMMED CELL DEATH AND APOPTOSIS

Embryologists have long recognized that regressive events play a major role in shaping organ development (Clarke and Clarke, 1996). About 50 years ago, the term *programmed cell death* (PCD) was coined. It evolved from detailed studies of the cellular degeneration during insect metamorphosis (Lockshin and Williams, 1965) and the morphogenesis of avian limbs (Saunders, 1966). PCD is a genetically regulated

mechanism that plays a critical role in specific stages of development, sculpting different organs during the formation and maturation of tissues (Ellis et al., 1991).

Apoptosis is the best known form of PCD, characterized originally by morphological changes observed by microscopy (Kerr et al., 1994). Apoptosis is characterized by nuclear size reduction, blebbing of the cellular membrane, chromatin condensation, and DNA fragmentation (Kerr et al., 1972; Wyllie et al., 1984). In the absence of inflammation, the apoptotic corpses are usually eliminated by phagocytes (Arends et al., 1990), which use the phosphatidylserine receptor (PSR) to identify and remove the dying cells (Zhuang et al., 1998, Wang et al., 2003). Apoptosis is considered a counterpoint to cell death by necrosis (Kerr et al., 1972). Necrosis is distinguished by early swelling and rupture of both intracellular organelles and the plasma membrane.

Although the definition of apoptosis is based on morphological criteria and PCD is characterized as a physiological event during development, both terms have been used interchangeably since their inception (Tomei et al., 1994). This use reflects an early consensus among scientists about the programmed nature of apoptosis, even when triggered by a non-physiological stimulus. It is important to emphasize that the often-neglected distinction between apoptosis and PCD has somewhat muddied the field, delaying the appreciation of other forms of PCD that are also relevant to development of the nervous system, such as autophagy (Dunn, 1994; Xue et al., 1999; Guimaraes et al., 2003). In this chapter, the term PCD refers to all forms of cell death associated with a developmental process.

GENETIC CONTROL OF
PROGRAMMED CELL DEATH

The original concept of PCD suggests an event during normal development that is under genetic control. Much of what we know about this regulation arises from the pioneering work by Sydney Brenner, John Sulston, and Robert Horvitz, who were awarded the 2002 Nobel Prize in Physiology or Medicine for elucidating mechanisms of cell death in the nematode *Caenorhabditis elegans.*

During nematode development, the generation of its 1090 somatic cells is followed by the death and elimination of 131 specified cells (Ellis and Horvitz, 1986). Most of these eliminated cells are neural precursors. In a series of elegant genetic experiments, Horvitz and colleagues defined the "central dogma" of PCD: that the expression of certain genes (*ced-3* and *ced-4* in nematode) is required for cell death, whereas other gene products (*ced-9*) can block the phenomenon.

In vertebrates, pro-death genes are the caspase family of cysteine proteases and the apoptotic protease-activating factor (APAF) 1, and anti-apoptotic proteins (including Bcl-2 and Bcl-xL) (see Chapter 6). The Bcl-2 family is critically involved in the regulation of mammalian cell death and survival and includes not only anti-apoptotic proteins, but also pro-apoptotic proteins acting through both caspase-dependent and caspase-independent pathways (Korsmeyer, 1999). This family is divided into three major subgroups based on the pattern of Bcl-2 homology (BH) domains (Korsmeyer, 1999). Anti-death Bcl-2 family members, including Bcl-2, Bcl-xL, Bcl-w, and Mcl-1,

contain four BH domains (termed BH1, BH2, BH3, and BH4). There are two pro-death subgroups of the Bcl-2 family: the multidomain subgroup contains the BH1 and BH2 domains and includes Bax, Bak, Bok, and Bcl-xS; the BH3-only subgroup includes Bim, Bid, Bcl-2-associated death protein (Bad), death protein 5/hara-kiri, Puma, and Noxa. Bcl-2 family members can interact with each other via their BH domains, and the final fate of a cell may depend on the intracellular balance between anti- and pro-death proteins (Akhtar et al, 2004).

NEUROTROPHIC THEORY AND
CLASSICAL CELL DEATH

During the 1940s–1950s, Viktor Hamburger, Rita Levi-Montalcini, and Stanley Cohen conducted pioneering studies on mechanisms controlling cell death that culminated with the identification of nerve growth factor (NGF; Cohen and Levi-Montalcini, 1957). In 1986, Levi-Montalcini and Cohen were awarded the Nobel Prize in Physiology or Medicine for their important discovery of NGF and its role in both neurite outgrowth and cell survival. Research on the function of NGF lead to the neurotrophic theory, which postulates that neuronal survival depends on competition for limited amounts of trophic factor(s) released by targets (Oppenheim, 1991). This early work has been the impetus for numerous research groups investigating novel neurotrophic factors that regulate the survival of developing neural cells. With the cloning of the gene for NGF (Scott et al, 1983), other related growth factors with similar amino acid sequences have been discovered. This family of proteins, collectively referred to as *neurotrophins*, consists of NGF and brain-derived neurotrophic factor (BDNF; Scott et al, 1983), neurotrophin (NT)-3 (Ernfors et al, 1990), NT-4/5 (Berkemeier et al, 1991; Hallbrook et al, 1991), and NT-6 and NT-7 (Gotz et al, 1994; Nilsson et al, 1998).

Two types of neurotrophin receptors have been identified on the basis of their pharmacological properties: a low-affinity receptor called p75, and a family of high-affinity receptors (trks) that are tyrosine protein kinases and the members of which bind selectively to different neurotrophins (Barbacid, 1994). In general, NGF activates trkA, BDNF and NT-4/5 are ligands for trkB, and NT-3 activates trkC, although there is some degree of cross-talk among them.

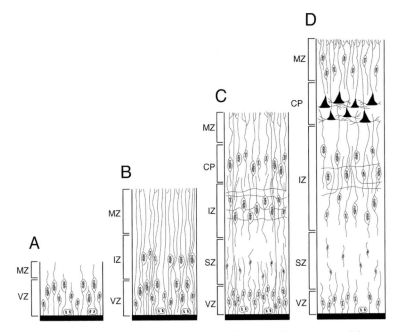

FIGURE 5–1 Zones in the developing cerebral cortex. The anatomy of the cerebral cortex changes as development proceeds (increasing age from left to right). **A.** The early proliferative age consists of a pseudostratified epithelium. **B, C.** With development, the cerebral wall increases in width. In some cells, neurites processes stretch from the ventricular surface (black bar) to the pial surface. **C, D.** With further development, more mature neurons (black triangular cells) begin to differentiate superficially in the cortical plate (CP), along with the ingrowth and outgrowth of axons in the intermediate zone (IZ; lines parallel to the black bar). MZ, marginal zone; SZ, subventricular zone; VZ, ventricular zone. (*Source:* Adapted from Cowan, 1979)

Activation of trk receptors initiates intracellular signaling cascades that can produce rapid, long-term effects on neuron growth and survival. Binding with p75 can promote either apoptosis or survival. It can facilitate neurotrophin signaling through trk receptors promoting cell survival. Interestingly, p75 is structurally related to the tumor necrosis factor receptors that regulate the onset of cell death in the immune system (Majdan et al, 1997). Constitutive expression of the intracellular p75 domain in transgenic mice leads to cell death in several neuronal populations. Readers wishing to learn more about neurotrophic factors and their receptors are referred to some of the many excellent recent reviews on this topic (e.g., Huang and Reichardt, 2001; Dechant and Barde, 2002; Hempstead, 2002).

DEVELOPING CEREBRAL CORTEX AS A MODEL FOR STUDYING MAMMALIAN NEURAL CELL DEATH

Neurons of the mammalian cerebral cortex first arise during embryonic development from neuroproliferative zones that surround the cavities, or ventricles, that contain cerebral spinal fluid. In the cerebral cortex these proliferative regions are known as the *ventricular zone* (VZ), which lines the ventricle, and the *subventricular zone* (SZ), which is immediately suprajacent to the VZ (Fig. 5–1). Developmental events in the VZ serve as an archetypal example of neurogenesis elsewhere in the neural tube, including the spinal cord.

During neurogenesis, cells undergo one of three general fates. They can continue to proliferate, become postmitotic, or die. Those neurons that become post-mitotic, a step referred to as the *birth of a neuron*, migrate out of the VZ, through a superficial region termed the *intermediate zone* (IZ), until they reach a position in the superficial aspect of the anlage of the cortical gray matter known as the *cortical plate* (CP). Once in the CP, neurons differentiate and make synaptic connections (Miller, 1988; Bayer and Altman, 1991) or die (e.g., Finlay and Slattery, 1983; Miller, 1995).

Death of Post-Mitotic Cells

Historically, one reason the contribution of PCD to development has not been well-recognized is that apoptotic bodies are susceptible to rapid clearance and phagocytosis in intact tissue. Thus, it is difficult to study the presence of cell death in static (fixed) tissue. A real-time approach could unequivocally determine the prevalence and distribution of dying cells in situ, however, this method is not currently practical since ex vivo systems produce artifactual changes in cellular behavior and induce premature cell death.

Approximately one-third or more of the post-mitotic neuronal population undergoes naturally occurring PCD during development related to insufficient access to trophic signals (e.g., NGF and BDNF) from targets and afferents (Oppenheim, 1991; Linden, 1994). The amount of neuronal death varies with time, location, and cell type (e.g., Miller, 1995). In cortex, for example, the incidence of death among different populations of post-migratory neurons can vary from 10% to 60%. Neurons in the deepest and most superficial cortex are more likely to die than those in mid-cortex. Moreover, local circuit neurons within a particular layer are twice as likely to die relative to laminar-cohort projection neurons.

PCD plays a crucial part in the developmental strategy of the cerebral cortex. An overabundance of neurons is generated to create a transient scaffold for the developing cortex and is subsequently eliminated as the cortex matures. During development of the mammalian telencephalon, the genesis of neurons destined for the six layers of the cerebral cortex is preceded by generation of a population of neurons that reside in the subplate (an anlage of the white matter) and the marginal zone (the anlage of cortical layer I). These neuropeptide-containing neurons (Chun et al., 1987; Al-Ghoul and Miller, 1989; Ghosh et al., 1990) are present in large numbers during development and function in early synaptic circuitry (Chun and Shatz, 1989a; 1989b). As the brain matures, their disappearance through neuronal death occurs in concert with the invasion of the cortical plate by axonal projections and with the elimination of synapses in the subplate. These observations suggest that during development the subplate (a) is a transient synaptic neuropil (Chun et al., 1987); and (b) serves as a guidepost for ingrowing thalamocortical axons subsequently eliminated by cell death. This idea of sculpting the cortex through an initial overproduction of neurons followed by paring back is in concert with the neurotrophic theory.

Most studies on PCD in the central nervous system (CNS) have focused on the period of target innervation (see below), when differentiating neurons are sending out axons and making synaptic connections with postmitotic neurons (Hamburger and Levi-Montalcini, 1949; Williams and Smith, 1993; Miller, 1995). An implicit assumption of many of these studies was that PCD played a minor role during embryonic CNS development. Indeed, elaborate mathematical models have been constructed that assume there is no PCD during neuronogenetic phases of development (Caviness et al., 1995).

Death of Proliferating Cells

Death can affect proliferating populations of cells, a phenomenon representing a distinct form and phase of cell death in the developing CNS. This population is best represented by neural progenitor and stem cells (NPCs). These cells, which have morphological and molecular characteristics of radial glia (Noctor et al., 2001), are located in the VZ and SZ. They also share similarities with mitotic immune cells such as T cells of the thymic cortex (Chun, 2001). Importantly, NPCs do not have synaptic contacts at this stage of development, and are still proliferative.

Thymic T cells are notable as a comparison population to NPCs. Developing T cells undergo several distinct cell selection mechanisms (positive selection, negative selection, and death by neglect) that result in elimination of 97% of the developing T-cell population (Egerton et al., 1990; Shortman et al., 1990; Shortman and Scollay, 1994). Nevertheless, for decades controversy existed following the proposal of intrathymic cell death (Metcalf, 1966), because of the absence of histological evidence for intrathymic cell death (Poste and Olsen, 1973). It was not until the development of novel hybridization techniques collectively termed *in situ end labeling*, or ISEL, that intrathymic cell death was convincingly demonstrated (Surh and Sprent, 1994; Chun, 2001). ISEL identifies breaks in double-stranded DNA produced during PCD by attaching labeled nucleotides to free DNA ends. The label can then be visualized in tissue sections (Gavrieli et al., 1992; Abrams et al., 1993; Wijsman et al., 1993; Wood et al., 1993; Homma et al., 1994; White et al., 1994). In situ end-labeling plus (ISEL+) improves the sensitivity of the original ISEL techniques to visualize PCD in the developing nervous system (Blaschke et al, 1996, 1998; Staley et al, 1997; Pompeiano et al, 1998, 2000; Zhu and Chun, 1998). The increased sensitivity of ISEL+ has been validated in several established mammalian models of PCD. For example, ISEL+ reveals normal PCD and quantitative increases in PCD within the thymic cortex following dexamethasone treatment of the thymus (Wyllie, 1980; Egerton et al, 1990; Shortman et al 1990; Surh and Sprent, 1994). Moreover, studies using ISEL+ in the small intestinal villus, a model of PCD where the entire population of cells turns over every two to four days, demonstrate that apoptotic DNA fragmentation can be identified in at least some dying cells several days before their actual elimination (Pompeiano et al, 1998).

The search for PCD in the developing cerebral cortex was prompted by the superficial similarities between thymocyte development and cortical neurogenesis, particularly in light of the lack of histological evidence for cell death in the thymus. The patterns of labeled cells revealed by ISEL+ in the embryonic rodent brain suggest that PCD occurs on a large scale throughout the neuraxis (Blaschke et al, 1998).

As expected from previous studies on target-dependent PCD, dying cells are present in the anticipated postmitotic neuronal compartments of the cerebral cortex (IZ and CP). Strikingly, a large amount of PCD is also present in the VZ. The time course of cell death in mouse cortex varies across development and is related to the progression of the cell cycle (Blaschke et al, 1996, 1998; Thomaidou et al, 1997). Most PCD is observed between gestational day (G) 12 and G18, when 25% to 70% of cells in the fetal cerebral cortex die (Fig. 5–2). Peak incidence of cell death occurs about G14. Prior to G10 and in the adult, less than 1% of cortical cells are dying. This pattern shows that there is a substantial amount of cell

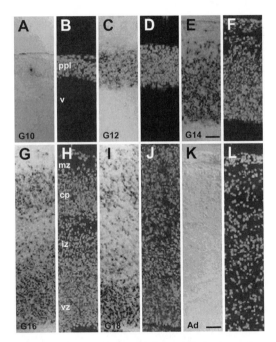

FIGURE 5–2 Distribution of dying cells in the embryonic mouse cortex. In situ end-labeling plus (ISEL+) from gestational day (G)10–G18 and in the adult cortex (A, C, E, G, I, and K), along with nuclear staining by 4,6-diamino-2-phenylindole of the same field (B, D, F, H, J, and L). **A, B.** G10. From this age through G14 (A–F), the neuroepithelium consists of a homogeneous-appearing proliferative layer (ppl). **C, D.** G12. **E, F.** G14. **G, H.** G16. The cerebral wall at G16 has stratified into additional layers (the marginal zone [MZ], cortical plate [CP], intermediate zone [IZ], and ventricular zone [VZ]) that are also apparent at G18 (**I, J**). **K, L.** Adult (Ad) cortex. The ventricle (v) is at the lower edge of each photograph. Note the sparse ISEL+ labeling at G10 that increases through G14, and then declines with further development. From G12 to G18, note the extensive labeling in the proliferative zones (ppl, VZ) as well as in the postmitotic zones (MZ, CP, and IZ). Only rare dying cells are detected by ISEL+ in the adult cortex. Thus cortical PCD is developmentally regulated and ceases by adulthood. Scale bars = 50 mm. (*Source:* Modified from Blaschke and colleagues, 1996)

death within proliferating NPC populations. These cells have not yet sent out axons to synaptic targets, hence, classical neurotrophic theory cannot account for this early phase of cell death. This phenomenon represents a novel form of PCD and is discussed below.

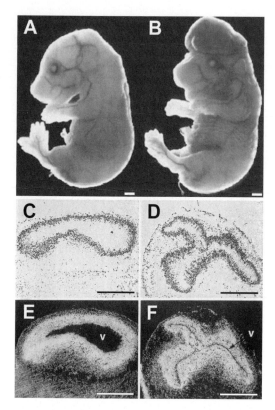

FIGURE 5–3 Examination of caspase-9 and caspase-3 knockout mice. Capase-9+/− (A) and caspase 9−/− (B) fetuses at G16.5, showing the larger and morphologically abnormal brain in the knockout. Scale bar = 1.0 mm. C–F. Caspase-3 mutants have an expanded proliferative zone. C, D. BrdU immunolabeling in a section through the developing cerebral cortex of a heterozygote and mutant embryo, respectively. E, F. DAPI staining of the adjacent section in a series from C and D, respectively. In the caspase-3 knockout fetus, the cortex is distorted into folds and the lateral ventricle is identifiable only as a thin slit in the center of the cortical mass. The thickness of the proliferative layer relative to the cortex looks very much alike in the two embryos. Statistics showed that the percentage of BrdU-labeled cells was only slightly increased in the −/− fetuses compared to the +/− fetuses. v, lateral ventricle. Scale bar = 500 μm. (Source: A, B: adapted from Kuida et al., 1998. C–F: adapted from Pompeiano et al., 2000)

Glial Death within the Developing Brain

The role of astrocytes or other glia in neuronal cell death is poorly understood. Interestingly, phagocytes of macrophage lineages such as microglia contribute to the elimination of dead cells in the brain. Phagocytes, from mice lacking the gene encoding PSR are defective in removing apoptotic cells. These PCR-deficient mice have developmental abnormalities, such as in the accumulation of dead cells in the lung and brain. Some of these animals also present a hyperplasic brain phenotype resembling that of mice deficient in the cell death–associated genes APAF-1, caspase-3, and caspase-9 (Fig. 5–3) suggesting that phagocytes may also be involved in promoting apoptosis (Li et al., 2003). Actually, in the developing cerebellum, the death of Purkinje neurons can be promoted by microglia. This finding suggests that a form of engulfment-related cell death may link PCD to the clearance of dead cells (Marin-Teva et al., 2004).

DIFFERENT PHASES OF DEVELOPMENT, DIFFERENT MECHANISMS OF PROGRAMMED CELL DEATH

Using an early molecular marker for post-mitotic neurons, Weiner and Chun (1997), found that PCD in neuroproliferative zones does not become pronounced until NPCs begin to differentiate into postmitotic cells. This correlation suggests that the initial generation of postmitotic neurons may trigger the onset of PCD in a given proliferative zone. The nature of this link; however, is currently unclear.

Similar to the developing cerebral cortex, the retina of newborn mice and rats is composed of two strata containing cells in various stages of development. One layer of differentiated cells is the ganglion cell layer and the other is the neuroblastic layer (NBL). Like the cortical VZ, the NBL is comprised of NPCs (Alexiades and Cepko, 1997). During differentiation, NPCs that are exiting the cell cycle, migrate from the NBL to form other layers of postmitotic neurons (Linden et al., 1999).

PCD can be induced in the NBL following inhibition of protein synthesis. Interestingly, as the retina matures, retinal cells become less sensitive to protein synthesis inhibitors, and in adult retinal tissue, these inhibitors have no effect on cell death (Rehen et al, 1996). When BrdU, a marker of proliferating cells (Miller and Nowakowski, 1988), is used in conjunction with protein synthesis inhibitors, the vast majority of cells undergoing PCD are not labeled with BrdU (Fig. 5.4). This result suggests that the population of newly postmitotic neurons is particularly sensitive to PCD through inhibition of protein synthesis. Continuous synthesis of anti-apoptotic proteins appears to be important in the regulation of PCD during neuronal migration and differentiation in the retina (Rehens et al, 1999). Consistent with this hypothesis, mouse embryos deficient for Bcl-x$_L$, an anti-apoptotic member of the Bcl-2 family, exhibit massive cell death of immature neurons in the cerebral cortex (Motoyama et al, 1995). Bcl-x$_L$ is up-regulated in early postmitotic neurons as they migrate from the VZ and this high level of expression is maintained through adulthood. On the other hand, Bcl-x$_L$ expression is low in NPCs (Motoyama et al, 1995).

In summary, ISEL+ results indicate that PCD is a common cell fate for NPCs throughout the neural tube. Studies involving inhibition of protein

FIGURE 5–4 Identification of newly postmitotic cells sensitive to apoptosis induced by inhibition of protein synthesis. Immunolabeling for BrdU in the proliferative zone of a retinal explant (arrows) after inhibition of protein synthesis. Notice that the majority of dying cells (arrowheads), identified as globular apoptotic bodies under differential interference contrast, is unlabeled with BrdU. Scale bar = 20 μm. (*Source*: Adapted from Rehen et al., 1999)

synthesis in the developing nervous system and targeted deletion of the anti-apoptotic gene Bcl-x$_L$ suggest that during migration and initial differentiation, the PCD machinery is controlled by suppressor proteins.

PROLIFERATIVE CELL DEATH, DNA BREAKS AND END JOINING

Thymic PCD occurs during the selection of functionally and molecularly distinct thymocytes (Surh and Sprent, 1994), based on somatic DNA rearrangements encoding T cell receptors and immunoglobulins in T and B lymphocytes, respectively. This process, known as V(D)J recombination (Weaver and Alt, 1997), is responsible for the unparalleled degree of immunological diversity that is fundamental to the immune response. As described above, a parallel exists between PCD in the thymus and the fetal brain, where cell death takes place in conjunction with cell proliferation (Shortman et al., 1990; Chun, 2001).

ISEL+ results suggest that a form of cell selection occurs in the neuroproliferative regions of the brain and that the occurrence of PCD is associated with the maturation process (Blaschke et al., 1996, 1998). In the fetal brain, the peak of cell death coincides with the period when the first neurons destined to comprise the mature cortex are being generated (Caviness, 1982). This spike in PCD might allow the selection of the first cortical neurons having desired phenotypes which would serve as a template for the selection of later-generated cells. This hypothetical scenario leaves open the question of how cells might be mechanistically selected.

Nearly a decade before genetic recombination was formally demonstrated in lymphocytes, Dreyer and colleagues (1967) postulated that recombined genes encoding cell-surface proteins might play a part in guiding the correct re-innervation of the goldfish tectum by retinal axons. These recombined proteins would act as a kind of molecular code to ensure that the topographically correct retinotectal mapping is achieved. Since this idea was put forward, however, no gene undergoing the requisite recombination in the nervous system has been found. This is perhaps not surprising, as the reagents that were instrumental in the discovery of lymphocyte V(D)J recombination—DNA sequences from a known candidate locus, and clonal cell lines in which the rearrangement event takes place—do not currently exist for the nervous system.

An indirect approach to this issue is to ask whether genes involved in immunological V(D)J recombination are expressed in the nervous system. In fact, a common feature shared by cortical thymocytes (Turka et al., 1991) and VZ NPCs (Chun et al., 1991) is expression of a range of genes involved in the initial cleavage of recombined genes and the rejoining of the free DNA ends to complete the recombination reaction. Part of the initial cleavage reaction in lymphocytes is driven by recombination-activating genes 1 and 2 (RAG1 and RAG2), which are involved in V(D)J recombination (Schatz et al., 1989). Rag1- knockout mice, however, have no obvious brain phenotype (Mombaerts et al., 1992), and Rag2 is not expressed in the CNS. It is notable that broken DNA ends that exist in cells that, like those produced by recombinase cleavage, have blunt ends that are 5′-phosphorylated, although most of these ends appear to be predominantly associated with cell death (Staley et al., 1997).

After cleavage, DNA end joining take place by means of several nonhomologous end-joining (NHEJ) proteins including Ku70, Ku80, DNA-dependent protein kinase catalytic subunit (DNA-PKcs), XRCC4, and DNA ligase IV (Lig IV). Through gene-targeting in the mouse, it has been shown that XRCC4 or Lig IV deficiency causes growth defects, premature senescence, immune response sensitivity, and inability to support V(D)J recombination in primary murine cells (Lieber, 1999).

Strikingly, XRCC4 or Lig IV deficiency in mice causes late embryonic lethality accompanied not only by defective lymphogenesis but also by defective neurogenesis, manifested by extensive apoptotic death of newly generated postmitotic neuronal cells (Gao et al., 1998). In the context of Lig IV and XRCC4 deficiency, embryonic lethality and neuronal apoptosis likely result from a p53-dependent response to unrepaired DNA damage (Frank et al., 2000; Gao et al., 2000). Ku70 and Ku80 deficiency results in dramatically increased death of developing neurons in mice though DNA-PKcs deficiency does not lead to any neuronal death phenotype. The Ku-deficient phenotype is

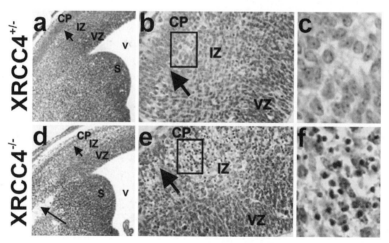

FIGURE 5–5 Massive cell death of newly postmitotic neurons in XRCC4 knockout mice. A–F. Hematoxylin and eosin staining of littermate XRCC4+/– and XRCC4–/– brain sections. Horizontal brain sections from G14.5 XRCC4+/– (A–C) and XRCC4–/– (D–F) mutants at a comparable level reveal severe acellularity (cavitation, long arrow) and thinner cortical plate (CP, small arrows) in the cerebral hemisphere of XRCC4–/– brain. Higher magnifications show relatively normal ventricular zone (VZ) of the mutant cortex (A, B vs. D, E), whereas in the intermediate zone (IZ) extending to the CP there are numerous pyknotic nuclei (dense hematoxylin stain) (E, F). CP, cortical plate; S, striatal analge or the ganglionic eminence; v, ventricle. Original magnifications: A and D x100; B, C, E, and F, x400. (*Source:* Adapted from Gao et al., 1998)

qualitatively similar to, but less severe, than that associated with XRCC4 and Lig IV deficiency (Gu et al., 2000). The lack of a neuronal death phenotype in DNA-PKcs–deficient fetuses, along with the milder phenotype of Ku deficiency (vs. XRCC4- or Lig IV–deficient fetuses), is likely related to relative low fidelity of DNA end-joining in the background strain of these mutants, shown by a V(D)J recombination end-joining assay.

A intriguing aspect of these studies is the consistency of abnormal cell death patterns in the developing cerebral cortex of mice deficient in DNA ligase IV, XRCC4 (Barnes et al., 1998; Frank et al., 1998; Gao et al., 1998), and Ku (Gu et al., 2000). Aberrant death is not observed at the earliest embryonic ages, and it is not until the period when most postmitotic neurons are generated that dead cells are clearly observed (Fig. 5–5). This general timing is seen in all examined regions of the neural tube, including the spinal cord (Gao et al., 1998).

These studies provide the first evidence that evolutionarily conserved genes required for completion of V(D)J recombination in lymphocytes are required for normal neural cell survival in the developing brain (Gao et al., 1998; Chun, 1999; Chun and Schatz, 1999). Several NHEJ proteins have roles in NPC survival during the onset of neural differentiation. The synthesis of these proteins could be crucial for the normal behavior of newly postmitotic neurons during their migration from proliferative zones to final destinations in the CNS (Rehen et al., 1996, 1999).

The absence of proteins important for the process of immunological V(D)J recombination promotes cell death in newly postmitotic neurons. This finding suggests the operation of a novel form of cell selection that distinguishes between neurons that make advantageous DNA rearrangements or other genomic alterations and those that do not. What kind of DNA alterations could occur in NPCs within the developing brain?

ANEUPLOIDY, CELL SELECTION, AND PROLIFERATIVE CELL DEATH IN THE BRAIN

As discussed above, there is indirect evidence for somatic alteration of the genome in neurons during neurogenesis based on a growing list of molecules that function in DNA recombination, repair, and surveillance (Gao et al, 1998, 2000; Chun, 1999; Chun and Schatz, 1999; Gu et al, 2000; Lee et al, 2000; Rolig and McKinnon, 2000; Allen et al, 2001). Many of these molecules are also implicated in the genetic alterations that are found in cancers. One prominent genetic abnormality in cancer cells is aneuloidy, a deviation from the normal diploid number of chromosomes. The association between cancer and neurodevelopment led to the search for aneuploidy as one expression of genomic change in neurons.

Direct assessment of chromosomes in dividing cells can be performed with spectral karyotyping (SKY) which uses fluorescent labels to uniquely identify each chromosome. This technique reveals that a large fraction of NPCs harbor chromosomal abnormalities. Remarkably, one-third of mouse NPCs have gained or lost at least one of their 40 chromosomes (Fig 5–6; Rehen et al, 2001). NPCs isolated from the VZ of the fetal mouse cerebral cortex are often observed with one or more chromosomes displaced from the mitotic spindle. Such chromosome displacement suggests that NPCs frequently mis-segregate their chromosomes, which may represent one way that neurons can become aneuploid during development (Yang et al, 2003).

Aneuploidy has also been detected in the adult cerebral cortex, using interphase fluorescent in situ hybridization (FISH) to visualize individual chromosomes. In adult male cerebral cortex, FISH for X and Y chromosomes shows that approximately 1% of neurons gained or lost a sex chromosome (Fig 5–7). This implies that at least some fraction of aneuploid cells that are produced during neurogenesis survive to adulthood. Theoretically, the overall percentage of aneuploid neurons in the adult could be much higher than 1%, assuming the rate of gain/loss is similar for all chromosomes (Kaushal et al, 2003), although further studies are required to address this issue.

Although some aneuploid cells survive, Aneuploid cells may account for a significant proportion of PCD during neurogenesis. Cell death is likely a common fate for aneuploid cells. In cancers, many cells that are thought to be dying have an altered genome. Further, the high amounts of PCD in neuroproliferative zones supports the idea of a selection process against undesirable genetic abnormalities. As a first approximation, aneuploidy appears to be generated in a stochastic fashion. One can speculate that random

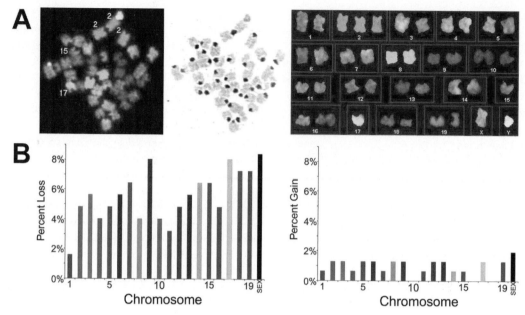

FIGURE 5–6 Aneuploid neural progenitor cells (NPCs) in the embryonic mouse brain. **A.** Spectral karyotyping (SKY) from a representative aneuploid embryonic NPC. Spectral (left) and inverse DAPI (center) images of the chromosome spread are shown, along with the karyotype table (right). Note that each different chromosome has a unique spectral color (indicated by shades of gray). Euploid chromosome number in mice is 40. The spread has an extra copy of chromosome 2, but has only one copy of chromosomes 15 and 17 (39, XY, +2, −15, −17). **B.** Graphs show the percentage of loss (left) and gain (right) of specific chromosomes in NPCs. Bars are coded on the basis of spectral color of each chromosome (except for sex chromosomes). Specific chromosomes are lost at rates of 1.6%–8.4% of cells analyzed and are gained at rates of less than 2%.

aneuploidy imparts diversity and complexity to neuronal populations, and that aneuploid NPCs are selected on the basis of their genomic contents, with one probable fate being cell death. The pervasiveness of adult neural aneuploidy may indicate a selective advantage acquired by some aneuploid neurons, as has been noted in certain aneuploid cancer cells (Lengauer et al, 1997). Thus, variation in chromosome number can be considered a new mechanism for generating cellular diversity in the CNS.

The main conclusion from these data is that aneuploid cells are found in the developing and adult nervous system, demonstrating that brain cells can differ at the level of their genome. Whether DNA rearrangements are also present in these cells remains an open question. These somatic changes in the DNA of a cell could affect a significant portion of the genome, altering hundreds of gene copies which would have important consequences for the physiology of that cell. The global effect of this process could result in a mature brain that is a unique genetic mosaic, characterized by a euploid population intermixed with a diverse aneuploid population of neurons (Rehen et al, 2001; Kaushal et al, 2003; Yang et al, 2003).

LYSOPHOSPHATIDIC ACID, CELL CYCLE EXIT, DECREASED PROGRAMMED CELL DEATH, AND INCREASES IN BRAIN DIMENSIONS

A variety of extracellular factors have been shown to influence NPCs and young neurons of the cortex. Neurotransmitters (LoTurco et al., 1995) and peptide factors (Drago et al., 1991; Ghosh and Greenberg, 1995; Temple and Qian, 1995) affect neurogenic parameters of developing cortical cells, although it is generally unclear how these signals influence the growth and morphology of the intact cerebral cortex.

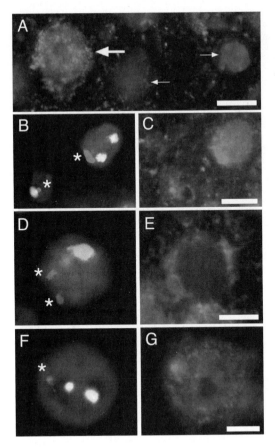

FIGURE 5–7 Aneuploid cells in the adult cortex are neurons. **A.** The presence of both microtuble-associated protein (MAP) 2-positive (large arrow) and MAP2-negative (small arrows) cells in a 10 μm section through adult cerebral cortex demonstrates the specificity of MAP2 labeling as a neuronal marker. Nuclei were counterstained with DAPI. **B–G.** Cells in 10 μm sections through the adult male cortex were hybridized with X and Y chromosome paints. **C, E, G.** Cells in these same 10 μm sections were then immunostained for MAP2. **B.** The cell on the left contains both an X and a Y chromosome (noted by an asterisk), whereas the cell on the right has an extra Y chromosome. **C.** The cell with two Y chromosomes is MAP2-positive. **D, E.** A cell in motor cortex contains an extra X chromosome (D) and is MAP2-positive (E). **F, G.** A cell in motor cortex contains an extra Y chromosome (F) and is MAP2-positive (G). Scale bars = 10 μm (D, F) and 5.0 μm (H, J). (*Source:* Adapted from Rehen et al., 2001)

Some trophic factors such as fibroblast growth factor 2 (FGF-2) and NT-3 are also known to regulate the transition from dividing NPCs to terminally differentiated neurons in the CNS, (Ghosh and Greenberg, 1995). That said, factors able to modulate PCD within the VZ are less well understood.

A lipid molecule, lysophosphatidic acid (LPA), has been implicated in the regulation of neurogenetic processes, including proliferative cell death. Many of the effects of LPA are mediated by G protein–coupled receptors that are members of the lysophospholipid receptor gene family (Fukushima et al., 2001; Chun et al., 2002; Anliker and Chun, 2004; Ishii et al., 2004). A role for LPA signaling in nervous system development was initially suggested by the discovery of the first lysophospholipid receptor, LPA_1, which shows enriched expression in the VZ (Hecht et al., 1996). Subsequent studies have identified LPA_2 expression in postmitotic cells of the embryonic cortex (Fukushima et al., 2002; McGiffert et al., 2002) and LPA_3 expression within the early postnatal brain (Contos et al., 2000). LPA, is also present in the brain (Das and Hajra, 1989; Sugiura et al., 1999) and can be produced by postmitotic neurons and Schwann cells in culture (Weiner and Chun, 1999; Fukushima et al., 2000).

In an *ex vivo* brain culture system, LPA exposure rapidly alters the organization of the developing cerebral cortex (Kingsbury et al., 2003). After just 17 hours, LPA-treated hemispheres display striking cortical folds and a widening of the cerebral wall, compared to untreated opposite hemispheres obtained from the same animals (Fig. 5–8) (Kingsbury et al., 2003, 2004). This expansion of cortical thickness is due to an increase in cells within both proliferative and postmitotic regions without a corresponding change in cell density. Whereas LPA is a mitogen for many cell types in culture (Moolenaar, 1995; Moolenaar et al., 1997), LPA exposure appears to decrease proliferation in an ex vivo brain culture system in favor of terminal mitosis (Kingsbury et al., 2003). In addition, LPA exposure in this ex vivo system promotes the survival of VZ cells. Therefore, the increase in cortical thickness following LPA treatment is due to (1) the increased survival of many NPCs, which enlarges the proliferating pool, and (2) the induction of terminal mitosis, which increases the number of postmitotic neurons. Most importantly from a mechanistic standpoint, neither folding nor increases in

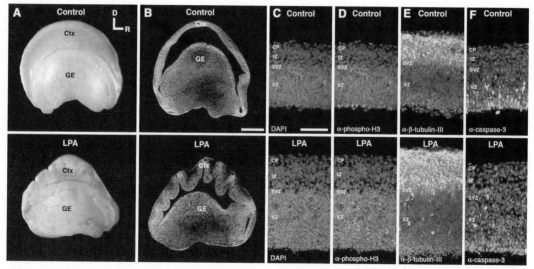

FIGURE 5–8 Effect of lysophosphatidic acid (LPA) on cortical development. Intact cerebral hemispheres exposed to (LPA) ex vivo exhibit cortical folding and widening of the cerebral wall compared to control hemispheres from the same animal. Whole-mount views (A) and sagittal sections (B) from gestational day (G) 14 hemispheres show dramatic cortical folding following culture with LPA, compared to control medium. D, dorsal; R, rostral; Ctx, cortex; GE, ganglionic eminence. Scale bar = 0.50 mm. C. G14 cortices labeled with the nuclear stain DAPI show increased thickness following LPA-treatment. CP, cortical plate; IZ, intermediate zone; SZ, subventricular zone; VZ, ventricular zone. Scale bar = 100 μm. LPA promotes terminal mitosis through an increase in M-phase cells immunolabeled with anti-phosphohistone H3 antibody (D), a decrease in S-phase cells (data not shown), and an increase in differentiating neurons immunolabeled with anti-β-tubulin III antibody (E). LPA decreases the number of dying cells immunolabeled for anti-active caspase-3 antibody (F). (*Source:* Modified from Kingsbury et al., 2004)

cortical thickness, mitosis, and cell survival are observed in LPA_1/LPA_2 receptor null mice (Kingsbury et al., 2003), results demonstrating that the effects of LPA in an *ex vivo* system are receptor mediated.

The rapid increase in cortical size following LPA exposure is consistent with studies showing that rescue of VZ cell death—likely multiple rounds of death, given the ~2-hour clearance time estimated for dying cells in the cortex (Thomaidou et al., 1997)—can have major consequences for cortical growth (Kuida et al., 1996; Pompeiano et al., 2000). Moreover, the increased presence of postmitotic neurons (β-tubulin-III–labeled cells) in the VZ following LPA treatment may represent premature differentiation of NPCs that contribute to increased VZ thickness. The switch to a postmitotic status could trigger the production of suppressor proteins (i.e., $Bcl-x_L$) able to abrogate PCD in cells migrating from VZ to CP.

LPA signaling can have major effects on cells within the embryonic cerebral cortex that are distinct from cell proliferation. Interestingly, the folding pattern observed in brains treated with LPA are superficially reminiscent of those observed in hyperplastic brains from knockout mice for caspases (Kuida et al., 1996; Roth et al., 2000) or PSR (Li et al., 2003). Despite these similarities, LPA-mediated cytoarchitectonic changes differ from those of caspase deletion in several aspects. Disruption of cell death by caspase deletion results in reduced NPC death and increased VZ size without a marked increase in CP thickness (Kuida et al., 1996; Haydar et al., 1999b; Pompeiano et al., 2000). Augmented cell cycle re-entry by overexpression of β-catenin produces folds via the tangential expansion of cortical surface area without increases in cortical width (Chenn and Walsh, 2002; Zechner et al., 2003). By comparison, receptor-mediated LPA signaling increases cortical thickness by altering both proliferative and postmitotic populations, and further produces regularly arranged cortical folds.

Future studies that involve the inhibition of specific G-proteins and downstream effectors in cortical progenitors should provide insight into how receptor-mediated LPA signaling promotes terminal mitosis and cell survival in the developing cerebral cortex. Such studies may also reveal links between cell death and suppressor proteins, including those related to V(D)J/NHEJ and Bcl-2 family molecules, for the survival and proper function of newly postmitotic neurons within the developing brain.

CONCLUSIONS

Tissue homeostasis is currently viewed as a careful balance between proliferation and cell death. The number, composition and distribution of cells within both adult and developing organs, including the CNS, critically depend on this balance. The dramatic increase in cerebral cortical size across mammalian evolution is paralleled by increased cell numbers and an expansion of cortical surface area due to changes in the regulation of proliferation, differentiation and PCD within the fetal brain (Rakic and Caviness, 1995; Caviness et al, 1995; Kuda et al 1996; Cecconi et al, 1998; Yoshida et al, 1998; Haydar et al, 1999b; Pompeiano et al, 2000; Roth et al, 2000; Chenn and Walsh, 2003; Li et al, 2003). The present chapter focused on the role of PCD in shaping the development of the cerebral cortex.

Collectively, the results discussed in the present chapter indicate that in the developing CNS, PCD is a significant cell fate for proliferating NPCs, and this PCD could be responsible for a selection process based on alterations of DNA, particularly involving chromosomal aneuploidy. During migration and initial differentiation, cell death is prevented or delayed by the expression of suppressor proteins, including members of the Bcl-2 family and the V(D)J/NHEJ factors, thus allowing these newly postmitotic cells to find their final positions and differentiate. After reaching their final destination, neural cells start to compete for limited trophic factor support to survive another round of PCD. A newly identified group of factors that affect NPCs are the lysophospholipids—small lipid signals acting through cognate G protein–coupled receptors. LPA signaling results in decreased cell death and induced cell cycle exit, which can be considered new influences on cerebral cortical growth and anatomy. Future studies will better define the mechanisms of selection and cell death during nervous system development.

Abbreviations

APAF   apoptotic protease-activating factor
BDNF   brain-derived neurotrophic factor
BH   bcl-2 homology
BrdU   bromodeoxyuridine
CNS   central nervous system
CP   cortical plate
DNA-PKcs   DNA-dependent protein kinase catalytic subunit
FGF   fibroblast growth factor
G   gestational day
ISEL   in situ end-labeling
IZ   intermediate zone
Lig IV   ligase IV
LPA   lysophosphatidic acid
MAP   microtuble-associated protein
NBL   neuroblastic layer
NGF   nerve growth factor
NHEJ   nonhomologous end-joining
NPC   neural progenitor cell
NT   neurotrophin
PCD   programmed cell death
PSR   phosphatidylserine receptor
SKY   spectral karyotyping
SZ   subventricular zone
trk   tyrosine protein kinase
VZ   ventricular zone

ACKNOWEDGMENTS   We are grateful to Amy Yang, Marcy Kingsbury, Brigitte Anliker, Christine Paczkowski, and Suzanne Peterson for the critical reading of this manuscript. This work was supported by the National Institute of Mental Health, National Institute for, and Pew Latin American Program in Biomedical Sciences.

References

Abrams JM, White K, Fessler LI, Steller H (1993) Programmed cell death during *Drosophila* embryogenesis. Development 117:29–43.

Akhtar RS, Ness JM, Roth KA (2004) Bcl-2 family regulation of neuronal development and neurodegeneration. Biochim Biophys Acta 1644:189–203.

Alexiades MR, Cepko C (1996) Quantitative analysis of proliferation and cell cycle length during development of the rat retina. Dev Dyn 205:293–307.

Alexiades MR, Cepko CL (1997) Subsets of retinal progenitors display temporally regulated and distinct biases in the fates of their progeny. Development 124:1119–1131.

Al-Ghoul WM, Miller MW (1989) Transient expression of Alz-50-immunoreactivity in developing rat neocortex: a marker for naturally occurring neuronal death? Brain Res 481:361–367.

Allen DM, van Praag H, Ray J, Weaver Z, Winrow CJ, Carter TA, Braquet R, Harrington E, Ried T, Brown KD, Gage FH, Barlow C (2001) Ataxia telangiectasia mutated is essential during adult neurogenesis. Genes Dev 15:554–566.

Anliker B, Chun J (2004) Lysophospholipid G protein–coupled receptors. J Biol Chem 279:20 555–20558.

Arends MJ, Morris RG, Wyllie AH (1990) Apoptosis; the role of the endonuclease. Am J Pathol 136: 593–608.

Barbacid M (1994) The Trk family of neurotrophin receptors. J Neurobiol 25:1386–1403.

Barnes DE, Stamp G, Rosewell I, Denzel A, Lindahl T (1998) Targeted disruption of the gene encoding DNA ligase IV leads to lethality in embryonic mice. Curr Biol 8:1395–1398.

Bayer SA, Altman J (1991) Neocortical Development. Raven Press, New York.

Berkemeier LR, Winslow JW, Kaplan DR, Nikolics K, Goeddel DV, Rosenthal A (1991) Neurotrophin-5: a novel neurotrophic factor that activates trk and trkB. Neuron 7:857–866.

Blaschke AJ, Staley K, Chun J (1996) Widespread programmed cell death in proliferative and postmitotic regions of the fetal cerebral cortex. Development 122:1165–1174.

Blaschke AJ, Weiner JA, Chun J (1998) Programmed cell death is a universal feature of embryonic and postnatal neuroproliferative regions throughout the central nervous system. J Comp Neurol 396: 39–50.

Boise LH, Gonzalez-Garcia M, Postema CE, Ding L, Lindsten T, Turka LA, Mao X, Nunez G, Thompson CB (1993) bcl-x, a bcl-2-related gene that functions as a dominant regulator of apoptotic cell death. Cell 74:597–608.

Caviness VS Jr (1982) Neocortical histogenesis in normal and reeler mice: a developmental study based upon [³H]thymidine autoradiography. Brain Res 256:293–302.

Caviness VS Jr, Takahashi T, Nowakowski RS (1995) Numbers, time and neocortical neuronogenesis: a general developmental and evolutionary model. Trends Neurosci 18:379–383.

Cecconi F, Alvarez-Bolado G, Meyer BI, Roth KA, Gruss P (1998) Apaf1 (CED-4 homolog) regulates programmed cell death in mammalian development. Cell 94:727–737.

Chenn A, Walsh CA (2002) Regulation of cerebral cortical size by control of cell cycle exit in neural precursors. Science 297:365–369.

—— (2003) Increased neuronal production, enlarged forebrains and cytoarchitectural distortions in β-catenin overexpressing transgenic mice. Cereb Cortex 13:599–606.

Chun J (1999) Developmental neurobiology: a genetic Cheshire cat? Curr Biol 9:R651–R654.

—— (2001) Selected comparison of immune and nervous system development. Adv Immunol 77: 297–322.

Chun J, Goetzl EJ, Hla T, Igarashi Y, Lynch KR, Moolenaar W, Pyne S, Tigyi G (2002) Intl Union Pharmacol XXXIV. Lysophospholipid receptor nomenclature. Pharmacol Rev 54:265–269.

Chun JJ, Nakamura MJ, Shatz CJ (1987) Transient cells of the developing mammalian telencephalon are peptide-immunoreactive neurons. Nature 325: 617–620.

Chun J, Schatz DG (1999) Developmental neurobiology: alternative ends for a familiar story? Curr Biol 9:R251–253.

Chun JJM, Schatz DG, Oettinger MA, Jaenisch R, Baltimore D (1991) The recombination activating gene-1 (RAG-1) transcript is present in the murine central nervous system. Cell 64:189–200.

Chun JJM, Shatz CJ (1989a) The earliest-generated neurons of the cat cerebral cortex: characterization by MAP2 and neurotransmitter immunohistochemistry during fetal life. J Neurosci 9:1648–1677.

—— (1989b) Interstitial cells of the adult neocortical white matter are the remnant of the early generated subplate neuron population. J Comp Neurol 282: 555–569.

Clarke PG, Clarke S (1996) Nineteenth century research on naturally occurring cell death and related phenomena. Anat Embryol 193:81–99.

Clarke PG, Rogers LA, Cowan WM (1976) The time of origin and the pattern of survival of neurons in the isthmo-optic nucleus of the chick. J Comp Neurol 167:125–142.

Cohen S, Levi-Montalcini R (1957) Purification and properties of a nerve growth–promoting factor isolated from mouse sarcoma. Cancer Res 17: 15–20.

Contos JJ, Ishii I, Chun J (2000) Lysophosphatidic acid receptors. Mol Pharmacol 58:1188–1196.

Cowan WM (1979) The development of the brain. Sci Am 241:113–133.

Cowan WM, Fawcett JW, O'Leary DDM, Stanfield BB (1984) Regressive events in neurogenesis. Science 225:1258–1265.

Danial NN, Korsmeyer SJ (2004) Cell death: critical control points. Cell 116:205–219.

Das AK, Hajra AK (1989) Quantification, characterization and fatty acid composition of lysophosphatidic acid in different rat tissues. Lipids 24:329–333.

Davies AM (1994) Neurobiology. Tracking neurotrophin function. Nature 368:193–194.

Dechant G, Barde YA (2002) The neurotrophin receptor p75(NTR): novel functions and implications for diseases of the nervous system. Nat Neurosci 5: 1131–1136.

Dechant G, Rodriguez-Tebar A, Barde YA (1994) Neurotrophin receptors. Prog Neurobiol 42:347–352.

Denham S (1967) A cell proliferation study of the neural retina in the two-day rat. J Embryol Exp Morphol 18:53–66.

Doetsch F, Caille I, Lim DA, Garcia-Verdugo JM, Alvarez-Buylla A (1999) Subventricular zone astrocytes are neural stem cells in the adult mammalian brain. Cell 97:703–716.

Drago J, Murphy M, Carroll SM, Harvey RP, Bartlett PF (1991) Fibroblast growth factor–mediated proliferation of central nervous system precursors depends on endogenous production of insulin-like growth factor I. Proc Natl Acad Sci USA 88:2199–2203.

Dreyer WJ, Gray WR, Hood L (1967) The genetic, molecular and cellular basis of antibody formation: some facts and a unifying hypothesis. Cold Spring Harbor Symp Quant Biol 32:353–367.

Dunn WA Jr (1994) Autophagy and related mechanisms of lysosome-mediated protein degradation. Trends Cell Biol 4:139–143.

Egerton M, Scollay R, Shortman K (1990) Kinetics of mature T-cell development in the thymus. Proc Natl Acad Sci USA 87:2579–2582.

Ellis HM, Horvitz HR (1986) Genetic control of programmed cell death in the nematode C. elegans. Cell 44:817–829.

Ellis RE, Yuan J, Horvitz RH (1991) Mechanisms and functions of cell death. Annu Rev Cell Biol 7: 663–698.

Ernfors P, Ibanez CF, Ebendal T, Olson L, Persson H (1990) Molecular cloning and neurotrophic activities of a protein with structural similarities to nerve growth factor: developmental and topographical expression in the brain. Proc Natl Acad Sci USA 87: 5454–5458.

Finlay BL, Slattery M (1983) Local differences in the amount of early cell death in neorcortex predict adult local specializations. Science 219:1349–1351.

Frank KM, Sekiguchi JM, Seidl KJ, Swat W, Rathbun GA, Cheng HL, Davidson L, Kangaloo L, Alt FW (1998) Late embryonic lethality and impaired V(D)J recombination in mice lacking DNA ligase IV. Nature 396:173–177.

Frank KM, Sharpless NE, Gao Y, Sekiguchi JM, Ferguson DO, Zhu C, Manis JP, Horner J, DePinho RA, Alt FW (2000) DNA ligase IV deficiency in mice leads to defective neurogenesis and embryonic lethality via the p53 pathway. Mol Cell 5:993–1002.

Fukushima N, Ishii I, Contos JA, Weiner JA, Chun J (2001) Lysophospholipid receptors. Annu Rev Pharmacol Toxicol 41:507–534.

Fukushima N, Weiner JA, Chun J (2000) Lysophosphatidic acid (LPA) is a novel extracellular regulator of cortical neuroblast morphology. Dev Biol 228:6–18.

Fukushima N, Weiner JA, Kaushal J, Contos JJA, Rehen SK, Kingsbury MA, Kim KY, Chun J (2002) Lysophosphatidic acid influences the morphology and motility of young, postmitotic cortical neurons. Mol Cell Neurosci 20:271–282.

Gao Y, Ferguson DO, Xie W, Manis JP, Sekiguchi J, Frank KM, Chaudhuri J, Horner J, DePinho RA, Alt FW (2000) Interplay of p53 and DNA-repair protein XRCC4 in tumorigenesis, genomic stability and development. Nature 404:897–900.

Gao Y, Sun Y, Frank KM, Dikkes P, Fujiwara Y, Seidl KJ, Sekiguchi JM, Rathbun GA, Swat W, Wang J, Bronson RT, Malynn BA, Bryans M, Zhu C, Chaudhuri J, Davidson L, Ferrini R, Stamato T, Orkin SH, Greenberg ME, Alt FW (1998) A critical role for DNA end-joining proteins in both lymphogenesis and neurogenesis. Cell 95:891–902.

Gavrieli Y, Sherman Y, Ben-Sasson SA (1992) Identification of programmed cell death in situ via specific labeling of nuclear DNA fragmentation. J Cell Biol 119:493–501.

Ghosh A, Antonini A, McConnell SK, Shatz CJ (1990) Requirement for subplate neurons in the formation of thalamocortical connections. Nature 347: 179–181.

Ghosh A, Greenberg ME (1995) Distinct roles for bFGF and NT-3 in the regulation of cortical neurogenesis. Neuron 15:89–103.

Gotz R, Koster R, Winkler C, Raulf F, Lottspeich F, Schartl M, Thoenen H (1994) Neurotrophin-6 is a new member of the nerve growth factor family. Nature 372:266–269.

Gu Y, Sekiguchi J, Gao Y, Dikkes P, Frank K, Ferguson D, Hasty P, Chun J, Alt FW (2000) Defective embryonic neurogenesis in Ku-deficient but not

DNA-dependent protein kinase catalytic subunit–deficient mice. Proc Natl Acad Sci USA 97:2668–2673.

Guimaraes CA, Benchimol M, Amarante-Mendes GP, Linden R (2003) Alternative programs of cell death in developing retinal tissue. J Biol Chem 278:41938–41946.

Hallbook F, Ibanez CF, Persson H (1991) Evolutionary studies of the nerve growth factor family reveal a novel member abundantly expressed in *Xenopus* ovary. Neuron 6:845–858.

Hamburger V (1975) Cell death in the development of the lateral motor column of the chick embryo. J Comp Neurol 160:535–546.

Hamburger V, Levi-Montalcini R (1949) Proliferation, differentiation and degeneration in the spinal ganglia of the chick embryo under normal and experimental conditions. J Exp Zool 111:457–502.

Haydar TF, Bambrick LL, Krueger BK, Rakic P (1999a) Organotypic slice cultures for analysis of proliferation, cell death, and migration in the embryonic neocortex. Brain Res Prot 4:425–437.

Haydar TF, Kuan CY, Flavell RA, Rakic P (1999b) The role of cell death in regulating the size and shape of the mammalian forebrain. Cereb Cortex 9:621–626.

Hecht JH, Weiner JA, Post SR, Chun J (1996) Ventricular zone gene-1 (*vzg-1*) encodes a lysophosphatidic acid receptor expressed in neurogenic regions of the developing cerebral cortex. J Cell Biol 135:1071–1083.

Hempstead BL (2002) The many faces of p75NTR. Curr Opin Neurobiol 12:260–267.

Homma S, Yaginuma H, Oppenheim RW (1994) Programmed cell death during the earliest stages of spinal cord developement in the chick embryo: a possible means of early phenotypic selection. J Comp Neurol 345:377–395.

Huang EJ, Reichardt LF (2001) Neurotrophins: roles in neuronal development and function. Annu Rev Neurosci 24:677–736.

Ishii I, Fukushima N, Ye X, Chun J (2004) Lysophospholipid receptors: signaling and biology. Annu Rev Biochem 73:321–354.

Kaushal D, Contos JJ, Treuner K, Yang AH, Kingsbury MA, Rehen SK, McConnell MJ, Okabe M, Barlow C, Chun J (2003) Alteration of gene expression by chromosome loss in the postnatal mouse brain. J Neurosci 23:5599–5606.

Kerr JF, Winterford CM, Harmon BV (1994) Apoptosis. Its significance in cancer and cancer therapy. Cancer 73:2013–2026.

Kerr JF, Wyllie AH, Currie AR (1972) Apoptosis: a basic biological phenomenon with wide-ranging implications in tissue kinetics. Br J Cancer 26:239–257.

Kerr JFR, Harmon BV (1991) Definition and incidence of apoptosis an historical perspective. In: Tomei LD, Cope FO (ed). *Apoptosis: The Molecular Basis of Cell Death*. Cold Spring Harbor Lab, New York, pp 5–29.

Kingsbury MA, Rehen SK, Contos JJ, Higgins CM, Chun J (2003) Non-proliferative effects of lysophosphatidic acid enhance cortical growth and folding. Nat Neurosci 6:1292–1299.

Kingsbury MA, Rehen SK, Ye X, Chun J (2004) Genetics and cell biology of lysophosphatidic acid receptor-mediated signaling during cortical neurogenesis. J Cell Biochem 92:1004–1012.

Korsmeyer SJ (1999) Bcl-2 gene family and the regulation of programmed cell death. Cancer Res 59:1693s–1700s.

Kuida K, Haydar TF, Kuan CY, Gu Y, Taya C, Karasuyama H, Su MS, Rakic P, Flavell RA (1998) Reduced apoptosis and cytochrome C–mediated caspase activation in mice lacking caspase 9. Cell 94:325–337.

Kuida K, Zheng TS, Na S, Kuan C, Yang D, Karasuyama H, Rakic P, Flavell RA (1996) Decreased apoptosis in the brain and premature lethality in CPP32-deficient mice. Nature 384:368–372.

Lee Y, Barnes DE, Lindahl T, McKinnon PJ (2000) Defective neurogenesis resulting from DNA ligase IV deficiency requires Atm. Genes Dev 14:2576–2580.

Lengauer C, Kinzler KW, Vogelstein B (1997) Genetic instability in colorectal cancers. Nature 386:623–627.

Levi-Montalcini R (1987) The nerve growth factor 35 years later. Science 237:1154–1162.

Li MO, Sarkisian MR, Mehal WZ, Rakic P, Flavell RA (2003) Phosphatidylserine receptor is required for clearance of apoptotic cells. Science 302:1560–1563.

Lieber MR (1999) The biochemistry and biological significance of nonhomologous DNA end joining: an essential repair process in multicellular eukaryotes. Genes Cells 4:77–85.

Lim DA, Alvarez-Buylla A (1999) Interaction between astrocytes and adult subventricular zone precursors stimulates neurogenesis. Proc Natl Acad Sci USA 96:7526–7531.

Linden R (1994) The survival of developing neurons: a review of afferent control. Neuroscience 58:671–682.

Linden R, Rehen SK, Chiarini LB (1999) Apoptosis in developing retinal tissue. Prog Retin Eye Res 18:133–165.

Lockshin RA, Williams CM (1965) Programmed cell death—I. Cytology of degeneration in the intersegmental muscles of the pernyi silkmoth. J Insect Physiol 11:123–133.

LoTurco JJ, Owens DF, Heath MJ, Davis MB, Kriegstein AR (1995) GABA and glutamate depolarize cortical progenitor cells and inhibit DNA synthesis. Neuron 15:1287–1298.

Majdan M, Lachance C, Gloster A, Aloyz R, Zeindler C, Bamji S, Bhakar A, Belliveau D, Fawcett J, Miller FD, Barker PA (1997) Transgenic mice expressing the intracellular domain of the p75 neurotrophin receptor undergo neuronal apoptosis. J Neurosci 17:6988–6998.

Marin-Teva JL, Dusart I, Colin C, Gervais A, van Rooijen N, Mallat M (2004) Microglia promote the death of developing Purkinje cells. Neuron 41: 535–547.

McGiffert C, Contos JJ, Friedman B, Chun J (2002) Embryonic brain expression analysis of lysophospholipid receptor genes suggests roles for s1p(1) in neurogenesis and s1p(1–3) in angiogenesis. FEBS Lett 531:103–108.

Metcalf D (1966) *The Structure of the Thymus*. Springer-Verlag, Berlin.

Miller MW (1988) Development of projection and local circuit neurons in cerebral cortex. In: Peters A, Jones EG (eds). *Cerebral Cortex, Vol. 7. Development and Maturation of Cerebral Cortex*. Plenum, New York, pp 133–175.

—— (1995) Relationship of time of origin and death of neurons in rat somatosensory cortex: barrel versus septal cortex and projection versus local circuit neurons. J Comp Neurol 355:6–14.

Miller MW, Nowakowski RS (1988) Use of bromodeoxyuridine-immunohistochemistry to examine the proliferation, migration, and time of origin of cells in the central nervous system. Brain Res 457: 44–52.

Mombaerts P, Iacomini J, Johnson RS, Herrup K, Tonegawa S, Papaioannou VE (1992) RAG-1 deficient mice have no mature B and T lymphocytes. Cell 68:869–877.

Moolenaar WH (1995) Lysophosphatidic acid signalling. Curr Opin Cell Biol 7:203–210.

Moolenaar WH, Kranenburg O, Postma FR, Zondag GCM (1997) Lysophosphatidic acid: G-protein signalling and cellular responses. Curr Opin Cell Biol 9:168–173.

Motoyama N, Wang F, Roth KA, Sawa H, Nakayama K, Nakayama K, Negishi I, Senju S, Zhang Q, Fujii S, Loh DY (1995) Massive cell death of immature hematopoietic cell and neurons in bcl-x-deficient mice. Science 267:1506–1510.

Nilsson AS, Fainzilber M, Falck P, Ibanez CF (1998) Neurotrophin-7: a novel member of the neurotrophin family from the zebrafish. FEBS Lett 424: 285–290.

Noctor SC, Flint AC, Weissman TA, Dammerman RS, Kriegstein AR (2001) Neurons derived from radial glial cells establish radial units in neocortex. Nature 409:714–720.

Oppenheim RW (1991) Cell death during development of the nervous system. Annu Rev Neurosci 14: 453–501.

Pompeiano M, Blaschke AJ, Flavell RA, Srinivasan A, Chun J (2000) Decreased apoptosis in proliferative and postmitotic regions of the caspase 3–deficient embryonic central nervous system. J Comp Neurol 423:1–12.

Pompeiano M, Hvala M, Chun J (1998) Onset of apoptotic DNA fragmentation can precede cell elimination by days in the small intestinal villus. Cell Death Differ 5:702–709.

Poste ME, Olsen IA (1973) An investigation of the sites of mitotic activities in the guinea-pig thymus using autoradiography and colcemid-induced mitotic arrest. Immunology 24:691–697.

Rakic P, Caviness VS Jr (1995) Cortical development: view from neurological mutants two decades later. Neuron 14:1101–1104.

Rehen SK, McConnell MJ, Kaushal D, Kingsbury MA, Yang AH, Chun J (2001) Chromosomal variation in neurons of the developing and adult mammalian nervous system. Proc Natl Acad Sci USA 98: 13361–13366.

Rehen SK, Neves DD, Fragel-Madeira L, Britto LR, Linden R (1999) Selective sensitivity of early postmitotic retinal cells to apoptosis induced by inhibition of protein synthesis. Eur J Neurosci 11:4349–4356.

Rehen SK, Varella MH, Freitas FG, Moraes MO, Linden R (1996) Contrasting effects of protein synthesis inhibition and of cyclic AMP on apoptosis in the developing retina. Development 122:1439–1448.

Rolig RL, McKinnon PJ (2000) Linking DNA damage and neurodegeneration. Trends Neurosci 23: 417–424.

Roth KA, Kuan C, Haydar TF, D'Sa-Eipper C, Shindler KS, Zheng TS, Kuida K, Flavell RA, Rakic P (2000) Epistatic and independent functions of caspase-3 and Bcl-X(L) in developmental programmed cell death. Proc Natl Acad Sci USA 97: 466–471.

Saunders JW (1966) Death in embryonic systems. Science 154:604–612.

Schatz DG, Oettinger MA, Baltimore D (1989) The V(D)J recombination activating gene (RAG-1). Cell 59:1035–1048.

Scott J, Selby M, Urdea M, Quiroga M, Bell GI, Rutter WJ (1983) Isolation and nucleotide sequence of a cDNA encoding the precursor of mouse nerve growth factor. Nature 302:538–540.

Shortman K, Egerton M, Spangrude GJ, Scollay R (1990) The generation and fate of thymocytes. Semin Immunol 2:3–12.

Shortman K, Scollay R (1994) Immunology. Death in the thymus. Nature 372:44–45.

Staley K, Blaschke AJ, Chun JJM (1997) Apoptotic DNA fragmentation is detected by a semi-quantitative ligation-mediated PCR of blunt DNA Ends. Cell Death Differ 4:66–75.

Sugiura T, Nakane S, Kishimoto S, Waku K, Yoshioka Y, Tokumura A, Hanahan DJ (1999) Occurrence of lysophosphatidic acid and its alkyl ether–linked analog in rat brain and comparison of their biological activities toward cultured neural cells. Biochim Biophys Acta 1440:194–204.

Surh CD, Sprent J (1994) T-cell apoptosis detected in situ during positive and negative selection in the thymus. Nature 372:100–103.

Temple S, Qian X (1995) bFGF, neurotrophins, and the control or cortical neurogenesis. Neuron 15:249–252.

Thomaidou D, Mione MC, Cavanagh JF, Parnavelas JG (1997) Apoptosis and its relation to the cell cycle in the developing cerebral cortex. J Neurosci 17:1075–1085.

Tomei LD, Cope FO, Barr PJ (1994) Apoptosis: aging and phenotypic fidelity. In: Cope FO (ed). *Apoptosis II: The Molecular Basis of Apoptosis in Disease.* Cold Spring Harbor Lab Press, Plainview NY, pp 377–398.

Turka LA, Schatz DG, Oettinger MA, Chun JJM, Gorka C, Lee K, McCormack WT, Thompson CB (1991) Thymocyte expression of RAG-1 and RAG-2: termination by T cell receptor cross-linking. Science 253:778–781.

Wang X, Wu FC, Fadok VA, Lee MC, Gengyo-Ando K, Cheng LC, Ledwich D, Hsu PK, Chen JY, Chou BK, Henson P, Mitani S, Xue D (2003) Cell corpse engulfment mediated by C. elegans phosphotidyl-sevine receptor through CED-5 and CED-12. Science 302:1563–1566.

Weaver DT, Alt FW (1997) V(D)J recombination. From RAGs to stitches. Nature 388:428–429.

Weiner JA, Chun J (1997) Png-1, a nervous system–specific zinc finger gene, identifies regions containing postmitotic neurons during mammalian embryonic development. J Comp Neurol 381:130–142.

—— (1999) Schwann cell survival mediated by the signaling phospholipid lysophosphatidic acid. Proc Natl Acad Sci USA 96:5233–5238.

White K, Grether ME, Abrams JM, Young L, Farrrel K, Steller H (1994) Genetic control of programmed cell death in *Drosophila*. Science 264:677–683.

Wijsman JH, Jonker RR, Keijzer R, Van De Velde CJH, Cornelisse CJ, Van Dierendonck JH (1993) A new method to detect apoptosis in paraffin sections: in situ end-labeling of fragmented DNA. J Histochem Cytochem 41:7–12.

Williams GT, Smith CA (1993) Molecular regulation of apoptosis: genetic controls on cell death. Cell 74:777–779.

Wood KA, Dipasquale B, Youle RJ (1993) In situ labeling of granule cells for apoptosis-associated DNA fragmentation reveals different mechanisms of cell loss in developing cerebellum. Neuron 11:621–632.

Wyllie AH (1980) Glucocorticoid-induced thymocyte apoptosis is associated with endogenous endonuclease activation. Nature 284:555–556.

Wyllie AH, Morris RG, Smith AL, Dunlop D (1984) Chromatin cleavage in apoptosis: association with condensed chromatin morphology and dependence on macromolecular synthesis. J Pathol 142:67–77.

Xue L, Fletcher GC, Tolkovsky AM (1999) Autophagy is activated by apoptotic signalling in sympathetic neurons: an alternative mechanism of death execution. Mol Cell Neurosci 14:180–198.

Yang AH, Kaushal D, Rehen SK, Kriedt K, Kingsbury MA, McConnell MJ, Chun J (2003) Chromosome segregation defects contribute to aneuploidy in normal neural progenitor cells. J Neurosci 23:10454–10462.

Yoshida H, Kong YY, Yoshida R, Elia AJ, Hakem A, Hakem R, Penninger JM, Mak TW (1998) Apaf1 is required for mitochondrial pathways of apoptosis and brain development. Cell 94:739–750.

Zechner D, Fujita Y, Hulsken J, Muller T, Walther I, Taketo MM, Crenshaw EB 3rd, Birchmeier W, Birchmeier C (2003) β-catenin signals regulate cell growth and the balance between progenitor cell expansion and differentiation in the nervous system. Dev Biol 258:406–418.

Zhu L, Chun J (1998) *Apoptosis Detection and Assay Methods.* Eaton, Natick, MA.

Zhuang J, Ren Y, Snowden RT, Zhu H, Gogvadze V, Savill JS, Cohen GM (1998) Dissociation of phagocyte recognition of cells undergoing apoptosis from other features of the apoptotic program. J Biol Chem 273:15628–15632.

6

Intracellular Pathways
of Neuronal Death

Sandra M. Mooney

George I. Henderson

Cell death is critical to normal development in multiple organ systems. For example, it is required during the formation of digits and during the generation of the middle ear space and the vaginal opening (e.g., Saunders, 1966; Rodriguez et al., 1997; Roberts and Miller, 1998). Likewise, in the central nervous system (CNS) of the normal developing mammal, an estimated 20%–80% more neurons than the final number are generated before the surplus is eliminated (Miller, 1995; Sastry and Rao, 2000). This loss of neurons varies by brain structure and by specific neuron populations.

In some brain structures there is a wholesale loss of transient neuronal populations. Such culling of populations is required for proper development to ensue. Two exemplary populations are subplate neurons (e.g., Kostovic and Rakic, 1980; Chun et al., 1987; Al-Ghoul and Miller, 1989), and Cajal-Retzius neurons (e.g., Derer and Derer, 1990; Meyer et al., 1998) in neocortex (Marin-Padilla, 1998; Super et al., 1998; Sarnat and Flores-Sarnat, 2002). It is believed that these populations die after they serve their role in cortical development. The subplate neurons provide a temporary target population for thalamocortical axons that arrive in the subplate before the neurons of their target layer (cortical layer IV) have migrated to their final position (Ghosh et al., 1990). Cajal-Retzius neurons express reelin, which is vital for normal migration of cortical neurons (Lambert de Rouvroit and Goffinet, 1998; Rice and Curran, 2001). This association is indicated by the disrupted cortical organization that occurs in *reeler* mice (Lambert de Rouvroit and Goffinet, 1998) and when Cajal-Retzius neurons are prematurely lost (Frotscher, 1998; Hartmann et al., 1999; Saftig et al., 1999).

Target-dependent neuronal death may be the most important process controlling neuronal death in the CNS. Through this mechanism the nervous system sculpts itself, matching the number of neurons in communicating parts of a system for optimal output and maximizing efficient function. Neuronal death occurs if (a) there is a lack of input/innervation,

(b) axons reach the wrong place within the target area, (c) axons project to the wrong target, (d) there are simply too many axons terminating within the target, or (e) no target exists. One example of the latter is the damaged trigeminal-somatosensory system; transection of the infraorbital nerve causes a loss of neurons in the trigeminal brain stem nuclei and the ventrobasal nucleus of the thalamus (Klein et al., 1988; Miller et al., 1991; Waite et al., 1992; Miller, 1999; Sugimoto et al., 1999; Baldi et al., 2000).

It is important to note that programmed neuronal death is a phenomenon mainly confined to developing invertebrates. As the term implies, neurons can die as a consequence of a genetic program. The best examples are provided by *Caenorhabditis elegans* (see Apoptosis, below). Thus, programmed cell death must be distinguished from naturally occurring neuronal death, which principally represents target-dependent neuronal death.

Many developing neurons die soon after they are generated (see Chapter 5), perhaps as a consequence of an error in DNA replication. This adaptive mechanism allows an organism to protect itself from basing its circuitry on a cadre of neurons with mutated or damaged DNA.

EXPERIMENTAL MODEL SYSTEMS

This chapter considers in vitro and in vivo studies of neuronal death. Each experimental approach has its own advantages and limitations. A major advantage of in vitro studies is that a homogeneous population of cells is addressed. This setting is crucial to studies of the induction of neuronal death by xenobiotics, because cells within the brain differ widely in their susceptibility (Watts et al., 2005). Additionally, the entire population is likely to respond to a manipulation in a similar manner and develop synchronously. This means that small changes in transcript and protein expression or post-translational modifications are more likely to be detectable. Disadvantages to this method are that culture conditions can influence the pathway(s) activated, and the model may not be physiologically relevant. In contrast, *in vivo* studies use a highly heterogenous system in which there are multiple cell types in diverse developmental stages at a given time. This temporal asynchrony makes it harder to differentiate transcript and protein changes from a background of ontogenetic noise. In addition,

changes that are seen may be difficult or impossible to interpret. Of course, the major advantage to this method is that it is the more physiologically and clinically relevant model.

Direct evidence of neuronal death is difficult to amass because the degenerative process can be rapid and the debris can be removed quickly (Reddien and Horvitz, 2004). Thus, cells can express death-related proteins (e.g., active caspase 3 and bax) for a long time before they die (e.g., Cheng and Zochodne, 2003), and not all cells rely on caspase as an effector of cell death (see Caspase-Independent Cell Death, below). Another widely used method of identifying dying cells is terminal deoxynucleotidyl transferase mediated deoxyuridine nick end labeling (TUNEL), in which free, adenylated ends of degenerating DNA are labeled. Unfortunately, TUNEL can generate false positive results; in at least one model system the amount of TUNEL exceeds cell loss (Gordon et al., 2002).

The only incontrovertible proof of neuronal death is documentation of a decrease in neuronal numbers in a longitudinal, population-based study. Final neuronal numbers are a function of three developmental events: generation, migration, and death. A study performed at a single time-point in a mature animal cannot determine the relative contributions of these developmental events. As a result of the potential of generating false positive results, a mathematical method was devised to determine the numbers of dying neurons (Miller, 2003). The great advantage of this approach is that the estimate of cell death depends on the documented cell numbers and the proliferative activity of the population.

MODES OF CELL DEATH

The modes of cell death include apoptosis, necrosis, and autophagy (e.g., Green and Reed, 1998; Lockshin and Zakeri, 2004). Apoptosis is a highly controlled mechanism, during which specific transcript and protein changes occur. Apoptosis has been called cellular suicide, as it only affects the cell undergoing it. In contrast, during necrosis, cells and their organelles swell and burst, releasing enzymes into the local environment. A result of this type of death is damage to neighboring cells, thus causing a cluster of dying cells. Autophagy involves lysosomal engulfment of damaged cells or cell fragments. In many models of disease or injury, dying cell neighbors may exhibit different modes of cell death and an individual cell may exhibit features of different modes.

One important point to consider in cell death is that the life of a critically damaged cell may be temporarily maintained, but it will likely die. That is, the blocking of one mode of cell death may merely cause a cell to shift to another mode of cell death. Thus, the outcome is that the cell still dies, but it may do so by a different sequence of events (e.g., D'Mello et al., 2000; Denecker et al., 2001; Zhou et al., 2005). Alternatively, blocking of cell death may allow cell survival, which is not necessarily a good thing. For example, in mice deficient in apoptosis protease-activating factor (APAF) 1, caspase 3, or caspase 9, there is a lack of cell death in the neural tube, and this prevents normal closure of the tube (Kuida et al., 1996, 1998; Cecconi et al., 1998; Hakem et al., 1998; Yoshida et al., 1998; Honarpour et al., 2000). It should also be considered that enhanced cell death is not the etiology of a pathological state, rather, neuronal death is a process or end point associated with a given disease.

Apoptosis

The term *apoptosis* was coined to describe a series of morphological steps through which dying cells pass (Kerr et al., 1972). With further study, apoptosis has become associated with a metabolically active process (e.g., Wyllie, 1997; Putcha and Johnson, 2004). Accordingly, chromosomal DNA is cleaved, the chromatin condenses, and the nucleus is broken into small pieces. Eventually the cell shrinks and breaks into small, membrane-bound apoptotic bodies that are engulfed by neighboring cells or macrophages. This mechanism ensures that proteolytic enzymes are contained within membrane-bound entities and that the apoptotic cell dies without causing death of neighboring cells.

Much of the initial fundamental information on the pathways of apoptosis came from studies of the nematode *C. elegans* (e.g., Horvitz et al., 1983; Hentgartner and Horvitz, 1994; Reddien and Horvitz, 2004). Of the 1090 cells produced during the development of *C. elegans*, 131 die. Products of two genes are essential for this death: Ced3 and Ced4 (Horvitz et al., 1983; Ellis and Horvitz, 1986). Loss or inactivation of either of these genes prevents cell death. In the 959 cells that do not die, the product of another gene, Ced9, binds to Ced4, and prevents it from

activating Ced3. Mammalian homologs of these critical genes have been identified. Ced3 is homologous with the caspase family, Ced4 with APAF-1, and Ced9 with the Bcl family. Although the genes and gene products involved in apoptosis are highly conserved across species, the mammalian pathways are considerably more complex and convoluted than those identified in *C. elegans*. For example, different pathways of apoptosis are invoked in cerebellar granule cells depending on whether the cells are pre- or postmigratory (Lossi et al., 2004).

As stated above, use of the term *apoptosis* has changed over the years. The definition has been reworked from a set of morphological features to include molecular and biochemical features. Putcha and Johnson (2004) suggest that *apoptosis* be reserved for a caspase-dependent cell death that causes the morphological features described by Kerr et al. (1972; see above). They contend that caspase-independent cell death is nonapoptotic, despite acknowledging that it would be possible to see apoptotic morpholgy without caspase activation. Many researchers use *apoptosis* and *programmed cell death* interchangeably, but this is inappropriate because a *program* connotes genetic determination, as in the case of *C. elegans*. In mammalian systems, this type of genetic death is rare, and most apoptotic death results from environmental factors. In this case, apoptotic death is best considered as naturally occurring cell death. In this chapter, *apoptosis* includes morpholgical and biochemical events.

Major Components of Apoptotic Pathways

Bcl Family

Bcl proteins play pivotal roles in cell death. In contrast to *C. elegans*, which only expresses a single gene, *Ced9*, many organisms have multiple members of this family. There are two functionally distinct groups within the Bcl family: those that induce death and those that protect against death. Bcl proteins can also be subdivided structurally: there are three subgroups defined by the number or type of Bcl-2 homology (BH) domains. Anti-apoptotic members of the family, including Bcl-2, Bcl-x_L, Bcl-w, Mcl-1, and A1/Bfl-1, contain four BH motifs: BH1, BH2, BH3, and BH4. Pro-apoptotic members may be in one of two subgroups: (1) those that contain multiple BH domains but lack BH4—e.g., Bax, Bcl-x$_S$, Bak, and Bok/Mtd, or (2) the BH3-only subgroup that includes Bid, Bim/Bod, Bad, Bmf, Bik/Nbk, Blk, Noxa, Puma/Bbc3, and Hrk/DP5.

Bcl family members form dimers. Homodimers of two anti-apoptotic members, or heterodimers formed by one pro-apoptotic and one anti-apoptotic member, for example, Bcl-2-Bax, are pro-survival. In contrast, homodimers of pro-apoptotic members, or heterodimers of two pro-apoptotic members, result in death. The BH3 domain appears to be the prime suspect for inducing apoptosis. Proteins with the BH3 domain have two functions: (1) to bind to and inactivate the survival-inducing Bcl proteins, and (2) to activate the pro-apoptotic Bcl proteins with multiple BH domains, such as bax and bak (Desagher et al., 1999; Wei et al., 2000, 2001; Degterev et al., 2001). According to one model of apoptosis, Bak is a trans-membrane protein in the outer mitochondrial membrane and Bax is in the cytoplasm (Lucken-Ardjomande and Martinou, 2005). An apoptotic signal causes a conformational change in both proteins that results in exposure of their N terminals and translocation of Bax to the mitochondrial outer membrane. Once in the membrane, Bak and Bax form oligomers that induce membrane permeability and thus allow movement of molecules such as cytochrome C, HtrA2/Omi, and Smac/DIABLO.

Caspases

Caspases are a group of structurally related enzymes in mammals. Genes for caspases have homology with the *C. elegans* gene *Ced3* (e.g., Jiang and Wang, 2004; Shiozaki and Shi, 2004). Like the gene product of Ced3, caspases are important for cell death. In contrast to Ced3, however, caspases are not required for death (see below). Caspases are proteases; at least 14 caspases have been identified. They have cysteines in their active sites and cleave their target protein adjacent to an aspartic acid residue. Caspases are synthesized as inactive isoforms and are cleaved into large and small subunits. Active caspases are tetramers composed of two large and two small subunits.

Caspases are grouped into three subfamilies: interleukin-1β-converting enzyme-like caspases, initiator caspases (e.g., caspase 8 or caspase 9), and effector caspases (e.g., caspase 3) (Shi, 2002). Initiator caspases can cleave themselves and effector caspases are cleaved by other enzymes, including initiator caspases. Activating initiator caspases can induce a caspase cascade in which effector caspases are cleaved and then other apoptosis-related downstream molecules are activated. Caspases can cleave more than 40 target proteins; of particular importance are an inhibitor of DNases, nuclear laminins, and cytoskeletal proteins. Inactivation of DNase inhibitors allows DNases to cut DNA into fragments that are multiples of 180–200 bp. The result of this serial snipping is the stereotypical DNA ladder on a Southern blot that is associated with apoptosis. Cleavage of nuclear laminins results in nuclear fragmentation. Similarly, cleavage of cytoskeletal elements results in membrane blebbing and, ultimately, cell fragmentation.

The importance of caspases in normal development is reflected in mice that lack effective caspase 3 or 9. Both mutants have craniofacial malformations and abnormal brain morphology (Kuida et al., 1996, 1998; Cecconi et al., 1998; Hakem et al., 1998). Specifically, these animals exhibit enlarged proliferative zones, heterotopic clusters of neurons, and increased numbers of neurons. Interestingly, caspase 3 deficiency can be offset by deficiency in the anti-apoptotic gene *Bcl-x$_L$* (Roth et al., 2000), implying that Bcl-x$_L$ can act through a caspase-3-independent mechanism.

Apoptosis Protease Activating Factor 1

APAF-1, homologous to Ced4, exists in the cytoplasm as an inactive protein (Ferraro et al., 2003; Shiozaki and Shi, 2004). Interaction with cytochrome C in the presence of adenosine triphosphate (ATP) results in a conformational change in APAF-1 that allows seven molecules of APAF-1 to assemble and form the central portion of the apoptosome. In addition, the conformational change exposes the caspase recruitment domain, which binds procaspase 9. In the absence of an inhibitory apoptotic protein (IAP) such as X-linked IAP (XIAP), caspase 9 is activated via an unknown mechanism. Active caspase 9 recruits and activates effector caspases 3 and 7.

APAF-1 knockout mice are embryolethal (Cecconi et al., 1998). They have craniofacial and CNS malformations that appear to result from insufficient cell death during development. Interestingly, their limbs are differentially affected. On gestational day (G) 15.5, the limbs are less mature those than in wild-type animals, as evidenced by the persistence of interdigital webbing. By G16.5, however, their limbs appear normal; the webbing is lost after undergoing a caspase-independent form of cell death. This finding implies that some tissue can overcome the loss of APAF-1, but the CNS cannot, and that death via the caspase-independent pathway takes longer.

Cytochrome C

Cytochrome C is normally found between the inner and outer mitochondrial membranes and is used for transporting electrons between the cytochrome B–C1 and cytochrome oxidase complexes in the electron transport chain. When the mitochondrial permeability transition pore is compromised, substances in the intramembrane space, including cytochrome C, are allowed to move into the cytoplasm. Once in the cytoplasm, cytochrome C interacts with APAF-1, ATP, and caspase 9 to form the apoptosome.

Poly-Adenosine Diphosphate Ribose Polymerase

Poly-adenosine diphosphate (ADP) ribose polymerase (PARP) 1 is found in the nucleus and mitochondria. It can be activated in response to DNA damage or to oxidative stress (e.g., Hong et al., 2004; Nguewa et al., 2005). Following DNA damage, PARP-1 becomes active and synthesizes poly(ADP-ribose) and catalyzes the addition of ADP-ribose to the DNA (e.g., Bouchard et al., 2003). Following poly(ADP-ribosyl)ation, DNA repair enzymes can be recruited and activated. Caspases 3 and 7 cleave PARP in its nuclear localization sequence, resulting in an inactive form of the enzyme that cannot add ADP-ribose, thus, the DNA cannot undergo repair.

During the synthesis of poly(ADP-ribose), nicotinamide-adenine dinucleotide (NAD) is cleaved into ADP-ribose and nicotinamide. To restore NAD levels (and thus the NAD/NADH ratio), the cell converts nicotinamide to NAD by means of two molecules of ATP, thus depleting the energy pool. Following severe DNA damage, the loss of cellular energy is likely responsible for a necrotic cell death after excessive DNA damage (Szabo and Dawson, 1998; Ha and Snyder, 1999; Fuertes et al., 2003). Interestingly, the loss of energy may be necessary, but is unlikely to be sufficient, for cell death (Wang et al., 2004).

Mitochondrial PARP-1 may be involved in apoptosis via release of apoptosis inducing factor (AIF) (Yu et al., 2002; Du et al., 2003). Genomic damage causes poly(ADP-ribosylation) in the nucleus, resulting in cellular NAD depletion, activation of mitochondrial PARP, AIF release, and subsequent cell death.

Apoptosis Inducing Factor

In normal, undamaged cells, AIF is important for protection against oxidative stress (Klein et al., 2002; Lindholm et al., 2004; Vahsen et al., 2004). Following PARP activation, AIF is released from the mitochondria into the cytosol (see Poly-Adenosine Diphosphate Polymerase, above). AIF translocates into the nucleus where it is involved in condensation of chromatin and DNA fragmentation (Hong et al., 2004). The PARP-dependent release of AIF is a caspase-independent mechanism of cell death (see Caspase-Independent Cell Death, below). In addition, caspases can cause release of AIF, as can changes in mitochondrial membrane permeability, for example, by Bax and Bak. Bcl-2 can interfere with AIF-mediated apoptosis by blocking the cellular redistribution of AIF that is necessary for death (Susin et al., 1996, 1999; Daugas et al., 2000).

Apoptosis-Related Receptors

Ligands (e.g., tumor necrosis factor [TNF]-α, Apo2/TRAIL, FasL, and possibly growth factors) that interact with receptors of the TNF family activate the extrinsic apoptotic pathway. TNF-α binds to the TNF receptor, Apo2/TRAIL binds to TNF-related apoptosis inducing ligand-receptor 1 (TRAIL-R1)/death receptor (DR) 4 and TRAIL-R2/DR5, and FasL binds to Fas (CD95, APO-1).

Effectors of Apoptosis

p53

p53 is a multifunctional housekeeping protein involved in cell cycle regulation, recognition of DNA damage and consequent repair, and cell death (Miller et al., 2000; Morrison et al., 2002). Although it is a transcription factor, it also responds to genotoxic stress (e.g. Bertrand et al., 2004). p53 activation can halt the cell cycle and initiate DNA repair or apoptosis (Harms et al., 2004).

p53 usually has a short half-life (Kim et al., 2004). When stabilized, for example, through phosphorylation on serine residues, p53 accumulates in the nucleus, where it has transcriptional activities. p53-regulated genes critical for normal brain development include cell cycle proteins p21 and murine double minute 2, the DNA repair protein growth arrest and DNA damage-inducible gene 45, and the apoptosis-related proteins insulin-like growth factor binding protein 3 and Bax (Levine, 1997). In addition, p53 regulates the Fas receptor (Somasundaram, 2000) and the hormone polyadenylate cyclase–activating polypeptide receptor 1 (e.g., Ciani et al., 1999; Johnson, 2001) (see Chapters 15 and 16).

p53 can play a direct role in cell death by interacting with the Bcl family of proteins (Chipuk et al., 2003, 2004; Mihara et al., 2003), APAF-1, and apoptosis-related receptors. These interactions are pro-apoptotic. p53 down-regulates pro-survival Bcl-2 and Bcl-x, and up-regulates Bax, Bid, and APAF-1. It also up-regulates TRAIL-R2/DR5, Fas, and FasL. In addition, p53 represses c-Fos (Kley et al., 1992), thus potentially interfering with activator protein 1 and, hence, transcription.

Oxidative Stress

Oxygen, though central to life, can be toxic. In its ground state, it possesses two unpaired electrons with parallel spin states. This setting makes a two-electron reduction kinetically unlikely; however, sequential one-electron reductions can occur, hence generating oxygen free radicals, reactive oxygen species (ROS). In the biological setting, the initial one-electron exchange generates the superoxide anion radical. The protonated two-electron reduction produces H_2O_2 (the protonated form of the peroxide ion), with the final protonated four-electron product being water. The oxygen radicals resulting from this process generate a plethora of reactive species with other molecules, such as nitrogen and iron, all of which can produce a pro-oxidant environment in cells, termed *oxidative stress*.

The central roles for ROS in apoptosis, both as initiators and as signaling events within the apoptotic process, are well documented (Curtin et al., 2002; Fleury et al., 2002; Polster and Fiskum 2004). Although the specific mechanisms by which ROS elicit and/or maintain apoptosis remain undefined, these compounds have an effect on a variety of cellular components: proteins, DNA bases and sugars, polysaccharides, and lipids. One ROS-related pathway that has been connected to ethanol-mediated neuron

apoptosis is the production of pro-apoptotic products of lipid peroxidation within mitochondria (Ramachandran et al., 2001, 2003). ROS react with unsaturated fatty acids, initiating a self-perpetuating peroxidation of membrane lipids (Kappus, 1985). In addition to direct damage to biomembranes, this ubiquitous process generates highly reactive aldehydes, the most studied and the most toxic being 4-hydroxynonenal (HNE) (Esterbauer et al., 1990; Uchida et al., 1993). Importantly, HNE formation generates apoptotic death of neurons, and its production, secondary to oxidative stress, has been compellingly linked to neuron death in a variety of neurodegenerative diseases (Zarkovic, 2003).

APOPTOTIC PATHWAYS

Caspase-Dependent: Intrinsic vs. Extrinsic Pathways of Apoptosis

The pathways of apoptosis can be divided into intrinsic and extrinsic on the basis of activation site (Budihardjo et al., 1999; Shiozaki and Shi, 2004). The intrinsic, mitochondria-associated pathway depends on Bcl proteins. The extrinsic pathway is mediated by activation of an apoptosis-related receptor. The pathways are not truly independent, as there is much cross-talk, and both can activate caspase 3 (Fig. 6–1). In addition, activation of the extrinsic pathway can activate a feedback loop to the intrinsic pathway.

Intrinsic Pathways

The fundamental feature of the intrinsic pathway is the release of pro-apoptotic compounds from mitochondria. This pathway is activated by intracellular stress signals including but not limited to oxidative stress or DNA damage. Thus, major effectors may be ROS and p53.

Mitochondrial permeability is affected by the Bcl family of proteins. Bax homodimers allow ion flux through the mitochondrial membrane, and this somehow allows movement of cytochrome C, possibly through enlargement of the voltage-dependent anion channels (Banerjee and Ghosh, 2004) or by opening the mitochondrial permeability transition pore (e.g., Marzo et al., 1998). Breach of the membrane causes a loss of membrane potential and release of cytochrome *c*, AIF, HtrA2/Omi, and/or second mitochondria-derived activator of caspase/direct IAP binding protein, which has a low isoelectric point (Smac/DIABLO). In normal cells, these substances are sequestered between the inner and outer mitochondrial membranes. Release into the cytoplasm initiates apoptotic pathways (Fig. 6–1). It should be noted that permeabilization of the mitochondrial membrane does not necessarily allow dumping of all intermembrane substances. Instead, there is some selectivity. For example, application of

n-methyl-D-aspartate to cultured primary mouse cortical neurons can cause release of AIF and cytochrome c (Wang et al., 2004). In contrast, α-amino-3-hydroxy-5-methyl-4-isoxazoleproprionic acid can induce the release of cytochrome c, but not AIF.

In response to DNA damage or ROS, p53 accumulates in the mitochondria (e.g., Marchenko et al., 2000; Erster et al., 2004), where it interacts with Bcl-family proteins in a transcriptional-independent manner.

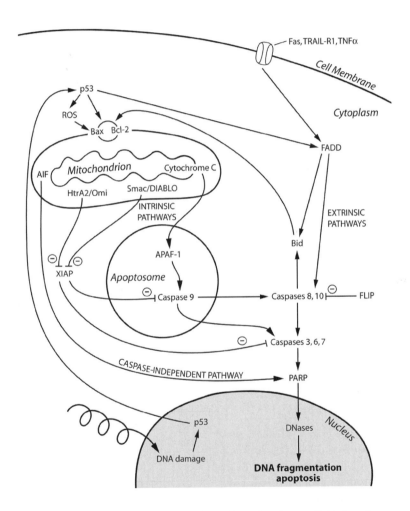

FIGURE 6–1 Pathways underlying neural cell death. Three cell death pathways tracing the flow of information from external effects to nuclear response are depicted: intrinsic and extrinsic caspase-dependent pathways and a caspase-independent pathway. Various players involved in these pathways are shown. Positive and negative effectors are depicted by lines ending in arrows and blunted tips, respectively. FADD, Fas-associated death domain; FLIP, FADD-like interleukin-1-converting enzyme inhibitory protein for other abbreviations see Abbreviations list. See text for details.

This interaction explains the rapid response of a cell to a death signal. P53 alters expression of Bcl family members in a pro-apoptotic manner, i.e., expression of Bax is increased and concurrently Bcl-2 is down-regulated. In addition, p53 up-regulates APAF-1 expression. Released cytochrome C forms a complex with seven APAF-1 molecules, and in the presence of ATP, caspase-9 is recruited into this complex, the apoptosome, and activated. Active caspase 9 cleaves and activates effector caspases 3, 6, and/or 7. Note that at this point, the intrinsic and extrinsic pathways merge as caspases 8 and 10, activated by receptors (see below), cleave and activate effector caspases.

Extrinsic Pathways

The extrinsic pathway is activated by factors outside the cell membrane via ligand-receptor binding (Muzio et al., 1996; Almasan and Ashkenazi, 2003; Choi and Benveniste, 2004). Binding of the ligand to the receptor causes recruitment of cytoplasmic elements such as Fas-associated death domain and TNF receptor–associated death domain that form the death-inducing signaling complex. This process results in recruitment and activation of initiator caspases 8 and 10 through proteolysis. Caspases 8 and 10 then activate effector caspases 3, 6, and 7, and can also cleave a member of the Bcl family of proteins, Bid. At this point, the intrinsic pathway also comes into play as Bid translocates to the mitochondrion and causes insertion of Bax-Bax homodimers into the mitochondrial membrane, thus allowing release of cytochrome *c* and the resulting downstream events, and effector caspase activation (Li et al., 1998; Luo et al., 1998; Wei et al., 2001; Scorrano and Korsmeyer, 2003).

Substrates of Caspases

Substrates of effector caspases may number in the hundreds (e.g., Earnshaw et al., 1999; Nicholson et al., 1999; Fischer et al., 2003; Fuentes-Prior and Salvesen, 2004). Three are of particular interest—Bid, PARP, and DFF40/CAD. Activated, i.e., cleaved, Bid translocates to the mitochondria, where it interacts with other pro-apoptotic members of the Bcl family, specifically Bax and Bak, thus causing membrane permeability, and leakage of cytochrome C (Li et al., 1998; Luo et al., 1998; Wei et al., 2001). Cleavage of PARP by caspases 3 and 7 inactivates the DNA repair mechanism (Lazebnik et al., 1994). Activation of DFF40/CAD by caspase 3 results in enzymatic cleavage of double-stranded DNA, the hallmark characteristic of fragmented DNA. This structure can be visualized on an agarose gel as a ladder or can be labeled in vivo by means of TUNEL.

Caspase-Independent Cell Death

There is some debate as to whether caspase-independent cell death is a form of apoptosis (Chipuk and Green, 2004; Putcha and Johnson, 2004), however, pathways of caspase-independent cell death are frequently activated concomitant with caspase-dependent pathways (Ramachandran et al., 2003). Caspase–independent cell death is initiated by the same effectors as those in typical apoptosis—for example, p53 and ROS (Hill et al., 2000; Godefroy et al., 2004), but the morphological outcome differs. Caspase-independent death does not result in DNA fragmentation or cell blebbing, nor do the mitochondria lose membrane potential. In addition, the caspase-independent pathway may be initiated by overactivation of PARP-1 (Hong et al., 2004).

As with caspase-dependent pathways, the release of mitochondrial intermembrane substances AIF, endonuclease G, HtrA2/Omi, and/or Smac/DIABLO appears to be pivotal for caspase-independent death (Susin et al., 1999; Cregan et al., 2002; Hong et al., 2004; Yakovlev and Faden, 2004). Release of AIF from the mitochondria results in activation of DNases that cause DNA fragmentation. Endonuclease G is a mitochondrial nuclease necessary for replication of mitochondrial DNA (Cote and Ruiz-Carrillo, 1993). If released into the cytoplasm, it translocates into the nucleus where it causes internucleosomal DNA fragmentation (Li et al., 2001). HtrA2/Omi and Smac/DIABLO also appear to induce caspase-independent death, although the exact mechanism is unknown (Yakovlev and Faden, 2004).

CONCLUSIONS AND SUMMARY

Misleadingly referred to as a regressive process, neuronal death is essential for normal CNS development. Without it, the nervous system can become overpopulated with poorly integrated neurons and circuitry that produces functional deficits. This observation is supported by studies of knockout mice deficient in caspase 3 or 9 (Oppenheim et al., 2001). In these animals, the amount of neuronal death is reduced and learning and memory is compromised.

Although neuronal death may be described as apoptotic or necrotic, dying cells commonly exhibit features of both (Evan and Littlewood, 1998; Green and Reed, 1998; Lockshin and Zakeri, 2004). More attention has been directed to understanding apoptosis. The pathways activated during apoptotic degeneration are complex and often appear to be conflicting. They include so-called intrinsic and extrinsic systems, both of which culminate in the activation of caspase 3. Some cells, however, die through a caspase-independent mechanism. The current and future understanding of neuronal death has been and will be garnered from studies of the actions of toxins (e.g., ethanol and neurotransmitter blockers), radiation, stress, and other challenges. Such studies provide valuable insight into the interplay between the various modes of cell death and the pathways underlying these degenerative events.

Abbreviations

ADP   adenosine diphosphate

AIF   apoptosis inducing factor

APAF   apoptosis protease-activating factor

ATP   adenosine triphosphate

BH   Bcl-2 homology

CNS   central nervous system

DIABLO   direct IAP binding protein

HNE   4-hydroxynonenal

IAP   inhibitory apoptotic protein

NAD   nicotinamide-adenine dinucleotide

PARP   poly-adenosine diphosphate ribose polymerase

ROS   reactive oxygen species

SMAC   second mitochondrial-derived activator of caspase

TNF   tumor necrosis factor

TUNEL   terminal deoxynucleotidyl transferase mediated deoxyuridine nick end labeling

ACKNOWLEDGMENTS Work on this chapter was supported by the National Institute of Alcohol Abuse and Alcoholism.

References

Al-Ghoul WM, Miller MW (1989) Transient expression of Alz-50-immunoreactivity in developing rat neocortex: a marker for naturally occurring neuronal death? Brain Res 481:361–367.

Almasan A, Ashkenazi A (2003) Apo2L/TRAIL: apoptosis signaling, biology, and potential for cancer therapy. Cytokine Growth Factor Rev 14:337–348.

Baldi A, Calia E, Ciampini A, Riccio M, Vetuschi A, Persico AM, Keller F (2000) Deafferentation-induced apoptosis of neurons in thalamic somatosensory nuclei of the newborn rat: critical period and rescue from cell death by peripherally applied neurotrophins. Eur J Neurosci 12:2281–2290.

Banerjee J, Ghosh S (2004) Bax increases the pore size of rat brain mitochondrial voltage-dependent anion channel in the presence of tBid. Biochem Biophys Res Comm 323:310–314.

Bertrand P, Rouillard D, Boulet A, Levalois C, Soussi T, Lopez BS (2004) p53's double life: transactivation-independent repression of homologous recombination. Trends Gen 20:235–243.

Bouchard VJ, Rouleau M, Poirier GG (2003) PARP-1, a determinant of cell survival in response to DNA damage. Exp Hematol 31:446–454.

Budihardjo I, Oliver H, Lutter M, Luo X, Wang X (1999) Biochemical pathways of caspase activation during apoptosis. Annu Rev Cell Dev Biol 15:269–290.

Cecconi F, Alvarez-Bolado G, Meyer BI, Roth KA, Gruss P (1998) Apaf1 (Ced-4 homolog) regulates programmed cell death in mammalian development. Cell 94:727–737.

Cheng C, Zochodne DW (2003) Sensory neurons with activated caspase-3 survive long-term experimental diabetes. Diabetes 52:2363–2371.

Chipuk JE, Green DR (2004) Cytoplasmic p53: Bax and forward. Cell Cycle 3:429–431.

Chipuk JE, Kuwana T, Bouchier-Hayes L, Droin NM, Newmeyer DD, Schuler M, Green DR (2004) Direct activation of Bax by p53 mediates mitochondrial membrane permeabilization and apoptosis. Science 303:1010–1014.

Chipuk JE, Maurer U, Green DR, Schuler M (2003) Pharmacologic activation of p53 elicits Bax-dependent apoptosis in the absence of transcription. Cancer Cell 4:371–381.

Choi C, Benveniste EN (2004) Fas ligand/Fas system in the brain: regulator of immune and apoptotic responses. Brain Res Rev 44:65–81.

Chun JJ, Nakamura MJ, Shatz CJ (1987) Transient cells of the developing mammalian telencephalon are peptide-immunoreactive neurons. Nature 325: 617–620.

Ciani E, Hoffmann A, Schmidt P, Journot L, Spengler D (1999) Induction of the PAC1-R (PACAP-type I receptor) gene by p53 and Zac. Mol Brain Res 69: 290–294.

Cote J, Ruiz-Carrillo A (1993) Primers for mitochondrial DNA replication generated by endonuclease G. Science 261:765–769.

Cregan SP, Fortin A, MacLaurin JG, Callaghan SM, Cecconi F, Yu SW, Dawson TM, Dawson VL, Park DS, Kroemer G, Slack RS (2002) Apoptosis-inducing factor is involved in the regulation of caspase-independent neuronal cell death. J Cell Biol 158:507–517.

Curtin JF, Donovan M, Cotter TG (2002) Regulation and measurement of oxidative stress in apoptosis. J Immunol Meth 265: 49–72.

Daugas E, Susin SA, Zamzami N, Ferri KF, Irinopoulou T, Larochette N, Prevost MC, Leber B, Andrews D, Penninger J, Kroemer G (2000) Mitochondrio-nuclear translocation of AIF in apoptosis and necrosis. FASEB J 14:729–739.

Degterev A, Lugovskoy A, Cardone M, Mulley B, Wagner G, Mitchison T, Yuan J (2001) Identification of small-molecule inhibitors of interaction between the BH3 domain and Bcl-xL. Nat Cell Biol 3:173–182.

Denecker G, Vercammen D, Declerq W, Vandenabeele P (2001) Apoptotic and necrotic cell death induced by death domain receptors. Cell Mol Life Sci 58: 356–370.

Derer P, Derer M (1990) Cajal-Retzius cell ontogenesis and death in mouse brain visualized with horseradish peroxidase and electron microscopy. Neuroscience 36:839–856.

Desagher S, Osen-Sand A, Nichols A, Eskes R, Montessuit S, Lauper S, Maundrell K, Antonsson B, Martinou JC (1999) Bid-induced conformational change of Bax is responsible for mitochondrial cytochrome c release during apoptosis. J Cell Biol 144:891–901.

D'Mello SR, Kuan CY, Flavell RA, Rakic P (2000) Caspase-3 is required for apoptosis-associated DNA fragmentation but not for cell death in neurons deprived of potassium. J Neurosci Res 59:24–31.

Du L, Zhang X, Han YY, Burke NA, Kochanek PM, Watkins SC, Graham SH, Carcillo JA, Szabo C, Clark RS (2003) Intra-mitochondrial poly(ADP-ribosylation) contributes to NAD$^+$ depletion and cell death induced by oxidative stress. J Biol Chem 278:18426–18433.

Earnshaw WC, Martins LM, Kaufmann SH (1999) Mammalian caspases: structure, activation, substrates, and functions during apoptosis. Annu Rev Biochem 68: 383–424.

Ellis HM, Horvitz HR (1986) Genetic control of programmed cell death in the nematode C. elegans. Cell 44:817–829.

Erster S, Mihara M, Kim RH, Petrenko O, Moll UM (2004) In vivo mitochondrial p53 translocation triggers a rapid first wave of cell death in response to DNA damage that can precede p53 target gene activation. Mol Cell Biol 24:6728–6741.

Esterbauer H, Zollner H, Schaur RJ (1990) Aldehydes formed by lipid peroxidation: mechanisms of formation, occurrence, and determination. In: Virgo-Peifrey C (ed). Membrane Lipid Oxidation. CRC Press, Boca Raton FL, pp 239–268.

Evan G, Littlewood T (2004) A matter of life and cell death. Science 28:1317–1322.

Fischer U, Jänicke RU, Schulze-Osthoff K (2003) Many cuts to ruin: a comprehensive update of caspase substrates. Cell Death Differ 10:76–100.

Fleury C, Mignotte B, Vayssiere JL (2002) Mitochondrial reactive oxygen species in cell death signaling. Biochemie 84: 131–141.

Frotscher M (1998) Cajal-Retzius cells, reelin, and the formation of layers. Curr Opin Neurobiol 8:570–575.

Fuentes-Prior P, Salvesen GS (2004) The protein structures that shape caspase activity, specificity, activation and inhibition. Biochem J 384:201–232.

Fuertes MA, Castilla J, Alonso C, Pérez, JM (2003) Cisplatin biochemical mechanism of action: from cytotoxicity to induction of cell death through interconnections between apoptotic and necrotic pathways. Curr Med Chem 10:257–266.

Ghosh A, Antonini A, McConnell SK, Shatz CJ (1990) Requirement for subplate neurons in the formation of thalamocortical connections. Nature 347:179–181.

Godefroy N, Bouleau S, Gruel G, Renaud F, Rincheval V, Mignotte B, Tronik-Le Roux D, Vayssiere JL (2004) Transcriptional repression by p53 promotes a Bcl-2-insensitive and mitochondria-independent pathway of apoptosis. Nucleic Acids Res 32:4480–4490.

Gordon WC, Casey DM, Lukiw WJ, Bazan NG (2002) DNA damage and repair in light-induced photoreceptor degeneration. Invest Ophthal Vis Sci 43: 3511–3521.

Green DR, Reed JC (1998) Mitochondria and apoptosis. Science 281:1309–1312.

Ha HC, Snyder SH (1999) Poly(ADP-ribose) polymerase is a mediator of necrotic cell death by ATP depletion. Proc Natl Acad Sci USA 96:13978–13982.

Hakem R, Hakem A, Duncan GS, Henderson JT, Woo M, Soengas MS, Elia A, de la Pompa JL, Kägi D, Shoo W, Potter J, Yoshida R, Kaufman SA, Lowe SW, Penninger JM, Mak TW (1998) Differential requirement for caspase-9 in apoptotic pathways in vivo. Cell 94:339–352.

Harms K, Nozell S, Chen X (2004) The common and distinct target genes of the p53 family transcription factors. Cell Mol Life Sci 61:822–842.

Hartmann D, De Strooper B, Saftig P (1999) Presenilin-1 deficiency leads to loss of Cajal-Retzius neurons and cortical dysplasia similar to human type 2 lissencephaly. Curr Biol 9:719–727.

Hengartner MO, Horvitz HR (1994) Programmed cell death in Caenorhabditis elegans. Curr Opin Gen Devel 4:581–586.

Hill IE, Murray C, Richard J, Rasquinha I, MacManus JP (2000) Despite the internucleosomal cleavage of DNA, reactive oxygen species do not produce other markers of apoptosis in cultured neurons. Exp Neurol 162:73–88.

Honarpour N, Du C, Richardson JA, Hammer RE, Wang X, Herz J (2000) Adult Apaf-1-deficient mice exhibit male infertility. Dev Biol 218:248–258.

Hong SJ, Dawson TM, Dawson VL (2004) Nuclear and mitochondrial conversations in cell death: PARP-1 and AIF signaling. Trends Pharm Sci 25:259–264.

Horvitz HR, Sternberg PW, Greenwald IS, Fixsen W, Ellis HM (1983) Mutations that affect neural cell lineages and cell fates during the development of the nematode Caenorhabditis elegans. Cold Spring Harb Symp Quant Biol 48:453–463.

Jiang XJ, Wang XD (2004) Cytochrome C-mediated apoptosis. Annu Rev Biochem 73:87–106.

Johnson S (2001) Micronutrient accumulation and depletion in schizophrenia, epilepsy, autism and Parkinson's disease? Med Hypotheses 56:641–645.

Kappus H (1985) Lipid peroxidation: mechanisms, analysis, enzymology and biological relevance. In: Sies H (ed). Oxidative Stress. Academic Press, London, pp 273–303.

Kerr JF, Wyllie AH, Currie AR (1972) Apoptosis: a basic biological phenomenon with wide-ranging implications in tissue kinetics. Br J Cancer 26:239–257.

Kim YY, Park BJ, Kim DJ, Kim WH, Kim S, Oh KS, Lim JY, Kim J, Park C, Park SI (2004) Modification of serine 392 is a critical event in the regulation of p53 nuclear export and stability. FEBS Letters 572:92–98.

Klein JA, Longo-Guess CM, Rossmann MP, Seburn KL, Hurd RE, Frankel WN, Bronson RT, Ackerman SL (2002) The harlequin mouse mutation downregulates apoptosis-inducing factor. Nature 419:367–374.

Klein BG, Renehan WE, Jacquin MF, Rhoades RW (1988) Anatomical consequences of neonatal infraorbital nerve transection upon the trigeminal ganglion and vibrissa follicle nerves in the adult rat. J Comp Neurol 268:469–488.

Kley N, Chung RY, Fay S, Loeffler JP, Seizinger BR (1992) Repression of the basal c-fos promoter by wild-type p53. Nucl Acids Res 20:4083–4087.

Kostovic I, Rakic P (1980) Cytology and time of origin of interstitial neurons in the white matter in infant and adult human and monkey telencephalon. J Neurocytol 9:219–242.

Kuida K, Haydar TF, Kuan CY, Gu Y, Taya C, Karasuyama H, Su MS, Rakic P, Flavell RA (1998) Reduced apoptosis and cytochrome c–mediated caspase activation in mice lacking caspase 9. Cell 94:325–337.

Kuida K, Zheng TS, Na S, Kuan C, Yang D, Karasuyama H, Rakic P, Flavell RA (1996) Decreased apoptosis in the brain and premature lethality in CPP32-deficient mice. Nature 384:368–372.

Lambert de Rouvroit C, Goffinet AM (1998) The reeler mouse as a model of brain development. Adv Anat Embryol Cell Biol 150:1–106.

Lazebnik YA, Kaufmann SH, Desnoyers S, Poirier GG, Earnshaw WC (1994) Cleavage of poly(ADP-ribose) polymerase by a proteinase with properties like ICE. Nature 371:346–347.

Levine AJ (1997) p53, the cellular gatekeeper for growth and division. Cell 88:323–331.

Li H, Zhu H, Xu CJ, Yuan J (1998) Cleavage of BID by caspase 8 mediates the mitochondrial damage in the Fas pathway of apoptosis. Cell 94:491–501.

Li LY, Luo X, Wang X (2001) Endonuclease G is an apoptotic DNase when released from mitochondria. Nature 412:95–99.

Lindholm D, Eriksson O, Korhonen L (2004) Mitochondrial proteins in neuronal degeneration. Biochem Biophys Res Commun 321:753–758.

Lockshin RA, Zakeri Z (2004) Apoptosis, autophagy, and more. Int J Biochem Cell Biol 36:2405–2419.

Lossi L, Gambino G, Mioletti S, Merighi A (2004) In vivo analysis reveals different apoptotic pathways in pre- and postmigratory cerebellar granule cells of rabbit. J Neurobiol 60:437–452.

Lucken-Ardjomande S, Martinou JC (2005) Newcomers in the process of mitochondrial permeabilization. J Cell Sci 118:473–483.

Luo X, Budihardjo I, Zou H, Slaughter C, Wang X (1998) Bid, a Bcl2 interacting protein, mediates cytochrome c release from mitochondria in response to activation of cell surface death receptors. Cell 94:481–490.

Marchenko ND, Zaika A, Moll UM (2000) Death signal-induced localization of p53 protein to mitochondria. A potential role in apoptotic signaling. J Biol Chem 275:16202–16212.

Marin-Padilla M (1998) Cajal-Retzius cells and the development of the neocortex. Trends Neurosci 21:64–71.

Marzo I, Brenner C, Zamzami N, Susin SA, Beutner G, Brdiczka D, Remy R, Xie ZH, Reed JC, Kroemer G (1998) The permeability transition pore complex: a target for apoptosis regulation by caspases and bcl-2-related proteins. J Exp Med 187:1261–1271.

Meyer G, Soria JM, Martinez-Galan JR, Martin-Clemente B, Fairen A (1998) Different origins and developmental histories of transient neurons in the marginal zone of the fetal and neonatal rat cortex. J Comp Neurol 397:493–518.

Mihara M, Erster S, Zaika A, Petrenko O, Chittenden T, Pancoska P Moll UM (2003) p53 has a direct apoptogenic role at the mitochondria. Mol Cell 11: 577–590.

Miller FD, Pozniak CD, Walsh GS (2000) Neuronal life and death: an essential role for the p53 family. Cell Death Differ 7:880–888.

Miller MW (1995) Relationship of time of origin and death of neurons in rat somatosensory cortex: barrel versus septal cortex and projection versus local circuit neurons. J Comp Neurol 355:6–14.

—— (1999) A longitudinal study of the effects of prenatal ethanol exposure on neuronal acquisition and death in the principal sensory nucleus of the trigeminal nerve: interaction with changes induced by transection of the infraorbital nerve. J Neurocytol 28:999–1015.

—— (2003) Balance of cell proliferation and death among dynamic populations: a mathematical model. J Neurobiol 57:172–182.

Miller MW, Al-Ghoul WM, Murtaugh M (1991) Expression of ALZ-50-immunoreactivity in the developing principal sensory nucleus of the trigeminal nerve: effect of transecting the infraorbital nerve. Brain Res 560:132–138.

Morrison RS, Kinoshita Y, Johnson MD, Ghatan S, Ho JT, Garden G (2002) Neuronal survival and cell death signaling pathways. Adv Exp Med Biol 513: 41–86.

Muzio M, Chinnaiyan AM, Kischkel FC, O'Rourke K, Shevchenko A, Ni J, Scaffidi C, Bretz JD, Zhang M, Gentz R, Mann M, Krammer PH, Peter ME, Dixit VM (1996) FLICE, a novel FADD-homologous ICE/CED-3-like protease, is recruited to the CD95 (Fas/APO-1) death-inducing signaling complex. Cell 85:817–827.

Nguewa PA, Fuertes MA, Valladares B, Alonso C, Perez JM (2005) Poly(ADP-ribose) polymerases: homology, structural domains and functions. Novel therapeutic applications. Prog Biophys Mol Biol 88: 143–172.

Nicholson DW (1999) Caspase structure, proteolytic substrates, and function during apoptotic cell death. Cell Death Differ 6:1028–1042.

Oppenheim RW, Flavell RA, Vinsant S, Prevette D, Kuan C-Y, Rakic P (2001) Programmed cell death of developing mammalian neurons after genetic deletion of caspases. J Neurosci 21:4752–4760.

Polster BM, Fiskum G (2004) Mitochondrial mechanisms of neural cell apoptosis. J Neurochem 90:1281–1289.

Putcha GV, Johnson EM Jr (2004) Men are but worms: neuronal cell death in C. elegans and vertebrates. Cell Death Differ 11:38–48.

Ramachandran V, Perez A, Chen J, Senthil D, Schenker S, Henderson GI (2001) In utero ethanol exposure causes mitochondrial dysfunction which can result in apoptotic cell death in fetal brain: A potential role for 4-hydroxynonenal. Alcohol Clin Exp Res 25:862–871.

Ramachandran V, Watt LT, Maffi S, Chen JJ, Schenker S, Henderson GI (2003) Ethanol-induced Oxidative stress precedes mitochondrially-mediated apoptotic death of cultured fetal cortical neurons. J Neurosci Res V74:577–588.

Reddien PW, Horvitz HR (2004) The engulfment process of programmed cell death in Caenorhabditis elegans. Annu Rev Cell Dev Biol 20:193–221.

Reed JC (1998) Bcl-2 family proteins. Oncogene 17:3225–3236.

Rice DS, Curran T (2001) Role of the reelin signaling pathway in central nervous system development. Annu Rev Neurosci 24:1005–1039.

Roberts DS, Miller SA (1998) Apoptosis in cavitation of middle ear space. Anat Rec 251:286–289.

Rodriguez I, Araki K, Khatib K, Martinou JC, Vassalli P (1997) Mouse vaginal opening is an apoptosis-dependent process which can be prevented by the overexpression of Bcl2. Dev Biol 184:115–121.

Roth KA, Kuan C, Haydar TF, D'Sa-Eipper C, Shindler KS, Zheng TS, Kuida K, Flavell RA, Rakic P (2000) Epistatic and independent functions of caspase-3 and Bcl-X(L) in developmental programmed cell death. Proc Natl Acad Sci USA 97: 466–471.

Saftig P, Hartmann D, De Strooper B (1999) The function of presenilin-1 in amyloid β-peptide generation and brain development. Eur Arch Psych Clin Neurosci. 249:271–279.

Sarnat HB, Flores-Sarnat L (2002) Role of Cajal-Retzius and subplate neurons in cerebral cortical development. Sem in Pediatr Neurol 9:302–308.

Sastry PS, Rao KS (2000) Apoptosis and the nervous system. J Neurochem 74:1–20.

Saunders JW Jr (1966) Death in embryonic systems. Science 154:604–612.

Scorrano L, Korsmeyer SJ (2003) Mechanisms of cytochrome *c* release by proapoptotic Bcl-2 family members. Biochem Biophys Res Commun 304: 437–444.

Shi Y (2002) Mechanisms of caspase activation and inhibition during apoptosis. Mol Cell 9:459–470.

Shiozaki EN, Shi Y (2004) Caspases, IAPs and Smac/DIABLO: mechanisms from structural biology. Trends Biochem Sci 29:486–494.

Somasundaram K (2000) Tumor suppressor p53: regulation and function. Front Biosci 5:D424–D437.

Sugimoto T, Xiao C, Takeyama A, He YF, Takano-Yamamoto T, Ichikawa H (1999) Apoptotic cascade of neurons in the subcortical sensory relay nuclei following the neonatal infraorbital nerve transection. Brain Res 824:284–290.

Super H, Soriano E, Uylings HB (1998) The functions of the preplate in development and evolution of the neocortex and hippocampus. Brain Res Rev 27: 40–64.

Susin SA, Lorenzo HK, Zamzami N, Marzo I, Snow BE, Brothers GM, Mangion J, Jacotot E, Costantini P, Loeffler M, Larochette N, Goodlett DR, Aebersold R, Siderovski DP, Penninger JM, Kroemer G (1999) Molecular characterization of mitochondrial apoptosis-inducing factor. Nature 397:441–446.

Susin SA, Zamzami N, Castedo M, Hirsch T, Marchetti P, Macho A, Daugas E, Geuskens M, Kroemer G (1996) Bcl-2 inhibits the mitochondrial release of an apoptogenic protease. J Exp Med 184:1331–1342.

Szabo C, Dawson VL (1998) Role of poly(ADP-ribose) synthetase in inflammation and ischaemia-reperfusion. Trends Pharmacol Sci 19: 287–298.

Uchida K, Szweda LI, Chae H-Z, Stadtman ER (1993) Immunochemical detection of 4-hydroxynonenal protein adducts in oxidized hepatocytes. Proc Natl Acad Sci USA 90:8742–8746.

Vahsen N, Cande C, Briere JJ, Benit P, Joza N, Larochette N, Mastroberardino PG, Pequignot MO, Casares N, Lazar V, Feraud O, Debili N, Wissing S, Engelhardt S, Madeo F, Piacentini M, Penninger JM, Schagger H, Rustin P, Kroemer G (2004) AIF deficiency compromises oxidative phosphorylation. EMBO J 23:4679–4689.

Wang H, Yu SW, Koh DW, Lew J, Coombs C, Bowers W, Federoff HJ, Poirier GG, Dawson TM, Dawson VL (2004) Apoptosis-inducing factor substitutes for caspase executioners in NMDA-triggered excitotoxic neuronal death. J Neurosci 24:10963–10973.

Waite PM, Li L, Ashwell KW (1992) Developmental and lesion induced cell death in the rat ventrobasal complex. Neuroreport 3:485–488.

Wang X, Abdel-Rahman AA (2004) An association between ethanol-evoked enhancement of c-jun gene expression in the nucleus tractus solitarius and the attenuation of baroreflexes. Alcohol Clin Exp Res 28:1264–1272

Watts LT, Rathinam ML, Schenker S, Henderson GI (2005) Astrocytes protect neurons from ethanol-induced oxidative stress and apoptotic death. J Neurosci Res 80:655–666.

Wei MC, Lindsten T, Mootha VK, Weiler S, Gross A, Ashiya M, Thompson CB, Korsmeyer SJ (2000) tBID, a membrane-targeted death ligand, oligomerizes BAK to release cytochrome *c*. Genes Dev 14: 2060–2071.

Wei MC, Zong WX, Cheng EH, Lindsten T, Panoutsakopoulou V, Ross AJ, Roth KA, MacGregor GR, Thompson CB, Korsmeyer SJ (2001) Proapoptotic Bax and Bak: a requisite gateway to mitochondrial dysfunction and death. Science 292:727–730.

Wyllie AH (1997) Apoptosis: an overview. Br Med Bull 53:451–465.

Yakovlev AG, Faden AI (2004) Mechanisms of neural cell death: implications for development of neuroprotective treatment strategies. Neurorx 1:5–16.

Yoshida H, Kong YY, Yoshida R, Elia AJ, Hakem A, Hakem R, Penninger JM, Ma TW (1998) Apaf1 is required for mitochondrial pathways of apoptosis and brain development. Cell 94:739–750.

Yu SW, Wang H, Poitras MF, Coombs C, Bowers WJ, Federoff HJ, Poirier GG, Dawson TM, Dawson VL (2002) Mediation of poly(ADP-ribose) polymerase-1-dependent cell death by apoptosis-inducing factor. Science 297: 259–263.

Zarkovic K (2003) 4-hydroxynonenal and neurodegenerative diseases. Mol Aspects Med 24:293–303.

Zhou P, Qian L, Iadecola C (2005) Nitric oxide inhibits caspase activation and apoptotic morphology but does not rescue neuronal death. J Cereb Blood Flow Metab 25:348–357.

7

Developmental Disorders and Evolutionary Expectations: Mechanisms of Resilience

Barbara L. Finlay

Jeremy C. Yost

Desmond T. Cheung

Every living organism can trace its lineage back to the unicellular organisms that first populated Earth. We are thus the descendants of creatures who have not only survived but have successfully reproduced in the face of gross atmospheric shifts, blasts of ionizing radiation, the impacts of comets, ice ages, global warming, earthquakes and hurricanes, plagues of any number of viral and bacterial forms, predation, starvation and drought, the toxins of plants and animals, parasites, competing tribes, jealous fathers, indifferent mothers, and everyday accidents of all kinds. Any survivor of this wildly improbable lineage is made of tough stuff. The point of the present chapter is to turn the usual discussion of developmental vulnerability on its head and, rather than discuss the effects of an "environmental insult(s)" on a fragile infant, examine the design features of the tough stuff of which we are made. We argue that only in this evolutionary context will the disorders of development that sometimes do emerge make mechanistic sense.

EVOLUTIONARY DRIVES

Catastrophe

Conservation of the building blocks of the embryo across the invertebrate and vertebrate lineages and the resilience of that embryo have been part of a general rethinking of the character of the evolutionary process to which our ancestors were subjected, along with greater awareness of the effects of periodic global catastrophes on the nature of the genome (Gerhart and Kirschner, 1997). Struggle for success among individuals in an evolutionary landscape of potential niches and their associated fitness peaks, success defined by better adaptation resulting in greater reproduction, is the essential Darwinian view. The kinds of adaptations highlighted by this process are both increasingly subtle organism and environment fits and enhancements important in sexual selection, a central aspect of evolutionary change.

Catastrophe, local or global, provides a force in which all organisms, across radiations and species, are

104

subjected to a severe filter; success arises from survival in suddenly changed environments (Alvarez et al., 1980; Albritton, 1989). Variation in gene transmission during catastrophe can arise from individual competition as well, but whole radiations may be lost. The best-known example, of course, is the extinction of the dinosaurs and survival of mammals in the late Cretaceous period. Selection will favor the robust and adaptable organism, able to weather disaster, to relocate or create its favored niche or get by in a new one, and to reproduce as much as possible. Our genomes carry the history of both types of change. Moreover, the nature of genetic change appears to make it likely that this history is not overwritten in such a way that it is inaccessible, but rather added to, as we will elaborate later.

Evolvability

"Evolvability" is a related, but distinct idea that carries import for how a genome can respond to challenge. This idea has been used in two distinct ways in the allied fields of evolutionary biology and artificial intelligence and robotics by means of genetic algorithms. The first, and somewhat stricter, sense of this concept arose from the hypothesis and later demonstration (in bacteria) that in times of extreme stress and crisis, "deliberate" additional variation and mutation would arise as an adaptive mechanism, suppressed in favored environments (Gerhart and Kirschner, 1997; Radman et al., 1999). The second, more general, sense is the observation that some types of genomic or informational structures more readily produce usable adaptive changes and the potential for evolution than others (Lipson and Pollack, 2000; Nolfi and Floreano, 2002; Baum, 2004). Everything else equal, the "evolvable" organism is more likely to be with us today. Both the strict and the general sense of evolvability will be important in understanding the response of organisms to developmental challenge.

Adaptive Response Or Pathology?

The third conceptual thread to be woven into the argument for evolutionary change is the recasting of some states usually viewed as illness or pathology as adaptations by the emerging field of evolutionary medicine (Nesse and Williams, 1996). A virus co-opting our genome for its own purposes is a bad thing. Consequently, an immune response disables the virus at the cellular level (antibodies), makes its environment inhospitable (fever), and expels it (all the various miseries of flu). Each of these symptoms can be viewed as adaptive responses, not as pathology. Of course, not every response to disease or trauma is adaptation, and the urge to tell such "just-so" stories must be strictly policed. For example, exsanguination when an artery is severed might cleanse the wound and quickly lessen metabolic load, but obviously it is not an adaptive response. Conceptual clarity in this domain gets particularly muddled when organisms are in close competition. For example, it would appear that the enterprising rhinovirus has co-opted the expulsion component of the immune response for its own adaptive purpose of spreading itself around the environment—whose adaptation is the sneeze?

Evolutionary medicine becomes particularly relevant to the developmental response to shortages and pathogens when the normal, tactical nature of the response of the adult organism to challenges is considered and applied to development (Bateson et al., 2004; Gluckman and Hanson, 2004). The best and most elaborated example in physiology is the balancing of requirements for short- and long-term survival in the hypothalamic–pituitary–adrenal axis in response to acute and chronic environmental stressors (Sapolsky et al., 1986). In order to survive an immediate threat, energy is mobilized by metabolic changes that, if they persist long-term, will damage the animal. Alterations in nervous systems and behavior in response to early environmental challenges, particularly commonly encountered ones, might also be tactical adaptations and should not automatically be construed as pathology. For example, perhaps it is a good bet to alter interest in food compared to general exploration in perpetuity if early experience shows food to be in unusually short supply (Smart and Dobbing, 1977; Levitsky, 1979; Bateson et al., 2004; Gluckman and Hanson, 2004).

Environmental Expectation

The fourth thread is environmental expectation. This is usually raised in the context of predictable environments and a genome predisposed to learn (Greenough and Black, 1992): if information about the future structure of visual information in the world is well predicted by present structure, and there is time to learn it, why waste genome specifying it? Considering one of the classic cases of ethology, if mother is the first large, moving thing any duck likely to survive sees, then learning the qualities of the first large, moving object is an efficient way to get the information. On the other hand, the physiological armamentarium available indicates that we also expect trauma, infection, and poor nutrition of all kinds. There is no reason to assume that the brain is not similarly prepared. Recent comparison of the genome of the chimpanzee and of the human, showing rather more changes in genes involved in food metabolism and immune response than in the brain-related genes, has underlined that genetic response to often-encountered challenges may be fairly rapid, and "diet and pathogens are dominant selective forces for all species" (Olson and Varki, 2004). Relevant to this chapter is the cultural history of alcohol. As alcohol has served as a common source of nutrition and food preservation in Western Europe, those populations (compared to Asian ones) have become equipped to metabolize alcohol, and there is some evidence that the incidence of alcoholism falls the longer fermented products have been used in a particular culture (Goedde et al., 1992; Whitfield, 1997). To understand a developmental response to an environmental challenge, it will make a great deal of difference whether the challenge is "expected," such as alcohol, or unprecedented—for example, a designer drug such as thalidomide that may mimic the form of an early regulatory gene.

A Warning and a Road Map

In the following section, we first examine a few central cases of the developmental consequences of alcohol and other substance abuse, and turn the usual style of presentation upside down to show the outrageous situations in which the typical embryo can survive. A strong caveat is necessary here: at no point should a demonstration that the "typical" infant can be born without defect—for example, following a persistent bath of alcohol—be mistaken as an argument endorsing alcoholism in pregnant mothers. A substantial percentage of infants exposed to ethanol do have defects, a probability no prospective parent should ignore. Nor are we in any way attempting to minimize the value of locating and ameliorating those defects caused by developmental insults described in many of the other chapters of this volume. Rather, our point is that if we fail to appreciate the robust nature of the developing embryo and consistently mislabel

deviations as pathology instead of adaptations (or just deviations), we will be in an explanatory realm that makes no sense if we try to understand the pathologies of development that can and do occur.

Next, we will turn to some general design features of development that are stable in the face of challenge, and consider some particular cases of nervous system development that show those principles. Overall, the guiding principal in this discussion is one that is true for all life sciences but is often ignored in medicine: "nothing in biology makes sense except in the light of evolution." (Dobzhansky, 1973)

CONTEXTUALIZING THE DEVELOPMENTAL EFFECTS OF ALCOHOL, NICOTINE, AND THALIDOMIDE

Alcohol

The human body has a variety of mechanisms for the screening and disposal of toxins. Alcohol is no exception. The presence of alcohol in our evolutionary and developmental environment has led to specific enzymes responsible for its metabolism: alcohol dehydrogenase and acetaldehyde dehydrogenase. Ethanol is naturally encountered in fermentation in fruit, and also is a direct result of fermentation of starches in the gut. In many human cultures, alcohol is sought not only for the obvious psychoactive consequences but also because it serves a useful role as a preservative and secondarily as a source of calories (Goedde et al., 1992; Whitfield, 1997; Dudley, 2000, 2002). Alcohol can thus be considered not simply a completely alien disruptive element but also a normal part of the developmental environment. This is not to downplay the dangers of ethanol to a developing organism but to place it in the context of a regulating system. We note in passing that this evolutionary history may have a significant impact on the relevance of animal models to human development, where frugivores and omnivores might be considerably better models than carnivores.

With the assumption of the robustness of the developmental system in mind, we turn to a recent study from Martinez-Frias and colleagues (2004) on the relationship between alcohol consumption during pregnancy and congenital anomalies, paying specific attention to those anomalies indicative of fetal alcohol spectrum disorders (FASD). From a corpus of data collected over 24 years, Martinez-Frias and colleagues drew a group of 4705 malformed infants and a comparable group of 4329 normal infants whose mothers reported alcohol consumption during pregnancy. These infants were examined in the first 3 days of life for a variety of congenital anomalies, including various nervous system defects and a set of craniofacial anomalies. These facial anomalies, including a hypoplastic nose, are indicative of several cognitive impairments (Swillen et al., 1999; Donnai and Karmiloff-Smith, 2000). In particular, they are typical of FASD and, in conjunction with maternal alcohol consumption, are considered reliable predictors of the condition (Astley and Clarren, 1997; Coles et al., 2000; Streissguth and O'Malley, 2000; Sood et al., 2001).

Subjects can be grouped by maternal alcohol consumption into five categories, ranging from Group 1, who experienced low, sporadic exposure through a range of daily doses, to Group 5, who were exposed to over 92 g of absolute alcohol per day throughout gestation, including several glasses of distilled spirits. Group 5 also included the offspring of those who self-identified as alcoholics. An odds ratio was calculated for each birth defect to indicate the effect of alcohol consumption on the risk of developing that defect.

To begin with the worst-case scenario, we should expect infants of Group 5 mothers to show severe deficits. In adults this level of alcohol consumption is associated with anoxia, the pathological deficiency of oxygen, as well as renal failure and severe nutritional deficiencies. As a result, it would be expected that this level of exposure would cause a variety of deficits in a developing organism. Among 87 infants exposed to this amount of ethanol, 67 had at least one physical defect. Thus, only 23% were normal at birth. Looking to the nervous system, however, 79% of the infants showed no central nervous system (CNS) defects under standard infant neurological examinations. Given a level of alcohol exposure known for its damaging effects on the physiology of adults, this is remarkable resilience. Because the neurological component of the suite of FASD-associated symptoms is not consistently detectable at this age, facial phenotypes alone are used as a proxy for FASD (Astley and Clarren, 1997); fully 60% of the infants in Group 5 had a normal facial phenotype. Although 40% damage is a tragic statistic, even in this extreme case of shockingly irresponsible alcohol consumption, more than one-half of the infants show evidence of being quite normal.

Normality dominates the rest of the groups. In Group 4 (the second-highest group), the offspring of mothers who consumed between 56 and 88 g ethanol per day, 95% of the infants showed normal facial phenotypes. According to the odds ratio, children of these mothers were twice as likely to develop the typical FAS characteristics, but the difference was not statistically significant. Only Group 3, with low daily consumption, showed a statistically significant relationship between alcohol consumption and this phenotype. At this consumption level, 97% of the infants showed the normal phenotype. In the sporadic alcohol consumption groups (1 and 2), not only were FASD-predictive anomalies present in only 3% and 2% of the infants, respectively, but the odds ratios suggested that alcohol consumption decreased the risk of anomalies, although these differences were not statistically significant.

An important consideration in this study, and generally in the field, is that of socioeconomic factors. Children of mothers of lower socioeconomic status are at greater risk, for a variety of reasons. These mothers are more likely to be exposed to other risk factors, including lead (Malcoe et al., 2002; Morello-Frosch et al., 2002), chemical solvents (Cordier et al., 1992), and illegal drugs (Hans, 1999). These risk factors are also associated with cognitive impairments. Hence, it is difficult to separate alcohol from other potential causative factors. Additionally, even given equivalent alcohol and drug exposure, children of higher socioeconomic status are more likely to be normal. A substantial review of neurobehavioral studies of alcohol-exposed children (Mattson and Riley, 1998) confirms the prevalence of low scores on cognitive tests in groups of low socioeconomic status (SES), but also includes startling examples of children who perform at normal levels and even above on cognitive tests (Streissguth et al., 1980; Fried and Watkinson, 1988, 1990; Fried et al., 1992). Indeed, the term *low-risk group* is used synonymously with higher socioeconomic status in these studies. Notably, given low to moderate consumption and a high level of maternal education, intelligence quotient and other cognitive scores fall well within the normal range, and occasionally with mean scores a full standard deviation above normal. Although these scores were lower than those achieved by children in the same socioeconomic level without fetal alcohol exposure, it is clear that multiple factors in the developmental environment beyond alcohol consumption are at work in children who show substantial deficits.

Further, studies of the effects of exposure to low (Forrest et al., 1991; Greene et al., 1991; Fried et al., 1992) or even moderate (Mau, 1980) amounts of alcohol fail to find a cognitive deficit. Although these studies focus on exposure to lower amounts of ethanol, they are significant in light of conventional wisdom that any and all alcohol consumption during pregnancy is an unacceptable risk. Rather than being a silver bullet capable of derailing normal neurological development, alcohol exposure at low levels has effects that are hard to demonstrate, which makes sense in terms of the long-term presence of alcohol in our ancestry. Even at pathologically high levels it does not have 100% penetrance.

Nicotine

Nicotine is certainly less common than alcohol in our evolutionary history. Indeed, consumption of any significant amount of nicotine is a recent development in human history. The suite of developmental effects caused by smoking (the most typical way of using nicotine) is complex, involving respiration and oxygen availability directly, peripheral vasoactive effects, and action on central neurotransmitter systems. Still, a number of its effects fall within a well-developed evolutionary context in development, that of reduced resource availability. Although we cannot review this context and its effects fully here, it is well established that the developmental program shows significant flexibility with regard to nutrient availability. Within limits, growth can be scaled back or delayed in times of poor nutrition, favoring the brain whose generation is largely prenatal, and caught up when conditions are favorable (Lucas and Campbell, 2000).

Tobacco exposure restricts the availability of nutrients to the developing fetus (Lambers and Clark, 1996). Carbon monoxide from tobacco smoke binds with hemoglobin, the oxygen-carrying molecule in blood, to form a stable carboxyhemoglobin, limiting oxygen transport in the mother and thereby depriving the fetus of oxygen as well. Nicotine increases heart rate and causes vasoconstriction, increasing blood pressure in the mother, reducing uterine blood flow, and therefore decreasing a fetus's access to all nutrients. Hypoxia, malnutrition, and the ensuing metabolic challenges force the fetus to make do with inadequate resources. As such, it is not surprising that the most common effect of nicotine exposure is low

birth weight (Ellard et al., 1996; Lambers and Clark, 1996). Low birth weight is independently associated with cognitive deficits (Chaudhari et al., 2004; Corbett and Drewett, 2004; Viggedal et al., 2004), regardless of the causative agent. Indeed, as a systematic problem, it is generally associated with growth deficits throughout the body, including osteopathic effects (Nelson et al., 1999), yielding a generally underdeveloped organism. As such, it is difficult to determine whether any cognitive deficits can be directly attributed to nicotine or tobacco or if they secondarily stem from anoxia and generally decreased resources.

The direct effects of nicotine on neurological development are controversial, and in a way that is reminiscent of the complex interactions of postnatal environment with prenatal malnutrition. A variety of studies indicate no cognitive deficits in infants and young children (Streissguth et al., 1980; Forrest et al., 1991), and there is some evidence of a transitive effect, with scores on the Bayley Scales of Development (BSID) that are low at 12 months coming up to normal levels by 24 months (Fried and Watkinson, 1988). Often tests that do indicate an effect in children of heavy smokers fail to separate it from postnatal exposure (Richardson et al., 1995), which has more reliably been associated with decreased scores on cognitive tests (DiFranza et al., 2004). Even so, this effect on BSID test scores is typically small when compared to other factors, including number of toys in the household, SES, number of infant illnesses, and even the identity of the examiner. Essentially, the data indicate that one would be better off spending the cigarette money on toys, as a deficiency of toys in the child's home is a more reliable predictor of decreased cognitive scores than nicotine and tobacco exposure.

Embryological Silver Bullets

In contrast to our relatively robust developmental defense against alcohol, for which we have evolved specific mechanisms dedicated to its detoxification and metabolism, and against nicotine, which may be subsumed under mechanisms already available to buffer resource limitations, there stands a new class of potential teratogens: designer drugs. These drugs are often evolutionarily novel, based on molecules never encountered by our ancestors in the natural environment. Or they can be similar to or even based on molecules naturally produced by the human body, potentially bypassing protective mechanisms, to manipulate the developmental process directly.

Though hardly typical of modern entries into the category, thalidomide is certainly the most infamous example of a designer drug. Introduced in 1957 as a sedative and anti-nausea agent, it was considered so safe as to be regularly prescribed to combat morning sickness and insomnia in pregnant women. Withdrawn from the market in 1961, in less than 4 years thalidomide had caused a worldwide epidemic of birth defects. While no accurate census was ever taken, it is estimated that between 10,000 and 20,000 babies were born disabled as a result of thalidomide (Knightley et al., 1979; see http://www.thalidomide .ca, http://www.marchofdimes.com/professional/681_ 1172.asp). Completely unknown is the rate of embryonic rejection in the face of this drug. Thus it is difficult to estimate the penetration of the teratogenic effects of thalidomide.

The methods of action responsible for the teratogenic effects of thalidomide are still under investigation nearly 50 years after its introduction. Indeed, study has increased drastically in recent years as new applications for the drug have been found in treatments for leprosy, lupus, rheumatoid arthritis, and other disorders. As a result, at least 30 different mechanisms have been proposed for the teratogenic effects (Stephens and Fillmore, 2000). Some have been discredited, others are contradictory, whereas others can coexist handily.

An affinity for DNA sequences rich in guanine has been established, such as those in the GC-box, a hexanucleotide promoter in the human genome (GGGCGG). Thalidomide can insert into such sequences, interfering with their function (Jonsson, 1972). Approximately 9% of the human genome uses G-rich promoters to the exclusion of other common promoters such as TATA and CCAAT boxes (Bucher, 1990). Additionally, thalidomide has been linked to the fibroblast growth factor (FGF) family of transcription factors. Wolpert (1976, 1999) champions the idea that thalidomide inhibits FGF-8, an initiator of sonic hedgehog (shh). Stephens (1988) implicated it in the insulin-like growth factor (IGF) I/FGF-2/ angiogenesis pathway. A follow-up to this work (Stephens and Fillmore, 2000) details the interrupted pathway and its promoter sequences, effectively tying together the leading theories on thalidomide embryopathy to make a strong case for intersecting vulnerabilities in certain systems.

Within the thalidomide-affected population, certain trends in the abnormalities are relevant to our discussion. Some defects are much more common in children that survived to birth. Limb outgrowth deficiencies are far and away the most common, present in approximately 90% of the group. Ear and eye defects are the second most common pathologies, affecting approximately 60% of the group (Yang et al., 1977; Quibell, 1981; Lenz, 1985).

In the developing limb, the IGF-I/FGF-2/angio genesis pathway is necessary for normal outgrowth. Of 10 genes in the pathway, nine rely on GC-box promoters lacking TATA or CCAAT promoter sequences. This pathway is particularly vulnerable to intercalation by thalidomide. A similar situation exists for the vascular endothelial growth factor–integrin pathway, which has been implicated in deformities of the ear. Regardless of which or how many of these mechanisms are eventually implicated in developmental disorders, it is notable that the explanations, as a class, directly implicate developmental control mechanisms.

FEATURES OF EVOLUTION AND DEVELOPMENT THAT MAXIMIZE STABILITY

The prior examples show that we have a phenomenon to account for developmental stability of most infants in the face of what would appear to be severe challenges, particularly in the case of "expected" challenges. Most of the other chapters in this volume give accounts of abnormality; here we make some argument for forces for normality.

A list of the features of the genome and development that produce "evolvability" and the list of those that produce stable solutions to developmental challenges are quite similar. Both problems have the defining feature of producing a functional consequence in the event of a deviation. In the case of evolution, the deviation to be assimilated comes from the genome; in the developmental cases we are discussing here, the deviation is introduced from the environment. The principal difference is that evolution lacks the tactical nature of some developmental solutions. Evolution has no plans for the future, and in the genome and life histories of current organisms we see the direct evidence of what is evolvable. Development, however, most certainly has intention and tactics, as they have been selected and written into the genome. No developmental program has as its end point a perfect, nonreproductive infant. Trade-offs and faults can be gambled on to produce an imperfect, reproductive adult.

Duplicate and Vary

An overall quantitative feature of evolution is that as organisms become more complex, from prokaryotes to eukaryotes and to plants and animals, they have more DNA and more genes (Lynch and Conery, 2003). That an increase in complexity should be part-nered with an increase in genes at first seems reasonable on its face, until the amount of conservatism in basic metabolic pathways is confronted and the actual history of genetic change is investigated (Szath-máry et al., 2001). It is not clear that increasing the number of gene products per se should necessarily lead to fancier animals—if Shakespeare had had a few more letters of the alphabet to work with, few would argue that the plays would thereby be deeper.

The historical record of the genome as viewed in current animals does not show linear increases of genetic material consistent with the notion of progressive addition of complexity. Rather, duplications occur many times over, gene duplication followed by variation of one of the duplicated genes, both at the level of the individual gene and at the level of the whole genome, as well as at various intermediate steps (Lynch and Conery, 2000). Below are a few examples. The trichomatic color vision of primates has arisen three separate times, by duplication of the "yellow" opsin followed by one or two minor amino acid changes in one of the genes producing a slight change in wavelength selectivity (Jacobs, 1998). A whole-genome duplication occurs at the chordate–vertebrate boundary, implicated particularly in the subsequent elaboration of the cranium, jaw, and forebrain (Northcutt, 1996).

The regulatory genes controlling body plan, which are conserved across vertebrates and invertebrates, show evidence of multiple replications in evolutionary history (Gerhart and Kirschner, 1997). The use of this strategy is clear—one gene can continue its essential roles, while a second can be free to vary, assume new functions, or be produced in different contexts. The ability to duplicate and vary "semantic" aspects of the genome—that is, aspects of the genome that relate to meaningful components of

the organisms—is a feature that allows evolvability, and has been employed to advantage in "genetic algorithms" in computer science (Lipson and Pollack, 2000; Nolfi and Floreano, 2002; Baum, 2004).

Duplicate-and-vary by its nature makes development responsive to local genetic accident. One frustrating aspect of early genetic work (to geneticists) is that when it became possible to "knock out" single genes (in the case of nonlethal omissions), the usual effect was often nil, largely because of the massive redundancy of gene copies. It should be emphasized that extra or slightly altered gene copies did not evolve in anticipation of future accident. Once in place, however, creatures with the duplications have had a developmental edge. Many other versions of the duplicate-and-vary strategy can be seen in addition to gene duplication and variation. For example, the segmental structure of the vertebrate and invertebrate brain and body plan is another version of duplicate-and-vary, at a higher level of complexity.

Large neural structures, such as the cortex and cerebellum, may also be cases of duplicate-and-vary (or multiply-and-vary), regardless of whether the unit duplicated is a cell assembly, a "cortical column," a region, or a cortical area. Cortical areas have the analogous strategic features of conserved structure throughout, such that cortical areas may be functionally substituted for each other, as shown from myriad examples of plasticity either early or late in life, but particular cortical areas, such as visual or somatosensory cortex, appear to have functionally relevant local features "wired in" (reviewed in Kingsbury and Finlay, 2001; Pallas, 2001). Finally, it is possible that some of the peculiar features of our bilateral body (and brain) plan might be placed in this context. The exact caloric requirements of each body part appear to be very tightly regulated. For example, the brain size and gut length (two metabolically expensive organs) co-vary negatively with each other very precisely in primates with the result of keeping basal metabolic rate unchanged (Aiello and Wheeler, 1995). Yet the amount of each organ we possess seems to be far from the bare minimum required, or even the amount required for everyday function. Jared Diamond calculates from various successful surgeries in humans that we can get by with one kidney, half of one lung, a third of a liver, half the cerebral cortex, and so on (Diamond, 1994). It has now been acknowledged that creative use of brain lateralization, in the duplicate-and-vary version, can be found throughout the invertebrate and vertebrate lineage, in fruit fly, fish, birds, and many arthropods, and, of course, ourselves (Vallortigara and Rogers, 2005). Humans do quite peculiarly well with early, full-hemispheric deletions.

Convergent Redundancy

Frank duplication and variation of identifiable developmental mechanisms seem to have occurred numerous times, as can be seen in the many isoforms and other variants of cell recognition molecules, signaling molecules, and trophic molecules. An absolute hallmark of development, however, is redundancy of a different type, where multiple distinct mechanisms are all directed toward the same outcome. The retinotectal system, in which the two-dimensional layout of cells in the retina is faithfully transferred to the two-dimensional surface of the tectum for the organization of eye and body movements, has served as a "model system" for the investigation of axon guidance, synaptogenesis, and topographic map formation since Roger Sperry first investigated it half a century ago (Sperry, 1963). This model system provides the clearest instance of mechanistic redundancy. Each proposed mechanism has had its researcher-champion, until the realization dawned that evolution had taken no vow of mechanistic parsimony.

There are a number of logical possibilities of mapping an array A–B–C–D onto a second array A*–B*–C*–D*, each of which alone can solve the developmental puzzle. A could recognize A*; B recognize B*, and so on, which is called "chemoaffinity," Sperry's first hypothesis (Sperry, 1963). Alternative to attraction, A could be repelled by D*, and less by C* (Bonhoeffer and Huf, 1992). Or, A might stick to B better than to C, preserving intrinsic order in the fiber array, and then have some rule about how to position itself relative to A*–D* (Fraser, 1980). Or, temporal order in development might be exploited, having A and A* mature first, then B and B*, and so on (Reese, 1996). Or, the elements in both arrays could be produced in excess, connected at random, and errors removed by some second rule, as cell death is a major component of brain development (Oppenheim, 1991). Or, the map could self-organize by a Hebbian rule, using the feature that the contrast level of neighboring elements in the visual world is more highly correlated than distant elements (Schmidt, 1985; Wong, 1999). The answer is, of course, that every single one

of these logically separate mechanisms cooperates to produce orderly maps. During development, it is possible to disable one or more of these mechanisms altogether, yet still preserve topographic map order, much as in gene knockout experiments, as residual mechanisms rescue the map.

These two separate forms of redundancy, duplicate-and-vary and convergent redundancy, contribute to a massively parallel, semimodular architecture of developmental mechanisms living beneath the surface of an organism maturing over time. Starting from scratch to build a complex organism, one might be predisposed to a sequential, assembly-line mechanism, producing one part at a time, and connecting it up, but the relatively greater vulnerability of such a system to loss of any component is obvious. It is interesting to observe the present-day parallel evolution of manufacturing systems from the strictly serial Ford assembly line to current, multiple-component "just-in-time" manufacturing systems. The fact that evolution *must* tinker with existing systems rather than design from scratch is often given as an argument for the unique, redundant nature of biological construction, but it is possible evolution has come upon solutions for efficient biological construction that we may not yet be able to recognize.

Catastrophe Curves

It will not do to make a large fraction of an organism: it is a waste of energy for the parents and certainly no good for the offspring. Restated, partial solutions are no good in development—if uncorrectable defects are detected, no more energy should be spent on the embryo to compound the metabolic loss. For this reason, bailing out is perhaps the most common response to developmental defect. For many species, particularly "reselected" animals who are specialized for rapid reproduction in challenging environments, embryos may be resorbed until late developmental stages in response to very small changes in environmental stress, or the fetuses may be aborted and cannibalized, as any researcher attempting to study the etiology of developmental disorders in rodents knows. Even for primates, who spend much energy on the growth and care of one or two infants, a large proportion of conceptions are aborted and resorbed in the first trimester; the common figure given in medical advisories about pregnancy is "up to 50%," although it is hard to locate the empirical basis of this claim.

Even if the number is much lower, the recognition of developmental disorder and termination of development, particularly in early stages, are as much an important facet of development as constructive mechanisms.

If a commitment to the offspring is unavoidable — for example, if it is the only chance at reproduction, or a life-threatening metabolic commitment has already been made — then every subsequent choice to preserve the offspring should be made as is physically possible. Particularly in shortage situations, clearly strategic choices are made — for example, to preserve the brain of the infant, which is generated only early in development, over and against the musculoskeletal system, whose growth can be delayed, or to favor the infant's nutritional needs over the caloric requirements of the mother (Martyn et al., 1996; Lucas and Campbell, 2000). One "difficulty" in research on developmental disorders, which may not be entirely obvious to those working in well-established paradigms, is to be able to find just those regimes that lie on the cusp between the plateaus of embryonic rejection and death, and full normality.

Analogous strategic similarities can be seen in various developmental mechanisms in the nervous system, for example, a certain number of neurons, a certain convergence ratio between neurons, or a feature of physiology. Central mechanisms can gird the system against environmental stressors, but at a critical value, this defense will suddenly and catastrophically collapse. For example, if the number of neurons in the cortex is progressively depleted by the mitotic inhibitor methylazoxymethanol during early development, the thalamus projecting to that cortex will show no loss of neurons until more than 70%–80% of its target is gone, and then collapse itself (Woo et al., 1996). Similar events may be at play with the antimitogen ethanol. Prenatal exposure to ethanol causes a <35% reduction in the number of cortical neurons (Miller and Potempa, 1990) and no loss of thalamic neurons (Mooney and Miller, 2000). Unfortunately, no studies have generated fetal damage sufficient to cause catastrophic loss of cortical neurons. If the convergence ratio in the retinotectal system is challenged, synaptic organization reconforms to simultaneously produce normal single-neuron response properties and normal gross topography, and at a critical point, both aspects of organization fail together (Xiong and Finlay, 1996).

The belief that developing organisms should produce a linear response in degree of malfunction to linear increases in environmental stressors is written very deeply into our experimental paradigms, and at best is a hypothesis to be demonstrated. The nature of malfunction-functions will depend on the evolutionary expectations and consequent strategic developmental choices of each separate species.

Self-Initiate, Self-Terminate

The nature of control and monitoring regimes to move animals through developmental stages should be evaluated routinely for developmental robustness. In the following sections, we examine some aspects of early neural development, particularly neurogenesis, neuron type specification, critical periods, and the features these periods appear to have to stabilize developmental outcomes. The bottom line is that most developmental mechanisms contain numerous (and redundant) logical checkpoints to determine if the correct complement of cells is being produced. Feedback-free, "I Love Lucy" assembly lines are virtually nonexistent.

Developmental mechanisms are initiated when multiple conditions for initiation are satisfied, and are terminated when the process initiated is completed, not with respect to arbitrary clocks. In evolution of mammals, in which the time taken to produce a brain scales by a factor well over 10, mechanisms like these simply allow graceful scaling (Clancy et al., 2001). As brains enlarge during evolution, investigators begin to observe "waiting periods" in the development of certain properties, as a set of cells or axon terminals go quiescent until appropriate environmental conjunctions appear to be reached. In the case of developmental challenges, the same ability to pause or delay may be employed to amass enough material or wait for the right conditions to occur to proceed.

ROBUSTNESS AND VULNERABILITIES IN FUNDAMENTAL DEVELOPMENTAL PROCESSES

Having introduced several features of development through which evolution and development produce stability, we now examine in detail instantiations of these principles at various developmental stages in the vertebrate nervous system.

Neurogenesis and the Process
of Cell Type Specification

Neurogenesis comprises the production of neurons and glia that will reside in a structure; this is analogous to *organogenesis*, which is the production of cells that will constitute an organ. Thus, neurogenesis includes the proliferation of neural precursors, the fate decision, the migration, differentiation, and sometimes death of the cells. Most neuronal precursor cells are generated in the proliferative zones that line the inner surface of the neural tube (see Chapters 2, 11, and 12). In these zones, precursor cells undergo mitosis, with "symmetric" divisions, producing more precursors. Eventually, some precursors begin "asymmetric" divisions, with one daughter cell exiting the cell cycle and the proliferative zone, and then beginning the transformation into particular types of neurons or glia (Caviness et al., 1995; Ohnuma and Harris, 2003). The original size of the progenitor pool combined with the duration of neurogenesis of any given part of the brain predicts its size (Finlay and Darlington, 1995; Finlay et al., 2001).

Not every precursor cell in the nervous system differentiates. In some regions of the brain, stem cells remain undifferentiated throughout the life of the animal, and recent work suggests that these cells can be pressed into service to effect repairs for damaged neural circuits even in the adult brain (e.g., Alvarez-Buylla and Garcia-Verdugo, 2002; Gage, 2002; Picard-Riera et al., 2004). That is, neuronal stem cells may provide a substrate for compensatory plasticity in some systems of the brains of adults.

We concentrate here on mechanisms that control the assignment of cell identity, with particular attention paid to how the process may regulate itself if disturbances occur. Researchers first framed the question of cell specification in terms of where cell specification occurs. Conceivably, this decision is (a) intrinsic, such that specific precursor populations give rise to particular subpopulations of cells only; (b) determined by a clock producing a certain cell type after a required number of precursor cell subdivisions or with regard to some externally specified stage; or (c) extrinsic, defined by the external milieu of the precursor cells, in either the proliferative zones or their eventual destination. The answer that may vary from one brain region to another is likely the usual developmental answer: all of the above. We give a few specific examples, and consider the implications of hybrid mechanisms for producing normal structures in response to challenge.

In vivo and in vitro experiments demonstrate that the order of neurogenesis and cell type are correlated. For example, in the vertebrate nervous system, most glia are produced after the completion of neuronal generation (Ohnuma and Harris, 2003). In the retina, the six types of cells are produced in order, although in all cases, the production of cell types overlaps (Polley et al., 1989). Evidence suggests that a combination of clock-like initiation of specification of particular cell types and feedback processes that assess how many cells of a class have been produced. One of these, p27^{Kip1}, a cell cycle inhibitor, gradually increases in progenitors until a critical level is reached, whereupon cells designated as oligodendrocytes exit the cell cycle and differentiate (Freeman, 2000; Dyer and Cepko, 2001; Ohnuma and Harris, 2003). Thus, the gradual accrual of p27^{Kip1} is a negative feedback mechanism that tells precursor cells when to start differentiating into glia as opposed to neurons.

Injury is capable of resetting the neurogenetic mechanism. In frogs and fishes, for example, Muller glia can re-enter the cell cycle in response to retinal injury, and can produce progeny that differentiate into neurons (Reh and Levine, 1998). In mature glia, p27^{Kip1} is expressed at high levels. Following retinal injury, however, p27^{Kip1} is down-regulated in cells that re-enter the cell cycle, allowing for the generation of new neurons. Regulation of specification of cell classes has also been shown to occur at a more detailed level—for example, if the retina is depleted of a particular class of amacrine cells while retinogenesis is ongoing, the subsequent production of that cell type is up-regulated (Reh, 1987).

Negative feedback control of the rate of histogenesis provides flexibility and robustness in the developing organism relative to more rigid developmental schemes that might plausibly have evolved. For instance, suppose that only glia are produced on a set day following the onset of neuronogenesis, or that glia are produced only after a certain number of cell cycles with no feedback regulation. In either of these cases, if anything interferes with cell production at a certain time point, an essential cell group might never be generated. On the other hand, if progression through cell classes is regulated only by feedback, in the case of low resource availability, neurogenesis could stall at an early point and never produce late-generated cell groups. Intrinsic clocks, overlapping distributions of cell production, and feedback regulation of the amount of each cell type in concert together virtually guarantee that some members of each cell class are generated, and their normal ratios defended.

Cell Migration

The migration of developing neurons to their adult positions in the brain is a critical step in the development of the nervous system. Several distinct developmental mechanisms, such as radial and tangential migration and cellular adhesion molecules, are thought to govern this process (Rosenweig et al., 1999; Corbin et al., 2001). This is a process that can go wrong, and "ectopia," cell groups lying elsewhere than their normal terminal site, is one of the principal morphological deviations associated with retardation (Evrard et al., 1989a, 1989b). Even if migration abnormalities result in misplaced cells, however, all is not lost.

One of the most striking demonstrations of developmental robustness comes from one model system of perturbed cell migration, in reeler mice. Reelin is a protein secreted by several neuronal populations during development, and is vital for allowing neurons to complete migration and adopt their ultimate positions in a number of laminar structures in the CNS (Rakic and Caviness, 1995; Rice and Curran, 2001). Mice lacking reelin (*reeler* mice, so named for their staggering gait, which results primarily from a cerebellar anomaly) show abnormal patterns of cerebral cortical lamination. The arrangement of the six layers of the cerebral cortex is inverted, so that the earliest-generated cells form the most superficial layers of the cortex and late-generated neurons tend to be distributed in deep cortex. Despite this perturbation, afferent projections to the visual, somatosensory, olfactory, and motor cortices find their correct target cells. In addition, the overall organization of major systems and the physiological responses of individual neurons in reeler mice are comparable to those in the normal brain. Reeler mice have other anatomical abnormalities relative to wild-type mice. These include changes in synaptic density, distribution, and topology that are present in a number of brain structures including the hippocampus, piriform cortex, and cerebellum. Nevertheless, although morphology is grossly abnormal, function is spared. This result suggests caution in any assumption that disturbed morphology has negative functional consequences.

Reeler mice provide an additional demonstration of the robustness of the "duplicate-and-vary" strategy. Only mice homozygous for the mutant *reelin* allele show the neuronal abnormalities listed above. Studies of mice heterozygous for *reelin* have neuronal and behavioral phenotypes virtually indistinguishable from those of wild-type mice (Salinger et al., 2003).

Maturation of Cell Types during Later Development

The maturation of neuronal morphology provides an example of convergent redundancy. In vitro experiments show that granule and Purkinje cells isolated from their normal connections grow in a typical manner (Seil et al., 1974). This finding implies that signals intrinsic to cells can regulate aspects of neuronal differentiation. The neural environment of developing cells, however, also influences cell morphology and connectivity. For instance, some spinal cells are directed to become motor neurons under the influence of cells ventral to the notochord (Roelink et al., 1994). If a second length of notochord is inserted above the spinal cord, cells begin to differentiate as motor neurons on either side of the notochord. Cell–cell interactions of this sort, in which cells influence the fates of adjacent precursor cells, are referred to as *induction*, and have been documented extensively in the vertebrate brain (Rosenweig et al., 1999). The ability of extrinsic cell–cell interactions to regulate cell fate is not restricted to precursor cells. Cortical transplant studies consistently show that sensory and motor cortex cells grafted onto distant cortical regions can assume morphological, connectional, and functional properties appropriate to that region. For instance, fetal visual cortex of rats transplanted into rat neonatal somatosensory cortex develops the barrel-like whisker representations characteristic of primary somatosensory cortex (Schlaggar and O'Leary, 1991), and the expression of the limbic system–associated membrane protein that marks specific functional regions of the cerebral cortex can be regulated by environmental stimuli (Levitt et al., 1997).

Patterned sensory activity can alter cell fate. Cross-modal rewiring of retinal axons into ferret auditory thalamus provides visually patterned activity to the auditory cortex (Pallas et al., 1999). Primary auditory cortex provided with early visual input resembles visual cortex topographically (Roe et al., 1990), physiologically (Roe et al., 1992), and perceptually (von Melchner et al., 2000). Neurons in this altered auditory cortex not only assume the functional properties and arrangement of neurons in the visual cortex but also are capable of mediating visually guided behavior (von Melchner et al., 2000).

Hence, intrinsic factors such as gene expression and extrinsic factors such as induction, neuron–neuron interactions, and patterned activity are all capable of regulating cell fate at various (and sometimes overlapping) points in development. Not all of these mechanisms are necessarily invoked or even necessary during the production of any given neuron.

Postnatal Development and Critical Periods

Critical periods are time windows in postnatal development during which neurons and circuitry are particularly receptive to acquiring certain kinds of information critical for normal development (Hensch, 2004). Critical periods have been extensively documented for sensory systems, motor systems, and multimodal functions such as imprinting, birdsong learning, sound localization, and human language learning. How are critical periods useful for ensuring normal development, when it seems that the unlucky absence of a particular experience at a particular time might permanently derail normal development? The answer is that the critical-period onset, duration, and termination are not regulated simply by age, but rather by experience. If appropriate neural activation is not provided at all, then developing circuits often remain in a waiting state until such input is available. For instance, the segregation of ocular dominance columns depends on visual experience. If all visual experience is denied, the representation of the two eyes does not begin its segregation and the special neurotransmitters and receptors that are responsible for this structural change are held in their initial state (Kirkwood et al., 1995). Within certain constraints, when experience is reinstated, anatomical, pharmacological, and physiological events then progress as they would have independent of the age of the animals. A similar phenomenon has also been observed in birds that learn their songs from tutors—for the unfortunate nestlings born too late in the season to hear any of the spring songs that establish territory, the critical period is held over until next spring, when singing begins again (Doupe and Kuhl, 1999). Critical periods have vulnerabilities. If activation is only partial, it may initiate the progression of the critical period, stabilizing an abnormal state, as has been seen in the production of ocular dominance columns: if both eyes are closed, the critical period is delayed. On the other hand, if just one eye is closed, the critical period proceeds, dedicating all resources to the open eye (Katz and Shatz, 1996).

ETHANOL AND THE DEVELOPING NERVOUS SYSTEM: EVOLUTIONARY CONSIDERATIONS

Here we look at a few of the cases in which the effects of ethanol on developing systems have been investigated and consider them in the context of self-regulation. The effects of ethanol on the nervous system—at any stage of development—are known to be numerous and varied (see Chapters 11–18). For instance, ethanol can both inhibit and stimulate neuron proliferation, depending on the physical location of the cells, and the concentration and even timing (day or night) of exposure (Luo and Miller, 1998; see Chapter 11).

Given that the effects of ethanol on the developing nervous system are numerous, complex, and contingent upon many factors, can we be sure that all these effects are malignant? To be sure, some are unambiguously deleterious. Ethanol can induce neuronal death *in vitro* and *in vivo*, oxidative stress, and excitotoxicity (Chapters 15 and 16); interfere with glucose transport and uptake; and reduce the expression and adhesive properties of cell adhesion molecules (Chapter 13). Other effects of ethanol, however, may not necessarily be maladaptive. For instance, in addition to causing neuronal death in developing cerebellum (Li et al., 2002) and cortex (Jacobs and Miller, 2001), ethanol can slow the production of developing cerebellar (Li et al., 2002) and cortical (Miller and Nowakowski, 1991; Miller, 2003) neurons, and it can increase the time during which postmitotic cortical neurons remain in the proliferative zone before commencing their migration while also decreasing the rate of neuronal migration (Miller, 1993). Given that development is dynamically regulated and sensitive to environmental cues, it is not implausible that these delays might be an adaptive response to a hostile developmental environment (high concentrations of ethanol) in which cell production and migration are retarded until a more favorable environment becomes available. This interpretation generates testable predictions. If cell-cycle and migration delays are a response to a hostile environment, then we should expect to see a restoration of these activities to normal (or even above-normal) rates once the normal developmental environment is restored. In practice, we might expect to see resumption of neuron proliferation and migration after transient exposure to ethanol (after the restoration of normal cellular environment). Certainly, research has demonstrated that the nervous system can and does recover from ethanol-related developmental insults (Anders and Persaud, 1980; Riley, 1990; Popova, 1997) but the precise mechanisms mediating recovery are poorly characterized. We suggest that some of the observed ethanol-induced changes in the developing nervous system may not be disorders, but remnants of processes that have mediated recovery.

SUMMARY AND CONCLUSIONS

Development can go wrong. One need only consider the appearance of a poorly placed or underfertilized garden plant compared to its well-nourished siblings to counteract the rosy glow that this chapter, with its relentless underscoring of mechanisms designed for developmental stability, may have produced. Nevertheless, there are many reasons for taking a view of pathology that begins with evolution, rather than with human development in isolation.

First, although due caution should be employed in advising pregnant mothers, communicating the wild improbability of gross developmental disorders from tiny infractions in alcohol consumption during pregnancy would relieve unnecessary anxiety.

Second, animal "models" should be examined for their appropriateness to understanding human pathology. Vertebrate nervous systems are quite conservative in structure; current work comparing the genomes of different species suggests that their defensive packaging is quite different, depending on such factors as "r" and "k" selection and the dietary and pathogen exposure in the evolutionary history of the species. The kind of modeling of development we do must change and is, in fact, in the process of change—from the assumption of linear dose–response curves to pathogens and teratogens, to multicomponent chaotic systems in which "normality" is the strongest attractor, or in which several attractors, each representing a developmentally stable strategy, may exist.

Finally, we need to establish better causal links in developmental models that go from fundamental physiology to morphology to behavior, in order to discriminate pathological change from compensatory change and from simple deviation. Evolutionary models can provide scaffolding for such understanding that pathology-based research can never provide.

Abbreviations

BSID   Bayley Scales of Development
CNS   central nervous system
FASD   fetal alcohol spectrum disorder
FGF   fibroblast growth factor
IGF   insulin-like growth factor

References

Aiello LC, Wheeler P (1995) The expensive-tissue hypothesis: the brain and digestive system in human and primate evolution. Curr Anthropol 36:199–221.

Albritton CC (1989) Catastrophic Episodes in Earth History. Chapman and Hall, London.

Alvarez LW, Alvarez W, Asaro F, Michel HV (1980) Extraterrestrial cause for the Cretaceous-Tertiary extinction. Science 208:1095–1108.

Alvarez-Buylla A, Garcia-Verdugo JM (2002) Neurogenesis in adult subventricular zone. J Neurosci 22:629–634.

Anders K, Persaud TV (1980) Compensatory embryonic development in the rat following maternal treatment with ethanol. Anat Anz 148:375–383.

Astley SJ, Clarren SK (1997) Diagnostic Guide for Fetal Alcohol Syndrome and Related Conditions. University of Washington, Seattle.

Bateson P, Barker D, Clutton-Brock T, Deb D, D'Udine B, Foley RA, Gluckman P, Godfrey K, Kirkwood T, Lahr MM, McNamara J, Metcalfe NB, Monaghan P, Spencer HG, Sultan SE (2004) Developmental plasticity and human health. Nature 430:419–421.

Baum EB (2004) What Is Thought? MIT Press, Boston.

Bonhoeffer F, Huf J (1992) Position-dependent properties of retinal axons and their growth cones. Nature 315:409–410.

Bucher P (1990) Weight matrix descriptions of four eukaryotic RNA polymerase II promoter elements derived from 502 unrelated promoter sequences. J Mol Biol 212:563–578.

Caviness VS, Takahashi T, Nowakowski RS (1995) Numbers, time and neocortical neuronogenesis: a general developmental and evolutionary model. Trends Neurosci 18:379–383.

Chaudhari S, Otiv M, Chitale A, Pandit A, Hoge M (2004) Pune low birth weight study—cognitive abilities and educational performance at twelve years. Indian Pediatr 41:121–128.

Clancy B, Darlington RB, Finlay BL (2001) Translating developmental time across mammalian species. Neuroscience 105:7–17.

Coles CD, Kable JA, Drews-Botsch C, Falek A (2000) Early identification of risk for effects of prenatal alcohol exposure. J Stud Alcohol 61:607–616.

Corbett SS, Drewett RF (2004) To what extent is failure to thrive in infancy associated with poorer cognitive development? A review and meta-analysis. J Child Psychol Psychiatry 45:641–654.

Corbin JG, Nery S, Fishell G (2001) Telencephalic cells take a tangent: non-radial migration in the mammalian forebrain. Nat Neurosci 4 (Suppl):1177–1182.

Cordier S, Ha MC, Ayme S, Goujard J (1992) Maternal occupational exposure and congenital malformations. Scand J Work Environ Health 18:11–17.

Diamond J (1994) Best size and number of body parts. Nat Hist 103:78–81.

DiFranza JR, Aligne CA, Weitzman M (2004) Prenatal and postnatal environmental tobacco smoke exposure and children's health. Pediatrics 113:1007–1015.

Dobzhansky T (1973) Nothing in biology makes sense except in light of evolution. American Teacher 35:125–129.

Donnai D, Karmiloff-Smith A (2000) Williams syndrome: from genotype through to the cognitive phenotype. Am J Med Genet 97:164–171.

Doupe AJ, Kuhl PK (1999) Birdsong and human speech: common themes and mechanisms. Annu Rev Neurosci 22:567–631.

Dudley R (2000) Evolutionary origins of human alcoholism in primate frugivory. Q Rev Biol 75:3–15.

—— (2002) Fermenting fruit and the historical ecology of ethanol ingestion: is alcoholism in modern humans an evolutionary hangover? Addiction 97:381–388.

Dyer MA, Cepko CL (2001) Regulating proliferation during retinal development. Nat Rev Neurosci 2:333–341.

Ellard GA, Johnstone FD, Prescott RJ, Ji-Xian W, Jian-Hua M (1996) Smoking during pregnancy: the dose dependence of birthweight deficits. Br J Obstet Gynecol 103:806–813.

Evrard P, de Saint-Georges P, Kadhim HJ, Gadisseux J-F (1989a) Pathology of prenatal encephalopathies. In: Brookes PH, (ed). Child Neurology and Developmental Disabilities. Paul H Brookes, Baltimore, pp 153–176.

Evrard P, Kadhim HJ, de Saint-Georges P, Gadisseux J-F (1989b.) Abnormal development and destructive processes of the human brain during the second half of gestation. In: Evrard P, Minkowski A (eds). Developmental Neurobiology. Raven Press, New York, pp 21–41.

Finlay BL, Darlington R (1995) Linked regularities in the development and evolution of mammalian brains. Science 268:1578–1584.

Finlay BL, Darlington RB, Nicastro N (2001) Developmental structure in brain evolution. Behav Brain Sci 24:263–307.

Forrest F, Florey CD, Taylor D, McPherson F, Young JA (1991) Reported social alcohol consumption during pregnancy and infants' development at 18 months. BMJ 303:22–26.

Fraser SE (1980) A differential adhesion approach to the patterning of nerve connections. Dev Biol 79:453–464.

Freeman M (2000) Feedback control of intercellular signalling in development. Nature 408:313–319.

Fried PA, O'Connell CM, Watkinson B (1992) 60- and 72-month follow-up of children prenatally exposed to marijuana, cigarettes, and alcohol: cognitive and language assessment. J Dev Behav Pediatr 13:383–391.

Fried PA, Watkinson B (1988) 12- and 24-month neurobehavioural follow-up of children prenatally exposed to marihuana, cigarettes and alcohol. Neurotoxicol Teratol 10:305–313.

—— (1990) 36- and 48-month neurobehavioral follow-up of children prenatally exposed to marijuana, cigarettes, and alcohol. J Dev Behav Pediatr 11:49–58.

Gage, FH (2002) Neurogenesis in the adult brain. J Neurosci 22:612–613.

Gerhart J, Kirschner M (1997) Cells, Embryos and Evolution. Blackwell, Malden, MA.

Gluckman PD, Hanson MA (2004) Living with the past: evolution, development and patterns of disease. Science 305:1733–1739.

Goedde HW, Agarwal DP, Fritze G, Meier-Tackmann D, Singh S, Beckmann G, Bhatia K, Chen LZ, Fang B, Lisker R, Paik YK, Rothhammer F, Saha N, Segal B, Srivastava LM, Czeizel A (1992) Distribution of ADH2 and ALDH2 genotypes in different populations. Hum Genet 88:344–346.

Greene T, Ernhart CB, Ager J, Sokol R, Martier S, Boyd T (1991) Prenatal alcohol exposure and cognitive development in the preschool years. Neurotoxicol Teratol 13:57–68.

Greenough W, Black J (1992) Induction of brain structure by experience: substrate for cognitive development. In: Gunnar MR, Nelson CA (eds). Developmental

Behavioral Neuroscience. Lawrence Erlbaum, Hillsdale, NJ, pp 155–299.

Hans SL (1999) Demographic and psychosocial characteristics of substance-abusing pregnant women. Clin Perinatol 26:55–74.

Hensch TK (2004) Critical period regulation. Annu Rev Neurosci 27:549–579.

Jacobs GH (1998) Photopigments and seeing—lessons from natural experiments. The Proctor Lecture. Invest Ophthalmol Vis Sci 39:2205–2216.

Jacobs JS, Miller MW (2001) Proliferation and death of cultured fetal neocortical neurons: effects of ethanol on the dynamics of cell growth. J Neurocytol 30:391–401.

Jonsson NA (1972) Chemical structure and teratogenic properties. IV. An outline of a chemical hypothesis for the teratogenic action of thalidomide. Acta Pharmacol Sin 9:543–562.

Katz LC, Shatz CJ (1996) Synaptic activity and the construction of cortical circuits. Science 274:1133–1138.

Kingsbury MA, Finlay BL (2001) The cortex in multidimensional space: where do cortical areas come from? Dev Science 4:125–156.

Kirkwood A, Lee HK, Bear MF (1995) Co-regulation of long-term potentiation and experience-dependent synaptic plasticity in visual cortex by age and experience. Nature 375:328–331.

Knightley P, Evans H, Potter E, Wallace M (1979) *Suffer the Children: The Story of Thalidomide.* Andre Deutsch, London.

Lambers DS, Clark KE (1996) The maternal and fetal physiologic effects of nicotine. Semin Perinatol 20:115–126.

Lenz W (1985) Thalidomide embryopathy in Germany, 1959–1961. Prog Clin Biol Res 163C:77–83.

Levitsky DA (1979) Malnutrition and the hunger to learn. In: Levitsky DA (ed). *Malnutrition, Environment, and Behavior.* Cornell University Press, Ithaca, pp 161–179.

Levitt P, Eagleson KL, Chan AV, Ferri RT, Lillien L (1997) Signaling pathways that regulate specification of neurons in developing cerebral cortex. Dev Neurosci 19:6–8.

Li Z, Miller MW, Luo J (2002) Effects of prenatal exposure to ethanol on the cyclin-dependent kinase system in the developing rat cerebellum. Dev Brain Res 139:237–245.

Lipson H, Pollack JB (2000) Automatic design and manufacture of robotic lifeforms. Nature 406:974–978.

Lucas WD, Campbell BC (2000) Evolutionary and ecological aspects of early brain malnutrition in humans. Hum Nat 11:1–26.

Luo J, Miller MW (1998) Growth factor–mediated neural proliferation: target of ethanol toxicity. Brain Res Rev 27:157–167.

Lynch M, Conery JH (2000) Evolutionary fate and consequences of duplicate genes. Science 290:1151–1155.

Lynch M, Conery JS (2003) The origins of genome complexity. Science 302:1401–1404.

Malcoe LH, Lynch RA, Keger MC, Skaggs VJ (2002) Lead sources, behaviors, and socioeconomic factors in relation to blood lead of native american and white children: a community-based assessment of a former mining area. Environ Health Perspect 110 (Suppl 2):221–231.

Martinez-Frias ML, Bermejo E, Rodriguez-Pinilla E, Frias JL (2004) Risk for congenital anomalies associated with different sporadic and daily doses of alcohol consumption during pregnancy: a case–control study. Birth Defects Res Part A Clin Mol Teratol 70:194–200.

Martyn CN, Gale CR, Sayer AA, Fall C (1996) Growth in utero and cognitive function in adult life: follow-up study of people born between 1920 and 1943. BMJ 312:1393–1396.

Mattson SN, Riley EP (1998) A review of the neurobehavioral deficits in children with fetal alcohol syndrome or prenatal exposure to alcohol. Alcohol Clin Exp Res 22:279–294.

Mau G (1980) Moderate alcohol consumption during pregnancy and child development. Eur J Pediatr 133:233–237.

Miller MW (1993) Migration of cortical neurons is altered by gestational exposure to ethanol. Alcohol Clin Exp Res 17:304–314.

—— (2003) Expression of transforming growth factor-beta in developing rat cerebral cortex: effects of prenatal exposure to ethanol. J Comp Neurol 460:410–424.

Miller MW, Nowakowski R (1991) Effect of prenatal exposure to ethanol on the cell cycle kinetics and growth fraction in the proliferative zones of fetal rat cerebral cortex. Alcohol Clin Exp Res 15:229–232.

Miller MW, Potempa G (1990) Numbers of neurons and glia in mature rat somatosensory cortex: effects of prenatal exposure to ethanol. J Comp Neurol 293:92–102.

Mooney SM, Miller M (1999) Effects of prenatal exposure to ethanol on systems matching: the number of neurons in the ventrobasal thalamic nucleus of the mature rat. Dev Brain Res 117:121–125.

Morello-Frosch R, Pastor M Jr, Porras C, Sadd J (2002) Environmental justice and regional inequality in southern California: implications for future research. Environ Health Perspect 110 (Suppl 2): 149–154.

Nelson E, Jodscheit K, Guo Y (1999) Maternal passive smoking during pregnancy and fetal developmental toxicity. Part 1: gross morphological effects. Hum Exp Toxicol 18:252–256.

Nesse R, Williams G (1996) *Why We Get Sick: The New Science of Darwinian Medicine*. Vintage Books, New York.

Nolfi S, Floreano D (2002) Synthesis of autonomous robots through evolution. Trends Cogn Sci 6:31–37.

Northcutt RG (1996) The agnathan ark: the origin of craniate brains. Brain Behav Evol 48:237–247.

Ohnuma S, Harris WA (2003) Neurogenesis and the cell cycle. Neuron 40:199–208.

Olson M, Varki A (2004) The chimpanzee genome—a bittersweet celebration. Science 305:191–192.

Oppenheim RW (1991) Cell death during development of the nervous system. Annu Rev Neurosci 14: 453–502.

Pallas SL (2001) Intrinsic and extrinsic factors that shape neocortical specification. Trends Neurosci 24:417–423.

Pallas SL, Littman T, Moore DR (1999) Cross-modal reorganization of callosal connectivity without altering thalamocortical projections. Proc Natl Acad Sci USA 96:8751–8756.

Picard-Riera N, Nait-Oumesmar B, Baron-Van Evercooren A (2004) Endogenous adult neural stem cells: limits and potential to repair the injured central nervous system. J Neurosci Res 76:223–231.

Polley EH, Zimmerman RP, Fortney RL (1989) Neurogenesis and maturation of cell morphology in the development of the mammalian retina. In: Finlay BL, Sengelaub DR (eds). *Development of the Vertebrate Retina*. Plenum, New York, pp 3–29.

Popova EN (1997) Dystrophic and reparative changes in cortical neurons in the offspring of rats with moderate prenatal alcoholism. Neurosci Behav Physiol 27:189–193.

Quibell EP (1981) The thalidomide embryopathy. An analysis from the UK. Practitioner 225:721–726.

Radman M, Matic I, Taddei F (1999) Evolution of evolvability. Ann NY Acad Sci 870:146–155.

Rakic P, Caviness V Jr (1995) Cortical development: view from neurological mutants two decades later. Neuron 14:1101–1104.

Reese BE (1996) The chronotopic reordering of optic axons. Perspect Dev Neurobiol 3:233–242.

Reh T (1987) Cell-specific regulation of neuronal production in the larval frog retina. J Neurosci 7:3317–3324.

Reh TA, Levine EM (1998) Multipotential stem cells and progenitors in the vertebrate retina. J Neurobiol 36:206–220.

Rice DS, Curran T (2001) Role of the reelin signaling pathway in central nervous system development. Annu Rev Neurosci 24:1005–1039.

Richardson GA, Day NL, Goldschmidt L (1995) Prenatal alcohol, marijuana, and tobacco use: infant mental and motor development. Neurotoxicol Teratol 17:479–487.

Riley EP (1990) The long-term behavioral effects of prenatal alcohol exposure in rats. Alcohol Clin Exp Res 14:670–673.

Roe AW, Pallas SL, Hahm JO, Sur M (1990) A map of visual space induced in primary auditory cortex. Science 250:818–820.

Roe AW, Pallas SL, Kwon YH, Sur M (1992) Visual projections routed to the auditory pathway in ferrets: receptive fields of visual neurons in primary auditory cortex. J Neurosci 12:3651–3664.

Roelink H, Augsburger A, Heemskerk J, Korzh V, Norlin S, Ruiz i Altaba A, Tanabe Y, Placzek M, Edlund T, Jessell TM, Dodd J (1994) Floor plate and motor neuron induction by vhh-1, a vertebrate homolog of hedgehog expressed by the notochord. Cell 76: 761–775.

Rosenweig MR, Leiman AL, Breedlove M (1999) *Biological Psychology*. Sinauer Associates, Sunderland, MA.

Salinger WL, Ladrow P, Wheeler C (2003) Behavioral phenotype of the reeler mutant mouse: effects of *RELN* gene dosage and social isolation. Behav Neurosci 117:1257–1275.

Sapolsky RM, Krey LC, McEwen BS (1986) The neuroendocrinology of stress and aging: the glucocorticoid cascade hypothesis. Endocrinol Rev 7:284–301.

Schlaggar BL, O'Leary DD (1991) Potential of visual cortex to develop an array of functional units unique to somatosensory cortex. Science 252:1556–1560.

Schmidt JT (1985) Formation of retinotopic connections: selective stabilization by an activity-dependent mechanism. Cell Mol Neurobiol 5:65–84.

Seil FJ, Kelly JM 3rd, Leiman AL (1974) Anatomical organization of cerebral neocortex in tissue culture. Exp Neurol 45:435–450.

Smart JL, Dobbing J (1977) Increased thirst and hunger in adult rats undernourished as infants: an alternative explanation. Br J Nutr 37:421–429.

Sood B, Delaney-Black V, Covington C, Nordstrom-Klee B, Ager J, Templin T, Janisse J, Martier S, Sokol RJ (2001) Prenatal alcohol exposure and childhood behavior at age 6 to 7 years: I. dose-response effect. Pediatrics 108:E34.

Sperry RW (1963) Chemoaffinity in the orderly growth of nerve fiber patterns and their connections. Proc Natl Acad Sci USA 50:703–710.

Stephens TD (1988) Proposed mechanisms of action in thalidomide embryopathy. Teratology 38:229–239.

Stephens TD, Fillmore BJ (2000) Hypothesis: thalidomide embryopathy-proposed mechanism of action. Teratology 61:189–195.

Streissguth AP, Barr HM, Martin DC, Herman CS (1980) Effects of maternal alcohol, nicotine, and caffeine use during pregnancy on infant mental and motor development at eight months. Alcohol Clin Exp Res 4:152–164.

Streissguth AP, O'Malley K (2000) Neuropsychiatric implications and long-term consequences of fetal alcohol spectrum disorders. Semin Clin Neuropsychiatry 5:177–190.

Swillen A, Devriendt K, Legius E, Prinzic P, Vogels A, Ghesquiere P, Fryns JP (1999) The behavioural phenotype in velo-cardio-facial syndrome (VCFS): from infancy to adolescence. Genet Couns 10:79–88.

Szathmáry E, Ferenc J, Csaba P (2001) Can genes explain biological complexity? Science 292:1315–1316.

Vallortigara G, Rogers LJ (2005) Survival with an asymmetrical brain: advantages and disadvantages of cerebral lateralization. Behav Brain Sci 28: 575–633.

Viggedal G, Lundalv E, Carlsson G, Kjellmer I (2004) Neuropsychological follow-up into young adulthood of term infants born small for gestational age. Med Sci Monit 10:CR8–CR16.

von Melchner L, Pallas SL, Sur M (2000) Visual behaviour mediated by retinal projections directed to the auditory pathway. Nature 404:871–876.

Whitfield JB (1997) Meta-analysis of the effects of alcohol dehydrogenase genotype on alcohol dependence and alcoholic liver disease. Alcohol Alcohol 32:613–619.

Wolpert L (1976) Mechanisms of limb development and malformation. Br Med Bull 32:65–70.

—— (1999) Vertebrate limb development and malformations. Pediatr Res 46:247–254.

Wong ROL (1999) Retinal waves and visual system development. Annu Rev Neurosci 22:29–47.

Woo TU, Niederer JK, Finlay BL (1996) Cortical target depletion and the developing lateral geniculate nucleus: implications for trophic dependence. Cereb Cortex 6:446–456.

Xiong M, Finlay BL (1996) What do developmental mapping rules optimize? Prog Brain Res 112:350–361.

Yang TS, Shen Cheng CC, Wang CM (1977) A survey of thalidomide embryopathy in Taiwan. Taiwan Yi Xue Hui Za Zhi 76:546–562.

II

ETHANOL-AFFECTED DEVELOPMENT

8

Prenatal Alcohol Exposure and Human Development

Claire D. Coles

Although a relationship between maternal drinking and reproductive problems had been suspected long ago (Warner and Rosett, 1975; Abel, 1984), it was the description of fetal alcohol syndrome (FAS) in 1973 (Jones and Smith, 1973; Jones et al., 1973) that initiated comprehensive studies of the effects of prenatal alcohol exposure on human development. Research over the last 30 years has confirmed the original observations that affected children show growth retardation; birth defects, particularly a characteristic facial dysmorphia; and behavioral deficits indicative of central nervous system (CNS) damage (Fig. 8.1). Animal models as well as epidemiological and clinical studies in humans have provided evidence of the effects on both physical and behavioral characteristics of exposed offspring, but the CNS effects and their personal and social consequences have received the most study in human samples. There have been a number of comprehensive reviews of the results of prenatal alcohol exposure on development, particularly in early childhood (e.g., Coles, 1992, Stratton et al., 1996;

Streissguth, 1997; Mattson and Riley, 1998; US Department of Health and Human Services, 2000). Recently, publications in this area have increased so much that it is now impossible to review the entire literature in a single chapter. For that reason, this chapter refers briefly to earlier findings and deals in more detail with recent studies.

A decade ago, the following areas were among those that seemed to have the most research potential: threshold effects, neuroimaging, long-term development in affected individuals, specific versus global effects, and what is now called "translation" among the different disciplines studying this problem (Coles, 1992). These areas have remained active. In addition, several other issues have come to the fore. With better diagnosis and identification of affected individuals by professionals and increasing demand for services and resources by families, the need for improving education and remediation of affected individuals has become evident. Also, as clinical and longitudinal research cohorts have matured, different areas of

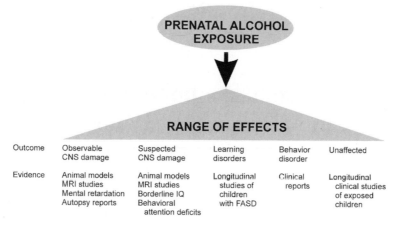

FIGURE 8–1 Range of effects of prenatal alcohol exposure on the central nervous system.

behavior have become salient. For instance, social and adaptive functions have been identified as impaired in individuals with FAS (Kelly et al., 2001), and patients from clinical samples are reported to have a high frequency of legal and mental health problems (Streissguth et al., 1996; Famy et al., 1998, Fast and Conroy, 2004). These issues are discussed below, in addition to recent research on neurodevelopmental outcomes in affected individuals.

METHODOLOGICAL CONSIDERATIONS

Despite 30 years of study, there remain significant disagreements in the literature and among the public and many professionals about the effects of prenatal alcohol exposure. Some of these discrepancies can be accounted for by differences in methodologies used to study this phenomenon. Before undertaking a review of the research literature in this area, it is important to understand how methodology affects outcomes and to acknowledge that these issues are not specific to this field.

It is obviously impossible, ethically and practically, to carry out true experimental studies of the effects of prenatal alcohol exposure on human growth, behavior, and cognition. For those aspects of development that cannot be modeled in animal studies, research must be done in either clinical samples of already affected individuals or in cohorts of offspring

of women who drink during pregnancy. Either approach has real value and real difficulties. As experimental control of the "independent" variable is not possible, such studies must be correlational and descriptive. In addition, it is usually not possible to control completely the confounders or effect modifiers in such situations. When conducting studies with samples of individuals drawn from clinical settings, researchers must take into account systematic biases and confounders. Children diagnosed with FAS or other effects of prenatal alcohol exposure come to the attention of professionals because of problems in behavior or development. Thus, it is inappropriate to use such samples to evaluate the relationship between alcohol exposure and these particular outcomes. Nevertheless, study of such children may be valuable for other research purposes. Also, many clinically identified alcohol-affected children have negative early caregiving histories resulting from maternal substance abuse, out-of-home placement, and other caregiving failures, and research with such groups must include similar contrast groups to avoid confusing the effects of pre- and postnatal environments on the outcomes of interest.

In addition to being very expensive and time consuming, exposure samples also have methodological limitations. Women who drink during pregnancy usually also smoke tobacco and may use other drugs (Day et al., 1993) (see Chapter 19), introducing other confounders into the research. They may have a genetic predisposition to alcoholism and associated mental health problems (Zucker et al., 1995), have a family history characterized by substance use and its social correlates, and be selected from a low socioeconomic status (SES) environment, as such women are more likely to be available for recruitment into exposure studies. Another limitation of the use of exposure samples is that most sample populations are composed of women drinking in the low to moderate range (e.g., Day et al., 1993; Jacobson et al., 1998). Although it is valuable to have information about the effects of lower amounts of ethanol exposure. The relative absence of exposure studies of infants of heavier drinkers is due in some part to the difficulty in recruiting such women.

For these reasons, when trying to understand the effect of alcohol exposure on offspring development, it is important to take into consideration the characteristics of the research sample and the resultant implications. Any single study may not be sufficient to understand these teratogenic effects, whereas the body of literature as a whole can provide considerable insight.

THRESHOLDS AND DOSE–RESPONSE EFFECTS OF PRENATAL ALCOHOL EXPOSURE

There is a great deal of interest in the question of the "dose" of alcohol necessary to cause negative outcomes. For public health reasons, it would be valuable to know if there is a "safe" level of prenatal exposure. This is a complicated question. Some researchers posit that the construct of threshold is not useful because it oversimplifies the real relationship between the teratogen and the multiple outcomes that are measured (Sampson et al., 2000). Sampson and colleagues argue in their review that there are no meaningful differences in behavior, standard scores, academic outcomes, and behavior between those individuals labeled as having FAS and those characterized as having alcohol-related neurodevelopment disorders (ARND). They believe that behavioral outcome does not vary with variation in physical teratogenic effects. In addition, these researchers present evidence from their large prospective exposure study suggesting that the relationship between prenatal exposure and neurodevelopmental outcomes is monotonic, or without meaningful threshold

effects "when dose and behavioral effects are quantified appropriately" (p. 421).

Other investigators have identified threshold effects in their samples. Jacobson and colleagues (1998) found that aspects of infant cognition show threshold effects. At 26 months in their cohort, psychomotor functioning and aspects of fine motor functioning are affected only in the offspring of heavier drinkers (Kaplin-Estrin et al., 1999), although none of these children exhibit physical dysmorphia. In another sample, Day and colleagues (1991, 1999, 2002) show that growth is affected in a dose–response fashion. Growth is more affected in individuals whose mothers drank most heavily (>1 drink/day); they average 14 pounds less than controls. Similar relationships are evident for cognition and achievement. When this cohort was 6 years old, a threshold of exposure to one drink daily is found for academic achievement in reading and spelling, whereas effects on mathematics skills are linear (Goldschmidt et al., 1996).

In addition, as discussed below, the morphological outcomes characteristic of prenatal alcohol exposure appear to be affected in a dose–response manner (Lynch et al., 2004). All of these reports suggest that heavier drinking is associated with greater physical and neurodevelopmental effects. The extent to which results can be described as monotonic or reflective of "thresholds" in alcohol use may depend on the type of samples recruited and the amount of exposure in the sample as well as by the methods used in the study and in the data analysis.

PHYSICAL EFFECTS OF PRENATAL ALCOHOL EXPOSURE

Facial Dysmorphia

The facial dysmorphia associated with heavy exposure is one of the three diagnostic features used to define FAS. These features include midface hypoplasia (anteverted nares), short palpebral fissures, and flattened or indistinct philtrum, usually associated with a thin or flattened upper vermillion border. Other minor anomalies also are commonly found in affected children, including epicanthal folds, low nasal bridge, ear anomalies (low set and rotated), and micrognathia. The craniofacial anomalies are believed to be the result of disturbances of cell migration during organogenesis (US Department of Health and Human Services, 2000; see Chapter 17). In practice, assessment of these anomalies is complicated by variance associated with age and ethnicity. When affected individuals are followed over childhood into early adulthood, some of the individual features that are salient during infancy and early childhood become harder to identify, particularly after puberty (Streissguth, 1997).

Several different "systems" of diagnosis are used in clinical diagnosis and research on FAS. Astley and Clarren (2001) have proposed a system that focuses on "sentinel features," which they have identified through analysis of a large sample of children who applied for diagnostic services. In this large clinical sample, several facial features have been found to be associated with the diagnosis at each stage of development. These features are (1) an absent or indistinct philthrum, (2) a thinned upper vermillion, and (3) shortened palpebral fissures. In their four-digit code method for diagnosis, these facial features constitute one dimension necessary for diagnosis (Astley, 2004). Other dimensions are growth (less than third percentile), maternal alcohol use, and evidence of CNS involvement.

The Collaborative Initiative on Fetal Alcohol Spectrum Disorders, sponsored by the National Institute on Alcoholism and Alcohol Abuse, has developed a Dysmorphia Core Physical Exam that is used in international studies to diagnosis participants of all ages and ethnicities (May et al., 2000; Hoyme et al., 2005). This method, developed by Jones and colleagues (1973), is based on the original descriptions of FAS and is a modification of the criteria offered by the Institute of Medicine (Stratton et al., 1996). As in other systems, the child is measured and examined for physical and facial anomalies, as well as height, weight, head circumference, and heart and neurological problems. Then a determination is made as to whether the child can be rated as (1) having FAS, (2) not having FAS, or (3) deferred. The classification "deferred" indicates that some characteristics are present but that the diagnosis cannot be made without more information (e.g., neurodevelopmental test results). This methodology has been used in Russia and South Africa as well as the United States (Hoyme et al., 2005).

Coles and colleagues (Fernhoff et al., 1980; Blackston et al., 2004; Lynch et al., 2004) have used a slightly different methodology. In a longitudinally followed exposure sample report, a dose–response pattern between alcohol exposure and physical characteristics can be identified both in the neonatal period and later in development. The same dysmorphic features, however, are not always salient over development. Rather, it is the total "dysmorphia score" that is reliable from infancy through middle adolescence. More longitudinal research is needed to determine the continuity of physical characteristics, particularly facial anomalies, to provide guidelines for making the diagnosis in older children and adults. This kind of research is important also because there may be ethnic differences in facial characteristics that can affect diagnosis. Finally, it is necessary to use a longitudinal approach because use of clinical samples in a cohort design exaggerates the salience of features that are expected to be part of the criteria and ignores individuals whose features are not consistent with these expectations.

Effect of Alcohol Exposure on Growth

Growth retardation is useful for the identification of FAS during infancy and the preschool period, but it is less consistently evident in older children and youth (Streissguth, 1997; Coles et al., 2002). It is difficult to evaluate this factor in clinical samples because the argument is necessarily circular. This criterion is used in making a clinical diagnosis, hence such individuals are necessarily growth retarded. Exposed individuals who present for diagnosis do not receive it if they are not growth retarded. Long-term follow-up of children identified early in life is necessary to confirm persistent growth deficits. For this reason, exposure studies provide a better method for evaluation of this outcome. Generally, children exposed to alcohol appear to be statistically smaller than controls or than national norms (Day et al., 1999, 2002). Often means are within normal ranges, however, so although this characteristic is statistically "real," it may or may not be of clinical significance, and it is not necessarily helpful in identification of specific individuals if prenatal alcohol exposure is not known. It is not yet established whether lower birth weight, height, and head circumference associated with prenatal alcohol exposure (and, perhaps, associated polydrug use) are risk factors for other conditions occurring later in life.

NEURODEVELOPMENTAL EFFECTS
OF PRENATAL
ALCOHOL EXPOSURE

Effects on Brain Structure:
Information from
Neuroimaging studies

The following section briefly reviews neuroimaging studies of the effects of prenatal alcohol exposure on brain structure. Brain morphology could be described as a "physical effect" of prenatal exposure, as well; a fuller discussion of this subject is provided in Chapter 9.

Both human studies of behavior and animal models leave no doubt that alcohol is a teratogen that has toxic effects on the brain. Until recently, it was impossible to evaluate directly its effect on human brain structure and functioning, but in the last decade, imaging studies of alcohol-affected patients have been conducted. Several research groups using clinical samples of patients with fetal alcohol spectrum disorders (FASD) have reported effects on the brain in older children and adults. Most of these published studies have used structural magnetic resonance imaging (sMRI) and have focused on morphology. Several studies (Bookstein et al., 2001, 2002; Sowell et al., 2001b) have correlated structural outcomes with neurobehavioral data. Although functional magnetic resonance imaging (fMRI) is being developed as a research tool in this area, no studies have been published as of this writing.

In sMRI studies, microcephaly has been the most consistent finding, with FAS patients having a general reduction in brain volume compared to that of contrast groups (Riley et al., 1995; Archibald et al., 2001; Sowell et al., 2001a, 2001b; Bhatara et al., 2002). More specifically, relative reductions in white matter have been noted the corpus callosum and the parietal lobe (Riikonen et al., 1999; Archibald et al., 2001; Sowell et al., 2001b) in patients with FAS. The corpus callosum has been a focus of interest because it is a midline structure and is readily identifiable. Agenesis and hypoplasia of this structure have been reported repeatedly, particularly in extremely dysmorphic individuals (Riley et al., 1995; Johnson et al., 1996; Swayze et al., 1997; Riikonen et al., 1999; Sowell et al., 2001b; Bhatara et al., 2002). Sowell and colleagues (2001b) reported reductions and displace-ments in the anterior region of the corpus callosum as well as in the splenium, which correlated with deficits in verbal learning and memory in the same patients. Bookstein and colleagues (2001, 2002) reported that there is greater variability in the shape of the corpus callosum among alcohol-affected patients and that thicker or thinner structures are related to specific patterns of neurodevelopmental deficits: a thicker corpus callosum is associated with deficits in executive functioning, whereas a thinner one accompanies motor deficits.

The cerebellum can be affected by prenatal exposure to ethanol. It is smaller in children with FAS (Riikonen et al., 1999; Autti-Ramo et al., 2002), particularly in the anterior vermis (lobules I–V) (Sowell et al., 1996). These findings are supported by animal studies (e.g., Goodlett and Lundahl, 1996). Many studies report other specific deficits in CNS morphology, although none as consistently as those of the corpus callosum and the cerebellum.

Studies on the structural effect of prenatal exposure on the brain indicate that significant morphological changes can be found. It is not clear, however, that a specific area of deficit is present in all cases. This finding suggests that the teratogenic effect is more general. Several candidates for further research have emerged from these data, but even the corpus callosum, which has been implicated frequently, does not show specific macrostructural patterns related to alcohol exposure across all studies. For instance, although callosal agenesis has been reported (Riley et al., 1995; Johnson et al., 1996; Bhatara et al., 2002), other studies find thinning of these areas or posterior displacement (Sowell et al., 2001b), and yet other studies find macrostructural anomalies only in a minority of individuals with FAS (Autti-Ramo et al., 2002). This situation is further complicated by a study in nonhuman primates showing that repeated, episodic exposure to ethanol during pregnancy can result in an increase in the size of the corpus callosum, especially the anterior segment (Miller et al., 1999). These outcomes suggest that, particularly in individuals whose alcohol effects are subtle, gross anatomical studies may not be observable.

A complementary imaging technique to sMRI is diffusion tensor imaging (DTI), which allows the measurement of white matter integrity. In FAS patients, sMRI studies frequently report effects on integrity of white matter tracts (Johnson et al., 1996;

Swayze et al., 1997; Clark et al., 2000; Archibald et al., 2001; Sowell et al., 2001b; Bhatara et al., 2002). Through DTI, Ma and colleagues (2005) found that fractional anistropy in the genu and splenium of the corpus callosum of alcohol-affected young adults was significantly lower than that of age-matched controls. This suggests an association of teratogenic exposure and white matter integrity.

Although in an early stage of exploration, neuroimaging procedures hold promise for understanding the teratogenic effects of prenatal exposure. When fMRI studies are published and functional outcomes are correlated with behavioral outcomes, knowledge of structure-function-behavior relationships in these patients will be greatly advanced.

Motor and Neuromotor Effects

Alcohol effects on psychomotor function have been observed regularly in infants and toddlers (Coles et al., 1985; Coles, 1993; Jacobson et al., 1993; see discussion of Jacobson et al., 1988, above). Problems in motor functioning in older children are less well documented but are reported (Aronson et al., 1985; Kyllerman et al., 1985; Janzen et al., 1995). Descriptive studies of children with FAS consistently note deficits in motor skills and coordination (Mattson and Riley, 1998). Among quasi-experimental research designs with children diagnosed with FAS are deficits in visual–motor integration (Conry, 1990; Coles et al., 1991; Mattson et al., 1993) and fine-motor strength and coordination (Barr et al., 1990; Conry, 1990). Kyllerman and colleagues (1985) found that children (mean age 70 months) born to women who abuse alcohol had lower motor development scores and did more poorly on tests of motor coordination than did those in a comparison group who were not prenatally exposed. Children with FAS also show deficits in balance (Marcus, 1987; Roebuck et al., 1998a, 1998b), increased clumsiness (Steinhausen et al., 1982), abnormal gait (Marcus, 1987; Conn-Blower, 1991) and tremors (Aronson et al., 1985; Marcus, 1987). Roebuck and colleagues (Roebuck et al., 1998a, 1998b) suggest that damage to the cerebellum from heavy prenatal alcohol exposure may interfere with efficient use of visual and somatosensory system cues. Using electromyography, these researchers concluded that this deficit was the result of damage to the CNS rather than to the peripheral nervous system controlling muscles or vestibular system.

Peripheral systems are affected by prenatal exposure to alcohol. Avaria and colleagues (2003) examined nerve conduction in median, ulnar, peroneal, and tibial nerves in newborns who were re-examined as toddlers at 12 and 14 months. Ulnar and tibial motor nerve velocities are slower and distal amplitudes are lower in ethanol-exposed children. The observed changes differed from those in alcoholic peripheral neuropathy of adults and reflected both myelin involvement (reduced velocity) and axonal damage (decreased amplitude). In contrast, assessment of sensory nerve conduction does not identify significant differences between alcohol-exposed infants and those in the control group. No clinical correlates are noted in either group of infants.

Although research in this area is limited, these studies and persistent clinical reports suggest that further exploration of effects on motor and sensory/ motor development is warranted. Deficits in these areas have a significant effect on early life, potentially affecting physical, cognitive, and social development. In addition, early motor deficits are often correlated with specific learning and academic problems at school age and later.

Global and Specific Effects on Neurocognitive Functioning

Global Cognitive Effects

Global intellectual deficits are the primary neurodevelopmental outcome associated with prenatal alcohol exposure. This is consistent with the results of other early neurological insults that, contrary to the adult pattern, tend to be more global than specific. Deficits in general intellectual function (that is, scores on intelligence or other ability tests) have been observed in sample populations composed of children diagnosed with FAS and in those drawn from longitudinal studies of heavy gestational alcohol exposure. Children meeting the diagnostic criteria for FAS show a relatively broad range of intellectual outcomes with sample estimates ranging from severe intellectual deficiency to average levels of functioning (e.g., IQs range from 20 to 120; Mattson and Riley, 1998; and from 16 to 105; Streissguth et al., 1978). Mean performance on standardized measures of intellectual function typically have been in the borderline to mildly deficient range (IQs range from 65 to 75) (Stratton et al., 1996). In large retrospective and prospective studies, half of the children with FAS meet criteria for mental retardation, an IQ < 70 on a standardized measure of intelligence (Abel, 1998). There has also been discussion of the effect of prenatal exposure to low or moderate levels of alcohol and most research studies have reported that in such cohorts there is a decrement of several IQ points (4 to 6) attributable to the exposure (e.g., Streissguth et al., 1993).

Specific Cognitive Effects

In addition to motor problems, functions that have been examined and appear to be affected by prenatal alcohol exposure include specific deficits in visual–spatial processing, arousal and regulation of attention, working memory, planning and organizational skills, mathematical achievement, and behavioral regulation. In reading the literature, it is important to examine the extent to which global deficits have been taken into consideration in the interpretation of "specific" deficits in outcome. Individuals showing mental retardation or borderline intellectual functioning (IQ < 85) cannot be compared to normal controls (IQ = 100) on specific neurocognitive tasks without accounting for global deficits. Those studies that have controlled for overall IQ or that have ascertained appropriate contrast groups are more convincing than those that have not.

Visual–Spatial Processing.   Evidence for a specific deficit in visual–spatial processing (Spohr et al., 1993; Ueckerer and Nadel, 1996; Coles et al., 2002) has been found. Mattson and Riley (1998) found that mean verbal IQ was 61.00 ± 12.82, whereas mean performance IQ was 55.33 ± 13.45. This pattern is similar to that seen in individuals with nonverbal learning disabilities (Rourke, 1995). Deficits in visual memory (Carmichael-Olson et al., 1998; Kaemingk and Paquette, 1999; Platzman et al., 2001), visual perceptual skills (Steinhausen et al., 1982; Aronson et al., 1985; Morse et al., 1992; Aronson and Hagberg, 1998), visual–motor integration (Janzen et al., 1995; Mattson et al., 1998; Kaemingk and Paquette, 1999), and spatial memory (Ueckerer and Nadel, 1998) have been reported. A specific deficit in visual processing, which is independent of the global intellectual deficit, is suggested by findings from a cohort of alcohol-exposed individuals seen during adolescence (Coles et al., 2002). In this study, visual and auditory sustained

attention were compared and adolescents with dysmorphic (i.e., FAS) and nondysmorphic FASD were less efficient at processing visual than auditory information. Sensitivity to the visual stimuli was significantly lower in alcohol-affected youth, a finding suggesting that the neurocognitive impact of alcohol exposure is more significant for tasks that involve visual stimuli than for auditory stimuli.

There are inconsistencies in reported outcomes on the effects of ethanol on sensory processing. Not all studies have found a specific or consistent impairment in visual or spatial processing of information, and some report that auditory information processing is more impaired (e.g., Janzen et al., 1995; Kerns et al., 1997; Connor et al., 1999). Certainly, there may be a real difference as a function of exposure in different groups of individuals; however, methodological differences among studies and in analysis strategies may also contribute to the variability. On the basis of a review of retrospective and prospective longitudinal studies and individual case studies, Mattson and Riley (1998) suggest that relative deficits in visual and verbal learning are equivalent. They compared studies of children with FASD and studies of children with low to moderate alcohol exposure for whom no diagnosis could be made. These groups of children may have different patterns of deficits. Studies of diagnosed individuals also vary in the extent to which they attempt to equate the discriminative power of the tasks by modality (auditory or visual) and whether they control for overall ability in the analyses. Differences in SES may also contribute to discrepancies in outcome across studies. Children with FAS from low SES environments have verbal IQs that are lower than their performance IQs (Conry, 1990; Kerns et al., 1997). Conry (1990), who included a low SES contrast group, concluded after examining discrepancy scores that "alcohol-involvement appeared to have greater effects on visual/spatial problem solving than on verbal effects" (p. 654).

Arousal and Attention.   The regulation of attention in prenatally exposed children has been a matter of persistent interest (Kopera-Frye et al., 1997). So commonly is attention deficit hyperactivity disorder (ADHD) diagnosed in children with FAS and associated disorders that some have suggested that ADHD is a hallmark of a behavioral phenotype associated with exposure (O'Malley and Nanson, 2002). Leaving aside the issue of the existence of such a phenotype, the regulation of attention is of great importance, as mastery of arousal and attention is a prerequisite for learning and social development (MacKintosh, 1975) and thus has the potential to mediate a number of long-term neurodevelopmental outcomes. Many children with FAS have difficulties with regulation of arousal; this problem may be associated with their ADHD diagnosis (Streissguth et al., 1986, 1995; Nanson and Hiscock, 1990; Kopera-Frye et al., 1997; Oesterheld and Wilson, 1997) or other alterations in attention (Streissguth et al., 1984; Coles et al., 1997).

Investigations into the effect of prenatal alcohol exposure on attentional regulation that have used prospective longitudinal designs have produced inconsistent results. Streissguth and colleagues (1984) found that prenatal alcohol exposure resulted in more errors and slower reaction times on a task of vigilance and sustained attention in preschool children with moderate alcohol exposure. In the same cohort, observations of children's behavior by trained observers and ratings by parents suggest that exposed children are less attentive, less compliant, and more fidgety (Landesman-Dwyer and Ragozin, 1981). These results have not always been confirmed by other prospective studies using exposure samples (i.e., Boyd et al., 1991; Coles et al., 1997). Brown and colleagues (1991) also show an association between gestational alcohol exposure and regulation of attention, but they attribute their results to the effects of the postnatal environment. A four-factor, multidimensional model of attentional regulation (Mirsky et al., 1991) was used to assess 7-year-olds prenatally exposed to alcohol (Coles et al., 1997). These children differ significantly from a contrast group of children diagnosed with ADHD in their ability to attend. Alcohol-affected children have more difficulty encoding information and in flexibility in problem solving, but they are similar to controls in their abilities to focus and sustain attention. The children diagnosed with ADHD have a contrasting pattern.

Hypothesizing that early difference in arousal levels noted in alcohol-exposed infants (Coles et al., 1985) might be associated with later problems in self-regulation and attention, Kable and Coles (2004) further examined the relationship of alcohol exposure and information processing in a different sample of high-risk, low-birth-weight infants who had been exposed to moderate amounts of alcohol. Behaviorally, at 6 and 12 months, these infants show small but significant developmental differences in mental and psychomotor development as well as in behavior regulation (Coles et al., 2000). When they were 6 months old, the infants' attention was evaluated by use of a habituation paradigm with cardiac orienting response as outcome. Infants with more alcohol exposure respond more slowly than "low-risk" controls to presentation of both visual and auditory stimuli and are rated as significantly higher in arousal level. This difference in information-processing speed is consistent with earlier work (Jacobson et al., 1994) showing that fixation duration (looking time) is longer in alcohol-exposed infants. The implication is that alcohol is related to the speed of information processing.

The relationship between attention and arousal regulation is suggestive. The ability to focus and sustain attention depends on the ability to moderate arousal to allow information to be processed efficiently (Ruff and Rothbart, 1996). It may be that alcohol-exposed infants cannot modulate arousal effectively and are therefore less efficient in processing environmental information. Findings among adolescents and adults of inefficiencies in information processing in the visual modality (e.g., Coles et al., 2002) or in both auditory and visual modalities (Connor et al., 1999) may be influenced by arousal level as well. This suggestion is supported by findings from a study of the effects of maternal substance abuse on attention. Suess and colleagues (1994) found that prenatal exposure to alcohol, but not opiates, influenced attention and psychophysiology (cardiac functioning and vagal tone) at school age. How this compromise is related to developmentally later and more complex cognitive functions and attention and behavioral regulation has not yet been investigated.

Executive Function Skills. Executive function is a construct referred to as, "perhaps the most appealing, yet least understood, aspect of cognition and metacognition" (Borkowski and Burke, 1996, p. 235). *Executive function* involves higher-order cognitive processes that range from attentional regulation, working memory skills, planning and organizational thinking and problem solving (Lyon, 1996; Morris, 1996). From an information-processing prospective, attention, memory, and executive function may be interrelated processes that affect cognitive functioning and the ability to carry out goal-oriented behaviors (Borkowski and Burke, 1996).

Both clinical descriptions of children with FAS and longitudinal exposure studies implicate ethanol in compromising executive function. Investigators have approached this construct from several theoretical positions. Some investigators aggregate measures to obtain an estimate of executive function (e.g., Sampson et al., 1997; Connor et al., 2000), whereas others evaluate specific areas thought to represent aspects of executive function (e.g., Kerns et al., 1997; Mattson et al., 1999; Schonfeld et al., 2001). It is difficult to compare studies because the construct per se is not well defined. Therefore, the following review will examine the effect of prenatal alcohol exposure on various components that are usually understood to be part of executive functioning.

Memory and Metamemory. Memory is a broad field of study, and only some aspects of memory are considered to be part of executive function. Children with FAS exhibit deficits in memory skills, but the impairments are not always stable and their extent seems to be influenced by modality of the task used and by the specific cognitive demands of tasks (Mattson and Roebuck, 2002). For instance, an interaction of age and task characteristics may determine whether effects are shown. Using the McCarthy Scales of Children's Abilities (McCarthy, 1972), Janzen and colleagues (1995) do not find differences in memory function between young children diagnosed with FAS and a contrast group selected from day-care settings. This finding contrasts with a study by Coles and colleagues (2004), who used a different test. They find that children in the same age range do have specific memory deficits.

The effect of presentation modality (i.e., visual–auditory) on memory has been investigated. Learning and recall on tasks presented visually or in narrative form were compared (Platzman et al., 2001). Adolescents with FAS have poorer recall of visual elements than controls and age mates in special education programs, whereas long-term recall of auditorily presented items is not impaired. Short-term memory for auditorily presented items (i.e., random strings of digits; Wechsler Intelligence Scale for Children–Revised, Digit Span) is also similar to that of contrast groups. In a different sample of clinically referred children, ages 3 to 9 years old, with a diagnosis of FASD, a similar auditory task and a visual/spatial analog were contrasted. Relative deficits for spatial span are evident, whereas performance on the digit span task is consistent with overall ability level (Coles et al., 2004). These findings suggest specific deficits in memory with

language-related or auditorily presented materials relatively spared. This pattern of performance is also noted by Mattson and Roebuck (2002) among school-aged and adolescent children diagnosed with FAS or having had heavy prenatal exposure. In this group, memory performance is compared to that of normal controls on five standardized measures of learning and memory: a verbal learning task (California Verbal Learning Test–Children's Version [CVLT-C]; Delis et al., 1987), the Biber Figure Learning Test, and three subtests from the Wide Range Assessment of Memory and Learning (WRAML; Sheslow and Adams, 1990). These subtests are Verbal Learning, Visual Learning, and Sound Symbol. The construction of the CVLT-C is important for understanding the results of these studies. This test is a verbal learning task with orally presented lists of words in several categories (i.e., clothing, fruits, and toys). Due to the list structure, an effective memory strategy (grouping by semantic category) can be used to aid learning and recall.

Through the use of tests of verbal and visual memory, it has been shown that alcohol-affected children learn fewer items (both words and figures) overall than controls (Mattson and Roebuck, 2002). After a standard delay period, however, the percentage recalled (of the material that *had* been learned) is not different between the groups for verbal material. On the nonverbal material, the alcohol-affected group show relative deficits in delayed recall. Thus, verbal memory is less affected than nonverbal memory. Data from these studies have been reanalyzed to examine the effect of stimulus differences in two of the verbal memory tasks (Roebuck-Spencer and Mattson, 2004). Accordingly, children with FASD demonstrate semantic clustering on the CVLT-C, indicating that they are able to take advantage of the list characteristics to aid recall. They perform better on this task than on the WRAML verbal memory task, which does not offer the same opportunity to use the "implicit" memory strategy inherent in the stimulus material. On the basis of these findings, the authors argue that previously observed differences in verbal and nonverbal memory may result from use of more effective memory strategies on verbal learning tasks. Other work (i.e., Platzman et al., 2001; Coles et al., 2004, see discussion above) does not support this explanation because visually and auditorially presented materials are equivalent in these studies.

Various studies report that children with FASD have memory deficits on verbal learning tasks (Mattson et al., 1996; Kerns et al., 1997; Schonfeld et al., 2001; Willford et al., 2004). A longitudinal follow-up study of 14-year-olds shows that verbal–auditory rather than visuospatial memory is affected with learning; short- and long-term memory deficits on a paired associate task are detected (Willford et al., 2004). In a sample of adolescents and young adults classified as having an "average IQ" or "below average IQ," Kerns and colleagues (1997) show that individuals with FAS perform below expectation on the CVLT-C. The greatest difference is not on initial learning trials, but on the fifth trial. These results suggest that affected individuals are not able to use semantic memory strategies appropriately to maintain a comparable learning slope over repeated trials. That is, the individuals with FAS do not use the categories inherent in the lists to organize and facilitate their recall and their responses do not show the clustering of semantically related items that is usually found if effective memory strategies are used. This finding contrasts to a lack of difference in primacy effect and serial clustering scores, which relies less on strategy use.

Mattson and Riley (1999) contrast intentional and incidental memory by measuring recall of information (a) when children with FAS are aware of the memory task involved and (b) when they learn information using effective memory strategies provided by the investigators without being aware of the need to learn the information in expectation of recall. The investigators conclude that incidental memory is not affected by prenatal alcohol exposure.

Coles and colleagues (1997) gave an alcohol-exposed and a contrast group of 7-year-olds a paired associate task requiring that the children continue with the list-learning process until they achieve mastery. At both immediate and delayed recall, alcohol-affected children are not different from controls with this methodology. The number of repetitions required to achieve list mastery, however, is significantly higher for alcohol-affected children.

Cumulatively, the above findings suggest that one aspect of the memory deficit observed in alcohol-affected individuals involves employing strategies. That is, they may not be exhibiting effective "metamemory" (an important aspect of executive functioning) in that they may have more difficulty in selecting and employing effective learning strategies and they may not be aware of the level of effort required to achieve mastery on a particular task. It may also be that because alcohol-affected individuals process information more

slowly, learning time is spent less efficiently and more trials are required. Whether these deficits are unique to individuals with FASD or are characteristic of slow learners in general is not clear and should be the subject of further study.

An aspect of memory that is considered a factor in executive processing is active working memory. This process involves mental manipulation of elements stored briefly in short-term memory and has been referred to as a "mental scratch pad" (Ashcraft, 1995). It requires that information be stored and processed in meaningful "units" at a given moment in time. Many of the cognitive tasks comprising neurodevelopmental test batteries include use of active working memory because higher-order processing or problem solving requires that several units of information be maintained simultaneously.

In alcohol-affected individuals, problems in active working memory have been identified early in infancy. Using a visual expectancy paradigm (Haith et al., 1988; Jacobson et al., 1992) as a measure of working memory, Wass and Haith (1999) show that 3-month-old infants exposed to alcohol prenatally have more difficulty than nonexposed controls in maintaining and manipulating three items of information simultaneously, a result implying a reduction in working memory capacity. On the same task, these infants have difficulties shifting from one rule to another (that is, learning to anticipate where items would be presented next) and with mastering complex spatial sequences. Kodituwakku and colleagues (1995) used several neurodevelopmental tasks tapping active working memory in older individuals. They conclude that a problem in managing goals in working memory is the mechanism underlying much of the cognitive impairment seen in children with FAS. In practical terms, such a deficit will affect daily functioning and academic performance as well as results of neuropsychological tests. For instance, children diagnosed with FAS consistently show impairments in doing mathematics, as demonstrated by performance on the arithmetic subtests from the Wechsler series (e.g., Wechsler, 1991) of intelligence tests. These tests rely heavily on active working memory skills by requiring the manipulation of numbers and arithmetic operations in short-term memory to generate correct answers.

Planning and Organization. People with FASD are described as having impairments in planning, organization, and problem-solving aspects of executive functioning (Streissguth, 1997). Two tasks that have been used to evaluate functioning in this area are progressive planning tasks (e.g., Tower of London; Shallice, 1982) and tasks assessing learning and reversal or shifts in discriminative stimuli (i.e., Wisconsin Card Sort Task [WCST]; Heaton et al., 1993). Both kinds of tasks were originally used to measure the effects of frontal lobe damage in adults (Shallice, 1982). Progressive planning tasks require that the person being tested replicate a visually presented design by rearranging circular disks or balls that are placed on vertical pegs. There are rules restraining the number and type of moves permitted. The task requires that the subject retain these rules as well as the sequence of moves in working memory to correctly solve the problem. Initially, the task is simple and requires little planning, but as task complexity increases, the individual must be able to visualize a multistep sequence of moves to complete the task successfully.

The WCST and similar tasks require the individual to identify or sort according to specific characteristics of the stimuli (i.e., color, number, or shape) presented to them, with feedback provided to facilitate learning. For the initial set of trials, the correct dimension may be color, so that all responses that match in color are rewarded. Once the correct dimension is reliably learned, a different dimension becomes "correct" so that, for instance, number becomes the correct solution and is rewarded. This task requires cognitive flexibility, because the individual must inhibit previously learned responses and shift sets or rules learned from previous trials.

Using both kinds of tasks, children with FAS have been found to perform more poorly than controls and to make perseveration errors (repetition of responses that are incorrect or not reinforced) (Kodituwakku et al., 1995; Coles et al., 1997; Kerns et al., 1997). These findings suggest that they have difficulty incorporating environmental feedback to correct a response. Children with FAS typically have more difficulty learning the shifts, particularly reversal shifts, than would be expected (Kodituwakku et al., 1995; Coles et al., 1997; Kerns et al., 1997), a pattern implying difficulties with inhibition of learned responses or an inattentiveness to new information.

Kodituwakku and colleagues (2001) used another paradigm to discriminate emotion-laden learning from conceptual set shifting (the reversal shift tasks discussed above) to further document neurodevelopmental impairments associated with FAS. These au-

thors expected performance of alcohol-exposed individuals to be impaired in tasks that involved an emotional component. In this study, performance on the WCST was contrasted with that on a different task that assessed visual-discrimination reversal learning as well as extinction of reward–response associations (Rolls et al., 1994). This second task was assumed to measure emotion-related learning because a reward was provided rather than the feedback provided in the WCST. After controlling for conceptual set shifting (performance on the WCST) and for general intellectual abilities, school-age, alcohol-exposed children perform more poorly than the reference sample on emotion-related learning; they achieve fewer reversals and show more variability in extinction. In addition, there is a significant relationship between these measures of emotion-related learning and conceptual shifting and parent-reported behavior problems. The ability to regulate arousal may have affected performance on this learning task, although this issue is not addressed in this study.

ACADEMIC ACHIEVEMENT

Given the neurocognitive problems identified in exposed individuals, it is not surprising that academic achievement is frequently affected. Learning problems, school failure, repeating grades, and dropping out of school have all been cited as negative outcomes associated with FAS in clinical samples (Streissguth et al., 1996; Autti-Ramo, 2000). It is important to bear in mind that for alcohol-exposed as well as for other children, academic achievement is determined by complex interactions between the child's neurodevelopmental status, environmental supports for academic success, and emotional stability.

Overall academic achievement is predicted by the individual's general intellectual ability and by SES. Academic problems consistent with global ability deficits are typically seen. There may also be specific areas of academic weakness for the child with FAS beyond those associated with cognitive deficit and social disadvantage. Research suggests that, relative to general intellectual ability, alcohol-exposed children and adolescents have specific learning problems with mathematics (Spohr and Steinhausen, 1984; Streissguth et al., 1994). Deficits in math achievement associated with prenatal alcohol exposure have been identified regularly in both longitudinal and clinical studies

(Streissguth et al., 1994; Kodituwakku et al., 1995; Goldschmidt et al., 1996; Mattson et al., 1996). Streissguth and colleagues (1993) report that arithmetic disabilities are related to prenatal alcohol exposure in their longitudinal cohort, particularly when there was "massed" or heavy drinking. These investigators also note that their findings in the longitudinal cohort are consistent with observations from their older, clinical sample of patients diagnosed with FAS. Other longitudinal samples have also found evidence of specific deficits in this area. Coles and colleagues (Coles et al., 1991, 1997; Howell et al., 2006) note specific deficits in math functioning in a cohort of African-American school children even when global delays are controlled. In this population, these problems appear to be related to deficits in visuospatial and visual–motor functioning. Jacobson (1999) note problems in math in a Detroit longitudinal cohort as well and attribute these difficulties to problems with working memory and executive functioning skills.

In a sample population including both inner-city and suburban 4½-year-old children with low birth weight, specific deficits in preacademic mathematical skills are identified among alcohol exposed children (Kable et al., 1999). Higher scores on a cumulative risk index related to alcohol and other drug use are significantly related to poorer performance on the Test of Early Mathematics Ability, 2nd Edition (Ginsburg and Baroody, 1990), on a number of specific preacademic skills, including cardinality, constancy, counting, and visual recognition of numbers. Apparently, problems with working memory, visual perception, and executive functioning underlie these functional problems. Adults with FAS also showed mathematics-related difficulties, including computation, and in solving problems requiring estimation of magnitude (Kopera-Frye et al., 1996). Thus, there is considerable evidence that this academic area is a problem in affected individuals, due, no doubt, to deficits in cognitive processes that support math achievement. Some candidate processes are those areas discussed above in this chapter—i.e., attention, executive functioning, and working memory as well as visuospatial skills (Geary, 1993; Ashcraft, 1995).

SOCIAL AND EMOTIONAL FUNCTIONING

Problems with behavior and emotional regulation are the most frequent reason for clinical referral of children

suspected of fetal alcohol exposure (e.g., Steinhausen et al., 1993; Janzen et al., 1995; Kopera-Frye et al., 1997; Oesterheld and Wilson, 1997; Roebuck et al., 1999; Mattson and Riley, 2000; Kodituwakku et al., 2001). Social and emotional problems are so commonly reported by parents and in clinical studies it has been suggested that "people with FAS appear to differ from the mentally retarded population because of additional problems in the social domain" (Kelly et al., 2001, p. 143). In a survey of a clinical population of individuals with FAS and ARND, Streissguth and colleagues (1996) report a high frequency of mental health, legal, and social problems among the secondary disabilities in this group. The vast majority (94%) of individuals are reported to have mental health problems of some kind, with the most common psychiatric problems being ADHD and depression. These reports are certainly a concern, but it may be too early to interpret these outcomes as the direct results of the teratogenic exposure, particularly as this survey did not include a comparison group and was drawn from a clinically referred population that should be expected to have such problems.

In interpreting reports from clinical samples or from samples that are self-referred (e.g., O'Connor et al., 2002), some other factors that might influence behavior should be taken into account. Many children with FASD experience environmental factors known to contribute to behavioral, social, and emotional problems, and it is disingenuous to ignore these issues to attribute problems to prenatal exposure. Children diagnosed with FAS often come from low-income or socially disadvantaged families and usually have limited access to educational or other resources. Caregiving disruptions are the norm rather than the exception in children referred to clinical settings, and many children are in foster care following a history of neglect and abuse.

To examine the frequency of behavior concerns in a clinical sample of alcohol-affected children, Coles and Kable (unpublished results) evaluated 287 patients (mean age, 4.5 years) referred for evaluation to a FAS specialty clinic. Of the 109 children diagnosed with FAS, 54.7% were described as "too active," 30.5% had difficulties with tantrums, and 41.1% were described as having problems with aggression. When these children are compared to those referred to the same clinic who have no evidence of dysmorphia or growth problems and to those with no history of prenatal alcohol exposure, the frequency of the same problems is 53.1%, 25.0%, and 43.8%, respectively. Upon further examination of the clinic sample and dividing it into four groups (FAS, ARND, nondysmorphic FASD, and unexposed), no significant relationship between diagnostic category and behavioral or emotional outcomes is evident. These findings suggest that problems with emotional and behavioral regulation, common in children with FAS, is associated as much with clinical referral status or adverse early experiences as with prenatal exposure.

The relationship between prenatal alcohol exposure and conduct disorder and delinquency in adolescence is an area of interest. Some researchers and FAS advocates have suggested that prenatal alcohol exposure is associated with delinquent or criminal behavior during adolescence (e.g., Streissguth et al., 1996; Fast et al., 1999; Fast and Conry, 2004). These conclusions are often based on studies of adolescents already referred to clinics for treatment or in the juvenile justice system. In a survey of secondary disabilities, Streissguth and colleagues (1996) describe that caregivers report that a majority of youth and young adults with FASD are involved in "delinquent" or problematic behaviors. Of 253 patients 12 years of age or older, 60% have disruptions in school experience (e.g., suspensions), 50% have demonstrated "inappropriate" sexual behavior, and 30%, alcohol and drug problems. Fast and colleagues (1999) also report an association between prenatal exposure and criminal behavior. In a sample of 287 adjudicated adolescents remanded for inpatient forensic psychiatric assessment, 23.3% were found to have some prenatal alcohol-related diagnosis.

In studies of the relationship of prenatal exposure and behavior in less high-risk groups, the results are more mixed. The Achenbach (1991) Child Behavior Checklist and the teacher version, the Teacher Report Form, have often been used to measure behavior problems. Elevated scores on problem indices have been reported in some studies (i.e., Olson et al., 1997; Mattson and Riley, 2000) but not others (Steinhausen et al., 1993). Even when scores for children with FASD are statistically higher than those of age-matched control groups, the scores do not always reach clinically significant levels (e.g., Brown et al., 1991). Lynch and colleagues (2003) specifically examine the question of delinquency and conduct problems in alcohol-exposed adolescents compared to contrast groups from the same population of low-income, urban youth. They show with a sample of 248 children, mean age of 15 years, males are more likely than females to report delinquent behavior, but there is no relationship between prenatal alcohol exposure and outcomes. Delinquent behavior is related to parenting factors and environmental stress. In the same group of young people, examination of academic and school records indicates no higher incidence of conduct problems, attendance problems, or suspensions in alcohol-exposed youth (Howell et al., 2006).

Methodological factors must be considered when assessing the results of research. Interpretation of reports from clinical studies is particularly speculative in the area of behavior and social/emotional functioning. Investigators must be very careful to identify appropriate contrast groups as well as the effects of confounding and mediating factors when attempting to understand observed outcomes. For the most part, these methodological restraints have not been observed in this area of study, and for these reasons, it is too early to draw conclusions about the effect of prenatal exposure on this area of functioning.

CURRENT ISSUES AND SUGGESTIONS FOR FUTURE RESEARCH

Despite greatly increased understanding of the consequences of prenatal exposure, some issues are still being debated. These areas of controversy and exploration suggest the direction for research during the next decade.

Description of Characteristics Over Time

Although some sample populations and a number of exposure studies have been followed longitudinally, there remains limited information about the trajectories of development resulting from prenatal alcohol exposure among those with either FAS or ARND. Even objective issues such as facial dysmorphia have not been studied in the same individuals over time to evaluate the saliency of features at different points in development. Outcomes from longitudinal cohorts in which repeated waves of data have been collected on the same individuals (Streissguth et al., 1993; Day et al., 2002) have often been reported by time period, as if these were cross-sectional cohorts, instead of examining them over time to evaluate developmental trajectories. Since these databases do exist, investigators have the opportunity to investigate the longitudinal aspects of development in alcohol-affected children and, when they have done so, to greatly increase understanding in this area.

Behavior and Conduct Disorders

A largely unresolved question is that of the relationship between prenatal exposure and later behavioral and emotional problems. Many of these problems as well as psychiatric disorders (Famy et al., 1998; O'Connor et al., 2002) have been identified in clinically referred samples. It is likely that the next decade will produce a number of studies on these relationships and further examinations of the effect of exposure on the risk for legal problems and substance abuse. If studies are carried out with the appropriate methodologies and control for the multiple confounding factors associated with maternal substance abuse, the contribution of prenatal exposure to such outcomes may be better understood.

Behavioral Phenotypes

In the real world, it is often difficult to ascribe observed outcomes to maternal alcohol use. There has been a good deal of interest in identifying a "behavioral phenotype" that characterizes people who are affected by prenatal exposure. Such a constellation of behavioral outcomes is believed to characterize both those with the full FAS and those who do not have identifying facial features. Clinicians would like to have a checklist of such behaviors that can be used by teachers, parents, and other observers to discriminate affected from unaffected children and to facilitate referral. The search for such a phenotype does not take into account the multiple factors that affect development and the many etiologies that can have a final common pathway in behavioral terms.

Intervention and Standards of Care

The most neglected area of research on the behavioral effects of alcohol is on methods for intervention to improve outcomes for affected individuals. Parents and caregivers of affected children state that their most urgent need is appropriate interventions. In 1996, a report by the Institute of Medicine (Stratton et al., 1996) recommended that studies be done in this area and that standards of care for affected individuals be written. To date, no reports of intervention studies in human samples have been published, although there are currently five such studies being carried out under the aegis of the Centers for Disease Control and Prevention. No standards of care have been proposed by any agency or professional organization. Although it is apparently difficult to carry out work in this area, it seems likely that as more information is accumulated about cognitive and behavioral consequences of prenatal exposure, intervention and treatment will be a focus of research in the future.

Abbreviations

ADHD   attention deficit, hyperactivity disorder

ARND   alcohol-related neurodevelopmental disorder

CNS   central nervous system

CVLT-C   California Verbal Learning Test-children's version

DTI   diffusion tensor imaging

FAS   fetal alcohol syndrome

FASD   fetal alcohol spectrum disorders

fMRI   functional magnetic resonance imaging

SES   socioeconomic status

sMRI   structural magnetic resonance imaging

WCST   Wisconsin Card Sort Task

WRAML   Wide Range Assessment of Memory and Learning

ACKNOWLEDGMENTS   The author would like to acknowledge the continuing contributions of the faculty and staff of the Maternal Substance Abuse and Child Development Laboratory, Department of Psychiatry and Behavioral Sciences, Emory University School of Medicine, and those of the research participants and their families who make research on these problems possible. Some of the work referred to in this chapter was supported by awards to the author from the following agencies: the Georgia Department of Human Resources (DHR), Maternal Substance Abuse Prevention Program, the National Institute of Alcohol Abuse and Alcoholism, and the Centers for Disease Control and Prevention.

References

Abel EL (1984) *Fetal Alcohol Syndrome and Fetal Alcohol Effects*. Plenum, New York.

—— (1998) *Fetal Alcohol Syndrome*. Plenum, New York.

Achenbach TM (1991) *Manual for the Child Behavior Checklist/4-18 and 1991 Profile*. University of Vermont, Burlington, VT.

Archibald SL, Fennema-Notestine C, Gamst A, Riley EP, Mattson SN, Jernigan TL (2001) Brain dysmorphology in individuals with severe prenatal alcohol exposure. Dev Med Child Neurol 43:148–154.

Aronson M, Hagberg B (1998) Neuropsychological disorders in children exposed to alcohol during pregnancy: a follow-up study of 24 children of alcoholic mothers in Goteborg, Sweden. Alcohol Clin Exp Res 22:321–324.

Aronson M, Kyllerman M, Sabel KG, Sandin B, Olegard R (1985) Children of alcoholic mothers. Developmental, perceptual and behavioral characteristics as compared to matched controls. Acta Paediatr Scand 74:27–35.

Ashcraft MH (1995) Cognitive psychology and simple arithmetic: a review and summary of new directions. Math Cognit 1:3–34.

Astley SJ (2004) *Diagnostic Guide for Fetal Alcohol Spectrum Disorders: The 4-Digit Diagnostic Code*, 3rd edition. University of Washington Public Service, Seattle, WA.

Astley SJ, Clarren SK (2001) Measuring the facial phenotype of individuals with prenatal alcohol exposure: correlations with brain dysfunction. Alcohol Alcohol 36:147–159.

Autti-Ramo IA (2000) Twelve-year follow-up of children exposed to alcohol in utero. Dev Med Child Neurol 421:406–411.

Autti-Ramo IA, Autti T, Korkman M, Kettunen S, Salonen O, Valanne L (2002) MRI findings in children with school problems who had been exposed prenatally to alcohol. Dev Med Child Neurol 44:98–106.

Avaria MD, Mills JL, Kleinsteuber K, Aros S, Conley MR, Cox C, Klebanoff M, Cassorla F (2003) Peripheral nerve conduction abnormalities in children exposed to alcohol in utero. J Pediatr 144:338–343.

Barr HM, Streissguth AP, Darby BL, Sampson PD (1990) Prenatal exposure to alcohol, caffeine, tobacco, and aspirin: effects on fine and gross motor performance in 4-year-old children. Dev Psychol 26:339–348.

Bhatara VS, Lovrein F, Kirkeby J, Swayze V, Unruh E, Johnson V (2002) Brain function in fetal alcohol syndrome assessed by single-photon emission computed tomography. South Dakota J Med 55:59–62.

Blackston RD, Coles CD, Kable JA, Seitz R (2004) Reliability and validity of the dysmorphia checklist: relating severity of dysmorphia to cognitive and behavioral outcomes in children with prenatal alcohol exposure. Poster at the annual meeting of the American Clinical Genetics Society.

Bookstein FL, Sampson PD, Streissguth AP, Connor PD (2001) Geometric morphometrics of corpus callosum and subcortical structures in the fetal-alcohol-affected-brain. Teratology 64:4–32.

Bookstein FL, Streissguth AP, Sampson PD, Connor PD, Barr HM (2002) Corpus callosum shape and neuropsychological deficits in adult males with heavy fetal alcohol exposure. Neuroimage 15:233–251.

Borkowski JG, Burke JE (1996) Theories, models and measurements of executive function: an information processing prospective. In: Lyon GR, Krasnegor NA (eds). *Attention, Memory, and Executive Function*. Paul Brookes Publishing, Baltimore, pp 235–262.

Boyd TA, Ernhart CB, Greene TH, Sokol RJ, Martier S (1991) Prenatal alcohol exposure and sustained attention in the preschool period. Neurotoxicol Teratol 13:49–55.

Brown RT, Coles CD, Smith IE, Platzman KA, Silverstein J, Erickson S, Falek A (1991) Effects of prenatal alcohol exposure at school age. II: Attention and behavior. Neurotoxicol Teratol 13:369–376.

Carmichael-Olson H, Feldman JJ, Streissguth AP, Sampson PD, Bookstein FL (1998) Neuropsychological deficits in adolescence with fetal alcohol syndrome: clinical findings. Alcohol Clin Exp Res 22:1998–2012.

Carmichael-Olson H, Streissguth AP, Sampson PD, Barr HM, Bookstein FL, Thiede K (1997) Association of prenatal alcohol exposure with behavioral and learning problems in early adolescence. J Am Acad Child Adolesc Psychiatry 36:1187–1194.

Clark CM, Li D, Conry J, Conry R, Loock C (2000) Structural and functional brain integrity of fetal alcohol syndrome in nonretarded cases. Pediatrics 105:1096–1099.

Coles CD (1992) Prenatal alcohol exposure and human development. In: Miller MW (ed). *Development of the Central Nervous System: Effects of Alcohol and Opiates*. Wiley-Liss, New York, pp 9–36.

—— (1993) Impact of prenatal alcohol exposure on the newborn and the child. Clin Obstet Gynecol 36:255–266.

Coles CD, Brown RT, Smith IE, Platzman KA, Erickson S, Falek A (1991) Effects of prenatal alcohol exposure at school age: I. Physical and cognitive development. Neurotoxicol Teratol 13:357–367.

Coles CD, Kable JA, Dent D, Lee D (2004) Socio-cognitive habilitation with children with FAS. Alcohol Clin Exp Res 28:719A.

Coles CD, Kable JA, Drews-Botsch C, Falek A (2000) Early identification of risk for effects of prenatal alcohol exposure. J Stud Alcohol 61:607–616.

Coles CD, Platzman KA, Lynch ME, Freides D (2002) Auditory and visual sustained attention in adolescents prenatally exposed to alcohol. Alcohol Clin Exp Res 26:263–271.

Coles CD, Platzman KA, Raskind-Hood CL, Brown RT, Falek A, Smith IE (1997) A comparison of children affected by prenatal alcohol exposure and attention deficit, hyperactivity disorder. Alcohol Clin Exp Res 21:150–161.

Coles CD, Smith IE, Fernhoff PM, Falek A (1985) Neonatal neurobehavioral characteristics as correlates of maternal alcohol use during gestation. Alcohol Clin Exp Res 9:1–7.

Conn-Blower EA (1991) Nurturing and educating children prenatally exposed to alcohol: the role of the counselor. Int J Adv Counsel 14:91–103.

Connor PD, Sampson PD, Bookstein FL, Barr HM, Streissguth AP (2000) Direct and indirect effects of prenatal alcohol damage on executive function. Dev Neuropsychol 18:331–354.

Connor PD, Streissguth AP, Sampson PD, Bookstein FL, Barr HM (1999) Individual differences in auditory and visual attention among fetal alcohol–affected adults. Alcohol Clin Exp Res 23:1395–1402.

Conry J (1990) Neuropsychological deficits in fetal alcohol syndrome and fetal alcohol effects. Alcohol Clin Exp Res 14:650–655.

Day NL, Cottreau CM, Richardson GA (1993) The epidemiology of alcohol, marijuana, and cocaine use among women of child bearing age and pregnant women. Clin Obstet Gynecol 36:232–245.

Day NL, Goldschmidt L, Robles N, Richardson GA, Cornelius M (1991) Prenatal alcohol exposure and offspring growth at eighteen months of age: the predictive validity of two measures of drinking. Alcohol Clin Exp Res 15:914–918.

Day NL, Leech SL, Richardson GA, Cornelius MD, Robles N, Larkby C (2002) Prenatal alcohol exposure predicts continued deficits in offspring size at 14 years of age. Alcohol Clin Exp Res 26:1584–1591.

Day NL, Zuo YU, Richardson GA, Goldschmidt L, Larkby CA, Cornelius MD (1999) Prenatal alcohol use and offspring size at 10 years of age. Alcohol Clin Exp Res 23:863–869.

Delis DC, Kramer JH, Kaplan E, Ober BA (1987) California Verbal Learning Test. Psychological Corp, San Antonio, TX.

Famy C, Streissguth AP, Unis AS (1998) Mental illness in adults with fetal alcohol syndrome or fetal alcohol effects. Am J Psychiatry 155:552–554.

Fast DK, Conry J (2004) The challenge of fetal alcohol syndrome in the criminal legal system. Addict Biol 9:167–168.

Fast DK, Conry J, Loock CA (1999) Identifying fetal alcohol syndrome among youth in the criminal justice system. J Dev Behav Pediatr 20:370–372.

Fernhoff PM, Smith IE, Falek A (1980) Dysmorphia Checklist. Document from the Maternal Substance Abuse and Child Development Project, Emory University School of Medicine, Atlanta.

Geary DC (1993) Mathematical disabilities: cognitive, neuropsychological, and genetic components. Psychol Bull 114:345–362.

Ginsburg HP, Baroody AJ (1990) Test of Early Mathematics Ability. Pro-ED, Austin.

Goldschmidt L, Richardson GA, Stoffer DS, Geva D, Day N (1996) Prenatal alcohol exposure and academic achievement at age six: a nonlinear fit. Alcohol Clin Exp Res 20:763–770.

Goodlett CR, Lundahl KR (1996) Temporal determinants of neonatal alcohol–induced cerebellar damage and motor performance deficits. Pharmacol Biochem Behav 55:531–540.

Grant DA, Berg EA (1980) The Wisconsin Card Sorting Test. Psychol Corp, San Antonio, TX.

Haith MM, Hazan C, Goodman GS (1988) Expectation and anticipation of dynamic visual events by 3.5-month-old babies. Child Dev 59:467–479.

Heaton RK, Chelune GJ, Talley JL, Kay GG, Curtiss G (1993) Wisconsin Card Sort Testing Manual: Revised and Expanded. Psychological Assessment Resources, Odessa, FL.

Howell KH, Platzman KA, Lynch ME, Smith GH, Coles CD (2006) Prenatal alcohol exposure and academic functioning in adolescence. J Pediatr Psychol. In press.

Hoyme HE, May PA, Kalberg WO, Kodituwakku P, Gossage JP, Trujillo PM, Buckley DG, Miller JH, Aragon AS, Khaole N, Viljoen DL, Jones KL, Robinson LK (2005) A practical clinical approach to diagnosis of fetal alcohol spectrum disorders: clarification of the 1996 Institute of Medicine criteria. Pediatrics 115:39–47.

Jacobson JL (1999) Cognitive processing deficits associated with poor mathematical performance in alcohol-exposed school-aged children. Alcohol Clin Exp Res 23(Suppl 5):4A.

Jacobson JL, Jacobson SW, Sokol RJ, Ager JW (1998) Relation of maternal age and pattern of pregnancy drinking to functionally significant cognitive deficit in infancy. Alcohol Clin Exp Res 22:345–351.

Jacobson SW, Jacobson JL, Sokol RJ (1994) Effects of fetal alcohol exposure on infant reaction time. Alcohol Clin Exp Res 18:1125–1132.

Jacobson SW, Jacobson JL, Sokol RJ, Martier SS, Ager JW (1993) Prenatal alcohol exposure and infant information processing ability. Child Dev 64:1706–1721.

Jacobson SW, Jacobson JL, O'Neill JM, Padgett RJ, Frankowski JJ, Bihun JT (1992) Visual expectation and dimensions of infant information processing. Child Dev 63:711–724.

Janzen LA, Nanson JL, Block GW (1995) Neuropsychological evaluation of preschoolers with fetal alcohol syndrome. Neurotoxicol Teratol 17:273–279.

Johnson VP, Swayze VW, Sato Y, Andreasen NC (1996) Fetal alcohol syndrome: craniofacial and central nervous system manifestations. Am J Med Genet 61:329–339.

Jones KL, Smith DW (1973) Recognition of the fetal alcohol syndrome in early infancy. Lancet 2:999–1001.

Jones KL, Smith DW, Ulleland CN, Streissguth AP (1973) Pattern of malformation in offspring of chronic alcoholic mothers. Lancet 1:1267–1271.

Kable JA, Coles CD (2004) The impact of prenatal alcohol exposure on neurophysiological encoding of environmental events at six months. Alcohol Clin Exp Res 28:489–496.

Kable JA, Coles CD, Drews-Botsch C, Falek A (1999) The effects of maternal drinking prenatally on patterns of pre-academic mathematical concept development. Paper presented at annual meeting of Research Society on Alcoholism as part of symposium "Prenatal alcohol exposure and developmental dyscalculia: Neurocognitive implications, Santa Barbara CA.

Kaemingk K, Paquette A (1999) Effects of prenatal alcohol exposure on neuropsychological functioning. Dev Neuropsychol 15:111–140.

Kaplan-Estrin M, Jacobson SW, Jacobson JL (1999) Neurobehavioral effects of prenatal alcohol exposure at 26 months. Neurotoxicol Teratol 21:503–511.

Kelly SJ, Day N, Streissguth AP (2001) Effects of prenatal alcohol exposure on social behavior in humans and other species. Neurotoxicol Teratol 22:143–149.

Kerns KA, Don A, Mateer CA, Streissguth AP (1997) Cognitive deficits in nonretarded adults with fetal alcohol syndrome. J Learn Disabil 30:685–693.

Kodituwakku PW, Handmaker NS, Cutler SK, Weathersby EK, Handmaker SD (1995) Specific impairments in self-regulation in children exposed to alcohol prenatally. Alcohol Clin Exp Res 19:1558–1564.

Kodituwakku PW, May PA, Clericuzio CL, Weers D (2001) Emotion-related learning in individuals prenatally exposed to alcohol: an investigation of the relation between set shifting, extinction of responses, and behavior. Neuropsychologia 39:699–708.

Kopera-Frye K, Dehaene S, Streissguth AP (1996) Impairments of number processing induced by prenatal alcohol exposure. Neuropsychologia 34:1187–1196.

Kopera-Frye K, Olson HC, Streissguth AP (1997) Teratogenic effects of alcohol on attention. In: Burack J, Enns JT (eds). Attention Development and Psychopathology. Guilford Press, New York, pp 171–204.

Kyllerman M, Aronson M, Sabel KG, Karlberg E, Sandin B, Olegard R (1985) Children of alcoholic mothers. Acta Paediatr Scand 74:2–26.

Landesman-Dwyer S, Ragozin AS (1981) Behavioral correlates of prenatal alcohol exposure: a four-year follow-up study. Neurobehav Toxicol Teratol 3:187–193.

Lyon GR (1996) The need for conceptual and theoretical clarity in the study of attention, memory, and executive function. In: Lyon GR, Krasnegor N (eds). Attention, Memory, and Executive Function. Paul Brookes Publishing, Baltimore, pp 3–10.

Lynch ME, Coles CD, Corley T, Falek A (2003) Examining delinquency in adolescents differentially prenatally exposed to alcohol: the role of proximal and distal risk factors. J Stud Alcohol 64:678–686.

Lynch ME, Coles CD, Fernhoff PD, Schmieding S (2004) Longitudinal effects of prenatal alcohol exposure on growth and dysmorphia. Alcohol Clin Exp Res 28(Suppl):42A.

Ma X, Coles CD, Lynch ME, LaConte SM, Zurkiya O, Wang D, Hu X (2005) Evaluation of corpus callosum anisotropy in young adults with fetal alcohol syndrome according to diffusion tensor imaging. Alcohol Clin Exp Res 29:1214–1222.

MacKintosh NJ (1975) A theory of attention: variations in the associability of stimuli with reinforcement. Psychol Rev 82:276–298.

Marcus JC (1987) Neurological findings in the fetal alcohol syndrome. Neuropediatrics 18:158–160.

Mattson SN, Carlos R, Riley EP (1993) The behavioral teratogenicity of alcohol is not affected by pretreatment with aspirin. Alcohol 10:51–57.

Mattson SN, Goodman AM, Caine C, Delis DC, Riley EP (1999) Executive functioning in children with heavy prenatal alcohol exposure. Alcohol Clin Exp Res 23:1808–1815.

Mattson SN, Riley EP (1998) A review of the neurobe-havioral deficits in children with fetal alchol syndrome or prenatal exposure to alcohol. Alcohol Clin Exp Res 22:279–294.

—— (1999) Implicit and explicit memory functioning in children with heavy prenatal alcohol exposure. J Int Neuropsychol Soc 5:462–471.

—— (2000) Parent ratings of behavior in children with heavy prenatal alcohol exposure and IQ-matched controls. Alcohol Clin Exp Res 24:226–231.

Mattson SN, Riley EP, Delis DC, Stern C, Jones KL (1996) Verbal learning and memory in children with fetal alcohol syndrome. Alcohol Clin Exp Res 20:810–816.

Mattson SN, Riley EP, Gramling L, Delis DC, Jones KL (1998) Neuropsychological comparison of alcohol-exposed children with or without physical features of fetal alcohol syndrome. Neuropsychology 12: 146–153.

Mattson SN, Roebuck TM (2002) Acquisition and retention of verbal and nonverbal information in children with heavy prenatal alcohol exposure. Alcohol Clin Exp Res 26:875–882.

May PA, Brooke L, Gossage JP, Croxford J, Adnams C, Jones KL, Robinson L, Viljoen D (2000) The epidemiology of fetal alcohol syndrome in a South African community in the Western Cape Province. Am J Public Health 90:1905–1912.

McCarthy D (1972) The McCarthy Scales of Children's Abilities. Psychological Corp, New York.

Miller MW, Astley SJ, Clarren SK (1999) Number of axons in the corpus callosum of the mature Macaca nemestrina: increases caused by prenatal exposure to ethanol. J Comp Neurol 412: 123–131.

Mirsky AF, Anthony BJ, Duncan CC, Ahern MB, Kellam SG (1991) Analysis of the elements of attention: a neuropsychological approach. Neuropsychol Rev 2: 75–88.

Morris RD (1996) Relationships and distinctions among the concepts of attention, memory and executive function: a developmental perspective. In: Lyon GR, Krasnegor N (eds). Attention, Memory, and Executive Function. Paul Brookes Publishing, Baltimore, pp 11–16.

Morse BA, Adams J, Weiner L (1992) FAS: neuropsychological manifestations. Alcohol Clin Exp Res 16:380.

Nanson JL, Hiscock M (1990) Attentional deficits in children exposed to alcohol prenatally. Alcohol Clin Exp Res 14:656–661.

O'Connor MJ, Shah B, Whaley S, Cronin P, Graham J, Gunderson B (2002) Psychiatric illness in a clinical sample of children with prenatal alcohol exposure. Am J Drug Alcohol Use 28:743–754.

Oesterheld JR, Wilson A (1997) ADHD and FAS. J Am Acad Child Adolesc Psychiatry 36:1163.

O'Malley KD, Nanson J (2002) Clinical implications of a link between fetal alcohol spectrum disorder and attention-deficit hyperactivity disorder. Can J Psychiatry 47:349–354.

Platzman KA, Friedes D, Lynch ME, Falek A (2001) Narrative and visual–spatial memory in adolescents prenatally exposed to alcohol. Alcohol Clin Exp Res 25(Suppl 5):122A.

Riikonen R, Salonen I, Partanen K, Verho S (1999) Brain perfusion SPECT and MRI in foetal alcohol syndrome. Dev Med Child Neurol 41:652–659.

Riley EP, Mattson SN, Sowell ER, Jernigan TL, Sobel DF, Jones KL (1995) Abnormalities of the corpus callosum in children prenatally exposed to alcohol. Alcohol Clin Exp Res 19:1198–1202.

Roebuck TM, Mattson SN, Riley EP (1998a) A review of the neuroanatomical findings in children with fetal alcohol syndrome or prenatal exposure to alcohol. Alcohol Clin Exp Res 22:339–344.

Roebuck TM, Simmons RW, Mattson SN, Riley EP (1998b) Prenatal exposure to alcohol affects the ability to maintain postural balance. Alcohol Clin Exp Res 22:1992–1997.

Roebuck TM, Mattson SN, Riley EP (1999) Behavioral and psychosocial profiles of alcohol-exposed children. Alcohol Clin Exp Res 23:1070–1076.

Roebuck-Spencer TM, Mattson SN (2004) Implicit strategy effects learning in children with heavy prenatal alcohol exposure. Alcohol Clin Exp Res 28:1424–1431.

Rolls ET, Hornack J, Wade D, McGrath J (1994) Emotion-related learning in patients with social and emotional changes associated with frontal lobe damage. J Neurol Neurosurg Psychiatry 57:1518–1524.

Rourke BP (1995) Syndrome of Nonverbal Learning Disabilities: Neurodevelopmental Manifestations. Guilford, New York.

Ruff HA, Rothbart MK (1996) Attention in Early Development: Themes and Variations. Oxford University Press, New York.

Sampson PD, Kerr B, Carmichael-Olson H, Streissguth AP, Hunt E, Barr H (1997) The effects of prenatal alcohol exposure on adolescent cognitive processing: a speed–accuracy tradeoff. Intelligence 24: 329–353.

Sampson PD, Streissguth AP, Bookstein FL, Barr HM (2000) On categorizations in analyses of alcohol teratogenesis. Environ Health Perspect 108(Suppl 3):421–428.

Schonfeld AM, Mattson SN, Lang A, Delis DC, Riley EP (2001) Verbal and nonverbal fluency in children with heavy prenatal alcohol exposure. J Stud Alcohol 62:239–246.

Shallice T (1982) Specific impairments in planning. In: Broadbent DE, Weiskrantz L (eds). *The Neuropsychology of Cognitive Function.* The Royal Society, London, pp 199–209.

Sheslow D, Adams W (1990) *Manual for the Wide Range Assessment of Memory and Learning.* Jastak Associates, Wilmington, DE.

Sowell ER, Jernigan TL, Mattson SN, Riley EP, Sobel DF, Jones KL (1996) Abnormal development of the cerebellar vermis in children prenatally exposed to alcohol: size reduction in lobules I–V. Alcohol Clin Exp Res 20:31–34.

Sowell ER, Mattson SN, Thompson PM, Jernigan TL, Riley EP, Toga AW (2001a) Mapping callosal morphology and cognitive correlates: effects of heavy prenatal alcohol exposure. Neurology 57:235–244.

Sowell ER, Thompson PM, Mattson SN, Tessner KD, Jernigan TL, Riley EP, Toga AW (2001b) Voxel-based morphometric analyses of the brain in children and adolescents prenatally exposed to alcohol. Cognit Neurosci Neuropsychol 12:515–523.

—— (2002a) Regional brain shape abnormalities persist into adolescence after heavy prenatal alcohol exposure. Cereb Cortex 12:856–865.

Spohr HL, Steinhausen JC (1984) Clinical, psychopathological, and developmental aspects in children with the fetal alcohol syndrome (FAS). CIBA Found Symp 105:197–217.

Spohr HL, Willms J, Steinhausen JC (1993) Prenatal alcohol exposure and long-term developmental consequences. Lancet 32:990–1006.

Steinhausen HC, Nestler V, Spohr HL (1982) Development and psychopathology of children with the fetal alcohol syndrome. Dev Behav Pediatr 3: 49–54.

Steinhausen HC, Willms J, Spohr HL (1993) Long-term psychopathology and cognitive outcome of children with fetal alcohol syndrome. J Am Acad Child Adolesc Psychiatry 32:990–994.

Stratton K, Howe C, Battaglia F (1996) *Fetal Alcohol Syndrome: Diagnosis, Epidemiology, Prevention and Treatment.* National Academy Press, Washington, DC.

Streissguth AP (1997) *Fetal Alcohol Syndrome: A Guide for Families and Communities.* Paul Brooks Publishing, Baltimore, MD.

Streissguth AP, Barr HM, Carmichael-Olson H, Sampson PD, Bookstein FL, Burgess DM (1994) Drinking during pregnancy decreases word attack and arithmetic scores on standardized tests: adolescent data from population-based prospective study. Alcohol Clin Exp Res 18:248–254.

Streissguth AP, Barr HM, Kogan J, Bookstein FL (1996) Understanding the occurrence of secondary disabilities in clients with fetal alcohol syndrome (FAS) and fetal alcohol effects (FAE). Centers for Disease Control and Prevention (CDC), Technical Report #96-06, Seattle, WA.

Streissguth AP, Barr HM, Sampson PD, Parrish-Johnson JC, Kirchner GL, Martin DC (1986) Attention, distraction and reaction time at 7 years and prenatal alcohol exposure. Neurobehav Toxicol Teratol 8: 717–725.

Streissguth AP, Bookstein FL, Sampson PD, Barr HM (1993) *The Enduring Effects of Prenatal Alcohol Exposure on Child Development: Birth Through Seven Years, a Partial Least-Square Solution.* University of Michigan Press, Ann Arbor.

—— (1995) Attention: prenatal alcohol and continuities of vigilance and attentional problems from 4 through 14 years. Dev Psychopathol 7:419–446.

Streissguth AP, Herman CS, Smith DW (1978) Intelligence, behavior and dysmorphogenesis in the fetal alcohol syndrome: a report on 20 patients. J Pediatr 92:363–367.

Streissguth AP, Martin DC, Barr HM, Sandman BM (1984) Intrauterine alcohol and nicotine exposure: attention and reaction time in 4-year-old children. Dev Psychol 20:533–541.

Suess PE, Porges S, Plude DJ (1994) Cardiac vagal tone and sustained attention in school-age children. Psychophysiology 31:17–22.

Swayze VM, Johnson VP, Hanson JW, Piven J, Sato Y, Giedd JN, Mosnik D, Andreason NC (1997) Magnetic resonance imaging of brain anomalies in fetal alcohol syndrome. Pediatrics 99:232–240.

Ueckerer A, Nadel L (1996) Spatial locations gone awry: object and spatial memory deficits in children with fetal alcohol syndrome. Neuropsychologia 34:209–223.

US Department of Health and Human Services (2000) Prenatal exposure to alcohol. In: *Tenth Special Report to the US Congress on Alcohol and Health: Highlights from Current Research,* pp 283–322.

Warner RH, Rosett HL (1975) The effects of drinking on offspring: an historical survey of the American and British literature. J Stud Alcohol 36:1395–1420.

Wass TS, Haith MM (1999) Executive function deficits in 3-month-old human infants exposed to alcohol in utero. Alcohol Clin Exp Res 23(Suppl):31A.

Wechsler D (1991) *Wechsler Intelligence Scale for Children–Revised.* Psychological Corp, New York.

Willford JA, Richardson GA, Leech SL, Day NL (2004) Verbal and visuospatial learning and memory function in children with moderate prenatal alcohol exposure. Alcohol Clin Exp Res 28:497–507.

Zucker RA, Fitzgerald HE, Moses HM (1995) Emergence of alcohol problems and the several alcoholisms: a developmental perspective on etiological theory and life course trajectory. In: Cicchetti D, Cohen DJ (eds). *Developmental Psychopathology: Risk, Disorder, and Adaption*, Vol. 2. Wiley, New York, pp 677–711.

9

Influence of Alcohol on Structure
of the Developing Human Brain

Susanna L. Fryer

Christie L. McGee

Andrea D. Spadoni

Edward P. Riley

A diagnosis of fetal alcohol syndrome (FAS) requires a combination of three clusters of symptoms: (1) a distinct craniofacial appearance, (2) growth deficiency, and (3) central nervous system (CNS) dysfunction. Characteristic FAS-related craniofacial dysmorphology includes short palpebral fissures (eye openings), a smooth philtrum (the area above the upper lip), a flat nasal bridge and mid-face, and thinness of the upper lip. The growth deficiency related to FAS manifests either prenatally and/or postnatally, and can necessitate neonatal care for failure to thrive. The third class of symptoms, CNS dysfunction and accompanying structural brain changes, are the subject of the present chapter. The effects of prenatal alcohol exposure on cognition and behavior are variable and wide-reaching. Common difficulties include attention deficits; decrements in general intelligence quotient (IQ); behavioral problems; visual, auditory, and perceptual disturbances; fine and gross motor problems; and learning disabilities (Streissguth and Connor, 2001). Indeed, the syndrome has been cited as the leading preventable cause of mental retardation (Pulsifer, 1996).

The study of brain structure in alcohol-exposed individuals offers a means to understand the etiological relationships that underlie the neurobehavioral abnormalities observed in these individuals. By examining relationships between brain structure and behavior, we gain insights into the mechanisms underlying alcohol teratogenicity. Before delving into a discussion of brain structural changes arising from fetal alcohol exposure, it is important to add a note on terminology. In recognition of the wide-ranging effects of prenatal alcohol exposure, the term *fetal alcohol spectrum disorders* (FASD) has been adopted to describe the entire range of outcomes from prenatal alcohol exposure (Bertrand et al., 2004). These effects vary from the pronounced facial, growth, and CNS abnormalities traditionally ascribed to FAS, to subtle neurobehavioral, growth, or physical deficits that may also occur as a result of such exposure. Using this classification, FAS corresponds to dysmorphic FASD (i.e., all three of the diagnostic criteria are met, including the combination of specific dysmophia required to meet FAS criteria). Therefore, individuals with a history of prenatal alcohol exposure and deficits thought to be related to the alcohol exposure, but without the necessary criteria for an FAS diagnosis, would be considered as nondysmorphic FASD. The terminology used throughout the present chapter refers to alcohol-exposed individuals as having FAS when they meet the three major criteria for the diagnosis, and nondysmorphic FASD when they do not. It is important to note that although there is a general consensus on the wide-ranging and variable effects of fetal alcohol exposure, diagnostic and classification terminology remains controversial. Thus, honing the diagnostic criteria that describe fetal alcohol effects is currently a priority for the field (Riley et al., 2003).

AUTOPSY STUDIES

Dysmorphic Fetal Alcohol Spectrum Disorder

Autopsy, which literally means, "to see for oneself," involves examination to determine the exact cause of death. Autopsies are useful in the study of brain disease processes. Postmortem examination permits a more direct study of neuroanatomy than *in vivo* techniques. Examination of expired tissue, however, presents a confound when attempting to generalize the findings to live cases. In other words, autopsies allow for a detailed description not possible with less invasive techniques, but the data they provide are not necessarily representative of living cohorts. Historically, autopsy case reporting was one of the initial methods used to examine teratogenic effects of alcohol on brain structure. In the autopsy cases of children with FAS, death usually occurred because of major CNS or cardiac dysfunction.

The handful of subsequent autopsy reports show that developing brains sufficiently exposed to alcohol have a host of structural abnormalities. These include gross microcephaly, cellular disorganization, and anomalies of specific brain structures such as the corpus callosum and cerebellum. The first autopsy of a FAS case was of an infant who died at 5 days of age (Jones, 1975). The infant's brain exhibited enlarged lateral ventricles and agenesis (absence) of the corpus callosum. In addition, neuroglial heterotopias, a type of microdysplasia in which abnormal neural and glial

tissue cover parts of the brain surface, were described. Notably, such microdysplasias are thought to result from aberrant cortical neural migration and are common in autopsy cases of prenatal alcohol exposure. For instance, in an autopsy report of five cases, heterotopias were noted in each case, although the amount of abnormal tissue was variable among individuals (Wisniewski et al., 1983). Another autopsy study that examined brains from fetuses, infants, and one child corroborated the presence of microdysplasias and commented on the diversity of malformations observed (Peiffer et al., 1979). Furthermore, the authors suspected that dosage, in addition to time course of exposure, likely influences the degree and nature of structural damage to the developing brain.

Recent neuropathological studies associate FAS with specific types of complex cerebral malformations (Coulter et al., 1993). Evaluation of a 2-month-old infant exposed to a binge pattern of alcohol exposure during the first trimester of pregnancy was the first observation associating fetal alcohol exposure with midline cerebral dysgenesis. Due to elements of septo-optodysplasia, midline cerebral dysgenesis is a type of midline malformation characterized by a lack of the septum pellucidum, optic nerve damage, and endocrine abnormalities. In addition to this midline damage, the case showed general microcephaly and cerebellar Purkinje neuron disruption. Specifically, the cerebellar neurons were unusually positioned and had abnormal dendritic structure.

Non-Dysmorphic Fetal Alcohol Spectrum Disorder

An early case study that examined the brains of four neonates included cases of both dysmorphic and nondysmorphic FASD (Clarren et al., 1978). Disruptions to brain structure were noted in addition to microcephaly, including heterotopias and histological structural aberrations associated with errors in neuronal and glial migration. The degree of structural damage to the alcohol-exposed brains prompted the authors to conclude "that problems of brain morphogenesis can occur as the predominant effect of ethanol exposure *in utero*" (p. 67). Brain alterations may more directly indicate damage from alcohol-related effects than facial dysmorphia.

As the consensus of initial autopsy reports indicating extensive and diffuse damage throughout the alcohol-exposed brain mounted, investigators began to speculate that no particular pattern of behavioral or intellectual functioning is characteristic of individuals with FAS (Clarren, 1986). Yet, neuropsychological studies suggest a syndrome-specific pattern of cognitive and behavioral deficits associated with fetal alcohol exposure (Mattson and Riley, 1998). The subjects that comprise autopsy studies likely represent the most severe cases of prenatal alcohol exposure, i.e., those with damage incompatible with life. Thus, findings from autopsy studies may not be representative of the majority of individuals with fetal alcohol effects. This is especially true in the case of FAS, because most of the brain damage caused by fetal alcohol exposure does not preclude viability (Clarren, 1986).

IMAGING STUDIES

Medical imaging technologies detect inherent differences in biological tissue density (e.g., gray brain matter vs. white brain matter vs. bone), displaying them as images with contrast differences. Imaging technologies offer the ability to examine structural brain damage in vivo and include larger, more representative samples than the descriptions of brain structure provided by autopsy. Given that CNS deficits are a hallmark feature of FASD, brain matter quantification through imaging studies provides a crucial insight into specifying how normative brain-behavior relationships might be affected by alcohol exposure. In contrast to autopsy, magnetic resonance imaging (MRI) and other in vivo techniques provide information, albeit indirectly, of living tissue. Moreover, as there is no inherent selection bias, the findings of these studies are likely more representative of the population of interest.

Structural brain image analyses reveal that children and adolescents prenatally exposed to alcohol, with or without dysmorphic facial features, have patterns of brain structure malformations consistent with the neuropsychological and behavioral effects found in this population. Most of the existing research on neurostructural changes associated with prenatal alcohol exposure relies on structural MRI techniques.

Total Brain Volume and Shape

Early MRI Studies

Most MRI studies of individuals prenatally exposed to alcohol have focused on measures of brain volume.

Reliably, quantitative volumetric analyses have confirmed the overall reductions in size of the brain and the cerebral vault (Swayze et al., 1997; Archibald et al., 2001; Autti-Ramo et al., 2002). Analytic techniques examining regional variations in brain size and shape have suggested that fetal alcohol exposure produces a pattern of differential brain damage. Specifically, the corpus callosum, cerebellar vermis, basal ganglia, and parietal regions may show particular sensitivity to the effects of prenatal alcohol. A discussion of findings from specific studies follows.

A series of imaging studies from a group of collaborators in San Diego has focused on images collected from a sample of children and adolescents prenatally exposed to alcohol, both with and without dysmorphic features (ALC) (Archibald et al., 2001). Analysis of total brain volume shows that there are lobar differences between ALC and control groups. After statistically controlling for overall brain reductions in the ALC group, the parietal lobe is disproportionately reduced, suggesting that this region is particularly vulnerable to alcohol exposure during development. Such data parallel findings in the mature rat, in which parietal cortex is reduced by one-third following prenatal exposure to ethanol (Miller and Potempa, 1990; Mooney and Napper, 2005), but occipital cortex is unaffected.

The regional tissue composition is affected by prenatal exposure to ethanol. Raw volume reductions are evident for both gray and white matter when FAS individuals are compared with controls. Yet, when overall reductions in brain volume were statistically accounted for, only white matter reductions reached statistical significance. Thus, global white matter hypoplasia appears to be more severe than global gray matter hypoplasia in brains of individuals with FAS. In addition, exploration of proportional tissue composition in each lobe revealed that parietal gray and white matter volumes are disproportionately reduced in individuals with FAS relative to controls, whereas occipital lobe white matter is proportionally larger in FAS subjects. These findings suggest relative sparing of white matter in this region.

Voxel-Based Morphometry

Whole-brain voxel-based morphometry (VBM) aims to localize cortical abnormalities by examining each voxel, or point, on the brain image. This methodology avoids the need to define boundaries on each image, as is often necessary with standard volumetric brain imaging methods. Thus, VBM allows for the study of brain regions without clear gyral or structural boundaries. As voxel intensity values are considered to be a proxy for tissue density, in VBM, statistical parametric maps depicting averaged tissue densities are created for both gray and white matter.

Results from a VBM analysis of children and adolescents with prenatal alcohol exposure (Sowell et al., 2001b) complement earlier volumetric findings on the same sample (Archibald et al., 2001). The VBM study reveals prominent abnormalities in the peri-Sylvian cortices of the left temporal and parietal lobes. Specifically, alcohol-exposed subjects have excess gray matter density and decreased white matter density in these regions, compared to age-matched controls.

Shape Analysis

Shape analysis determines the size of the brain by measuring the distance from the center to various landmark points on the brain surface. Accordingly, the average brain surface extent is smaller for the alcohol-exposed subjects than for controls (Sowell et al., 2002a). This result is consistent with myriad studies showing that prenatal exposure to alcohol causes microcephaly. Further examination reveals prominent regional patterns in alcohol-induced size and shape differences. Specifically, large group differences are evident in the peri-Sylvian and parietal regions, with characteristic narrowing observed in the alcohol-exposed subjects and increases in gray matter density. In addition, portions of the anterior and orbital frontal cortex, particularly in the left hemisphere, are affected in ALC subjects. These patterns confirm that alcohol-induced abnormalities are specific rather than reflecting diffuse damage or global microencephaly.

The surfaced-based analytic methods used by Sowell and colleagues (2002a) allow researchers to locate relatively small regions of gray matter volume increases masked by reductions in gray matter. In other words, gross volumetric studies have missed subtle anomalies by taking the total brain volume into account. Regional shape abnormalities may occur in alcohol-exposed subjects because of abnormal myelin deposition that (a) prevents normal growth and (b) leads to cortical thinning in select areas. Evidence of frontal lobe abnormalities are consistent with

findings from the cognitive and behavioral literature citing deficits in executive functions such as planning, cognitive flexibility, and response inhibition following prenatal exposure to alcohol (Mattson et al., 1999; Connor et al., 2000; Kodituwakku et al., 2001).

Brain shape has been explored with surface-based image analysis techniques designed to match cortical anatomy between hemispheres based on delineated landmarks (Sowell et al., 2002b). From this study of differences in brain shape and gray matter density, the authors note that the left hemisphere appears to be more affected than the right hemisphere and speculate that ALC subjects might have altered hemispheric symmetry compared to the pattern seen in typically developing subjects. Specifically, gray matter asymmetry is more prominent in the temporal lobe for nonexposed controls, with the right hemisphere having more gray matter than the left. This asymmetry is significantly reduced in alcohol-exposed subjects. The suggestion of altered brain asymmetry as a consequence of prenatal alcohol exposure is provocative, although further studies are needed before this claim can be substantiated and its implications for possible behavioral effects understood.

Taken together, data from the San Diego group show that aside from global reductions in brain volume, parietal regions are disproportionately affected and white matter is more affected than gray matter.

Cerebellum

Several MRI studies describe cerebellar hypoplasia in individuals prenatally exposed to alcohol with and without FAS (Mattson et al., 1996; Riikonen et al., 1999; Archibald et al., 2001; Autti-Ramo et al., 2002). Both cerebellar gray and white matter are reduced in alcohol-exposed individuals (Archibald et al., 2001). Reductions are particularly evident in vermal cortex of earlier maturing lobules (Sowell et al., 1996). The methodology used to generate these results is as follows. For each subject, the midsagittal section is identified and the vermis is divided into three regions: the anterior vermis (lobules I–V), lobules VI and VII, and lobules VIII–X. Alcohol-induced differences are only evident in the anterior vermis, where the alcohol-exposed children showed significant reductions. This pattern of cerebellar vermal dysmorphology is distinct from the patterns found in children with other disorders, such as autism, William syndrome, and Down syndrome (Raz et al., 1995; Courchesne et al., 2001; Schmitt et al., 2001).

Animal models of fetal alcohol exposure consistently show abnormalities of the cerebellar vermis and hemispheres. Various investigators have examined the effects of episodic ethanol exposure during the first postnatal week (see Goodlett et al., 1990; Light et al., 2002). Following such exposure, the number of Purkinje neurons is reduced. As in human studies, the greatest differences are apparent in early-maturing regions of the cerebellar vermis. Thus, ethanol-induced changes in the animal studies not only concur with the findings in humans but also show that the Purkinje cell is a key target of ethanol toxicity.

Corpus Callosum

The corpus callosum is a bundle of fibers that connects the two cerebral hemispheres. It develops during the second trimester of gestation. Autopsy reports document agenesis of this structure in infants exposed to alcohol in utero. Partial or complete agenesis is described in several imaging studies (Riley et al., 1995; Johnson et al., 1996; Swayze et al., 1997; Riikonen et al., 1999; Clark et al., 2000), and it is suggested that prenatal alcohol exposure is a leading cause of this condition (Jeret et al., 1986). Most individuals exposed to alcohol prenatally do not have such severe alterations. Careful evaluation indicates that alcohol induces subtle yet significant changes in the size and shape of this structure. Studies on the morphology of the corpus callosum reveal that anomalies within specific cortical regions often correspond to particular callosal subregions through which those regions send white matter fibers (Barkovich and Norman, 1988).

Authors of the first study to systematically evaluate the corpus callosum divide a midsagittal area section of the callosum into five subregions (Riley et al., 1995). After excluding two subjects with complete agenesis and controlling for overall brain size, group differences emerge in three callosal subsections. The alcohol-exposed group displays disproportionate area reductions in the genu (most anterior section) and two areas that correspond to the splenium (most posterior region). These data are consistent with a study by Autti-Ramo and colleagues (2002), who show that the splenium of corpus callosum is reduced in area, length, and diameter in children prenatally exposed

to alcohol. Striking differences are evident on maps charting the average corpus callosum displacement in alcohol-exposed subjects (Sowell et al., 2001a). Specifically, the posterior portion of the corpus callosum is the section most significantly displaced, lying more inferior and anterior in the alcohol-exposed subjects. This alcohol-induced change in callosal placement correlates with performance on a verbal learning task. Indeed, displacement is a better predictor of performance than testing of verbal IQ. In other words, individuals with greater callosal displacement exhibit increased verbal learning impairments.

A series of studies on a large sample of adolescents and adults exposed to alcohol prenatally evaluates the corpus callosum by means of landmark strategies (Bookstein et al., 2001, 2002a, 2002b). This work develops useful discrimination protocols to distinguish ALC from control subjects, a goal distinct from that of other image analysis research, which analyzes mean group differences for the purpose of description. Variability in the corpora callosa is greater in adolescents (Bookstein et al., 2002a) and adults (Bookstein et al., 2001) that were prenatally exposed to alcohol than in age-matched controls. The authors suggest that hypervariation in callosal shape within the ALC group is a function of the timing and amounts of exposure during the development of this structure. Thus, differences in the manner of the fetal alcohol exposure may explain the numerous patterns deviating from normal callosal variation. In addition, the dysmorphic and nondysmorphic FASD groups are indistinguishable with regard to callosal hypervariance. This finding is consistent with research in the behavioral domain (Mattson and Riley, 1998; Connor et al., 2000) and speaks to the utility of augmenting the use of facial features associated with FAS with MRI findings as markers of alcohol-related brain damage.

Two callosal summary scores and four landmark points can be used to create a classification algorithm that discriminates the sample (alcohol-exposed vs. nonexposed) with high sensitivity (100 out of 117 subjects) and specificity (49 out of 60 subjects) (Bookstein et al., 2002a). This type of discrimination protocol may be especially useful as a diagnostic tool for the age range studied as many conventional signs used in the diagnosis of young children become less apparent by adolescence and adulthood.

A subsample from the Seattle studies was used to examine the relationship between the alcohol-induced callosal hypervariance and decreased neuropsychological performance (Bookstein et al., 2002b). The relation of callosal shape and neuropsychological performance was analyzed using partial least-squares (PLS) analysis. Briefly, a PLS analysis applies traditional multiple regression methods to latent variables (LVs), which are variables created from a factor analytic procedure to combine and summarize multiple measures of a construct. The data reduction capabilities of PLS can be used to combat both the complexity brought about by large numbers of outcome variables and the statistical problems (e.g., multicollinearity) associated with multiple, indirect measurement of complex constructs. On the basis of this analysis, excess shape variation correlates with two different profiles of cognitive deficit that are unrelated to IQ or the dysmophic/nondysmoprhic group distinction. A relatively thick callosal tract is associated with deficits in executive function, whereas a relatively thin callosum is related to motor deficits.

The effect of ethanol on the corpus callosum has been examined in nonhuman primates (Miller et al., 1999). MRI studies and analyses of postmortem tissue show that the callosum is larger in some ethanol-exposed animals, the most affected segment being the anterior part (including the rostrum). This segment interconnects the frontal cortices and is involved in executive function. Moreover, the number of axons in the anterior callosum is increased in ethanol-exposed monkeys. It is important to note (a) that these ethanol-induced changes are dose-dependent and (b) that they are evident in monkeys with dysmorphic and nondysmorphic FASD.

Basal Ganglia

MRI studies show that the volume of the basal ganglia is reduced in individuals prenatally exposed to alcohol (Mattson et al., 1996). Although both the caudate and the lenticular nuclei are reduced in volume, only the caudate is reduced after brain size is taken into account. A larger study that further delineates subcortical structures (Archibald et al., 2001) describes significant differences in children with FAS. No differences are evident in children with nondysmorphic FASD. The latter data concur with findings of a MRI analysis of the basal ganglia showing no abnormalities in children with dysmorphic and nondysmorphic FASD (Autti-Ramo et al., 2002).

Hippocampus

The hippocampus is associated with short-term memory and learning. According to neuropsychological studies of children with FASD, it appears that the hippocampus is damaged by prenatal alcohol exposure. In a recent study, evaluating spatial learning and memory in children with fetal alcohol exposure (Hamilton et al., 2003), a virtual Morris maze task based on approaches routinely used in animal studies was used as a measure of hippocampal function (Sutherland et al., 2001; Johnson and Goodlett, 2002). Alcohol-exposed children have impaired place learning relative to controls but are equally proficient during the cue-navigation phase. Thus the results of the human studies, like those with animals, implicate that ethanol interferes with hippocampal-mediated place learning.

Imaging studies show hippocampal damage in alcohol-exposed subjects, although not all studies confirm this finding. In a small sample of Finnish adolescents prenatally exposed to alcohol, some children have hippocampal abnormalities including hypoplasia and regional thinning (Autti-Ramo et al., 2002). Moreover, it appears that the hippocampi in these individuals is asymmetrical; specifically, the right hippocampus are significantly larger than the left hippocampus (Riikonen et al., 1999). No lateralization is evident in controls. In contrast, another study describes relative sparing of the alcohol-exposed hippocampus in an otherwise hypoplastic brain (Archibald et al., 2001). Attempts to replicate existing MRI studies are needed to clarify such conflicting findings. Particularly, longitudinal studies will assist in assessing developmental trends; it is difficult to meaningfully compare cross-sectional samples that differ on crucial variables such as age.

Optic Nerve

Eye abnormalities are frequently documented in individuals with FAS. Optic nerve hypoplasia is the most frequent form of ocular dysmorphology associated with prenatal alcohol exposure (Strömland and Pinazo-Durán, 2002). Ten of 11 children diagnosed with FAS showed evidence of optic nerve hypoplasia when evaluated with MRI, ophthamological examinations, and electroretinogram (ERG) (Hug et al., 2000). In addition to the structural damage to the optic nerve, visual acuity was decreased in all but one subject. Reports of the frequency of vision problems in FAS vary; over half of the children studied in a Swedish sample had visual impairment, and >10% showed severe acuity problems (Strömland, 1985, in Strömland and Pinazo-Durán, 2002). This finding indicates that prenatal alcohol exposure has detrimental consequences on the developing visual system, a conclusion corroborated by ERG results. Ten of 11 subjects in the study by Hug and colleagues (2000) had abnormal ERG results, attributable to a lack of sufficient retinal sensitivity. Data from ophthalmological studies of FAS subjects suggest that ocular deficits should be considered among the constellation of presenting symptoms of an alcohol-exposed individual. Thus, an eye examination may be of diagnostic use in identifying individuals with prenatal alcohol exposure (Strömland and Pinazo-Durán, 2002).

OTHER IMAGING APPROACHES

Ultrasonography

In ultrasonography, sound waves are recorded to produce images of internal organs and body tissues. This imaging modality has been used to examine the consequences of prenatal alcohol exposure on the fetal development of the frontal cortex (Wass et al., 2001). The sample consists of 167 women, almost half of whom consumed varying amounts of alcohol while pregnant. Results from this study represent the spectrum of fetal alcohol exposure effects; the prospectively identified sample relies on neither spontaneously aborted fetuses nor severely affected children identified through retrospective methods, scenarios that overrepresent cases of heavy exposure. The frontal lobe measurement was operationalized as the linear distance from the posterior cavum septum pellucidum to the inner surface of the calvarium. It should be noted that this measurement is logically less comprehensive and precise than area or volume measurements of brain structure. Regression analyses were used to determine which of several variables studied were predictive of in vivo fetal frontal lobe size. In general, alcohol exposure is a significant predictor of reduced frontal lobe size. Interestingly, other brain measurements taken from the ultrasonographs, such as the distance between the posterior thalamus and the inner calvarium, are less sensitive to alcohol exposure than the frontal cortex.

There is an interaction between the effect of alcohol exposure on the developing frontal cortex and maternal age (Wass et al., 2001). Within the alcohol-exposed women, a maternal age of greater than 30 years old increases the risk of a fetus having a significantly smaller frontal lobe. This finding is consistent with previous research identifying advanced maternal age as a risk factor for having a child born with FAS (May and Gossage, 2001). Thus, it appears that the deleterious effects of alcohol exposure on the developing frontal cortex are exacerbated with increased maternal age.

Emission Computed Tomography

Emission computed tomography (CT) technologies, such as positron emission tomography (PET) and single photon emission computed tomography (SPECT), can be used to measure cerebral metabolism. Accordingly, a radiotracer is injected into a subject's body and images of a nonsedated individual, who might be asked to perform a behavioral task, are taken. The images are reconstructed to appreciate the activity within nuclei of the brain. For the purposes of the research discussed in the present chapter, measurements obtained in this way are a proxy for brain function in that increased metabolic rates within a brain region indicate more neural activity in that region.

The effect of prenatal alcohol exposure on brain function was assessed via PET analysis in 19 young adults diagnosed with FAS (Clark et al., 2000). Glucose metabolism in subcortical areas, including the thalamic and caudate nuclei, is decreased. In the most severe situations, ethanol causes gross structural deficits, whereas other cases show subtle effects that vary by region or cell type. These changes are reminiscent of ethanol-induced reductions in glucose utilization among specific subcortical structures in the rat brain (Vingan et al., 1986; Miller and Dow-Edwards, 1993). Thus, fetal alcohol exposure causes a continuum of damage to the developing brain.

SPECT has been used to evaluate the brain function of 11 children (mean age, 8.6 years) with FAS (Riikonen et al., 1999). These children exhibit moderate decreases in cerebral blood flow in the left parieto-occipital region. This is consistent with the abnormalities identified by structural MRI studies. Altered function within this region may be related to difficulties that children with FAS have with arithmetic and speech. Additionally, the sample of children with FAS shows an asymmetrical pattern of frontal lobe perfusion, or the pattern in which the radiotracer is incorporated by the tissue. Specifically, the right frontal region showed slight hyperperfusion compared to the pattern in the left region. This difference may relate to the attention deficits commonly seen in chidren with FAS, although this finding contrasts with the hypoperfusion in the left frontal and prefrontal lobes of children with attention deficit hyperactivity disorder (Sieg et al., 1995; Amen and Carmichael, 1997; Langleben et al., 2001). Notably, structural imaging in the children with FAS showed that the brains of 6 of the 11 subjects had gross structural abnormalities, including cortical atrophy and anomalies of the corpus callosum and cerebellum.

A recent SPECT study evaluated cerebral blood flow in three individuals diagnosed with FAS (one child, one adolescent, and one adult) (Bhatara et al., 2002). All three cases not only have structural abnormalities but also reduced cerebral blood flow in the temporal cortex. Similar to the findings of Riikonen and colleagues (1999), the case study report noted left hemisphere hyperfusion, which is consistent with left hemisphere dysfunction.

SUMMARY AND CONCLUSIONS

Teratogenic exposure to alcohol (1) causes permanent changes in brain structure and (2) differentially affects specific components and regions of the brain. These structural changes likely underlie deficits in the cognitive ability and adaptive functioning of exposed individuals. Structural brain deficits revealed by quantitative image analyses of alcohol-exposed individuals include reductions in overall brain volume and alterations in brain shape, density, and bilateral symmetry. Additionally, some structures are especially vulnerable to the teratogenic effects of alcohol, notably the cerebellum, corpus callosum, and the various structures that make up the basal ganglia.

From a neurobehavioral point of view, fetal alcohol effects comprise a continuum, resulting in a range of devastating behavioral and cognitive disabilities. Targeted research defining the degree of insult to a structure and the continuum of neurobehavioral effects will be of great clinical utility. Given that individuals with histories of heavy prenatal alcohol exposure face long-lasting deficits affecting multiple aspects of cognitive and behavioral functioning, identification of brain areas likely associated with such deficits will improve diagnostic and treatment strategies.

Multidisciplinary research is needed to fill in the gaps in our current knowledge and open new light on how structural deficits in the alcohol-exposed brain relate to neurobehavioral outcome. Accordingly, a recent meeting of international collaborators highlighted the critical importance of research focusing on the relationship between brain structure and function in FASD (Riley et al., 2003). In particular, functional imaging studies will provide an in vivo account of how prenatal alcohol exposure affects neural resource allocation, on a cognitive task-by-task basis. It is possible that future research will show that a pathognomonic FASD brain does not exist. Regardless of the wide-ranging neural complications that fetal alcohol effects may exhibit, the keystone of effective intervention rests on explicating how behavioral sequelae result from teratogenic alteration of the brain.

Abbreviations

ALC prenatally exposed to alcohol, both with and without dysmorphic features

CNS central nervous system

CT computed tomography

FAS fetal alcohol syndrome

FASD fetal alcohol spectrum disorders

IQ intelligence quotient

LV latent variable

MRI magnetic resonance imaging

PET positron emission tomography

PLS partial least squares analysis

SPECT single photon emission computed tomography

VBM voxel-based morphometry

ACKNOWLEDGMENTS This work was supported by the National Institutes of Heath (AA013525 and AA01 0417).

References

Abel EL (1984) *Fetal Alcohol Syndrome and Fetal Alcohol Effects.* Plenum, New York, pp 1–28.
——— (1995) An update on incidence of FAS: FAS is not an equal opportunity birth defect. Neurotoxicol Teratol 17:437–443.
Amen DG, Carmichael BD (1997) High resolution brain SPECT imaging and ADHD. Ann Clin Psychiatry 9:81–86.

Archibald SL, Fennema-Notestine C, Gamst A, Riley EP, Mattson SN, Jernigan TL (2001) Brain dysmorphology in individuals with severe prenatal alcohol exposure. Dev Med Child Neurol 43:148–154.

Autti-Ramo I, Autti T, Korkman M, Kettunen S, Salonen O, Valanne L (2002) MRI findings in children with school problems who had been exposed prenatally to alcohol. Dev Med Child Neurol 44:98–106.

Barkovich AJ, Norman D (1988) Anomalies of the corpus callosum: correlation with further anomalies of the brain. Am Roentgen 151:171–179.

Bertrand J, Floyd RL, Weber MK, O'Connor M, Riley EP, Johnson KA, Cohen DE (2004) *National Task Force on FAS/FAE: Guidelines for Referral and Diagnosis.* Centers for Disease Control and Prevention, Atlanta, GA.

Bhatara VS, Lovrein F, Kirkeby J, Swayze V 2nd, Unruh E, Johnson V (2002) Brain function in fetal alcohol syndrome assessed by single photon emission computed tomography. South Dakota J Med 55:59–62.

Bookstein FL, Sampson PD, Connor PD, Streissguth AP (2002a) Midline corpus callosum is a neuroanatomical focus of fetal alcohol damage. Anat Rec 269:162–174.

Bookstein FL, Sampson PD, Streissguth AP, Connor PD (2001) Geometric morphometrics of corpus callosum and subcortical structures in the fetal-alcohol-affected brain. Teratology 64:4–32.

Bookstein FL, Streissguth AP, Sampson PD, Connor PD, Barr HM (2002b) Corpus callosum shape and neuropsychological deficits in adult males with heavy fetal alcohol exposure. Neuroimage 15:233–251.

Clark CM, Li D, Conry J, Conry R, Loock C (2000) Structural and functional brain integrity of fetal alcohol syndrome in nonretarded cases. Pediatrics 105:1096–1099.

Clarren SK (1986) Neuropathology in fetal alcohol syndrome. In: West JR (ed). *Alcohol and Brain Development.* Oxford University Press, New York, pp 158–166.

Clarren SK, Alvord EC Jr, Sumi SM, Streissguth AP, Smith DW (1978) Brain malformations related to prenatal exposure to ethanol. J Pediatr 92:64–67.

Connor PD, Sampson PD, Bookstein FL, Barr HM, Streissguth AP (2000) Direct and indirect effects of prenatal alcohol damage on executive function. Dev Neuropsychol 18:331–354.

Coulter CL, Leech RW, Schaefer GB, Scheithauer BW, Brumback RA (1993) Midline cerebral dysgenesis, dysfunction of the hypothalamic-pituitary axis, and fetal alcohol effects. Arch Neurol 50:771–775.

Courchesne E, Karns CM, Davis HR, Ziccardi R, Carper RA, Tigue ZD, Chisum HJ, Moses P, Pierce K, Lord C, Lincoln AJ, Pizzo S, Schreibman L,

Haas RH, Akshoomoff NA, Courchesne RY (2001) Unusual brain growth patterns in early life in patients with autistic disorder: an MRI study. Neurology 57:245–254.

Goodlett CR, Marcussen BL, West JR (1990) A single day of alcohol exposure during the brain growth spurt induces brain weight restriction and cerebellar Purkinje cell loss. Alcohol 7:107–114.

Hamilton, DA, Kodituwakku, P, Sutherland, RJ, Savage, DD (2003) Children with fetal alcohol syndrome are impaired at place learning but not cued-navigation in a virtual Morris water task. Behav Brain Res 143:85–94.

Hug TE, Fitzgerald KM, Cibis GW (2000) Clinical and electroretinographic findings in fetal alcohol syndrome. J AAPOS 4:200–204.

Jeret JS, Serur D, Wisniewski K, Fisch C (1986) Frequency of agenesis of the corpus callosum in the developmentally disabled population as determined by computerized tomography. Pediatr Neurosci 12:101–103.

Johnson TB, Goodlett CR (2002) Selective and enduring deficits in spatial learning after limited neonatal binge alcohol exposure in male rats. Alcohol Clin Exp Res 26:83–93.

Johnson VP, Swayze VW 2nd, Sato Y, Andreasen NC (1996) Fetal alcohol syndrome: craniofacial and central nervous system manifestations. Am J Med Genet 61:329–339.

Jones KL (1975) Aberrant neuronal migration in the fetal alcohol syndrome. Birth Defects 11:131–132.

Kodituwakku PW, Kalberg W, May PA (2001) The effects of prenatal alcohol exposure on executive functioning. Alcohol Res Health 25:192–198.

Langleben DD, Austin G, Krikorian G, Ridlehuber HW, Goris ML, Strauss HW (2001) Interhemisphereic asymmetry of regional blood flow in prepubescent boys with attention deficit hyperactivity disorder. Nucl Med Commun 22:1333–1340.

Light KE, Belcher SM, Pierce DR (2002) Time course and manner of Purkinje neuron death following a single ethanol exposure on postnatal day 4 in the developing rat. Neuroscience 114:327–337.

Mattson SN, Goodman AM, Caine C, Delis DC, Riley EP (1999) Executive functioning in children with heavy prenatal alcohol exposure. Alcohol Clin Exp Res 23:1808–1815.

Mattson SN, Riley EP (1998) A review of the neurobehavioral deficits in children with fetal alcohol syndrome or prenatal exposure to alcohol. Alcohol Clin Exp Res 22:279–294.

Mattson SN, Riley EP, Sowell ER, Jernigan TL, Sobel DF, Jones KL (1996) A decrease in the size of the basal ganglia in children with fetal alcohol syndrome. Alcohol Clin Exp Res 20:1088–1093.

May PA, Gossage JP (2001) Examining the prevalence of fetal alcohol syndrome. Alcohol Res Health 25: 159–167.

Miller MW, Astley SJ, Clarren SK (1999) Number of axons in the corpus callosum of the mature *Macaca nemestrina*: increases caused by prenatal exposure to ethanol. J Comp Neurol 412:123–131.

Miller MW, Dow-Edwards DL (1993) Vibrissal stimulation affects glucose utilization in the rat trigeminal/somatosensory system both in normal rats and in rats prenatally exposed to ethanol. J Comp Neurol 335:283–294.

Miller MW, Potempa G (1990) Numbers of neurons and glia in mature rat somatosensory cortex: effects of prenatal exposure to ethanol. J Comp Neurol 293: 92–102.

Mooney SM, Napper RM, West JR (1996) Long-term effect of postnatal alcohol exposure on the number of cells in the neocortex of the rat: a stereological study. Alcohol Clin Exp Res 20:615–623.

Mooney SM, Napper RMA (2005) Early postnatal exposure to ethanol affects rat neocortex in a spatiotemporal manner. Alcohol Clin Exp Res 29:683–691.

Peiffer J, Majewski F, Fischbach H, Bierich JR, Volk B (1979) Alcohol embryo- and fetopathy. Neuropathology of 3 children and 3 fetuses. J Neurol Sci 41:125–137.

Pulsifer MB (1996) The neuropsychology of mental retardation. J Int Neuropsychol Soc 2:159–176.

Raz N, Torres IJ, Briggs SD, Spencer WD, Thornton AE, Loken WJ, Gunning FM, McQuain JD, Driesen NR, Acker JD (1995) Selective neuroanatomic abnormalities in Down's syndrome and their cognitive correlates: evidence from MRI morphometry. Neurology 45:356–366.

Riikonen R, Salonen I, Partanen K, Verho S (1999) Brain perfusion SPECT and MRI in foetal alcohol syndrome. Dev Med Child Neurol 41:652–659.

Riley EP, Guerri C, Calhoun F, Charness ME, Foroud TM, Li TK, Mattson SN, May PA, Warren KR (2003) Prenatal alcohol exposure: advancing knowledge through international collaborations. Alcohol Clin Exp Res 27:118–135.

Riley EP, Mattson SN, Sowell ER, Jernigan TL, Sobel DF, Jones KL (1995) Abnormalities of the corpus callosum in children prenatally exposed to alcohol. Alcohol Clin Exp Res 19:1198–1202.

Schmitt JE, Eliez S, Warsofsky IS, Bellugi U, Reiss AL (2001) Enlarged cerebellar vermis in Williams syndrome. J Psychiatr Res 35:225–229.

Sieg KG, Gaffney GR, Preston DF, Hellings JA (1995) SPECT brain imaging abnormalities in attention deficit hyperactivity disorder. Clin Nucl Med 20: 55–60.

Sowell ER, Jernigan TL, Mattson SN, Riley EP, Sobel DF, Jones KL (1996) Abnormal development of the cerebellar vermis in children prenatally exposed to alcohol: size reduction in lobules I–V. Alcohol Clin Exp Res 20:31–34.

Sowell ER, Mattson SN, Thompson PM, Jernigan TL, Riley EP, Toga AW (2001a) Mapping callosal morphology and cognitive correlates: effects of heavy prenatal alcohol exposure. Neurology 57:235–244.

Sowell ER, Thompson PM, Mattson SN, Tessner KD, Jernigan TL, Riley EP, Toga AW (2001b) Voxel-based morphometric analyses of the brain in children and adolescents prenatally exposed to alcohol. Neuroreport 12:515–523.

—— (2002a) Regional brain shape abnormalities persist into adolescence after heavy prenatal alcohol exposure. Cereb Cortex 12:856–865.

Sowell ER, Thompson PM, Peterson BS, Mattson SN, Welcome SE, Henkenius AL, Riley EP, Jernigan TL, Toga AW (2002b) Mapping cortical gray matter asymmetry patterns in adolescents with heavy prenatal alcohol exposure. Neuroimage 17:1807–1819.

Streissguth AP, Connor PD (2001) Fetal alcohol syndrome and other effect of prenatal alcohol: developmental cognitive neuroscience implications. In: Nelson CA, Luciana M (eds). *Handbook of Developmental Cognitive Neuroscience*. MIT Press, Cambridge, MA, pp 505–518.

Strömland K, Pinazo-Durán MD (2002) Ophthalmic involvement in the fetal alcohol syndrome: clinical and animal model studies. Alcohol Alcohol 37: 2–8.

Sutherland RJ, Weisend MP, Mumby D, Astur RS, Hanlon FM, Koerner A, Thomas MJ, Wu Y, Moses SN, Cole C, Hamilton DA, Hoesing JM (2001) Retrograde amnesia after hippocampal damage: recent vs. remote memories in two tasks. Hippocampus 11:27–42.

Swayze VW 2nd, Johnson VP, Hanson JW, Piven J, Sato Y, Giedd JN, Mosnik D, Andreasen NC. (1997) Magnetic resonance imaging of brain anomalies in fetal alcohol syndrome. Pediatrics 99:232–240.

Vingan RD, Dow-Edwards DL, Riley EP (1986) Cerebral metabolic alterations in rats following prenatal alcohol exposure: a deoxyglucose study. Alcohol Clin Exp Res 10:22–26.

Wass TS, Persutte WH, Hobbins JC (2001) The impact of prenatal alcohol exposure on frontal cortex development in utero. Am J Obstet Gynecol 185: 737–742.

Wisniewski K, Dambska M, Sher JH, Qazi Q (1983) A clinical neuropathological study of the fetal alcohol syndrome. Neuropediatrics 14:197–201.

10

Prenatal Ethanol Exposure and Fetal Programming: Implications for Endocrine and Immune Development and Long-Term Health

Joanna H. Sliwowska

Xingqi Zhang

Joanne Weinberg

Ethanol use and abuse result in clinical abnormalities of endocrine function and neuroendocrine regulation (Morgan, 1982; Adler, 1992). Direct and indirect effects of ethanol on many hormone systems, including the adrenal, gonadal, and thyroid axes, as well as on aldosterone, growth hormone, parathyroid hormone, calcitonin, insulin, and glucagon, have been reported. Secondary complications such as liver disease, malnutrition, and other medical conditions often present in alcoholics may in and of themselves have endocrine consequences and can potentially exacerbate the adverse effects of ethanol.

Whether ethanol-induced endocrine imbalances contribute to the etiology of fetal alcohol spectrum disorders (FASD) is unknown, but it is certainly a possibility (Anderson, 1981). The effects of ethanol on interactions between the pregnant female and fetus are complex (Rudeen and Taylor, 1992; Weinberg, 1993a, 1993b, 1994), and both direct and indirect effects of ethanol on fetal development occur. Ethanol readily crosses the placenta, thus directly affecting developing fetal cells and tissues, including those related to endocrine function. In addition, ethanol-induced changes in endocrine function can disrupt the hormonal interactions between the pregnant female and fetal systems, altering the normal hormone balance and indirectly affecting the development of fetal metabolic, physiological, and endocrine functions. Ethanol-induced changes in metabolic and/or endocrine function can also affect a female's ability to maintain a successful pregnancy, resulting in miscarriage or, if the fetus is carried to term, possible congenital defects. Of particular relevance to the present Chapter is the notion that disturbances of the reciprocal interconnections between (a) the pregnant female and fetus or (b) the maternal and neonatal hypothalamic–pituitary–adrenal (HPA) axes, may provide a common pathway by which perinatal exposure to different agents results in fetal programming (Angelucci et al., 1985). *Fetal* or *early programming* refers to the concept that early environmental or nongenetic factors, including pre- or perinatal exposure to drugs or other toxic agents, can permanently organize or imprint physiological and behavioral systems and increase vulnerability to illnesses or disorders later in life (Matthews, 2000, 2002; Bakker et al., 2001; Welberg and Seckl, 2001).

The present Chapter focuses on the adverse effects of prenatal ethanol exposure on neuroendocrine and immune function, with particular emphasis on the concept of fetal programming and the HPA axis, a key player in the stress response. The HPA axis is highly susceptible to programming during fetal and neonatal development (Matthews, 2000, 2002; Welberg and Seckl, 2001). Early environmental experiences, including exposure to ethanol, can reprogram the HPA axis such that HPA tone is increased throughout life. This chapter presents data demonstrating that gestational ethanol exposure increases HPA activity in both the pregnant female and the offspring. Evidence suggesting that increased exposure to endogenous glucocorticoids over the lifespan can alter behavioral and physiological responsiveness and predispose the organism to development of certain diseases later in life is also described. Alterations in immune function may be one of the consequences of fetal HPA programming. The chapter discusses studies demonstrating that ethanol is an immunoteratogenic agent and that programming of HPA activity may mediate some of the adverse effects of prenatal ethanol exposure on immune competence in later life.

THE CONCEPT OF STRESS

The term *stress*, used in the biological sense, was popularized by Hans Selye, who proposed that stress can be understood within the context of the "general adaptation syndrome." This concept grew out of Selye's observations that a wide variety of physically noxious stimuli, such as cold or heat exposure, surgery, muscular exercise, bacteria, toxins, or X-irradiation, resulted in essentially the same triad of symptoms: (1) adrenal cortical enlargement, (2) thymic involution or atrophy, and (3) gastrointestinal ulcers (Selye, 1936, 1950).

The response triad holds despite the fact that a highly specific adaptive response exists for any one of these agents by itself. These symptoms are considered a nonspecific adaptive response of the body to a physical stressor and part of the "alarm reaction," the first

stage of the general adaptation syndrome. This stage is characterized by activation of the HPA system, and the corresponding changes in immune function and gastric ulceration are thought to be mediated to some extent by this HPA activation. If the stressful stimulus persists, the organism enters the second, or resistance, phase of the general adaptation syndrome, during which adrenocortical activation is maintained. After repeated or constant exposure to the stressor the organism enters the third phase, when the capacity of the adrenal cortex to synthesize, store, and secrete glucocorticoids is exceeded (Selye, 1946). Although not all aspects of the general adaptation syndrome are supported by subsequent experimental evidence, this concept has provided a powerful context for stress research for many years.

The concept of nonspecificity (Selye 1936, 1950) has raised a critical question: through what mechanisms could so many diverse agents transmit the common "message" of stress? Selye speculated that there must be some physiological "first mediator" of stress, i.e., some nonspecific chemical or byproduct of biological reactions that produced these symptoms indicative of stress (Mason, 1975). The search for physiological first mediators was largely unproductive. By the 1960s, stress researchers became increasingly aware that (a) psychological and social factors had effects similar to and perhaps even more potent than those of physical stressors and (b) that the HPA axis was particularly sensitive to these psychological stimuli (Mason, 1968). This growing understanding of the role of psychological variables led Mason (1975) to suggest that the unrecognized first mediators in many of Selye's experiments may have been the substrate in the central nervous system (CNS) involved in emotional arousal. That HPA activation frequently occurred during novel or aversive stimulation is not surprising because the HPA axis is an excellent indicator of arousal (Hennessy and Levine, 1979). This understanding altered the concept of nonspecificity, at least in terms of the HPA response. Instead of viewing hormonal responses as being elicited by a great diversity of stimuli, they could be viewed as being elicited largely by the emotional arousal or activation common to most if not all novel and aversive situations.

A concept of stress emphasizing the "emergency" function of the sympathetic nervous system and the adrenal medulla and their roles in maintaining internal homeostasis comes from the work of Cannon

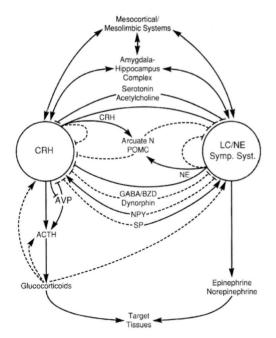

FIGURE 10–1 Schematic representation of circuitry of the stress system. The two major systems central to the stress response are the hypothalamic-pituitary-adrenal (HPA) axis and the locus coeruleus noradrenergic sympathetic adrenal medullary (LC-NE) system, which interact to maintain homeostasis. The HPA axis consists of a cascade of responses. Corticotropin-releasing hormone (CRH), secreted by the hypothalamus, stimulates the release of adrenocorticotropic hormone (ACTH) from the anterior pituitary, which in turn stimulates release of the glucocorticoid hormones from the adrenal cortex. The glucocorticoids feed back at multiple levels of the axis to inhibit activity. In the LC-NE system, norepinephrine (NE), released primarily from sympathetic nerve terminals, and epinephrine, released primarily from the adrenal medulla, activate sympathetic responses. Homeostasis is restored by activation of the parasympathetic system. The LC-NE system allows the organism to react rapidly, while the HPA hormones act over a longer time frame. There are intimate reciprocal interactions between the HPA axis and the LC-NE system, as well as reciprocal neural connections between the two systems. CRH and NE stimulate each other, and the two systems are regulated by similar neurotransmitters and by mesocortical and mesolimbic influences. Glucocorticoids are thought to restrain both systems to prevent the consequences of prolonged or excessive activation. Finally, activity and sensitivity of both systems are modulated by stress and circadian influences. AVP, arginine vasopressin; BZD, benzodiazepine; GABA, γ-aminobutyric acid; NPY, neuropeptide Y; POMC, proopiomelanocortin;

and colleagues (Cannon 1914, 1929; Cannon and de la Paz, 1911). Accordingly, homeostasis is viewed as the operation of coordinated physiological processes that maintain the steady state of the organism. These authors also recognize the importance of psychological over physical stimuli in eliciting a stress response.

In modern stress research, it is now widely accepted that the response to stress is mediated by both the HPA axis and the locus coeruleus noradrenergic sympathetic adrenal medullary system (referred to as the LC-NE system) and that these systems interact to maintain homeostasis (Fig. 10–1). The LC-NE system is involved in the "fight-or-flight" response and enables the organism to react rapidly. Two major players in this rapid response are norepinephrine (NE), secreted from sympathetic nerve terminals, and epinephrine, released from the adrenal medulla. In contrast, the HPA axis acts over a longer time frame and helps orchestrate the response and adaptation of the body to the stressor through various physiological and metabolic changes.

The term *stress* has prevailed over decades because it attempts to address a basic principle of nature: (1) the maintenance of balance, equilibrium, or harmony in the face of disturbing stimuli and (2) the counteracting, re-establishing responses that re-establish homeostasis (Chrousos et al., 1988). Many definitions and meanings have been and still are ascribed to the term *stress*, largely because the term has been used to refer to the disturbing stimuli, the state of disturbed equilibrium, and/or the results of the counteracting responses. This chapter uses the following definitions (Johnson et al., 1992; Miller and O'Callaghan, 2002). *Stress* is a state of threatened internal balance or homeostasis. The threatening or disturbing forces are defined as *stressors*. These can range from real threats to survival (e.g., immune challenges or physical stressors) to perceived threats (e.g., psychological or social stressors). The counteracting forces activated to neutralize the effects of a stressor are *adaptive responses*, which can be both behavioral and physical or physiological, and serve to re-establish homeostasis.

SP, substance P. Activation is represented by solid lines, inhibition by dashed lines. (*Source*: Reprinted from Chrousos (1998) with permission from New York Academy of Sciences)

In recent years, the concepts of allostasis and allostatic load have been added to the stress literature and have extended our thinking about homeostasis (McEwen, 1998; McEwen and Wingfield, 2003). In this framework, the term *homeostasis* refers to the stability of physiological systems that are essential for life and applies strictly to a limited number of systems, such as pH, body temperature, glucose contents, and oxygen tension, that are maintained within narrow ranges optimal for current life conditions. In contrast, the term *allostasis* means the achieving of stability through change and refers to systems such as the HPA axis, catecholamines, and cytokines that maintain homeostatic systems in balance. These systems are typically not required for immediate survival and have much broader boundaries than those of homeostatic systems. Further, as environments or life circumstances change, the set points or boundaries of these allostatic systems may also change.

Allostatic systems enable us to respond to our physical states—for example, awake, asleep, exercising, etc.—and to cope with challenges such as noise, crowding, isolation, extremes of temperature, danger, and infection (McEwen, 1998). The body responds to challenges by turning on allostatic responses (most commonly, for example, activation of the HPA axis and/or LC-NE system) that initiate complex adaptive responses and then shutting off these responses when the threat is past. The term *allostatic state* refers to altered and sustained activities of the primary response mediators, the HPA and catecholamine hormones, that integrate physiological and behavioral responses to challenge. Allostatic states can be sustained for limited periods, however, if inactivation is inefficient or the organism is exposed repeatedly to intense challenges. The cumulative result of an allostatic state is allostatic load, which can have pathophysiologic consequences.

The HPA Axis and β-Endorphin System

The HPA axis includes a number of brain areas, such as the paraventricular nucleus of the hypothalamus (PVN), the anterior pituitary, and adrenal cortex, that act together to produce a hormonal cascade in response to stressors (Fig. 10.1). Corticotropin-releasing hormone (CRH) and arginine vasopressin (AVP) are synthesized in the parvocellular PVN and released into the median eminence, reaching the anterior pituitary via the hypophysial portal system. CRH and AVP act synergistically at the anterior pituitary to stimulate the synthesis of proopiomelanocortin (POMC), a large precursor hormone that when cleaved results in the subsequent release of adrenocorticotropic hormone (ACTH) and the endogenous opioid β-endorphin (β-EP) (Guillemin et al., 1977; Gillies et al., 1982). ACTH then acts at the adrenal cortex to stimulate the synthesis and release of glucocorticoids—cortisol in humans and corticosterone (CORT) in rats. In addition to a variety of important physiological and metabolic functions, the glucocorticoids have a negative feedback action, causing inhibition of HPA activity by acting at the anterior pituitary, the PVN, and other brain regions, particularly the hippocampus and prefrontal cortex. During normal endocrine adaptation to stressors, CRH, ACTH, and glucocorticoid concentrations are kept within levels that promote health. When coping fails, an imbalance develops between drive and feedback mechanisms, resulting in the release of too much or too little of these hormones and increased vulnerability to disease (Chrousos et al., 1988).

The Concept of Fetal Programming

Both epidemiological data and experimental studies suggest that environmental factors operating early in life markedly affect developing systems, permanently altering structure and function throughout life (Fig. 10–2). Although the idea that early experiences can have long-term effects is not new, it is really only in the past decade or so that the concept of fetal or early programming has emerged as a key concept in development. This concept arises from a large body of data showing that low birth weight and other indices of fetal growth are associated with increased biological risk for coronary heart disease, hypertension, and type II diabetes or impaired glucose tolerance in adult life. Adult lifestyle factors such as smoking, ethanol consumption, and exercise appear to be additive to early life influences, thus the early life effects may have distinct roles and causes. These findings have led to the hypothesis that common adult diseases might originate during fetal development, i.e., the "fetal origins of adult disease" hypothesis.

The biological significance of physiological and behavioral programming is not known. It has been suggested that environmental factors acting on the pregnant female and fetus can alter the set point or responsiveness of physiological systems and thus prepare the organism for the environment into which it will be born and develop. If, however, this process is initiated by adverse factors during pregnancy (e.g., placental insufficiency or prenatal ethanol exposure) or if the environmental circumstances later in life differ from what was anticipated, then the physiological adaptations might alone result in maladaptive responses and ultimately predispose the organism to disease (Welberg and Seckl, 2001; Matthews, 2002).

The underlying processes that link early growth restriction with these long-term health consequences are not fully understood. It is generally accepted that low birth weight per se is unlikely to cause these increased risks for disease. Rather, birth weight likely serves as a marker for the effects of early life events, and common factors probably underlie both the intrauterine growth retardation and altered physiological responsiveness (Welberg and Seckl, 2001). The resetting of key hormonal systems by early environmental events may be one mechanism linking early life experiences with long-term health consequences. Studies have identified the HPA axis as one of the key systems likely involved (Fig. 10–2). The HPA axis is highly susceptible to programming during development (Phillips et al., 1998, 2000; Matthews, 2000, 2002) and studies demonstrate strong correlations between birth weight, plasma cortisol concentrations, and the development of hypertension and type II diabetes. Thus, it has been suggested that intrauterine programming of the HPA axis is a mechanism underlying the observed associations between low birth weight and increased risk for disease. In order to understand fetal programming more fully, it is important to describe how the HPA axis develops.

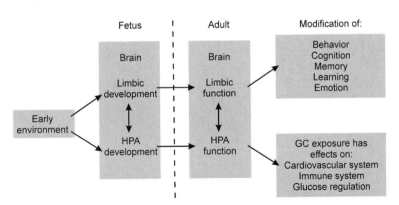

FIGURE 10–2 Routes by which the fetal and early neonatal environment can program adult hypothalamic–pituitary–adrenal (HPA) function and behavior. The developing limbic system, hypothalamus, and pituitary synthesize high levels of corticosteroid receptors and are sensitive to glucocorticoids (GCs). Early exposure to GCs alters the development and subsequent activity and function of both the limbic system and the HPA axis. In the periphery, the overall effect of programming during development is altered exposure to endogenous GCs throughout life. Increased exposure has long-term effects on behavior, cognition, learning, and memory, and predisposes the individual to neurological, metabolic, and immune diseases and disorders in later life. Conversely, if programming reduces exposure to GCs over the lifespan, this might act to protect against these pathological changes. (*Source*: Reprinted from Matthews (2002) with permission from Elsevier)

DEVELOPMENT OF THE HPA AXIS

The HPA Axis in
Human Development

As a result of the difficulty of sampling and measuring ACTH, few data exist on regulation of ACTH secretion in the human fetus. By 9 weeks of gestation, the human fetal pituitary contains measurable corticotropic activity and the content and concentration of ACTH increases with gestational age (Kastin et al., 1968; Pavlova et al., 1968). By 12 weeks of gestation, ACTH is detectable by radioimmunoassay in human placenta. ACTH concentration is high prior to 34 weeks and then falls significantly in late gestation (Winters et al., 1974). Infusion of ACTH to the pregnant female at term does not affect the concentrations of plasma ACTH in the fetus, providing evidence that this hormone does not cross the placenta (Miyakawa et al., 1976).

In contrast to ACTH, concentrations of cortisol are high in the blood of the pregnant woman and there is transplacental transfer of cortisol (Pasqualini et al., 1970). Fetal exposure to cortisol is minimized, however, because cortisol is rapidly inactivated by the placental enzyme 11 β-hydroxysteroid dehydrogenase type 2 (Seckl, 2004a, 2004b). About 80% of cortisol derived from the pregnant female is converted to CORT (Beitins et al., 1973; Murphy et al., 1974). The remaining fraction makes an important contribution to fetal plasma cortisol. Children exposed to dexamethasone (a synthetic glucocorticoid) during early pregnancy because of a risk of congenital adrenal hyperplasia show increased emotionality, unsociability, avoidance, and behavioral problems (Trautman et al., 1995). The role of prenatal glucocorticoids in animal models of FASD is discussed in the section Prenatal Ethanol Exposure Alters the Immune System of Offspring (below).

The HPA Axis in Rodents

Studies on rats show that CORT secretion in response to stressors is very high during the late fetal period (Milkovic and Milkovic, 1963). In contrast, beginning on about postnatal day (P) 2 and continuing into the second week of life, the HPA response is markedly suppressed in rat pups. The pioneering work of Schapiro (1962) identifies this developmental stage and calls it the "stress nonresponsive period" (SNRP). Later studies show that HPA responsiveness is not actually abolished during this period but simply suppressed, and this period has been renamed the "stress hyporesponsive period" (SHRP). The SHRP is characterized by blunted adrenal CORT secretion, despite normal pituitary ACTH responses to a variety of stressors. Hypothalamic CRH content is decreased to about 20% of that found in 21-day-old animals, and there is also a decrease in functionally active glucocorticoid receptors to about 20% of those found in adults (Levine et al., 1967; Meaney et al., 1985a, 1985b; Walker et al., 1986a, 1991; Witek-Janusek, 1988). This blunted basal and stimulated CORT secretion is believed to be due in part to a decrease in adrenal sensitivity to ACTH (Levine et al., 1967) and increase in sensitivity to HPA feedback (Walker et al., 1986b). The low circulating glucocorticoid concentrations during the SHRP appear to have a protective function and are essential for normal brain and behavioral development (Rosenfeld et al., 1992; Walker et al., 2002). For example, rats treated with glucocorticoids during the first week of life have reduced brain weights, alterations in neurons (e.g., reduced numbers of dendritic spines), glia, and myelin, and behavioral changes (Sapolsky and Meaney, 1986). Similarly, CORT treatment during the first postnatal week results in lowered adult basal CORT concentrations (Turner and Taylor, 1976) and neonatal treatment with ACTH on P7–P9 and P17–P19 suppresses the CORT circadian rhythm in adult rats (Taylor et al., 1976). The presence of the dam appears to be critical for maintaining the SHRP, and separation from the mother "releases" the pup HPA axis from inhibition. In 10-day-old pups, for example, maternal separation (removing active sensory stimulation, food, and passive contact) enhanced basal and stimulated ACTH and CORT secretion after exposure to ether vapors and insulin-induced hypoglycemia (Walker, 1995). Thus it appears that the first 2 postnatal weeks represent a critical period corresponding to specific stages in the normal development of hypothalamic and forebrain structures that modulate ACTH and CORT secretion as well as CNS structures involved in circadian regulation.

By weaning age (P21–P25), the plasma ACTH and CORT responses to stressors appear to be at essentially adult concentrations. Measures of CRH have shown a similar developmental pattern, with adult responsiveness being reached by weaning age (Hiroshige and Sato, 1970). In contrast, negative feedback mechanisms continue to increase in effectiveness between weaning age and adulthood. When exposed to ether or shock, for example, the plasma CORT response of the weanling shows a later peak and delayed return to resting concentrations compared with the pattern in adulthood (Goldman et al., 1973).

In summary, in the rat, the postnatal period is critical for the development and integration of the CNS and peripheral nervous system mechanisms necessary to maintain homeostasis. In contrast, many of these systems reach a greater degree of organization at birth in guinea pigs, sheep, nonhuman primates, and humans (Weaver et al., 2004).

GESTATIONAL ETHANOL EXPOSURE AND HPA ACTIVITY

Human Studies

Compared to the fairly large literature on the effects of ethanol consumption on the HPA axis of adults following acute or chronic ethanol intake, only a few human studies have examined the effects of drinking during pregnancy on the HPA axis of the developing child. In case studies by Root and colleagues (1975), plasma cortisol concentrations are within normal range in children with FASD. By contrast, data from Jacobson and colleagues (1999) show that heavy drinking during pregnancy and at conception are associated with higher basal and post-stress (blood draw) cortisol concentrations in 13-month-old infants. Basal cortisol concentrations are also higher in 2-month-old infants exposed in utero to ethanol or cigarettes (Ramsay et al., 1996). Animal studies strongly support this finding that ethanol exposure in utero can have major effects on development and function of the offspring HPA axis. Not surprisingly, HPA activity in the pregnant female is also altered by ethanol consumption.

Animal Studies

Effects of Ethanol Consumption on HPA Activity of the Pregnant Female

Data from rodent models indicate that gestational ethanol consumption increases adrenal weights, basal CORT concentrations, the CORT stress response, and the CORT stress increment in the pregnant dam (Weinberg and Bezio, 1987). This occurs as early as gestational day (G) 11, persists throughout gestation, may increase as gestation progresses, and occurs even with low concentrations of ethanol in the diet (Weinberg and Bezio, 1987; Weinberg and Gallo, 1982). Importantly, this activation appears to be related to ethanol rather than to nutritional factors as maternal nutritional status has no major impact on these effects (Weinberg and Bezio, 1987). The stimulatory effects of ethanol on basal hormone concentrations and the corticoid response to stressors also can extend through parturition, even when ethanol administration is discontinued prior to parturition (Weinberg, 1989). Thus regular consumption of high doses of ethanol during pregnancy not only raises the set point of HPA function in the pregnant female by increasing both basal and stress concentrations of CORT but also results in HPA hyperresponsiveness to stressors. The additional finding that binding capacity of corticosterone binding globulin (CBG) in ethanol-consuming females is similar to or less than that in control females, both during pregnancy and at parturition, indicates that the elevated CORT concentrations are functionally important and supports the conclusion that prenatal ethanol exposure results in both hypersecretion and hyperresponsiveness of the HPA axis (Weinberg and Bezio, 1987; Weinberg, 1989).

The pregnant female and the fetus constitute an interrelated functional unit. Hence, ethanol-induced alterations in HPA activity in the pregnant female have implications for fetal HPA development. CORT crosses the placenta, at least to some extent (Eguchi, 1969), resulting in suppression of endogenous fetal HPA activity. At the same time, ethanol can cross the placenta and directly activate the fetal HPA axis. Together these influences may have permanent organizational effects on neural structures that regulate HPA activity throughout life (Levine and Mullins, 1966). Whether the increased plasma CORT concentration in pregnant females plays a role in mediating HPA hyperresponsiveness in fetal ethanol-exposed (FEE) offspring is as yet unresolved. Adrenalectomy (ADX) of the pregnant dam has no effect on the increased CORT responses to restraint stress in FEE female offspring (Slone and Redei, 2002). Similarly, CORT treatment of ADX dams does not mimic the effect of prenatal ethanol exposure on HPA activity of offspring (Lee and Rivier, 1992) On the basis of these data, it appears that the increased stress responsiveness of FEE offspring is not mediated primarily by increased CORT concentrations in pregnant females.

In contrast, ADX of the pregnant female can reverse the effects of prenatal ethanol exposure on pituitary POMC mRNA concentrations in FEE offspring (Redei et al., 1993). Furthermore, Tritt and colleagues (1993) have suggested that removal of the adrenal cortex, but not the medulla, in the pregnant female prevents the growth-retarding effects of prenatal ethanol and may reverse the delay in postpartum weight gain in FEE offspring. Thus the adverse effects of ethanol on birth weight are mediated at least partially through the adrenal gland. Further studies must be done to resolve the role of corticosteroids derived from the pregnant female in mediating the adverse effects of ethanol on their offspring. It is likely, however, that a complex interaction between direct and indirect effects of ethanol mediates the adverse consequences of ethanol consumption during pregnancy on fetal development and programming of fetal HPA activity.

Effects of Prenatal Ethanol Exposure on HPA Activity in Offspring

The Preweaning Period. The complex interaction of direct and indirect effects of ethanol is apparent in the offspring following parturition. FEE fetuses exhibit decreased CORT concentrations compared to control fetuses on G19 (Revskoy et al., 1997). In contrast, at birth, FEE neonates have elevated plasma and brain contents of CORT, decreased CBG binding capacity, elevated plasma and pituitary concentrations of β-EP, and reduced pituitary concentrations of β-EP (Kakihana et al., 1980; Taylor et al., 1983; Weinberg et al., 1986; Angelogianni and Gianoulakis, 1989; Weinberg, 1989). Throughout the preweaning period, FEE offspring exhibit blunted HPA and β-EP responses to a wide range of stressors, including ether, novelty, saline injection, and cold stress (Taylor et al., 1986; Weinberg et al., 1986; Angelogianni and Gianoulakis, 1989; Weinberg, 1989). In addition, prenatal ethanol exposure alters the ontogenetic expression of mRNAs for CRH and POMC, delaying and exaggerating the rise in CRH expression in female (but not male) pups, and suppresses POMC mRNA concentrations in male (but not female) pups throughout the preweaning period (Aird et al., 1997). The implication is that sexually dimorphic effects of prenatal ethanol exposure on these two important glucocorticoid-regulated genes contribute to both the immediate and the long-term effects of prenatal ethanol on stress responsiveness of the offspring.

The significance of the reduced hormonal responsiveness described in FEE pups during early development remains to be determined. Evidence indicates that in addition to the reduced adrenocortical responses to stressors, plasma CBG binding capacity is also reduced in FEE compared to that in controls, at least during the first week of life (Weinberg, 1989). Thus it is possible that although the CORT stress response is reduced in FEE pups, the ratio of bound-to-free steroids may not be altered. The reduction in CBG binding capacity may represent a compensatory response to maintain normal neuroendocrine function in FEE offspring. This possibility remains to be tested.

Long-Term Effects of Prenatal Ethanol Exposure. Importantly, the reduced HPA and β-EP responsiveness in FEE rat pups early in life is a transient phenomenon. Following weaning, FEE rats are typically hyperresponsive to stressors and to drugs such as ethanol and morphine (Taylor et al., 1988; Weinberg, 1993a, 1993b; Kim et al., 1996; Lee et al., 1990, 2000). Similar results have been described in non-human primates (Schneider et al., 2004). In rhesus monkeys, prenatal exposure to moderate amounts of ethanol induced higher plasma ACTH and marginally higher plasma cortisol responses to the stress of maternal separation.

An interesting finding from rodent models is that the sexual dimorphism in the effects of prenatal ethanol exposure seen during the ontogeny of the HPA axis (Aird et al., 1997) extends into adulthood. Sex differences in responses of male and female offspring compared to those of their control counterparts are often observed and may vary depending on the nature of the stressor and the time course and hormonal end point measured (Weinberg, 1988, 1992a, 1995; Halasz et al., 1993; Lee and Rivier, 1996). For example, in adulthood, FEE males and females exhibit increased CORT, ACTH, and/or β-EP responses to stressors, such as repeated restraint, footshock, and immune challenges (Taylor et al., 1988; Weinberg, 1993b; Kim et al., 1996, 1999b; Lee and Rivier, 1996; Weinberg et al., 1996; Lee et al., 2000). Both males and females show increased expression of mRNAs for immediate early genes and CRH following stressors (Lee et al., 2000) as well as deficits in habituation to repeated restraint (Weinberg et al., 1996). In contrast, in response to prolonged restraint or cold stress, HPA hyperactivity is seen primarily in FEE males (Weinberg, 1992a; Kim et al., 1999a), whereas in response to acute restraint or acute ethanol or morphine challenge, increased CORT and ACTH concentrations occur primarily in FEE females (Taylor et al., 1982, 1988; Weinberg et al., 1986; Weinberg, 1988). Similarly, altered responses in a consummatory task (Weinberg, 1988) and to predictable and unpredictable restraint stress (Weinberg, 1992b) suggest deficits in the ability of FEE females but not males to use or respond to environmental cues.

Possible Mechanisms Mediating Ethanol-Induced HPA Hyperresponsiveness

The mechanisms underlying HPA hyperresponsiveness in FEE offspring are unknown at present but could reflect changes at all levels of the axis. Increased HPA activity could result from increased secretion of secretagogues (e.g., POMC, CRH, and AVP), increased pituitary and/or adrenal responsiveness to these secretagogues, increased drive to the hypothalamus, deficits in feedback regulation of HPA activity, and/or alterations in central neurotransmitters regulating the HPA axis. Indeed, it is likely that multiple mechanisms play a role. Furthermore, the finding that prenatal ethanol exposure differentially alters HPA responsiveness in males and females compared to that in their control counterparts suggests that the gonadal hormones or altered adrenal–gonadal interactions play a significant role in mediating prenatal ethanol effects on HPA activity. This chapter focuses on four possible mechanisms considered important in mediating HPA hyperresponsiveness in FEE animals: (1) alterations in HPA drive, (2) alterations in HPA feedback regulation, (3) altered neurotransmitter regulation of HPA activity, and (4) possible interactions between the HPA and hypothalamic–pituitary–gonadal (HPG) axes.

Altered HPA Drive and/or Feedback

A number of studies show that stimulatory inputs or drive to the PVN of the hypothalamus are enhanced by prenatal ethanol exposure. Weanling FEE male and female pups exhibit increased basal concentrations of CRH mRNA in the PVN (Lee et al., 1990), and adult FEE males have increased basal concentrations of both hypothalamic CRH mRNA and pituitary POMC

mRNA (Redei et al., 1993) compared to those of controls. Not all studies, however, show these alterations in central HPA regulation of basal activity. Kim and colleagues (1996) reported no differences in basal CRH or AVP mRNA concentrations among adult FEE and control animals. Lee and colleagues (2000) showed no differences in basal CRH heteronuclear (hn) RNA or in basal CRH and AVP median eminence protein concentrations in FEE rats compared to controls. Importantly, however, the latter investigators also showed that in response to both footshock and lipopolysaccharide (LPS; an endotoxin used to mimic infection or inflammation) challenge, FEE animals exhibit enhanced hypothalamic neuronal activity compared to that in controls, reflected in increased mRNA concentrations of two immediate early genes (c-*fos* and NGFI-B), as well as significantly increased CRH hnRNA content. Thus, although there is some controversy in the literature as to whether HPA regulation is altered in FEE animals under basal conditions, the data of Lee and colleagues (2000) provide the first evidence of a selective stress- and cytokine-induced increase in activity of hypothalamic CRH neurons in FEE animals, indicating a potential hypothalamic mechanism through which ethanol up-regulates the HPA axis.

Weinberg and colleagues (Glavas et al., 2001; Zhang et al., 2005b) undertook studies to resolve conflicting findings on whether FEE animals show changes in central HPA regulation under basal or nonstressed conditions. Steady-state HPA function and the role of CORT in mediating changes in HPA regulation were examined in ADX rats with or without CORT replacement. In addition to hormonal concentrations, these investigators assessed the concentrations of mRNA for (a) hypothalamic CRH and AVP as measures of hypothalamic activity, (b) CRH type 1 receptor (CRH-R_1) and POMC as indices of pituitary activity, and (c) hippocampal mineralocorticoid receptor (MR) and glucocorticoid receptor (GR) mRNA concentrations as measures of feedback regulation.

As expected, following ADX, animals exhibit an increase in basal plasma ACTH concentrations compared to those in sham-operated animals (Glavas et al., 2001, Zhang et al., 2005b). Importantly, ACTH elevations are greater in FEE males but not females, compared to those in their control counterparts. These data suggest that a CORT-independent alteration in HPA regulation is unmasked by removal of the CORT feedback signal, at least in males. ADX also reveals significant alterations in gene expression in FEE animals. Following ADX, hypothalamic CRH mRNA concentrations are significantly higher in FEE males and females than in their control counterparts, despite the finding that plasma ACTH concentrations are elevated only in FEE males. FEE males also have blunted AVP mRNA responses to ADX and lower pituitary CRH-R_1 mRNA expression overall compared to controls, but there are no significant differences among groups in pituitary POMC mRNA levels. In addition, CORT replacement is less effective in normalizing ADX-induced alterations in FEE than in control animals at several levels of the HPA axis, including hippocampal MR mRNA concentrations in both males and females, hippocampal GR and hypothalamic AVP mRNA in males, and anterior pituitary CRH-R_1 mRNA in females. The alterations in MR and GR mRNA concentrations are particularly noteworthy, as previous studies have found no ethanol-induced differences in MR and GR receptor concentrations or binding affinity in the hippocampus and other brain regions among FEE and control animals (Weinberg and Petersen, 1991; Kim et al., 1999c). These data are the first to provide direct evidence for possible deficits in sensitivity to CORT regulation of HPA feedback in FEE animals. They suggest an alteration in the balance between HPA drive and CORT feedback and extend previous work supporting alterations in feedback sensitivity in the intermediate (Osborn et al., 1996), but not the fast (Hofmann et al., 1999) feedback time domain.

An altered balance between HPA drive and feedback in FEE compared to control animals is also suggested by data on HPA responsiveness following glucocorticoid receptor blockade (Zhang et al., 2005). Adult female offspring from FEE and control groups were injected with the MR antagonist spironolactone, the GR antagonist RU38486, or vehicle. Following collection of basal blood samples, rats were subjected to a 1 hr restraint stress, and additional samples were collected during and following stress. Both MR and GR blockades increased basal ACTH concentrations in FEE but not control animals, compared to vehicle injection. Furthermore, MR blockade increased ACTH concentrations in control but not FEE females during restraint, whereas GR blockade increased ACTH concentrations in FEE females during restraint and in control females during restraint and recovery, compared to their vehicle-injected counterparts. This differential pattern of responses under both

basal and stress conditions suggests that prenatal ethanol exposure enhances HPA drive and alters sensitivity to feedback regulation by MR and GR, possibly reflecting an altered balance between HPA drive and feedback.

In summary, ethanol-exposed animals exhibit HPA dysregulation under basal conditions, even in the face of similar basal hormone levels, and differences are further unmasked following perturbations of the system by stress, ADX, or receptor blockade. Dysregulation occurs at multiple sites, including the hippocampus, hypothalamus, and pituitary, and reflects changes both in HPA drive and CORT feedback regulation and/or in the balance between drive and feedback. Although FEE animals initiate compensatory mechanisms to maintain normal basal hormone concentrations under most circumstances, perturbations of the system reveal that tonic or basal HPA tone increases and likely plays a key role in raising the set point of responsiveness following stress. The altered CRH-R_1 mRNA responses and the lack of differences in POMC mRNA concentrations in FEE animals suggest compensatory mechanisms, probably at the level of the pituitary, such that the enhanced activation in the hypothalamus does not translate directly into enhanced pituitary activity. This may be protective for FEE animals, minimizing enhanced basal pituitary activity in the face of enhanced hypothalamic drive. Finally, prenatal ethanol exposure has sexually dimorphic effects on HPA regulation. This finding implies a role for the gonadal steroids or possibly an alteration in adrenal–gonadal interactions mediating these effects of ethanol on HPA activity and regulation.

Ethanol Effects on Neurotransmitters Regulating HPA Activity

Fetal ethanol exposure may alter HPA responsiveness through effects on central neurotransmitter systems that regulate HPA function. Data indicate that CRH release is stimulated by acetylocholine and epinephrine in a dose-dependent manner, by low doses of NE, and by serotonin (5-HT), and is inhibited by β-EP, γ-aminobutyric acid (GABA), dynorphin, and substance P (Assenmacher et al., 1987; Plotsky, 1987). Prenatal ethanol exposure alters the development of central neurotransmitter systems in offspring (Druse, 1992). Of particular relevance to this review are data demonstrating long-term changes in NE, 5-HT, nitric oxide

(NO), glutamate, and GABA in FEE rats in brain regions critical for HPA regulation.

Norepinephrine. Ethanol-induced changes in steady-state concentrations of NE appear to vary by brain region as well as the timing of the exposure. Basal concentrations of hippocampal NE were not altered by prenatal ethanol exposure (Rudeen and Weinberg, 1993), whereas exposure through both prenatal and early postnatal development (equivalent of all three trimesters) increased hippocampal NE content in males and females in adulthood (Tran and Kelly, 1999). Whether prenatal ethanol exposure alters hypothalamic NE concentrations is not yet resolved. No differences in hypothalamic NE concentrations were detected between FEE and controls of either sex (Rudeen and Weinberg, 1993). On the other hand, Detering and colleagues (1980, 1981) showed that hypothalamic NE concentrations are decreased in both young and adult rats exposed to ethanol either pre- or postnatally. Unique to the three-trimester model (Tran and Kelly, 1999), however, ethanol-induced increases in basal hypothalamic NE are found in females, but not males.

Exposure to stressors differentially alters NE concentrations in FEE compared to control animals. Ethanol exposure increases hippocampal NE in females (Kelly, 1996b) and decreases cortical and hypothalamic NE concentrations, but it increases hippocampal NE content in both males and females (Rudeen and Weinberg, 1993). These data suggest that the NEergic system in the hippocampus and hypothalamus is particularly vulnerable to ethanol and that alterations in NE regulation in these areas may contribute to the ethanol-induced alterations in HPA activity observed in FEE animals.

Serotonin. The effects of prenatal ethanol exposure on the 5-HTergic system have received special attention because 5-HT also acts as a neurotrophic factor and early insult to this system may affect its own development as well as that of other neurotransmitter systems. Prenatal ethanol exposure results in decreased concentrations of 5-HT or its metabolites during fetal life and in weanling animals (Druse et al., 1991; Rathbun and Druse, 1985). Importantly, prenatal administration of buspirone or ipsapirone, partial $5-HT_{1A}$ agonists, in conjunction with ethanol, ameliorated some of these deficits (Tajuddin and Druse, 1993). On the other hand,

postnatal ethanol exposure increased hypothalamic 5-HT contents in adult rats of both sexes, with females showing greater overall concentrations than males (Kelly, 1996a). Exposure during pre- and postnatal life did not differentially alter hypothalamic 5-HT concentrations (Tran and Kelly, 1999). Fetal ethanol exposure also increased the number of binding sites for the serotonin transporter in some areas of the developing rat brain but decreased transporter binding site numbers in other areas. This finding indicates that ethanol exposure in utero permanently alters 5-HT transmission in discrete brain regions (Zafar et al., 2000). In addition, Sari and Zhou (2004) show that prenatal ethanol exposure results in long-lasting 5-HT deficits in mice and propose that ethanol or its metabolites cause loss of serotonergic neurons through apoptosis.

Animals prenatally exposed to ethanol exhibit physiological and behavioral abnormalities consistent with altered 5-HT function, including lack of response inhibition and increased anxiety and aggression. FEE animals have altered hypothermic responses to 8-hydroxy-2-(di-*n*-propylamino)tetralin (8-OH-DPAT), a $5-HT_{1A}$ receptor agonist, and FEE females, but not males, show an increased rate of "wet dog shakes" to 1-(2, 5-dimethoxy-4-iodophenyl)-2-aminopropane hydrochloride (DOI), a $5-HT_{2A/C}$ receptor agonist. These effects are consistent with ethanol-induced alterations in 5-HT receptor function (Hofmann et al., 2002). Furthermore, FEE females exhibit blunted ACTH responses to 8-OH-DPAT but increased ACTH responses to DOI compared to controls, which suggests an altered interaction between the HPA axis and the 5-HTergic system in FEE animals (Hofmann et al., 2001).

Nitric Oxide. Alterations in NO concentrations induced by prenatal ethanol exposure may play a role in mediating HPA hyperresponsiveness in FEE animals. NO is an intercellular gaseous signaling molecule that has multiple biological functions, including regulation of vascular tone, modulation of neurotransmission, involvement in cell–cell communication and killing of pathogens in nonspecific immune responses (Lamas et al., 1998; Moncada, 1997a, 1997b). NO is generated from L-arginine by NO synthase (NOS), an enzyme found in magnocellular neurons of the PVN and to some extent also in the parvocellular division (Lee and Rivier, 1993; Siaud et al., 1994; Hatakeyama et al., 1996). NO acts within the hypothalamus to activate the HPA axis, with specific stimulatory effects exerted on CRH-producing neurons (Rivier, 1999).

Ethanol-induced brain damage is closely related to glutamate-induced exitotoxicity, mediated through N-methyl-D-aspartate (NMDA) receptors. Chronic ethanol exposure increases NMDA receptors and Ca^{2+} channel activity, events associated with seizures during alcohol withdrawal (Lancaster, 1992). It has also been postulated that chronic prenatal ethanol exposure changes glutamate–NMDA receptor–NOS signal transduction in the developing guinea pig brain (Kimura et al., 2000). Kimura and coworkers (Kimura et al., 1996, 1999; Kimura and Brien, 1998) reported decreased fetal hippocampal NOS activity and, consequently, decreased formation of NO, but those changes are not accompanied by a loss of NOS-containing neurons in the hippocampal CA1 or CA3 areas or changes in localization of hippocampal NOS protein in the near-term guinea pig. The critical period for prenatal ethanol-induced loss of hippocampal CA1 neurons in the guinea pig brain appears to be between G62 and P12 (McGoey et al., 2003). Glutamate and NMDA binding sites decrease in the hippocampus of near-term fetal guinea pigs chronically exposed to ethanol (Abdollah and Brien, 1995). Thus it has been proposed that chronic prenatal exposure to ethanol suppresses the function of the glutamate–NMDA receptor–NO signal transduction system in the developing hippocampus. Furthermore, it has been postulated that persistent suppression of this signaling system disrupts or delays normal neuronal development, which temporally precedes the loss of hippocampal CA1 pyramidal cells in postnatal life (Gibson et al., 2000; Kimura et al., 2000; McGoey et al., 2003). In view of the important role of the hippocampus in HPA feedback, such alterations could underlie the ethanol-induced changes in HPA feedback regulation that have been observed.

Changes in NO synthesis in FEE animals may mediate the altered HPA responses to immune signals reported in FEE rats compared to those in controls. Gottesfeld (1998) report increased NO formation in response to LPS in FEE rats. Furthermore, blockade of NO synthesis prevents the blunted sympathetic response to LPS or interleukin (IL)-1 in FEE rats but not in control rats (Gottesfeld, 1998). Similarly, changes in hypothalamic responsiveness to NO may mediate the increased HPA responsiveness of

FEE animals to stressors. Intracerebroventricular injection of the NO donor 3-morpholinosydnonimine (SIN)-1 increases the ACTH response and the concentration of mRNA for the immediate early gene *NGFI-B* in FEE males (Lee et al., 2003). Moreover, blockade of NO formation abolishes differences between FEE and control animals in response to IL-1 (Rivier, 1995). In normal (no ethanol exposure) rats, SIN-1 also up-regulates CRH, AVP, and CRH-R$_1$ gene expression in the PVN. The functional importance of the increased concentrations of CRH and AVP transcripts is evidenced by immunoneutralization of endogenous CRH and AVP, which abolishes or blunts, respectively, the ACTH response to SIN-1 (Lee et al., 1999). It would be fascinating to study these relationships in animals prenatally exposed to ethanol.

Altered HPA–HPG Interactions

There are bidirectional interactions between the stress system and the HPG axis (Fig. 10–3). Hormones of the HPA axis have inhibitory effects on HPG activity. In turn, the gonadal steroids feed back to activate (estradiol) or inhibit (testosterone) HPA activity. Recent studies have investigated a possible role of ethanol-induced alterations in HPA–HPG interactions in mediating the sexually dimorphic effects of ethanol on male and female offspring. Studies have examined the effects of gonadectomy (GDX), with or without hormone replacement, on concentrations of the HPA hormones in both sexes under basal conditions and following stress. Preliminary data show that FEE males have higher plasma ACTH concentrations than controls following restraint stress, and that GDX eliminates the differences among groups (Lan et al., 2004). Thus, HPA hyperresponsiveness in FEE males appears to be mediated, at least in part, by ethanol-induced changes in testosterone regulation or in HPA sensitivity to testosterone. That is, the suppressive effects of testosterone and/or the stimulatory effects of GDX on stress-induced ACTH release are altered in FEE compared to control males. In contrast, the role of the gonadal hormones in HPA regulation in FEE females is more complex. Preliminary data (Yamashita et al., 2004) show that overall, FEE females are less responsive than controls to the effects of estradiol on both reproductive and nonreproductive measures. Furthermore, FEE females appear to

REPRODUCTION
&
STRESS

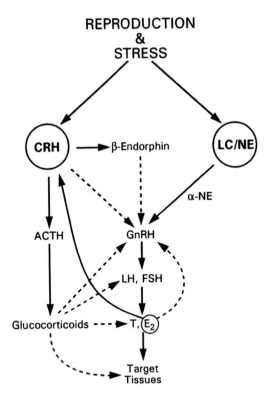

FIGURE 10–3 Interactions between the stress system and reproductive axis. The stress system consists of the hypothalamic–pituitary–adrenal (HPA) axis and the locus coeruleus noradrenergic sympathetic adrenal medullary (LC-NE) system (described in detail in Fig. 10.1). The reproductive axis consists of gonadotropin-releasing hormone (GnRH) neurons which stimulate secretion of luteinizing hormone (LH) and follicle stimulating hormone (FSH) from the pituitary, which in turn stimulate secretion of estrogens (mainly estradiol) and androgens (mainly testosterone) from the gonads. The reproductive axis is stimulated by the LC-NE system, primarily through α-noradrenergic (α_1-NE) receptors, and is inhibited at all levels by components of the HPA axis. Activation is represented by solid lines, inhibition by dashed lines. ACTH, adrenocorticotropic hormone; CRH, corticotropin releasing hormone; E_2, estradiol; T, testosterone. (*Source*: Reprinted from Stratakis and Chrousos (1995) with permission from New York Academy of Sciences)

have decreased tissue responsiveness to estradiol and altered HPG sensitivity to acute stress. Further studies are needed to elucidate the effects of prenatal ethanol exposure on interactions between the HPA and HPG axes.

PRENATAL ETHANOL EXPOSURE ALTERS THE IMMUNE SYSTEM OF THE OFFSPRING

Impairments in immune competence of children with FAS have been demonstrated broadly in both innate and adaptive immunity. Innate immunity is not major histocompatibility complex (MHC) restricted. It provides a first line of defense against many common pathogens through phagocytes such as monocytes, macrophages, polymorphonuclear leukocytes, natural killer cells, and soluble mediators such as complement and C-reactive protein. Adaptive immunity is MHC restricted and classified as cellular or humoral, mediated by T or B lymphocytes, respectively. Immune responses against microorganisms are mediated by multiple cell types, and interactions between the innate and adaptive immune systems are necessary to launch an effective immune response. An understanding of the timeline and events in normal development of the immune system, a complicated and multisystem process, is important to an understanding of the effect of ethanol on the developing immune system.

Normal Timing of the Ontogeny of the Immune System

Although development of the immune system takes place throughout life, the basic framework of immunity develops before birth. The misconception that the newborn is immunologically naive has been corrected with data demonstrating that neonatal T and B cells are matured to a stage that they can mount an antigen-specific immune response to antigens encountered in utero, such as the parasite *Ascaris* and tetanus toxoid vaccination (Gill et al., 1983; King et al., 1998).

Hematopoietic stem cells form and develop in the yolk sack until 4 weeks of gestation, migrate to the liver 3 to 4 weeks later, and then further migrate to the thymus and spleen. Stem cells are in the bone marrow at 11–12 weeks of gestation (Migliaccio et al., 1986; Holt and Jones, 2000). Susceptibility of early lympho-hematopoiesis and cell migration to environmental influences can occur as early as 7–10 weeks postconception (West, 2002). As early as 14 weeks of gestation, differentiated T and B cells can be identified in fetal blood (Goldblatt, 1998) and spleen (Peakman et al., 1992). The spleen is considered completely immunocompetent by 18 weeks of gestation. At this time, splenic T cells have adult levels of expression of CD3, CD4, and CD8 and are able to respond to mitogens (Kay et al., 1970), and splenic accessory cells are fully functional in delivering co-stimulatory signals (Holt and Jones, 2000). Fetuses still have fewer memory T cells than adults do at this time (Holt and Jones, 2000). Yolk sack–derived pro-B cells develop in the liver and acquire surface immunoglobulin (Ig) M, IgD, and CD20 expression by 10–13 weeks of gestation (Hofman et al., 1984). B cells are detectable in lymph nodes from 16–17 weeks, in spleen at 16–21 weeks, and are abundant in bone marrow at 16–20 weeks of gestation (West, 2002).

The structure of the thymus develops as a result of epitheliomesenchymal interactions. Endoderm of the third pharyngeal pouch differentiates into thymic epithelium. Neural crest cells then migrate through the branchial arches and become the mesenchyme that will form the layers around the epithelial primordium of the thymus and the connective tissue framework. T cell progenitors arrive in the thymus from the liver during the ninth week of gestation, and the structure of the thymus differentiates into a cortex and a medulla at 10–12 weeks (West, 2002). Prothymocytes express CD7 in the fetal liver at 7 weeks and CD3 at 8–9 weeks of gestation, when these cells migrate to the thymus (Holt and Jones, 2000). Gene rearrangement starts at around week 11, and expression of the T cell receptors (TCR), CD4, and CD8 follows. Thymic "education" of immature CD4+/CD8+ (double-positive) T cells takes place in the second trimester by positive selection, with the ability of TCR to bind to polymorphic parts of nonagonist MHC-encoded molecules on nonlymphoid cells, and by negative selection of TCR, with high affinity to self-antigens to avoid autoimmunity (von Boehmer et al., 2003). Export of mature CD4+ or CD8+ (single positive) cells begins after week 13, and a rapid expansion of the T cell pool happens during 14–16 weeks (Kay et al., 1970; Berry et al., 1992). At 13–14 weeks, thymocytes acquire proliferative ability to most mitogens. During the second trimester, susceptibility to environmental factors causes disruption of the thymic education processes and cell proliferation, leading to a defective T cell repertoire.

As rodent gestation (~3 weeks) is substantially shorter than that of humans (~40 weeks), immune system development of newborn rat and mouse pups occurs at a time equivalent to the end of the second trimester in humans (Zajac and Abel, 1992).

Therefore, studies in rodent models of prenatal ethanol exposure have focused primarily on the early events in ontogeny of the immune system, i.e., during the late gestational period and early postnatal life.

Impaired Immunity following Prenatal Exposure to Ethanol

Children prenatally exposed to alcohol have an increased incidence of bacterial infections, such as meningitis, pneumonia, recurrent otitis media, gastroenteritis, sepsis, urinary tract infections, and frequent upper respiratory tract infections (Johnson et al., 1981; Church and Gerkin, 1988). These children also have lower cell counts of eosinophils and neutrophils, decreased circulating E-rosette–forming lymphocytes, reduced mitogen-stimulated proliferative responses by peripheral blood leukocytes, and hypo-γ-globulinemia (Johnson et al., 1981).

Research using animal models to investigate immune function of FEE offspring has (a) substantiated the clinical evidence of impaired immunity associated with FASD and (b) greatly increased our understanding of these immune deficits in terms of both the spectrum of effects in different organ systems and the mechanisms mediating the immunoteratogenic effects of ethanol. Deficits in innate immunity have typically not been observed in animal studies. For example, one large study on nonhuman primates (*Macaca nemestrina*) shows that in utero ethanol exposure does not result in significant differences in total numbers of white blood cells, leukocyte subsets, or monocyte phagocytic activity compared to that in control subjects (Grossmann et al., 1993). In contrast, marked deficits in adaptive immunity involving both cell-mediated and humoral immunity are evident in FEE animals. Furthermore, as described in the discussion below, a marked sexual dimorphism in ethanol effects has been observed, with the majority of deficits occurring in male offspring.

Deficits in Adaptive Immunity

Inborn errors of immunocompetent cells in children with FASD result in immunodefiency disorders or increased susceptibility to infections. Recurrent opportunistic infection and infection caused by ubiquitous microorganisms, such as bacteria, viruses, and fungi, typically occur with deficits in cell-mediated immunity, whereas deficits in B cells, immunoglobulins, complement, and phagocytes usually lead to infection by encapsulated and pyrogenic bacteria, such as *Haemophilus influenzae*, *Streptococcus pneumoniae*, and *Staphylococcus aureus*. In children with FASD both types of recurrent infections have been reported, suggesting that both T and B cell–mediated immunity are compromised (Johnson et al., 1981).

Work with animal models confirms the findings in human subjects. For example, the immune response of FEE neonates to the intestinal parasite *Trichinella spiralis* indicates a diminished capacity to respond to the pathogen, demonstrated by an increased intestinal worm count (Steven et al., 1992; Seelig et al., 1996). The abnormalities involve depressed T and B cell–mediated responses such as lower serum IL-2 and tumor necrosis factor (TNF) contents, and lower IgM and IgG antibody titers. Interestingly, the detrimental effects of ethanol appear to increase across generations. That is, FEE pups (second generation) mothered by FEE adult offspring (first generation) who themselves consumed ethanol during pregnancy show reduced proliferative responses to *T. spiralis* antigen and stimulation with concanavalin A (Con A), lower titers of serum IgM and IgG anti–*T. spiralis*, and lower percentages of T cells and cytotoxic T cells, compared to the first-generation FEE and pair-fed groups (Seelig et al., 1999). The next two sections review studies that describe specific deficits in either cell-mediated or humoral immunity.

Deficits in Cell-Mediated Immunity

Prenatal ethanol exposure alters development of the thymus in rats and mice. Delayed thymic ontogeny (Ewald and Walden, 1988), decreased total numbers of thymocytes, and diminished mitogen-induced cell proliferation have been reported in near-term fetuses (Ewald and Frost, 1987). Decreased thymus weight, size, and cell counts have also been observed at birth (Redei et al., 1989). These changes persisted through the preweaning period and even into adolescence (Ewald and Frost, 1987; Ewald, 1989; Giberson and Blakley, 1994; Taylor et al., 1999a), although one study of mice found that total thymocyte numbers could return to control levels as early as P6 (Ewald, 1989). Similarly, mitogen-induced proliferative responses of thymic cells was suppressed in FEE males at weaning (Redei et al., 1989), but may be increased in adolescent (44-day-old) rats (Chiappelli et al., 1992; Wong et al., 1992). This increase in thymocyte

proliferation during adolescence does not appear to be mediated by changes in number of GRs on the thymocytes; further studies are needed to elucidate the mechanisms underlying these varying effects of ethanol.

The adverse effects of ethanol on thymic development have been confirmed by in vitro studies using organotypic cultures. Total cell numbers and percentages of immature fetal thymocytes ($CD4^+/CD8^+$) decrease in a concentration-responsive manner in ethanol-treated organ cultures (Bray et al., 1993). This decrease is a consequence of accelerated apoptosis, which then results in an increased percentage of more mature thymocytes expressing $CD4^+/CD8^-$ and γ/δ TCR (Ewald and Walden, 1988; Ewald et al., 1991; Bray et al., 1993; Ewald and Shao, 1993). Similar outcomes are observed in 20- to- 40-day-old FEE animals. That is, thymic cell counts and total numbers of $CD4^+$ and $CD8^+$ cells are decreased throughout this period, and immature $CD8^+/TCR^+$ and $CD8^+/CD45RC^+$ thymocytes are reduced by P35 (Taylor et al., 1999a), findings suggesting that prenatal ethanol treatment alters the later stages of thymocyte maturation, such as after double-positive ($CD4^+/CD8^+$) thymocytes acquire TCR expression.

Prenatal ethanol exposure has long-term adverse effects on the immune system that last well into adulthood. FEE animals have decreased numbers of $Thy1.2^+$, $CD4^+$, $CD8^+$, and IgG^+ splenocytes (Ewald and Huang, 1990; Giberson and Blakley, 1994; Giberson et al., 1997). Decreased percentages of $Thy1.2^+$ splenocytes are also evident in pups born to mothers consuming ethanol during pregnancy and lactation or during lactation alone, indicating direct effects of ethanol on postnatal development of the immune system (Giberson and Blakley, 1994). Similarly, rodent and primate studies indicate that splenic lymphocytes from FEE males have decreased proliferative responses to mitogens from adolescence through young adulthood (Norman et al., 1989; Redei et al., 1989; Gottesfeld et al., 1990; Weinberg and Jerrells, 1991; Grossmann et al., 1993; Jerrells and Weinberg, 1998) and that the response normalizes by 8 months of age (Gottesfeld and Ullrich, 1995; Norman et al., 1991). Furthermore, deficits not only in the response of freshly isolated splenic T cells but also in the response of T blast cells (obtained following treatment with Con A) to IL-2 or further Con A stimulation (Gottesfeld et al., 1990; Norman et al., 1991; Weinberg and Jerrells, 1991; Jerrells and Weinberg, 1998) have been observed. In contrast, the changes in mitogen-induced proliferation of thymocytes observed in FEE animals normalized in young adulthood (Chiappelli et al., 1992).

Deficits in Humoral Immunity

Humoral immunity is less affected by fetal ethanol exposure than is cell-mediated immunity. Prepubertal FEE rats do not differ from controls in serum immunoglobulin content after primary and secondary immunization (Gottesfeld and Ullrich, 1995). Similar results are evident in nonhuman primates after immunization with tetanus toxin (Grossmann et al., 1993). On the other hand, deficits in humoral immunity do occur. Abnormal development of B cell lineages in murine hematopoietic organs, including bone marrow, spleen, and liver, occur from fetal ages through adolescence. The total number of splenic B cells and their proliferative response to LPS is decreased at birth and throughout the preweaning period (Wolcott et al., 1995). In addition, B cell maturation in fetal liver is delayed (Biber et al., 1998) and the number of B220-positive hematopoietic cells in liver is decreased in rat fetuses at the end of gestation (Robinson and Seelig, 2002). At birth, the numbers of both immature (IgM+/IgD−) and mature (IgM+/IgD+) B cells in spleen and bone marrow are decreased, but most recover to normal levels by 3 to 4 weeks after birth, except for pre-B cells (B220+/IgM−) in bone marrow, which remain at low levels through 5 weeks of life (Moscatello et al., 1999).

Ethanol Exposure and Vulnerability to Stress-Induced Suppression of Immune Function

The nervous, endocrine, and immune systems exist within a complex regulatory network in which bidirectional communication occurs via shared receptors and hormonal mediators to maintain homeostasis (Fig. 10–4). The CNS can modulate both the endocrine and immune systems through release of neurotransmitters and through direct innervation of organs. Feedback to the CNS occurs through hormones and cytokines, many of which are similar or even identical in structure. Immune signals can activate the HPA axis and the glucocorticoids play a major role in the stress-induced suppression of immune and inflammatory reactions.

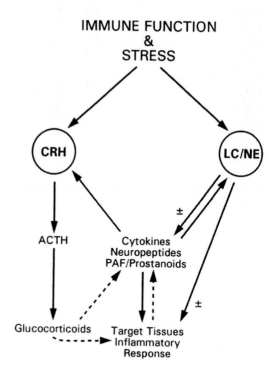

FIGURE 10–4 Interactions between the stress system and immune system. The long-term stress response is maintained via secretion of stress hormones (corticotropin releasing hormone [CRH], adrenocorticotropic hormone [ACTH], and glucocorticoids). The locus coeruleus noradrenergic (LC-NE) system participates in the effects of stress on the immune response through both its interaction with the hypothalamic–pituitary–adrenal (HPA) axis and its ability to transmit neural signals from the periphery to the immune system. Activation of the HPA axis occurs during the stress of infection, inflammation, or autoimmune processes, as well as accidental or operative trauma. During this activation, cytokines, neuropeptides, platelet-activating factor (PAF)/prostanoids are secreted and cause stimulation of the HPA axis. The glucocorticoids, end hormones of the HPA axis, play a major role in the stress-induced suppression of immune and inflammatory reactions. Activation is represented by solid lines, inhibition by dashed lines. (*Source:* Reprinted from Stratakis and Chrousos (1995) with permission from New York Academy of Sciences)

Chronic stress in adulthood provides a challenge to the immune system that differentially affects FEE and control animals. Similar to the data demonstrating that basal hormone concentrations are typically normal in FEE animals, specific deficits in the immune system may not be observed under nonstressed conditions, and become apparent only when FEE animals are exposed to stressors. In addition, sexually dimorphic effects of prenatal ethanol exposure may be observed.

In FEE males, exposure to chronic intermittent stressors selectively down-regulates the numbers of thymic and peripheral blood CD43+ cells as well as peripheral blood CD4+ T cells, and marginally decreases the number of peripheral blood MHC Class II Ia+ (antigen presenting) cells. In contrast, CD43 antigen expression on peripheral blood T cells is selectively up-regulated (Giberson and Weinberg, 1995). Stress does not differentially alter these immune measures in FEE females. The finding that FEE males exhibit greater stress-induced immune abnormalities than FEE females, despite showing less adrenal hypertrophy, suggests that males are more sensitive to small changes in glucocorticoid concentrations than females. Roles for estrogen as an immunoprotective hormone and testosterone as an immunosuppresive hormone in these sexually dimorphic immune responses remain to be determined.

One of the first demonstrations that stress differentially alters immune function in FEE and control females is the finding of an interaction between prenatal ethanol and chronic cold stress in female offspring (Giberson et al., 1997). After 1 day of cold stress, FEE females exhibit increased lymphocyte proliferation in response to pokeweed mitogen (PWM; a T cell–dependent B cell mitogen) and Con A challenge. No ethanol-induced differences in immune responsiveness are detected among males. In contrast, FEE males exposed to 1 or 3 days of cold stress have increased basal CORT concentrations compared to those of FEE males not exposed to cold. These findings are consistent with data from Halasz and colleagues (1993), who found that the challenge of chronic ethanol exposure in adulthood selectively increased Con A–induced lymphocyte proliferation in FEE females but not in males. These data have important implications for understanding the mechanisms underlying immune deficits induced by prenatal exposure to ethanol, because defective interactions between T and B cells would significantly hinder the development of a normal immune response.

Cytokines and the HPA Axis

Prenatal ethanol exposure blunts the LPS-induced febrile response in male rats (Taylor et al., 1999b,

2002a). This effect of ethanol may be mediated by a decreased response of central thermoregulatory systems to IL-1β, which could be mediated by a decreased hypothalamic IL-1β response to LPS administration, possibly through an impaired release of endogenous pyrogens (Ylikorkala et al., 1988; Yirmiya et al., 1993, 1996). Interestingly, both ADX and sham surgery in the pregnant female abrogate the effect of ethanol on the febrile response of female offspring to IL-1β, but only ADX has an effect on male offspring. This observation implies that maternal adrenal mediators play an important role in the blunted febrile response of FEE males and that nonadrenal mediators participate in modulation of thermoregulatory systems in FEE females (Taylor et al., 2002a, 2002b).

Parallel to blunted hormonal responses to stressors observed in FEE animals during the preweaning period, FEE preweanlings exhibit reduced ACTH, β-EP, and TNF-α responses to immune challenges (IL-1β, LPS). This reduction persists into adolescence in FEE males but not in females (Lee and Rivier, 1993, 1996; Chiappelli et al., 1997; Kim et al., 1999b). An altered ability of IL-1 to stimulate secretion of POMC-related peptides may underlie this reduced responsiveness (Lee and Rivier, 1993). Interestingly, ovariectomy prior to puberty eliminates the difference in ACTH response between FEE and control females (Lee and Rivier, 1996), a finding suggesting that ethanol and female sex hormones regulate HPA activity through a common pathway.

In contrast to the preweaning period, ACTH and CORT responses to immune signals such as LPS or IL-1β increase in FEE animals by adulthood (Kim et al., 1999b). This response parallels their HPA hyperresponsiveness to stressors. The finding that prenatal ethanol exposure does not alter cytokine responses to immune challenges suggests that cytokines probably do not mediate the ethanol-induced increase in HPA responsiveness to immune signals. On the other hand, FEE males exhibit increased plasma concentrations of pro-inflammatory cytokines to LPS challenge following repeated restraint stress (Eskes and Weinberg, 2003; Eskes et al., 2004). Whereas CORT responses to LPS are comparable among groups, FEE animals have greater and more sustained elevations of IL-1β, TNF-α, and IL-6 than those in controls. These data support and extend previous studies suggesting that although FEE animals may not differ in cytokine responses under basal or nonstressed conditions, they may in fact be more vulnerable to the adverse effects of stress on immune function (Eskes et al., 2004).

Mechanisms Underlying the Effects of Ethanol on the Developing Immune System

Direct and Indirect Effects of Ethanol on the Fetus

Ethanol can directly disrupt the development of the fetal thymus. The highly specified microenvironment of the thymus provided by epithelial and mesenchymal cells is pivotal in attracting immature lymphoid precursors to enable them to be selected and differentiated into mature T cells. Excess ethanol exposure during the development of the thymus inhibits the ontogeny of the thymic epithelium and disrupts the microenvironment for maturation of T cells, which leads to impaired T cell immunity (Bockman, 1997). These data are interesting in light of the shared clinical characteristics of FASD and DiGeorge syndrome (Ammann et al., 1982). The latter is a congenital immune deficiency syndrome involving mainly T cells and caused by an abnormality in the development of neural crest–derived components of the thymus and parathyroid glands (Kirby and Bockman, 1984). Targeted effects of ethanol on neural crest are described in Chapter 17.

Selective effects of ethanol on thymic CRH and POMC gene expression in male fetuses have been reported. Significant increases in thymic CRH and a decrease in thymic POMC gene expression have been observed on G19 (Revskoy et al., 1997). These changes do not appear to be related to CORT concentrations in the fetus or pregnant female, but possibly are induced by the fetal testosterone surge. Similarly, the ontogeny of GR sites per thymocyte in FEE animals in the first 2 months of life differs from that in control animals (Chiappelli et al., 1992). This indicates a role for the glucocorticoid hormones in the differential thymic development described in FEE and control animals.

Altered IL-2/IL-2 receptor interactions may play a role in the development of altered immune function in FEE animals (Weinberg and Jerrells, 1991; Taylor et al., 1993; Chang et al., 1994). For example, despite showing a reduced proliferative response to mitogens,

FEE animals have normal amounts of IL-2 production, IL-2 receptor expression and distribution, calcium influx in T cells, and binding of IL-2 to its receptor. The internalization and/or utilization of IL-2 by lymphoblasts, however, is reduced, and the half-time for dissociation of IL-2 from its receptor is increased in T cells from FEE animals. Therefore, impaired intracellular signaling events, mediated by IL-2/IL-2R interactions, may underlie the immune deficits observed in FEE animals. In contrast, direct treatment of lymphocytes with acetaldehyde-serum protein, which forms in vivo as a metabolite of ethanol consumption, results in decreased IL-2 production but not IL-2 receptor expression (Braun et al., 1995). This result suggests that, at least under some conditions, decreased IL-2 production contributes to impaired proliferative responses.

Altered neurotransmitter regulation of immune function may play a role in altered immune function of FEE animals. Prenatal exposure to ethanol decreases concentrations of NE and β-adrenoreceptors in the lymphoid organs and diminishes synaptic transmission in the spleen and thymus, but not the heart (Gottesfeld et al., 1990). Altered NEergic synaptic transmission, including a higher rate of NE turnover leading to reduced NE concentration and reduced β-adrenoreceptor density, could affect immune capacity in terms of NE-mediated IL-2 secretion and cytotoxic T cell responses.

Immunity at the Fetoplacental Interface

Immunity at the fetal–placental interface is biased toward humoral immunity; cell-mediated immunity is suppressed to prevent fetal rejection. Cell-mediated immunity is skewed toward Th2 responses and production of cytokines such as IL-3, IL-4, and IL-5, rather than toward Th1 responses and production of cytokines such as IL-2 and IFN-γ (Lin et al., 1993). It has been suggested that progesterone and CD4[+] regulatory T cells are the key factors enabling the fetus to evade immune rejection by the pregnant female, thus allowing the female to maintain pregnancy. Progesterone suppresses cytotoxic activity of lymphocytes from pregnant women via progesterone receptors (Szekeres-Bartho et al., 1990). A timely increase in CD4[+]/CD25[+] regulatory T cells, systematically and locally at the interface between the fetus and pregnant female, plays an important role in maintaining tolerance via suppression of an allogeneic response directed against the fetus (Szekeres-Bartho et al., 1990; Aluvihare et al., 2004). In utero exposure to ethanol could alter the balance between regulatory T cells and T effector cells, and thus contributes to the increased incidence of spontaneous abortions and premature births. This conclusion is supported by observations of elevated cord blood IgE concentrations in ethanol-exposed infants, indicating increased activity of Th2-type responses (Somerset et al., 2004). Long-term alterations in CD4+ regulatory T cells in FEE males may play a role in mediating deficits in T cell function (Zhang et al., 2005a). Dexamethasone-induced apoptosis and rescue by IL-2 of CD4+/CD25+ T regulatory cells from FEE animals and controls have been examined. CD4+/CD25+ regulatory T cells from FEE males were more resistant to dexamethasone-induced apoptosis in the presence of IL-2, resulting in increased survival of T regulatory cells. As T regulatory cells are suppressive in nature, the increased numbers of surviving T regulatory cells could play a role in ethanol-induced immune deficits.

Neuroendocrine–Immune Interactions

The CNS is critical for the development and maturation of the fetal immune system through both sympathetic activity and neuroendocrine mediators, such as growth hormone and the HPA and HPG hormones (Fig. 10.4). The sympathetic nervous system innervates lymphoid organs, and lymphocytes express receptors for CRH, ACTH, cortisol, NE, and epinephrine. The glucocorticoid hormones can exert profound influences on T cell function through their interaction with GRs on T cells, which modulate trafficking and homing, proliferation, activation, and apoptosis (Gonzalo et al., 1994; Dhabhar et al., 1996). For example, transgenic mice with decreased GR binding capacity but normal basal concentrations of ACTH and CORT show a partial blockage of T cell differentiation and decreased apoptosis in the fetal period but not in adult life (Sacedon et al., 1999). In addition, glucocorticoids cause a shift from Th1 to Th2 responses and a change from a pro-inflammatory cytokine pattern (e.g., IL-1 and TNF-α) to an anti-inflammatory cytokine pattern (e.g., IL-10 and IL-4) (DeRijk et al., 1997; Elenkov and Chrousos, 1999).

Growth hormone increases IFN-γ production and MHC class I and II expression by thymic epithelial cells, macrophages, dendritic cells, fibroblasts, and extracellular matrix (Savino and Dardenne, 2000). These results suggest that growth hormone facilitates MHC-mediated influences on thymocyte differentiation. Thymic epithelial cells and lymphocytes in rats express estrogen and androgen receptors from G16 (Tanriverdi et al., 2003) and thus are influenced by circulating sex steroid hormones. Furthermore, administration of gonadotropin releasing hormone (GnRH) restores fetal thymic and liver-derived T cell proliferative responses after surgical ablation of the forebrain or the entire brain including the hypothalamus and pituitary in 18-day-old fetuses (Zakharova et al., 2000). Thus, GnRH appears to be involved in regulation of T cell development even during prenatal ontogenesis. These examples show how closely development of the thymus is regulated by the neuroendocrine system.

Cytokines secreted by immune cells, such as IL-1, IL-2, IL-4, and IL-6, influence the function of hypothalamic neurosecretory and thermoregulatory neurons and pituitary cells (Cunningham and De Souza, 1993; Rivier, 1994; Zalcman et al., 1994; Dunn and Wang, 1995), resulting in activation of the HPA axis and inducing "sickness behavior" (Watkins and Maier, 2000; Dantzer, 2001). IL-1, IL-6, and TNF-α are also produced in the hypothalamus by microglia and macrophages (Hetier et al., 1988; Sebire et al., 1993) and thus can directly influence neuroendocrine function. For example, IL-1 stimulates the release of CRH and AVP from the hypothalamus (Suda et al., 1990; Chover-Gonzalez et al., 1994), and IL-1, IL-6, and TNF-α stimulate ACTH secretion from the anterior pituitary (Kehrer et al., 1988; Sharp et al., 1989; Lyson and McCann, 1991).

Given the intimate interactions between the neuroendocrine and immune systems (Fig. 10.4) during development and in adulthood, fetal ethanol-related developmental changes in neuroendocrine activity could affect immune competency. In turn, fetal ethanol-induced changes in cytokine secretion by immune cells can affect neuroendocrine activity. Therefore, the altered HPA responses to immune signals (Lee and Rivier, 1993) and differential vulnerability to stress-induced immune suppression (Giberson and Weinberg, 1995; Giberson et al., 1997) shown by FEE rats compared to that of controls could be mediated by the altered neuroendocrine–immune interactions.

PRENATAL ETHANOL EXPOSURE REPROGRAMS FETAL HPA AND IMMUNE FUNCTION

The routes by which the fetal and early neonatal environment can program adult HPA function and behavior are described eloquently by Matthews (2002) (Fig. 10.2) and Welberg and Seckl (2001). The developing limbic system, primarily the hippocampus, hypothalamus, and anterior pituitary, synthesize high amounts of GRs and are highly sensitive to glucocorticoids. Exposure to high concentrations of glucocorticoids during early life can alter the development and subsequent function of both the limbic system and the HPA axis. The limbic system, particularly the hippocampus, regulates HPA activity, and in turn, endogenous glucocorticoids modify numerous limbic system functions. Mechanisms underlying these mutual effects involve modification of developing neurotransmitter systems, their transporter mechanisms in the brain stem, the development of GR expression in the hippocampus, and the development and responsiveness of the hypothalamic PVN, which regulates glucocorticoid secretion. Prenatal events that can program HPA function include stress during pregnancy, exposure to synthetic glucocorticoids, and nutrient restriction. Postnatal events that can program HPA function include early handling, alterations in maternal behavior, and exposure to exogenous glucocorticoids and infection.

The overall effect of early developmental programming is altered exposure to endogenous glucocorticoids throughout life (Liu et al., 2001; Matthews, 2002). This altered exposure in turn modifies behavior, cognition, learning, memory, and emotion, and predisposes the individual to cardiovascular, metabolic, and immune disorders. Although environmental factors play an important role in fetal programming, it is likely that perinatal environmental and genetic factors mutually influence each other in determining HPA activity and behavior later in life. Moreover, although the effects of programming are often long-lasting, postnatal and later environmental events can modulate the effects of prenatal programming.

What is the mechanism underlying fetal or neonatal programming by early life experiences? Early experiences result in long-term consequences from the behavioral to the molecular level through epigenetic processes (Weaver et al., 2004). In the model of Weaver and colleagues, naturally occurring variations in maternal behavior are associated with the development of individual differences in behavioral and HPA responses to stressors. Thus, offspring of mothers showing high levels of maternal behavior (large amounts of licking, grooming, and arched-back nursing of their young) are less fearful and show better-modulated HPA responses to stressors than offspring of mothers showing low levels of maternal behavior. This outcome is not due to a change in the underlying genetic profile; if pups are cross-fostered from low– to high–maternal behavior mothers at birth, the offspring profile is associated with the adoptive rather than the biological mother. Therefore, variations in maternal behavior can serve as a mechanism for nongenomic transmission of individual differences in stress reactivity across generations. At least two major epigenomic mechanisms are thought to be involved: demethylation of one key site in the NGFI-A binding sequence of the first exon of the GR gene, and increased acetylation of the histones surrounding the GR gene (Weaver et al., 2004). These two alterations result in increased expression of GRs and increased access of transcription factors to GRs, thus increasing HPA feedback regulation and altering the physiological and behavioral profiles of the offspring.

In our model, prenatal ethanol exposure is an environmental variable that causes long-term alterations in the physiological and behavioral profile of the offspring (e.g., Weinberg and Jerrells, 1991; Giberson and Weinberg, 1995; Kim et al., 1996; Glavas et al., 2001; Hofmann et al., 2002; Lan et al., 2004; Zhang et al., 2005b). We hypothesize that prenatal ethanol exposure reprograms the fetal HPA axis, resulting in long-term alterations in HPA regulation and responsiveness under basal and stress conditions and increasing HPA tone throughout life. In view of the evidence (Phillips et al., 1998, 2000) that fetal programming of the HPA axis, at least in part, underlies the connection between the early environment and adult stress-related and behavioral disorders in humans, further studies are essential to elucidate the mechanisms underlying prenatal ethanol effects on programming of HPA activity.

SUMMARY AND CONCLUSIONS

The present chapter discusses the adverse effects of prenatal exposure to ethanol on neuroendocrine and immune function in the offspring, with particular emphasis on the HPA axis and the concept of fetal programming. Ethanol-induced disturbances of the reciprocal interconnections between the pregnant female and the fetus may provide a common pathway by which perinatal exposure to different agents results in fetal programming. The fetal HPA axis is reprogrammed by ethanol exposure such that HPA tone is increased throughout life. HPA activity is increased and HPA regulation is altered under both basal and stress conditions. Increased exposure to endogenous glucocorticoids over the lifespan can alter behavioral and physiological responsiveness and increase vulnerability to illnesses later in life. Deficits in immune competence may be one of the long-term consequences of fetal HPA programming. Prenatal ethanol exposure compromises offspring immune function and increases vulnerability to the immunosuppressive effects of stress.

It is now essential to explore possible epigenomic mechanisms mediating altered physiological and behavioral function following prenatal ethanol exposure. The fact that ethanol causes alterations in the methylation state within cells supports the possibility that mechanisms similar to those described by Weaver and colleagues (2004) mediate the changes induced by ethanol exposure in utero. Data from such investigations will have important implications for the development of therapeutic interventions focused on reversing the long-term adverse effects of prenatal alcohol exposure.

Abbreviations

ACTH   adrenocorticotropic hormone

ADX   adrenalectomy

AVP   arginine vasopressin

β-EP   β-endorphin

CBG   corticosterone-binding globulin

CNS   central nervous system

CON A   concanavalin A

CORT   corticosterone

CRH   corticotropin-releasing hormone

CRH-R$_1$ corticotropin-releasing hormone type 1 receptor

DOI   1-(2, 5-dimethoxy-4-iodophenyl)-2-aminopropane hydrochloride

8-OH-DPAT   8-hydroxy-2-(di-n-propylamino)-tetralin

FASD   fetal alcohol spectrum disorders

FEE   fetal ethanol-exposed

5-HT   serotonin

G   gestational day

GABA   γ-aminobutyric acid

GDX   gonadectomy

GnRH   gonadotropin-releasing hormone

GR   glucocorticoid receptor

hn   heteronuclear

HPA   hypothalamic-pituitary-adrenal

HPG   hypothalamic-pituitary-gonadal

Ig   immunoglobulin

IL   interleukin

LC-NE   locus coeruleus noradrenergic (sympathetic adrenal medullary)

LPS   lipopolysaccharide

MHC   major histocompatibility complex

MR   mineralocorticoid receptor

NE   norepinephrine

NMDA   N-methyl-D-aspartate

NO   nitric oxide

NOS   nitric oxide synthase

P   postnatal day

POMC   pro-opiomelanocortin

PVN   paraventricular nucleus

PWM   pokeweed mitogen

SHRP   stress hyporesponsive period

SIN-1   3-morpholinosydnonimine

SNRP   stress nonresponsive period

TCR   T cell receptors

TNF   tumor necrosis factor

ACKNOWLEDGMENTS   The research from our laboratory that is reported in this review was supported by grants from the National Institute of Alcohol Abuse and Alcoholism and from the University of British Columbia Human Early Learning Partnership to J.W. J.H.S. was supported by a Bluma Tischler postdoctoral fellowship.

References

Abdollah S, Brien JF (1995) Effect of chronic maternal ethanol administration on glutamate and N-methyl-D-aspartate binding sites in the hippocampus of the near-term fetal guinea pig. Alcohol 12:377–382.

Adler RA (1992) Clinical review 33: clinically important effects of alcohol on endocrine function. J Clin Endocrinol Metab 74:957–960.

Aird F, Halasz I, Redei E (1997) Ontogeny of hypothalamic corticotropin-releasing factor and anterior pituitary pro-opiomelanocortin expression in male and female offspring of alcohol-exposed and adrenalectomized dams. Alcohol Clin Exp Res 21: 1560–1566.

Aluvihare VR, Kallikourdis M, Betz AG (2004) Regulatory T cells mediate maternal tolerance to the fetus. Nat Immunol 5:266–271.

Ammann AJ, Wara DW, Cowan MJ, Barrett DJ, Stiehm ER (1982) The DiGeorge syndrome and the fetal alcohol syndrome. Am J Dis Child 136:906–908.

Anderson RA Jr (1981) Endocrine balance as a factor in the etiology of the fetal alcohol syndrome. Neurobehav Toxicol Teratol 3:89–104.

Angelogianni P, Gianoulakis C (1989) Prenatal exposure to ethanol alters the ontogeny of the β-endorphin response to stress. Alcohol Clin Exp Res 13: 564–571.

Angelucci L, Patacchioli FR, Scaccianoce S, Di Sciullo A, Cardillo A, Maccari S (1985) A model for later-life effects of perinatal drug exposure: maternal hormone mediation. Neurobehav Toxicol Teratol 7: 511–517.

Assenmacher I, Szafarczyk A, Alonso G, Ixart G, Barbanel G (1987) Physiology of neural pathways affecting CRH secretion. Ann NY Acad Sci 512: 149–161.

Bakker JM, van Bel F, Heijnen CJ (2001) Neonatal glucocorticoids and the developing brain: short-term treatment with life-long consequences? Trends Neurosci 24:649–653.

Beitins IZ, Bayard F, Ances IG, Kowarski A, Migeon CJ (1973) The metabolic clearance rate, blood production, interconversion and transplacental passage of cortisol and cortisone in pregnancy near term. Pediatr Res 75:509–519.

Berry SM, Fine N, Bichalski JA, Cotton DB, Dombrowski MP, Kaplan J (1992) Circulating lymphocyte subsets in second- and third-trimester fetuses: comparison with newborns and adults. Am J Obstet Gynecol 167:895–900.

Biber KL, Moscatello KM, Dempsey DC, Chervenak R, Wolcott RM (1998) Effects of in utero alcohol exposure on B-cell development in the murine fetal liver. Alcohol Clin Exp Res 22:1706–1712.

Bockman DE (1997) Development of the thymus. Microsc Res Tech 38:209–215.

Braun KP, Pearce RB, Peterson CM (1995) Acetaldehyde-serum protein adducts inhibit interleukin-2 secretion in concanavalin A-stimulated murine splenocytes: a potential common pathway for ethanol-induced immunomodulation. Alcohol Clin Exp Res 19: 345–349.

Bray LA, Shao H, Ewald SJ (1993) Effect of ethanol on development of fetal mouse thymocytes in organ culture. Cell Immunol 151:12–23.

Cannon WB (1914) The interrelation of emotions as suggested by recent physiological researches. Am J Physiol 25:256–282.

—— (1929) Bodily Changes in Pain, Hunger, Fear and Rage. Applegate, New York.

Cannon WB, de la Paz D (1911) Emotionl stimulation of adrenal secretion. Am J Physiol 28:64–70.

Chang MP, Yamaguchi DT, Yeh M, Taylor AN, Norman DC (1994) Mechanism of the impaired T-cell proliferation in adult rats exposed to alcohol in utero. Int J Immunopharmacol 16:345–357.

Chiappelli F, Kung MA, Tio DL, Tritt SH, Yirmiya R, Taylor AN (1997) Fetal alcohol exposure augments the blunting of tumor necrosis factor production in vitro resulting from in vivo priming with lipopolysaccharide in young adult male but not female rats. Alcohol Clin Exp Res 21:1542–1546.

Chiappelli F, Tio D, Tritt SH, Pilati ML, Taylor AN (1992) Selective effects of fetal alcohol exposure on rat thymocyte development. Alcohol 9:481–487.

Chover-Gonzalez AJ, Lightman SL, Harbuz MS (1994) An investigation of the effects of interleukin-1β on plasma arginine vasopressin in the rat: role of adrenal steroids. J Endocrinol 142:361–366.

Chrousos GP (1995) The hypothalamic-pituitary-adrenal axis and immune-mediated inflammation. N Engl J Med 332:1351–1362.

Chrousos GP, Loriaux DL, Gold PW (1988) The concept of stress and its historical development. Adv Exp Med Biol 245:3–7.

Church MW, Gerkin KP (1988) Hearing disorders in children with fetal alcohol syndrome: findings from case reports. Pediatrics 82:147–154.

Cunningham ET Jr, De Souza EB (1993) Interleukin 1 receptors in the brain and endocrine tissues. Immunol Today 14:171–176.

Dantzer R (2001) Cytokine-induced sickness behavior: where do we stand? Brain Behav Immun 15:7–24.

DeRijk R, Michelson D, Karp B, Petrides J, Galliven E, Deuster P, Paciotti G, Gold PW, Sternberg EM (1997) Exercise and circadian rhythm–induced variations in plasma cortisol differentially regulate interleukin-1β (IL-1β), IL-6, and tumor necrosis factor-α (TNFα) production in humans: high sensitivity of TNF α and resistance of IL-6. J Clin Endocrinol Metab 82:2182–2191.

Detering N, Collins R, Hawkins RL, Ozand PT, Karahasan AM (1980) The effects of ethanol on developing catecholamine neurons. Adv Exp Med Biol 132:721–727.

Detering N, Collins RM Jr., Hawkins RL, Ozand PT, Karahasan A (1981) Comparative effects of ethanol and malnutrition on the development of catecholamine neurons: a long-lasting effect in the hypothalamus. J Neurochem 36:2094–2096.

Dhabhar FS, Miller AH, McEwen BS, Spencer RL (1996) Stress-induced changes in blood leukocyte distribution. Role of adrenal steroid hormones. J Immunol 157:1638–1644.

Druse MJ (1992) Effects of in utero ethanol exposure on the development of neurotransmitter systems. In: Miller MW (ed). *Development of the Central Nervous System: Effects of Alcohol and Opiates*. Wiley-Liss, New York, pp 139–167.

Druse MJ, Kuo A, Tajuddin N (1991) Effects of in utero ethanol exposure on the developing serotonergic system. Alcohol Clin Exp Res 15:678–684.

Dunn AJ, Wang J (1995) Cytokine effects on CNS biogenic amines. Neuroimmunomodulation 2:319–328.

Eguchi Y (1969) Interrelationships between the foetal and maternal hypophysial adrenal axes in rats and mice. In: Bajusz E (ed). *Physiology and Pathology of Adaptation Mechanisms*. Pergamon Press, New York, pp 3–27.

Elenkov IJ, Chrousos GP (1999) Stress hormones, Th1/Th2 patterns, pro/anti-inflammatory cytokines and susceptibility to disease. Trends Endocrinol Metab 10:359–368.

Eskes J, Weinberg J (2003) Prenatal ethanol exposure differentially alters cytokine release in chronically stressed male rats. Abs Soc Neurosci 33:927.3.

Eskes J, Yu WK, Ellis L, Weinberg J (2004) Prenatal exposure to ethanol differentially affects cytokine - release but not pituitary c-Fos levels in chronically stressed male rats. Alcohol Clin Exp Res 28:165A.

Ewald SJ (1989) T lymphocyte populations in fetal alcohol syndrome. Alcohol Clin Exp Res 13:485–489.

Ewald SJ, Frost WW (1987) Effect of prenatal exposure to ethanol on development of the thymus. Thymus 9:211–215.

Ewald SJ, Huang C (1990) Lymphocyte populations and immune responses in mice prenatally exposed to ethanol. Prog Clin Biol Res 325:191–200.

Ewald SJ, Huang C, Bray L (1991) Effect of prenatal alcohol exposure on lymphocyte populations in mice. Adv Exp Med Biol 288:237–244.

Ewald SJ, Shao H (1993) Ethanol increases apoptotic cell death of thymocytes in vitro. Alcohol Clin Exp Res 17:359–365.

Ewald SJ, Walden SM (1988) Flow cytometric and histological analysis of mouse thymus in fetal alcohol syndrome. J Leukoc Biol 44:434–440.

Giberson PK, Blakley BR (1994) Effect of postnatal ethanol exposure on expression of differentiation antigens of murine splenic lymphocytes. Alcohol Clin Exp Res 18:21–28.

Giberson PK, Kim CK, Hutchison S, Yu W, Junker A, Weinberg J (1997) The effect of cold stress on lymphocyte proliferation in fetal ethanol-exposed rats. Alcohol Clin Exp Res 21:1440–1447.

Giberson PK, Weinberg J (1995) Effects of prenatal ethanol exposure and stress in adulthood on lymphocyte populations in rats. Alcohol Clin Exp Res 19:1286–1294.

Gibson MA, Butters NS, Reynolds JN, Brien JF (2000) Effects of chronic prenatal ethanol exposure on locomotor activity, and hippocampal weight, neurons, and nitric oxide synthase activity of the young postnatal guinea pig. Neurotoxicol Teratol 22:183–192.

Gill TJ 3rd, Repetti CF, Metlay LA, Rabin BS, Taylor FH, Thompson DS, Cortese AL (1983) Transplacental immunization of the human fetus to tetanus by immunization of the mother. J Clin Invest 72:987–996.

Gillies GE, Linton EA, Lowry PJ (1982) Corticotropin releasing activity of the new CRF is potentiated several times by vasopressin. Nature 299:355–357.

Glavas MM, Hofmann CE, Yu WK, Weinberg J (2001) Effects of prenatal ethanol exposure on hypothalamic-pituitary-adrenal regulation after adrenalectomy and corticosterone replacement. Alcohol Clin Exp Res 25:890–897.

Goldblatt D (1998) Immunisation and the maturation of infant immune responses. Dev Biol Stand 95:125–132.

Goldman L, Winget C, Hollingshead GW, Levine S (1973) Postweaning development of negative feedback in the pituitary-adrenal system of the rat. Neuroendocrinology 12:199–211.

Gonzalo JA, Gonzalez-Garcia A, Baixeras E, Zamzami N, Tarazona R, Rappuoli R, Martinez C, Kroemer G, Terezone R (1994) Pertussis toxin interferes with superantigen-induced deletion of peripheral T cells without affecting T cell activation in vivo. Inhibition of deletion and associated programmed cell death depends on ADP-ribosyltransferase activity. J Immunol 152:4291–4299.

Gottesfeld Z (1998) Sympathetic neural response to immune signals involves nitric oxide: effects of exposure to alcohol in utero. Alcohol 16:177–181.

Gottesfeld Z, Ullrich SE (1995) Prenatal alcohol exposure selectively suppresses cell-mediated but not humoral immune responsiveness. Intl J Immunopharmacol 17:247–254.

Gottesfeld Z, Christie R, Felten DL, LeGrue SJ (1990) Prenatal ethanol exposure alters immune capacity and noradrenergic synaptic transmission in lymphoid organs of the adult mouse. Neuroscience 35:185–194.

Grossmann A, Astley SJ, Liggitt HD, Clarren SK, Shiota F, Kennedy B, Thouless ME, Maggio-Price L (1993) Immune function in offspring of nonhuman primates (Macaca nemestrina) exposed weekly to 1.8 g/kg ethanol during pregnancy: preliminary observations. Alcohol Clin Exp Res 17:822–827.

Guillemin R, Vargo T, Rossier J, Minick S, Ling N, Rivier C, Vale W, Bloom F (1977) β-endorphin and adrenocorticotropin are selected concomitantly by the pituitary gland. Science 197:1367–1369.

Halasz I, Aird F, Li L, Prystowsky MB, Redei E (1993) Sexually dimorphic effects of alcohol exposure in utero on neuroendocrine and immune functions in chronic alcohol-exposed adult rats. Mol Cell Neurosci 4:343–353.

Hatakeyama S, Kawai Y, Ueyama T, Senba E (1996) Nitric oxide synthase–containing magnocellular neurons of the rat hypothalamus synthesize oxytocin and vasopressin and express Fos following stress stimuli. J Chem Neuroanat 11:243–256.

Hennessy JW, Levine S (1979) Stress, arousal, and the pituitary-adrenal system: a psychoendocrine hypothesis. In: Sprague JM, Epstein AN (ed). Progress in Psychobiology and Physiological Psychology. Academic Press, New York, pp 133–178.

Hetier E, Ayala J, Denefle P, Bousseau A, Rouget P, Mallat M, Prochiantz A (1988) Brain macrophages synthesize interleukin-1 and interleukin-1 mRNAs in vitro. J Neurosci Res 21:391–397.

Hiroshige T, Sato T (1970) Circadian rhythm and stress-induced changes in hypothalamic content of corticotropin-releasing activity during postnatal development in the rat. Endocrinology 86:1184–1186.

Hofman FM, Danilovs J, Husmann L, Taylor CR (1984) Ontogeny of B cell markers in the human fetal liver. J Immunol 133:1197–1201.

Hofmann C, Glavas M, Yu W, Weinberg J (1999) Glucocorticoid fast feedback is not altered in rats prenatally exposed to ethanol. Alcohol Clin Exp Res 23:891–900.

Hofmann CE, Simms W, Yu WK, Weinberg J (2002) Prenatal ethanol exposure in rats alters serotonergic-mediated behavioral and physiological function. Psychopharmacology 161:379–386.

Hofmann CE, Yu W, Ellis L, Weinberg J (2001) Prenatal ethanol exposure alters hormonal responses to 5-HT1A and 5-HT2A/C agonist. Abs Soc Neurosci 31:732.12.

Holt PG, Jones CA (2000) The development of the immune system during pregnancy and early life. Allergy 55:688–697.

Jacobson SW, Bihun JT, Chiodo LM (1999) Effects of prenatal alcohol and cocaine exposure on infant cortisol levels. Dev Psychopathol 11:195–208.

Jerrells TR, Weinberg J (1998) Influence of ethanol consumption on immune competence of adult animals exposed to ethanol in utero. Alcohol Clin Exp Res 22:391–400.

Johnson EO, Kamilaris TC, Chrousos GP, Gold PW (1992) Mechanisms of stress: a dynamic overview of hormonal and behavioral homeostasis. Neurosci Biobehav Rev 16:115–130.

Johnson S, Knight R, Marmer DJ, Steele RW (1981) Immune deficiency in fetal alcohol syndrome. Pediatr Res 15:908–911.

Kakihana R, Butte JC, Moore JA (1980) Endocrine effects of maternal alcoholization: plasma and brain testosterone, dihydrotestosterone, estradiol, and corticosterone. Alcohol Clin Exp Res 4:57–61.

Kastin AJ, Gennser G, Arimura A, Miller MC 3rd, Schally AV (1968) Melanocyte-stimulating and corticotrophic activities in human foetal pituitary glands. Acta Endocrinol 58:6–10.

Kay HE, Doe J, Hockley A (1970) Response of human foetal thymocytes to phytohaemagglutinin (PHA). Immunology 18:393–396.

Kehrer P, Turnill D, Dayer JM, Muller AF, Gaillard RC (1988) Human recombinant interleukin-1β and -α, but not recombinant tumor necrosis factor α stimulate ACTH release from rat anterior pituitary cells in vitro in a prostaglandin E2 and cAMP independent manner. Neuroendocrinology 48:160–166.

Kelly SJ (1996a) Alcohol exposure during development alters hypothalamic neurotransmitter concentrations. J Neural Transm 103:55–67.

—— (1996b) Effects of alcohol exposure and artificial rearing during development on septal and hippocampal neurotransmitters in adult rats. Alcohol Clin Exp Res 20:670–676.

Kim CK, Giberson PK, Yu W, Zoeller RT, Weinberg J (1999a) Effects of prenatal ethanol exposure on hypothalamic-pituitary-adrenal responses to chronic cold stress in rats. Alcohol Clin Exp Res 23:301–310.

Kim CK, Osborn JA, Weinberg J (1996) Stress reactivity in fetal alcohol syndrome. In: Abel E (ed). *Fetal Alcohol Syndrome: From Mechanism to Behavior.* CRC Press, Boca Raton, FL, pp 215–236.

Kim CK, Turnbull AV, Lee SY, Rivier CL (1999b) Effects of prenatal exposure to alcohol on the release of adenocorticotropic hormone, corticosterone, and proinflammatory cytokines. Alcohol Clin Exp Res 23:52–59.

Kim CK, Yu W, Edin G, Ellis L, Osborn JA, Weinberg J (1999c) Chronic intermittent stress does not differentially alter brain corticosteroid receptor densities in rats prenatally exposed to ethanol. Psychoneuroendocrinology 24:585–611.

Kimura KA, Brien JF (1998) Hippocampal nitric oxide synthase in the fetal guinea pig: effects of chronic prenatal ethanol exposure. Dev Brain Res 106:39–46.

Kimura KA, Chiu J, Reynolds JN, Brien JF (1999) Effect of chronic prenatal ethanol exposure on nitric oxide synthase I and III proteins in the hippocampus of the near-term fetal guinea pig. Neurotoxicol Teratol 21:251–259.

Kimura KA, Parr AM, Brien JF (1996) Effect of chronic maternal ethanol administration on nitric oxide synthase activity in the hippocampus of the mature fetal guinea pig. Alcohol Clin Exp Res 20: 948–953.

Kimura KA, Reynolds JN, Brien JF (2000) Ethanol neurobehavioral teratogenesis and the role of the hippocampal glutamate-N-methyl-D-aspartate receptor-nitric oxide synthase system. Neurotoxicol Teratol 22:607–616.

King CL, Malhotra I, Mungai P, Wamachi A, Kioko J, Ouma JH, Kazura JW (1998) B cell sensitization to helminthic infection develops in utero in humans. J Immunol 160:3578–3584.

Kirby ML, Bockman DE (1984) Neural crest and normal development: a new perspective. Anat Rec 209:1–6.

Lamas S, Perez-Sala D, Moncada S (1998) Nitric oxide: from discovery to the clinic. Trends Pharmacol Sci 19:436–438.

Lan N, Yamashita F, Halpert AG, Yu WK, Ellis L, Weinberg J (2004) The modulatory role of testosterone in the HPA responsiveness of male rats prenatally exposed to ethanol. Alcohol Clin Exp Res 28:165A.

Lancaster FE (1992)Alcohol, nitric oxide, and neurotoxicity: is there a connection? a review. Alcohol Clin Exp Res 16:539–541.

Lee S, Blanton CA, Rivier C (2003) Prenatal ethanol exposure alters the responsiveness of the rat hypothalamic-pituitary-adrenal axis to nitric oxide. Alcohol Clin Exp Res 27:962–969.

Lee S, Imaki T, Vale W, Rivier C (1990) Effect of prenatal exposure to ethanol on the activity of the hypothalamic-pituitary-adrenal axis of the offspring: importance of the time of exposure to ethanol and possible modulating mechanisms. Mol Cell Neurosci 1:168–177.

Lee S, Kim CK, Rivier C (1999) Nitric oxide stimulates ACTH secretion and the transcription of the genes encoding for NGFI-B, corticotropin-releasing factor, corticotropin-releasing factor receptor type 1, and vasopressin in the hypothalamus of the intact rat. J Neurosci 19:7640–7647.

Lee S, Rivier C (1992) Administration of corticosterone to pregnant adrenalectomized dams does not alter the hypothalamic-pituitary-adrenal axis activity of the offspring. Mol Cell Neurosci 3:118–123.

—— (1993) Prenatal alcohol exposure blunts interleukin-1-induced ACTH and β-endorphin secretion by immature rats. Alcohol Clin Exp Res 17:940–945.

—— (1996) Gender differences in the effect of prenatal alcohol exposure on the hypothalamic-pituitary-adrenal axis response to immune signals. Psychoneuroendocrinology 21:145–155.

Lee S, Schmidt D, Tilders F, Rivier C (2000) Increased activity of the hypothalamic-pituitary-adrenal axis of rats exposed to alcohol in utero: role of altered pituitary and hypothalamic function. Mol Cell Neurosci 16:515–528.

Levine S, Glick D, Nakane PK (1967) Adrenal and plasma corticosterone and vitamin A in rat adrenal glands during postnatal development. Endocrinology 80:910–914.

Levine S, Mullins RF Jr (1966) Hormonal influences on brain organization in infant rats. Science 152: 1585–1592.

Lin H, Mosmann TR, Guilbert L, Tuntipopipat S, Wegmann TG (1993) Synthesis of T helper 2-type cytokines at the maternal–fetal interface. J Immunol 151:4562–4573.

Liu L, Li A, Matthews SG (2001) Maternal glucocorticoid treatment programs HPA regulation in adult offspring: sex-specific effects. Am J Physiol Endocrinol Metab 280:E729–739.

Lyson K, McCann SM (1991) The effect of interleukin-6 on pituitary hormone release in vivo and in vitro. Neuroendocrinology 54:262–266.

Mason JW (1968) A review of psychoendocrine research on the pituitary–thyroid system. Psychosom Med 30(Suppl):666–681.

—— (1975) A historical view of the stress field. J Hum Stress 1:22–36.

Matthews SG (2000) Antenatal glucocorticoids and programming of the developing CNS. Pediatr Res 47:291–300.

—— (2002) Early programming of the hypothalamo-pituitary-adrenal axis. Trends Endocrinol Metab 13:373–380.

McEwen BS (1998) Protective and damaging effects of stress mediators. N Engl J Med 338:171–179.

McEwen BS, Wingfield JC (2003) The concept of allostasis in biology and biomedicine. Horm Behav 43:2–15.

McGoey TN, Reynolds JN, Brien JF (2003) Chronic prenatal ethanol exposure–induced decrease of guinea pig hippocampal CA1 pyramidal cell and cerebellar Purkinje cell density. Can J Physiol Pharmacol 81:476–484.

Meaney MJ, Sapolsky RM, McEwen BS (1985a) The development of the glucocorticoid receptor system in the rat limbic brain. I. Ontogeny and autoregulation. Brain Res 350:159–164.

—— (1985b) The development of the glucocorticoid receptor system in the rat limbic brain. II. An autoradiographic study. Brain Res 350:165–168.

Migliaccio G, Migliaccio AR, Petti S, Mavilio F, Russo G, Lazzaro D, Testa U, Marinucci M, Peschle C (1986) Human embryonic hemopoiesis. Kinetics of progenitors and precursors underlying the yolk sac-liver transition. J Clin Invest 78:51–60.

Milkovic K, Milkovic S (1963) Functioning of the pituitary-adrenocortical axis in rats at and after birth. Endocrinology 73:535–539.

Miller DB, O'Callaghan JP (2002) Neuroendocrine aspects of the response to stress. Metabolism 51:5–10.

Miyakawa I, Ikeda I, Maeyama M (1976) Transport of ACTH across human placenta. J Clin Endocrinol Metab 39:440–442.

Moncada S (1997a) Nitric oxide in the vasculature: physiology and pathophysiology. Ann NY Acad Sci 811:60–69.

—— (1997b) "Ottorino Rossi" Award 1997. The biology of nitric oxide. Funct Neurol 12:134–140.

Morgan MY (1982) Alcohol and the endocrine system. Br Med Bull 38:35–42.

Moscatello KM, Biber KL, Jennings SR, Chervenak R, Wolcott RM (1999) Effects of in utero alcohol exposure on B cell development in neonatal spleen and bone marrow. Cell Immunol 191:124–130.

Murphy BE, Clark SJ, Donald IR, Pinsky M, Vedady D (1974) Conversion of maternal cortisol to cortisone during placental transfer to the human fetus. Am J Obstet Gynecol 118:538–541.

Norman DC, Chang MP, Castle SC, Van Zuylen JE, Taylor AN (1989) Diminished proliferative response of Con A-blast cells to interleukin 2 in adult rats exposed to ethanol in utero. Alcohol Clin Exp Res 13:69–72.

Norman DC, Chang MP, Wong CM, Branch BJ, Castle S, Taylor AN (1991) Changes with age in the proliferative response of splenic T cells from rats exposed to ethanol in utero. Alcohol Clin Exp Res 15:428–432.

Osborn JA, Kim CK, Yu W, Herbert L, Weinberg J (1996) Fetal ethanol exposure alters pituitary–adrenal sensitivity to dexamethasone suppression. Psychoneuroendocrinology 21:127–143.

Pasqualini JR, Marfil J, Garnier F, Wiqvist N, Diczfalusy E (1970) Studies on the metabolism of corticosteroids in the human foeto-placental unit. 4. Metabolism of deoxycorticosterone and corticosterone administered simultaneously into the intact umbilical circulation. Acta Endocrinol 64:385–397.

Pavlova EB, Pronina TS, Skebelskaya YB (1968) Histostructure of adenohypophysis of human fetuses and contents of somatotropic and adrenocorticotropic hormones. Genet Comp Endocrinol 10:269–276.

Peakman M, Buggins AG, Nicolaides KH, Layton DM, Vergani D (1992) Analysis of lymphocyte phenotypes in cord blood from early gestation fetuses. Clin Exp Immunol 90:345–350.

Phillips DI, Barker DJ, Fall CH, Seckl JR, Whorwood CB, Wood PJ, Walker BR (1998) Elevated plasma cortisol concentrations: a link between low birth weight and the insulin resistance syndrome? J Clin Endocrinol Metab 83:757–760.

Phillips DI, Walker BR, Reynolds RM, Flanagan DE, Wood PJ, Osmond C, Barker DJ, Whorwood CB (2000) Low birth weight predicts elevated plasma cortisol concentrations in adults from 3 populations. Hypertension 35:1301–1306.

Plotsky PM (1987) Regulation of hypophysiotropic factors mediating ACTH secretion. Ann NY Acad Sci 512:205–217.

Ramsay DS, Bendersky MI, Lewis M (1996) Effect of prenatal alcohol and cigarette exposure on two- and six-month-old infants' adrenocortical reactivity to stress. J Pediatr Psychol 21:833–840.

Rathbun W, Druse MJ (1985) Dopamine, serotonin, and acid metabolites in brain regions from the developing offspring of ethanol-treated rats. J Neurochem 44:57–62.

Redei E, Clark WR, McGivern RF (1989) Alcohol exposure in utero results in diminished T-cell function and alterations in brain corticotropin-releasing factor and ACTH content. Alcohol Clin Exp Res 13:439–443.

Redei E, Halasz I, Li LF, Prystowsky MB, Aird F (1993) Maternal adrenalectomy alters the immune and endocrine functions of fetal alcohol-exposed male offspring. Endocrinology 133:452–460.

Revskoy S, Halasz I, Redei E (1997) Corticotropin-releasing hormone and proopiomelanocortin gene expression is altered selectively in the male rat fetal thymus by maternal alcohol consumption. Endocrinology 138:389–396.

Rivier C (1994) Stimulatory effect of interleukin-1β on the hypothalamic-pituitary-adrenal axis of the rat: influence of age, gender and circulating sex steroids. J Endocrinol 140:365–372.

—— (1995) Adult male rats exposed to an alcohol diet exhibit a blunted adrenocorticotropic hormone response to immune or physical stress: possible role of nitric oxide. Alcohol Clin Exp Res 19:1474–1479.

—— (1999) Gender, sex steroids, corticotropin-releasing factor, nitric oxide, and the HPA response to stress. Pharmacol Biochem Behav 64:739–751.

Robinson RS, Seelig LL Jr (2002) Effects of maternal ethanol consumption on hematopoietic cells in the rat fetal liver. Alcohol 28:151–156.

Root AW, Reiter EO, Andriola M, Duckett G (1975) Hypothalamic–pituitary function in the fetal alcohol syndrome. J Pediatr 87:585–588.

Rosenfeld P, Suchecki D, Levine S (1992) Multifactorial regulation of the hypothalamic-pituitary-adrenal axis during development. Neurosci Biobehav Rev 16:553–568.

Rudeen PK, Taylor JA (1992) Fetal alcohol neuroendocrinopathies. In: Watson RR (ed). *Alcohol and Neurobiology: Brain Development and Hormone Regulation*. CRC Press, Boca Raton, FL, pp 109–138.

Rudeen PK, Weinberg J (1993) Prenatal ethanol exposure: changes in regional brain catecholamine content following stress. J Neurochem 61:1907–1915.

Sacedon R, Vicente A, Varas A, Morale MC, Barden N, Marchetti B, Zapata AG (1999) Partial blockade of T-cell differentiation during ontogeny and marked alterations of the thymic microenvironment in transgenic mice with impaired glucocorticoid receptor function. J Neuroimmunol 98:157–167.

Sapolsky RM, Meaney MJ (1986) Maturation of the adrenocortical stress response: neuroendocrine control mechanisms and the stress hyporesponsive period. Brain Res 396:64–76.

Sari Y, Zhou FC (2004) Prenatal alcohol exposure causes long-term serotonin neuron deficit in mice. Alcohol Clin Exp Res 28:941–948.

Savino W, Dardenne M (2000) Neuroendocrine control of thymus physiology. Endocrinol Rev 21:412–443.

Schapiro S (1962) Pituitary ACTH and compensatory adrenal hypertrophy in stress-non-responsive infant rats. Endocrinology 71:986–989.

Schneider ML, Moore CF, Kraemer GW (2004) Moderate level alcohol during pregnancy, prenatal stress, or both and limbic-hypothalamic-pituitary-adrenocortical axis response to stress in rhesus monkeys. Child Dev 75:96–109.

Sebire G, Emilie D, Wallon C, Hery C, Devergne O, Delfraissy JF, Galanaud P, Tardieu M (1993) In vitro production of IL-6, IL-1β, and tumor necrosis factor-α by human embryonic microglial and neural cells. J Immunol 150:1517–1523.

Seckl JR (2004a) Prenatal glucocorticoids and long-term programming. Eur J Endocrinol 151:U49–U62.

—— (2004b) 11β-hydroxysteroid dehydrogenases: changing glucocorticoid action. Curr Opin Pharmacol 4:597–602.

Seelig LL Jr, Steven WM, Stewart GL (1996) Effects of maternal ethanol consumption on the subsequent development of immunity to *Trichinella spiralis* in rat neonates. Alcohol Clin Exp Res 20:514–522.

—— (1999) Second-generation effects of maternal ethanol consumption on immunity to *Trichinella spiralis* in female rats. Alcohol Alcohol 34:520–528.

Selye H (1936) A syndrome produced by diverse noxious agents. Nature 138:32–44.

—— (1946) The general adaptation syndrome and the diseases of adaptation. J Clin Endocrinol 6:117–230.

—— (1950) *The Physiology and Pathology of Exposure to Stress*. Acta Inc Medical Publishing, Montreal.

Sharp BM, Matta SG, Peterson PK, Newton R, Chao C, McAllen K (1989) Tumor necrosis factor-α is a potent ACTH secretagogue: comparison to interleukin-1β. Endocrinology 124:3131–3133.

Siaud P, Mekaouche M, Ixart G, Balmefrezol M, Givalois L, Barbanel G, Assenmacher I (1994) A subpopulation of corticotropin-releasing hormone neurosecretory cells in the paraventricular nucleus of the hypothalamus also contain NADPH-diaphorase. Neurosci Lett 170:51–54.

Slone JL, Redei EE (2002) Maternal alcohol and adrenalectomy: asynchrony of stress response and forced swim behavior. Neurotoxicol Teratol 24:173–178.

Somerset DA, Zheng Y, Kilby MD, Sansom DM, Drayson MT (2004) Normal human pregnancy is associated with an elevation in the immune suppressive CD25+ CD4+ regulatory T-cell subset. Immunology 112:38–43.

Steven WM, Stewart GL, Seelig LL (1992) The effects of maternal ethanol consumption on lactational transfer of immunity to *Trichinella spiralis* in rats. Alcohol Clin Exp Res 16:884–890.

Stratakis CA, Chrousos GP (1995) Neuroendocrinology and pathophysiology of the stress system. NY Acad Sci 711:1–18.

Suda T, Tozawa F, Ushiyama T, Sumitomo T, Yamada M, Demura H (1990) Interleukin-1 stimulates corticotropin-releasing factor gene expression in rat hypothalamus. Endocrinology 126:1223–1228.

Szekeres-Bartho J, Philibert D, Chaouat G (1990) Progesterone suppression of pregnancy lymphocytes is not mediated by glucocorticoid effect. Am J Reprod Immunol 23:42–43.

Tajuddin NF, Druse MJ (1993) Treatment of pregnant alcohol-consuming rats with buspirone: effects on serotonin and 5-hydroxyindoleacetic acid content in offspring. Alcohol Clin Exp Res 17:110–114.

Tanriverdi F, Silveira LF, MacColl GS, Bouloux PM (2003) The hypothalamic-pituitary-gonadal axis: immune function and autoimmunity. J Endocrinol 176:293–304.

Taylor AN, Ben-Eliyahu S, Yirmiya R, Chang MP, Norman DC, Chiappelli F (1993) Actions of alcohol on immunity and neoplasia in fetal alcohol exposed and adult rats. Alcohol Alcohol Suppl 2:69–74.

Taylor AN, Branch BJ, Kokka N, Poland RE (1983) Neonatal and long-term neuroendocrine effects of fetal alcohol exposure. Monogr Neural Sci 9:140–152.

Taylor AN, Branch BJ, Liu SH, Kokka N (1982) Long-term effects of fetal ethanol exposure on pituitary-adrenal response to stress. Pharmacol Biochem Behav 16:585–589.

Taylor AN, Branch BJ, Nelson LR, Lane LA, Poland RE (1986) Prenatal ethanol and ontogeny of pituitary-adrenal responses to ethanol and morphine. Alcohol 34:255–259.

Taylor AN, Branch BJ, Van Zuylen JE, Redei E (1988) Maternal alcohol consumption and stress responsiveness in offspring. Adv Exp Med Biol 245:311–317.

Taylor AN, Lorenz RJ, Turner BB, Ronnekleiv OK, Casady RL, Branch BJ (1976) Factors influencing pituitary-adrenal rhythmicity: its ontogeny and circadian variations in stress responsiveness. Psychoneuroendocrinology 1:291–301.

Taylor AN, Tio DL, Chiappelli F (1999a) Thymocyte development in male fetal alcohol-exposed rats. Alcohol Clin Exp Res 23:465–470.

Taylor AN, Tio DL, Heng NS, Yirmiya R (2002a) Alcohol consumption attenuates febrile responses to lipopolysaccharide and interleukin-1β in male rats. Alcohol Clin Exp Res 26:44–52.

Taylor AN, Tio DL, Yirmiya R (1999b) Fetal alcohol exposure attenuates interleukin-1β-induced fever: neuroimmune mechanisms. J Neuroimmunol 99:44–52.

Taylor AN, Tritt SH, Tio DL, Romeo HE, Yirmiya R (2002b) Maternal adrenalectomy abrogates the effect of fetal alcohol exposure on the interleukin-1β-induced febrile response: gender differences. Neuroendocrinology 76:185–192.

Tran TD, Kelly SJ (1999) Alterations in hippocampal and hypothalamic monoaminergic neurotransmitter systems after alcohol exposure during all three trimester equivalents in adult rats. J Neural Transm 106:773–786.

Trautman PD, Meyer-Bahlburg HF, Postelnek J, New MI (1995) Effects of early prenatal dexamethasone on the cognitive and behavioral development of young children: results of a pilot study. Psychoneuroendocrinology 20:439–449.

Tritt SH, Tio DL, Brammer GL, Taylor AN (1993) Adrenalectomy but not adrenal demedullation during pregnancy prevents the growth-retarding effects of fetal alcohol exposure. Alcohol Clin Exp Res 17:1281–1289.

Turner BB, Taylor AN (1976) Persistent alteration of pituitary–adrenal function in the rat by prepuberal corticosterone treatment. Endocrinology 98:1–9.

von Boehmer H, Aifantis I, Gounari F, Azogui O, Haughn L, Apostolou I, Jaeckel E, Grassi F, Klein L (2003) Thymic selection revisited: how essential is it? Immunol Rev 191:62–78.

Walker CD (1995) Chemical sympathectomy and maternal separation affect neonatal stress responses and adrenal sensitivity to ACTH. Am J Physiol 268:R1281–1288.

Walker CD, Perrin M, Vale W, Rivier C (1986a) Ontogeny of the stress response in the rat: role of the pituitary and the hypothalamus. Endocrinology 118:1445–1451.

Walker CD, Sapolsky RM, Meaney MJ, Vale WW, Rivier CL (1986b) Increased pituitary sensitivity to glucocorticoid feedback during the stress nonresponsive period in the neonatal rat. Endocrinology 119:1816–1821.

Walker CD, Scribner KA, Cascio CS, Dallman MF (1991) The pituitary–adrenocortical system of neonatal rats is responsive to stress throughout development in a time-dependent and stressor-specific fashion. Endocrinology 128:1385–1395.

Walker CD, Welberg L, Plotsky P (2002) Glucocorticoids, stress, and development. In: Pfaff D (ed). Hormones, Brain and Behavior. Academic Press, New York, pp 487–534.

Watkins LR, Maier SF (2000) The pain of being sick: implications of immune-to-brain communication for understanding pain. Annu Rev Psychol 51:29–57.

Weaver IC, Cervoni N, Champagne FA, D'Alessio AC, Sharma S, Seckl JR, Dymov S, Szyf M, Meaney MJ (2004) Epigenetic programming by maternal behavior. Nat Neurosci 7:847–854.

Weinberg J (1988) Hyperresponsiveness to stress: differential effects of prenatal ethanol on males and females. Alcohol Clin Exp Res 12:647–652.

—— (1989) Prenatal ethanol exposure alters adrenocortical development of offspring. Alcohol Clin Exp Res 13:73–83.

—— (1992a) Prenatal ethanol effects: sex differences in offspring stress responsiveness. Alcohol 9:219–223.

—— (1992b) Prenatal ethanol exposure alters adrenocortical response to predictable and unpredictable stressors. Alcohol 9:427–432.

—— (1993a) Prenatal alcohol exposure: endocrine function of offspring. In: Zakhari S (ed). *Alcohol and the Endocrine System*. NIH Press, Bethesda, MD, pp 363–382.

—— (1993b) Neuroendocrine effects of prenatal alcohol exposure. Ann NY Acad Sci 697:86–96.

—— (1994) Recent studies on the effects of fetal alcohol exposure on the endocrine and immune systems. Alcohol Alcohol Suppl 2:401–409.

—— (1995) In utero alcohol exposure and hypothalamic-pituitary-adrenal activity: gender differences in outcome. In: Zakhari S, Hunt WA (eds). *Stress, Gender and Alcohol-Seeking Behavior*. NIH Press, Bethesda, MD, pp 343–353.

Weinberg J, Bezio S (1987) Alcohol-induced changes in pituitary-adrenal activity during pregnancy. Alcohol Clin Exp Res 11:274–280.

Weinberg J, Gallo PV (1982) Prenatal ethanol exposure: pituitary-adrenal activity in pregnant dams and offspring. Neurobehav Toxicol Teratol 4:515–520.

Weinberg J, Jerrells TR (1991) Suppression of immune responsiveness: sex differences in prenatal ethanol effects. Alcohol Clin Exp Res 15:525–531.

Weinberg J, Nelson LR, Taylor AN (1986) Hormonal effects of fetal alcohol exposure. In: West JR (ed). *Alcohol and Brain Development*. Oxford University Press, New York, pp 310–342.

Weinberg J, Petersen TD (1991) Effects of prenatal ethanol exposure on glucocorticoid receptors in rat hippocampus. Alcohol Clin Exp Res 15:711–716.

Weinberg J, Taylor AN, Gianoulakis C (1996) Fetal ethanol exposure: hypothalamic-pituitary-adrenal and β-endorphin responses to repeated stress. Alcohol Clin Exp Res 20:122–131.

Welberg LA, Seckl JR (2001) Prenatal stress, glucocorticoids and the programming of the brain. J Neuroendocrinol 13:113–128.

West LJ (2002) Defining critical windows in the development of the human immune system. Hum Exp Toxicol 21:499–505.

Winters AJ, Oliver C, Colston C, MacDonald PC, Porter JC (1974) Plasma ACTH levels in the human fetus and neonate as related to age and parturition. J Clin Endocrinol Metab 39:269–273.

Witek-Janusek L (1988) Pituitary-adrenal response to bacterial endotoxin in developing rats. Am J Physiol 255:E525–530.

Wolcott RM, Jennings SR, Chervenak R (1995) In utero exposure to ethanol affects postnatal development of T- and B-lymphocytes, but not natural killer cells. Alcohol Clin Exp Res 19:170–176.

Wong CM, Chiappelli F, Chang MP, Norman DC, Cooper EL, Branch BJ, Taylor AN (1992) Prenatal exposure to alcohol enhances thymocyte mitogenic responses postnatally. Int J Immunopharmacol 14:303–309.

Yamashita F, Lan N, Yu W, Ellis L, Halpert AG, Weinberg J (2004) Role of estradiol in stress hyperresponsiveness seen in female rats prenatally exposed to ethanol. Neurotoxicol Teratol 26:502.

Yirmiya R, Pilati ML, Chiappelli F, Taylor AN (1993) Fetal alcohol exposure attenuates lipopolysaccharide-induced fever in rats. Alcohol Clin Exp Res 17:906–910.

Yirmiya R, Tio DL, Taylor AN (1996) Effects of fetal alcohol exposure on fever, sickness behavior, and pituitary-adrenal activation induced by interleukin-1β in young adult rats. Brain Behav Immun 10:205–220.

Ylikorkala O, Stenman UH, Halmesmaki E (1988) Testosterone, androstenedione, dehydroepiandrosterone sulfate, and sex-hormone-binding globulin in pregnant alcohol abusers. Obstet Gynecol 71:731–735.

Zafar H, Shelat SG, Redei E, Tejani-Butt S (2000) Fetal alcohol exposure alters serotonin transporter sites in rat brain. Brain Res 856:184–192.

Zajac CS, Abel EL (1992) Animal models of prenatal alcohol exposure. Int J Epidemiol 21(Suppl 1):S24–32.

Zakharova LA, Malyukova IV, Proshlyakova EV, Potapova AA, Sapronova AY, Ershov PV, Ugrumov MV (2000) Hypothalamo-pituitary control of the cell-mediated immunity in rat embryos: role of LHRH in regulation of lymphocyte proliferation. J Reprod Immunol 47:17–32.

Zalcman S, Green-Johnson JM, Murray L, Nance DM, Dyck D, Anisman H, Greenberg AH (1994) Cytokine-specific central monoamine alterations induced by interleukin-1, -2 and -6. Brain Res 643:40–49.

Zhang X, Yu W, Lam J, Jitratkosol M, Weinberg J (2005a) Effect of prenatal ethanol exposure on CD4+CD25+ regulatory T cells. Alcohol Clin Exp Res. 29:87A.

Zhang X, Sliwowska JH, Weinberg J. (2005b) Prenatal alcohol exposure and fetal programming: Effects on neuroendocrine and immune function. Exp Biol Med 230:376–388.

11

Early Exposure to Ethanol Affects the Proliferation of Neuronal Precursors

Michael W. Miller

The number of neurons constituting the brain is a direct reflection of the number of cells produced during early development. The present chapter explores the effects of ethanol on spatiotemporal patterns and systems regulating cell proliferation. During development more neurons are generated than the number comprising the mature brain. A "correction" occurs through the natural death of many neurons (see Chapter 5). This process is also affected by exposure to ethanol. The consequent effects are addressed in Chapters 15, 16, and 17.

SPATIOTEMPORAL PATTERNS

The proliferation of neuronal populations occurs in defined sites over restricted periods of time. These spatiotemporal patterns are affected by early exposure to ethanol. Various structures involved have been examined, including segments of the telencephalon (the neocortex and hippocampal formation) and brain stem (cerebellum and pons).

Telencephalic Structures

Neocortex

Patterns of Neuronal Generation. Neocortical neurons are largely generated over a protracted, but defined prenatal period. It has also been argued that neocortical neurons continue to be generated at a low rate in the mature cortex (see Gould and Gross, 2002; Rakic, 2002). For the purposes of this review, any potential contribution from adult neuronogenesis in neocortex can be considered to be too low as to have an impact on neuronal number. A possible model of postnatal neuronal generation may be the proliferative activity in the intrahilar zone (IHZ; also known as hippocampal field CA4) of hippocampal formation wherein the generation of granule neurons continues throughout life (see Hippocampal Formation, below).

In the rat, after production of the pallial preplate cortical neuronogenesis begins on gestational day (G) 11 and ends on G21 (Brückner et al., 1976; Lund and Mustari, 1977; Miller, 1985, 1988; Al-Ghoul and Miller, 1989). This process is orderly and follows a well-defined inside-out sequence. Accordingly, the first neurons generated become layer VIa neurons; later generations of neurons are destined for progressively more superficial laminae.

Ethanol exposure alters the number and sequence of neuronogenesis (Miller, 1986, 1988), delaying and extending the period of neuronal generation by 1 day each (Fig. 11–1). On each day, the number of neurons with a particular time of origin is reduced. The exception to this pattern is the substantial increase in neuronal generation as cortical neuronogenesis is winding down (after G19). The early depression in neuronal generation is followed by a late surge in terms of as neuronal density; on G20 and succeeding days, neuronal generation is significantly greater in the cortices of ethanol-treated rats than in controls. Interpretation of these data leads to four conclusions.

The first is that the delayed onset of cortical neuronal generation suggests an ethanol-related retarding effect on the acquisition of critical numbers of proliferating cells required to initiate neuronal generation. That is, the population of proliferating neural precursors has to reach a threshold size before neuronal precursors begin to pass through their final cell division and the young neurons begin to leave the proliferative population. This pattern is consistent with the concept of founder cells (see Chapter 2).

The second conclusion is that ethanol has complex effects on cell proliferation. Initially, the proliferation of neuronal precursors is depressed and later it is promoted. This conclusion is supported by various studies discussed below (see Sites of Proliferation, below).

The third observation, from the complex time-dependent effects of ethanol on the number of neurons being generated, is that the late surge may be an effort of the proliferative population to compensate for the early depression. Indeed, the density of neurons generated over the entire period of neuronogenesis is unaffected by ethanol exposure. This is an interesting finding in that the total number of cortical neurons, at

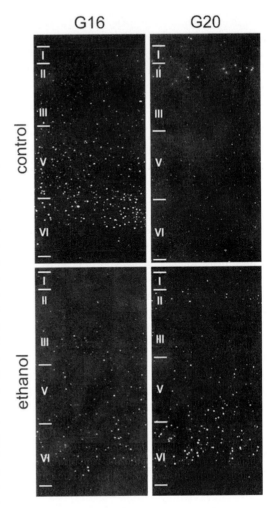

FIGURE 11–1 Neuronal generation in motor cortex. These dark-field micrographs show that in control rats, neurons generated on gestational day (G) 16 and on G20 are distributed in deep and superficial cortex, respectively. In ethanol-treated rats, neurons born on G16 are also distributed in deep cortex, although their numbers are fewer and they tend to be more deeply disposed. Neurons generated on G20 that are properly distributed in superficial cortex are also of fewer number. Many late-generated neurons, however, are ectopically distributed in deep cortex. (*Source:* Images taken, with permission, from Miller (1986), Science 233:1308–1311.)

least in somatosensory cortex, is significantly lower in ethanol-treated rats (Miller and Potempa, 1990). The implication is that ethanol does not affect the number of neurons produced from an ontogenetic column; rather, it reduces the number of columns. An ontogenetic column is a hypothetical unit of developing cortex that includes the proliferative cells and the radial array of the progeny (e.g., Rakic, 1978, 2000). This conclusion is supported by data showing that the density of radial glial fibers (the guides commonly used to coordinate neuronal migration) is unaffected by prenatal exposure to ethanol (Miller and Robertson, 1993).

Finally, the inside-out sequence is largely maintained until the end of cortical neuronal generation. At this time, many neurons destined for superficial cortex end up in deep cortex because of a defect in neuronal migration (see Chapter 13). The effects of ethanol on neuronal generation may be best appreciated by tracing the ontogeny of select populations of cortical neurons, for example, corticospinal (Miller, 1987) and callosal projection (Miller, 1997) neurons. In general, they are distributed in laminae that are normal for their phenotype, with the notable exception of the late-generated callosal neurons. Many of these neurons reside in infragranular laminae. Thus, in addition to the conclusions described above, it appears that (a) ethanol does not affect the connectional phenotype of a particular neuron (regardless of a migration defect) and (b) the decision about neuronal lineage occurs at the time of neuronal origin. Similar cortical disorganization of neuronal phenotypes occurs in cortices in which cells in the proliferative zones are heterochronically transplanted (McConnell, 1988).

Sites of Proliferation. The proliferation of neuronal precursors occurs in specific sites generally located proximal to the ventricular system (see Chapter 2). For neocortex, cell proliferation occurs in three sites (Fig. 11–2). The ventricular zone (VZ) is a pseudostratified epithelium lining the lateral ventricles (Sauer, 1936; Watterson et al., 1956; Sauer and Chittenden, 1959; Jacobson, 1991). The subventricular zone (SZ) is a stratified epithelium external to the neocortical VZ (Ramon y Cajal, 1909–1911; Rakic et al., 1974; Shoukimas and Hinds, 1978). The ganglionic eminence (GE) generates some local circuit neurons (Tamamaki et al., 1997; Zhu et al., 1999; Anderson et al., 2001; Wichterle et al., 2001).

The two primary neocortical proliferation zones are the VZ and SZ, and there is some controversy about the contribution of the VZ and SZ in the generation of neocortical neurons. Some investigators

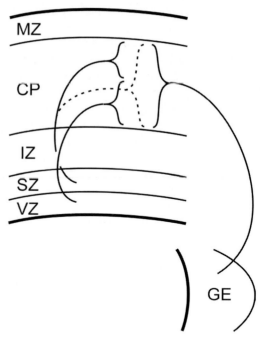

FIGURE 11–2 Effects of ethanol on the three sources of neocortical neurons. Neurons that populate the cortical plate (CP) are derived from the ventricular zone (VZ), subventricular zone (SZ), and ganglionic eminence (GE). In normal rats, VZ and SZ cells principally give rise to infra- and supragranular neurons, respectively (solid lines). The GE generates local circuit neurons that are distributed throughout neocortex. Following prenatal exposure to ethanol, many late-generated neurons (originating largely in the SZ) complete their migrations in deep cortex (dashed line). IZ, intermediate zone; MZ, marginal zone.

argue that the VZ is the site of neuronal origin and that the SZ generates glia and glial precursors (Gomes et al., 2003; Samuelson et al., 2003). In contrast, others argue that all neurons are derived from the SZ and that the VZ is merely a self-replacing population (Doetsch et al., 1997, 1999; Alvarez-Buylla and Garcia-Verdugo, 2002; Martens et al., 2000, 2002). Other studies support a different model of cortical development, that both the VZ and SZ give rise to cortical neurons (Miller, 1992; Luo and Miller, 1998).

Studies on the consequences of prenatal exposure to moderate amounts of ethanol (sufficient to produce peak blood ethanol concentrations of 150 mg/dl) provide unique insight into the controversy over the contribution of the VZ and SZ to the population of neocortical neurons. Daily neuronal production during the first half of the period of neuronongenesis is depressed by prenatal exposure to ethanol (Miller, 1986, 1988). During this time, the VZ is the prominent neocortical proliferative zone. Changes in cell proliferation within the VZ parallel the early reductions in neuronal generation. Prenatal exposure to ethanol reduces the total number of cells and the number of cycling cells in the VZ (Miller, 1989) and it increases the time cells need to transit through the cell cycle (Miller and Nowkowski, 1991).

The ethanol-induced late surge in neuronal generation occurs when the SZ becomes the predominant proliferative zone. The SZ is affected by ethanol in a way opposite that of the VZ. The total number of cells in the SZ and the number of cycling cells are increased by ethanol (Miller, 1989; Miller and Nowakowski, 1991).

Taken together, the correlative data on the birth dates of cortical neurons and characteristics of VZ and SZ cells show that both the VZ and SZ produce neurons. This thesis was tested in an experiment in which fetuses were exposed to ethanol for only 4 days during the period of (a) SZ prominence (between G18 and G21), (b) VZ prominence (between G12 and G15), or (c) stem cell production (between G6 and G9) (Miller, 1996a). SZ cell proliferation and the production of late-generated neurons are only affected when the ethanol exposure occurs between G18 and G21 (Fig. 11–3). Moreover, this late exposure to ethanol increases both cell proliferation and production. VZ cell proliferation and early-generated neurons, by contrast, are maximally affected by exposure to ethanol that occurs between G12 and G15, i.e., when the VZ is most prominent. This exposure to ethanol inhibits VZ cell proliferation and reduces the number of neurons generated on G15. Exposure to ethanol between G6 and G9 does not affect the proliferation of cells in either proliferative zone or the number of early- or late-generated neurons. Furthermore, based on timing, it appears that the VZ gives rise to neurons distributed in infragranular cortex and the SZ generates supragranular neurons. This conclusion is supported by the tracing of derivatives of cells that express transcripts for the genes Svet1 (Tarabykin et al., 2001) and cux (Nieto

et al., 2004) from the SZ to the supragranular laminae.

Radial Glia.   Radial glia, thought to serve as guides for neuronal migration (Rakic, 1971, 1978), are among the first cortical cells to be generated. Traditionally, radial glia have been considered transitional astrocytes (e.g., Schmechel and Rakic, 1979; Lu et al., 1980; Voigt, 1989; de Lima et al., 1997), however, more recent evidence shows that some radial glia can differentiate into neurons (Malatesta et al., 2000; Hartfuss et al., 2001; Levers et al., 2001; Noctor et al., 2001, 2002; Alvarez-Buylla and Garcia-Verdugo, 2002; Götz et al., 2002; Sanai et al., 2004). This dual lineage is consistent with glial expression of nestin, a cytoskeletal protein associated with neural stem cells (Hockfield and McKay, 1985; Miller and Robertson, 1993). Although no studies have directly assessed the effects of ethanol on the proliferation of radial glia, it appears that the periodicity of the network of radial glial fibers is unaffected by ethanol (Miller and Robertson, 1993; Valles et al., 1996; Miñana et al., 2000). This finding implies that these cells proliferate to maintain a consistent density within the expanding telencephalic vesicle. A discussion of the effects of ethanol on radial glia and their role in neuronal migration is provided in Chapter 3.

Hippocampal Formation

Neurons in the hippocampal formation are generated over a protracted period of time: in the rat, from G15 to adulthood (Altman, 1962; Angevine, 1965; Schlessinger et al., 1978; Bayer, 1980; Miller, 1995a). Most neurons in the three hippocampal fields, CA1–CA3, and the dentate gyrus are generated prenatally. The site of origin of these neurons is the VZ. A notable exception is that most (~85%) granule neurons in the dentate gyrus are generated postnatally. Postnatal granule cell generation occurs in the IHZ.

Hippocampal cell numbers are substantially affected by ethanol exposure. These effects are spatially and temporally defined. Total DNA and protein content in hippocampal formation is lower in animals exposed to ethanol prenatally (Miller, 1996b). In contrast, postnatal exposure increases both DNA and protein content. Anatomical studies have provided more detailed information on these ethanol-induced effects. Animals exposed to ethanol prenatally have

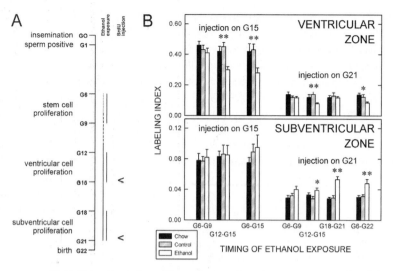

FIGURE 11–3 Time-dependent effects of ethanol on the two neocortical proliferative zones. **A.** Exposure to ethanol during three prenatal time periods was
examined: during the period of neocortical stem cell generation (gestational
day [G] 6 to G9), prominence of the ventricular zone (VZ) (G12–G15), and
prominence of the subventricular zone (SZ) (G18–G21). **B.** Exposure during
the period of stem cell generation does not affect the proportion of cells proliferating on G15 and G21 (when the VZ and SZ predominate, respectively).
Later exposures, by contrast, have specific effects on the zone most active during the time of exposure, i.e., the VZ between G12 and G15 and the SZ between G18 and G21. (*Source:* Images taken, with permission, from Miller
(1996a), Alcohol Clin Exp Res 20:139–143.)

fewer neurons in the pyramidal cell layer of CA1 and
granule cell layer of the dentate gyrus than do controls (Miller, 1995a). Interestingly, whereas postnatal
exposure generally has little effect on the number
of these neurons, it can increase the number of granule neurons in the dentate gyrus (Miller, 1995b;
Pawlak et al., 2002). This effect on granule neurons is
concentration-dependent. Moderate amounts of
ethanol are stimulatory and high concentrations of
ethanol are depressive.

The ethanol-induced changes in neuronal number
directly reflect alterations in neuronal generation. For
example, the generation of dentate granule neurons is
reduced by prenatal ethanol exposure and promoted
by postnatal exposure. Thus, ethanol affects developing hippocampal formation in the same manner that
it affects the generation of neocortical neurons. As
postnatal generation of granule neurons occurs in the
IHZ, it appears that ethanol affects all telencephalic
auxiliary (derived) proliferative zones similarly.

Brain Stem

The effect of chronic gestational exposure to ethanol
on the principal sensory nucleus of the trigeminal
nerve (PSN) and cerebellum has been examined. The
PSN is a simple structure. All of its neurons are derived
from the pontine VZ. Prenatal exposure to ethanol reduces the number of neurons in the PSN (Miller and
Muller, 1989; Miller, 1995b). This reduction is partially (two-thirds) due to decreased cell generation and
partially (one-third) to exacerbation of mechanisms of
naturally occurring neuronal death (Miller, 1999a). The
reduction in cell generation appears to be equivalent for
neurons and glia and neuronal generation is delayed by
about 1 day (Miller and Muller, 1989).

The cerebellar cortex is also vulnerable to ethanol
toxicity. A gross indication that ethanol affects cell generation in the cerebellum is the effect of ethanol on its
size (Bauer-Moffett and Altman, 1975; Kornguth et al.,
1979; Diaz and Samson, 1980; Pierce and West,

1986; Bonthius and West, 1988). Exposure to moderate amounts of ethanol (blood ethanol concentrations of ~150 mg/dl) causes reductions (15%–20%) in cerebellar size similar to that evident for cerebral cortex (Miller, 1996b). Following exposure to high amounts (sufficient to produce blood ethanol concentrations of >250 mg/dl), the size of the cerebellum is more adversely affected.

Cerebellar neurons are generated in two sites—the VZ and a derived proliferative zone, the external granular layer (EGL). Attention has been directed toward the EGL because it is most prominent in the rat postnatally and it gives birth to a populous neuron type in the central nervous system (CNS), the cerebellar granule neuron. Postnatal exposure to high amounts of ethanol prolongs the existence of the EGL and delays its depletion (Bauer-Moffett and Altman, 1977; Kornguth et al., 1979). Moreover, cell proliferation in the EGL is reduced. These data suggest that the EGL is different from other derived proliferative zones in that its proliferative activity is not stimulated by ethanol. The EGL differs from the SZ and IHZ insofar as it is the sole source of granule neurons, whereas the SZ and IHZ produce neurons that can be generated in the VZ. Nonetheless, this conclusion remains unconfirmed until dose–response data analysis of the EGL is performed.

CELL CYCLE KINETICS

In vivo and In Situ Studies

As cells proliferate they pass through a defined set of steps, cumulatively known as the *cell cycle*. The cell cycle has four phases: G1, S, G2, and M. During the G1 phase the cells either prepare for another pass through the cell cycle or exit from the cell cycle. Durings, cells replicate their nuclear DNA. G2 is a short period when preparation for mitosis takes place, which occurs during M. Data on the cell cycle are best appreciated for VZ cells. The somata of VZ cells move rhythmically as the cells pass through the four phases (Sauer, 1936; Watterson et al., 1956; Sauer and Chittenden, 1959; Atlas and Bond, 1965). Through this process, called *interkinetic nuclear migration*, mitotic cells that are at the ventricular surface reconstitute and move their nuclei to positions in the external third of the VZ where they replicate their DNA during S.

Ethanol does not affect the pattern of interkinetic nuclear migration in the VZ per se (Kennedy and Elliott, 1985; Miller, 1989). On the other hand, ethanol does affect the time a VZ cell takes to pass through the cell cycle. For example, in the neocortical VZ of a 21-day-old rat fetus (Miller and Nowakowski, 1991) or a slice of cortex explanted from a 17-day-old fetus (Siegenthaler and Miller, 2005a), the total length of the cell cycle (T_C) is increased 26%–29%. This increase has a direct negative effect on the number of cells produced in the VZ. An increase in the T_C is also evident in the EGL of the cerebellum (Borges and Lewis, 1983). Ethanol-induced increases in T_C primarily result from a lengthening of G1. These effects of ethanol are not the same for all proliferative populations. For example, the T_C of the neocortical SZ is not affected by moderate exposures to ethanol (Miller and Nowkowski, 1991).

In addition to cell cycle kinetics, the production of new cells is defined by three other features of proliferating populations: the growth fraction (GF), the proportion of cells that exit the cell cycle, and the leaving fraction (LF). The GF is the proportion of total cell population that is actively cycling. Overall, the GF for the cerebral wall extends over the period of neocortical neuronongenesis (Miller and Kuhn, 1995; Takahashi et al., 1995, 1996). Although there is no ethanol-induced difference in the GF at the beginning of this period, as neuronal generation proceeds a significant difference takes place. Ethanol causes an increase in the GF. The effect of ethanol on the overall GF is largely due to ethanol-induced increases in the SZ. Both the specific GF for the SZ (Miller and Nowkowski, 1991) and the number of cells in the SZ (Miller, 1989) are increased by ethanol. The GF for the VZ is either unaffected by ethanol in vivo (Miller and Nowakowski, 1991) or subtly, but significantly, reduced in the VZ of an organotypic slice preparation (Siegenthaler and Miller, 2005a). The effect of the increases in GF in the SZ is accentuated with time as the SZ becomes the major neocortical proliferative zone.

After cells pass through M, the daughter cells either re-enter the cycle or exit the cell cycle. The number of cells that exit the cell cycle can be determined by tracing the proportion of cells that have incorporated a DNA precursor during S relative to the total population of cycling cells, for example, cells that express Ki-67 (Chenn and Walsh, 2002, 2003; Siegenthaler and Miller, 2005a; 2005b). Accordingly, an in situ study shows that ethanol increases the number of cells that exit the cell cycle (Siegenthaler and Miller, 2005a).

A third feature contributing to neuronal production is the LF. This differs from the exit fraction in that it encompasses cell cycle exit and the process of moving from the proliferative zones. The LF rises steadily over the period of neuronal generation (Miller, 1993, 1999b; Takahashi et al., 1996). Ethanol does not affect the LF during this period (Miller, 1993). Inasmuch as ethanol does affect the number of exiting cells, this lack of increase in the LF implies that ethanol induces postmitotic cells to remain in the proliferative zones for a longer time before commencing their migration.

Various cell cycle–related proteins are affected by ethanol: the expression of cyclin A (a regulator of S and G2), cyclin D1, and cdk2 (proteins that regulate the progression of cells from G1 to S) is reduced by ethanol exposure (Li et al., 2001, 2002; Siegenthaler and Miller, 2005a). Cerebellar expression of cyclin D2, cdk4, and cdk6 (regulators of G1) are unaffected by ethanol (Li et al., 2002). By contrast, p27 (a protein involved in moving cells from G1 out of the cycle) is depressed by ethanol in the VZ of cortical explants (Siegenthaler and Miller, 2005a) and in developing rat cerebellum (Li et al., 2002). Thus, the effects of ethanol on cell cycle–related proteins not only corroborate, but provide a mechanism for ethanol-induced increases in the T_C and cell cycle exit and a decrease in the GF.

Cell Culture Studies

Studies in cell culture models replicate the in vivo data and provide systems in which to explore cellular and molecular mechanisms underlying the ethanol-induced changes. Various cells have been used as models of proliferating neural precursors—primary cultures of neurons (Jacobs and Miller, 2001; Miller, 2003a) and astrocytes (Kennedy and Mukerji, 1985; Guerri et al., 1990; Snyder et al., 1992; Kötter and Klein, 1999; Luo and Miller, 1999a; Costa and Guizzetti, 2002; Miller and Luo, 2002a) and neuronal (Luo and Miller, 1997a, 1999b; Miller and Luo, 2002b) or glial (Waziri et al.,1981; Isenberg et al., 1992; Resnicoff et al., 1994, 1996b; Luo and Miller, 1996) cancer cell lines. There is consensus that ethanol increases the time these neural cells take to double the size of their populations.

Doubling time is a complex yardstick reflecting the sum of simpler parameters. One of these parameters is an increase in the T_C, and most of this increase is from a lengthened G1 (Guerri et al., 1990; Luo and Miller, 1997a; Jacobs and Miller, 2001). Remarkably, the effects of ethanol on the proliferation of dissociated neurons and B104 neuroblastoma cells strongly parallel those of VZ cells in vivo (cf. Miller and Nowakowski, 1991; Luo and Miller, 1997a; Jacobs and Miller, 2001). Another factor is the GF. Alteration in the GF has an inverse effect on doubling time. For example, as in the case of B104 cells, an ethanol-induced decrease in the number of cycling cells contributes to an increase in doubling time (Luo and Miller, 1997a). A third factor defining the doubling time is the incidence of cell death. Death normally occurs among proliferating populations (Blaschke et al., 1996; Thomaidou et al., 1997; Jacobs and Miller, 2000) (see Chapter 5). Ethanol affects the balance between cell proliferation and death (Jacobs and Miller, 2001; Miller, 2003a). For example, ethanol causes a steady decrease in the number of primary cultured cortical neurons. Most (two-thirds) of the decrease is due to compromised cell proliferation, whereas the remainder is from ethanol-induced cell death. Ethanol affects neuronal generation and death in the immature PSN in a similar manner (Miller, 1999a).

LIGAND-MEDIATED SYSTEMS

Many factors may contribute to the differential effect of ethanol on specific populations of proliferating cells. A major player is the myriad of growth factors that tightly regulate cell proliferation. This section focuses on a small number of growth factors that has been studied in relation to the effects of ethanol. These factors include platelet-derived growth factor (PDGF), basic fibroblast growth factor (bFGF or FGF-2), insulin-like growth factor (IGF)-1 and IGF-2, and transforming growth factor (TGF) β1. They can be classified as mitogenic (FGF-2, IGF-1, and PDGF) or anti-mitogenic (TGFβ).

Mitogenic Factors

Platelet-Derived Growth Factor

The cycling activity of neural cells is potently promoted by PDGF. It is noteworthy that PDGF receptors are expressed in the SZ of normal rodents (Sasahara et al., 1991; Yeh et al., 1991). The growth-promoting effect of PDGF has also been described for astrocytes (Luo and Miller, 1999a) and B104 neuroblastoma cells (Luo and Miller, 1997a).

PDGF is active as a dimer, formed as a combination of the two isoforms, PDGF-A and PDGF-B. PDGF-BB is the most potent ligand, doubling or trebling the growth of B104 cells and astrocytes, respectively, over 3 days (Luo and Miller, 1997a, 1999a). In contrast, PDGF-AA only increases cell growth by ~50% (B104 neuroblastoma cells) or ~70% (astrocytes) over the same period. Although the total length of the cell cycle is reduced, most of the growth results from the recruitment of cells into the cycling population— i.e., through an increase in the GF. This pattern is reminiscent of the response of SZ cells to ethanol (Miller and Nowakowski, 1991; Miller and Kuhn, 1995).

The PDGF-mediated increase in cell proliferation is mediated through two intracellular signal transduction cascades: the *ras–raf* pathway and the protein kinase C (PKC) pathway (Fig. 11–4) (Luo and Miller, 1999a). The ultimate effects of PDGF are the transient (phasic) activation of mitogen-activated protein kinase and extracellular signal regulated kinase (ERK) and the transcription of proliferation-associated genes.

PDGF-mediated growth is compromised by ethanol, the growth among B104 cells (Luo and Miller, 1997a) and astrocytes (Luo and Miller, 1999a) being reduced in a concentration-dependent manner. Interestingly, the effects of ethanol on the two ligand isoforms are cell type–specific. The action of PDGF-BB on B104 cells is twice as sensitive to ethanol as it is to PDGF-AA (Luo and Miller, 1997a), and the inverse situation is evident for neocortical astrocytes (Luo and Miller, 1999a). This may mean that PDGF differentially affects cell lineages in vivo. Moreover, the variation in effects may underlie the differential activity of SZ cells, which in the rat are largely neuronogenetic prenatally and gliogenetic postnatally.

The effect of ethanol on ligand-mediated activity apparently reflects ethanol-induced changes in receptor expression and activation. Two receptors can bind PDGF ligands: PDGF-αr and PDGF-βr. In B104 cells, ethanol targets the PDGF-αr, which ultimately leads to a change in ERK activation (Luo and Miller, 1999a). Ethanol does not stop ERK phosphorylation; rather, it induces a sustained ERK activation, which in turn can lead to changes in gene transcription.

Fibroblast Growth Factor-2

FGF-2 is an important regulator of cell proliferation in the VZ and derived zones of developing rodents. An immunohistochemical study shows that FGF-2 receptors are predominantly expressed in VZ during normal, cortical development (Weise et al., 1993). SZ cells in the neonatal rat brain are also FGF-2 responsive (Bartlett et al., 1994; Gritti et al., 1999; Wagner et al., 1999; Decker et al., 2002). For example, intraperitoneal injection of FGF-2 stimulates the proliferation of neuronal precursors in the SZ (Lachapelle et al., 2002). Similarly, intraventricular administration of FGF-2 expands the population of SZ neuronal progenitors (Kuhn et al., 1997) and increases mitotic activity in the SZ and IHZ in adult rats (Wagner et al., 1999).

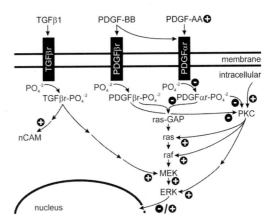

FIGURE 11–4 Signal transduction triggered by ethanol-sensitive growth factors. Cell proliferation is regulated by platelet-derived growth factor (PDGF) and transforming growth factor (TGF) β1. PDGF acts as a dimer of A or B isoforms. These growth factors bind to specific *trans*-membrane receptors that autophosphorylate. This process triggers a cascade of phosphorylation events through various intermediaries. Interestingly, although PDGF and TGFβ1 induce opposite effects (mitogenic and anti-mitogenic actions, respectively), they both stimulate extracellular signal–related kinase (ERK). The circled plus and minus signs identify the actions of ethanol. Briefly, ethanol has a specific effect on a single PDGF receptor isoform (PDGF-αr) and, through both pro- and antimitogenic factors, ethanol stimulates ERK activity. This in turn can alter nuclear gene transcription. MEK, methylethylketone; nCAM, nerve cell adhesion molecule; PKC, protein kinase C.

Dissociated cultures provide model systems to illuminate the effects of FGF-2 on proliferating populations. Cell cycle kinetics among B104 cells is affected by FGF-2 (Luo and Miller, 1997a). The T_C and GF are equally affected by FGF-2. These data are consistent with the mixed expression of FGF-2 response by VZ and SZ cells. Other preparations that presumably model VZ and SZ cells imply that FGF-2 promotes the proliferation of VZ and SZ derivatives (Martens et al., 2000, 2002).

The effects of ethanol on FGF-2-mediated cell proliferation are not well understood. Studies exploring this interaction have examined C6 glioma cells (Luo and Miller, 1996; Miller and Luo, 2002a) and telencephalic neuroepithelial cells (Ma et al., 2003). They show that ethanol eliminates the FGF-2-promoted increase in cell proliferation such that the effects of FGF-2 and ethanol nullify each other.

The depressive effects of ethanol are mediated through the FGF-2 receptor, flg (Luo and Miller, 1996b, 1997b). ERK phosphorylation, a downstream event of flg activation, increases in cortical astrocytes (Smith and Navratilova, 2003) and stem cells (Ma et al., 2003) treated with ethanol. Although ethanol does not alter protein expression of FGF-2 receptors, ERK activity remains elevated, implying that ethanol affects receptor phosphorylation.

Insulin–like Growth Factor-1

Prenatal exposure to ethanol inhibition of intrauterine and early postnatal growth correlates with the effect of ethanol on the IGF system (Breese et al., 1993; Singh et al., 1994). Ethanol halves plasma IGF-1 content in the pregnant dam (Singh et al., 1994; Breese and Sonntag, 1995) and in the fetal brain (Singh et al., 1996). Data on the effects of prenatal exposure to ethanol on IGF-2 are mixed. One report states that the amount of IGF-2 is doubled (Breese and Sontag, 1995), whereas others show that IGF-2 expression is halved (Singh et al., 1994, 1996). Likewise, the effect of ethanol on binding protein (IGF-BP) is also mixed. Some evidence shows that IGF-BP expression is reduced (Breese and Sontag, 1995), and other studies show that it is increased (Singh et al., 1994, 1996). Although the reasons for these disparate data are unclear, it is agreed that (1) ethanol affects circulating plasma and fetal expression of IGF-2 and IGF-BP and (2) ethanol causes opposing effects on the expression of these two proteins. The reduction in IGF-1 persists in the young

offspring (up to 3 weeks old), but it abates by 40 days of age (Breese et al., 1993). In contrast, IGF-2 and IGF-BP are unaffected in preweanling rats.

The effect of IGF-1 has been studied in C6 glioma cells (e.g., Resnicoff et al., 1994, 1996a, 1996b). These cells have the advantage of being able to proliferate in a serum-free medium and in the absence of any priming growth factors (e.g., Isenberg et al., 1992; Resnicoff et al., 1994; Luo and Miller, 1996). IGF-1 is a potent mitogen for proliferating C6 cells (Resnicoff et al., 1994, 1996a, 1996b). This effect is at least partially growth factor–specific, as proliferation of these cells is unaffected by PDGF (Resnicoff et al., 1994). It is worth noting that this differential response to growth factors may be a quality of the cells because primary culture astrocytes and B104 neuroblastoma cells are highly regulated by PDGF (Luo and Miller, 1997a, 1999a) (see Platelet-Derived Growth Factor, above).

Ethanol inhibits the proliferation of C6 cells (Waziri et al., 1981; Isenberg et al., 1992; Resnicoff et al., 1994, 1996a, 1996b; Luo and Miller, 1996), and it has been suggested that this inhibition is mediated by ethanol-induced disruptions of IGF-1 receptor (IGF-1r; Resnicoff et al., 1994, 1996a, 1996b). Ethanol blocks the mitogenic effect of the ligand (IGF-1) and interferes with receptor (IGF-1r) activation. Autophosphorylation of the IGF-1r is inhibited by low concentrations of ethanol. Also, ethanol inhibits the anti-apoptotic effects of IGF-1 (Cui et al., 1997).

Anti-mitogenic Factor

TGFβ ligands are intracortical factors that turn off neural cell growth (Cameron et al., 1998; Böttner et al., 2000). Exogenous TGFβ1 inhibits the growth of various cells, including C6 cells, astrocytes (Rozovsky et al., 1998; Rich et al., 1999; Robe et al., 2000; Miller and Luo, 2002a), B104 neuroblastoma cells (Luo and Miller, 1999b), and neural progenitors (Miller and Luo, 2002b). TGFβ1 does this by removing cells from the proliferative population, i.e., reducing the GF (Siegenthaler and Miller, 2005b). Interestingly, it does not affect cell cycle kinetics.

Transforming Growth Factor-Mediated Signal Transduction

The effect of TGFβ1 on cell proliferation is mediated through ERK activation (Fig. 11–4). TGFβ1 induces sustained (>90 min) activation (Luo and Miller, 1999b), an anti-intuitive result in that ERK is generally associated with mitogenic activity. A recent study of proliferating cells in organotypic cultures of fetal cortex shows that cycling cells in the VZ respond to TGFβ1 (Siegenthaler and Miller, 2005b). As with the dissociated cells, TGFβ1 inhibits VZ cell proliferation *in situ* by increasing the exit of cells from the cycling population and concomitantly decreasing the GF.

Combined treatment of cortical slices with ethanol and TGFβ1 affects the expression of cell cycle–related proteins (Siegenthaler and Miller, 2005b). For example, total cyclin D1 expression is reduced in the VZ, and because ethanol and TGFβ1 do not affect the frequency of cyclin D1-positive cells, it appears that the amount of cyclin D1 per cell is reduced. A similar decrement in p27 expression has been detected. As for p21, co-treatment with ethanol and TGFβ1 eliminated the increase in p21 expression promoted by TGFβ1 alone. Thus, three proteins involved in the transition of cells from G1 (to either S or G0) are depressed by combined exposure to ethanol and TGFβ1. It appears that ethanol interferes with TGFβ1 regulation of cell cycle activity.

In Vivo *Transforming Growth Factor Systems*

Various immunohistochemical analyses have shown that the developing nervous system contains an endogenous TGFβ system (Flanders et al., 1991; Pelton et al., 1991; Miller, 2003b). TGFβ ligands are expressed in the VZ and SZ of the cerebral vesicle *in vivo* (Fig. 11–5). TGFβ1 is expressed in the VZ pre- and postnatally and TGFβ2 is expressed during the first postnatal week. Potentially more important than ligand expression is the distribution of the two chief TGFβ receptors, TGFβIr and TGFβIIr. The TGFβIr is expressed in both neocortical proliferative zones throughout life, whereas the TGFβIIr is only expressed in the VZ. Moreover, both TGFβ2 and TGFβIr are expressed by radial glia.

Prenatal exposure to ethanol affects endogenous TGFβ system expression in vivo (Miller, 2003b). TGFβ1 expression falls in immature and mature rats, whereas TGFβ2 expression rises only in perinates. Changes in receptor expression are most evident for the TGFβIr; its expression is significantly higher in ethanol-treated rats, regardless of age. These ethanol-

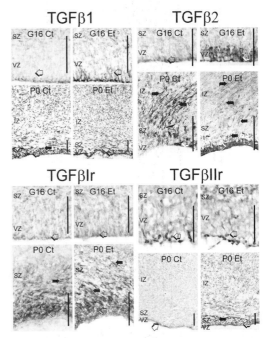

FIGURE 11–5 Transforming growth factor (TGF) β ligands and receptors in the developing ventricular and subventricular zones. Pairs of images depict the distribution of immunolabeling for TGFβ1 (top left), TGFβ2 (top right), TGFβIr (bottom left), and TGFβIIr (bottom right) in control (Ct) and ethanol-treated (Et) perinates. Ethanol markedly affects ligand and TGFβIIr expression in the subventricular zone (SZ). Open and solid arrows identify immunolabeling in the ventricular zone (VZ) and SZ, respectively. Curved arrows label radial glia in the intermediate zone (IZ). Scale bars = 100 μm. (*Source:* Images taken, with permission, from Miller (2003b), J Comp Neurol 460:410–424.)

induced changes are associated with alterations in the distribution of cells that are TGFβ1, TGFβ2, TGFβIr, and TGFβIIr immunoreactive. The most marked changes are increases in SZ expression of TGFβ ligands and especially receptors. This finding may underlie the increase in gliosis that occurs following early postnatal ethanol exposure (Fletcher and Shain, 1993; Goodlett et al., 1993).

Lineage Specificity

Studies of the effects of exogenous TGFβ1 imply that the endogenous TGFβ system in the developing and/or adult brain is affected by ethanol. In general, ethanol blocks TGFβ1 inhibition, however, this effect is lineage-dependent. For astrocytes and C6 cells, the combined effect of ethanol and TGFβ1 is competitive (Miller and Luo, 2002a), that is, in the presence of ethanol and TGFβ1, the proliferation of either of these cell types is the same as that occurring in untreated cultures. In contrast, the individual inhibitory effects of ethanol and TGFβ1 in B104 cells (Luo and Miller, 1999b) and cells determined to be neurons (Miller and Luo, 2002b) are additive. Treatment of B104 cells with an agent that blocks ERK activity largely eliminates the inhibition of [³H]thymidine incorporation. This result implies that both ethanol and TGFβ1-mediated inhibition of neuronal progenitors is transduced through ERK.

Interestingly, the T_C for *in situ* VZ cells treated with TGFβ1 and ethanol is the same as the T_C for untreated preparations. The same effect is evident for the GF: TGFβ1 and ethanol cancel the inhibitory action of the other anti-mitogen. Thus, VZ cells in organotypic cultures behave the same way as cultured cortical astrocytes. This finding is particularly interesting in light of data showing that radial glia, at least in cortex, are stem cells that can give rise to neurons or astrocytes (see Radial Glia, above). This phenomenon begs the question of how astrocytes are identified — i.e., is the commonly used marker, glial fibrillary acidic protein, astrocyte-specific (see Chapters 13 and 18)? Equally, if not more important, is the finding that after a cell is determined as becoming a neuron, even though it may retain mitotic ability (Jacobs and Miller, 2000), its reaction to its environment, such as combined TGFβ1 and ethanol, has changed. The implications of this shift in responsivity may frame our understanding of stem cells and progenitors and their future utility in transplantation.

Interactions among Growth Factors

Growth factors do not act *in vivo* in isolation. They are multiply expressed, and cells express multiple receptors. The effects of PDGF, FGF-2, IGF-1, and TGFβ1 are affected by the medium in which the cells are raised. The action of each factor is amplified, or only expressed, when the medium contains fetal serum (Luo and Miller, 1997a, 1999b; Miller and Luo, 2002a). (Serum is rich in a plethora of growth factors.) A specific example of an interaction among growth factors is that between FGF-2 and TGFβ1 (Miller and Luo, 2002a). In cultures of neocortical astrocytes and C6 cells, these two factors effectively cancel out the action of each other. Likewise, ethanol inhibits the primary action of each factor. The amount of cell growth that occurs among cells treated with FGF 2 and TGFβ1, with or without ethanol, is the same as that evident in untreated cultures.

The multiple effects of ethanol and/or growth factors on cell proliferation appear to depend on a single gatekeeper, ERK. With our current understanding, however, it is difficult to decipher the action of this transduction funnel. Ethanol can inhibit cell proliferation by altering ERK activity (Luo and Miller, 1999a, 1999b). Furthermore, both mitogenic (e.g., PDGF and IGF-1) and antimitogenic (TGFβ1) growth factors activate ERK. It seems parsimonious to conclude that ERK is not a simple switch that is either on or off; ERK is activated by a mitogen and turned off by an anti-mitogen. Instead, ERK is a complex switch that can be activated by substances with opposing effects, and the character of that activation (acute or sustained) defines the effect on subsequent transcription.

The effects of ethanol are not ubiquitous, they are quite specific. For example, ethanol affects the expression and activity of the PDGF-αr, but not the PDGF-βr. Potentially, this differential effect of ethanol depends on the distribution of the receptors. Could it be that one receptor is associated with a lipid raft, whereas another is not?

WHAT CONTROLS CELL NUMBER?

Ethanol studies suggest that, at least in some telencephalic structures, there is a dynamic interaction between the two proliferative zones. At low and moderate exposures to ethanol, cell proliferation in the VZ is reduced, but proliferation in the SZ and IHZ is increased (Miller, 1989, 1995a). Hence, the implication is that there is a set point, an implicit goal for cell number, and that the stimulated proliferation in the SZ and IHZ is compensating for the early depression of VZ proliferation.

The number of neurons in a defined cylinder of neocortex is unaffected by moderate ethanol exposure (Miller and Potempa, 1990). Nevertheless, cortex is smaller (Miller, 1987, 1996b). This decrease in size likely results from the ethanol-induced elimination of ontogenetic columns. Presumably, this alteration is a result of the goal of the developing nervous system to maintain the integrity of ontogenetic columns, even if the number of columns is reduced. Exposures to high concentrations of ethanol overwhelm the compensatory response.

The changes in the telencephalon contrast with those in regions of the brain derived from only the VZ. In the absence of a derived proliferative zone, no compensatory response is possible and reduction in cell number occurs regardless of ethanol concentration. The depression of proliferative activity in the VZ can occur through two nonmutually exclusive mechanisms. Ethanol can inhibit the action of mitogenic growth factors and/or ethanol potentiates the action of anti-mitogenic factors. Empirical evidence from cell culture studies supports both of these theses.

Derived proliferating populations, for example, the SZ, are affected by ethanol in a complex, bimodal fashion. This provides a mechanism for the SZ to offset primary damage to the VZ in an attempt to generate a structure with "proper" cell density. The ability of the SZ to compensate for reductions in VZ proliferation may result from the differential sensitivity of the two cell populations to ethanol. As such, it would reflect differential responsivity to particular growth factors. Key support for this conclusion is that the two zones respond to different combinations of growth factors and they express different receptors. By pulling together all of the data on the effects of ethanol on growth factor activity, we postulate that ethanol affects SZ cells in defined ways.

Take the example of cell proliferation in the SZ. The SZ contains receptors for PDGF and TGFβ. Ethanol blocks PDGF binding with an ED_{50} of 100–200 mg/dl, depending on the receptor isoform (Luo and Miller, 1999a). This results in a reduced mitogenic effect of PDGF. Ethanol interferes with TGFβ-induced inhibition with an ED_{50} of <50 mg/dl (Luo and Miller, 1999b). The interaction of ethanol and TGFβ results in a loss of the inhibition. Thus, the combined effects of ethanol, PDGF, and TGFβ are as follows. First, at relatively low concentrations, ethanol inhibits TGFβ-mediated inhibition in the relative absence of ethanol-induced interference with PDGF-promoted cell proliferation. Second, at high concentrations, ethanol eliminates the mitogenic effects of PDGF that supersede the loss of TGFβ-mediated inhibition. Finally, at intermediate concentrations, ethanol produces a mixed response.

Thus, the concentration-dependent effects of ethanol on two growth factor systems can explain the bimodal response of ethanol on SZ cells *in vivo*.

Abbreviations

bFGF (FGF-2)   basic fibroblast growth factor

EGL   external granular layer of the cerebellum

ERK   extracellular signal regulated kinase

G   gestational day

GE   ganglionic eminence

GF   growth fraction

IGF   insulin-like growth factor

IGF-BP   insulin-like growth factor binding protein

IGF-1r   insulin-like growth factor-1 receptor

IHZ   intrahilar zone, or hippocampal field CA4

LF   leaving fraction

PDGF   platelet-derived growth factor

PKC   protein kinase C

PSN   principal sensory nucleus of the trigeminal nerve

SZ   subventricular zone

T_C total length of the cell cycle

TGF   transforming growth factor

TGFβIr   transforming growth factor βI receptor

TGFβIIr   transforming growth factor βII receptor

VZ   ventricular zone

ACKNOWLEDGMENTS This work was supported by the National Institute on Alcohol Abuse and Alcoholism and the Department of Veterans Affairs.

References

Al-Ghoul WM, Miller MW (1989) Transient expression of Alz-50 immunoreactivity in developing rat neocortex: a marker for naturally occurring neuronal death? Brain Res 481:361–367.

Altman J (1962) Are new neurons formed in the brains of adult mammals? Science 135:1127–1128.

Alvarez-Buylla A, Garcia-Verdugo JM (2002) Neurogenesis in adult subventricular zone. J Neurosci 22: 629–634.

Anderson SA, Marin O, Horn C, Jennings K, Rubenstein JL (2001) Distinct cortical migrations from the medial and lateral ganglionic eminences. Development 128:353–363.

Angevine JB Jr (1965) Time of origin in the hippocampal region: an autoradiographic study in the mouse. Exp Neurol Suppl 2:1–70.

Atlas M, Bond VP (1965) The cell generation cycle of the eleven-day mouse embryo. J Cell Biol 26:19–24.

Bartlett PF, Dutton R, Likiardopoulos V, Brooker G (1994) Regulation of neurogenesis in the embryonic and adult brain by fibroblast growth factors. Alcohol Alcohol 2(Suppl):387–394.

Bauer-Moffett C, Altman J (1975) Ethanol-induced reductions in cerebellar growth of infant rats. Exp Neurol 48:378–382.

—— (1977) The effect of ethanol chronically administered to preweanling rats on cerebellar development: a morphological study. Brain Res 119:249–268.

Bayer SA (1980) Development of the hippocampal region of the rat. I. Neurogenesis examined with ^{3}H-thymidine autoradiography. J Comp Neurol 190: 87–114.

Blaschke AJ, Staley K, Chun J (1996) Widespread programmed cell death in proliferative and postmitotic regions of the fetal cerebral cortex. Development 122:1165–1174.

Bonthius DJ, West JR (1988) Blood alcohol concentration and microencephaly: a dose–response study in the neonatal rat. Teratology 37:223–231.

Borges S, Lewis PD (1983) The effect of ethanol on the cellular composition of the cerebellum. Neuropathol Appl Neurobiol 9:53–60.

Böttner M, Krieglstein K, Unsicker K (2000) The transforming growth factor-betas: structure, signaling, and roles in nervous system development and functions. J Neurochem 75:2227–2240.

Breese CR, D'Costa A, Ingram RL, Lenham J, Sonntag WE (1993) Long-term suppression of insulin-like growth factor-1 in rats after in utero ethanol exposure: relationship to somatic growth. J Pharmacol Exp Ther 264:448–456.

Breese CR, Sonntag WE (1995) Effect of ethanol on plasma and hepatic insulin-like growth factor regulation in pregnant rats. Alcohol Clin Exp Res 19: 867–873.

Brückner G, Mareš V, Biesold D (1976) Neurogenesis in the visual system of the rat. An autoradiographic investigation. J Comp Neurol 166:245–255.

Cameron HA, Hazel TG, McKay RD (1998) Regulation of neurogenesis by growth factors and neurotransmitters. J Neurobiol 36:287–306.

Chenn A, Walsh CA (2002) Regulation of cerebral cortical size by control of cell cycle exit in neural precursors. Science 297:365–369.

—— (2003) Increased neuronal production, enlarged forebrains and cytoarchitectural distortions in β-

catenin overexpressing transgenic mice. Cereb Cortex 13:599–606.

Costa LG, Guizzetti M (2002) Inhibition of muscarinic receptor-induced proliferation of astroglial cells by ethanol: mechanisms and implications for the fetal alcohol syndrome. Neurotoxicology 23:685–691.

Cui SJ, Tewari M, Schneider T, Rubin R (1997) Ethanol promotes cell death by inhibition of the insulin-like growth factor I receptor. Alcohol Clin Exp Res 21: 1121–1127.

Decker L, Picard-Riera N, Lachapelle F, Baron-Van Evercooren A (2002) Growth factor treatment promotes mobilization of young but not aged adult subventricular zone precursors in response to demyelination. J Neurosci Res 69:763–771.

de Lima AD, Merten MD, Voigt T (1997) Neuritic differentiation and synaptogenesis in serum-free neuronal cultures of the rat cerebral cortex. J Comp Neurol 382:230–246.

Diaz J, Samson HH (1980) Impaired brain growth in neonatal rats exposed to ethanol. Science 208: 751–753.

Doetsch F, Garcia-Verdugo JM, Alvarez-Buylla A (1997) Cellular composition and three-dimensional organization of the subventricular germinal zone in the adult mammalian brain. J Neurosci 17:5046–5061.

—— (1999) Regeneration of a germinal layer in the adult mammalian brain. Proc Natl Acad Sci USA 96:11619–11624.

Flanders KC, Ludecke G, Engels S, Cissel DS, Roberts AB, Kondaiah P, Lafyatis R, Sporn MB, Unsicker K (1991) Localization and actions of transforming growth factor–βs in the embryonic nervous system. Development 113:183–191.

Fletcher TL, Shain W (1993) Ethanol-induced changes in astrocyte gene expression during rat central nervous system development. Alcohol Clin Exp Res 17:993–1001.

Gomes WA, Mehler MF, Kessler JA (2003) Transgenic overexpression of BMP4 increases astroglial and decreases oligodendroglial lineage commitment. Dev Biol 255:164–177.

Goodlett CR, Leo JT, O'Callaghan JP, Mahoney JC, West JR (1993) Transient cortical astrogliosis induced by alcohol exposure during the neonatal brain growth spurt in rats. Dev Brain Res 72: 85–97.

Götz M, Hartfuss E, Malatesta P (2002) Radial glial cells as neuronal precursors: a new perspectives on the correlation of morphology and linage restriction in the developing cerebral cortex of mice. Brain Res Bull 57:777–788.

Gould E, Gross CG (2002) Neurogenesis in adult mammals: some progress and problems. J Neurosci 22:619–623.

Gritti A, Frolichsthal-Schoeller P, Galli R, Parati EA, Cova L, Pagano SF, Bjornson CR, Vescovi AL (1999) Epidermal and fibroblast growth factors behave as mitogenic regulators for a single multipotent stem cell–like population from the subventricular region of the adult mouse forebrain. J Neurosci 19:3287–3297.

Guerri C, Sáez R, Sancho-Tello M, Martin de Aquilera E, Renau-Piqueras J (1990) Ethanol alters astrocyte development: a study of critical periods using primary cultures. Neurochem Res 15:559–565.

Hartfuss E, Galli R, Heins N, Gotz M (2001) Characterization of CNS precursor subtypes and radial glia. Dev Biol 229:15–30.

Hockfield S, McKay RD (1985) Identification of major cell classes in the developing mammalian nervous system. J Neurosci 5:3310–3328.

Isenberg K, Zhou X, Moore BW (1992) Ethanol inhibits C6 cell growth: fetal alcohol syndrome model. Alcohol Clin Exp Res 16:695–699.

Jacobs JS, Miller MW (2000) Cell cycle kinetics and immunohistochemical characterization of dissociated fetal cortical cultures: evidence that differentiated neurons have mitotic capacity. Dev Brain Res 122:67–80.

—— (2001) Proliferation and death of cultured fetal neocortical neurons: effects of ethanol on the dynamics of cell growth. J Neurocytol 30:391–401.

Jacobson M (1991) Developmental Neurobiology, 3rd edition. Plenum Press, New York.

Kennedy LA, Elliot MJ (1985) Cell proliferation in the embryonic mouse neocortex following acute maternal alcohol intoxication. Int J Dev Neurosci 3:311–315.

Kennedy LA, Mukerji S (1986) Ethanol neurotoxicity. 1. Direct effects on replicating astrocytes. Neurobehav Toxicol Teratol 8:11–15.

Kornguth SE, Rutledge JJ, Sunderland E, Siegel F, Carlson I, Smollens J, Juhl U, Young B (1979) Impeded cerebellar development and reduced serum thyroxine levels associated with fetal alcohol intoxication. Brain Res 177:347–360.

Kötter K, Klein J (1999) Ethanol inhibits astroglial cell proliferation by disruption of phospholipase D-mediated signaling. J Neurochem 73:2517–2523.

Kuhn HG, Dickinson-Anson H, Gage FH (1996) Neurogenesis in the dentate gyrus of the adult rat: age-related decrease of neuronal progenitor proliferation. J Neurosci 16:2027–2033.

Kuhn HG, Winkler J, Kempermann G, Thal LJ, Gage FH (1997) Epidermal growth factor and fibroblast growth factor-2 have different effects on neural progenitors in the adult rat brain. J Neurosci 17:5820–5829.

Lachapelle F, Avellana-Adalid V, Nait-Oumesmar B, Baron-Van Evercooren A (2002) Fibroblast growth factor-2 (FGF-2) and platelet-derived growth factor AB (PDGF AB) promote adult SVZ-derived oligodendrogenesis in vivo. Mol Cell Neurosci 20:390–403.

Levers TE, Edgar JM, Price DJ (2001) The fates of cells generated at the end of neurogenesis in developing mouse cortex. J Neurobiol 48:265–277.

Li Z, Lin H, Zhu Y, Wang M, Luo J (2001) Disruption of cell cycle kinetics and cyclin-dependent kinase system by ethanol in cultured cerebellar granule progenitors. Dev Brain Res 132:47–58.

Li Z, Miller MW, Luo J (2002) Effects of prenatal exposure to ethanol on the cyclin-dependent kinase system in the developing rat cerebellum. Dev Brain Res 139:237–245.

Lu EJ, Brown WJ, Cole R, deVellis J (1980) Ultrastructural differentiation and synaptogenesis in aggregating rotation cultures of rat cerebral cells. J Neurosci Res 5:447–463.

Lund RD, Mustari MJ (1977) Development of the geniculocortical pathway in rats. J Comp Neurol 173:289–306.

Luo J, Miller MW (1996) Ethanol inhibits basic fibroblast growth factor–mediated proliferation of C6 astrocytoma cells. J Neurochem 67:1448–1456.

—— (1997a) Basic fibroblast growth factor– and platelet-derived growth factor–mediated cell proliferation in B104 neuroblastoma cells: effect of ethanol on cell cycle kinetics. Brain Res 770:139–150.

—— (1997b) Differential sensitivity of human neuroblastoma cell lines to ethanol: correlations with their proliferative responses to mitogenic growth factors and expression of growth factor receptors. Alcohol Clin Exp Res 21:1186–1194.

—— (1998) Growth factor-mediated neural proliferation: target of ethanol toxicity. Brain Res Rev 27:157–167.

—— (1999a) Platelet-derived growth factor–mediated signal transduction underlying astrocyte proliferation: site of ethanol action. J Neurosci 19:10014–10025.

—— (1999b) Transforming growth factor β1–regulated cell proliferation and expression of neural cell adhesion molecule in B104 neuroblastoma cells: differential effects of ethanol. J Neurochem 72:2286–2293.

Ma W, Li BS, Maric D, Zhao WQ, Lin HJ, Zhang L, Pant HC, Barker JL (2003) Ethanol blocks both basic fibroblast growth factor–and carbachol-mediated neuroepithelial cell expansion with differential effects on carbachol-activated signaling pathways. Neuroscience 118:37–47.

Malatesta P, Hartfuss E, Gotz M (2000) Isolation of radial glial cells by fluorescent-activated cell sorting reveals a neuronal lineage. Development 127:5253–5263.

Martens DJ, Seaberg RM, van der Kooy D (2002) In vivo infusions of exogenous growth factors into the fourth ventricle of the adult mouse brain increase the proliferation of neural progenitors around the fourth ventricle and the central canal of the spinal cord. Eur J Neurosci 16:1045–1057.

Martens DJ, Tropepe V, van der Kooy D (2000) Separate proliferation kinetics of fibroblast growth factor–responsive and epidermal growth factor–responsive neural stem cells within the embryonic forebrain germinal zone. J Neurosci 20:1085–1095.

McConnell SK (1988) Fates of visual cortical neurons in the ferret after isochronic and heterochronic transplantation. J Neurosci 8:945–974.

Miller MW (1985) Co-generation of projection and local circuit neurons in neocortex. Dev Brain Res 23:187–192.

—— (1986) Effects of alcohol on the generation and migration of cerebral cortical neurons. Science 233:1308–1311.

—— (1987) Effect of prenatal exposure to alcohol on the distribution and time of origin of corticospinal neurons in the rat. J Comp Neurol 257:372–382.

—— (1988) Effect of prenatal exposure to ethanol on the development of cerebral cortex: I. Neuronal generation. Alcohol Clin Exp Res 12:440–449.

—— (1989) Effects of prenatal exposure to ethanol on neocortical development: II. Cell proliferation in the ventricular and subventricular zones of the rat. J Comp Neurol 287:326–338.

—— (1992) Effects of prenatal exposure to ethanol on cell proliferation and neuronal migration. In: Miller MW (ed). *Development of the Central Nervous System: Effects of Alcohol and Opiates.* Wiley-Liss, New York, pp 47–69.

—— (1993) Migration of cortical neurons is altered by gestational exposure to ethanol. Alcohol Clin Exp Res 17:304–314.

—— (1995a) Generation of neurons in the rat dentate gyrus and hippocampus: effects of prenatal and postnatal treatment with ethanol. Alcohol Clin Exp Res 19:1500–1509.

—— (1995b) Effect of pre- or postnatal exposure to ethanol on the total number of neurons in the principal sensory nucleus of the trigeminal nerve: cell proliferation and neuronal death. Alcohol Clin Exp Res 19:1359–1363.

—— (1996a) Limited ethanol exposure selectively alters the proliferation of precursor cells in the cerebral cortex. Alcohol Clin Exp Res 20:139–143.

—— (1996b) Effects of early exposure to ethanol on the protein and DNA contents of specific brain regions. Brain Res 734:286–294.

—— (1997) Effects of prenatal exposure to ethanol on callosal projection neurons in rat somatosensory cortex. Brain Res 766:121–128.

—— (1999a) A longitudinal study of the effects of prenatal ethanol exposure on neuronal acquisition and death in the principal sensory nucleus of the trigeminal nerve: interaction with changes induced by transection of the infraorbital nerve. J Neurocytol 28:999–1015.

—— (1999b) Kinetics of the migration of neurons to rat somatosensory cortex. Dev Brain Res 115:111–122.

—— (2003a) Balance of cell proliferation and death among dynamic populations: a mathematical model. J Neurobiol 57:172–182.

—— (2003b) Expression of transforming growth factor β in developing rat cerebral cortex: effects of prenatal exposure to ethanol. J Comp Neurol 460:410–424.

Miller MW, Kuhn PE (1995) Cell cycle kinetics in fetal rat cerebral cortex: effects of prenatal exposure to ethanol assessed by a cumulative labeling technique with flow cytometry. Alcohol Clin Exp Res 19:233–237.

Miller MW, Luo J (2002a) Effects of ethanol and basic fibroblast growth factor on the transforming growth factor β1 regulated proliferation of cortical astrocytes and C6 astrocytoma cells. Alcohol Clin Exp Res 26:671–676.

—— (2002b) Effects of ethanol and transforming growth factor β (TGFβ) on neuronal proliferation and nCAM expression. Alcohol Clin Exp Res 26:1281–1285.

Miller MW, Muller SJ (1989) Structure and histogenesis of the principal sensory nucleus of the trigeminal nerve: effects of prenatal exposure to ethanol. J Comp Neurol 282:570–580.

Miller MW, Nowakowski RS (1991) Effect of prenatal exposure to ethanol on the cell cycle kinetics and growth fraction in the proliferative zones of fetal rat cerebral cortex. Alcohol Clin Exp Res 15:229–232.

Miller MW, Potempa G (1990) Numbers of neurons and glia in mature rat somatosensory cortex: effects of prenatal exposure to ethanol. J Comp Neurol 293:92–102.

Miller MW, Robertson S (1993) Prenatal exposure to ethanol alters the postnatal development and transformation of radial glia to astrocytes in the cortex. J Comp Neurol 337:253–266.

Miñana R, Climent E, Barettino D, Segui JM, Renau-Piqueras J, Guerri C (2000) Alcohol exposure alters the expression pattern of neural cell adhesion molecules during brain development. J Neurochem 75:954–964.

Nieto M, Monuki ES, Tang H, Imitola J, Haubst N, Khoury SJ, Cunningham J, Gotz M, Walsh CA

(2004) Expression of Cux-1 and Cux-2 in the subventricular zone and upper layers II–IV of the cerebral cortex. J Comp Neurol 479:168–180.

Noctor SC, Flint AC, Weissman TA, Dammerman RS, Kriegstein AR (2001) Neurons derived from radial glial cells establish radial units in neocortex. Nature 409:714–720.

Noctor SC, Flint AC, Weissman TA, Wong WS, Clinton BK, Kriegstein AR (2002) Dividing precursor cells of the embryonic cortical ventricular zone have morphological and molecular characteristics of radial glia. J Neurosci 22:3161–3173.

Pawlak R, Skrzypiec A, Sulkowski S, Buczko W (2002) Ethanol-induced neurotoxicity is counterbalanced by increased cell proliferation in mouse dentate gyrus. Neurosci Lett 327:83–86.

Pelton RW, Saxena B, Jones M, Moses HL, Gold LI (1991) Immunohistochemical localization of TGFβ1, TGFβ2, and TGFβ3 in the mouse embryo: expression patterns suggest multiple roles during embryonic development. J Cell Biol 115:1091–1105.

Pierce DR, West JR (1986) Alcohol-induced microencephaly during the third trimester equivalent: relationship to dose and blood alcohol concentration. Alcohol 3:185–191.

Rakic P (1971) Neuron-glia relationship during granule cell migration in developing cerebellar cortex. A Golgi and electronmicroscopic study in *Macacus rhesus*. J Comp Neurol 141:283–312.

—— (1978) Neuronal migration and contact guidance in the primate telencephalon. Postgrad Med J 54 (Suppl 1):25–40.

—— (2000) Radial unit hypothesis of neocortical expansion. Novartis Found Symp 228:30–42.

—— (2002) Neurogenesis in adult primates. Prog Brain Res 138:3–14.

Rakic P, Stensaas LJ, Sayre E, Sidman RL (1974) Computer-aided three-dimensional reconstruction and quantitative analysis of cells from serial electron microscopic montages of foetal monkey brain. Nature 250:31–34.

Ramon y Cajal S (1909–1911) *Histology of the Nervous System*. (Trans. by Swanson N, Swanson LW) Oxford University Press, New York.

Resnicoff M, Cui S, Coppola D, Hoek JB, Rubin R (1996a) Ethanol-induced inhibition of cell proliferation is modulated by insulin-like growth factor-I receptor levels. Alcohol Clin Exp Res 20:961–966.

Resnicoff M, Li W, Basak S, Herlyn D, Baserga R, Rubin R (1996b) Inhibition of rat C6 glioblastoma tumor growth by expression of insulin-like growth factor I receptor antisense mRNA. Cancer Immunol Immunother 42:64–68.

Resnicoff M, Rubini M, Baserga R, Rubin R (1994) Ethanol inhibits insulin-like growth factor-1-mediated signalling and proliferation of C6 rat glioblastoma cells. Lab Invest 71:657–662.

Rich JN, Zhang M, Datto MB, Bigner DD, Wang XF (1999) Transforming growth factor-beta–mediated p15 (INK4B) induction and growth inhibition in astrocytes is SMAD3-dependent and a pathway prominently altered in human glioma cell lines. J Biol Chem 274:35053–35058.

Robe PA, Rogister B, Merville MP, Bours V (2000) Growth regulation of astrocytes and C6 cells by TGFβ1: correlation with gap junctions. Neuroreport 11:2837–2841.

Rozovsky I, Finch CE, Morgan TE (1998) Age-related activation of microglia and astrocytes: in vitro studies show persistent phenotypes of aging, increased proliferation, and resistance to down-regulation. Neurobiol Aging 19:97–103.

Samuelsen GB, Larsen KB, Bogdanovic N, Laursen H, Graem N, Larsen JF, Pakkenberg B (2003) The changing number of cells in the human fetal forebrain and its subdivisions: a stereologic analysis. Cereb Cortex 13:115–122.

Sanai N, Tramontin AD, Quiñones-Hinojosa A, Barbaro NM, Gupta N, Kunwar S, Lawton MT, McDermott MW, Parsa AT, Garcia-Verdugo JM, Berger MS, Alvarez-Buylla A (2004) Unique astrocyte ribbon in adult human brain contains neural stem cells but lacks chain migration. Nature 427: 740–744.

Sasahara M, Fries JW, Raines EW, Gown AM, Westrum LE, Frosch MP, Bonthron DT, Ross R, Collins T (1991) PDGF B-chain in neurons of the central nervous system, posterior pituitary, and in a transgenic model. Cell 64:217–227.

Sauer FC (1936) The interkinetic migration of embryonic epithelial nuclei. J Morphol 60:1–11.

Sauer ME, Chittenden AC (1959) Deoxyribonucleic acid content of cell nuclei in the neural tube of the chick embryo: evidence for intermitotic migration of nuclei. Exp Cell Res 16:1–6.

Sauer ME, Walker BE (1959) Radiographic study of interkinetic nuclear migration in the neural tube. Proc Soc Exp Biol 101:557–560.

Schlessinger AR, Cowan WM, Swanson LW (1978) The time of origin of neurons in Ammon's horn and the associated retrohippocampal fields. Anat Embryol 154:153–173.

Schmechel DE, Rakic P (1979) A Golgi study of radial glial cells in developing monkey telencephalon: morphogenesis and transformation into astrocytes. Anat Embryol 156:115–152.

Shoukimas GM, Hinds JW (1978) The development of the cerebral cortex in the embryonic mouse: an electron microscopic serial section analysis. J Comp Neurol 179:795–830.

Siegenthaler JA, Miller MW (2005a) Ethanol disrupts cell cycle regulation in developing rat cortex: interaction with transforming growth factor β1. J Neurochem 95:902–912.

—— (2005b) TGFβ1 promotes cell cycle exit through the CKI p21in the developing cerebral cortex. J Neursci 25:8627–8636.

Singh SP, Ehmann S, Snyder AK (1996) Ethanol-induced changes in insulin-like growth factors and IGF gene expression in the fetal brain. Proc Soc Exp Biol Med 212:349–354.

Singh SP, Srivenugopal KS, Ehmann S, Yuan XH, Snyder AK (1994) Insulin-like growth factors (IGF-I and IGF-II), IGF-binding proteins, and IGF gene expression in the offspring of ethanol-fed rats. J Lab Clin Med 124:183–192.

Smith TL, Navratilova E (2003) The effect of ethanol exposure on mitogen-activated protein kinase activity and expression in cultured rat astrocytes. Neurosci Lett 341:91–94.

Snyder AK, Singh SP, Ehmann S (1992) Effects of ethanol on DNA, RNA, and protein synthesis in rat astrocyte cultures. Alcohol Clin Exp Res 16:295–300.

Takahashi T, Nowakowski RS, Caviness VS Jr (1995) The cell cycle of the pseudostratified ventricular epithelium of the embryonic murine cerebral wall. J Neurosci 15:6046–6057.

—— (1996) The leaving or Q fraction of the murine cerebral proliferative epithelium: a general model of neocortical neuronogenesis. J Neurosci 16:6183–6196.

Tamamaki N, Fujimori KE, Takauji R (1997) Origin and route of tangentially migrating neurons in the developing neocortical intermediate zone. J Neurosci 17:8313–8323.

Tarabykin V, Stoykova A, Usman N, Gruss P (2001) Cortical upper layer neurons derive from the subventricular zone as indicated by Svet1 gene expression. Development 128:1983–1993.

Thomaidou D, Mione MC, Cavanagh JF, Parnavelas JG (1997) Apoptosis and its relation to the cell cycle in the developing cerebral cortex. J Neurosci 17:1075–1085.

Valles S, Sancho-Tello M, Miñana R, Climent E, Renau-Piqueras J, Guerri C (1996) Glial fibrillary acidic protein expression in rat brain and in radial glia culture is delayed by prenatal ethanol exposure. J Neurochem 67:2425–2433.

Voigt T (1989) Development of glial cells in the cerebral wall of ferrets: direct tracing of their transformation from radial glia into astrocytes. J Comp Neurol 289:74–88.

Waechter R, Jaensch B (1972) Generation times of the matrix cells during embryonic brain development: an autoradiographic study in rats. Brain Res 46:235–250.

Wagner JP, Black IB, DiCicco-Bloom E (1999) Stimulation of neonatal and adult brain neurogenesis by subcutaneous injection of basic fibroblast growth factor. J Neurosci 19:6006–6016.

Watterson RL, Veneziano P, Bartha A (1956) Absence of a true germinal zone in neural tubes of young chick embryos as demonstrated by the colchicine technique. Anat Rec 124:379.

Waziri R, Kamath SH, Sahu S (1981) Alcohol inhibits morphological and biochemical differentiation of C6 glial cells in culture. Differentiation 18:55–59.

Weise B, Janet T, Grothe C (1993) Localization of bFGF and FGF-receptor in the developing nervous system of the embryonic and newborn rat. J Neurosci Res 34:442–453.

Wichterle H, Turnbull DH, Nery S, Fishell G, Alvarez-Buylla A (2001) In utero fate mapping reveals distinct migratory pathways and fates of neurons born in the mammalian basal forebrain. Development 128:3759–3771.

Yeh HJ, Ruit KG, Wang YX, Parks WC, Snider WD, Deuel TF (1991) PDGF A-chain gene is expressed by mammalian neurons during development and in maturity. Cell 64:209–216.

Zhu Y, Li H, Zhou L, Wu JY, Rao Y (1999) Cellular and molecular guidance of GABAergic neuronal migration from an extracortical origin to the neocortex. Neuron 23:473–485.

12

Effects of Ethanol on the Regulation of Cell Cycle in Neural Stem Cells

W. Michael Zawada
Mita Das

The effects of early exposure to ethanol on the proliferation of neuronal precursors are described in Chapter 11. The present chapter discusses the effects of ethanol on the cell cycle with the particular reference to neural stem cells (NSCs) in the developing brain. Relatively little is known about the mechanism by which ethanol affects the cell cycle machinery in NSCs because most studies focus on the effects of ethanol on other cell types. Understanding how ethanol affects the cell cycle of NSCs might be valuable in the context of treatment of ethanol-induced developmental defects, such as those observed in fetal alcohol spectrum disorders (FASD). Before delving into the effects of ethanol on the progression of the cell cycle, NSCs and the major molecular components of cell cycle are defined.

DEFINITION OF NEURAL STEM CELLS

Origin of Neural Stem Cells

Stem cells make the development and maintenance of mammalian tissues and hence organs possible. Embryonic stem (ES) cells reside in the inner mass of a blastocyst, are pluripotent, and are capable of generating cells of all three primary germ lineages (endoderm, mesoderm, and ectoderm.) A subdivision of the ectoderm, neuroectoderm, gives rise to the central nervous system (CNS). In the developing CNS, a subset of stem cells known as NSCs shapes the structural and functional layout of the brain.

Neural stem cells are defined as cells with a high proliferative capacity that allows for self-renewal, retention of multilineage potential (multipotency), and clonality, which permits a single NSC to generate progeny with the same multi-lineage potential as its own. In contrast, neuronal precursors are probably best defined as a type of stem cell that is oligopotent, that is, capable of generating only a few selected types of cells, in this case neurons. Although adult brain NSCs are less abundant and generally characterized by a reduced proliferative potential (see Cell Cycle of Stem Cells), they maintain the homeostasis of cell pools with high turnover rates, such as granule cell neurons of the hippocampus and granule and periglomerular interneurons of the olfactory bulb.

Characteristics of Neural Stem Cells

During development of the CNS, two distinct populations of NSCs exist. The first population consists of relatively homogenous population that participates in neural tube formation. These cells are primarily located in the ventricular zone (VZ) and lack expression of markers typical of differentiated neural cells. Their proliferation and survival are controlled by transmissible proteins such as basic fibroblast growth factor (bFGF or FGF-2) (Kilpatrick and Bartlett, 1995).

Mitotically active cells derived from the VZ contribute to derived proliferative zones such as the subventricular zone (SZ; also known as the subependymal zone) in the case of the telencephalon. This zone grows as the VZ diminishes in thickness (Miller, 1989). With the rise of the SZ, a second identifiable population of NSCs appears (Reynolds and Weiss, 1992, 1996). These stem cells proliferate in response to both bFGF and epidermal growth factor (Vescovi et al., 1993). Thus, during the second half of telencephalic generation, two populations of NSCs exist, a principal population in the VZ and a growing population in the SZ.

Despite differences in the VZ and SZ, both populations share similarities in protein expression. Cells in these zones express nestin, ATP-binding cassette protein (ABCG2), telomerase reverse transcriptase (TERT), telomerase-repeat-binding factor (TRF) 1, and TRF2 (Klapper et al., 2001). Moreover, telomerase activity is detectable in both the VZ and SZ. A fuller description of telomerase is provided in the sections Stem Cells, and Telomerase.

In addition to the VZ and SZ, NSCs, some radial glia, and cells expressing glial fibrillary acidic protein (GFAP) have been postulated to be stem cells (Doetsch et al., 1997; Garcia-Verdugo et al., 1998;

Hartfuss et al., 2001; Alvarez-Buylla and Garcia-Verdugo, 2002). It should be noted that expressing GFAP does not necessarily mean that a cell is an astrocyte. Rather, it means that a cell expresses an intermediate filament also expressed by astrocytes. For example, radial glia can express GFAP, but they do not appear to be astrocytes. Instead, they have traits associated with NSCs, such as the ability to generate neurons and glia. Consequently, the effects of ethanol exposure on GFAP-positive cells and radial glia during development also have wide-ranging consequences for NSCs (see Chapters 13 and 18).

In adult rodents, four distinct cell types have been identified in the SZ (Doetsch et al., 1997). They can be discriminated on the basis of the length of their cell cycle and ultrastructural characteristics. These are (1) proliferating migratory neuroblasts (type A cells), (2) slowly dividing astrocytes (type B cells), (3) rapidly dividing progenitors (type C cells), and (4) ependyma (type D cells) that line the ventricular wall. Whether ependymal cells themselves are stem cells is contested (Chiasson et al., 1999; Johansson et al., 1999; Spassky et al., 2005). Furthermore, parenchymal cells positive for neural cell adhesion molecule and transdifferentiated cells are candidates for NSCs (Pevny and Rao, 2003).

Symmetric and Asymmetric Cell Division among Neural Stem Cells

Like other types of stem cells, NSCs undergo either symmetric or asymmetric cell divisions (Zhong, 2003). During a symmetric cell division both daughter cells share the same fate. Accordingly, both cells remain in the proliferative population or both exit the cell cycle. In contrast, an asymmetric division produces two cells with different fates. For example, one remains a stem cell and the other assumes a defined phenotype such as that of a neuronal progenitor. How is this fate determination possible?

Although mitotic cell division produces two daughter cells containing identical genetic material, the epigenetic molecules within the cytoplasm can be distributed unequally between the two daughter cells. Such differential distribution of cytoplasmic determinants is postulated to affect cell fate decisions (Zhong, 2003). Asymmetric cell division is indeed a fundamental attribute of stem cells, because for a stem cell both to self-renew and to produce differentiated progeny, the cell must have an ability to divide asymmetrically. A specific example of asymmetric cell division comes from the *Drosophila* CNS in which a neuroblast gives rise to a smaller daughter cell known as the ganglion mother cell (GMC). A GMC in turn produces two neurons or glial/neuronal siblings (Doe et al., 1998).

Among several component proteins that participate in asymmetric divisions in *Drosophila*, prospero and Numb are retained in the basal region of a dividing neuroblast at metaphase and preferentially segregate into the ganglion mother cell (Knoblich et al., 1995). Although tracing cell lineage trees is currently impossible in vertebrates in vivo, it is feasible to trace the progeny of single cells labeled retrovirally. Other methodologies for tracing stem cells in vivo, such as transplantation of labeled cells, are discussed below in the section Use of Neural Stem Cell Transplantation to Examine the Effects of Ethanol on Cell Regulation In Vivo. A discussion on the asymmetric cell division is particularly relevant here, because asymmetric distribution of cytoplasmic determinants is cell-cycle dependent. Although it is not known whether ethanol can disrupt this distribution, the possibility exists because the asymmetric cell division occurs early in the process of fate determination. Thus, even small changes during this period might result in substantial abnormalities later in development.

Markers of NSC Populations

No discussion of NSCs is complete without an attempt to define them by means of unique stem cell markers. Although no absolute marker for NSCs exists, the presence of a hematopoietic stem cell marker, CD (cell determinant) 133 (known as prominin in rodents), is required for the clonogenic NSCs that self-renew and retain multilineage differentiation properties (Uchida et al., 2000). Such clonogenic NSCs can be derived from human fetal brain tissues by fluorescence-activated cell sorting for cells that are CD133+, CD34-, CD45-, and CD23-/lo. These cells appear to be the only human fetal brain cells that display clonogenic characteristics, retain the ability to differentiate into both neurons and glia, and participate in a neurogenetic program following transplantation into the rodent CNS (Uchida et al., 2000; Tamaki et al., 2002).

Evidence of the importance of CD133 as an indicator of "stemness" (i.e., their proliferative and differentiative potential) was discovered when testing the cancer stem cell hypothesis. As few as 100 CD133+ cells isolated from human brain tumors give rise to phenotypically identical tumors when transplanted into brains of immunodeficient mice (Singh et al., 2004). By contrast, the CD133- cells fail to produce tumors in these transplants, even when engrafted as a bolus of 10^5 cells. These findings do not imply that all NSCs are tumorigenic, but that stem cells introduced into the brain ectopically and/or at an inappropriate time have a capacity for tumor generation. Although CD133 labeling has been used mostly for detection of human NSCs, expression of other potentially useful markers for NSCs such as Sox-1, Sox-2, nestin, musashi, Hu, neuralstemnin, LeX (trisaccharide 3-frucosyl-N-acetyllactosamine)/stage-specific embryonic antigen 1, and ABCG2 has been used to identify NSCs in a variety of species (Capela and Temple, 2002; Pevny and Rao, 2003).

CELL CYCLE

The most fundamental property of living organisms is their ability to reproduce themselves. This property is based upon the feature that cells are able to duplicate by a process known as the cell or mitotic cycle. Mammalian brain development depends on a precise sequence of cell divisions controlled by the cell cycle. Sculpting of the CNS and other organs in the embryo is greatly affected by the kinetics of the cell cycle and the quality of chromosomal replication that occurs during this process. Alterations in the amounts of necessary trophic factors (e.g., glucose and growth factors), mutations in the genes that control the cell cycle (e.g., cyclins and cyclin-dependent kinases [Cdks]), and various biophysical stresses (e.g., excessive hypoxia and acidemia) occur naturally. These alterations can affect the cell cycle and result in stunted or abnormal development, and they cannot be easily controlled. Cell cycle regulation, and hence, development can be also affected by unnatural causes such as excessive ethanol consumption. Before discussing the specific effects of ethanol on the cell cycle, it is important to review the components of cell cycle machinery and the differences between the cell cycles of somatic and ES cells.

Cell Cycle of Somatic Cells

As mentioned above, the cell cycle is the means by which organisms reproduce themselves. In virtually all cells, the cell cycle is composed of four discrete phases:

(1) the DNA synthesis phase (the S phase), (2) the cell division phase (the M phase), and two gap phases, (3) the G1 phase between M and S and (4) the G2 phase between S and M (Fig. 12–1). During G1, the cell prepares for DNA replication that results in duplication of the chromosomes during S. The second gap period, G2, is the post-DNA synthetic phase during which the cell prepares for mitosis. The term *cell cycle checkpoint* refers to a mechanism by which the cell actively halts the progression of the cell cycle until it can ensure that an earlier process, such as DNA replication or mitosis, is complete. Such cell cycle checkpoints are mediated by p53 at the end of G1 and during G2 (Table 12–1). P53 is also known as a tumor suppressor and when inactivated permits oncogenes to promote transformation and tumorigenesis (Lowe et al., 2004).

Cyclins and their partners, the Cdks, constitute the basis of the molecular mechanism that controls cell cycle regulation (Fig. 12–1) (Murray, 2004). Cdks are serine/threonine protein kinases that require binding of a cyclin to become activated. Mammalian cells contain multiple Cdks that are activated by multiple cyclins. Much of the difference between the behavior of different cyclins reflects their location and timing of expression rather than their direct effects on substrate specificity. The activity of Cdks is highly regulated by a number of mechanisms: (1) the level of their respective partner proteins, the cyclins, (2) the amounts of inhibitory proteins of the Cip/Kip (e.g., p21, p27, and p57) and Ink4 (e.g., p15, p16, p18, and p19) families (Cdk inhibitors or CKIs), and (3) inhibitory and stimulatory phosphorylation of various Cdk residues (Table 12–1) (Cheng, 2004; Siegenthaler and Miller, 2005). High concentrations of cyclins therefore generally stimulate cell-cycle progression and proliferation through activation of Cdks, whereas high amounts of CKIs antagonize these processes.

Cyclins are activating subunits that interact with specific Cdks to regulate their activity and substrate specificity. In mammals, these complexes include: (1) the D-type cyclins (cyclins D1, D2, and D3) that activate Cdk4 and Cdk6 to execute critical regulatory events in G1; (2) the E- and A-type cyclins that activate Cdk2 to affect events in S including DNA replication; and (3) the A-type cyclins and B-type cyclins that activate Cdk1 to direct structural and regulatory events in M (Fig. 12–1). Inactivation of Cdk1 in late M contributes to progression into G1.

In somatic cells, movement through G1 and into S is driven by the active forms of the cyclin D1, D2,

or D3 complexing with Cdk4 or Cdk6. This triggers an intricate cascade of events. Formation of a cyclin D-Cdk complex induces the phosphorylation of retinoblastoma (Rb) protein (Fig. 12–2) (Classon and Harlow, 2002). Before a cell prepares to enter a new cell cycle during the G1/S transition, a critical transcription factor, E_2F-1 is inactive and bound to Rb. Once the new cell cycle begins, Rb is phosphorylated and E_2F-1 is partially released from Rb inhibition. This activates cell cycle regulators including cyclin A and cyclin E that complex with Cdk2 and Cdc25A phosphatase. Cdc25A phosphatase removes phosphates that inhibit Cdk2 and the resultant cyclin E/Cdk2 complex further phosphorylates Rb. The result is a complete release of E_2F and the transcription of a series of genes essential for progression into S and DNA synthesis. Paralleling this activity is the direct contribution of the c-*myc* pathway to the G1/S transition by elevating the transcription for cyclin E and Cdc25A (Fig. 12–2).

In addition to the positive regulation by cyclins, Cdks are regulated (1) by multiple phosphorylation and dephosphorylation events and (2) by several CKIs that physically associate with the cyclin-Cdk complexes to inhibit their activities and promote cell cycle arrest or delay. Since phosphorylation is fundamental to the regulation of cell cycle progression, a large subset of *Drosophila* protein kinases (kinome) studied for their necessity in the normal cell cycle was examined by silencing genes with RNA-mediated interference (Bettencourt-Dias et al., 2004). Of 228 protein kinases that are down-regulated by this silencing, down-regulation of 80 of them can induce cell cycle dysfunction. Many of these enzymes were already known to phosphorylate microtubules, actin, and associated proteins, but as a consequence of these studies, the protein kinases have been assigned new functions in cell cycle. These findings underscore the complexity of cell cycle regulation and the multitude of potential targets that ethanol might affect during development.

Cell cycle progression is regulated by growth factors (see Chapter 11), the extracellular matrix, and cell-cell contacts. Upon deprivation of cells from an essential component (nutrients or growth factors) the cells become quiescent and enter the so-called G0-phase. This exit from the cell cycle can be reversible in astrocytes (Li et al., 1996; MacFarlane and Sontheimer, 2000) or irreversible, as evident in many types of postmitotic neurons (Zawada et al., 1996). In mammalian

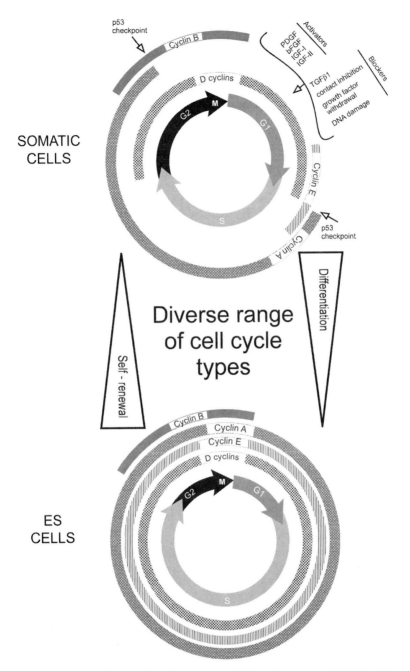

FIGURE 12–1 Cell cycle of embryonic stem (ES) and somatic cells. Note that ES cells have greatly shortened gap phases, exhibit constant expression of cyclins A, E, and D, and lack p53 checkpoints that allow for rapid cell division. bFGF, basic fibrobalst growth factor; IGF, insulin-like growth factor; PDGF, platelet-derived growth factor; TGFβ1, transforming growth factor β1.

TABLE 12–1 Endogenous cell cycle inhibitors slow down cell cycle at different stages by acting on various cyclin-CDK complexes.

Cell Cycle Stage	Cyclin-Cdk Complexes	Ink4 Family				Cip/Kip Family			
		p15	p16	p18	p19	p21	p27	p57	p53
G1	cyclin D-Cdk 4/6	+	+	+	+	+	+/−	+/−	−
G1/S	cyclin E-Cdk2	−	−	−	−	+	+	+	+
S	cyclin A-Cdk2	−	−	−	−	+	−	+	−
G2/M	cyclin B-Cdk2	−	−	−	−	+	−	−	+

cells, the cell cycle machinery that determines whether cells continue proliferating or cease dividing and differentiate appears to operate mainly in the G1.

Cell Cycle of Stem Cells

Embryonic Cells

In stem cells, there is a distinct cell cycle control that operates in order to maintain their stemness. The need for higher rates of proliferation is met by minimizing the length of time that ES cells spend in G1 and G2 (Fig. 12–1). Mouse ES cells have a defective Rb pathway and a nonresponsive p53 pathway (Savatier and Malashicheva, 2004). Furthermore, ES cells have constitutive phosphatidyl-inositol-3-kinase activity and ectopic cyclin E/Cdk2 kinase activity, features often evident in tumors (Sherr, 1996). The uncoupling of G1 from the influence of extrinsic stimuli might explain in part the rapid proliferation rate of ES cells. Another method through which stem cells are able to maintain a high rate of self-renewal is reduction in expression of CKIs, particularly p21 and p27 (Cheng and Scadden, 2004; Siegenthaler and Miller, 2005). It is likely that the distinct cell cycle profile in stem cells is mediated either by distinct upstream intracellular mediators or by unique combinatorial relationships of common

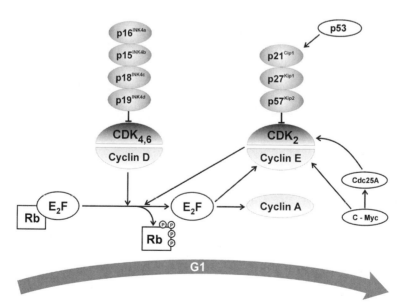

FIGURE 12–2 Major regulators of cell cycle initiation in G1. See text for details. Cdk, cyclin-dependent kinase, RB, retinoblastoma.

biochemical mediators that limit the intensity of signals to exit the cell cycle.

Stem cells are not only key building blocks in normal development but they are also candidates as the cell of origin for cancer because of their pre-existing capacity of self-renewal and unlimited replication (Beachy et al., 2004). Cancer most often emerges in those tissues undergoing constant renewal by the proliferation of stem cells. By retaining or re-acquiring stem cell behavior, malignant cells may be able to re-create a tumor during metastasis or after therapeutic elimination of the bulk of the tumor population (Beachy et al., 2004).

Neural Stem Cells

During normal development of the CNS, the division rates of NSCs within the germinal zones vary with brain region and with time (see Chapters 2 and 11). The principle of the cell cycle of ES cells (described above) composed solely of S and M no longer applies. By contrast, as the development of CNS progresses, a multitude a cell cycle "types" emerges (Fig. 12–1). These cell cycles differ in length, which is most commonly determined by the period of time that the cell is in G1 and/or G2.

Studies of murine cortical neurogenesis detail the cell cycle over the 6-day long process (Caviness et al., 1999). Founder cells and their progeny undergo 11 cell cycles. The proportion of the cells becoming postmitotic increases with each successive cell cycle and the length of the cycle increases due to a gradual prolongation of G1. G1 is characterized by two main enzymatic activities: Cdk4 in mid-G1 and Cdk2 in late G1 just prior to initiation of S (Fig. 12–2). As described above in Origin of Neural Stem Cells, the SZ cells can be subdivided into slowly dividing GFAP-positive (type B) cells, rapidly dividing transit-amplifying progenitors (type C cells), and proliferating migratory neuroblasts (type A cells). One proposed model of neurogenic program defines the flowing lineage progression: type B to type C to type A cells (Doetsch et al., 1997).

The CKI p27 is an inhibitor of Cdk2 that can prolong the entry of a proliferating cell into S. During neurogenesis, loss of p27 has no effect on the number of stem cells (type B cells), but selectively increases the number of transit-amplifying type C cells, while concomitantly reducing the number of type A neuroblasts (Doetsch et al., 2002). By contrast, NSCs in transgenic mice over-expressing p27 have longer G1 (Mitsuhashi et al., 2001). The length of cell cycle (T_C) in germinal zones is under temporal and spatial control. For example, in the mouse, division rates can be as rapid as 7–10 hr in early gestation and up to 18 hr long at the end of cortical neuronogenesis (Takahashi et al., 1995). Likewise, the length of the cell cycle increases in rat cortex from 11 to 17 hr across the period of neuronogenesis (Miller and Kuhn, 1995). Cell cycle varies by location, too. The T_C for the rat neocortical VZ on G21 is 19 hr and 16 hr for SZ cells (Miller and Nowakowski, 1991). In the adult brain, the frequency of cell proliferation can be as infrequent as days or months (Garcia-Verdugo et al., 1998; Morshead et al., 1998; Doetsch et al., 1999). In addition to the apparent differences in cell cycle lengths, the details of molecular controls dictating characteristics of various cell cycles of NSCs are speculative.

EFFECTS OF ETHANOL ON CELL CYCLE

Somatic Cells

Reports on the effects of ethanol on cell cycle regulatory molecules suggest that the ethanol-mediated effects on key regulators of cell cycle are tissue-specific and cell type dependent. For example, in human lymphocytes, ethanol-induced inhibition of mitosis is mediated through G2/M blockade (Ahluwalia et al., 1995). In human epithelial cells, ethanol delays cell cycle progression by up-regulating the expression of transcripts for p21 (a key CKI) and inhibiting Cdk2 kinase activity in G1 (Guo et al., 1997). In epithelial cells, these ethanol-mediated effects on the cell cycle are independent of the cellular status of a checkpoint mediator, p53. Other studies in a variety of tissues corroborate the findings that specific CKIs serve as targets of ethanol actions. For example, an increase in *p21* gene expression upon ethanol infusion has been reported in the isolated perfused heart (Jankala et al., 2001). Hepatocyte proliferation after partial hepatectomy is also inhibited by ethanol through amplification of G1 checkpoint mechanism involving induction of *p21* gene and inhibition of cyclin D (Koteish et al., 2002). Yet the effects of ethanol might not influence only a single phase of the cell cycle. Transient blockade of cell cycle at G2/M and prevention of the cell from exiting the cycle by ethanol exposure have been shown in a fibroblastic cell line derived from actively dividing mouse connective tissue (Mikami et al., 1997).

Ethanol intake by pregnant rats inhibits growth of the intestinal epithelia (Peres et al., 2004). Ethanol substantially attenuates crypt cell proliferation in both the jejunum and ileum and prolongs cell cycle time among crypt cells. In ethanol-fed rabbits, neo-intimal hyperplasia in coronary arteries following balloon angioplasty is diminished (Merritt et al., 1997). Similarly, local delivery of ethanol by balloon catheters in balloon-injured coronary arteries inhibits intimal hyperplasia (Liu et al., 1997). In cultured vascular smooth muscle cells, ethanol inhibits the progression of cells from the G1 to S by modulating the expression/activity of key regulatory molecules of the cycle (Sayeed et al., 2002). In particular, ethanol induces the expression of p21, inhibits Cdk2 activity, and halts the induction of cyclin A, resulting in a decrease of hyperphosphorylation of Rb and failure to initiate a new cell cycle. Cumulatively, reports on ethanol-mediated effects on the cell cycle of somatic cells suggest that p21, the key negative regulator of mammalian cell cycle, is an important target of ethanol.

Despite an overwhelming number of reports supporting the anti-proliferative role of ethanol, instead of perturbing the cell cycle progression, its actions can actually induce the cell cycle in certain cell types under particular conditions. In such cases, reduced expression of cell cycle inhibitors upon exposure to ethanol accelerates progression from the G1 to S. Indeed, ethanol-mediated inhibition of p18, p19, and p21 expression, increased Rb phosphorylation and increased proliferation have been reported in squamous cell carcinoma cell lines of the head and neck (Hager et al., 2001; Kornfehl et al., 2002). Increased hepatocyte proliferation in rats after chronic ethanol feeding has also been demonstrated by several investigators (Chung et al., 2001). Immortalized NSCs, grown under proliferation-encouraging conditions, also respond to ethanol by increasing the rate of their division (Morgan et al., 2003) (described in more detail below). Likewise, following prenatal exposure to moderate amounts of ethanol, SZ cell proliferation increased (Miller and Nowakowski, 1991) because of recruitment of cells into the cycling population, not because of a decrease in the T_C or the length of the G1. Taken together, these findings indicate that the effects of ethanol on cell cycle progression are highly variable and depend on the molecular, cellular, and system contexts under which they occur.

Stem Cells

Neural Stem Cells

Mechanisms of neuronogenesis during development (Miller, 1986) and adulthood (Herrera et al., 2003) are affected by ethanol (see Chapters 11 and 13). Much of the following discussion is based on findings from adult NSCs, as studies examining molecular details of cell cycle modulation by ethanol during brain development are few. Nonetheless, approaches and findings presented here should be useful in studying effects of ethanol on the characteristics of cell cycle in the course of neurogenesis.

Both binge (Nixon and Crews, 2002) and chronic (Miller, 1995; Rice et al., 2004; He et al., 2005) ethanol consumption reduce the postnatal proliferation of neural progenitor cells in the SZ of the lateral ventricle and the intrahilar zone (IHZ; also known as the subgranular zone) of the dentate gyrus. Adult rats receiving liquid diet containing ethanol (6.5% v/v) for 3 days reduced their neural progenitor proliferation in the IHZ as evidenced by a decrease in the number of cells that incorporate bromodeoxyuridine (BrdU) (Rice et al., 2004). In contrast, animals receiving an ethanol diet for 10 or 30 days no longer display reduced progenitor proliferation, indicating activation of a compensatory response to the action of ethanol. At least during the early postnatal period, the effects of ethanol are concentration-dependent (Miller, 1995); high doses inhibit cell proliferation and lower doses are stimulatory. During fetal development, ethanol might also stimulate proliferation of neural progenitors as illustrated by enhanced proliferation of cerebral cortical neuroepithelial precursors upon exposure to alcohol (Miller and Nowakowski, 1991; Miller, 1995; Santillano et al., 2005). Treatment with ethanol for 4 days increases the size, variation, and number of cortical precursor neurospheres, induces S, and increases progression through G2/M (Santillano et al., 2005).

Analysis of the effects of ethanol on postnatal neurogenesis should be conducted in terms of the final numbers of cells generated and retained. This measure is affected by not only the rate of cell proliferation, but also by the rate of cell death (Miller, 2003). The importance of this approach has been documented by studies reporting that ethanol actually increases cell proliferation and concomitantly increases cell death as determined with terminal deoxynucleotide transferase-mediated deoxyuridine triphosphate nick-end labeling

(TUNEL) (Pawlak et al., 2002; Miller, 2003). TUNEL identifies nucleosome-sized products of DNA degradation. These findings underscore the complexity of the effects of ethanol on cell cycle and cell survival. One study explores the effects of a 24 hr exposure to ethanol on C17.2 cells, a line of NSCs derived from a postnatal mouse cerebellum (Morgan et al., 2003). Exposure to ethanol doubled the number of surviving NSCs when grown under proliferation-favoring culture conditions (10% serum/uncoated culture plate). In contrast, ethanol reduces the number of NSCs grown under differentiating conditions (1.0% serum/poly-L-lysine-coated culture plate). As this NSC line has been immortalized with v-*myc*, it is conceivable that the increase in proliferation of C17.2 during exposure to ethanol is related to the effects of ethanol on the activity of the oncogene, v-*myc*. Oncogenes are known activators of telomerase, which in turn maintains telomere length necessary for unabated proliferation (see Stem Cells, and Telomerase, below).

Mechanisms Underlying Cell Cycle

Despite the abundance of literature describing the effects of ethanol on neural progenitor proliferation during neurogenesis, only a few studies have examined the molecular mechanisms mediating these changes. One of the few models used to date is that of cerebellar neurogenesis. Cerebellar granule neurons represent a major neuronal type in the cerebellum and arise from the proliferating external germinal layer during the first 2–3 postnatal weeks in the rat (Miale and Sidman, 1961; Altman, 1972). Cyclin A and Cdk2, two positive regulators of the cell cycle, exert control over neurogenesis in the developing cerebellum (Li et al., 2002). Cerebellar granule progenitors express predominantly Cdk2 (Courtney and Coffey, 1999; Li et al., 2001). Li and colleagues (2002) report that in cerebellar granule progenitors derived from 3-day-old rat pups, ethanol exposure decreases the expression of Cdk2 and cyclin A. This ethanol-mediated reduction of Cdk2/cyclin A expression may induce cell cycle arrest in neuronal precursors by increasing the duration of G1 and S.

P27, a negative regulator of the cell cycle, plays an important role during neurogenesis of the developing cerebellum. In the neonatal cerebellum, p27 is severely down-regulated after early postnatal exposure to ethanol (Li et al., 2002). P27 induces cell cycle arrest in neuronal precursors and accelerates differentiation

of neurons (Perez-Juste and Aranda, 1999; Farah et al., 2000; Miyazawa et al., 2000). Repression of p27 by ethanol exposure may reactivate postmitotic neurons and evoke apoptotic cell death. Collectively, reports on the effects of ethanol on neurogenesis suggest that p27, Cdk2, and cyclin A are primary targets of the ethanol in the developing cerebellum. Unfortunately, such detailed analysis of cell cycle proteins during prenatal exposure to ethanol is unavailable.

Different neuronal populations from diverse locations in the developing brain exhibit different degrees of susceptibility to ethanol toxicity (Maier et al., 1999). Ethanol also inhibits carbachol-induced DNA synthesis of astroglia (Guizzetti et al., 2003). Muscarinic agonist-driven progression from the G1 to S also can be affected by ethanol in these cells (Guizzetti and Costa, 1996; Guizzetti et al., 2003). Taken together, these reports on ethanol-induced effects on the cell cycle of different neuronal and astroglial populations suggest that S and G1 are the primary targets of ethanol-induced effects.

Not only can cell cycle pathways be studied in vitro and in vivo (see Use of Neural Stem Cell Transplantation to Examine the Effects of Ethanol on Cell Cycle Regulation In Vivo), but gene array technology makes it possible to screen stem cells for ethanol-mediated gene expression patterns in an effort to discover new ethanol-responsive genes. A report by Treadwell and Singh (2004), who used microarrays of adult mouse brain gene expression following acute ethanol exposure, suggests that a significant proportion of ethanol-responsive genes have roles in cell cycle transition and arrest. The genes, *p21* and the growth arrest and DNA damage-inducible gene (*Gadd45r*), are up-regulated in response to ethanol. P21 and Gadd45r are implicated in both p53-mediated and p53-independent induction of G1 growth arrest in response to ethanol and oxidative stress (Guo et al., 1997; Kitamura et al., 1999).

The molecular mechanisms of ethanol-induced effects on cell cycle involve ethanol-responsive elements on promoters of target genes. Ethanol alters the expression and DNA binding activity of various transcription factors, such as activating protein 1 (AP-1), nuclear factor κ-B, and early growth response gene (Beckmann et al., 1997; Cebers et al., 1999; Fried et al., 2001; Acquaah-Mensah et al., 2002). These transcription factors regulate the transcription of genes encoding cyclins, Cdks, and CKIs (Sylvester et al., 1998; Beier et al., 2000; Milde-Langosch et al.,

2000; Passegue and Wagner, 2000; Hennigan and Stambrook, 2001). AP-1 binds to the cAMP-responsive element in the promoter of cyclin A gene (Sylvester et al., 1998; Beier et al., 2000) and enhances transcription of cyclin A. Suppression of AP-1 activity by prenatal ethanol exposure (Acquaah-Mensah et al., 2002) inhibits the transcription of cyclin A in developing cerebellum. Given the critical role of Cdks and CKIs in neurogenesis, disruption of the Cdk/CKI system may be the mechanism underlying ethanol-induced damage of many developing CNS nuclei, including the cerebellum.

Telomerase

A potential opportunity for ethanol to influence stem cell proliferation is to affect the chromosomal termini, the telomeres. In all vertebrates, telomeres consist of non-coding G-rich DNA repeats (TTAGGG). These specialized chromatin structures are necessary for successful cell division and are shortened with each round of DNA replication. They can also be preserved by elongation mediated by an enzyme called *telomerase*. In normal human somatic cells, consecutive rounds of telomere shortening induce replicative senescence, particularly in the absence of telomerase. Loss of TTAGGG sequences leads to telomere dysfunction characterized by end-to-end chromosome fusion that results in genomic instability. Telomeres are protected by a collection of proteins that, in addition to telomerase, include several other proteins regulating telomere length, including protection of telomeres 1 (Lei et al., 2004) and others (Bekaert et al., 2004). Telomerase activity requires (1) the reverse transcriptase TERT and (2) an RNA component that adds TTAGGG repeats to the ends of chromosomes to prevent chromosomal shortening.

Telomerase activity in the developing rodent brain is high on gestational day (G) 13 but declines by G18, remains low until postnatal day (P) 3, and finally becomes undetectable by P10 (Klapper et al., 2001). These observations are consistent with a role of telomerase in proliferation of NSCs. Interestingly, accelerated shortening of telomeres in mice deficient in telomerase abrogates proliferation of adult NSCs isolated from the SZ, however, it does not have that effect in the NSCs isolated from the fetal brain despite severe telomere erosion resulting in chromosomal abnormalities and nuclear accumulation of p53 (Ferron et al., 2004). This observation parallels the finding

that mouse ES cells lack p53-dependent checkpoints (Savatier and Malashicheva, 2004). Whether fetal NSCs at various stages of development share independence is not clear, but various "types" of cell cycles differ in length and differing expression patterns of cell cycle regulatory proteins have been identified both in somatic cells and ES cells (Fig. 12–1).

At least some NSCs display cell cycle characteristics like those of somatic cells. This is evident in adult NSCs, which can have a prolonged G0 (Takahashi et al., 1995; Garcia-Verdugo et al., 1998; Morshead et al., 1998; Doetsch et al., 1999) and those dependent on the p53 checkpoints (Meletis et al., 2005). In neurospheres derived from the SZ of p53-null mice, the number of BrdU-positive cells is increased as much as 20%, whereas p21 content is reduced (Meletis et al., 2005). Concomitant with this increased capacity for self-renewal is a reduction in cell death, evidenced by reduced caspase 3 activity and annexin V staining.

When examining neurogenesis, it is important not to presume that the proteins involved share the same function at all stages of development. Such is the case for caspase 3, a pro-apoptotic protease, in later stages of brain organogenesis and adulthood. Caspase 3 is necessary for normal growth of morula and blastocyst embryos, as its inhibition stalls the growth of such embryos (Zwaka et al., 2005). NSCs undergoing telomere shortening, invariably enter an irreversible growth arrest, and eventually senesce. Development of perpetual NSC lines for studies on human fetal NSCs has been successfully attempted using transfection with a proto-oncogene, v-*myc* (Villa et al., 2004). In such immortalized NSCs, v-*myc* maintains high telomerase activity and allows culturing of NSCs for up to 4 years with preservation of short, but stable and homogenous telomeres.

Ethanol affects the expression of a proto-oncogene, c-*myc*, but it fails to change the amounts of p53 in the skeletal muscle of rats exposed to chronic ethanol (Nakahara et al., 2003). Prenatal exposure to ethanol increases gestational expression of p53 in the cerebral cortex (Kuhn and Miller, 1998). This finding parallels the effects of ethanol on SZ cells, but whether ethanol alters the expression and activity of oncogenes and p53 in NSCs remains to be examined.

Ionic and Metabolic Homeostasis

Calcium and magnesium are both believed to play an important role in cell proliferation (Wolf and

Cittadini, 1999; Ziesche et al., 2004). Ethanol can cause a decrease in cytosolic-free Ca^{2+} (Zhang et al., 1992) and a rapid depletion of intracellular Mg^{2+} in vascular smooth muscle cells (Altura et al., 1995). In addition, ethanol can adversely affect mitochondrial cytochrome oxidase (Kennedy, 1998) and ATP synthesis (Devi et al., 1994). Therefore, the effects of ethanol on ion distribution and/or cellular bioenergetic metabolism should not be overlooked as possible modulators of cell cycle regulatory molecules and cellular proliferation.

USE OF NEURAL STEM CELL TRANSPLANTATION TO EXAMINE THE EFFECTS OF ETHANOL ON CELL CYCLE REGULATION IN VIVO

Labeling Neural Stem Cells for In Vivo Studies

Cultured cells are much more amenable to the study of cell cycle regulators than are cells in situ. Therefore, most studies have examined NSCs that have been derived from the CNS and experimentally manipulated in culture. Both the removal of cells from their natural surrounding in the brain and artificial culture conditions contribute to a degree of uncertainty as to whether observations from tissue culture truly reflect the natural responses of stem cells in the intact brain. This issue can only be addressed through examination of NSCs in live animals. Many novel techniques are currently available to study NSCs in situ.

The initial step of any such study is to develop a method for identifying the cells of interest in vivo. A review of these methods is beyond the scope of this chapter. Nonetheless, one approach is to use genetic techniques that allow creation of transgenic mice with expression of marker genes under NSC promoters such as nestin or CD133. Viral vectors delivering a label such as green fluorescent protein or LacZ β-galactosidase, or the exhaustively used BrdU-labeling can be used as well (Zawada et al., 1998; Ourednik et al., 2001). Another approach is transplantation of NSCs into the brain, following their ex vivo labeling and/or genetic modification. Potential advantages of this approach include the ability to control the number of cells to be studied, their placement, and the ability to follow their movement and differentiation in

vivo. In such labeled, transplanted stem cells and their progeny, one can assess the effects of ethanol intake on cell cycle regulatory proteins. A suitable model of neurogenesis that is as close as possible to human neurogenesis (i.e., transplantation of human NSCs into a pregnant primate that is available for examination of effects of ethanol on cell cycle of stem cells) has been developed (Ourednik et al., 2001) (for details see section below).

Transplanted Human Neural Stem Cells Participate in Brain Development

It has been hypothesized that multiple bonafide stem cell pools exist and represent descendants of a common NSC (Ourednik et al., 2001). These cells emerge, by design, in the context of a single developmental process of allocation and segregation during the earliest stages of cerebrogenesis and then establish a lifelong reservoir, presumably for use in homeostasis and repair. This phenomenon could represent a developmental strategy in which plasticity is "programmed" into the CNS at the single cell level from the earliest stages of embryogenesis. This program depends on both progenitor proliferation and differentiation.

A clone of NSCs of human derivation (hNSCs) was grafted into developing brains of fetal bonnet monkeys (*Macaca radiata*), an Old World monkey species (as close as feasible experimentally to the human condition) (Ourednik et al., 2001). Unilaterally injected hNSCs distribute themselves evenly throughout both cerebral hemispheres and at all levels of the neural axis, settling in diverse widespread regions of the telencephalon, principally at the frontal and frontoparietal levels. Although individual hNSCs are clonally related, they appear to segregate into two subpopulations.

Cells in subpopulation 1 traverse great distances through the developing cerebrum by migrating from the periventricular germinal zones along host radial glia to terminate at developmentally and temporally appropriate cortical laminae and differentiate accordingly into several neuronal and glial cell types. Those hNSCs that migrated to the more distant superficial neurogenic lamina become neurons, identified by dual immunoreactivity to antibodies against neuron-specific nuclear protein, calbindin, and neurofilament, intermixed seamlessly with the monkey's own neurons.

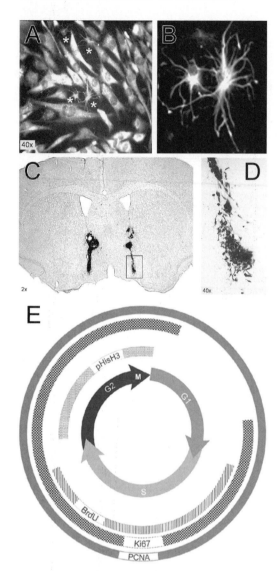

Most hNSC-derived neurons are found in superficial cortical layers II/III (which, at the time of transplant, profited from an intensive supply of newly formed neurons) (Frantz and McConnell, 1996). hNSC-derived cells, that stop and integrate within the cortical layers IV–VI, differentiate appropriately into glia, as identified by immunoreactivity to GFAP (for astrocytes) or to 2′,3′-cyclic-nucleotide phosphodiesterase (for oligodendrocytes). Glia of donor origin are also observed in the marginal zone (MZ; layer I) and in subcortical regions. Some donor cells also contribute to the population of radial glia.

Cells in subpopulation 2 are small, non–process-bearing, undifferentiated BrdU-positive cells dispersed throughout the SZ as single cells or as small clusters intermingled with the germinal cells of the host. When double-stained for cell type-specific antigens, these cells express vimentin (an immature progenitor/stem cell marker), but are negative for all other markers of differentiation. A small number of subpopulation 2 cells, however, are present within the striatum and cortex, intermixed with the differentiated cells appropriate to the specific lamina.

The transplantation experiment answers a number of important questions concerning NSCs and provides a model for studying individual NSCs during neurogenesis. (1) The data provide a plausible explanation for the generation of multiple, disparate stem cell populations as part of a unitary strategy of NSC allocation. (2) The clonal progeny of a given NSC segregate to yield differentiated cells for organogenesis (e.g., subpopulation 1), whereas others (e.g., subpopulation 2) are deposited in germinal zones (e.g., the SZ) as a reservoir. (3) Grafted hNSCs can integrate into the morphogenetic program of the developing primate host brain.

Examination of Cell Cycle Machinery In Vivo

Although the model of neurogenesis described above is instructive, it is very labor intensive and costly. Simpler models have been developed. A prototypical NSC-line, C17.2, has been derived from postnatal murine cerebellum. These cells are nestin-positive and differentiate into neurons, astrocytes (Fig. 12–3), and oligodendrocytes in culture. C17.2 cells are

FIGURE 12–3 Transplanted neural stem cells (NSC). Neural stem cells can be grown in vitro and successfully transplanted into mammalian brain for studies examining their survival, proliferation, differentiation, and migration. A. C17.2 murine NSCs cultured in low serum differentiate into astrocytes (large GFAP-positive cells), whereas some remain undifferentiated and positive for nestin (four cells above the asterisks). B. Enlargement of the two nestin-positive C17.2 stem cells from panel A. C. Ten days after transplantation into striatum and nucleus accumbens of adult C57BL/6 mice, C17.2 NSCs survive and express active β-galactosidase as evidenced by staining this 40 μm-thick coronal section for 5-bromo-4-chloro-3-indolyl β-d-galactopyranoside (X-gal). D. Enlargement of X-gal-positive cells in boxed area in panel C. E. Four markers of various stages of cell cycle. Shown here are:

proliferating cell nuclear antigen (PCNA) that labels the entire cell cycle, Ki-67 (nearly entire cycle), bromodeoxyuridine (BrdU) (a marker for DNA synthesis), and phosphorylated histone H3 (pHisH3, for G2/M).

highly engraftable in the brain and can be identified by their expression of β-galactosidase (Fig. 12–3). Immunocytochemical determination of the particular phase in which NSCs are present is also possible. Four common cell cycle markers, proliferating cell nuclear antigen that labels the entire cell cycle, Ki-67 (nearly entire cycle), BrdU (DNA synthesis), and phosphorylated histone H3 (pHisH3, for G_2/M), have been commonly used (Fig. 12–3). In one elegant study, these markers were used to determine that morphine induces premature mitosis in proliferating cells in the adult mouse SZ (Mandyam et al., 2004). Commercially available antibodies against cyclins, Cdks, and CKIs are useful for exploration of expression of cell cycle mediators in even greater detail.

SUMMARY AND CONCLUSIONS

Prenatal exposure to ethanol can lead to FASD. Ethanol in the developing brain not only triggers cell death, but also negatively affects cell division. Since the length of the cell cycle differs for ES cells, NSCs, and somatic cells, the effect of ethanol on cell cycle progression varies in these cell populations and is developmentally controlled. Taken together, ethanol generally reduces proliferation of NSCs during brain development by affecting the expression of Cdks, cyclins, and CKIs such as p21 and p27. Although these complex responses are cell-type dependent, and spatially and temporarily controlled, the net result generally is prolongation of gap phases of the cell cycle, particularly G1. Other potential cell cycle-altering targets of ethanol in NSCs might be telomerases, transcription factors, and proteins regulating cellular bioenergetics. With the advent of novel technologies, many new cell cycle regulators are being discovered and will become important players in future studies examining how ethanol affects NSC proliferation and differentiation in vivo.

Abbreviations

ABCG2   ATP-binding cassette protein

AP-1   activating protein-1

bFGF   basic fibroblast growth factor (also known as FGF-2)

BrdU   bromodeoxyuridine

CD133   cell determinant

Cdk   cyclin-dependent kinase

CKI   cyclin-dependent kinase inhibitor

CNS   central nervous system

ES   embryonic stem

FASD   fetal alcohol spectrum disorders

G   gestational day

Gadd45   growth arrest and DNA damage inducible

GFAP   glial fibrillary acidic protein

GMC   ganglion mother cell

hNSC   human neural stem cell

IHZ   intrahilar zone

Ki-67   proliferation-associated nuclear antigen

MZ   marginal zone

NSC   neural stem cell

P   postnatal day

Rb   retinoblastoma

SZ   subventricular zone

T_C total length of the cell cycle

TERT   telomerase reverse transcriptase

TRF   telomerase-repeat-binding factor

TUNEL   terminal deoxynucleotide transferase-mediated deoxyuridine triphosphate nick-end labeling

VZ   ventricular zone

ACKNOWLEDGMENTS The authors thank Andy Poczobutt for figure design and the National Institute of Alcohol Abuse and Alcoholism and the Integrative Neuroscience Initiative on Alcoholism for support of our research.

References

Acquaah-Mensah GK, Kehrer JP, Leslie SW (2002) In utero ethanol suppresses cerebellar activator protein-1 and nuclear factor-6 B transcriptional activation in a rat fetal alcohol syndrome model. J Pharmacol Exp Ther 301:277–283.

Ahluwalia BS, Westney LS, Rajguru SU (1995) Alcohol inhibits cell mitosis in G2-M phase in cell cycle in a human lymphocytes in vitro study. Alcohol 12:589–592.

Altman J (1972) Postnatal development of the cerebellar cortex in the rat. I. The external germinal layer and the transitional molecular layer. J Comp Neurol 145:353–397.

Altura BM, Zhang A, Cheng TP, Altura BT (1995) Alcohols induce rapid depletion of intracellular free

Mg^{2+} in cerebral vascular muscle cells: relation to chain length and partition coefficient. Alcohol 12: 247–250.

Alvarez-Buylla A, Garcia-Verdugo JM (2002) Neurogenesis in adult subventricular zone. J Neurosci 22: 629–634.

Beachy PA, Karhadkar SS, Berman DM (2004) Tissue repair and stem cell renewal in carcinogenesis. Nature 432:324–331.

Beckmann AM, Matsumoto I, Wilce PA (1997) AP-1 and Egr DNA-binding activities are increased in rat brain during ethanol withdrawal. J Neurochem 69:306–314.

Beier R, Burgin A, Kiermaier A, Fero M, Karsunky H, Saffrich R, Moroy T, Ansorge W, Roberts J, Eilers M (2000) Induction of cyclin E-cdk2 kinase activity, E$_2$F-dependent transcription and cell growth by Myc are genetically separable events. EMBO J 19:5813–5823.

Bekaert S, Derradji H, Baatout S (2004) Telomere biology in mammalian germ cells and during development. Dev Biol 274:15–30.

Bettencourt-Dias M, Giet R, Sinka R, Mazumdar A, Lock WG, Balloux F, Zafiropoulos PJ, Yamaguchi S, Winter S, Carthew RW, Cooper M, Jones D, Frenz L, Glover DM (2004) Genome-wide survey of protein kinases required for cell cycle progression. Nature 432:980–987.

Capela A, Temple S (2002) LeX/ssea-1 is expressed by adult mouse CNS stem cells, identifying them as nonependymal. Neuron 35:865–875.

Caviness VS Jr, Takahashi T, Nowakowski RS (1999) The G1 restriction point as critical regulator of neocortical neuronogenesis. Neurochem Res 24: 497–506.

Cebers G, Hou Y, Cebere A, Terenius L, Liljequist S (1999) Chronic ethanol enhances muscarinic receptor-mediated activator protein-1 (AP-1) DNA binding in cerebellar granule cells. Eur J Pharmacol 383:203–208.

Cheng T (2004) Cell cycle inhibitors in normal and tumor stem cells. Oncogene 23:7256–7266.

Cheng T, Scadden DT (2004) Cell cycle regulators in stem cells. In: Lanza R (ed). *Handbook of Stem Cells*. Academic Press, New York, pp 73–82.

Chiasson BJ, Tropepe V, Morshead CM, van der Kooy D (1999) Adult mammalian forebrain ependymal and subependymal cells demonstrate proliferative potential, but only subependymal cells have neural stem cell characteristics. J Neurosci 19:4462–4471.

Chung J, Liu C, Smith DE, Seitz HK, Russell RM, Wang XD (2001) Restoration of retinoic acid concentration suppresses ethanol-enhanced c-Jun expression

and hepatocyte proliferation in rat liver. Carcinogenesis 22:1213–1219.

Classon M, Harlow E (2002) The retinoblastoma tumour suppressor in development and cancer. Nat Rev Cancer 2:910–917.

Courtney MJ, Coffey ET (1999) The mechanism of Ara-C-induced apoptosis of differentiating cerebellar granule neurons. Eur J Neurosci 11:1073–1084.

Devi BG, Henderson GI, Frosto TA, Schenker S (1994) Effect of acute ethanol exposure on cultured fetal rat hepatocytes: relation to mitochondrial function. Alcohol Clin Exp Res 18:1436–1442.

Doe CQ, Fuerstenberg S, Peng CY (1998) Neural stem cells: from fly to vertebrates. J Neurobiol 36:111–127.

Doetsch F, Caille I, Lim DA, Garcia-Verdugo JM, Alvarez-Buylla A (1999) Subventricular zone astrocytes are neural stem cells in the adult mammalian brain. Cell 97:703–716.

Doetsch F, Garcia-Verdugo JM, Alvarez-Buylla A (1997) Cellular composition and three-dimensional organization of the subventricular germinal zone in the adult mammalian brain. J Neurosci 17:5046–5061.

Doetsch F, Verdugo JM, Caille I, Alvarez-Buylla A, Chao MV, Casaccia-Bonnefil P (2002) Lack of the cell-cycle inhibitor p27Kip1 results in selective increase of transit-amplifying cells for adult neurogenesis. J Neurosci 22:2255–2264.

Farah MH, Olson JM, Sucic HB, Hume RI, Tapscott SJ, Turner DL (2000) Generation of neurons by transient expression of neural bHLH proteins in mammalian cells. Development 127:693–702.

Ferron S, Mira H, Franco S, Cano-Jaimez M, Bellmunt E, Ramirez C, Farinas I, Blasco MA (2004) Telomere shortening and chromosomal instability abrogates proliferation of adult but not embryonic neural stem cells. Development 131:4059–4070.

Frantz GD, McConnell SK (1996) Restriction of late cerebral cortical progenitors to an upper-layer fate. Neuron 17:55–61.

Fried U, Kotarsky K, Alling C (2001) Chronic ethanol exposure enhances activating protein-1 transcriptional activity in human neuroblastoma cells. Alcohol 24:189–195.

Garcia-Verdugo JM, Doetsch F, Wichterle H, Lim DA, Alvarez-Buylla A (1998) Architecture and cell types of the adult subventricular zone: in search of the stem cells. J Neurobiol 36:234–248.

Guizzetti M, Costa LG (1996) Inhibition of muscarinic receptor-stimulated glial cell proliferation by ethanol. J Neurochem 67:2236–2245.

Guizzetti M, Moller T, Costa LG (2003) Ethanol inhibits muscarinic receptor-mediated DNA synthesis and signal transduction in human fetal astrocytes. Neurosci Lett 344:68–70.

Guo W, Baluda MA, Park NH (1997) Ethanol upregulates the expression of p21 WAF1/CIP1 and prolongs G1 transition via a p53-independent pathway in human epithelial cells. Oncogene 15:1143–1149.

Hager G, Formanek M, Gedlicka C, Knerer B, Kornfehl J (2001) Ethanol decreases expression of p21 and increases hyperphosphorylated pRb in cell lines of squamous cell carcinomas of the head and neck. Alcohol Clin Exp Res 25:496–501.

Hartfuss E, Galli R, Heins N, Gotz M (2001) Characterization of CNS precursor subtypes and radial glia. Dev Biol 229:15–30.

He J, Nixon K, Shetty AK, Crews FT (2005) Chronic alcohol exposure reduces hippocampal neurogenesis and dendritic growth of newborn neurons. Eur J Neurosci 21:2711–2720.

Hennigan RF, Stambrook PJ (2001) Dominant negative c-jun inhibits activation of the cyclin D1 and cyclin E kinase complexes. Mol Biol Cell 12:2352–2363.

Herrera DG, Yague AG, Johnsen-Soriano S, Bosch-Morell F, Collado-Morente L, Muriach M, Romero FJ, Garcia-Verdugo JM (2003) Selective impairment of hippocampal neurogenesis by chronic alcoholism: protective effects of an antioxidant. Proc Natl Acad Sci USA 100:7919–7924.

Jankala H, Eklund KK, Kokkonen JO, Kovanen PT, Linstedt KA, Harkonen M, Maki T (2001) Ethanol infusion increases ANP and p21 gene expression in isolated perfused rat heart. Biochem Biophys Res Commun 281:328–333.

Johansson CB, Momma S, Clarke DL, Risling M, Lendahl U, Frisen J (1999) Identification of a neural stem cell in the adult mammalian central nervous system. Cell 96:25–34.

Kennedy JM (1998) Mitochondrial gene expression is impaired by ethanol exposure in cultured chick cardiac myocytes. Cardiovasc Res 37:141–150.

Kilpatrick TJ, Bartlett PF (1995) Cloned multipotential precursors from the mouse cerebrum require FGF-2, whereas glial restricted precursors are stimulated with either FGF-2 or EGF. J Neurosci 15:3653–3661.

Kitamura Y, Ota T, Matsuoka Y, Tooyama I, Kimura H, Shimohama S, Nomura Y, Gebicke-Haerter PJ, Taniguchi T (1999) Hydrogen peroxide-induced apoptosis mediated by p53 protein in glial cells. Glia 25:154–164.

Klapper W, Shin T, Mattson MP (2001) Differential regulation of telomerase activity and TERT expression during brain development in mice. J Neurosci Res 64:252–260.

Knoblich JA, Jan LY, Jan YN (1995) Asymmetric segregation of Numb and Prospero during cell division. Nature 377:624–627.

Kornfehl J, Hager G, Gedlicka C, Formanek M (2002) Ethanol decreases negative cell-cycle-regulating proteins in a head and neck squamous cell carcinoma cell line. Acta Otolaryngol 122:338–342.

Koteish A, Yang S, Lin H, Huang J, Diehl AM (2002) Ethanol induces redox-sensitive cell-cycle inhibitors and inhibits liver regeneration after partial hepatectomy. Alcohol Clin Exp Res 26:1710–1718.

Kuhn PE, Miller MW (1998) Expression of p53 and ALZ-50 immunoreactivity in rat cortex: effect of prenatal exposure to ethanol. Exp Neurol 154:418–429.

Lei M, Podell ER, Cech TR (2004) Structure of human POT1 bound to telomeric single-stranded DNA provides a model for chromosome end-protection. Nat Struct Mol Biol 11:1223–1229.

Li V, Kelly K, Schrot R, Langan TJ (1996) Cell cycle kinetics and commitment in newborn, adult, and tumoral astrocytes. Dev Brain Res 96:138–147.

Li Z, Lin H, Zhu Y, Wang M, Luo J (2001) Disruption of cell cycle kinetics and cyclin-dependent kinase system by ethanol in cultured cerebellar granule progenitors. Dev Brain Res 132:47–58.

Li Z, Miller MW, Luo J (2002) Effects of prenatal exposure to ethanol on the cyclin-dependent kinase system in the developing rat cerebellum. Dev Brain Res 139:237–245.

Liu MW, Anderson PG, Luo JF, Roubin GS (1997) Local delivery of ethanol inhibits intimal hyperplasia in pig coronary arteries after balloon injury. Circulation 96:2295–2301.

Lowe SW, Cepero E, Evan G (2004) Intrinsic tumour suppression. Nature 432:307–315.

MacFarlane SN, Sontheimer H (2000) Changes in ion channel expression accompany cell cycle progression of spinal cord astrocytes. Glia 30:39–48.

Maier SE, Miller JA, Blackwell JM, West JR (1999) Fetal alcohol exposure and temporal vulnerability: regional differences in cell loss as a function of the timing of binge-like alcohol exposure during brain development. Alcohol Clin Exp Res 23:726–734.

Mandyam CD, Norris RD, Eisch AJ (2004) Chronic morphine induces premature mitosis of proliferating cells in the adult mouse subgranular zone. J Neurosci Res 76:783–794.

Meletis K, Berg SM, Frisen J, Nister M (2005) Neurosphere characteristics in p53 null mice. Keystone Symp Abs Mol Regul Stem Cells, 86.

Merritt R, Guruge BL, Miller DD, Chaitman BR, Bora PS (1997) Moderate alcohol feeding attenuates postinjury vascular cell proliferation in rabbit angioplasty model. J Cardiovasc Pharmacol 30:19–25.

Miale IL, Sidman RL (1961) An autoradiographic analysis of histogenesis in the mouse cerebellum. Exp Neurol 4:277–296.

Mikami K, Haseba T, Ohno Y (1997) Ethanol induces transient arrest of cell division (G2 + M block) followed by G0/G1 block: dose effects of short- and longer-term ethanol exposure on cell cycle and cell functions. Alcohol Alcohol 32:145–152.

Milde-Langosch K, Bamberger AM, Methner C, Rieck G, Loning T (2000) Expression of cell cycle-regulatory proteins rb, p16/MTS1, p27/KIP1, p21/WAF1, cyclin D1 and cyclin E in breast cancer: correlations with expression of activating protein-1 family members. Int J Cancer 87:468–472.

Miller MW (1986) Effects of alcohol on the generation and migration of cerebral cortical neurons. Science 233:1308–1311.

—— (1989) Effects of prenatal exposure to ethanol on neocortical development: II. Cell proliferation in the ventricular and subventricular zones of the rat. J Comp Neurol 287:326–338.

—— (1995) Generation of neurons in the rat dentate gyrus and hippocampus: effects of prenatal and postnatal treatment with ethanol. Alcohol Clin Exp Res 19:1500–1509.

—— (2003) Describing the balance of cell proliferation and death: a mathematical model. J Neurobiol 57:172–182.

Miller MW, Kuhn PE (1995) Cell cycle kinetics in fetal rat cerebral cortex: effects of prenatal exposure to ethanol assessed by a cumulative labeling technique with flow cytometry. Alcohol Clin Exp Res 19:233–237.

Miller MW, Nowakowski RS (1991) Effect of prenatal exposure to ethanol on the cell cycle kinetics and growth fraction in the proliferative zones of the fetal rat cerebral cortex. Alcohol Clin Exp Res 15:229–232.

Mitsuhashi T, Aoki Y, Eksioglu YZ, Takahashi T, Bhide PG, Reeves SA, Caviness VS Jr (2001) Overexpression of p27Kip1 lengthens the G1 phase in a mouse model that targets inducible gene expression to central nervous system progenitor cells. Proc Natl Acad Sci USA 98:6435–6440.

Miyazawa K, Himi T, Garcia V, Yamagishi H, Sato S, Ishizaki Y (2000) A role for p27/Kip1 in the control of cerebellar granule cell precursor proliferation. J Neurosci 20:5756–5763.

Morgan MA, Jones SM, Zawada WM (2003) Neural stem cells' response to chronic alcohol exposure in vitro. Abs Soc Neurosci 29:632.2.

Morshead CM, Craig CG, van der KD (1998) In vivo clonal analyses reveal the properties of endogenous neural stem cell proliferation in the adult mammalian forebrain. Development 125:2251–2261.

Murray AW (2004) Recycling the cell cycle: cyclins revisited. Cell 116:221–234.

Nakahara T, Hashimoto K, Hirano M, Koll M, Martin CR, Preedy VR (2003) Acute and chronic effects of alcohol exposure on skeletal muscle c-myc, p53, and Bcl-2 mRNA expression. Am J Physiol Endocrinol Metab 285:E1273–E1281.

Nixon K, Crews FT (2002) Binge ethanol exposure decreases neurogenesis in adult rat hippocampus. J Neurochem 83:1087–1093.

Ourednik V, Ourednik J, Flax JD, Zawada WM, Hutt C, Yang C, Park KI, Kim SU, Sidman RL, Freed CR, Snyder EY (2001) Segregation of human neural stem cells in the developing primate forebrain. Science 293:1820–1824.

Passegue E, Wagner EF (2000) JunB suppresses cell proliferation by transcriptional activation of p16(INK4a) expression. EMBO J 19:2969–2979.

Pawlak R, Skrzypiec A, Sulkowski S, Buczko W (2002) Ethanol-induced neurotoxicity is counterbalanced by increased cell proliferation in mouse dentate gyrus. Neurosci Lett 327:83–86.

Peres WA, Carmo MG, Zucoloto S, Iglesias AC, Braulio VB (2004) Ethanol intake inhibits growth of the epithelium in the intestine of pregnant rats. Alcohol 33:83–89.

Perez-Juste G, Aranda A (1999) The cyclin-dependent kinase inhibitor p27(Kip1) is involved in thyroid hormone-mediated neuronal differentiation. J Biol Chem 274:5026–5031.

Pevny L, Rao MS (2003) The stem-cell menagerie. Trends Neurosci 26:351–359.

Reynolds BA, Weiss S (1992) Generation of neurons and astrocytes from isolated cells of the adult mammalian central nervous system. Science 255:1707–1710.

—— (1996) Clonal and population analyses demonstrate that an EGF-responsive mammalian embryonic CNS precursor is a stem cell. Dev Biol 175:1–13.

Rice AC, Bullock MR, Shelton KL (2004) Chronic ethanol consumption transiently reduces adult neural progenitor cell proliferation. Brain Res 1011:94–98.

Santillano DR, Kumar LS, Prock TL, Camarillo C, Tingling JD, Miranda RC (2005) Ethanol induces cell-cycle activity and reduces stem cell diversity to alter both regenerative capacity and differentiation potential of cerebral cortical neuroepithelial precursors. BMC Neurosci 6:5–9.

Savatier P, Malashicheva A (2004) Cell-cycle control in embryonic stem cells. In: Lanza R (ed). Handbook of Stem Cells. Academic Press, New York, pp 53–62.

Sayeed S, Cullen JP, Coppage M, Sitzmann JV, Redmond EM (2002) Ethanol differentially modulates the expression and activity of cell cycle regulatory proteins in rat aortic smooth muscle cells. Eur J Pharmacol 445:163–170.

Sherr CJ (1996) Cancer cell cycles. Science 274: 1672–1677.

Singh SK, Hawkins C, Clarke ID, Squire JA, Bayani J, Hide T, Henkelman RM, Cusimano MD, Dirks PB (2004) Identification of human brain tumour initiating cells. Nature 432:396–401.

Spassky N, Merkle FT, Flames N, Tramontin AD, Garcia-Verdugo JM, Alvarez-Buylla A (2005) Adult ependymal cells are postmitotic and are derived from radial glial cells during embryogenesis. J Neurosci 25:10–18.

Sylvester AM, Chen D, Krasinski K, Andres V (1998) Role of c-fos and E_2F in the induction of cyclin A transcription and vascular smooth muscle cell proliferation. J Clin Invest 101:940–948.

Takahashi T, Nowakowski RS, Caviness VS Jr (1995) The cell cycle of the pseudostratified ventricular epithelium of the embryonic murine cerebral wall. J Neurosci 15:6046–6057.

Tamaki S, Eckert K, He D, Sutton R, Doshe M, Jain G, Tushinski R, Reitsma M, Harris B, Tsukamoto A, Gage F, Weissman I, Uchida N (2002) Engraftment of sorted/expanded human central nervous system stem cells from fetal brain. J Neurosci Res 69: 976–986.

Treadwell JA, Singh SM (2004) Microarray analysis of mouse brain gene expression following acute ethanol treatment. Neurochemical Res 29:357–369.

Uchida N, Buck DW, He D, Reitsma MJ, Masek M, Phan TV, Tsukamoto AS, Gage FH, Weissman IL (2000) Direct isolation of human central nervous system stem cells. Proc Natl Acad Sci USA 97:14720–14725.

Vescovi AL, Reynolds BA, Fraser DD, Weiss S (1993) bFGF regulates the proliferative fate of unipotent (neuronal) and bipotent (neuronal/astroglial) EGF-generated CNS progenitor cells. Neuron 11: 951–966.

Villa A, Navarro-Galve B, Bueno C, Franco S, Blasco MA, Martinez-Serrano A (2004) Long-term molecular and cellular stability of human neural stem cell lines. Exp Cell Res 294:559–570.

Wolf FI, Cittadini A (1999) Magnesium in cell proliferation and differentiation. Front Biosci 4:D607–D617.

Zawada WM, Cibelli JB, Choi PK, Clarkson ED, Golueke PJ, Witta SE, Bell KP, Kane J, Ponce de Leon FA, Jerry DJ, Robl JM, Freed CR, Stice SL (1998) Somatic cell cloned transgenic bovine neurons for transplantation in parkinsonian rats. Nat Med 4:569–574.

Zawada WM, Kirschman DL, Cohen JJ, Heidenreich KA, Freed CR (1996) Growth factors rescue embryonic dopamine neurons from programmed cell death. Exp Neurol 140:60–67.

Zhang A, Cheng TP, Altura BM (1992) Ethanol decreases cytosolic-free calcium ions in vascular smooth muscle cells as assessed by digital image analysis. Alcohol Clin Exp Res 16:55–57.

Zhong W (2003) Diversifying neural cells through order of birth and asymmetry of division. Neuron 37: 11–14.

Ziesche R, Petkov V, Lambers C, Erne P, Block LH (2004) The calcium channel blocker amlodipine exerts its anti-proliferative action via p21(Waf1/Cip1) gene activation. FASEB J 18:1516–1523.

Zwaka TP, Smuga-Otto K, Murphy KR, Ludwig TE, Jones JM, Thomson JA (2005) Programmed cell death pathways are essential for maintaining pluripotency. Keystone Symp Abs Mol Regul Stem Cells, 115.

13

Mechanisms of Ethanol-Induced Alterations in Neuronal Migration

Julie A. Siegenthaler

Michael W. Miller

Neuronal migration is the process by which postmitotic neurons translocate from their birthplace in proliferative zones to the appropriate target structure where the neurons integrate into the emerging network. In the cerebral cortex, for example, neurons generated in one of two germinal zones adjacent to a lateral ventricle, the ventricular and subventricular zones (see Chapters 2 and 11), migrate in an orderly fashion to a defined laminar residence (Angevine and Sidman, 1961; Berry and Rogers, 1965; Rakic, 1972, 1974; Rakic et al., 1994).

The inability of neurons to properly migrate is one cause of neurological disorders. The cerebral cortex is the brain region most frequently described as exhibiting malformations designated as neuronal migration disorders (NMDs). Two likely reasons for this are (1) its immense size and the large number of constituent neurons and (2) its highly laminated structure. These features make morphological disruptions more readily identifiable.

Structural Malformations in Human Brain

Two types of cortical malformations are evident in humans with NMDs: lissencephaly or heterotopias. Both malformations are often associated with debilitating cognitive defects in individuals who are mentally retarded and/or epileptic (Andermann, 2000; Pilz et al., 2002).

The term *lissencephaly*, meaning "smooth brain," is derived from the even appearance of the surface of the brain caused by a reduction (pachygyria) or absence (agyria) of cortical gyri. Other defects associated with lissencephaly include increased cortical thickness and reduced or poorly defined cortical lamination (Crome, 1956; Friede, 1989).

Heterotopia refers to a cluster of neurons that is abnormally distributed relative to neurons with a common phenotype, such as birthdate or connectivity. Heterotopias can be detected at four sites. Clusters of ectopic neurons may be distributed within the cortical gray (Miller, 1986; Anton et al., 1999). Heterotopias can also be distributed in the subcortical white matter. A common example is a subcortical band heterotopia, a thick strip of ectopic cells beneath the cortex. A band heterotopia is often associated with lissencephaly (Chevassus-au-Louis and Represa, 1999; Kato and Dobyns, 2003). Heterotopias are also found outside the cortex beyond the ventricular (Eksioglu et al., 1996) or pial surface (Williams et al., 1984; Saito et al., 1999; Takeda et al., 2003).

Ethanol-Induced Malformations

Neuronal migration disorders in humans have genetic and/or epigenetic roots. Mutations in genes that transcribe proteins regulating neuronal migration lead to a spectrum of defects, including cortical lissencephaly and heterotopias (Mochida and Walsh, 2004). Exposure to drugs of abuse, in particular ethanol, can lead to NMDs. Fetal brains exposed to ethanol in utero may exhibit a diminution of gyri and sulci and disruptions in cortical lamination (Fig.13–1) (Clarren et al., 1978; Wisniewski et al., 1983; Konovalov et al., 1997; Roebuck et al., 1998). Morphological defects caused by gestational ethanol exposure likely contribute to the cognitive defects and mental retardation associated with fetal alcohol syndrome (FAS).

Several brain regions in animal models of FAS display morphological defects, including heterotopias and structural disorganization (Fig. 13–2A), similar to those reported in humans. These regions include the cerebral cortex (Miller, 1986; Kotkoskie and Norton, 1988; Komatsu et al., 2001; Mooney et al., 2004), striatum (Heaton et al., 1996), midbrain (Sari et al., 2001; Zhou et al., 2001), and cerebellum (Kornguth et al., 1979; Borges and Lewis, 1983; Quesada et al., 1990a, 1990b). The similarities between humans and laboratory animals establish the utility of animal models for examining the effect of ethanol on neuronal migration. Rigorous measures of all aspects of cell migration are required to evaluate the effect of ethanol on neuronal migration. Due to the obvious limitations of human studies, animal models of FAS have been used (a) to further document the phenomenon of ethanol-induced defects in neuronal migration and (b) to study underlying mechanisms.

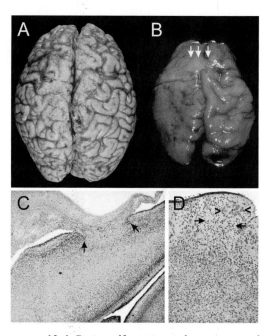

FIGURE 13–1 Brain malformations in humans exposed to ethanol in utero. The gyral pattern of the normal human infant brain **A.** contrasts with the smoother cortical surface in the brain of an infant with FAS **B.** The brain is marked by its small size, which is likely caused by ethanol-induced defects in both neuronal proliferation and cell death. The brain also exhibits a paucity of gyri, and these gyri tend to be broad. These features are signs of lissencephaly. Moreover, the brain is covered by sheets of heterotopic cells over the surface of the brain. The lissencephaly and heterotopias are consistent with defects in neuronal migration. **C.** Ethanol exposure can also induce heterotopias to form in other regions of the brain, including the brain stem. Arrows depict the breach in pial surface through which the migrating neurons presumably streamed to form the heterotopia. **D.** Heterotopias are also collections of cells that presumably terminate their migrations in inappropriate locations. Such neurons are often found in the cerebral cortex. Cells with large (arrow) and small (arrowhead) somata form a heterotopia within a portion of layer I, a region of the cortex that is normally cell-sparse. (*Source:* Images provided courtesy of Sterling Clarren.)

MIGRATION DEFECTS IN ANIMAL MODELS OF FETAL ALCOHOL SYNDROME

A method commonly used to study neuronal migration is mapping of spatiotemporal changes of cells with [³H]thymidine autoradiography. Through this method, proliferating cells can be permanently radio-labeled and the migration of tagged cells traced from their "birth" through the completion of their migration. During normal development, most neurons labeled with [³H]thymidine early in corticogenesis eventually are distributed in deep layers, whereas neurons labeled later in development occupy superficial layers (Angevine and Sidman, 1961; Berry and Rogers, 1965; Rakic, 1974; Miller and Nowakowski, 1988). Thus, cortical layers are formed in an orderly inside-out manner, during which migrating neurons move past those that have already completed cell migration.

Migration can be divided into three phases. The first is the onset of migration, which occurs in the proliferative zones. Second, young neurons actively migrate through the intermediate zone (IZ; the anlage of the white matter) to the superficial limit of the cortical plate, the predecessor of the cortical gray matter. The final step is the termination of neuronal migration in the developing structure.

Although the basic inside-out development of the cortex is largely preserved in rodent models of FAS, each phase of migration is affected by ethanol. The birth of cells that will occupy analogous sites in cortex is 1 to 2 days later in ethanol-treated rats than in controls (see Fig. 11–1, Chapter 11) (Miller, 1986, 1987, 1993). Part of this delay (as much as 31 hr) is due to postmitotic cells lingering longer in the proliferative zones before initiating their migrations. This likely contributes to the increase in size of the subventricular zone, which contains many young neurons beginning their migrations (Miller, 1989). On the other hand, the number of neurons beginning migration at any one time, the leaving fraction, is not affected by ethanol.

Ethanol also reduces the rate of migration throughout development (Fig. 13–2B) (Miller, 1993). For example, in the cortices of 17-day-old fetuses, the mean rate of migration is 138 μm/day, whereas in ethanol-treated fetuses the mean rate is 82 μm/day. Studies using slice cultures of cortex show that ethanol has a similar effect in vitro (Siegenthaler and Miller, 2004) and the rate of migration is reduced in a concentration-dependent manner (Hirai et al., 1999b). The finding that the rate of migration in situ is the same as that *in vivo* suggests that neuronal migration is regulated by local microenvironment—i.e., that extracortical signals (monoamines) may not be critical regulators.

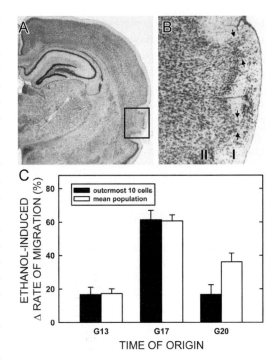

FIGURE 13–2 Animal models of fetal alcohol syndrome (FAS). **A.** Malformations incidental to prenatal alcohol exposure, including cortical heterotopias (box indicates area magnified in B), can be replicated in animal models of FAS. **B.** This particular heterotopia appears to be caused by cells streaming through layer 1 at multiple sites (arrows), forming a layer of ectopic cells outside the cortex. **C.** The rate of migration throughout corticogenesis is particularly vulnerable to ethanol. Pulse-chase experiments using [³H] thymidine show that ethanol causes significant decreases in the rate of migration of cells generated on gestational day (6) 13, G17, and G20. The migration of cells generated on G17 is most effected by ethanol. On G13 and G17, the cells that begin migration first (outermost 10) and the total migrating population (mean population) are similarly slowed by ethanol. In contrast, migration of the outermost 10 cells generated on G20 is less sensitive to alcohol than that of the total population. (*Source*: Images A and B provided courtesy of William Shoemaker and Gordon Sherman.)

During later stages of cortical development, ethanol causes migrating neurons to finish their migration in inappropriate locations. For instance, neurons in the cortex of mature, normal rats that are generated on gestational day (G) 20 are destined for layer II/III. Following prenatal exposure to ethanol, however, most of these neurons either terminate their migrations in deep laminae (layers IV, V, and VI) or they overmigrate into layer I (Miller, 1986, 1993). Other studies show that ethanol can cause the production of suprapial heterotopias, or warts (Kotkoskie and Norton, 1988; Komatsu et al., 2001; Mooney et al., 2004). The implication is that ethanol disrupts mechanisms involved in stopping neuronal migration.

MIGRATION MACHINERY: PROTEIN TARGETS OF ETHANOL TOXICITY

The three phases of neuronal migration are regulated by a number of different protein complexes and signaling pathways that work in concert to move young neurons from the proliferative zones to their targets. Each phase of neuronal migration is vulnerable to the effects of ethanol. Therefore, proteins that regulate migration, including cell adhesion proteins (CAPs), cytoskeletal proteins, extracellular matrix (ECM) proteins, and growth factors, are likely candidates as targets of ethanol toxicity.

Cell Adhesion Proteins

The migration of most cortical neurons begins soon after their birth in a zone proximal to the lateral ventricle (see Chapter 3). The neuron migrates out of the germinal area using radial fibers that span the width of the cerebral wall and remains apposed to the guiding fiber throughout its migratory trek (Rakic, 1971, 1972; Edmondson and Hatten, 1987). Appropriate adherence to the glial guide is regulated by cell adhesion receptors that link the neural cytoskeleton to CAPs, components of the ECM, and membrane-bound moities of the glial fiber.

Cell Adhesion Proteins Regulate Neuronal Migration in Normal Animals

Adhesion proteins from both the cell adhesion molecule (CAM) and integrin families are particularly important for neuronal migration (Ronn et al., 1998; Clegg et al., 2003; Schmid and Anton, 2003). Neural CAM (nCAM) and L1 mediate neuronal migration through homophilic binding and consequent activation of intracellular signaling cascades central to

cytoskeleton reorganization (Panicker et al., 2003). Integrin receptors bind integrins and ECM components (e.g., laminin, fibronectin, and glycoproteins). Integrin binding triggers cytoskeletal changes through a cascade of phosphorylation events (Juliano, 2002).

Up-regulating expression of CAPs is an important part of initiating and propelling neuronal migration. CAPs are richly expressed in regions of the cerebral wall, the IZ, and the cortical plate (CP), containing migrating neurons (Edmondson et al., 1988; Seki and Arai, 1991; Anton et al., 1999; Siegenthaler and Miller, 2004). Disruption of normal cell adhesion slows the progression of glial-guided migration and can lead to detachment of neurons from the glial fiber (Chuong et al., 1987; Anton et al., 1996, 1999).

Ethanol-Induced Changes in Cell Adhesion Proteins

Ethanol exposure reduces the rate of migration and causes neurons to be marooned in ectopic cortical locales (Miller, 1986, 1987; Miller and Robertson, 1993). A likely mechanism underlying ethanol-induced defects in neuronal migration is disrupted cell adhesion. For example, ethanol inhibits L1–L1 mediated cell adhesion by physically blocking L1–L1 homophilic binding (Charness et al., 1994; Ramanathan et al., 1996; Wilkemeyer et al., 1999, 2000, 2002a, 2002b). Ethanol treatment also inhibits L1-mediated neurite outgrowth by cultured cerebellar granule cells; however, ethanol apparently does not affect L1–L1 binding per se (Bearer et al., 1999). The implications of this finding are that ethanol can disrupt L1-mediated cell adhesion through mechanisms other than the L1 protein–protein interaction.

Unlike L1, the effects of ethanol on nCAM appear to be at the level of protein expression. Ethanol treatment increases nCAM protein expression in primary cortical neurons and in slices from fetal cortex (Fig. 13–3A) (Miller and Luo, 2002a; Siegenthaler and Miller, 2004). Specifically, ethanol-induced increases in nCAM expression are noted on the surface of migrating neurons in cortical explants (Fig. 13–3B, 3C) (Hirai et al., 1999b; Siegenthaler and Miller, 2004). The expression and post-translational processing of the three isoforms of nCAM in the postnatal brain are differentially affected by prenatal ethanol exposure, however, there are no significant changes in nCAM mRNA expression with ethanol,

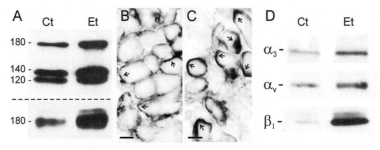

FIGURE 13–3 Expression of cell adhesion proteins is effected by ethanol.
A. Expression of three isoforms (120, 140, and 180 kDa isoforms) of neural
cell adhesion molecule (nCAM) is increased in primary cortical cultures
(top) and organotypic slice cultures (180 kDa only) (bottom). **B.** Cells in the
intermediate zone (IZ) from untreated organotypic slices immunolabel with
nCAM antibody. nCAM expression is highest proximal to the cell membrane
and appears to localize to patches (arrows). **C.** Patches of nCAM immunoreactivity appear to be larger, denser, and more frequent in IZ cells exposed to
ethanol. Ethanol exposure also increases the expression of integrin subunits
α_3, α_v, and β_1 in organotypic cortical cultures **D.** Large increases in nCAM
and integrin receptors, like those observed with ethanol exposure, may cause
a migrating cell to adhere too tightly to the surrounding environ and thus slow
motility. (*Source:* From Siegenthaler and Miller, 2004, with permission).

suggesting a defect in nCAM translation (Miñana
et al., 2000).

Ethanol-induced changes in integrin expression
and function are only beginning to be investigated. A
compelling reason to explore integrins is the similarities between cortical migration defects in mice lacking specific integrin subunits and animal models of
FAS. In mice lacking integrin α_3 and in animals exposed prenatally to ethanol, cortical neurons destined
for superficial layers lie in ectopic, deep-layer positions (Miller, 1986, 1993; Anton et al., 1999). Neural-
specific integrin β_1 knockout mice also display
abnormal neuronal migration. Ectopic cells are common in the marginal zone and the pial surface is disrupted, analogous to the heterotopias seen with
prenatal ethanol exposure (Graus-Porta et al., 2001).

Despite the similarities between animal models of
FAS and integrin knockout animals, *in vitro* studies
indicate that ethanol potentiates integrin protein content (Fig. 13–3D) (Siegenthaler and Miller, 2004).
Interestingly, this finding is similar to the effect observed with nCAM expression (Hirai et al., 1999b;
Luo and Miller, 1999; Miller and Luo, 2002a; Siegenthaler and Miller, 2004). Ethanol increases the ex-
pression of integrin subunits α_3, α_v, and β_1 in cortical

explants (Siegenthaler and Miller, 2004). In cultured
neurophils (Bautista, 1995) and hepatocytes (Schaf-
fert et al., 2001), integrin α_1, α_5, and β_1 are increased
following treatment with ethanol, setting up the
possibility that too much integrin, like too much
nCAM, is detrimental to neuronal migration. Indeed,
neurons that overexpress integrin receptors have impaired migration (Palecek et al., 1997). Presumably,
excess CAP causes increased cell adhesion and prevents migrating neurons from breaking adhesions at
the rear of the cell. Essentially, the adhesion is too
sticky.

Alterations in integrin expression may also contribute to ethanol-induced defects in the radial glial
scaffold. Radial glial fibers traverse the migration pathway in the developing cortex and provide a guide for
neurons during their migration to their ultimate residence. After neuronal migration is complete, radial
glia transform into stellate astrocytes (Schmechel and
Rakic, 1979; Voigt, 1989; Culican et al., 1990; Miller
and Robertson, 1993). Ethanol exposure in utero
leads to the premature differentiation of radial glia
into astrocytes in both the cortex (Miller and Robertson, 1993; Miller, 2003) and cerebellum (Shetty and
Phillips, 1992). Neurons actively migrating on these

transforming radial glia are stranded in deep cortical layers, unable to complete their migration. This finding is further supported by [³H]thymidine studies in which neurons intended for superficial layers are found in deep cortex following ethanol exposure (Miller, 1986, 1993). Incidentally, absence of integrin α_3 also causes premature transformation of radial glial (Anton et al., 1999) and attachment of radial glial endfeet is disrupted in integrin-β_1 knockout mice (Graus-Porta et al., 2001). Thus, ethanol-induced disruptions in integrin function or expression may precede the premature withdrawal of radial glia.

Disruptions in Ca^{2+} channel flux during neuronal migration may contribute to the ethanol-induced reduction in the rate of migration. Ca^{2+} currents in migrating neurons are mediated by N-methyl-D-aspartate (NMDA) subtype of glutamate receptors. Cell migration decreases following treatment with NMDA antagonists (Komuro and Rakic, 1992, 1993; Hirai et al., 1999a). Ethanol affects both the expression and function of NMDA receptors. Chronic ethanol exposure up-regulates specific subunits of the NMDA receptor in fetal cortical neurons (Kumari, 2001). In contrast, acute treatment with ethanol blocks NMDA-dependent Ca^{2+} currents in cultured hippocampal neurons and slices (Lovinger et al., 1989, 1990). Ca^{2+} currents are particularly important at the trailing edge of migrating cells. Loss of integrin-dependent cell adhesion at the rear edge of motile cells depends on increases in intracellular Ca^{2+} (Marks and Maxfield, 1990; Lawson and Maxfield, 1995). Thus, ethanol-dependent changes in normal Ca^{2+} currents might slow neuronal migration by preventing normal separation at the rear edge of the cell.

Extracellular Matrix

The pial membrane (PM) (or pial basement membrane) is an ECM-rich region. The ECM contributes to the role of the PM in the normal developing cortex as a barrier (chemical and physical) around developing neural tissue and an attachment point for radial glia (Sievers et al., 1994). Breaches in the PM allow neurons to migrate beyond the pial surface and form heterotopias (Marin-Padilla, 1996).

Prenatal ethanol exposure can induce formation of heterotopias in humans exposed prenatally to ethanol (Clarren et al., 1978). Rodent models of prenatal ethanol exposure also show heterotopias in both the cerebellum and cortex (Kotkoskie and Norton,

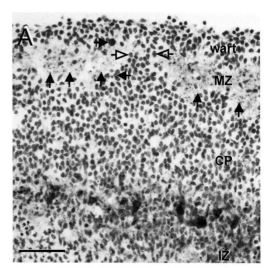

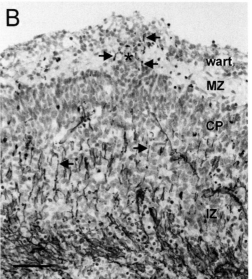

FIGURE 13–4 Ethanol-induced heterotopias are associated with disruptions in the marginal zone (MZ) of organotypic cortical cultures. **A.** Several cell soma occupy a breach (open arrows) in calretinin-positive fibers within the MZ. The cells appear to be streaming through the break and contributing to the heterotopia, or "wart," forming outside the cerebral wall. Cajal-Retzius cell bodies (closed arrow with line) and processes (closed arrows) that occupy the MZ immunolabel with calretinin antibodies (closed arrows). CP, cortical plate. **B.** Breaches in the MZ (*) contain nestin-positive radial glial fibers (arrows). These fibers normally terminate at the pial membrane (PM) adjacent to the MZ. Ethanol-induced disruptions in the MZ and/or PM likely allow the fibers to course inappropriately into the heterotopia. (*Source*: From Mooney et al., 2004, with permission).

1988; Komatsu et al., 2001; Sakata-Haga et al., 2001; Mooney et al., 2004). In rodents, breaches in the glial limitans and marginal zone, a superficial cortical region adjacent to the PM, are often found at the base of ethanol-induced heterotopias (Fig. 13–4) (Komatsu et al., 2001; Sakata-Haga et al., 2001; Mooney et al., 2004).

Despite repeated reports of heterotopias associated with prenatal ethanol exposure, a clear link between defects in the ECM constituents of the PM and ethanol has not been made. Nevertheless, the appearance of heterotopias in animals in which specific ECM proteins are dysfunctional strongly indicates that these proteins are disrupted by ethanol. Deletion or dysfunction of PM proteins laminin (Halfter et al., 2002), perlecan (Costell et al., 1999), and chondroitin sulfate proteoglycans (Blackshear et al., 1997) leads to overmigration of neurons and formation of ectopias reminiscent of ethanol-induced heterotopias. Integrin receptors bind to and organize ECM proteins. Mice lacking the integrin α_6 or integrin β_1 feature defects in the cortical pial membrane that lead to the appearance of ectopic cell bodies (Georges-Labouesse et al., 1998; Graus-Porta et al., 2001). As noted above, ethanol does affect the expression of integrin subunits, including β_1 (Siegenthaler and Miller, 2004). Conceivably, ethanol targeting of these integrins is key to the generation of heterotopias and, by deduction, these integrins are key to the integrity of the PM.

Reelin, a large glycoprotein component of the marginal zone ECM, is produced and secreted by Cajal-Retzius cells (D'Arcangelo et al., 1995; Hirotsune et al., 1995; Ogawa et al., 1995; Soda et al., 2003). Reelin is believed to act as a stop signal causing migrating neurons to end migration and detach from their glial guides (Pearlman and Sheppard, 1996; Marin-Padilla, 1998; Dulabon et al., 2000; Hack et al., 2002). Immunohistochemistry studies show that reelin is abnormally distributed in ethanol induced-heterotopias (Mooney et al., 2004). It is absent directly below heterotopias, but it is distributed toward the perimeter of a heterotopia. Conceivably, the peripheral displacement of reelin underlies continued migration of neurons into a heterotopia.

Cytoskeleton

Successful cell adhesion and release during neuronal migration depends on the rapid reorganization of the cytoskeleton. This reorganization is essential for the initiation and maintenance of neuronal migration (Lambert de Rouvroit and Goffinet, 2001; Marin and Rubenstein, 2003). The two main cytoskeletal elements in neurons are actin and microtubules, proteins that can polymerize into long chains of individual subunits that comprise the intracellular scaffold. Actin filaments are enriched at the leading edge of migrating neurons. Microtubules, in contrast, form a cage-like structure within the cell somata and are aligned longitudinally in the leading process (Rivas and Hatten, 1995). The importance of both actin and microtubule assembly is emphasized by findings that several genetic NMDs are caused by defects in proteins that bind and organize cytoskeletal proteins (Sapir et al., 1997; Gleeson et al., 1999).

Ethanol negatively affects the cytoskeleton in neural and non-neural cells. Actin assembly is aberrant in cultured neural crest cells treated with ethanol outgrowth (Hassler and Moran, 1986a, 1986b). Ethanol induces the formation of thick bundles of actin fibers that prevent the normal process. The actin cytoskeleton in astrocytes is also sensitive to treatment with ethanol (see Chapter 18). The normal organization of actin filaments in cultured astrocytes is severely disrupted by ethanol in a concentration-dependent manner (Allansson et al., 2001; Guasch et al., 2003; Tomas et al., 2003). Ethanol promotes the transformation of actin stress fibers into dysfunctional actin rings. Interestingly, the effect of ethanol on the actin cytoskeleton is alleviated by overexpression of RhoA, a small GTPase that induces actin stress fiber assembly (Guasch et al., 2003). This effect suggests that ethanol exposure may disrupt signaling pathways regulating cytoskeletal reorganization. Microtubule polymerization is also affected by ethanol exposure in astrocytes and hepatocytes (Yoon et al., 1998; Tomas et al., 2003). After treatment with the microtubule-disrupting agent nocodazole, the speed of microtubule repolymerization is reduced in the presence of ethanol.

Growth Factors

Role in Neuronal Migration

Growth factors are proteins that regulate cell ontogeny via extracellular mechanisms. Growth factors that affect neuronal migration include members of the transforming growth factor (TGF) β superfamily (TGFβ1 and bone morphogenic protein [BMP] 4) and brain-derived neurotrophic factor (BDNF). Several studies imply that these factors are active endogenously. Each ligand and the relevant receptors are expressed in proliferative zones during cortical development (Flanders et al., 1991; Fukumitsu et al., 1998; Li et al., 1998; Miller, 2003).

Functional studies relying on exogenous growth factor further indicate that TGFβ1, BMP-4, and BDNF are involved in the initiation and/or maintenance of neuronal migration. Both TGFβ1 and BMP-4 decrease cell proliferation and promote neuronal migration (Li et al., 1998; Luo and Miller, 1999; Siegenthaler and Miller, 2004, 2005a). Complimentary lines of evidence indicate that BDNF, though not classically associated with neuronal migration, promotes the initiation of neuronal migration. First, studies show that cerebellar granule cells from BDNF$^{-/-}$ mice are able to attach to glial fibers but fail to begin migrating (Borghesani et al., 2002). Also, addition of exogenous BDNF enables BDNF$^{-/-}$ granule cells to migrate properly. Finally, injection of BDNF into the lateral ventricles of embryonic animals induces the premature initiation of migration of neurons destined for deep cortex (Ohmiya et al., 2002).

Effect of Ethanol on Growth Factor–Mediated Neuronal Migration

Ethanol effects both the expression of the endogenous TGFβ system and the function of exogenously applied TGFβ1 in vitro. Rats prenatally exposed to ethanol exhibit altered TGFβ ligand and receptor expression (Miller, 2003) Specifically, ethanol increases TGFβ1 and TGFβ2 content in the proliferative zones prenatally, but it diminishes perinatal TGFβ2 expression in the internal segments of radial glia. In contrast, ethanol increases TGFβ receptor type 1 expression in radial glial fibers. The presence of an endogenous TGFβ system in the proliferative and intermediate zones suggests that TGFβ is important for at least the initiation and propagation of neuronal migration through the inner half of the cerebral wall. Further, the vulnerability of this portion of the TGFβ system to ethanol may contribute to ethanol-induced defects in neuronal migration.

Ethanol disrupts TGFβ1-mediated neuronal migration. In slice cultures of cerebral cortex, ethanol impedes the effects of exogenously applied TGFβ1 on both cell migration and CAP expression (Siegenthaler and Miller, 2004, 2005b). In vitro studies of dissociated cortical cells and neural tumorgenic cells describe a similar effect of TGFβ1 and ethanol on a specific CAP, nCAM. nCAM expression is increased with TGFβ1 treatment alone but is reduced to control levels by combined treatment with ethanol (Luo and Miller, 1999; Miller and Luo, 2002a, 2002b). Collectively, these studies show that (1) ethanol interferes with TGFβ1-mediated promotion of cell migration and (2) it may do so by blocking TGFβ1-dependent increases in expression of nCAM and other CAPs.

BMP signaling is involved in the initiation of cell migration in the developing cerebral cortex (Li et al., 1998). BMP-4 specifically is expressed by cells about to begin migration (e.g., at the ventricular surface). Although the effect of ethanol on BMP-mediated initiation of migration is not established per se, ethanol does block BMP-4-induced cell adhesion among cultured neuroglioblastoma cells (Wilkemeyer et al., 1999). Presumably, such inhibition may be involved in delay of the initiation of neuronal migration.

BDNF promotes the initiation of glial-guided migration (Borghesani et al., 2002). Incidentally, the endogenous BDNF system is perturbed by ethanol. Perinatal ethanol exposure down-regulates BDNF mRNA and its receptor, trkB, in the developing cerebellum (Heaton et al., 2000; Light et al., 2001) and olfactory bulb (Maier et al., 1999). A similar down-regulation of BDNF protein accompanied by a ethanol-induced decrease in BDNF signaling is evident in prenatal cortex (Climent et al., 2002). An ethanol-induced reduction in BDNF activity in the developing brain likely affects BDNF-regulated processes including the initiation of neuronal migration.

SUMMARY AND CONCLUSIONS

Neuronal migration is a unique and critical component of neural development. It provides a bridge between the birth of a cell and its proper integration into an evolving structure. NMDs are caused by breakdowns in the commencement, completion, and/or cessation of neuronal migration. The NMDs detected in cases of FAS are likely caused by ethanol interfering with each phase of neuronal migration.

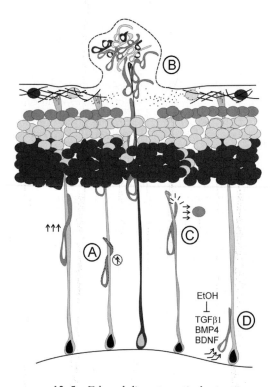

Ethanol-induced defects in neuronal migration have serious consequences for downstream developmental events. For example, exposure to ethanol during the period of neuronal migration can cause neurons to land in the wrong cortical layers (Miller, 1986, 1987). Despite this, the neurons may retain their destined phenotype, for example, as corticospinal (Miller, 1987) or callosal (Miller, 1997) projection neurons. As the cell bodies are distributed in inappropriate locations, they integrate into the synaptic web incorrectly (Al-Rabiai and Miller, 1989). Consequently, abnormalities in cortical metabolism and activity occur (Vingan et al., 1986; Miller and Dow-Edwards, 1988, 1993). Flawed synaptic connections due to heterotopias can cause a myriad of problems, the foremost being epilepsy (Chevassus-au-Louis and Represa, 1999), a neurological symptom prevalent in children with FAS (Burd et al., 2003).

Over the last two decades, studies of neuronal migration have identified a number of possible mechanisms for ethanol-induced defects in migration. Ethanol alters both the microenvironment encountered by the migrating neuron (e.g., radial glial fibers, CAPs, ECM proteins, and growth factors) and the motility of neurons within that environment (e.g., CAPs and cytoskeletal proteins) (Fig. 13–5). The diversity of cellular pathways affected by ethanol speaks to the complexity of ethanol-induced disturbances in neuronal migration.

FIGURE 13–5 Ethanol disrupts cortical migration at many levels. **A.** Ethanol reduces the rate of neuronal migration in the developing cerebral cortex. Migrating neurons depend on proper cell adhesion (e.g., cell adhesion molecules and integrins) and cytoskeletal reorganization (e.g., microtubules and actin) for motility along glial guides. Ethanol-dependent increases in cell adhesion protein expression and abnormal cytoskeletal organization are a likely cause of reduced cortical cell motility. **B.** Heterotopia formation has been linked to disruptions in both the extracellular matrix components of the pial membrane (PM) and their organization by integrin receptors. The resulting "holes" in the PM and adjacent MZ permit overmigration of neurons that would normally stop and incorporate into the cortical plate. In particular, absence of the stop-signal reelin within the breaches likely contributes to heterotopia formation. Evidence of radial glial fibers coursing into the heterotopia may mean that migrating neurons migrate into the wart on overextended glial fibers. **C.** Ethanol exposure causes premature transformation of radial glia into astrocytes. Neurons still migrating on these retracting fibers would be stranded inappropriately in deeper cortical layers. This phenomenon may explain the appearance of layer II/III neurons are found in layers IV, V, and VI in ethanol-exposed brains. **D.** Various growth factors (e.g., TGFβ1, BMP-4, and BDNF) are involved in

Abbreviations

BDNF   brain-derived neurotrophic factor

BMP   bone morphogenic protein

CAM   cell adhesion molecule

CAP   cell adhesion protein

CP   cortical plate

ECM   extracellular matrix

FAS   fetal alcohol syndrome

G   gestation day

IZ   intermediate zone

the initiation of neuronal migration. Ethanol disrupts the normal function of these growth factors. The delay in initiation of migration seen with ethanol exposure likely results from inhibition of growth factor–mediated activities.

nCAM   neural cell adhesion molecule

NMD   neuronal migration disorder

NMDA   N-methyl-D-aspartate

PM   pial membrane

TGF   transforming growth factor

References

Allansson L, Khatibi S, Olsson T, Hansson E (2001) Acute ethanol exposure induces [Ca²⁺]i transients, cell swelling and transformation of actin cytoskeleton in astroglial primary cultures. J Neurochem 76: 472–479.

Al-Rabiai S, Miller MW (1989) Effect of prenatal exposure to ethanol on the ultrastructure of layer V of mature rat somatosensory cortex. J Neurocytol 18: 711–729.

Andermann F (2000) Cortical dysplasias and epilepsy: a review of the architectonic, clinical, and seizure patterns. Adv Neurol 84:479–496.

Angevine JB Jr, Sidman RL (1961) Autoradiographic study of cell migration during histiogenesis of cerebral cortex in the mouse. Nature 192:766–768.

Anton ES, Cameron RS, Rakic P (1996) Role of neuronglial junctional domain proteins in the maintenance and termination of neuronal migration across the embryonic cerebral wall. J Neurosci 16: 2283–2293.

Anton ES, Kreidberg JA, Rakic P (1999) Distinct functions of α3 and α(v) integrin receptors in neuronal migration and laminar organization of the cerebral cortex. Neuron 22:277–289.

Bautista AP (1995) Chronic alcohol intoxication enhances the expression of CD18 adhesion molecules on rat neutrophils and release of a chemotactic factor by Kupffer cells. Alcohol Clin Exp Res 19: 285–290.

Bearer CF, Swick AR, O'Riordan MA, Cheng G (1999) Ethanol inhibits L1-mediated neurite outgrowth in postnatal rat cerebellar granule cells. J Biol Chem 274:13264–13270.

Berry M, Rogers AW (1965) The migration of neuroblasts in the developing cerebral cortex. J Anat 99: 691–709.

Blackshear P, Silver J, Nairn A, Sulik KK, Squier MV, Stumpo D, Tuttle J (1997) Widespread neuronal ectopia associated with secondary defects in cerebrocortical chondroiten sulfate proteoglycans and basal lamina in MARCKS-deficient mice. Exp Neurol 145:46–61.

Borges S, Lewis PD (1983) The effect of ethanol on the cellular composition of the cerebellum. Neuropathol Appl Neurobiol 9:53–60.

Borghesani PR, Peyrin JM, Klein R, Rubin J, Carter AR, Schwartz PM, Luster A, Corfas G, Segal RA (2002) BDNF stimulates migration of cerebellar granule cells. Development 129:1435–1442.

Burd L, Cotsonas-Hassler TM, Martsolf JT, Kerbeshian J (2003) Recognition and management of fetal alcohol syndrome. Neurotoxicol Teratol 25:681–688.

Charness ME, Safran RM, Perides G (1994) Ethanol inhibits neural cell–cell adhesion. J Biol Chem 269: 9304–9309.

Chevassus-au-Louis N, Represa A (1999) The right neuron at the wrong place: biology of heterotopic neurons in cortical neuronal migration disorders, with special reference to associated pathologies. Cell Mol Life Sci 55:1206–1215.

Chuong CM, Crossin KL, Edelman GM (1987) Sequential expression and differential function of multiple adhesion molecules during the formation of cerebellar cortical layers. J Cell Biol 104: 331–342.

Clarren SK, Alvord EC Jr, Sumi SM, Streissguth AP, Smith DW (1978) Brain malformations related to prenatal exposure to ethanol. J Pediatr 92:64–67.

Clegg DO, Wingerd KL, Hikita ST, Tolhurst EC (2003) Integrins in the development, function and dysfunction of the nervous system. Front Biosci 8: 723–750.

Climent E, Pascual M, Renau-Piqueras J, Guerri C (2002) Ethanol exposure enhances cell death in the developing cerebral cortex: role of brain-derived neurotrophic factor and its signaling pathways. J Neurosci Res 68:213–225.

Costell M, Gustafsson E, Aszodi A, Morgelin M, Bloch W, Hunziker E, Addicks K, Timpl R, Fassler R (1999) Perlecan maintains the integrity of cartilage and some basement membranes. J Cell Biol 147: 1109–1122.

Crome L (1956) Pachygyria. J Pathol Bacteriol 71: 335–352.

Culican SM, Baumrind NL, Yamamoto M, Pearlman AL (1990) Cortical radial glia: identification in tissue culture and evidence for their transformation to astrocytes. J Neurosci 10:684–692.

D'Arcangelo G, Miao GG, Chen SC, Soares HD, Morgan JI, Curran T (1995) A protein related to extracellular matrix proteins deleted in the mouse mutant reeler. Nature 374:719–723.

Dulabon L, Olson EC, Taglienti MG, Eisenhuth S, McGrath B, Walsh CA, Kreidberg JA, Anton ES (2000) Reelin binds α₃β₁ integrin and inhibits neuronal migration. Neuron 27:33–44.

Edmondson JC, Hatten ME (1987) Glial-guided granule neuron migration in vitro: a high-resolution time-lapse video microscopic study. J Neurosci 7: 1928–1934.

Edmondson JC, Liem RK, Kuster JE, Hatten ME (1988) Astrotactin: a novel neuronal cell surface antigen that mediates neuron–astroglial interactions in cerebellar microcultures. J Cell Biol 106:505–517.

Eksioglu YZ, Scheffer IE, Cardenas P, Knoll J, DiMario F, Ramsby G, Berg M, Kamuro K, Berkovic SF, Duyk GM, Parisi J, Huttenlocher PR, Walsh CA (1996) Periventricular heterotopia: an X-linked dominant epilepsy locus causing aberrant cerebral cortical development. Neuron 16:77–87.

Flanders KC, Ludecke G, Engels S, Cissel DS, Roberts AB, Kondaiah P, Lafyatis R, Sporn MB, Unsicker K (1991) Localization and actions of transforming growth factor-β in the embryonic nervous system. Development 113:183–191.

Friede R (1989) Developmental Neuropathology. Berlin, Springer.

Fukumitsu H, Furukawa Y, Tsusaka M, Kinukawa H, Nitta A, Nomoto H, Mima T, Furukawa S (1998) Simultaneous expression of brain-derived neurotrophic factor and neurotrophin-3 in Cajal-Retzius, subplate and ventricular progenitor cells during early development stages of the rat cerebral cortex. Neuroscience 84:115–127.

Georges-Labouesse E, Mark M, Messaddeq N, Gansmuller A (1998) Essential role of α_6 integrins in cortical and retinal lamination. Curr Biol 8:983–986.

Gleeson JG, Lin PT, Flanagan LA, Walsh CA (1999) Doublecortin is a microtubule-associated protein and is expressed widely by migrating neurons. Neuron 23:257–271.

Graus-Porta D, Blaess S, Senften M, Littlewood-Evans A, Damsky C, Huang Z, Orban P, Klein R, Schittny JC, Muller U (2001) β_1-class integrins regulate the development of laminae and folia in the cerebral and cerebellar cortex. Neuron 31:367–379.

Guasch RM, Tomas M, Minambres R, Valles S, Renau-Piqueras J, Guerri C (2003) RhoA and lysophosphatidic acid are involved in the actin cytoskeleton reorganization of astrocytes exposed to ethanol. J Neurosci Res 72:487–502.

Hack I, Bancila M, Loulier K, Carroll P, Cremer H (2002) Reelin is a detachment signal in tangential chain-migration during postnatal neurogenesis. Nat Neurosci 5:939–945.

Halfter W, Sucai D, Yip Y, Willem M, Mayer U (2002) A critical function of the pial basement membrane in cortical histogenesis. J Neurosci 22:6029–6040.

Hassler JA, Moran DJ (1986a) The effects of ethanol on embryonic actin: a possible role in teratogenesis. Experientia 42:575–577.

—— (1986b) Effects of ethanol on the cytoskeleton of migrating and differentiating neural crest cells: possible role in teratogenesis. J Craniofac Genet Dev Biol Suppl 2:129–136.

Heaton MB, Mitchell JJ, Paiva M, Walker DW (2000) Ethanol-induced alterations in the expression of neurotrophic factors in the developing rat central nervous system. Dev Brain Res 121:97–107.

Heaton MB, Swanson DJ, Paiva M, Walker DW (1996) Influence of prenatal ethanol exposure on cholinergic development in the rat striatum. J Comp Neurol 364:113–120.

Hirai K, Yoshioka H, Kihara M, Hasegawa K, Sakamoto T, Sawada T, Fushiki S (1999a) Inhibiting neuronal migration by blocking NMDA receptors in the embryonic rat cerebral cortex: a tissue culture study. Dev Brain Res 114:63–67.

Hirai K, Yoshioka H, Kihara M, Hasegawa K, Sawada T, Fushiki S (1999b) Effects of ethanol on neuronal migration and neural cell adhesion molecules in the embryonic rat cerebral cortex: a tissue culture study. Dev Brain Res 118:205–210.

Hirotsune S, Takahara T, Sasaki N, Hirose K, Yoshiki A, Ohashi T, Kusakabe M, Murakami Y, Muramatsu M, Watanabe S, Nakao K, Katski M, Hayashizaki Y (1995) The reeler gene encodes a protein with an EGF-like motif expressed by pioneer neurons. Nat Genet 10:77–83.

Juliano RL (2002) Signal transduction by cell adhesion receptors and the cytoskeleton: functions of integrins, cadherins, selectins, and immunoglobulin-superfamily members. Annu Rev Pharmacol Toxicol 42:283–323.

Kato M, Dobyns WB (2003) Lissencephaly and the molecular basis of neuronal migration. Hum Mol Genet 12 (Spec No 1): R89–96.

Komatsu S, Sakata-Haga H, Sawada K, Hisano S, Fukui Y (2001) Prenatal exposure to ethanol induces leptomeningeal heterotopia in the cerebral cortex of the rat fetus. Acta Neuropathol 101:22–26.

Komuro H, Rakic P (1992) Selective role of N-type calcium channels in neuronal migration. Science 257: 806–809.

—— (1993) Modulation of neuronal migration by NMDA receptors. Science 260:95–97.

Konovalov HV, Kovetsky NS, Bobryshev YV, Ashwell KW (1997) Disorders of brain development in the progeny of mothers who used alcohol during pregnancy. Early Hum Dev 48:153–166.

Kornguth SE, Rutledge JJ, Sunderland E, Siegel F, Carlson I, Smollens J, Juhl U, Young B (1979) Impeded cerebellar development and reduced serum thyroxine levels associated with fetal alcohol intoxication. Brain Res 177:347–360.

Kotkoskie LA, Norton S (1988) Prenatal brain malformations following acute ethanol exposure in the rat. Alcohol Clin Exp Res 12:831–836.

Kumari M (2001) Differential effects of chronic ethanol treatment on N-methyl-D-aspartate R1 splice variants in fetal cortical neurons. J Biol Chem 276: 29764–29771.

Lambert de Rouvroit C, Goffinet AM (2001) Neuronal migration. Mech Dev 105:47–56.

Lawson MA, Maxfield FR (1995) $Ca^{(2+)}$– and calcineurin-dependent recycling of an integrin to the front of migrating neutrophils. Nature 377: 75–79.

Li W, Cogswell CA, LoTurco JJ (1998) Neuronal differentiation of precursors in the neocortical ventricular zone is triggered by BMP. J Neurosci 18:8853–8862.

Light KE, Ge Y, Belcher SM (2001) Early postnatal ethanol exposure selectively decreases BDNF and truncated TrkB-T2 receptor mRNA expression in the rat cerebellum. Mol Brain Res 93: 46–55.

Lovinger DM, White G, Weight FF (1989) Ethanol inhibits NMDA-activated ion current in hippocampal neurons. Science 243:1721–1724.

—— (1990) NMDA receptor–mediated synaptic excitation selectively inhibited by ethanol in hippocampal slice from adult rat. J Neurosci 10: 1372–1379.

Luo J, Miller MW (1999) Transforming growth factor β1–regulated cell proliferation and expression of neural cell adhesion molecule in B104 neuroblastoma cells: differential effects of ethanol. J Neurochem 72:2286–2293.

Maier SE, Cramer JA, West JR, Sohrabji F (1999) Alcohol exposure during the first two trimesters equivalent alters granule cell number and neurotrophin expression in the developing rat olfactory bulb. J Neurobiol 41:414–423.

Marin O, Rubenstein JL (2003) Cell migration in the forebrain. Annu Rev Neurosci 26:441–483.

Marin-Padilla M (1996) Developmental neuropathology and impact of perinatal brain damage: hemorrhagic lesions of neocortex. J Neuropathol Exp Neurol 55:758–773.

—— (1998) Cajal-Retzius cells and the development of the neocortex. Trends Neurosci 21:64–71.

Marks PW, Maxfield FR (1990) Transient increases in cytosolic free calcium appear to be required for the migration of adherent human neutrophils. J Cell Biol 110:43–52.

Miller MW (1986) Effects of alcohol on the generation and migration of cerebral cortical neurons. Science 233:1308–1311.

—— (1987) Effect of prenatal exposure to alcohol on the distribution and time of origin of corticospinal neurons in the rat. J Comp Neurol 257: 372–382.

—— (1989) Effects of prenatal exposure to ethanol on neocortical development: II. Cell proliferation in the ventricular and subventricular zones of the rat. J Comp Neurol 287:326–338.

—— (1993) Migration of cortical neurons is altered by gestational exposure to ethanol. Alcohol Clin Exp Res 17:304–314.

—— (1997) Effects of prenatal exposure to ethanol on callosal projection neurons in rat somatosensory cortex. Brain Res 766:121–128.

—— (2003) Expression of transforming growth factor-β in developing rat cerebral cortex: effects of prenatal exposure to ethanol. J Comp Neurol 460:410–424.

Miller MW, Dow-Edwards DL (1988) Structural and metabolic alterations in rat cerebral cortex induced by prenatal exposure to ethanol. Brain Res 474: 316–326.

—— (1993) Vibrissal stimulation affects glucose utilization in the trigeminal/somatosensory system of normal rats and rats prenatally exposed to ethanol. J Comp Neurol 335:283–284.

Miller MW, Luo J (2002a) Effects of ethanol and transforming growth factor β (TGFβ) on neuronal proliferation and nCAM expression. Alcohol Clin Exp Res 26:1281–1285.

—— (2002b) Effects of ethanol and basic fibroblast growth factor on the transforming growth factor-β1 regulated proliferation of cortical astrocytes and C6 astrocytoma cells. Alcohol Clin Exp Res 26: 671–676.

Miller MW, Nowakowski RS (1988) Use of bromodeoxyuridine-immunohistochemistry to examine the proliferation, migration and time of origin of cells in the central nervous system. Brain Res 457: 44–52.

Miller MW, Robertson S (1993) Prenatal exposure to ethanol alters the postnatal development and transformation of radial glia to astrocytes in the cortex. J Comp Neurol 337:253–266.

Miñana R, Climent E, Barettino D, Segui JM, Renau-Piqueras J, Guerri C (2000) Alcohol exposure alters the expression pattern of neural cell adhesion molecules during brain development. J Neurochem 75:954–964.

Mochida GH, Walsh CA (2004) Genetic basis of developmental malformations of the cerebral cortex. Arch Neurol 61:637–640.

Mooney SM, Siegenthaler JA, Miller MW (2004) Ethanol induces heterotopias in organotypic cultures of rat cerebral cortex. Cereb Cortex 14:1071–1080.

Ogawa M, Miyata T, Nakajima K, Yagyu K, Seike M, Ikenaka K, Yamamoto H, Mikoshiba K (1995) The reeler gene–associated antigen on Cajal–Retzius neurons is a crucial molecule for laminar organization of cortical neurons. Neuron 14:899–912.

Ohmiya M, Shudai T, Nitta A, Nomoto H, Furukawa Y, Furukawa S (2002) Brain-derived neurotrophic factor alters cell migration of particular progenitors in the developing mouse cerebral cortex. Neurosci Lett 317:21–24.

Palecek SP, Loftus JC, Ginsberg MH, Lauffenburger DA, Horwitz AF (1997) Integrin–ligand binding properties govern cell migration speed through cell-substratum adhesiveness. Nature 385:537–540.

Panicker AK, Buhusi M, Thelen K, Maness PF (2003) Cellular signalling mechanisms of neural cell adhesion molecules. Front Biosci 8:d900–911.

Pearlman AL, Sheppard AM (1996) Extracellular matrix in early cortical development. Prog Brain Res 108: 117–134.

Pilz D, Stoodley N, Golden JA (2002) Neuronal migration, cerebral cortical development, and cerebral cortical anomalies. J Neuropathol Exp Neurol 61: 1–11.

Quesada A, Prada FA, Espinar A, Genis-Galvez JM (1990a) Effect of ethanol on the cerebellar cortex of the chick embryo. Histol Histopathol 5: 315–324.

—— (1990b) Effect of ethanol on the morphohistogenesis and differentiation of cerebellar granule cells in the chick embryo. Alcohol 7:419–428.

Rakic P (1971) Neuron–glia relationship during granule cell migration in developing cerebellar cortex. A Golgi and electronmicroscopic study in *Macaca rhesus*. J Comp Neurol 141:283–312.

—— (1972) Mode of cell migration to the superficial layers of fetal monkey neocortex. J Comp Neurol 145:61–83.

—— (1974) Neurons in rhesus monkey visual cortex: systematic relation between time of origin and eventual disposition. Science 183:425–427.

Rakic P, Bourgeois JP, Goldman-Rakic PS (1994) Synaptic development of the cerebral cortex: implications for learning, memory, and mental illness. Prog Brain Res 102:227–243.

Ramanathan R, Wilkemeyer MF, Mittal B, Perides G, Charness ME (1996) Alcohol inhibits cell–cell adhesion mediated by human L1. J Cell Biol 133: 381–390.

Rivas RJ, Hatten ME (1995) Motility and cytoskeletal organization of migrating cerebellar granule neurons. J Neurosci 15:981–989.

Roebuck TM, Mattson SN, Riley EP (1998) A review of the neuroanatomical findings in children with fetal alcohol syndrome or prenatal exposure to alcohol. Alcohol Clin Exp Res 22:339–344.

Ronn LC, Hartz BP, Bock E (1998) The neural cell adhesion molecule (NCAM) in development and plasticity of the nervous system. Exp Gerontol 33: 853–864.

Saito Y, Murayama S, Kawai M, Nakano I (1999) Breached cerebral glia limitans–basal lamina complex in Fukuyama-type congenital muscular dystrophy. Acta Neuropathol 98:330–336.

Sakata-Haga H, Sawada K, Hisano S, Fukui Y (2001) Abnormalities of cerebellar foliation in rats prenatally exposed to ethanol. Acta Neuropathol 102:36–40.

Sapir T, Elbaum M, Reiner O (1997) Reduction of microtubule catastrophe events by LIS1, platelet-activating factor acetylhydrolase subunit. EMBO J 16:6977–6984.

Sari Y, Powrozek T, Zhou FC (2001) Alcohol deters the outgrowth of serotonergic neurons at midgestation. J Biomed Sci 8:119–125.

Schaffert CS, Sorrell MF, Tuma DJ (2001) Expression and cytoskeletal association of integrin subunits is selectively increased in rat perivenous hepatocytes after chronic ethanol administration. Alcohol Clin Exp Res 25:1749–1757.

Schmechel DE, Rakic P (1979) A Golgi study of radial glial cells in developing monkey telencephalon: morphogenesis and transformation into astrocytes. Anat Embryol 156:115–152.

Schmid RS, Anton ES (2003) Role of integrins in the development of the cerebral cortex. Cereb Cortex 13: 219–224.

Seki T, Arai Y (1991) Expression of highly polysialylated NCAM in the neocortex and piriform cortex of the developing and the adult rat. Anat Embryol 184: 395–401.

Shetty AK, Phillips DE (1992) Effects of prenatal ethanol exposure on the development of Bergmann glia and astrocytes in the rat cerebellum: an immunohistochemical study. J Comp Neurol 321: 19–32.

Siegenthaler JA, Miller MW (2005a) Transforming growth factor β1 promotes cell cycle exit through the cyclin-dependent kinase inhibitor P21 in the developing cerebral cortex. J Neurosci 25: 8627–8636.

—— (2005b) Ethanol disrupts cell cycle regulation in developing rat cortex: interaction with transforming growth factor β1. J Neurochem.

—— (2004) Transforming growth factor β1 modulates cell migration in rat cortex: effects of ethanol. Cereb Cortex 14:791–802.

Sievers J, Phlemann F, Gude S, Berry M (1994) Meningeal cells organize the superficial glial limitans of the cerebellum and produce both the interstitial matrix and basement membrane. J Neurocytol 23:135–149.

Soda T, Nakashima R, Watanabe D, Nakajima K, Pastan I, Nakanishi S (2003) Segregation and coactivation of developing neocortical layer 1 neurons. J Neurosci 23:6272–6279.

Takeda S, Kondo M, Sasaki J, Kurahashi H, Kano H, Arai K, Misaki K, Fukui T, Kobayashi K, Tachikawa M, Imamura M, Nakamura Y, Shimizu T, Murakami T, Sunada Y, Fujikado T, Matsumura K, Terashima T, Toda T (2003) Fukutin is required for maintenance of muscle integrity, cortical histiogenesis and normal eye development. Hum Mol Genet 12:1449–1459.

Tomas M, Lazaro-Dieguez F, Duran JM, Marin P, Renau-Piqueras J, Egea G (2003) Protective effects of lysophosphatidic acid (LPA) on chronic ethanol-induced injuries to the cytoskeleton and on glucose uptake in rat astrocytes. J Neurochem 87:220–229.

Vingan RD, Dow-Edwards DL, Riley EP (1986) Cerebral metabolic alterations in rats following prenatal alcohol exposure: a deoxyglucose study. Alcohol Clin Exp Res 10:22–26.

Voigt T (1989) Development of glial cells in the cerebral wall of ferrets: direct tracing of their transformation from radial glia into astrocytes. J Comp Neurol 289:74–88.

Wilkemeyer MF, Menkari CE, Charness ME (2002a) Novel antagonists of alcohol inhibition of L1-mediated cell adhesion: multiple mechanisms of action. Mol Pharmacol 62:1053–1060.

Wilkemeyer MF, Menkari CE, Spong CY, Charness ME (2002b) Peptide antagonists of ethanol inhibition of l1-mediate cell–cell adhesion. J Pharmacol Exp Ther 303:110–116.

Wilkemeyer MF, Pajerski M, Charness ME (1999) Alcohol inhibition of cell adhesion in BMP-treated NG108-15 cells. Alcohol Clin Exp Res 23:1711–1720.

Wilkemeyer MF, Sebastian AB, Smith SA, Charness ME (2000) Antagonists of alcohol inhibition of cell adhesion. Proc Natl Acad Sci USA 97:3690–3695.

Williams RS, Swisher CN, Jennings M, Ambler M, Caviness VS Jr (1984) Cerebro-ocular dysgenesis (Walker-Warburg syndrome): neuropathologic and etiologic analysis. Neurology 34:1531–1541.

Wisniewski K, Dambska M, Sher JH, Qazi Q (1983) A clinical neuropathological study of the fetal alcohol syndrome. Neuropediatrics 14:197–201.

Yoon Y, Torok N, Krueger E, Oswald B, McNiven MA (1998) Ethanol-induced alterations of the microtubule cytoskeleton in hepatocytes. Am J Physiol 274:G757–766.

Zhou FC, Sari Y, Zhang JK, Goodlett CR, Li T-K (2001) Prenatal alcohol exposure retards the migration and development of serotonin neurons in fetal C57BL mice. Brain Res Dev Brain Res 126:147–155.

14

Effects of Ethanol on Mechanisms Regulating Neuronal Process Outgrowth

Tara A. Lindsley

Establishment of normal neural circuitry in the central nervous system (CNS) requires spatial and temporal control of the outgrowth of neurites. This outgrowth and the specification of axons and dendrites are among the earliest events in the development of postmigratory neurons.

Three decades of research show that exposure to ethanol disrupts the development of axons and dendrites and alters neural circuitry in diverse brain regions. The primary actions of ethanol on developing neurons are still largely unknown, however, in part, because the endogenous mechanisms and extracellular signaling pathways regulating process outgrowth and guidance during normal development are not fully understood (see Chapter 4). For comprehensive descriptions of effects of ethanol on the microscopic structure of the developing brain, the reader is referred to reviews by Pentney and Miller (1992) and Berman and Hannigan (2000), respectively.

The present chapter summarizes the effects of ethanol on the outgrowth and maturation of dendrites and axons, focusing on CNS neurons developing in vivo or in vitro. The selected observations highlight both well-established and emerging insights regarding the effects of ethanol on axonal and dendritic growth. Although not exhaustive, one section describes how recent advances in developmental neural cell biology are informing work aimed at understanding the mechanisms underlying disruption of neuronal development by ethanol.

EFFECTS OF ETHANOL ON DEVELOPMENT OF DENDRITES

In Vivo Studies

The complex and characteristic shape of a dendritic arbor, where neurons receive and integrate input from multiple synaptic partners, is a critical determinant of the electrophysiological properties of a neuron. Ethanol-induced changes in dendritic morphology could severely affect neuronal function. Results of morphometric studies in rodents exposed to ethanol during development suggest that regions of the brain are not equivalently affected by ethanol. Even within a brain region vulnerable to ethanol-induced changes in dendritic shape, the specific parameters of the dendritic arbor (e.g., length of dendritic segments, number of primary dendrites, or branching) may be differentially affected.

The expanse of dendritic arbors is determined by the number and length of its primary dendrites (which extend directly from the cell body) and dendritic branches. In young mice exposed to ethanol pre- and perinatally, pyramidal neurons in the CA1 region of the hippocampus have shorter basal dendrites, but the length of apical dendrites is unaffected (Davies and Smith, 1981; Smith and Davies, 1990). Parallel results have been reported for the dendrites of pyramidal neurons in the sensorimotor cortex (Hammer and Scheibel, 1981; Fabregues et al., 1985). The number of primary dendrites and the extent of their branching are also decreased in other areas including chick spinal cord serotonergic neurons (Mendelson and Driskill, 1996), rat dopaminergic neurons of the substantia nigra (Shetty et al., 1993), and rat cerebellar granule neurons (Smith and Davies, 1986). That ethanol may differentially affect distinct parameters of dendritic morphology is a potentially important observation given evidence that the number, length, and branching of dendrites may be independently regulated (Scott and Luo, 2001).

Although many reports emphasize the inhibitory effects of prenatal ethanol exposure on the size of dendritic arbors in various regions of immature rodent brain, studies indicate that ethanol can *increase* the size of dendritic arbors. For example, ethanol increases the number and length of apical and basilar dendritic branches of callosal projection neurons in the rat (Qiang et al., 2002). The stimulatory effect of ethanol on dendrites appears to involve N-methyl-D-aspartate (NMDA) receptors, since dendrites are normal in ethanol-exposed transgenic mice with deletion of the NR1 subtype of NMDA receptor (Deng and Elberger, 2003).

Notably, the data cited above exemplify effects of developmental exposure to ethanol observed when neonatal or immature animals are examined. In some cases, however, when prenatal ethanol-exposed animals are examined at other young ages, or as adults, areas that had stunted dendrites are found to be either normal (Pentney et al., 1984) or have significantly larger and more complex dendrites than controls (Miller et al., 1990). These data are generally believed to indicate that ethanol-induced reduction in dendritic arbor size reflects delayed dendritic development or that initial inhibition of growth is followed by an abnormal compensatory growth response when the animal is no longer exposed to ethanol. Another possibility is that ethanol interferes with dendritic pruning, a process associated with a glutamatergic–NMDA receptor mechanism (Kozlowski et al., 1997). This concept is supported by evidence that ethanol can cause axonal hypertrophy as well (see Effects of Ethanol on Development of Axons).

That dendritic morphology could change so significantly is not surprising, given that dendrite development is a highly dynamic process. Dendritic growth in vivo is characterized by extensive remodeling, as exemplified by the postnatal retraction of the apical dendrites of some layer V callosal projection neurons, from cortical layer I to layer IV (Koester and O'Leary, 1992). Thus, assessment of prenatal ethanol effects on dendrites over extended development, and after withdrawal from ethanol, is important. More studies are needed to explore the possibility that ethanol affects the cellular events whereby exuberant early growth is followed by partial pruning, or initially stunted development is later reversed by compensatory growth.

Dendritic remodeling can be directly visualized by time-lapse imaging, as performed on neurons from frog optic tectum, in which rapid addition and retraction of new branches and remodeling of existing branches, as well as the differential regulation of these events during maturation, has been documented (Wu et al., 1999). It is now possible to image neurons in complex environments over extended time periods (Danuser and Waterman-Storer, 2003). Such time-lapse studies could help distinguish whether ethanol delays or alters one or more features of dendritic growth in the intact developing brain (e.g., outgrowth, elongation, branching, or remodeling).

In Vitro Studies

Several neuron culture systems have been used to examine the effects of ethanol on developing neurons. Some cell culture models are poorly suited to exploring effects of ethanol specifically on dendrites or axons. For example, in some dissociated cultures,

(1) the neurons are too dense or there are various cell types present, limiting both morphometric and molecular analyses; (2) the neurons do not survive or develop long enough for researchers to investigate the persistence of ethanol effects or the capacity of the neuron to recover normal morphology, or (3) the neurons are not the types sensitive to ethanol damage in vivo. Not surprisingly, an inconsistent picture of ethanol effects on neuromorphogenesis has emerged. Some reports show that ethanol inhibits process outgrowth (Dow and Riopelle, 1985; Kentroti and Vernadakis, 1991; Heaton et al., 1994; Saunders et al., 1995; Bearer et al., 1999), whereas others report a stimulatory effect (Messing et al., 1991; Wooten and Ewald, 1991; Roivainen et al., 1993; Zou et al., 1993). The following discussion focuses on studies for which there is reasonable certainty that the processes being studied are either dendrites or axons.

Unique characteristics of low-density cultures of fetal rat hippocampal pyramidal neurons make them a valuable model for examining the molecular mechanism(s) by which ethanol interferes with dendritic and axonal growth. These cultures, detailed in Chapter 4, are the most extensively characterized primary culture of mammalian CNS neurons, and numerous studies have been conducted comparing them to pyramidal neurons developing in situ (Craig and Banker, 1994; Goslin et al., 1998). Neurons in these cultures are nearly homogeneous; typically 94% are readily distinguished as pyramidal neurons. They live for up to 4 weeks, undergoing stereotypical, nearly synchronous development, each neuron having a single axon and several dendrites of well-defined shape and characteristic molecular constituents. The cultured neurons form synaptic relationships that are representative of those normally present in the hippocampus (e.g., Schaffer collaterals interconnecting pyramidal neurons). This pattern parallels hippocampal development in situ, which is largely complete by the end of the third postnatal week (Minkwitz and Holz, 1975). Moreover, the developmental progression that occurs during the elaboration of axons, dendrites, and synapses can be readily quantified by time-lapse microscopy of individual neurons (Dotti et al., 1988; Goslin and Banker, 1989).

Some of the inhibitory effects of ethanol on dendrite development are supported by results from studies using these cultures, in which definitive dendrites can be identified by their characteristic proximal–distal taper and by immunolocalization of microtubule-associated protein (MAP) 2, a protein distributed in the somatodendritic compartment (Goslin et al., 1998). In hippocampal cultures, quantitative morphometric analyses of MAP2-stained, pyramidal neurons 6 days in vitro (DIV), exposed continuously to 43–87 mM ethanol, show concentration-dependent decreases in total dendritic length, in the number of primary dendrites and dendritic branches, and in the length of individual dendrites (Yanni and Lindsley, 2000; Yanni et al., 2002). Ethanol also decreases the number of synapses formed by these neurons (Yanni and Lindsley, 2000). Nevertheless, synaptic density is not affected. Hence, it is likely secondary to effects on dendrites and not a direct effect on synapse formation per se. Delaying the addition of ethanol until 1 DIV, when most neurons have developed an axon, results in significantly shorter, less-branched dendrites at 6 DIV, relative to the neurons exposed to ethanol at the time of plating (Lindsley et al., 2002). Thus the maturity of hippocampal neurons influences their vulnerability to morphoregulatory effects of ethanol.

The duration of ethanol exposure and the timing of withdrawal have variable effects on dendrite development in hippocampal cultures (Lindsley and Clarke, 2004). When ethanol is added to the medium shortly after plating, continuous exposure for up to 14 DIV decreases the length and number of dendrites formed, but it has no effect on neuron survival. When ethanol exposure is limited to the first day post-plating and withdrawal occurs before dendrites elongate, individual dendrites achieve normal length by 14 DIV. The arbors, however, are still smaller than controls because of a persistent reduction in the number of primary dendrites. These findings are consistent with in vivo observations that inhibitory effects of prenatal ethanol on dendritic length may not endure after withdrawal from ethanol (Pentney et al., 1984; Lopez-Tejero et al., 1986), but the effect on the number of primary dendrites may persist even after limited exposure to ethanol (Durand et al., 1989).

The addition of ethanol at any time point prior to 6 DIV does not affect neuron survival. In contrast, addition of ethanol on Day 6 (after rapid growth of dendrites and synapses has begun) triggers cell death, despite the shorter duration of ethanol exposure (Lindsley et al., 2002). Developmental stage–dependent sensitivity to ethanol-induced cell death has also been reported for cerebellar neurons in vivo and in vitro (Goodlett and Johnson, 1999) and may involve the nitric oxide–cyclic guanosine 5′-monophosphate–dependent protein kinase pathway (Bonthius et al., 2004). Elucidating the mechanisms by which the timing of ethanol exposure influences the nature and severity of its effects on dendrites and on neuronal survival is a goal of ongoing research.

EFFECTS OF ETHANOL ON DEVELOPMENT OF AXONS

In Vivo Studies

The effect of prenatal ethanol on axonal growth in various brain regions is less well characterized than its effects on dendrites. It is most often reported as an overall hypertrophy of axons from projection neurons, such as those comprising the corticospinal tract and the mossy fiber tract in the hippocampus. This hypertrophic effect of ethanol is not as consistently observed in axon tracts that cross the midline in the brain, such as the corpus callosum and anterior commissure.

Axons of Projection Neurons

Prenatal exposure to ethanol markedly alters the number and distribution of axons of projection neurons in various brain regions. In most cases, changes in the number of axons cannot be attributed to corresponding changes in the number of neurons in the brain region from which the tract extends. For example, prenatal exposure to ethanol increases the number of neurons projecting from rat somatosensory cortex to the spinal cord (Miller, 1987), the number of axons in the caudal pyramidal tract (Miller and Al-Rabiai, 1994), and the total axoplasmic volume in layer V of the somatosensory cortex (Al-Rabiai and Miller, 1989). Although the absolute number of corticospinal neurons is not affected, because the total number of neurons in layer V is reduced by one-third (Miller and Potempa, 1990), the relative number is substantially increased. It has been suggested that these exuberant projections are persistent, immature connections and may indicate that ethanol inhibits the pruning of axons that normally refines over time (Miller, 1987).

A hypertrophic axonal projection has been observed in axons extending from granule cells in the dentate gyrus (mossy fibers) to apical dendrites of the pyramidal neurons in the CA3 region of the hippocampus. Adult rats prenatally exposed to ethanol have a conspicuous abnormal band of infrapyramidal mossy fibers in hippocampal subfield CA3a at middle and temporal levels (West et al., 1981). In addition, the band of suprapyamidal mossy fibers in the stratum lucidum is disorganized. This exposure period coincides with the birth of pyramidal neurons in CA3, but it is before most granule cells or their axons appear. Therefore, it has been postulated that alterations in the terminal field induce hypertrophic growth of mossy fibers.

As with the corticospinal tract, mossy fibers in the hippocampus undergo stereotyped pruning of axonal branches that sculpts the connections into the mature pattern. Although the mechanisms controlling mossy fiber axon pruning are not fully understood, recent evidence points to a role for the repulsive guidance molecule Sema 3F (Bagri et al., 2003). There are intriguing similarities between the abnormal mossy fiber trajectories of prenatal ethanol-exposed rats and mice deficient in the axon guidance molecule semaphorin 3F (Sahay et al., 2003) or in members of the holoreceptor for semaphorins, neuropilin-2 (Chen et al., 2000) and plexin A3 (Cheng et al., 2001). It is appealing to speculate that ethanol interference with mossy fiber pruning is mediated by altered semaphorin signaling.

Axons That Cross the Midline

During brain development, axons from specific regions within each cerebral hemisphere are guided by extracellular signals to grow across the midline to synapse on neurons in the opposite hemisphere. The largest axon tract crossing the midline is the corpus callosum. It consists of axons projecting to the contralateral cortex, thereby allowing sensory and motor integration between the left and right sides of the brain. A higher than normal incidence of corpus callosum abnormalities has been reported for individuals with fetal alcohol syndrome (FAS) (Riley et al., 1995).

Magnetic resonance imaging and autopsy studies in humans exposed prenatally to ethanol show that ethanol decreases the cross-sectional area of the corpus callosum, especially the posterior region (splenium), and displaces it relative to other brain structures (e.g., Clarren et al., 1978; Peifer et al., 1979; Pratt and Doshi, 1984; Schaefer et al., 1991; Riley et al., 1995; Roebuck et al., 1998; Swayze et al., 1997; Sowell et al., 2001). In contrast, prenatal ethanol can increase the size of the corpus callosum in children prenatally exposed to ethanol (Bookstein et al., 2002) and in a nonhuman primate (*Macaca nemestrina*) (Miller et al., 1999). Indeed, the total number of axons is increased. The most labile segment is the rostral portion (genu), without affecting the thickness of axons or their myelin sheaths. The differences in the primates may reflect concentration-dependent effects of ethanol: at lower exposures, ethanol leads to hypertrophic effects, whereas at higher exposures it is fully depressive. Results in rodent models are similarly inconsistent, with some studies showing ethanol-induced decreases in various measures of corpus callosum size (Chernoff, 1977; Zimmerberg and Mickus, 1990; Moreland et al., 2002) and others showing no effect (Livy and Elberger, 2001) or an increase in the number of callosal projection neurons (Miller, 1997).

Noncallosal axon tracts that cross the midline are vulnerable to disruption by ethanol. Prolonged exposure to relatively high doses of alcohol can reduce the size of the hippocampal commissure (Livy and Elberger, 2001). The midsagittal area of the anterior commissure is reduced by prenatal ethanol exposure in some inbred mice (Cassells et al., 1987), however, this effect has not been observed in studies of rats (Zimmerberg and Mickus, 1990; Livy and Elberger, 2001). Granato et al. (1995) reported reduced terminal axonal arbors of corticothalamic projections, in which the most severe damage is in the selective absence of corticothalamic projections that cross the midline, a characteristic of rat corticothalamic systems that is not seen in humans.

Some of these inconsistencies may reflect differences in species, strain differences in the developmental sensitivity of commissural axons, differences in the dose or timing of ethanol administration, or other methodologic factors (Miller et al., 1999). In any case, the susceptibility of crossing fibers to disruption by ethanol has some important mechanistic implications because the midline is a unique developmental field where the response of axons to attractive and repulsive cues is finely regulated by precise molecular mechanisms now being identified (Tessier-Lavigne and Goodman, 1996; Huber et al., 2003).

In Vitro Studies

Partial to complete agenesis of the corpus callosum, as seen in FAS, is also common in people with mutations in L1, the so-called CRASH syndrome (Fransen

et al., 1995; Bearer, 2001). This finding led to the hypothesis that disruption of L1 function may contribute to neuropathologic effects of prenatal ethanol exposure (Charness et al., 1994). L1 is a neural cell adhesion molecule expressed on axons that facilitates axon growth through both heterophilic and homophilic binding (Brummendorf and Rathjen, 1996).

Some in vitro evidence is consistent with ethanol disruption of L1-mediated axon outgrowth from CNS neurons. Rat cerebellar granule neuron cultures extend neurites when cultured on substrates coated with L1. Ethanol inhibits L1-mediated outgrowth of the longest neurite formed 12 hr after plating (presumably the axon) in these cultures, even at concentrations as low as 3–5 mM (Bearer et al., 1999). Apparently, this is not due to inhibition of L1-mediated adhesion per se, because the same effect of ethanol on axon growth is observed when the cells are plated on poly-lysine substrates and treated with a soluble form of the extracellular domain of L1. This result was taken to indicate that ethanol disrupts signaling downstream of L1 that influences organization of the growth cone cytoskeleton.

There is growing evidence from *in vitro* experiments that second messenger cascades and cytoskeletal reorganization are triggered by L1, either directly or via its interactions with co-receptors (Burden-Gulley et al., 1997; Castellani et al., 2000; Watanabe et al., 2004). Other subsets of axons in the developing CNS express L1 in high amounts, including pyramidal tract axons (Joosten and Gribnau, 1989), which are sensitive to ethanol disruption during development (see Axons of Projection Neurons, above). Thus, elucidating the mechanisms by which ethanol disrupts L1 regulated axon growth is an important focus of future studies. Various studies have shown that L1 is but one of many cell adhesion proteins affected by ethanol (Luo and Miller, 1999; Miller and Luo, 2002; Siegenthaler and Miller, 2004). These proteins are regulated by factors such as transforming growth factor β1, which is known to promote neurite outgrowth (Ishihara et al., 1994) and is a target of ethanol (e.g., Luo and Miller, 1999; Miller and Luo, 2002; Siegenthaler and Miller, 2004).

Although studies *in vivo* have not focused on the effects of ethanol on early stages of process outgrowth, some in vitro studies point to effects of ethanol on the timing of initial axon outgrowth (axon specification). In cultures of hippocampal pyramidal neurons, the proportion of neurons that reach Stage 2 (extended neurites, but before axon specification) and the proportion that reach Stage 3 (axon specification) are both increased when ethanol is added to the medium, beginning shortly after plating (Clamp and Lindsley, 1998). Subsequent time-lapse studies, which include only cells that achieved Stage 3, show that ethanol delays axonal outgrowth (Lindsley et al., 2003). Both observations indicate that the increase in the proportion of cells with undifferentiated neurites is responsible for the final increase in the proportion of polarized cells at 1 DIV, and that ethanol may increase the likelihood of forming an axon even as it decreases the rate at which this occurs.

Some caution is required when interpreting studies of ethanol effects on process outgrowth that compare neurite morphology at a selected time after plating. Differences in the length of processes measured at a single time point do not take into account effects on the time it takes for a neuron to initiate axon extension and the rate of elongation once the axon is formed. A time course of ethanol effects during initial stages of neurite outgrowth, or time-lapse analyses on live cells, is needed to make this distinction.

An even higher-resolution time course is required to assess the effects of ethanol on the rate of axon growth after an axon emerges. This is because once axons are formed, they grow in a saltatory manner characterized by cycling between periods of growth (when length increases) and periods of relative quiescence ("non-growth"; when short retraction occurs) (Fig. 14–1). Molecular and pharmacologic treatments can selectively alter specific aspects of process outgrowth, such as the relative duration of periods of growth, the timing of axon establishment, or the magnitude of retraction during pauses (Esch et al., 1999; Ruthel and Banker, 1999; Shea and Beerman, 1999; Walker et al., 2001; Lindsley et al., 2003). These findings suggest that these features of process growth dynamics are independently regulated under normal conditions and could be differentially sensitive to ethanol.

Time-lapse analysis of living neurons has demonstrated saltatory axonal growth in dissociated cultures (Katz et al., 1984; Aletta and Greene, 1988; Ruthel and Banker, 1999; Lindsley et al., 2003), tissue slices (Halloran and Kalil, 1994), and the intact brain (Kaethner and Stuermer, 1992). In some axons, such as those comprising the corpus callosum, this can be quite

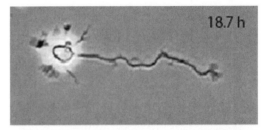

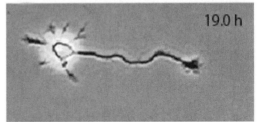

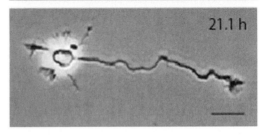

FIGURE 14–1 Axonal growth of a hippocampal pyramidal neuron. Phase-contrast images of a rat hippocampal pyramidal neuron, captured at various times postplating (shown in hr). The distal tip of the axon advances and retracts during elongation. Scale bar = 15 μm.

dramatic, with extensive lengths of axon retracting or sprouting rapidly (Dent et al., 1999). Dendrites also undergo significant retractions during outgrowth and remodeling, as demonstrated by withdrawal of the apical dendrite from subsets of pyramidal neurons in the developing cortex (Koester and O'Leary, 1992). Aside from affecting net growth rate, saltatory growth is associated with other important features of neural development, including branch formation (Szebenyi et al., 2001), branch growth alternation (Futerman and Banker, 1996), and growth cone responses to attractive and repulsive guidance cues (Song and Poo, 1999; Ming et al., 2002).

Time-lapse analysis of the effects of ethanol on the saltatory growth dynamics in hippocampal cultures shows that ethanol increases the overall rate of axon elongation by decreasing the extent of retractions during pauses in growth. Ethanol does not increase the rate of extension during growth spurts or the relative time axons spend growing and pausing (Lindsley et al., 2003).

MECHANISMS UNDERLYING ETHANOL-INDUCED CHANGES IN DENDRITIC AND AXONAL MORPHOLOGY

As described above, in vivo and in vitro data indicate that specific morphologic features that make up the overall shape of dendrites and specific features of axonal growth dynamics may not be equally affected by ethanol. They also indicate that the morphoregulatory effects of ethanol may be correlated with the earliest stages of process outgrowth. More studies are needed to identify the molecular basis for such specific vulnerability to ethanol-induced damage. Advances in understanding key cellular regulators of growth cone motility provide new opportunities to speculate on how ethanol exposure might modulate morphogenesis of axons and dendrites during development. Two of these emerging ideas are discussed below.

Small Rho Guanosine Triphosphatases

Although regulatory mechanisms underlying dendritic remodeling are not fully understood, the molecules and signals involved are thought to influence the actin and microtubule cytoskeleton, since significant cytoskeletal rearrangement occurs. The Rho family, small guanosine triphosphatases (GTPases), Rac, Cdc42, and RhoA, are essential components of signaling pathways that transduce a variety of extracellular signals (e.g., neurotrophins and integrins) into morphological changes. Rho guanosine 5'-triphosphatases (GTPases) do this by regulating downstream kinases that alter the activity of actin and tubulin binding proteins involved in actin-based cytoskeletal remodeling in growth cones (Luo et al., 1997; Mackay and Hall, 1998; Luo, 2000; Redmond and Ghosh, 2001; Lundquist, 2003).

Different members of Rho-family GTPases regulate distinct features of dendritic development, including initial outgrowth, rate of growth, number of primary dendrites, and extent of branching (Redmond and Ghosh, 2001). For example, results of experimentally altered Rac1 or Cdc42 expression in cortical neurons indicates that these proteins are important for dendritic branching and remodeling, but that they have little effect on dendritic growth rate per se (Threadgill et al., 1997; Li et al., 2000). In contrast, overexpression or activation of RhoA inhibits dendritic growth and underexpression or inactivation of RhoA leads to an increase in dendritic length (Lee et al., 2000; Li et al., 2000).

Studies focused on the cellular mechanisms regulating extension and retraction behavior of axons during growth and in response to guidance factors (e.g., semaphorins) also point to Rho family GTPases and their downstream effectors (Luo et al., 1997; Kuhn et al., 2000; Luo, 2000; Redmond and Ghosh, 2001). In general, process extension is correlated with increased formation of lamellipodia and filopodia at the leading edge of the growth cone, which requires activation of Cdc42 and Rac1, whereas retraction is correlated with increased RhoA signaling (Hall, 1998; Luo, 2000).

Two studies show that ethanol can dramatically rearrange F-actin structures in some non-neuronal cells and that activation of small Rho GTPases may mediate these effects. Ethanol induces actin reorganization and shape change in astrocytes in vitro, and it has been suggested that these effects are mediated by decreased RhoA activity, since they could be reverted by expression of constitutively active RhoA (Guasch et al., 2003). In the endothelial cell line, SVEC4-10, ethanol induces actin reorganization and motility. Since these effects can be blocked by expression of dominant negative Cdc42, it has been suggested that they are mediated by activation of Cdc42 (Qian et al., 2003). On the other hand, the effect of ethanol on F-actin distribution in the growth cones of developing neurons has not been reported. Some preliminary data are consistent with altered F-actin organization in axonal growth cones of hippocampal neurons maintained for 1 DIV with ethanol (Shah and Lindsley, unpublished observations). Figure 14–2 contains examples of confocal images showing F-actin rich structures in axonal growth cones of control and ethanol-treated hippocampal neurons 1 DIV that are fixed and stained with phalloidin-Alexa 568. Continuous exposure to low doses of ethanol induces extensive elaboration of lamellipodia and numerous thickened filopodia in axonal growth cones, and high doses only increase

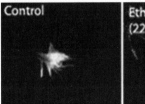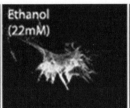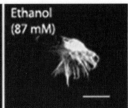

FIGURE 14–2 Effect of ethanol on F-actin distribution in growth cones. Representative confocal images of F-actin distribution in axonal growth cones of 1-day-old hippocampal neurons cultured for 1 day in vitro without or with ethanol (concentrations shown). Images were captured at 0.20 μm intervals using 8-image jump averaging. Each image is the lowest section from the z-series stack. The low dose of ethanol increased the extent of lamellipodia and filopodia compared to controls, and the high dose increased filopodia only. Scale bar = 5.0 μm.

filopodia formation. Moreover, the involvement of small GTPases in reorganization of growth cone actin in neurons exposed to ethanol is indicated by pull-down experiments showing changes in Rac1 activation in whole-cell lysates of hippocampal cultures exposed to ethanol for 1 day during axon elongation.

Important advances in understanding the effects of ethanol on growth-related signaling in axons and dendrites can be expected, given the availability of appropriate model systems amenable to measuring the effects of expression of relevant dominant-negative or constitutively active mutant Rho GTPases on ethanol-induced disruption of morphogenesis. Interestingly, many of the signaling pathways known to control growth cone extension–retraction and attraction–repulsion behaviors appear to be differentially regulated in axons and dendrites. Some evidence suggests that Rho GTPases are differentially distributed in growth cones (Renaudin et al., 1999), and experimental manipulations to over- or underexpress Rho-family proteins have differential effects on the number and length of dendrites compared to their effects on axonal growth (Threadgill et al., 1997; Lee et al., 2000; Luo, 2000). Thus, if Rho-family GTPase modulation is indeed involved in the morphoregulatory effects of ethanol, then differential effects of the various Rho-family members on axonal vs. dendritic effects may help explain the various effects of ethanol on these distinct process types.

If ethanol-induced changes in growth dynamics and/or cytoskeletal reorganization do indeed involve altered GTPase signaling, then one could ask what upstream modulators of Rho GTPases are particularly important in morphoregulatory effects of ethanol. In NIH 3T3 cells, growth factor–induced Rac1 activation is sensitive to protein kinase C (PKC) inhibition, placing PKC upstream of Rac in that system (Buchanan et al., 2000). The relationship between Rho GTPase signaling and PKCs is potentially quite interesting. In PC12 cells, exposure to 25–200 mM ethanol for 2–8 days stimulates neurite growth via upregulation of PKCε (Messing et al., 1991; Hundle et al., 1997).

What role might downstream effectors of Rho GTPases have in mediating the effects of ethanol on neuronal process growth? Among a number of known effectors, several are of particular interest. In hippocampal neuron cultures, axon specification is linked to activation of Cdc42 and Rac1 in a positive feedback loop involving a highly localized complex of mPar3/mPar6, PKC, and phosphoinositide 3 kinase (PI3K), which modulates actin and microtubule cytoskeletal dynamics in the growth cone of the nascent axon (Shi et al., 2003). It is not yet clear, however, whether PI3K initiates signals that activate Rac1/Cdc42 downstream or whether Rac1/Cdc42 are upstream signals for PI3K in this cascade. Other known downstream effectors of potential interest include actin cytoskeleton-regulating proteins, such as ezrin, radixin, and moesin, and regulators of mitogen-activated protein kinase pathways (Hall, 1998; Redmond and Ghosh, 2001).

Some insight into the regulation of neurite outgrowth may come from studies of neuronal migration, as common proteins are involved in both processes (see Chapters 3 and 13). Reduced F-actin at the leading edge of migrating neurons is associated with modulation of RhoA, Rac1, and Cdc42 activity (Kholmanskikh et al., 2003). Since abnormal neuronal migration is a key neuropathologic feature of prenatal alcohol exposure (Miller, 1986, 1993; Hirai et al., 1999; Mooney et al., 2004; Siegenthaler and Miller, 2004), an understanding of the effects of ethanol on Rho GTPase signaling in neurons may shed light on cellular mechanisms contributing to prenatal ethanol-induced neuronal migration errors.

Intracellular Calcium

Results of numerous studies of the molecular pathways linking activation of specific Rho-family proteins and their effectors point to involvement of Ca^{2+} influx (Kuhn et al., 1998). Thus it is likely that effects of ethanol on dynamic growth cone behavior might ultimately be linked mechanistically through Rho-family effectors acting on the growth cone cytoskeleton, either directly or indirectly, to Ca^{2+} signaling.

It has long been appreciated that intracellular Ca^{2+} is a critical second messenger that modulates growth cone behavior during neuronal development by communicating growth-related signals to the cytoskeleton and vesicular apparatus of the growth cone (Kater and Mills, 1991; Letourneau and Cypher, 1991; Neely and Nicholls, 1995). Ethanol can alter the function and expression of L-type Ca^{2+} channels in neural cells (Walter and Messing, 1999). The effects of ethanol on Ca^{2+} signaling in neurons have focused primarily on mature neurons, in which Ca^{2+} channels and receptors figure importantly into cellular adaptations to ethanol and to withdrawal-induced neuronal damage (Fadda and Rossetti, 1998). Ethanol affects Ca^{2+} homeostasis in mature neurons by altering the expression or function of voltage-dependent Ca^{2+} channels (VDCCs), ionotropic receptors, and Ca^{2+}-induced Ca^{2+} release from intracellular stores (Leslie et al., 1990; Bergamaschi et al., 1993). Unfortunately, far fewer studies have pursued the idea that ethanol disrupts Ca^{2+} signaling

regulating neuronal development. The potential importance of this distinction is suggested by evidence that the effect of ethanol on VDCCs may not be constant during neuronal differentiation (Bergamashi et al., 1995; Webb et al., 1997).

The "set-point hypothesis" proposes that process growth occurs within a narrow range of intracellular Ca^{2+} concentration $[Ca^{2+}]_i$, and that sustained increases or decreases in $[Ca^{2+}]_i$ lead to growth cone collapse and/or cell damage (Kater and Mills, 1991). In contrast, oscillations or transient increases in $[Ca^{2+}]_i$ are associated with signaling induced by effector pathways, similar to those thought to be involved in effects of ethanol on process growth. Some of these transient Ca^{2+} signals are highly localized. For example, growth cones generate transient increases in $[Ca^{2+}]_i$ as they migrate in vivo (Gomez and Spitzer, 1999) and *in vitro* (Gomez et al., 1995; Ciccolini et al., 2003; Tang et al., 2003). The frequencies and amplitudes of these $[Ca^{2+}]_i$ transients are inversely related to the rate of axon elongation and increase several-fold when axons pause during periods of nongrowth. These transients are likely to alter growth cone extension by reorganizing the cytoskeleton, perhaps by disassembling local actin and microtubule networks. In cortical neurons, these transients are spontaneous and Ca^{2+}-dependent and act primarily through L-type VDCCs (Tang et al., 2003). Signaling to the cytoskeleton appears, at least in part, to involve the phosphatase calcinerin (Lautermilch and Spitzer, 2000).

The results of time-series, confocal imaging of Ca^{2+} flux in axons of hippocampal neurons exposed to ethanol under conditions that alter axonal growth dynamics have been recently reported (Gillis and Lindsley, 2004). In these studies, the frequency and kinetics of spontaneous $[Ca^{2+}]_i$ transients in axonal growth cones of hippocampal neurons at 1 DIV in control medium were compared to those of neurons maintained in medium to which ethanol (22, 43, or 87 mM) was added at the time of plating. Figure 14–3 illustrates typical time-series images of axonal growth cones from control and ethanol-exposed cultures, and corresponding plots of relative fluorescence intensity in the subscribed region of the growth cone over a 10 min recording period. As described by Gomez and colleagues (1995), a *transient* is defined by an increase in $[Ca^{2+}]_i$ of >200% of baseline, slow kinetics (~20 sec to peak), and return to baseline.

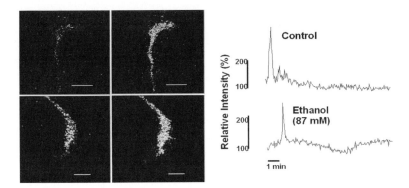

FIGURE 14–3 Time-series confocal images of axonal growth cones. The growth cones of 1-day-old neurons were loaded with Fluo-3. A growth cone from a control culture (top row) and one from a culture exposed to 87 mM ethanol (bottom row) are shown. For each growth cone two images from the time series are presented, one depicting baseline fluorescence (left), and the other, peak fluorescence during a spontaneous calcium transient (right). Peak calcium elevations are imaged in white. The plots on the right show the relative fluorescence intensity as a percent of baseline for the growth cones in the panels (left). Scale bar = 5.0 μm.

Results of recording more than 100 neurons from 10 cultures showed that only 18% of axons in control cultures exhibited one or more transients during the 10 min recording period. Exposure to low doses of ethanol reduced the number of neurons with one or more transients to 8% ($p < 0.005$), but exposure to the highest dose of ethanol increased the proportion of growth cones with transients to 39% ($p < 0.005$). Ethanol, at any concentration tested, had no effect on the peak amplitude, time to peak, or total duration of the transients. These findings suggest that ethanol modulates the frequency of spontaneous Ca^{2+} transients in axonal growth cones. It is yet to be determined whether dendritic growth dynamics and Ca^{2+} transients are similarly altered by ethanol. In hippocampal cultures, a global increase in $[Ca^{2+}]_i$ can inhibit dendritic growth but promotes or has no effect on axonal growth (Mills and Kater, 1990; Mattson et al., 1988; Mattson and Kater, 1987). This finding indicates potential differences in Ca^{2+}-dependent, growth-related signaling in axons and dendrites. The modulation of transient Ca^{2+} flux in the growth cone could be an important cellular target of ethanol that mediates its differential effects on axons and dendrites, considering the sensitivity of growth cones to elevated free Ca^{2+} and the number of Ca^{2+}-activated

proteins expressed differentially by axons and dendrites.

SUMMARY AND CONCLUSIONS

Descriptive studies detailing specific morphological features of neuronal development that are sensitive to disruption by ethanol in a variety of neuronal cell cultures are essential in laying the groundwork for identifying cellular mechanisms underlying the effects of ethanol on neuronal morphogenesis. Many ethanol-sensitive developmental phenomena discovered so far—the altered growth dynamics and stage-specific effects of ethanol—could not have been so readily derived from fixed sections taken from animals exposed to ethanol in utero. Neuronal development in vivo involves a diversity of interactions between neurons and their environment that experimental conditions in vitro cannot fully reproduce. Therefore, an important goal for the future should be to test specific mechanistic hypotheses arising from cell culture experiments in model systems that preserve the endogenous spatiotemporal expression of extracellular growth-regulating molecules. Such model systems might provide opportunities to manipulate the expression of specific molecules through the use of genetically modified animals and optical methods that enable the visualization of axons and dendrites growing *in situ*.

Abbreviations

$[Ca^{2+}]_i$ intracellular concentration of Ca^{2+}

CNS   central nervous system

DIV   days in vitro

FAS   fetal alcohol syndrome

GTPase   guanosine 5′-triphosphatase

PI3K   phosphoinositide 3 kinase

PKC   protein kinase C

MAP   microtubule-associated protein

NMDA   N-methyl-D-aspartate

VDCC   voltage-dependent Ca^{2+} channel

ACKNOWLEDGMENTS   The author thanks Samit Shah and Jessica Gillis for their assistance in preparing the figures for this chapter and agreeing to share their unpublished observations. This work was supported by the National Institute of Alcohol Abuse and Alcoholism.

References

Aletta JM, Greene LA (1988) Growth cone configuration and advance: a time-lapse study using video-enhanced differential interference contrast microscopy. J Neurosci 8:1425–1435.

Al-Rabiai S, Miller MW (1989) Effect of prenatal exposure to ethanol on the ultrastructure of layer V of mature rat somatosensory cortex. J Neurocytol 18: 711–729.

Bagri A, Cheng HJ, Yaron A, Pleasure SJ, Tessier-Lavigne M (2003) Stereotyped pruning of long hippocampal axon branches triggered by retraction inducers of the semaphorin family. Cell 113: 285–299.

Bearer CF (2001) L1 cell adhesion molecule signal cascades: targets for ethanol developmental neurotoxicity. Neurotoxicology 22:625–633.

Bearer CF, Swick AR, O'Riordan MA, Cheng G (1999) Ethanol inhibits L1-mediated neurite outgrowth in postnatal rat cerebellar granule cells. J Biol Chem 274:13264–13270.

Bergamaschi S, Battaini F, Trabucchi M, Parenti M, Lopez CM, Govoni S (1995) Neuronal differentiation modifies the effect of ethanol exposure on

voltage-dependent calcium channels in NG 108-15 cells. Alcohol 12:497–503.

Bergamaschi S, Govoni S, Battaini F, Parenti M, Trabucchi M (1993) Effect of ethanol exposure on voltage dependent calcium channels in *in vitro* cellular models. Alcohol Alcohol Suppl 2:403–407.

Berman RF, Hannigan JH (2000) Effects of prenatal alcohol exposure on the hippocampus: spatial behavior, electrophysiology, and neuroanatomy. Hippocampus 10:94–110.

Bonthius DJ, Karacay B, Dai D, Hutton A, Pantazis J (2004) The NO-cGMP-PKG pathway plays an essential role in the acquisition of ethanol resistance by cerebellar granule neurons. Neurotox Teratol 26:47–57.

Bookstein FL, Streissguth AP, Sampson PD, Connor PD, Barr HM (2002) Corpus callosum shape and neuropsychological deficits in adult males with heavy fetal alcohol exposure. Neuroimage 15: 233–251.

Brummendorf T, Rathjen FG (1996) Structure/function relationships of axon-associated adhesion receptors of the immunoglobulin superfamily. Curr Opin Neurobiol 6:584–593.

Buchanan FG, Elliot CM, Gibbs M, Exton JH (2000) Translocation of the Rac1 guanine nucleotide exchange factor Tiam1 induced by platelet-derived growth factor and lysophosphatidic acid. J Biol Chem 275:9742–9748.

Burden-Gulley SM, Pendergast M, Lemmon V (1997) The role of cell adhesion molecule L1 in axonal extension, growth cone motility, and signal transduction. Cell Tissue Res 290:415–422.

Cassells B, Wainwright P, Blom K (1987) Heredity and alcohol-induced brain anomalies: effects of alcohol on anomalous prenatal development of the corpus callosum and anterior commissure in BALB/c and C57BL/6 mice. Exp Neurol 95:587–604.

Castellani V, Chedotal A, Schachner M, Faivre-Sarrailh C, Rougon G (2000) Analysis of the L1-deficient mouse phenotype reveals cross-talk between Sema3A and L1 signaling pathways in axonal guidance. Neuron 27:237–249.

Charness M, Safran R, Perides G (1994) Ethanol inhibits neural cell–cell adhesion. J Biol Chem 269: 9304–9309.

Chen H, Bagri A, Zupicich JA, Zou Y, Stoeckli E, Pleasure SJ, Lowenstein DH, Skarnes WC, Chedotal A, Tessier-Lavigne M (2000) Neuropilin-2 regulates the development of selective cranial and sensory nerves and hippocampal mossy fiber projections. Neuron 25:43–56.

Cheng HJ, Bagri A, Yaron A, Stein E, Pleasure SJ, Tessier-Lavigne M (2001) Plexin-A3 mediates semaphorin signaling and regulates the development of hippocampal axonal projections. Neuron 32:249–263.

Chernoff GF (1977) The fetal alcohol syndrome in mice: an animal model. Teratology 15:223–230.

Ciccolini F, Collins TJ, Sudhoelter J, Lipp P, Berridge MJ, Bootman MD (2003) Local and global spontaneous calcium events regulate neurite outgrowth and onset of GABAergic phenotype during neural precursor differentiation. J Neurosci 23:103–111.

Clamp PA, Lindsley TA (1998) Early events in the development of neuronal polarity in vitro are altered by ethanol. Alcohol Clin Exp Res 22:1277–1284.

Clarren SK, Alvord EC, Sumi SM, Streissguth AP, Smith DW (1978) Brain malformations related to prenatal exposure to ethanol. J Pediatr 92:64–67.

Craig AM, Banker G (1994) Neuronal polarity. Annu Rev Neurosci 17:267–310.

Danuser G, Waterman-Storer CM (2003) Quantitative fluorescent speckle microscopy: where it came from and where it is going. J Microsc 211:191–207.

Davies DL, Smith DE (1981) A Golgi study of mouse hippocampal CA1 pyramidal neurons following perinatal ethanol exposure. Neurosci Lett 26: 49–54.

Deng J, Elberger AJ (2003) Corpus callosum and visual cortex of mice with deletion of the NMDA-NR1 receptor. II. Attenuation of prenatal alcohol exposure effects. Dev Brain Res 144:135–150.

Dent EW, Callaway JL, Szebenyi G, Baas PW, Kalil K (1999) Reorganization and movement of microtubules in axonal growth cones and developing interstitial branches. J Neurosci 19:8894–8908.

Dotti CG, Sullivan CA, Banker GA (1988) The establishment of polarity by hippocampal neurons in culture. J Neurosci 8:1454–1468.

Dow KE, Riopelle RJ (1985) Ethanol neurotoxicity: effects on neurite formation and neurotrophic factor production in vitro. Science 228:591–593.

Durand D, Saint-Cyr JA, Gurevich N, Carlen PL (1989) Ethanol-induced dendritic alternations in hippocampal granule cells. Brain Res 477:373–377.

Esch T, Lemmon V, Banker G (1999) Local presentation of substrate molecules directs axon specification by cultured hippocampal neurons. J Neurosci 19:6417–1626.

Fabregues I, Ferrer I, Gairi JM, Cahuana A, Giner P (1985) Effects of prenatal exposure to ethanol on the maturation of the pyramidal neurons in the cerebral cortex of the guinea-pig: a quantitative Golgi study. Neuropathol Appl Neurobiol 11:291–298.

Fadda F, Rossetti ZL (1998) Chronic ethanol consumption: from neuroadaptation to neurodegeneration. Prog Neurobiol 56:385–431.

Fransen E, Lemmon V, Van Camp G, Vits L, Coucke P, Willems PJ (1995) CRASH syndrome: clinical spectrum of corpus callosum hypoplasia, retardation, adducted thumbs, spastic paraparesis and hydrocephalus due to mutations in one single gene, L1. Eur J Human Genet 3:273–284.

Futerman AH, Banker GA (1996) The economics of neurite outgrowth—the addition of new membrane to growing axons. Trends Neurosci 19:144–149.

Gillis J, Lindsley TA (2004) Ethanol modulates growth cone calcium treatments in rat hippocampal neurons in vitro. Alcohol Clin Exp Res 28:167A.

Gomez TM, Snow DM, Letourneau PC (1995) Characterization of spontaneous calcium transients in nerve growth cones and their effect on growth cone migration. Neuron 14:1233–1246.

Gomez TM, Spitzer NC (1999) In vivo regulation of axon extension and pathfinding by growth-cone calcium transients. Nature 397:350–355.

Goodlett CR, Johnson TB (1999) Temporal windows of vulnerability within the third trimester equivalent: why "knowing when" matters. In: Hannigan J, Spear LP, Spear NE, Goodlett CR (eds). Alcohol: Effects on Brain and Development. Lawrence Erlbaum Associates, Mahwah NJ, pp 59–91.

Goslin K, Assumssen H, Banker G (1998) Rat hippocampal neurons in low density culture. In: Banker G, Goslin K (eds). Culturing Nerve Cells. MIT Press, Cambridge, MA, pp 339–390.

Goslin K, Banker G (1989) Experimental observations on the development of polarity by hippocampal neurons in culture. J Cell Biol 108:1507–1516.

Granato A, Santarelli M, Sbriccoli A, Minciacchi D (1995) Multifaceted alterations of the thalamo-cortico-thalamic loop in adult rats prenatally exposed to ethanol. Anat Embryol 191:11–23.

Guasch RM, Tomas M, Minambres R, Valles S, Renau-Piqueras J, Guerri C (2003) RhoA and lysophosphatidic acid are involved in the actin cytoskeleton reorganization of astrocytes exposed to ethanol. J Neurosci Res 72:487–502.

Hall A (1998) Rho GTPases and the actin cytoskeleton. Science 279:509–514.

Halloran MC, Kalil K (1994) Dynamic behaviors of growth cones extending in the corpus callosum of living cortical brain slices observed with video microscopy. J Neurosci 14:2161–2177.

Hammer RP, Scheibel AB (1981) Morphologic evidence for a delay of neuronal maturation in fetal alcohol exposure. Exp Neurol 74:587–596.

Heaton MB, Paiva M, Swanson DJ, Walker DW (1994) Responsiveness of cultured septal and hippocampal neurons to ethanol and neurotrophic substances. J Neurosci Res 39:305–318.

Hirai K, Yoshioka H, Kihara M, Hasegawa K, Sawada T, Fushiki S (1999) Effects of ethanol on neuronal migration and neural cell adhesion molecules in the embryonic rat cerebral cortex: a tissue culture study. Dev Brain Res 118:205–210.

Huber AB, Kolodkin AL, Ginty DD, Cloutier J-F (2003) Signaling at the growth cone: ligand-receptor complexes and the control of axon growth and guidance. Annu Rev Neurosci 26:509–563.

Hundle B, McMahon T, Dadgar J, Chen CH, Mochly-Rosen D, Messing RO (1997) An inhibitory fragment derived from protein kinase C-ε prevents enhancement of nerve growth factor responses by ethanol and phorbol esters. J Biol Chem 272:15028–15035.

Ishihara A, Saito H, Abe K (1994) Transforming growth factor-β1 and -β2 promote neurite sprouting and elongation of cultured rat hippocampal neurons. Brain Res 639:21–25.

Joosten EA, Gribnau AA (1989) Immunocytochemical localization of cell adhesion molecule L1 in developing rat pyramidal tract. Neurosci Lett 100:94–98.

Kaethner RJ, Stuermer CA (1992) Dynamics of terminal arbor formation and target approach of retinotectal axons in living zebrafish embryos: a time-lapse study of single axons. J Neurosci 12:3257–3271.

Kater SB, Mills LR (1991) Regulation of growth cone behavior by calcium. J Neurosci 11:891–899.

Katz MJ, George EB, Gilbert LJ (1984) Axonal elongation as a stochastic walk. Cell Motil 4:351–370.

Kentroti S, Vernadakis A (1991) Correlation between morphological and biochemical effects of ethanol on neuroblast-enriched cultures derived from three-day-old chick embryos. J Neurosci Res 30:484–492.

Kholmanskikh SS, Dobrin JS, Wynshaw-Boris A, Letourneau PC, Ross ME (2003) Disregulated RhoGTPases and actin cytoskeleton contribute to the migration defect in Lis1-deficient neurons. J Neurosci 23:8673–8681.

Killisch I, Dotti CG, Laurie DJ, Luddens H, Seeburg PH (1991) Expression patterns of GABA$_A$ receptor subtypes in developing hippocampal neurons. Neuron 7:927–936.

Koester SE, O'Leary DD (1992) Functional classes of cortical projection neurons develop dendritic distinctions by class-specific sculpting of an early common pattern. J Neurosci 12:1382–1393.

Kozlowski DA, Hilliard S, Schallert T (1997) Ethanol consumption following recovery from unilateral damage to the forelimb area of the sensorimotor cortex: reinstatement of deficits and prevention of dendritic pruning. Brain Res 763:159–166.

Krahl SE, Berman RF, Hannigan JH (1999) Electrophysiology of hippocampal CA1 neurons after prenatal ethanol exposure. Alcohol 17:125–131.

Kuhn TB, Meberg PJ, Brown MD, Bernstein BW, Minamide LS, Jensen JR, Okada K, Soda EA, Bamburg JR (2000) Regulating actin dynamics in neuronal growth cones by ADF/cofilin and rho family GTPases. J Neurobiol 44:126–144.

Kuhn TB, Williams CV, Dou P, Kater SB (1998) Laminin directs growth cone navigation via two temporally and functionally distinct calcium signals. J Neurosci 18:184–194.

Lautermilch NJ, Spitzer NC (2000) Regulation of calcineurin by growth cone calcium waves controls neurite extension. J Neurosci 20:315–325.

Lee T, Winter C, Marticke SS, Lee A, Luo L (2000) Essential roles of *Drosophila* RhoA in the regulation of neuroblast proliferation and dendritic but not axonal morphogenesis. Neuron 25:307–316.

Leslie SW, Brown LM, Dildy JE, Sims JS (1990) Ethanol and neuronal calcium channels. Alcohol 7:233–236.

Letourneau PC, Cypher C (1991) Regulation of growth cone motility. Cell Motil Cytoskeleton 20:267–271.

Li Z, Van Aelst L, Cline HT (2000) Rho GTPases regulate distinct aspects of dendritic arbor growth in *Xenopus* central neurons in vivo. Nat Neurosci 3:217–225.

Lindsley TA, Clarke S (2004) Ethanol withdrawal influences survival and morphology of developing rat hippocampal neurons in vitro. Alcohol Clin Exp Res 28:85–92.

Lindsley TA, Comstock LL, Rising LJ (2002) Morphologic and neurotoxic effects of ethanol vary with timing of exposure in vitro. Alcohol 28:197–203.

Lindsley TA, Kerlin AM, Rising LJ (2003) Time-lapse analysis of ethanol's effects on axon growth in vitro. Dev Brain Res 147:191–199.

Livy DJ, Elberger AJ (2001) Effect of prenatal alcohol exposure on midsagittal commissure size in rats. Teratology 63:15–22.

Lopez-Tejero D, Ferrer I, Llobera M, Herrera E (1986) Effects of prenatal ethanol exposure on physical growth, sensory reflex maturation and brain development in the rat. Neuropathol Appl Neurobiol 12:251–260.

Lundquist EA (2003) Rac proteins and the control of axon development. Curr Opin Neurobiol 13:384–390.

Luo J, Miller MW (1999) Transforming growth factor β1 (TGFβ1) mediated inhibition of B104 neuroblastoma cell proliferation and neural cell adhesion molecule expression: effect of ethanol. J Neurochem 72:2286–2293.

Luo L (2000) Rho GTPases in neuronal morphogenesis. Nat Rev Neurosci 1:173–180.

Luo L, Jan LY, Jan YN (1997) Rho family GTP-binding proteins in growth cone signalling. Curr Opin Neurobiol 7:81–86.

Mackay DJ, Hall A (1998) Rho GTPases. J Biol Chem 273:20685–20688.

Mattson MP, Dou P, Kater SB (1988) Outgrowth-regulating actions of glutamate in isolated hippocampal pyramidal neurons. J Neurosci 8:2087–20100.

Mattson MP, Kater SB (1987) Calcium regulation of neurite elongation and growth cone motility. J Neurosci 7:4034–4043.

Mendelson B, Driskill A (1996) Ethanol exposure alters the development of sertonergic neurons in chick spinal cord. Alcohol 13:431–441.

Messing RO, Henteleff M, Park JJ (1991) Ethanol enhances growth factor–induced neurite formation in PC12 cells. Brain Res 565:301–311.

Miller MW (1986) Fetal alcohol effects on the generation and migration of cerebral cortical neurons. Science 233:1308–1311.

—— (1987) Effect of prenatal exposure to alcohol on the distribution and time of origin of corticospinal neurons in the rat. J Comp Neurol 257:372–382.

—— (1993) Migration of cortical neurons is altered by gestational exposure to ethanol. Alcohol Clin Exp Res 17:304–314.

—— (1997) Effects of prenatal exposure to ethanol on callosal projection neurons in rat somatosensory cortex. Brain Res 766:121–128.

Miller MW, Al-Rabiai S (1994) Effects of prenatal exposure to ethanol on the number of axons in the pyramidal tract of the rat. Alcohol Clin Exp Res 18:346–354.

Miller MW, Astley SJ, Clarren SK (1999) Number of axons in the corpus callosum of the mature *Macaca nemestrina*: increases caused by prenatal exposure to ethanol. J Comp Neurol 412:123–131.

Miller MW, Chiaia NL, Rhoades RW (1990) Intracellular recording and injection study of corticospinal neurons in the rat somatosensory cortex: effect of prenatal exposure to ethanol. J Comp Neurol 297:91–105.

Miller MW, Luo J (2002) Effects of ethanol and transforming growth factor β (TGFβ) on neuronal proliferation and nCAM expression. Alcohol Clin Exp Res 26:1073–1079.

Miller MW, Potempa G (1990) Numbers of neurons and glia in mature rat somatosensory cortex: effects of prenatal exposure to ethanol. J Comp Neurol 293:92–102.

Mills LR, Kater SB (1990) Neuron-specific and state-specific differences in calcium homeostasis regulate the generation and degeneration of neuronal architecture. Neuron 4:149–163.

Ming GL, Wong ST, Henley J, Yuan XB, Song HJ, Spitzer NC, Poo MM (2002) Adaptation in the chemotactic guidance of nerve growth cones. Nature 417:411–418.

Minkwitz HG, Holz L (1975) The ontogenetic development of pyramidal neurons in the hippocampus (CA1) of the rat. J Hirnforsch 16:37–54.

Mooney SM, Siegenthaler JA, Miller MW (2004) Ethanol induces heterotopias in organotypic cultures of rat cerebral cortex. Cereb Cortex 14:1071–1080.

Moreland N, La Grange L, Montoya R (2002) Impact of in utero exposure to EtOH on corpus callosum development and paw preference in rats: protective effects of silymarin. BMC Compl Altern Med 2:10.

Neely MD, Nicholls JG (1995) Electrical activity, growth cone motility and the cytoskeleton. J Exp Biol 198:1433–1446.

Peifer J, Majewski F, Fischbach H, Beirich JR, Volk B (1979) Alcohol embryo- and fetopathy: neuropathology of 3 children and 3 fetuses. J Neurol Sci 41:125–137.

Pentney RJ, Cotter JR, Abel EL (1984) Quantitative measures of mature neuronal morphology after in utero ethanol exposure. Neurobehav Toxicol Teratol 6:59–65.

Pentney RJ, Miller MW (1992) Effects of ethanol on neuronal morphogenesis. In: Miller MW (ed). *Development of the Central Nervous System: Effects of Alcohol and Opiates.* Wiley, New York, pp 71–107.

Pratt OE, Doshi R (1984) Range of alcohol-induced damage in the developing central nervous system. CIBA Found Symp 105:142–156.

Qian Y, Luo J, Leonard SS, Harris GK, Millecchia L, Flynn DC, Shi X (2003) Hydrogen peroxide formation and actin filament reorganization by Cdc42 are essential for ethanol-induced in vitro angiogenesis. J Biol Chem 278:16189–16197.

Qiang M, Wang MW, Elberger AJ (2002) Second trimester prenatal alcohol exposure alters development of rat corpus callosum. Neurotoxicol Teratol 24:719–732.

Redmond L, Ghosh A (2001) The role of Notch and Rho GTPase signaling in the control of dendritic development. Curr Opin Neurobiol 11:111–117.

Renaudin A, Lehmann M, Girault J, McKerracher L (1999) Organization of point contacts in neuronal growth cones. J Neurosci Res 55:458–471.

Riley EP, Mattson SN, Sowell ER, Jernigan TL, Sobel DF, Jones KL (1995) Abnormalities of the corpus callosum in children prenatally exposed to alcohol. Alcohol Clin Exp Res 19:1198–1202.

Roebuck TM, Mattson SN, Riley EP (1998) A review of the neuroanatomical findings in children with fetal alcohol syndrome or prenatal exposure to alcohol. Alcohol Clin Exp Res 22:339–344.

Roivainen R, McMahon T, Messing RO (1993) Protein kinase C isozymes that mediate enhancement of neurite outgrowth by ethanol and phorbol esters in PC12 cells. Brain Res 624:85–93.

Ruthel G, Banker G (1999) Role of moving growth cone-like "wave" structures in the outgrowth of cultured hippocampal axons and dendrites. J Neurobiol 39: 97–106.

Sahay A, Molliver ME, Ginty DD, Kolodkin AL (2003) Semaphorin 3F is critical for development of limbic system circuitry and is required in neurons for selective CNS axon guidance events. J Neurosci 23:6671–6680.

Saunders DE, Zajac CS, Wappler NL (1995) Alcohol inhibits neurite extension and increases N-myc and c-myc proteins. Alcohol 12:475–483.

Schaefer GB, Shuman RM, Wilson DA, Saleeb S, Domek DB, Johnson SF, Bodensteiner JB (1991) Partial agenesis of the anterior corpus callosum: correlation between appearance, imaging, and neuropathology. Pediatr Neurol 7:39.

Scott EK, Luo L (2001) How do dendrites take their shape? Nat Neurosci 4:359–365.

Shea TB, Beermann ML (1999) Neuronal intermediate filament protein α-internexin facilitates axonal neurite elongation in neuroblastoma cells. Cell Motil Cytoskeleton 43:322–333.

Shetty AK, Burrows RC, Phillips DE (1993) Alterations in neuronal development in the substantia nigra pars compacta following in utero ethanol exposure: immunohistochemical and Golgi studies. Neuroscience 52:311–322.

Shi SH, Jan LY, Jan YN (2003) Hippocampal neuronal polarity specified by spatially localized mPar3/mPar6 and PI 3-kinase activity. Cell 112:63–75.

Siegenthaler JA, Miller MW (2004) Transforming growth factor β1 regulates cell migration in rat cortex: effects of ethanol. Cereb Cortex 14:602–613.

Smith DE, Davies DL (1990) Effect of perinatal administration of ethanol on the CA1 pyramidal cell of the hippocampus and Purkinje cell of the cerebellum: an ultrastructural survey. J Neurocytol 19:708–717.

Smith DE, Foundas A, Canales J (1986) Effect of perinatally administered ethanol on the development of the cerebellar granule cell. Exp Neurol 92:491–501.

Song HJ, Poo MM (1999) Signal transduction underlying growth cone guidance by diffusible factors. Curr Opin Neurobiol 9:355–363.

Sowell ER, Mattson SN, Thompson PM, Jernigan TL, Riley EP, Toga AW (2001) Mapping callosal morphology and cognitive correlates: effect of heavy prenatal alcohol exposure. Neurology 57:235–244.

Swayze VW II, Johnson VP, Hanson JW, Piven J, Sato Y, Giedd JN, Mosnik D, Andreasen NC (1997) Magnetic resonance imaging of brain anomalies in fetal alcohol syndrome. Pediatrics 99:232–240.

Szebenyi G, Dent EW, Callaway JL, Seys C, Lueth H, Kalil K (2001) Fibroblast growth factor-2 promotes axon branching of cortical neurons by influencing morphology and behavior of the primary growth cone. J Neurosci 21:3932–3941.

Tang F, Dent EW, Kalil K (2003) Spontaneous calcium transients in developing cortical neurons regulate axon outgrowth. J Neurosci 23:927–936.

Tessier-Lavigne M, Goodman CS (1996) The molecular biology of axon guidance. Science 274:1123–1133.

Threadgill R, Bobb K, Ghosh A (1997) Regulation of dendritic growth and remodeling by Rho, Rac, and Cdc42. Neuron 19:625–634.

Walker KL, Yoo HK, Undamatla J, Szaro BG (2001) Loss of neurofilaments alters axonal growth dynamics. J Neurosci 21:9655–9666.

Walter HJ, Messing RO (1999) Regulation of neuronal voltage-gated calcium channels by ethanol. Neurochem Int 35:95–101.

Watanabe H, Yamazaki M, Miyazaki H, Arikawa C, Itoh K, Sasaki T, Maehama T, Frohman MA, Kanaho Y (2004) Phospholipase D2 functions as a downstream signaling molecule of MAP kinase pathway in L1-stimulated neurite outgrowth of cerebellar granule neurons. J Neurochem 89:142–151.

Webb B, Suarez SS, Heaton MB, Walker DW (1997) Cultured postnatal rat septohippocampal neurons change intracellular calcium in response to ethanol and nerve growth factor. Brain Res 778: 354–366.

West JR, Hodges CA, Black AC (1981) Prenatal exposure to ethanol alters the organization of hippocampal mossy fibers in rats. Science 211:957–958.

Wooten MW, Ewald SJ (1991) Alcohols synergize with NGF to induce early differentiation of PC12 cells. Brain Res 550:333–339.

Wu GY, Zou DJ, Rajan I, Cline H (1999) Dendritic dynamics in vivo change during neuronal maturation. J Neurosci 19:4472–4483.

Yanni PA, Lindsley TA (2000) Ethanol inhibits development of dendrites and synapses in rat hippocampal pyramidal neuron cultures. Dev Brain Res 120:233–243.

Yanni PA, Rising LJ, Ingraham CA, Lindsley TA (2002) Astrocyte-derived factors modulate the inhibitory effect of ethanol on dendritic development. Glia 38:292–302.

Zimmerberg B, Mickus LA (1990) Sex differences in corpus callosum: influence of prenatal alcohol exposure and maternal undernutrition. Brain Res 537:115–122.

Zou J, Rabin RA, Pentney RJ (1993) Ethanol enhances neurite outgrowth in primary cultures of rat cerebellar macroneurons. Dev Brain Res 72:75–84.

15

Neuronal Survival Is Compromised by Ethanol: Extracellular Mediators

Michael W. Miller

Marla B. Bruns

Paula L. Hoffman

A salient characteristic of fetal alcohol spectrum disorder (FASD) is microcephaly and the associated microencephaly (Lemoine et al., 1968; Jones and Smith, 1973; Stratton et al., 1996; see Chapters 1, 8, and 9). Major contributors to this microencephaly are ethanol-induced reductions in the additive ontogenetic processes (cell proliferation and neuronal migration) and increases in the amount of neuronal death. The effects of ethanol on the additive processes are addressed in Chapters 11, 12, and 13. The present and following chapter (Chapter 16) describe the effects of ethanol on neuronal death and, conversely, neuronal survival. This chapter deals with the effects of ethanol on the incidence of neuronal death and the extracellular mediators that define this death, and the next chapter covers intracellular mechanisms that underlie this death.

Neuronal death is a natural process in the developing nervous system (Jacobson, 1991; Martin, 2001; Lossi and Merighi, 2003). It affects proliferating and postmitotic, postmigratory neurons (see Chapter 5).

The amount of neuronal death in the nervous system can vary from 20% to 80%. Factors that contribute to the amount of death are the location and the maturational state of the vulnerable neurons. One example is the cerebral cortex, in which the incidence of neuronal death is lamina- and neuron type–dependent (Miller, 1995a). Two- to threefold more neurons die in superficial layer VI (or layer VIa) than in layer IV and local circuit neurons (which, in part, differentiate on a later time line) are twice as likely to die as projection neurons in the same layer.

EFFECTS OF ETHANOL ON BRAIN STRUCTURES IN VIVO

In vivo studies show that ethanol affects the spatiotemporal pattern of neuronal death throughout the nervous system. Most studies have focused on the outcome, i.e., the effect of ethanol on total neuronal number. Few have teased out the effects on neuronal death from the effects of ethanol on other developmental events. The present review describes the limitations and advances in our understanding of such effects on four structures: the principal sensory nucleus of the trigeminal nerve (PSN), cerebellum, hippocampal formation, and neocortex. Each structure has a different developmental history that provides a distinctive platform for understanding the mechanism of ethanol toxicity.

Principal Sensory Nucleus of the Trigeminal Nerve

Documentation of neuronal death in vivo has consisted of two challenges: difficulties in identifying dying neurons and distinguishing the effects of ethanol on cell proliferation from those on neuronal death. The PSN is an ideal structure for separating these issues because it is a small, pontine nucleus that lends itself to quantitative studies. The PSN is largely surrounded by fiber bundles, facilitating the delineation of borders and comprises a relatively homogeneous population of neurons (Miller and Muller, 1989). Furthermore, the role of the PSN in neuronal development implicates it in FASD because it is a key site for the passage of information from somatosensory afferents arising in facial skin to higher centers—a primary characteristic of FASD is craniofacial malformations (Lemoine et al., 1968; Smith and Jones, 1973; Sulik et al., 1988; Johnston and Bronsky, 1995; Astley et al., 1999).

The PSN in the normal rat has 28,000 neurons. Following prenatal exposure to ethanol, the nucleus has only 19,600 neurons (Miller and Muller, 1989). This exposure occurs during the periods when PSN neurons proliferate and migrate (Nornes and Morita, 1979; Miller and Muller, 1989; Al-Ghoul and Miller, 1993a). A longitudinal study of the temporal effects of prenatal exposure to ethanol showed that one-third of this difference is a latent effect on neuronal survival (Miller, 1999) (Fig. 15–1). This finding was documented by two changes in the neonate: (1) a decrease in the total number of neurons and (2) increases in the number of pyknotic and silver-stained cells. PSN neurons also die when exposure occurs during the periods of primary synapse formation and naturally occurring neuronal death (NOND) (Miller, 1995b)—i.e., postnatally before postnatal day (P) 10 (Ashwell and Waite, 1991; Al-Ghoul and Miller, 1993b; Miller and Al-Ghoul, 1993). In contrast, ethanol exposure during adolescence does not have a significant effect

on neuronal number (Miller, 1995b). Thus, the critical window for ethanol-induced neuronal death in the PSN is framed by the periods of neuronal generation and synaptogenesis.

A prime afferent of the PSN is the infraorbital nerve. A neonatal lesion of this nerve causes massive neuronal death, confined to the ventral portion of the PSN where the infraorbital nerve terminates (Miller et al., 1991). Exposure to ethanol doubles the amount of this *trans*-synaptic death (Miller, 1999). Furthermore, this death is rapid, as the expression of Fos (a marker of cellular activity) and ALZ-50 (a marker of dying neurons) increases within 2 hr of placing the lesion (Miller and Kuhn, 1997).

Cerebellum

The cerebellum is susceptible to ethanol-induced damage in a dose-dependent manner; ethanol-exposed rats have smaller cerebella than controls (Diaz and Samson, 1981; West et al., 1989). A key factor contributing to the degree of damage is the peak blood ethanol concentration (BEC; Pierce and West, 1986; Bonthius et al., 1988). Rat pups exposed to the same amount of ethanol daily do not have the same amount of damage if the schedule of ethanol delivery differs. Exposures to relatively large boli of ethanol are significantly more deleterious than a constant delivery of low doses of ethanol.

The study of neuron numbers in the cerebellum has centered on Purkinje neurons (Goodlett and Horn, 2001; Light et al., 2002). Adult rats exposed to ethanol during the period from P4 to P10 have significantly fewer neurons than controls. The amount of Purkinje cell loss can vary from 10% to 70% depending on the developmental history and cerebellar compartment (Fig. 15–2). For example, lobules I–V, IX, and X are more vulnerable to ethanol exposure than lobules VI and VII (Pierce et al., 1989; Goodlett et al., 1990). The development of neurons in lobules I, II, IX, and X precedes that of neurons in the intervening lobules VI and VII (Miale and Sidman, 1961; Altman and Das, 1966; Altman and Bayer, 1978). Exposure to ethanol during the restricted period of P4 or P5 causes as much of a difference as does exposure between P4 and P10 (Light et al., 2002). This effect is concentration-dependent. Thus, exposure to a high BEC, even for a short time, can result in the loss of vulnerable neurons in the cerebellum (West et al., 1989; Miller, 1996b; Thomas et al., 1996).

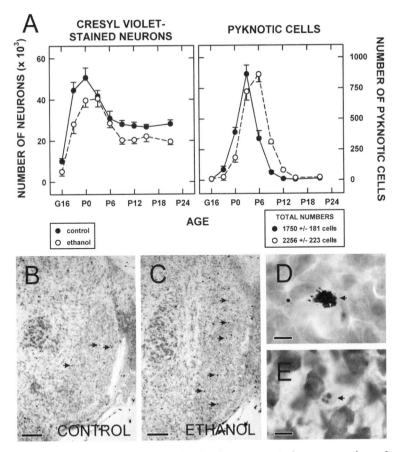

FIGURE 15–1 Neuronal death in the developing principal sensory nucleus of the trigeminal nerve (PSN). **A.** The numbers of neurons in the PSN rises prenatally and falls during the first 2 postnatal weeks (left). This decrease coincides with an increase in the frequency of pyknotic cells (right). Prenatal exposure to ethanol delays the period of neuronal death. **B.** Presumptive dying neurons (arrows) can be identified in a silver-stained section from the pons of a 3-day-old rat. They are distributed throughout the PSN. **C.** More argyrophilic neurons are evident in the PSN of an ethanol-treated 3-day-old pup. **D.** An argyrophilic cell (arrow) has a dense core and often is surrounded by granules. These are presumed to be blebs and released nucleosomes. **E.** A pyknotic cell is characterized by a condensed nucleus that often is broken into small bodies. Scale bars = 100 μm (B and C) and 10 μm (D and E). (*Source:* Data in A are taken with permission from Miller, 1999.)

Ethanol-induced differences in cell number may result from reductions in neuronal number and/or increases in neuronal death. The cerebella of rats exposed to ethanol during gestation alone or during the pre- and early postnatal period weigh less and have no fewer Purkinje neurons than rats exposed during the postnatal period alone (West et al., 1994; Miller, 1996b; Light et al., 2002). These data have been interpreted as evidence that ethanol does not affect neuronal generation. This may in part be true, as ethanol may not affect the generation of Purkinje cells which occurs prenatally (Miale and Sidman, 1961; Altman and Bayer, 1978). The possibility still exists, however, that ethanol does reduce the generation of

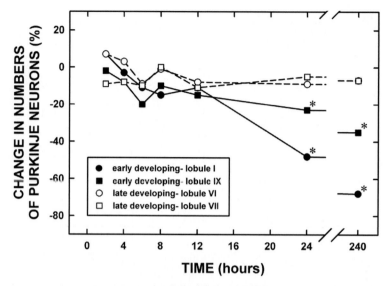

FIGURE 15–2 Effect of ethanol exposure on numbers of Purkinje neurons. Rats were exposed to ethanol by gavage on postnatal day 4. The numbers of Purkinje neurons in various cerebellar lobules were determined. The data for two pairs of lobules are presented: lobules I and IX, which are early developing lobules, and lobules VI and VII, which develop relatively late. Each point describes the change in the number of Purkinje neurons relative to the number identified in controls on P4. No significant changes were detected for late-developing lobules. Both of the early-developing lobules, however, were vulnerable to ethanol toxicity. Significant differences (p < 0.05; noted by asterisks) were detected only 24 hr or 10 days after exposure. (*Source:* Data taken from Light and colleagues, 2002.)

granule neurons produced postnatally, which can secondarily lead to the degeneration of Purkinje neurons dependent on their afferents (Rezai and Yoon, 1972; Herrup and Trenkner, 1987).

Recent evidence, from studies of restricted ethanol exposure, supports the notion that ethanol causes the death of Purkinje neurons. It is unlikely that a 1-day exposure to ethanol affects granule cell generation so profoundly and rapidly as to cause the short-term death of Purkinje neurons. Moreover, various studies show that ethanol increases the expression of two indices of apoptotic death by Purkinje neurons (Light et al., 2002)—the expression of activated caspase-3, an enzyme involved in the clipping of DNA into packets during apoptotic death, and evidence of terminal uridylated nick-end labeling (TUNEL), an index of DNA fragments. Moreover, exposure to ethanol on P4 leads to an increase in whole cerebellar catalase and reactive oxygen species (Horn, personal comm.).

Activated caspase-3 expression is markedly increased in many Purkinje cells and in a smattering of small cells in the internal granule cell layer. The sensitivity of the granule neurons per se to ethanol-induced death remains a question, as does the mechanism of ethanol-induced loss of Purkinje neurons (West et al., 1994; Goodlett and Horn, 2001). Suffice it to say that ethanol can compromise neuronal survival. Intracellular events underlying this death are reviewed in Chapters 6 and 16. The molecular mechanism of Purkinje cell death deserves more detailed analysis, given recent evidence that Purkinje neurons may die by a process of autophagy following removal of trophic support (Florez-McClure et al., 2004).

Hippocampal Formation

The hippocampal formation is a complex structure containing at least two major subdivisions, the hippocampus and the dentate gyrus. The axons of granule cells in the dentate gyrus synapse with pyramidal neurons in the hippocampus. These neuronal populations develop differently. For example, hippocampal pyramidal neurons are generated prenatally in the ventricular zone, whereas most (85%) granule neurons are generated postnatally in the intrahilar zone (Schlessinger et al., 1978; Nowakowski and Rakic, 1981).

Prenatal and postnatal exposure to ethanol has differential effects on the numbers of cells in the hippocampal formation. The amount of DNA in the hippocampal formation is not affected following prenatal exposure; however, postnatal exposure leads to an increase in DNA content (Miller, 1996a). Although this result suggests that ethanol does not affect neuronal survival, these biochemical measures do not discriminate between neurons and glia or differentiate the specific effects of ethanol on the hippocampus or dentate gyrus. Careful anatomical studies have shown that prenatal exposure to ethanol reduces the number of neurons in the hippocampus (Miller, 1995c). It is likely that some of this reduction results from a decrease in cell proliferation. Early postnatal exposure does not affect neuronal number unless the ethanol exposure is high (BEC >300 mg/dl; Miller, 1995c). Thus, it appears that ethanol does not induce the death of neurons in the hippocampal formation beyond that occurring naturally.

Neocortex

In Vivo Studies

Cortex contrasts with the cerebellum and hippocampus in that the generation of its neuronal subpopulations, such as projection and local circuit neurons, occurs concurrently (Miller, 1985). Likewise, the periods of NOND and synaptogenesis are largely synchronized for all cortical neurons (Rakic et al., 1986; Miller, 1988). In these aspects, neocortex is more like the PSN than the cerebellum and hippocampal formation.

Pre- and postnatal exposures to ethanol induce a difference in the number of cortical cells. Overall, total DNA content is 29% lower in the cortices of ethanol-treated rats than that of controls (Miller, 1996a). If the same mechanisms are at work in the developing cortex as in the PSN (Miller, 1999), one-third of the difference caused by prenatal exposure to ethanol is due to latent death. Prenatal exposure to

ethanol causes a ~33% difference in the number of neurons in somatosensory cortex (Miller and Potempa, 1990) and no difference in the number of neurons in visual cortex (Mooney et al., 1996; Mooney and Napper, 2005). Apparently, not all parts of the pallium are equally affected by ethanol. Postnatal exposure to ethanol also causes a significant difference in DNA content, although this difference is only 13% (Miller, 1996b), a difference expected to have equal effect on neurons and glia (Miller and Potempa, 1990). Interestingly, the amount of neuronal death (estimated at $29\% \times \frac{1}{3} = 10\%$) caused by exposure during the period of neuronogenesis (between gestational day [G] 11 and G21) is similar to that caused by exposure during early synaptogenesis (between P4 and P10). Does this mean that ethanol causes an equivalent amount of cell death regardless of the time of exposure, i.e., that there is no critical period for ethanol toxicity? No. Exposure to ethanol after the end of the periods of NOND and synaptogenesis does not affect the number of cortical neurons (Miller, unpublished results).

Changes in cell number are paralleled by alterations in the expression of proteins associated with neuronal death. These include ALZ-50 (Kuhn and Miller, 1998), bcl proteins, and activated caspase-3 (Mooney and Miller, 2000). The expression of each of these markers rises during the first and second postnatal weeks. Ethanol significantly affects each marker, mostly by delaying the period of expression (Kuhn and Miller, 1996; Mooney and Miller, 2001a).

A prime source of cortical afferents and target of cortical efferents is the thalamus. It is noteworthy that although ethanol-induced neuronal death occurs in the neocortex, apparently no such death occurs in at least some thalamic nuclei (Livy et al., 2001), including the ventrobasal thalamus (VB; Mooney and Miller, 1999a). Not only is the number of VB neurons the same in mature ethanol-treated and control rats, but there appears to be no difference in the temporal change in numbers during the periods of NOND and synaptogenesis (Mooney and Miller, 2001b). This phenomenon is particularly interesting in that the differential effect of ethanol sets up a potential mismatch in thalamocortical afferents and their target and with corticothalamic afferents and their target.

A series of studies by Olney and colleagues (e.g., Ikonomidou et al., 1999, 2000) describe the effects of early postnatal exposure to ethanol on the death of cortical cells. The authors claim that early developmental exposure to ethanol causes massive neuronal death when the exposure selectively occurs during synaptogenesis. In cortex, this process begins on P3 and peaks after P30 (Miller, 1988). Allegedly, transient exposure to ethanol causes a wave of neuronal death that is initially greatest in deep laminae and progresses superficially. Their work suggests that the vast majority of cortical neurons die as a consequence of early postnatal exposure to ethanol. These data are in conflict with a wealth of data (some of which are referenced above) and must be interpreted with caution.

As the data of Olney and colleagues have received considerable attention, they deserve comment. The data are based on a silver-staining method (de Olmos and Ingram, 1971; Friedman and Price, 1986) that purportedly identifies dying neurons. It is difficult to assess the applicability of this method because sections from the brains of control animals have virtually no label. This lack of labeling is disturbing because the consensus is that the first postnatal week is part of the period of NOND in the normal rat brain (e.g., Finlay and Slattery, 1983; Ferrer et al., 1990; Miller, 1995a; Spreafico et al., 1995). The data from the ethanol-treated rats are equally disturbing. Massive numbers of neurons in the cortices of ethanol-treated rats are argyrophilic (Ikonomidou et al., 1999). Recent evidence shows that neurons that exhibit a "marker" of cell death (e.g., TUNEL or caspase immunoreactivity) are not obliged to die (Gordon et al., 2002; Cheng and Zochodne, 2003; Ishida et al., 2004; Oomman et al., 2004). Furthermore, if all of the cortical neurons that exhibit ethanol-induced silver staining indeed do die, then early postnatal exposure to ethanol would cause a collapse of the cerebral wall. Careful studies show, however, that less than one sixth of all cortical neurons die as a result of ethanol exposure (Miller, 1996a; Mooney et al., 1996; Mooney and Napper, 2005).

According to Olney and colleagues, the ravages of ethanol are not confined to cerebral cortex. For example, various thalamic nuclei also exhibit widespread neuronal degeneration following early postnatal exposure to ethanol. It appears that most neurons in the anterior nuclei and ventral thalamus of 8-day-old rats are argyrophilic. Studies of mature rat thalami, however, show that rats exposed to ethanol pre- or postnatally have robust anterior nuclei and stereological data show that ethanol does not affect the number of neurons in thalamic nuclei (Mooney and Miller, 1999a; Livy et al., 2001, 2002).

Finally, Olney and colleagues conclude, incorrectly, that the temporal window of ethanol toxicity is restricted to the period of synaptogenesis. Indeed, exposure to ethanol during these ontogenetic events can cause neuronal death during the period of synaptogenesis (Miller, 1995b, 1999; Kuhn and Miller, 1998; Mooney and Miller, 1999b). Prenatal exposure to ethanol can also cause neuronal death (see above). Furthermore, ethanol has profound effects on cell proliferation (see Chapters 11 and 12) and neuronal migration (see Chapter 13).

Cell Culture Studies

Cultured cortical neurons obtained from 17-day-old fetuses exhibit a 25% loss over the first 2 days postplating (Fig. 15–3) (Seabold et al., 1998; Jacobs and Miller, 2001; Miller et al., 2003; Ramachandran et al., 2003). This loss is equivalent to the amount of natural death occurring among post-migratory neurons in cortex *in vivo* (Finlay and Slattery, 1983; Ferrer et al., 1990; Miller, 1995a; Spreafico et al., 1995). Ethanol exposure causes an additional 25% loss. Interpretation of these data is confounded because at least some of the neurons in fetal cortical cultures have the ability to proliferate (Jacobs and Miller, 1999). This confounding variable can be addressed by applying a mathematical model that determines the total amounts of cell proliferation and death (Miller, 2003). A particular strength of this model is that it does not rely on a method for identifying dying cells, which can bias the results. Accordingly, ethanol causes a 30% difference in the number of cultured cortical neurons or B104 neuroblastoma cells. Of this difference, two-thirds result from decreases in cell proliferation and one-third from ethanol-induced cell loss. Thus, the in vitro studies of cortical neurons concur with the in vivo data.

SURVIVAL-PROMOTING FACTORS

Evidence that neuronal death occurs during the period of synaptogenesis supports the hypothesis that neuronal death is driven by neurons failing to compete for an entity (a growth factor and/or synaptic sites) in limited supply. Among the factors that have

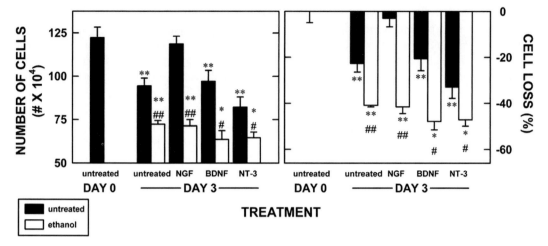

FIGURE 15–3 Effect of ethanol on neurotrophin-supported neuronal survival. Cortical neurons derived from 17-day-old fetuses were cultured in the presence of a neurotrophin (0 or 10 ng/ml) and ethanol (0 or 400 mg/dl). Over 3 days postplating, one-quarter of the untreated cortical neurons were lost. Nerve growth factor (NGF) prevented this loss, whereas brain-derived neurotrophic factor (BDNF) and neurotrophin 3 (NT-3) did not. Ethanol exacerbated the "natural" death observed in untreated cultures. Ethanol also eliminated the ability of NGF to maintain viability. Asterisks and pound signs denote significant differences relative to the untreated controls on day 0 and day 3, respectively. A single sign identifies data that are different at a level of $p < 0.05$ and a double sign designates differences at the $p < 0.01$ level of significance.

most commonly been implicated as promoting neuronal survival are nerve growth factor (NGF), brain-derived neurotrophic factor (BDNF), insulin-like growth factor-1 (IGF-1), N-methyl-D-aspartate (NMDA), and pituitary adenylyl cyclase activating polypeptide (PACAP).

Neurotrophins

Neurotrophins are secreted, diffusible signaling proteins known to exert neuromodulatory effects on adaptive processes such as synaptic plasticity, required for learning and memory, and neuronal survival. This family of proteins acts in an autocrine and anterograde fashion similar to that of neurotransmitters (Pitts and Miller, 1995, 2000; Miller and Pitts, 2000; Neet and Campenot, 2001). A number of neurotrophic factors have been identified, including NGF, BDNF, neurotrophin (NT)3, and NT-4/5, each of which supports distinct populations of neurons. To perform their functions, the neurotrophins bind to tyrosine kinase receptors (trks). NGF binds to trkA with high affinity, whereas BDNF and NT-4/5 bind to trkB. NT-3 binds primarily to trkC, but has also been associated with trkA or trkB in certain populations. A low-affinity receptor, p75, may also bind to any of the neurotrophins. This receptor may act in cooperation with or independently of the trks.

The tyrosine kinase associated with the high-affinity trks can activate at least three different signaling pathways to support differentiation, process outgrowth, cell survival, and activity-dependent plasticity (Bibel and Barde, 2000). The p75 receptor has no kinase activity associated with it per se, but it is now known to have signaling capability. The mechanisms of p75 signaling are far less characterized.

Depending on the extracellular environment and the composition and abundance of receptors on the membrane surface, neurotrophins can have beneficial or deleterious effects on neurons. The trks and p75 form homo- and heterodimers with each other, and these dynamic complexes can cooperate to exert varied effects (Chao, 2003; Huang and Reichardt, 2003). Receptor interactions can also be antagonistic, depending on which ligands are available.

The expression of neurotrophins changes in a time-dependent manner during development. That is, certain populations of neurons are dependent on one neurotrophin for a period of time. Then, after a critical period, these neurons become dependent on another neurotrophin(s). For example, Purkinje cells switch from BDNF dependence to NT-3 dependence between P4 and P6 (Davies, 1997). Coincidentally, this is the period of highest vulnerability of Purkinje cells to ethanol (Light et al., 2002; see above). Ethanol neurotoxicity may be mediated by changes in neurotrophin systems.

The distribution of neurotrophin ligands in various brain tissues during normal development is critical to appropriate signal transduction for survival. Alterations in the abundance of the neurotrophin ligands and receptors may result after ethanol exposure. In other words, withdrawal from or an inadequate supply of neurotrophins may underlie decreased cell survival. Conversely, ethanol may down-regulate receptor expression below a threshold required to initiate signals, interfere with ligand–receptor binding, or render neurotrophin receptors nonfunctional. Most likely, several mechanisms are at play, depending, of course, on the population of neurons and the time of ethanol exposure. The differential effects of ethanol on distinct populations of neurons can offer valuable insight to the normal interactions of neurotrophins during development.

Nerve Growth Factor

NGF prevents NOND—i.e., it is an anti-thanatopic factor (e.g., Majdan and Miller, 1999; Bibel and Barde, 2000; Morrison et al., 2002). This is particularly evident among cultures of cortical cells in which NGF uniquely supports cell survival (Fig. 15–3) (Seabold et al., 1998; Miller et al., 2003). NGF can also affect other developmental phenomena, notably the cell cycle and the survival of cells that exit the cycling population (Lopez-Sanchez and Frade, 2002).

Ethanol can interfere with NGF-mediated function both in vitro and in vivo. It disrupts the NGF-mediated survival of primary cultured cortical neurons (Seabold et al., 1998; Miller et al., 2003). A neuroprotective role of NGF is supported by studies of NGF over-expression in mice (Heaton et al., 2000b). Early postnatal exposure to ethanol kills fewer Purkinje cells in these mice than in wild-type controls. Altered NGF abundance could have pathological consequences, for example, NGF can potentiate free radical–induced apoptosis in vitro (Spear et al., 1998).

The effects of gestational ethanol exposure on NGF expression have also been examined in vivo. The amount of NGF protein was measured at P1 and P10 after gestational ethanol exposure. NGF is increased in the cortex and striatum of ethanol exposed animals at P1, but does not differ from controls at P10. No other neurotrophins are affected in any brain region at P1 (Heaton et al., 2000c). Expression of NGF protein is also increased in the hippocampal formation transiently at P15 after gestational ethanol exposure (Angelucci et al., 1997).

In addition to affecting neurotrophin ligand expression, ethanol can alter receptor expression. Ethanol-induced cell death in vitro is associated with a selective decrease in p75 expression; the expression of all trk isoforms is unaffected by ethanol (Seabold et al., 1998). This pattern reverberates in other cells, including septohippocampal neurons (Angelucci et al., 1997) and PC12 pheochromocytoma cells (Luo et al., 1996, 1999). In cerebellar Purkinje cells, following early postnatal ethanol exposure, there is a significant decrease in trkA and p75 receptor expression in vivo, despite there being no change in the amount of NGF (Dohrman et al., 1997). Selective down-regulation of the neurotrophin receptors by ethanol during the early postnatal development period is fatal to Purkinje cells (Light et al., 2002). The differential effect of ethanol on receptors may reflect the distribution of these receptors in the plasma membrane. Conceivably, p75 is distributed in lipid rafts (Higuchi et al., 2003), the fluidity of which is affected by ethanol (Peoples et al., 1996), whereas trks are relatively protected from ethanol because they appear not to be dispersed within rafts (Mutoh et al., 2004).

In addition, glia offer a critical supply of neurotrophins. Under normal homeostatic conditions, glia do not express NGF, however, they may elevate NGF under pathological conditions (Pitts and Miller, 1995; Miller and Pitts, 2000). This glial production of neurotrophins may be an attempt at neuroprotection. For example, astrocytes increase NGF expression after ethanol exposure in vitro (Vallés et al., 1994). C6 glioma cells secrete increased amounts of NGF and BDNF, quantities that are sufficient to protect cerebellar granule neurons from ethanol insult (Pantazis et al., 2000). Antibodies specific to neurotrophins and trk receptors block this ethanol-induced neuroprotection of the granule cells. Interestingly, trkA receptors are not localized in cerebellar granule cells, and they express only low amounts of p75. The implication is that NGF must be acting through a promiscuous trk isoform.

A downstream effect of ethanol toxicity in cortical cultures is the quashing of the expression of a gene up-regulated by NGF, *neg* (*ne*rve growth factor-stimulated, *e*thanol-depressed *g*ene) (Miller et al., 2003). The function of the gene product is unknown, although it appears that Neg is involved in NGF-mediated cell survival. The gene product has protein domains suggesting that it is a mitochondrial transmembrane protein (Nagase et al., 1996). This finding is intriguing in light of evidence that ethanol affects other mitochondrial proteins that regulate cell survival, for example, bcl-2 and bax (Mooney and Miller, 2001a) (see Chapter 16).

Brain-Derived Neurotrophic Factor

BDNF promotes cell survival in vivo and *in vitro*. During critical periods of normal development, BDNF is necessary for both neurite outgrowth and synaptic pruning. Developing neuronal processes compete for a limited supply of BDNF. Those neurons that are unable to obtain a sufficient amount of BDNF or that have insufficient trkB receptors undergo cell death.

Like NGF, BDNF is also thought to play a neuroprotective role in response to ethanol exposure. Indeed, BDNF may play a role in the tissue- and age-dependent components of ethanol-induced neuronal cell death. The striatum is a good example. In the normal striatum, NOND is more common on P3 than P14 (Heaton et al., 2003). This sequence is the inverse of the pattern of endogenous BDNF expression; striatal BDNF content is higher on P14 (Fig. 15–3). Early postnatal exposure to ethanol increases striatal BDNF content (Heaton et al., 2000c). Cerebellar Purkinje cells reveal a contrasting situation: Purkinje cells decrease BDNF expression after early postnatal ethanol exposure (Ge et al., 2004). Within hours of ethanol exposure, there is also decreased expression of cerebellar trkB. After P9, ethanol exposure does not affect BDNF or trkB expression. Compromised, time-dependent BDNF support in cerebellum may underlie high rates of Purkinje cell apoptosis during its period of ethanol sensitivity (P4 to P5).

Manipulation of available BDNF support *in vivo* can further demonstrate neurotrophin system–specific vulnerability to ethanol. Transgenic mice lacking BDNF expression in the cerebellum show significant losses of Purkinje cells after early postnatal ethanol exposure (Heaton et al., 2002). There are also concurrent decreases in anti-apoptotic factors (e.g., bcl-2) in these mice, suggesting that BDNF signals mediate neuronal survival. The contrasting results observed in cerebellum and striatum illustrate that ethanol can exert tissue-specific effects dependent on BDNF regulation.

In cortical tissue, the effects of ethanol on BDNF and trkB expression are also specific to the *time* of exposure. Early postnatal exposure causes significant increases in neocortical BDNF abundance, similar to changes observed in hippocampus and striatum (Heaton et al., 2000c). In contrast, gestational exposure results in significant decreases in BDNF and trkB receptor expression in cortex, which correlate with significant increases in apoptosis of cortical neurons (Climent et al., 2002). Both of these observations support the hypothesis that a sufficient amount of BDNF must be present to promote cell survival in response to ethanol.

Insulin-Like Growth Factor-1

IGF-1 is another survival-promoting factor that is target of ethanol (Zhang et al., 1998). Activation of the IGF-1 receptor can inhibit cell death in vitro (Wu et al., 1996) and *in vivo* (Resnicoff et al., 1995). An *in vivo* model in which transplanted tumor cells overexpressed IGF-1 receptors shows that IGF-1 plays a major protective role. In contrast, a decrease in IGF-1 receptor expression results in heavy amounts of apoptosis *in vivo*. The cytotoxic effects are more dramatic than when tumor cells are manipulated *in vitro*.

Like the neurotrophins, IGF-1 expression fluctuates during development. Normal changes of IGF-1 receptor distribution indicate that different populations of cells have different periods of IGF-1 dependence during the postnatal period of brain maturation (Breese et al., 1991). Normal neonates express the greatest abundance of IGF-1 protein at birth; IGF-1 content falls 61% by P20.

Gestational ethanol exposure alters IGF-1 abundance and distribution during postnatal brain development (Breese et al., 1994). In offspring of ethanol-exposed mothers, the decrease in IGF-1 expression is attenuated, falling only by 25% during the first 20 days after birth. Localization of IGF-1 and IGF-1 receptors, however, is not affected. Thus, ethanol may disrupt the regulation of IGF-1 availability (i.e., production and secretion) rather than the ligand–receptor signals.

Ethanol can reverse the anti-apoptotic effects of IGF-1 receptor signaling (Resnicoff et al., 1996). Fibroblasts lacking IGF-1 receptors are completely insensitive to ethanol-induced cell death *in vitro*. Cerebellar granule neurons can normally be rescued from apoptosis in the presence of IGF-1 (D'Mello et al., 1993). Ethanol can inhibit this neuroprotection even when excess IGF-1 is available (Zhang et al., 1998).

The amount of IGF-1 in maternal plasma is reduced after ethanol exposure (Breese and Sonntag, 1995). Insufficient IGF-1 ligand or receptors can cause massive amounts of apoptosis. Thus, the consequences of insufficient plasma IGF-1 on metabolism and hormone physiology may contribute to body growth deficiencies that compound the pathological microcephalic brain development associated with FAS.

The vulnerability of an individual IGF-1 receptor to ethanol can vary in that the affinity of the receptor for its ligand may be altered. The enzyme activity of the IGF-1 receptor can also be disrupted. Several subclones of 3T3 cells generated to express equal amounts of IGF-1 receptor demonstrated that not all IGF-1 receptors are created equal (Seiler et al., 2000). IGF-1 receptors in some subclones resisted the effects of ethanol; ethanol did not inhibit the autophosphorylation of the IGF-1 receptor. Like the tissue-specific distribution of neurotrophin receptors and variable expression of trk isoforms, relative abundance of IGF-1 receptors and their variable resistance to ethanol may explain the differential effects of ethanol on various cell populations.

N-Methyl-D-Aspartate

Glutamate is a major excitatory neurotransmitter in the mammalian nervous system. Its actions are mediated by interaction with both metabotropic and ionotropic receptors (Hollman and Heinemann, 1994; Ozawa et al., 1998). The NMDA subtype of ionotropic glutamate receptor plays an important role in synaptic plasticity (e.g., learning and memory), but hyperactivation of NMDA receptors can lead to excitotoxic, primarily necrotic, death of mature neurons (Choi, 1992).

During neuronal development, NMDA receptor function is necessary for the activity-dependent organization of synapses (Collingridge and Lester, 1989; McDonald and Johnston, 1990). In addition, activation of

NMDA receptors can have a trophic or protective effect on developing neurons. This protective effect has been most extensively studied with cultured cerebellar granule neurons. Cerebellar granule neurons isolated from 7-day-old rats require a growth medium containing a depolarizing concentration of K^+ (25 mM KCl) for survival (Gallo et al., 1987; Balázs et al., 1988). The dependence of cell survival on depolarization develops over a narrow time frame. This period includes the time when the glutamatergic mossy fibers innervate postmitotic granule neurons. Treatment of cerebellar granule neurons with NMDA also can protect these postmitotic neurons from cell death when they are grown in medium containing a physiological concentration of K^+ (5 mM KCl) (Balázs et al., 1988; Burgoyne et al., 1993; Bhave and Hoffman, 1997). This neuroprotective action of NMDA apparently mimics the effect of innervation of the granule neurons by mossy fiber afferents *in vivo*.

Two models of cultured cerebellar granule cells have been used to explore the neuroprotective property of NMDA. In the first model, neurons from postnatal rats are cultured in a medium containing a physiological concentration of KCl (see above). These cells undergo spontaneous death. In the second model, the cells are grown in medium containing 25 mM KCl and after several days in culture, the medium is replaced with medium containing a low KCl concentration and often is serum-free (Yan et al., 1994). Under both of these conditions, neurons die over a period of 1 or 2 days, and can be protected by the addition of NMDA (Yan et al., 1994; Bhave and Hoffman, 1997) or polyamines (Harada and Sugimoto, 1997). Polyamines modulate the function of NMDA receptors (Dodd et al., 2000) and act in part through an NMDA receptor–dependent mechanism (Harada and Sugimoto, 1997). In both instances, NMDA has a neuroprotective effect on cerebellar granule neurons, however, the molecular mechanism of cell death differs in the two models (Kharlamov et al., 1995; Bhave et al., 1999; Bonni et al., 1999).

It is well-established that ethanol acutely inhibits NMDA receptor function. This action has been demonstrated in vivo and in vitro, and in recombinant systems where the NMDA receptor is expressed in heterologous cells (Hoffman, 2003). These findings led to the proposal that ethanol can promote the death of cerebellar granule neurons by interfering with the protective effect of NMDA. Interestingly, ethanol not only reduces the protective effect of

NMDA on cerebellar granule neurons grown in the presence of a low concentration of K^+ but also reduces the toxic effect of NMDA on cerebellar granule neurons grown in a high concentration of K^+ (Wegelius and Korpi, 1995). Neurons grown in low K^+-containing medium are thought to have the characteristics of immature neurons, thus cerebellar granule neurons grown under these conditions represent a model in which the effects of ethanol and NMDA on neuronal survival during development can be assessed in a mechanistic manner.

Cerebellar granule neurons grown in low K^+, or subjected to removal of high KCl, exhibit apoptotic features, such as DNA fragmentation, nuclear condensation, somatic blebbing, and caspase activation (Yan et al., 1994; Bhave and Hoffman, 1997; Bhave et al., 1999). The death of these neurons in culture appears to mimic the apoptosis observed in the developing rat cerebellum *in vivo* between P5 and P11 (Wood et al., 1993). Many factors, such as activation of various caspases, the proteasome and accumulation of ubiquinated proteins, mitochondrial function, Bcl-family proteins, and oxidative stress, have been implicated in apoptotic cell loss (Atabay et al., 1996; Alavez et al., 2000; Canu et al., 2000; Vogel, 2002; Konishi and Bonni, 2003). Treatment of cerebellar granule neurons with NMDA prevents this apoptotic death (Yan et al., 1994; Bhave and Hoffman, 1997; Bhave et al., 1999).

Ethanol promotes apoptosis by interfering with the protective effect of NMDA (Bhave and Hoffman, 1997). Neurons grown in low KCl–containing medium for 4 days prior to addition of ethanol and/or NMDA for 24 hr experience the same amount of apoptotic death as neurons treated with ethanol alone. Ethanol also inhibits the neuroprotective effect of NMDA when cerebellar granule neurons are switched from high- to low-KCl medium (Castoldi et al., 1998). NMDA protects cerebellar granule neurons from apoptosis by increasing the expression of BDNF, which in turn activates phosphatidylinositol 3-phosphokinase (PI3K) and Akt phosphorylation (Bhave et al., 1999). Ethanol inhibits the first step of this pathway, the NMDA-stimulated increase in BDNF expression, which is mediated by NMDA-induced increases in intracellular calcium (Zafra et al., 1990, 1991; Ghosh et al., 1994). This action of ethanol is specific, i.e., ethanol does not affect later steps in the neuroprotective pathway (Bhave et al., 1999). Thus, ethanol apparently does not interfere with the

protective effect of BDNF (Hoffman et al., 1994; Seabold et al., 1998). The site of action of ethanol at the NMDA receptor is further supported by studies of cerebellar granule neurons showing that the inhibitory effect of ethanol on NMDA receptor function (measured as an increase in intracellular calcium) and that on the protective role of NMDA are both attenuated in the presence of a high concentration of glycine, the co-agonist at the NMDA receptor (Bhave and Hoffman, 1997).

Although ethanol acutely inhibits NMDA receptor function, chronic exposure of *mature* neurons to ethanol up-regulates NMDA receptor function (Hoffman, 2003). This change, *in vivo*, is thought to contribute to ethanol withdrawal hyperexcitability and the brain damage associated with long-term ethanol ingestion. By contrast, chronic treatment of cultured "immature" cerebellar granule neurons (grown in 5.0 mM KCl) with ethanol *decreases* the neuroprotective effect of NMDA, similar to the effect of short-term ethanol treatment (Bhave et al., 2000). The effect of chronic (3 day) exposure to ethanol persists even after ethanol is removed (Castoldi et al., 1998; Bhave et al., 2000), attributed to decreased expression of NMDA receptor subunits by the ethanol-treated "immature" neurons, resulting in decreased NMDA receptor–mediated stimulation of BDNF expression (Bhave et al., 2000). Similarly, chronic prenatal ethanol treatment *in vivo* reduces the expression of NMDA receptor subunits in the offspring (Hughes et al., 1998).

The age of the cultured cerebellar granule neurons defines the response to ethanol and NMDA. For example, ethanol exposure induces the death of cerebellar granule neurons harvested on P10 and treated with ethanol (50 or 200 mM) for 1 day (Pantazis et al., 1995). This death can be prevented by adding NMDA to the cultures (Pantazis et al., 1995). In contrast, if cells are maintained in culture (5.0 mM or 25 mM KCl) for 7 days and then exposed to ethanol for 24 hr, there is no evidence of increased cell death. The underlying mechanism of this phenomenon is unknown. It must be considered that the ethanol-induced death of neurons on the first day in culture could reflect interference with cellular adhesion to the culture dishes and thus be an artifact of the culture system. Nevertheless, under conditions in which ethanol alone produces neuronal death, a number of anti-apoptotic agents (e.g., NMDA, neurotrophins, and PACAP) can prevent ethanol-induced death

(Pantazis et al., 1995; Heaton et al., 1999; 2000a, 2000b; de la Monte et al., 2000; Vaudry et al., 2002). Whether these results are indicative of the mechanism by which ethanol itself induces neuronal death or reflect algebraically additive effects of ethanol and protective agents has yet to be determined. Such studies of the temporal vulnerability of cultured cerebellar granule neurons to ethanol-induced death are reminiscent of the *in vivo* studies demonstrating windows of vulnerability of the cerebellum to ethanol-induced neuronal loss during development in vivo (e.g., Hamre and West, 1993).

An in vivo interaction of ethanol and the NMDA receptor with respect to neuronal death is not well established. Studies reported by Olney and colleagues (2002b) suggest such an interaction. They found that a single treatment with ethanol produces apoptotic degeneration in mouse or rat brain (Ikonomidou et al., 2000). On the basis of patterns of neurodegeneration and comparisons with the effects of NMDA receptor antagonists, they proposed that the pro-apoptotic action of ethanol is mediated through NMDA (and γ-aminobutyric acid A) receptors (Ikonomidou et al., 1999, 2000; Olney et al., 2002a). In the cerebellum, the fact that cerebellar granule neurons undergo apoptosis at a specific time during development (Wood et al., 1993) and the possibility that this apoptosis is a consequence of the lack of innervation by the glutamatergic mossy fiber afferents (Balázs et al., 1988) suggest that inhibition of NMDA receptor function by ethanol at this critical period of development *in vivo* would result in inappropriate cell loss. Although the mechanism of cell death proposed by Olney and colleagues is consistent with results from the *in vitro* studies, the caveats raised earlier in this chapter, that the massive amount of cell death reported by Olney and colleagues is not consistent with studies of the number of neurons in adult animals treated pre- or postnatally with ethanol, cast doubt on the interpretation of the *in vivo* studies.

Pituitary Adenylyl Cyclase Activating Polypeptide

Activation of the transcription factor cyclic adenosine monophosphate (cAMP) response element binding protein (CREB) may be a downstream mediator of stimulus-dependent neuronal survival (Fig. 15–4) (Shaywitz and Greenberg, 1999; Finkbeiner, 2000; Walton and Dragunow, 2000). Persistent phosphorylation of CREB is considered necessary to increase the expression of genes needed for cell survival. Therefore, activation of several signal transduction pathways that contribute to CREB phosphorylation may provide optimal conditions for survival. One such pathway is the cAMP/protein kinase A (PKA) pathway. Activation of the intracellular messenger cAMP can increase neuronal proliferation, differentiation, and survival (Tojima et al., 2003; Fujioka et al., 2004). Many studies of the role of the cAMP/PKA/CREB pathway in neuronal death have used cerebellar granule neurons as a model. Raising cAMP concentration in cerebellar granule neurons in many (D'Mello et al., 1993; Chang et al., 1996; Kienlen Campard et al., 1997; Moran et al., 1999; Li et al., 2000) but not all (Yan et al., 1995) instances has prevented apoptosis.

PACAP, a cAMP generator, is a neuropeptide originally isolated from an ovine hypothalamic extract (Miyata et al., 1989). This peptide exists in two isoforms (PACAP-27 and PACAP-38) that are members of the vasoactive intestinal polypeptide (VIP)/secretin/glucagon family. Both isoforms of PACAP have similar biochemical effects. They interact with high-affinity PAC_1 receptors (which have high specific affinity for PACAP) and with two forms of VPAC receptors (which have equal affinity for PACAP and VIP; Harmar et al., 1998). Both PACAP and several splice variants of the PAC_1 receptor (Spengler et al., 1993) are found in the cerebellum and expressed by cultured cerebellar granule neurons (Basille et al., 1995; Favit et al., 1995; Tabuchi et al., 2001). In these neurons, activation of the PAC_1 receptor leads both to cAMP accumulation and polyphosphoinositide hydrolysis (Basille et al., 1995; Favit et al., 1995). Treatment of cerebellar granule neurons with PACAP attenuates apoptosis produced either by growing the neurons in low KCl-containing medium or by switching them from a high to low KCl-containing medium (Cavallaro et al., 1996; Campard et al., 1997; Villalba et al., 1997; Bhave and Hoffman, 2004). PACAP is likely an endogenous factor that promotes cerebellar granule neuron survival because treatment of granule neurons grown in a high KCl–containing medium with a PACAP receptor antagonist reduces neuronal survival (Tabuchi et al., 2001).

The mechanism by which PACAP promotes cerebellar granule neuron survival has been evaluated in several studies. The cAMP/PKA pathway and the mitogen-activated protein kinase (MAPK) pathway (Villalba et al., 1997) have been implicated

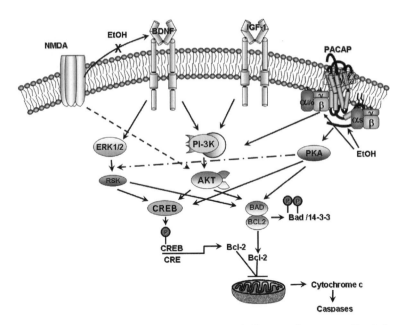

FIGURE 15–4 Neuroprotective pathways in cerebellar granule neurons. Cerebellar granule neurons from postnatal rats, cultured in medium containing 5 mM KCl, undergo spontaneous apoptosis. These neurons can be protected by addition of *n*-methyl-D-aspartate (NMDA), brain-derived neurotrophic factor (BDNF), insulin-like growth factor 1 (IGF-1), or pituitary adenylyl cyclase activating polypeptide (PACAP) to the culture medium. The anti-apoptotic effect of NMDA depends on NMDA-induced expression of BDNF, which is inhibited by ethanol. The protective effects of NMDA and BDNF are mediated through activation of phosphatidylinositol-3′ hydroxy kinase (PI3K), which in turn activates Akt. NMDA has also been suggested to activate Akt directly via Ca^{2+}/calmodulin-dependent protein kinase kinase (CaM-KK) (dotted line). BDNF can also promote cerebellar granule neuron survival by activation of microtubule-associated protein kinase (MAPK) extracellular signal-related kinase (ERK) 1/2. Activation of this pathway results in phosphorylation of the pro-apoptotic protein Bad on the Ser[112], which is mediated by Rsk-2, a member of the MAPK–activated pp90 ribosomal S6 kinase family. Phosphorylation of Bad results in dissociation of Bad from the anti-apoptotic Bcl-2 protein, allowing the survival function of Bcl-2 to be expressed. Activation of the PI3K/Akt pathway results in phosphorylation of Bad on Ser[136], and phosphorylation on both sites may be necessary to reduce apoptosis (Bonni et al., 1999). Although treatment of cells with NMDA activates MAPK, an inhibitor of this pathway does not block the protective effect of NMDA. There is also evidence that the anti-apoptotic actions of the MAPK and PI 3-kinase pathways may converge at the level of cyclic AMP response element binding protein (CREB). CREB activation can increase the expression of bcl-2 mRNA. The overall effect of activation of these pathways is to release Bcl-2 from dimerization with Bad and to increase Bcl-2 levels. The anti-apoptotic effect of PACAP in cerebellar granule neurons is mediated through activation of PKA by cAMP and by activation of the PI3K pathway via a pertussis toxin–sensitive G protein. Ethanol enhances both of these PACAP-stimulated pathways. Protein Kinase A (PKA) can phosphorylate Bad at Ser[112] while Akt phosphorylates Bad at Ser[136], as discussed above. Activation of PKA and PI3K also leads to CREB activation. Therefore, the protective effect of PACAP may depend on the convergence of two signaling pathways at the level of phosphorylation of Bad and/or CREB.

(Campard et al., 1997; Vaudry et al., 1998). Ethanol acutely enhances receptor-stimulated cAMP production in various neuronal and non-neuronal systems (Tabakoff and Hoffman, 1998). If ethanol also enhances PACAP-stimulated cAMP production, one could postulate that ethanol has a neuroprotective effect when granule neurons are treated simultaneously with ethanol and PACAP.

The signaling pathways that mediate the anti-apoptotic effect of PACAP on cerebellar granule neurons have been examined. In cells grown in the absence or presence of ethanol in a medium contain-

ing 5 mM KCl, the anti-apoptotic effect of PACAP was reduced by inhibitors of the cAMP/PKA pathway and the PI3K pathway (Bhave and Hoffman, 2004). The anti-apoptotic effect of PACAP is evident within 4 hr. Ethanol (100 mM) accelerates this process as the anti-apoptotic effect of PACAP is maximal after only 1 hr of exposure to ethanol and PACAP. The effect of ethanol is blocked by inhibitors of both the cAMP/PKA and the PI3K pathways, and ethanol stimulates PACAP-induced production of cAMP and phosphorylation of Akt (Bhave and Hoffman, 2004). In addition, ethanol enhances PACAP-induced

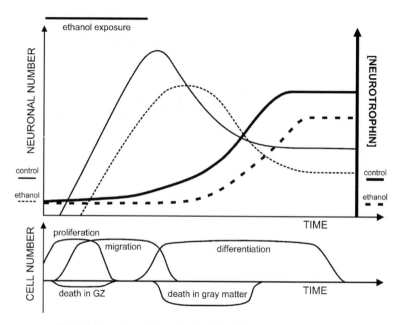

FIGURE 15–5 Schematic of the relationship of neurotrophin expression and neuronal ontogeny. There are two periods of cell death during neural ontogeny: during the period of cell proliferation (in the germinal zone [GZ]) and during the period of neuronal differentiation (in the gray matter). At least the latter is associated with neurotrophin expression. Neurotrophin expression increases during the period of neuronal differentiation to support the growth of neurites and promote synaptogenesis. Nevertheless, neurotrophin expression is limited, hence it defines the number of neurons that can successfully compete for enough neurotrophin to maintain their survival. Ethanol delays the numbers of neurons that are generated and successfully migrate to the CNS structure and reduces the amount of available neurotrophin. The consequence of this reduction is that fewer neurons survive. Solid and broken lines identify changes for control and ethanol-treated subjects, respectively. Thicker lines depict changes in the numbers of neurons in a CNS structure and thinner lines describe changes in neurotrophin expression. The graphs at the bottom depict changes in the numbers of cells involved in a particular ontogenetic event (for a control subject).

CREB phosphorylation. These results indicated that ethanol treatment of cerebellar granule neurons can *increase* neuroprotection induced by PACAP.

Although exposure of the developing brain to ethanol is associated with an overall loss of neurons, and the cerebellum is particularly sensitive to ethanol-induced neuronal loss (Goodlett et al., 1990; West et al., 1990; Miller, 1992, 1996b; Maier et al., 1999), the findings for PACAP offer a possible approach for amelioration of the overall deleterious effect of ethanol. Since PACAP is endogenously present in cerebellar granule neurons, the presence of ethanol at critical times of development could enhance the protective effect of this endogenous factor. Neuronal survival during development depends on the interplay of various neurotrophic factors. Ethanol can affect the balance among the effects of these factors. One approach to alleviating the damaging effects of ethanol during central nervous system development is to increase the contribution of neuroprotective pathways that are targeted by ethanol.

SUMMARY AND CONCLUSIONS

Ethanol-induced neuronal death occurs during defined periods of the developmental time line (Fig. 15–5). These time periods coincide with those of neuronogenesis and primary synaptogenesis, which are periods of NOND (see Chapter 5). Exposure to ethanol at this time may exacerbate processes involved in NOND. This pattern applies to parts of the brain in which the development of the constituent neurons is relatively synchronized, as in the PSN and cerebral cortex. An interesting counterpoint is the cerebellum, in which populations of neurons follow nonoverlapping ontogenetic time lines. For example, the proliferation of granule cell precursors coincides with the synaptogenesis of Purkinje neurons. In this case, the window of vulnerability to ethanol is narrow; it is only 2 days (P4 and P5), early during the period of Purkinje neuron synaptogenesis.

Ethanol has multiple targets, including extracellular components of growth factor systems, i.e., ligands and receptors. Ethanol is not a promiscuous toxin; rather, it affects the actions of specific ligands (e.g., for fetal cortical neurons, NGF, but not BDNF or NT-3). Ligands may be temporally expressed and overlaid upon pre-existing systems. This situation is evident in the developing peripheral nervous system (Davies, 1997). Potentially, neurons are more susceptible when only a single neurotrophin system is active, but they become more resistant to ethanol toxicity as additional intercellular communication systems are established. How this affects intracellular processing is currently unknown. An alternative but not mutually exclusive mechanism is that ethanol targets receptors (e.g., p75, but not trk isoform content). Receptor selectivity may reflect the differential distribution of p75 and trks in the plasma membrane, for example, in lipid rafts.

In summary, ethanol vulnerability is determined by extracellularly initiated events. The effects of ethanol on ligands and receptors may be additive or synergistic. Regardless, the differential effects are instructive about the role of neurotrophin systems during early development.

Abbreviations

BDNF   brain-derived neurotrophic factor

BEC   blood ethanol concentration

cAMP   cyclic adenosine monophosphate

CREB   cAMP response element binding protein

ERK   extracellular signal-related kinase

FASD   fetal alcohol spectrum disorders

G   gestational day

IGF-1   insulin-like growth factor-1

MAPK   mitogen-activated protein kinase

NGF   nerve growth factor

NMDA   N-methyl-D-aspartate

NOND   naturally occurring neuronal death

NT   neurotrophin

P   postnatal day

PACAP   pituitary adenylyl cyclase activating polypeptide

PI3K   phosphatidylinositol 3′-phosphokinase

PKA   protein kinase A

PSN   principal sensory nucleus of the trigeminal nerve

trk   tyrosine kinase receptor

TUNEL   terminal uridylated nick-end labeling

VB   ventrobasal nucleus of the thalamus

VIP   vasoactive intestinal polypeptide

ACKNOWLEDGMENTS This chapter was written with the support of the National Institutes of Alcohol Abuse and Alcoholism (MBB, PLH, and MWM) and the Department of Veterans Affairs (MWM).

References

Alavez S, Pedroza D, Moran J (2000) Role of heat shock proteins in the effect of NMDA and KCl on cerebellar granule cells survival. Neurochem Res 25:341–347.

Al-Ghoul WM, Miller MW (1993a) Orderly migration of neurons to the principal sensory nucleus of the trigeminal nerve of the rat. J Comp Neurol 330:464–475.

Al-Ghoul WM, Miller MW (1993b) Development of the principal sensory nucleus of the trigeminal nerve of the rat and evidence for a transient synaptic field in the trigeminal sensory tract. J Comp Neurol 330:476–490.

Altman J, Bayer SA (1978) Prenatal development of the cerebellar system in the rat. I. Cytogenesis and histogenesis of the deep nuclei and the cortex of the cerebellum. J Comp Neurol 179:23–48.

Altman J, Das GD (1966) Autoradiographic and histological studies of postnatal neurogenesis. I. J Comp Neurol 126:337–390.

Angelucci F, Cimino M, Balduini W, Piltillo L, Aloe L (1997) Prenatal exposure to ethanol causes differential effects in nerve growth factor and its receptor in the basal forebrain of preweaning and adult rats. J Neural Transplant Plast 6:63–71.

Ashwell KW, Waite PM (1991) Cell death in the developing trigeminal nuclear complex of the rat. Dev Brain Res 63:291–295.

Astley SJ, Magnuson SI, Omnell LM, Clarren SK (1999) Fetal alcohol syndrome: changes in craniofacial form with age, cognition, and timing of ethanol exposure in the macaque. Teratology 59:163–172.

Atabay C, Cagnoli CM, Kharlamov E, Ikonomovic MD, Mancv H (1996) Removal of serum from primary cultures of cerebellar granule neurons induces oxidative stress and DNA fragmentation: protection with antioxidants and glutamate receptor antagonists. J Neurosci Res 43:465–475.

Balázs R, Jorgensen OS, Hack N (1988) N-methyl-D-aspartate promotes the survival of cerebellar granule cells in culture. Neuroscience 27:437–451.

Basille M, Gonzalez BJ, Leroux P, Jeandel L, Fournier A, Vaudry H (1993) Localization and characterization of PACAP receptors in the rat cerebellum during development: evidence for a stimulatory effect of PACAP on immature cerebellar granule cells. Neuroscience 57:329–338.

Bhave SV, Hoffman PL (1997) Ethanol promotes apoptosis in cerebellar granule cells by inhibiting the trophic effect of NMDA. J Neurochem 68:578–586.

Bhave SV, Ghoda L, Hoffman PL (1999) Brain-derived neurotrophic factor mediates the anti-apoptotic effect of NMDA in cerebellar granule neurons: signal transduction cascades and site of ethanol action. J Neurosci 19:3277–3286.

Bhave SV, Hoffman PL (2004) Phosphatidylinositol 3′-OH kinase and protein kinase A pathways mediate the anti-apoptotic effect of pituitary adenylyl cyclase-activating polypeptide in cultured cerebellar granule neurons: modulation by ethanol. J Neurochem 88:359–369.

Bhave SV, Snell LD, Tabakoff B, Hoffman PL (2000) Chronic ethanol exposure attenuates the anti-apoptotic effect of NMDA in cerebellar granule neurons. J Neurochem 75:1035–1044.

Bibel M, Barde YA (2000) Neurotrophins: key regulators of cell fate and cell shape in the vertebrate nervous system. Genes Dev 14:2919–2937.

Bonni A, Brunet A, West AE, Datta SR, Takasu MA, Greenberg ME (1999) Cell survival promoted by the Ras-MAPK signaling pathway by transcription-dependent and independent mechanisms. Science 286:1358–1362.

Bonthius DJ, Goodlett CR, West JR (1988) Blood alcohol concentration and severity of microencephaly in neonatal rats depend on the pattern of alcohol administration. Alcohol 5:209–214.

Breese CR, D'Costa A, Booze RM, Sonntag WE (1991) Distribution of insulin-like growth factor 1 (IGF-1) and 2 (IGF-2) receptors in the hippocampal formation of rats and mice. Adv Exp Med Biol 293:449–458.

Breese CR, D'Costa A, Sonntag WE (1994) Effect of in utero ethanol exposure on the postnatal ontogeny of insulin-like growth factor-1, and type-1 and type-2 insulin-like growth factor receptors in the rat brain. Neuroscience 63:579–589.

Breese CR, Sonntag WE (1995) Effect of ethanol on plasma and hepatic insulin-like growth factor regulation in pregnant rats. Alcohol Clin Exp Res 19:867–873.

Burgoyne RD, Graham ME, Cambray-Deakin M (1993) Neurotrophic effects of NMDA receptor activation on developing cerebellar granule cells. J Neurocytol 22:689–695.

Campard PK, Crochemore C, Rene F, Monnier D, Koch B, Loeffler JP (1997) PACAP type I receptor activation promotes cerebellar neuron survival through the cAMP/PKA signaling pathway. DNA Cell Biol 16:323–333.

Canu N, Barbato C, Ciotti MT, Serafino A, Dus L, Calissano P (2000) Proteasome involvement and accumulation of ubiquitinated proteins in cerebellar granule neurons undergoing apoptosis. J Neurosci 20:589–599.

Castagne V, Gautschi M, Lefevre K, Posada A, Clarke PG (1999) Relationships between neuronal death and the cellular redox status. Focus on the developing nervous system. Prog Neurobiol 59:397–423.

Castoldi AF, Barni S, Randine G, Costa LG, Manzo L (1998) Ethanol selectively interferes with the trophic action of NMDA and carbachol on cultured cerebellar granule neurons undergoing apoptosis. Dev Brain Res 111:279–289.

Cavallaro S, Copani A, D'Agata V, Musco S, Petralia S, Ventra C, Stivala F, Travali S, Canonico PL (1996) Pituitary adenylate cyclase activating polypeptide prevents apoptosis in cultured cerebellar granule neurons. Mol Pharmacol 50:60–66.

Chang JY, Korolev VV, Wang JZ (1996) Cyclic AMP and pituitary adenylate cyclase-activating polypeptide (PACAP) prevent programmed cell death of cultured rat cerebellar granule cells. Neurosci Lett 206:181–184.

Chao MV (2003) Neurotrophins and their receptors: a convergence point for many signalling pathways. Nat Rev Neurosci 4:299–209.

Cheng C, Zochodne DW (2003) Sensory neurons with activated caspase-3 survive long-term experimental diabetes. Diabetes 52:2363–2371.

Choi DW (1992) Excitotoxic cell death. J Neurobiol 23:1261–1276.

Climent E, Pascual M, Renau-Piqueras J, Guerri C (2002) Ethanol exposure enhances cell death in the developing cerebral cortex: role of brain-derived neurotrophic factor and its signaling pathways. J Neurosci Res 68:213–225.

Collingridge GL, Lester RA (1989) Excitatory amino acid receptors in the vertebrate central nervous system. Pharmacol Rev 41:143–210.

Davies AM (1997) Neurotrophin switching: where does it stand? Curr Opin Neurobiol 7:110–118.

de la Monte SM, Ganju N, Banerjee K, Brown NV, Luong T, Wands JR (2000) Partial rescue of ethanol-induced neuronal apoptosis by growth factor activation of phosphoinositol-3-kinase. Alcohol Clin Exp Res 24:716–726.

de Olmos JS, Ingram WR (1971) An improved cupric-silver method for impregnation of axonal and terminal degeneration. Brain Res 33:523–529.

Diaz J, Samson HH (1980) Impaired brain growth in neonatal rats exposed to ethanol. Science 208:751–753.

D'Mello SR, Galli C, Ciotti T, Calissano P (1993) Induction of apoptosis in cerebellar granule neurons by low potassium: inhibition of death by insulin-like growth factor I and cAMP. Proc Natl Acad Sci USA 90:10989–10993.

Dodd PR, Beckmann AM, Davidson MS, Wilce PA (2000) Glutamate-mediated transmission, alcohol, and alcoholism. Neurochem Int 37:509–533.

Dohrman DP, West JR, Pantazis NJ (1997) Ethanol reduces expression of the nerve growth factor receptor, but not nerve growth factor protein levels in the neonatal rat cerebellum. Alcohol Clin Exp Res 21:882–893.

Favit A, Scapagnini U, Canonico PL (1995) Pituitary adenylate cyclase-activating polypeptide activates different signal transducing mechanisms in cultured cerebellar granule cells. Neuroendocrinology 61:377–382.

Ferrer I, Bernet E, Soriano E, Del Rio T, Fonseca M (1990) Naturally occurring cell death in the cerebral cortex of the rat and removal of dead cells by transitory phagocytes. Neuroscience 39:451–458.

Finkbeiner S (2000) CREB couples neurotrophin signals to survival messages. Neuron 25:11–14.

Finlay BL, Slattery M (1983) Local differences in the amount of early cell death in neocortex predict adult local specializations. Science 19:1349–1351.

Florez-McClure ML, Linseman DA, Chu CT, Barker PA, Bouchard RJ, Le SS, Laessig TA, Heidenreich KA (2004) The p75 neurotrophin receptor can induce autophagy and death of cerebellar Purkinje neurons. J Neurosci 24:4498–4509.

Friedman B, Price JL (1986) Age-dependent cell death in the olfactory cortex: lack of transneuronal degeneration. J Comp Neurol 246:20–31.

Fujioka T, Fujioka A, Duman RS (2004) Activation of cAMP signaling facilitates the morphological maturation of newborn neurons in adult hippocampus. J Neurosci 24:319–328.

Gallo V, Kingsbury A, Balazs R, Jorgensen OS (1987) The role of depolarization in the survival and differentiation of cerebellar granule cells in culture. J Neurosci 7:2203–2213.

Ge Y, Belcher SM, Light KE (2004) Alterations of cerebellar mRNA specific for BDNF, p75^{NTR}, and trkB receptor isoforms occur within hours of ethanol administration to 4-day-old rat pups. Dev Brain Res 151:99–109.

Ghosh A, Carnahan J, Greenberg ME (1994) Requirement for BDNF in activity-dependent survival of cortical neurons. Science 263:1618–1623.

Goodlett CR, Horn KH (2001) Mechanisms of alcohol-induced damage to the developing nervous system. Alcohol Res Health J NIAAA 25:175–184.

Goodlett CR, Marcussen BL, West JR (1990) A single day of alcohol exposure during the brain growth spurt induces brain weight restriction and cerebellar Purkinje cell loss. Alcohol 7:107–114.

Gordon WC, Casey DM, Lukiw WJ, Bazan NG (2002) DNA damage and repair in light-induced photoreceptor degeneration. Invest Ophthal Vis Sci 43: 3511–3521.

Hamre KM, West JR (1993) The effects of the timing of ethanol exposure during the brain growth spurt on the number of cerebellar Purkinje and granule cell nuclear profiles. Alcohol Clin Exp Res 17:610–622.

Harada J, Sugimoto M (1997) Polyamines prevent apoptotic cell death in cultured cerebellar granule neurons. Brain Res 753:251–259.

Harmar AJ, Arimura A, Gozes I, Journot L, Laburthe M, Pisegna JR, Rawlings SR, Robberecht P, Said SI, Sreedharan SP, Wank SA, Waschek JA (1998) International Union of Pharmacology. XVIII. Nomenclature of receptors for vasoactive intestinal peptide and pituitary adenylate cyclase-activating polypeptide. Pharmacol Rev 50:265–270.

Heaton MB, Kim DS, Paiva M (2000a) Neurotrophic factor protection against ethanol toxicity in rat cerebellar granule cell cultures requires phosphatidylinositol 3-kinase activation. Neurosci Lett 291:121–125.

Heaton MB, Madorsky I, Paiva M, Mayer J (2002) Influence of ethanol on neonatal cerebellum of BDNF gene–deleted animals: analyses of effects on Purkinje cells, apoptosis-related proteins, and endogenous antioxidants. J Neurobiol 51:160–176.

Heaton MB, Mitchell JJ, Paiva M (2000b) Overexpression of NGF ameliorates ethanol neurotoxicity in the developing cerebellum. J Neurobiol 45:95–104.

Heaton MB, Mitchell JJ, Paiva M, Walker DW (2000c) Ethanol-induced alterations in the expression of neurotrophic factors in the developing rat central nervous system. Dev Brain Res 121:97–107.

Heaton MB, Moore DB, Paiva M, Gibbs T, Bernard O (1999) Bcl-2 overexpression protects the neonatal cerebellum from ethanol neurotoxicity. Brain Res 817:13–18.

Heaton MB, Paiva M, Madorsky I, Mayer J, Moore DB (2003) Effects of ethanol on neurotrophic factors, apoptosis-related proteins, endogenous antioxidants, and reactive oxygen species in neonatal striatum: relationship to periods of vulnerability. Dev Brain Res 140:237–252.

Herrup K, Trenkner E (1987) Regional differences in cytoarchitecture of the Weaver cerebellum suggest a new model for Weaver gene action. Neuroscience 23:871–885.

Higuchi H, Yamashita T, Yoshikawa H, Tohyama M (2003) PKA phosphorylates the p75 receptor and regulates its localization to lipid rafts. EMBO J 22:1790–1800.

Hoffman PL (2003) NMDA receptors in alcoholism. Int Rev Neurobiol 56:35–82.

Hoffman PL, Snell LD, Bhave SV, Tabakoff B (1994) Ethanol inhibition of NMDA receptor function in primary cultures of rat cerebellar granule cells and cerebral cortical cells. Alcohol Alcohol 2:199–204.

Hollmann M, Heinemann S (1994) Cloned glutamate receptors. Annu Rev Neurosci 17:31–108.

Huang EJ, Reichardt LF (2003) Trk receptors: roles in neuronal signal transduction. Annu Rev Biochem 72:609–642.

Hughes PD, Kim YN, Randall PK, Leslie SW (1998) Effect of prenatal ethanol exposure on the developmental profile of the NMDA receptor subunits in rat forebrain and hippocampus. Alcohol Clin Exp Res 22:1255–1261.

Ikonomidou C, Bittigau P, Ishimaru MJ, Wozniak DF, Koch C, Genz K, Price MT, Stefovska V, Horster F, Tenkova T, Dikranian K, Olney JW (2000) Ethanol-induced apoptotic neurodegeneration and fetal alcohol syndrome. Science 287:1056–1060.

Ikonomidou C, Bosch F, Miksa M, Bittigau P, Vockler J, Dikranian K, Tenkova TI, Stefovska V, Turski L, Olney JW (1999) Blockade of NMDA receptors and apoptotic neurodegeneration in the developing brain. Science 283:70–74.

Ishida K, Shimizu H, Hida H, Urakawa S, Ida K, Nishino H (2004) Argyrophilic dark neurons represent various states of neuronal damage in brain insults: some come to die and others survive. Neuroscience 125: 633–644.

Jacobs JS, Miller MW (1999) Expression of nerve growth factor and neurotrophin receptors in the trigeminal system: evidence for autocrine regulation. J Neurocytol 28:571–595.

Jacobs JS, Miller MW (2001) Proliferation and death of cultured fetal neocortical neurons: effects of ethanol on the dynamics of cell growth. J Neurocytol 30: 391–401.

Jacobson M (1991) Developmental Neurobiology. Plenum, New York.

Johnston MC, Bronsky PT (1995) Prenatal craniofacial development: new insights on normal and abnormal mechanisms. Crit Rev Oral Biol Med 6:25–79.

Jones KL, Smith DW (1973) Recognition of the fetal alcohol syndrome in early infancy. Lancet 2:999–1001.

Kharlamov E, Cagnoli CM, Atabay C, Ikonomovic S, Grayson DR, Manev H (1995) Opposite effect of protein synthesis inhibitors on potassium deficiency–induced apoptotic cell death in immature and mature neuronal cultures. J Neurochem 65:1395–1398.

Kienlen Campard P, Crochemore C, Rene F, Monnier D, Koch B, Loeffler JP (1997) PACAP type I receptor activation promotes cerebellar neuron survival through the cAMP/PKA signaling pathway. DNA Cell Biol 16:323–333.

Konishi Y, Bonni A (2003) The E2F-Cdc2 cell-cycle pathway specifically mediates activity deprivation-induced apoptosis of postmitotic neurons. J Neurosci 23:1649–1658.

Kuhn PE, Miller MW (1998) Expression of p53 and ALZ-50 immunoreactivity in rat cortex: effect of prenatal exposure to ethanol. Exp Neurol 154:418–429.

Lemoine P, Harousseau H, Borteyru J-P, Menuet J-C (1968) Les enfants de parents alcooliques: Anomalies observées à propos de 127 cas. Ouest Medical 21:476–482.

Li M, Wang X, Meintzer MK, Laessig T, Birnbaum MJ, Heidenreich KA (2000) Cyclic AMP promotes neuronal survival by phosphorylation of glycogen synthase kinase 3β. Mol Cell Biol 20:9356–9363.

Light KE, Belcher SM, Pierce DR (2002) Time course and manner of Purkinje neuron death following a single ethanol exposure on postnatal day 4 in the developing rat. Neuroscience 114:327–337.

Light KE, Brown DP, Newton BW, Belcher SM, Kane CJM (2002) Ethanol-induced alterations of neurotrophin receptor expression on Purkinje cells in the neonatal rat cerebellum. Brain Res 924:71–81.

Livy DJ, Maier SE, West JR (2001) Fetal alcohol exposure and temporal vulnerability: effects of binge-like alcohol exposure on the ventrolateral nucleus of the thalamus. Alcohol Clin Exp Res 25:774–780.

Lopez-Sanchez N, Frade JM (2002) Control of the cell cycle by neurotrophins: lessons from the p75 neurotrophin receptor. Hist Histopathol 17:1227–1237.

Lossi L, Merighi A (2003) In vivo cellular and molecular mechanisms of neuronal apoptosis in the mammalian CNS. Prog Neurobiol 69:287–312.

Luo J, West JR, Cook RT, Pantazis NJ (1999) Ethanol induces cell death and cell cycle delay in cultures of pheochromocytoma PC12 cells. Alcohol Clin Exp Res 23:644–656.

Luo J, West JR, Pantazis NJ (1996) Ethanol exposure reduces the density of the low-affinity nerve growth factor receptor (p75) on pheochromocytoma (PC12) cells. Brain Res 737:34–44.

Maier SE, Miller JA, Blackwell JM, West JR (1999) Fetal alcohol exposure and temporal vulnerability: regional differences in cell loss as a function of the timing of binge-like alcohol exposure during brain development. Alcohol Clin Exp Res 23:726–734.

Majdan M, Miller FD (1999) Neuronal life and death decisions functional antagonism between the Trk and p75 neurotrophin receptors. Int J Dev Neurosci 17:153–161.

Martin LJ (2001) Neuronal cell death in nervous system development, disease, and injury. Int J Mol Med 7:455–478.

McDonald JW, Johnston MV (1990) Physiological and pathophysiological roles of excitatory amino acids during central nervous system development. Brain Res Rev 15:41–70.

Miale IL, Sidman RL (1961) An autoradiographic analysis of histogenesis in the mouse cerebellum. Exp Neurol 2:277–296.

Miller MW (1985) Co-generation of projection and local circuit neurons in neocortex. Dev Brain Res 23:187–192.

Miller MW (1988) Effect of prenatal exposure to ethanol on the development of cerebral cortex: I. Neuronal generation. Alcohol Clin Exp Res 12:440–449.

Miller MW (1992) Effects of prenatal exposure to ethanol on cell proliferation and neuronal migration. In: Miller MW (ed). Development of the Central Nervous System: Effects of Alcohol and Opiates. Wiley-Liss, New York, pp 47–69.

Miller MW (1995a) Relationship of time of origin and death of neurons in rat somatosensory cortex: barrel versus septal cortex and projection versus local circuit neurons. J Comp Neurol 355:6–14.

Miller MW (1995b) Effect of pre- or postnatal exposure to ethanol on the total number of neurons in the principal sensory nucleus of the trigeminal nerve: cell proliferation versus neuronal death. Alcohol Clin Exp Res 19:1359–1364.

Miller MW (1995c) Generation of neurons in the rat dentate gyrus and hippocampus: effects of prenatal and postnatal treatment with ethanol. Alcohol Clin Exp Res 19:1500–1509.

Miller MW (1996a) Effects of early exposure to ethanol on the protein and DNA contents of specific brain regions. Brain Res 734:286–294.

Miller MW (1996b) Mechanisms of ethanol-induced neuronal death during development: from the molecule to behavior. Alcohol Clin Exp Res 20:128A–132A.

Miller MW (1999) A longitudinal study of the effects of prenatal ethanol exposure on neuronal acquisition and death in the principal sensory nucleus of the trigeminal nerve: interaction with changes induced by transection of the infraorbital nerve. J Neurocytol 28:999–1015.

Miller MW (2003) Describing the balance of cell proliferation and death: a mathematical model. J Neurobiol 57:172–182.

Miller MW, Al-Ghoul WM (1993) Numbers of neurons in the developing principal sensory nucleus of the trigeminal nerve: evidence of naturally occurring neuronal death. J Comp Neurol 330:491–501.

Miller MW, Al-Ghoul WM, Murtaugh M (1991) Expression of ALZ-50-immunoreactivity in the developing principal sensory nucleus of the trigeminal nerve: effect of transecting the infraorbital nerve. Brain Res 560:132–138.

Miller MW, Jacobs JS, Yokoyama R (2003) Neg, a nerve growth factor-stimulated gene expressed by fetal neocortical neurons that is down-regulated by ethanol. J Comp Neurol 460:212–222.

Miller MW, Kuhn PE (1997) Neonatal transection of the infraorbital nerve increases the expression of proteins related to neuronal death in the principal sensory nucleus of the trigeminal nerve. Brain Res 769:233–244.

Miller MW, Muller SJ (1989) Structure and histogenesis of the principal sensory nucleus of the trigeminal nerve: effects of prenatal exposure to ethanol. J Comp Neurol 282:570–580.

Miller MW, Pitts AF (2000) Neurotrophin receptors in the somatosensory cortex of the mature rat: co-localization of p75, *trk* isoforms, and c-*neu*. Brain Res 852:355–366.

Miller MW, Potempa G (1990) Numbers of neurons and glia in mature rat somatosensory cortex: effects of prenatal exposure to ethanol. J Comp Neurol 293:92–102.

Milligan CE, Li L, Barnes NY, Urioste AS (2000) Mechanisms of neuronal death during development—insights from chick motoneurons. In Vivo 14:61–82.

Miyata A, Arimura A, Dahl RR, Minamino N, Uehara A, Jiang L, Culler MD, Coy DH (1989) Isolation of a novel 38 residue-hypothalamic polypeptide which stimulates adenylate cyclase in pituitary cells. Biochem Biophys Res Commun 164:567–574.

Mooney SM, Miller MW (1999a) Effects of prenatal exposure to ethanol on systems matching: the number of neurons in the ventrobasal thalamic nucleus of the mature rat thalamus. Dev Brain Res 117:121–125.

—— (1999b) Processes associated with naturally occurring neuronal death are exacerbated by ethanol treatment. Rec Res Dev Neurochem 2:573–586.

—— (2000) Expression of bcl-2, bax, and caspase-3 in the CNS of the developing rat. Dev Brain Res 123:103–117.

—— (2001a) Effects of prenatal exposure on the expression of bcl-2, bax, and caspase-3 in the developing rat cerebral cortex and thalamus. Brain Res 911:71–81.

—— (2001b) Effect of prenatal exposure to ethanol on the ventrobasal nucleus of the thalamus: a longitudinal study. Alcohol Clin Exp Res 25:72A.

Mooney SM, Napper RMA (2005) Early postnatal exposure to ethanol affects rat neocortex in a spatio-temporal manner. Alcohol Clin Exp Res 29:683–691.

Mooney SM, Napper RM, West JR (1996) Long-term effect of postnatal alcohol exposure on the number of cells in the neocortex of the rat: a stereological study. Alcohol Clin Exp Res 20:615–623.

Moran J, Itoh T, Reddy UR, Chen M, Alnemri ES, Pleasure D (1999) Caspase-3 expression by cerebellar granule neurons is regulated by calcium and cyclic AMP. J Neurochem 73:568–577.

Morrison RS, Kinoshita Y, Johnson MD, Ghatan S, Ho JT, Garden G (2002) Neuronal survival and cell death signaling pathways. Ad Exp Med Biol 513:41–86.

Mutoh T, Yano S, Yamamoto H (2004) Signal transduction mechanisms for the survival and death of neurons and muscle cells: modulation by membrane lipid rafts and their abnormality in the disorders of the nervous system. Nihon Shin Seish Yak Zass 24:199–203.

Nagase T, Seki N, Ishikawa K, Ohira M, Kawarabayashi Y, Ohara O, Tanaka A, Kotani H, Miyajima N, Nomura N (1996) Prediction of the coding sequences of unidentified human genes. VI. The coding sequences of 80 new genes (KIAA0201-KIAA0280) deduced by analysis of cNDA clones from cell line KG-1 and brain. DNA Res 3:321–329.

Neet KE, Campenot RB (2001) Receptor binding, internalization, and retrograde transport of neurotrophic factors. Cell Mol Life Sci 58:1021–1035.

Nornes HO, Morita M (1979) Time of origin of the neurons in the caudal brain stem of rat. An autoradiographic study. Dev Neurosci 2:101–114.

Nowakowski RS, Rakic P (1981) The site of origin and route and rate of migration of neurons to the hippocampal region of the rhesus monkey. J Comp Neurol 196:129–154.

Olney JW, Tenkova T, Dikranian K, Muglia LJ, Jermakowicz WJ, D'Sa C, Roth KA (2002a) Ethanol-induced caspase-3 activation in the in vivo developing mouse brain. Neurobiol Dis 9:205–219.

Olney JW, Wozniak DF, Farber NB, Jevtovic-Todorovic V, Bittigau P, Ikonomidou C (2002b) The enigma of fetal alcohol neurotoxicity. Ann Med 34:109–119.

Oomman S, Finckbone V, Dertien J, Attridge J, Henne W, Medina M, Mansouri B, Singh H, Strahlendorf H, Strahlendorf J (2004) Active caspase-3 expression during postnatal development of rat cerebellum is not systematically or consistently associated with apoptosis. J Comp Neurol 476:154–173.

Ozawa S, Kamiya H, Tsuzuki K (1998) Glutamate receptors in the mammalian central nervous system. Prog Neurobiol 54:581–618.

Pantazis NJ, Dohrman DP, Luo J, Thomas JD, Goodlett CR, West JR (1995) NMDA prevents alcohol-induced neuronal cell death of cerebellar granule cells in culture. Alcohol Clin Exp Res 19:846–853.

Pantazis NL, Zaheer A, Dai D, Zaheer S, Green SH, Lim R (2000) Transfection of C6 glioma cells with glia maturation factor upregulates brain-derived neurotrophic factor and nerve growth factor: trophic effects and protection against ethanol toxicity in cerebellar granule cells. Brain Res 865:59–76.

Peoples RW, Li C, Weight FF (1996) Lipid vs protein theories of alcohol action in the nervous system. Annu Rev Pharmacol Toxicol 36:185–201.

Pierce DR, Goodlett CR, West JR (1989) Differential neuronal loss following early postnatal alcohol exposure. Teratology 40:113–126.

Pierce DR, West JR (1986) Alcohol-induced microencephaly during the third trimester equivalent: relationship to dose and blood alcohol concentration. Alcohol 3:185–191.

Pitts AF, Miller MW (1995) Expression of nerve growth factor, p75, and *trk* in the somatosensory-motor cortices of mature rats: evidence for local cortical support circuits. Somatosensory Motor Res 12:329–342.

—— (2000) Expression of nerve growth factor, brain-derived neurotrophic factor, and neurotrophin-3 in the somatosensory cortex of the rat: co-expression with high affinity neurotrophin receptors. J Comp Neurol 418:241–254.

Rakic P, Bourgeois JP, Eckenhoff MF, Zecevic N, Goldman-Rakic PS (1986) Concurrent overproduction of synapses in diverse regions of the primate cerebral cortex. Science 232:232–235.

Ramachandran V, Watts LT, Maffi SK, Chen J, Schenker S, Henderson G (2003) Ethanol-induced oxidative stress precedes mitochondrially mediated apoptotic death of cultured fetal cortical neurons. J Neurosci Res 74:577–588.

Resnicoff M, Abraham D, Yutanawiboonchai W, Rotman HL, Kajstura J, Rubin R, Zoltick P, Baserga R (1995) The insulin-like growth factor I receptor protects tumor cells from apoptosis *in vivo*. Cancer Res 55:2463–2469.

Resnicoff M, Cui S, Coppola D, Hoek JB, Rubin R (1996) Ethanol-induced inhibition of cell proliferation is modulated by insulin-like growth factor-I receptor levels. Alcohol Clin Exp Res 20:961–966.

Rezai Z, Yoon CH (1972) Abnormal rate of granule cell migration in the cerebellum of "weaver" mutant mice. Dev Biol 29:17–26.

SchlessingerAR, Cowan MW, Swanson LW (1978) The time of origin of neurons in Ammon's horn and the associated retrohippocampal fields. Anat Embryol 154:153–173.

Seabold G, Luo J, Miller MW (1998) Effect of ethanol on neurotrophin-mediated cell survival and receptor expression in cortical neuronal cultures. Dev Brain Res 128:139–145.

Seiler AE, Ross BN, Green JS, Rubin R (2000) Differential effects of ethanol on insulin-like growth factor-I receptor signaling. Alcohol Clin Exp Res 24:140–148.

Shaywitz AJ, Greenberg ME (1999) CREB: a stimulus-induced transcription factor activated by a diverse array of extracellular signals. Annu Rev Biochem 68:821–861.

Spear N, Estevez AG, Johnson GV, Bredesen DE, Thompson JA, Beckman JS (1998) Enhancement of peroxynitrite-induced apoptosis in PC12 cells by fibroblast growth factor-1 and nerve growth factor requires p21Ras activation and is suppressed by bcl-2. Arch Biochem Biophys 356:41–45.

Spengler D, Waeber C, Pantaloni C, Holsboer F, Bockaert J, Seeburg PH, Journot L (1993) Differential signal transduction by five splice variants of the PACAP receptor. Nature 365:170–175.

Spreafico R, Frassoni C, Arcelli P, Selvaggio M, De Biasi S (1995) In situ labeling of apoptotic cell death in the cerebral cortex and thalamus of rats during development. J Comp Neurol 363:281–295.

Stratton K, Howe C, Battaglia F (1996) *Fetal Alcohol Syndrome: Diagnosis, Epidemiology, Prevention and Treatment*. Natl Acad Sci Press, Washington DC.

Sulik KK, Cook CS, Webster WS (1988) Teratogens and craniofacial malformations: relationships to cell death. Development 103(Suppl):213–231.

Tabakoff B, Hoffman PL (1998) Adenylyl cyclases and alcohol. Adv Second Messenger Phosphoprotein Res 32:173–193.

Tabuchi A, Koizumi M, Nakatsubo J, Yaguchi T, Tsuda M (2001) Involvement of endogenous PACAP expression in the activity-dependent survival of mouse cerebellar granule cells. Neurosci Res 39:85–93.

Thomas JD, Wasserman EA, West JR, Goodlett CR (1996) Behavioral deficits induced by bingelike exposure to alcohol in neonatal rats: importance of developmental timing and number of episodes. Dev Psychobiol 29:433–452.

Tojima T, Kobayashi S, Ito E (2003) Dual role of cyclic AMP–dependent protein kinase in neuritogenesis and synaptogenesis during neuronal differentiation. J Neurosci Res 74:829–837.

Vallés S, Lindo L, Montoliu C, Renau-Piqueras JR, Guerri C (1994) Prenatal exposure to ethanol induces changes in the nerve growth factor and its receptor in proliferating astrocytes in primary culture. Brain Res 656:281–286.

Vaudry D, Gonzalez BJ, Basille M, Anouar Y, Fournier A, Vaudry H (1998) Pituitary adenylate cyclase-activating polypeptide stimulates both c-fos gene expression and cell survival in rat cerebellar granule neurons through activation of the protein kinase A pathway. Neuroscience 84:801–812.

Vaudry D, Rousselle C, Basille M, Falluel-Morel A, Pamantung TF, Fontaine M, Fournier A, Vaudry H, Gonzalez BJ (2002) Pituitary adenylate cyclase-activating polypeptide protects rat cerebellar granule neurons against ethanol-induced apoptotic cell death. Proc Natl Acad USA 99:6398–6403.

Villalba M, Bockaert J, Journot L (1997) Pituitary adenylate cyclase-activating polypeptide (PACAP-38) protects cerebellar granule neurons from apoptosis by activating the mitogen-activated protein kinase (MAP kinase) pathway. J Neurosci 17:83–90.

Vogel MW (2002) Cell death, Bcl-2, Bax, and the cerebellum. Cerebellum 1:277–287.

Walton MR, Dragunow I (2000) Is CREB a key to neuronal survival? Trends Neurosci 23:48–53.

Wegelius K, Korpi ER (1995) Ethanol inhibits NMDA-induced toxicity and trophism in cultured cerebellar granule cells. Acta Physiol Scand 154:25–34.

West JR, Chen WJ, Pantazis NJ (1994) Fetal alcohol syndrome: the vulnerability of the developing brain and possible mechanisms of damage. Metab Brain Dis 9:291–322.

West JR, Goodlett CR, Bonthius DJ, Hamre KM, Marcussen BL (1990) Cell population depletion associated with fetal alcohol brain damage: mechanisms of BAC-dependent cell loss. Alcohol Clin Exp Res 14:813–818.

West JR, Goodlett CR, Bonthius DJ, Pierce DR (1989) Manipulating peak blood alcohol concentrations in neonatal rats: review of an animal model for alcohol-related developmental effects. Neurotoxicology 10:347–365.

Wood KA, Dipasquale B, Youle RJ (1993) In situ labeling of granule cells for apoptosis-associated DNA fragmentation reveals different mechanisms of cell loss in developing cerebellum. Neuron 11:621–632.

Wu Y, Tewari M, Cui S, Rubin R (1996) Activation of the insulin-like growth factor-I receptor inhibits tumor necrosis factor-induced cell death. J Cell Physiol 168:499–509.

Yan GM, Lin SZ, Irwin RP, Paul SM (1995) Activation of G proteins bidirectionally affects apoptosis of cultured cerebellar granule neurons. J Neurochem 65:2425–2431.

Yan GM, Ni B, Weller M, Wood KA, Paul SM (1994) Depolarization or glutamate receptor activation blocks apoptotic cell death of cultured cerebellar granule neurons. Brain Res 656:43–51.

Zafra F, Castren E, Thoenen H, Lindholm D (1991) Interplay between glutamate and gamma-aminobutyric acid transmitter systems in the physiological regulation of brain-derived neurotrophic factor and nerve growth factor synthesis in hippocampal neurons. Proc Natl Acad Sci USA 88:10037–10041.

Zafra F, Hengerer B, Leibrock J, Thoenen H, Lindholm D (1990) Activity dependent regulation of BDNF and NGF mRNAs in the rat hippocampus is mediated by non-NMDA glutamate receptors. EMBO J 9:3545–3550.

Zhang FX, Rubin R, Rooney TA (1998) Ethanol induces apoptosis in cerebellar granule neurons by inhibiting insulin-like growth factor 1 signaling. J Neurochem 71:196–204.

16

Intracellular Events in Ethanol-Induced Neuronal Death

Sandra M. Mooney

Michael W. Miller

George I. Henderson

Developmental exposure to ethanol can significantly reduce the number of neurons in specific areas of the brain. This may result from a decrease in the additive processes of cell generation and migration (Chapters 11, 12, and 13) and/or an increase in the subtractive process of cell death (see Chapter 15). The present Chapter explores the effects of ethanol on intracellular pathways involved in neuronal death.

Before embarking on a description of the various pathways and the effects of ethanol on them, it is important to acknowledge caveats that may affect interpretation of the relevant data. Exposure to ethanol alters expression and/or activation of many proteins involved in apoptosis. Evidence shows that ethanol can trigger intrinsic and extrinsic apoptotic pathways. For example, ethanol-induced cell death in vivo can be mediated by Bcl proteins, i.e., the intrinsic pathway (Mooney and Miller, 2001; Young et al., 2003). Studies with organotypic cultures, by contrast, show that Fas receptor expression can also be affected by ethanol (e.g., Cheema et al., 2000; de la Monte and

Wands, 2002), thus implicating the extrinsic pathway. Part of the resolution of this riddle is that ethanol may trigger death through both pathways. The relevant research is thus based on a variety of (in vivo and in vitro) models that encompass multiple variables, such as the peak concentration of ethanol, the duration of the exposure, the type of cell or tissue being examined, and the time after exposure that the cells or tissues were examined. Although these different models may provide complementary approaches, they may also generate nonphysiological, model-dependent responses. Thus, it is challenging to reconstruct the mechanisms of ethanol-induced apoptosis.

When reviewing the literature on the effects of ethanol on neuronal death, it must be kept in mind that developmental exposure to ethanol interferes with other developmental events, notably cell proliferation and migration (see Chapters 11, 12, and 13). Without including the effects of ethanol on these early ontogenetic events the data may be confounded and misinterpretations may result. For example, longitudinal studies of the effects of ethanol on neural cell number in vitro (Jacobs and Miller, 2001; Miller, 2003) or in vivo (Miller, 1999) document a significant reduction in cell number. Two-thirds of this change is due to a depression in cell proliferation; the remaining third results from ethanol-induced cell death. The consequent lesson must be heeded by alcohol investigators examining cell number: reductions in cell number are not necessarily due to cell death.

CELL DEATH PATHWAYS

The effects of ethanol on three pathways of neuronal death are discussed below: (1) the intrinsic caspase-dependent pathway, (2) the extrinsic caspase-dependent pathway, and (3) the caspase-independent pathway (Fig. 16–1). These pathways are described in greater detail in Chapter 6, but a brief outline is included below.

The intrinsic pathway is mitochondrially mediated, typically in response to an apoptotic signal such as DNA damage or reactive oxygen species (ROS). An initial event is release of proapoptotic proteins from the mitochondrial intermembrane space. Permeabilization of the mitochondrial outer membrane appears to be mediated by Bcl-2 family proteins and may include direct binding of p53 to one or more anti-apoptotic proteins, such as Bcl-X_L or Bax. Up-regulation of Bax may allow insertion of Bax-Bax homodimers into the mitochondrial membrane, which alters membrane permeability and allows intermembrane substances to escape into the cytoplasm. One such substance, Cytochrome C, associates with apoptotic protease activating factor 1 and caspase-9 in the presence of adenosine triphosphate (ATP) to form an apoptosome. This activates caspase-9, which in turn activates caspase-3. Active caspase-3 inactivates poly-adenosine diphosphate ribose polymerase (PARP) 1, thus repressing DNA repair mechanisms. In combination with activation of enzymes such as DNA fragmentation factor 40, the result is DNase-mediated fragmentation of DNA and cell death.

The extrinsic pathway is activated by binding of a ligand to a cell surface receptor. One example is the binding of Fas ligand (FasL) to its receptor Fas. This binding causes receptor oligomerization, and

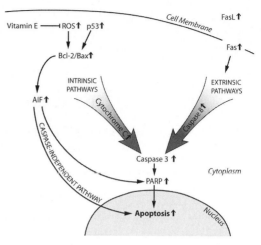

FIGURE 16–1 Schematic of three pathways leading to cell death. Three pathways of cell death, outlining the flow of information from external effects to nuclear response, are depicted: intrinsic and extrinsic caspase-dependent pathways and a caspase-independent pathway. A subset of the molecules involved in these pathways is shown; a more comprehensive figure detailing the pathways is shown in Figure 6–1 in Chapter 6. Factors known to be affected by ethanol are identified. Small arrows show the effect of developmental exposure to ethanol on each factor. The blunted line signifies an inhibitory effect. AIF, apoptosis inducing factor; PARP, poly-adenosine diphosphate ribose polymerase; ROS, reactive oxygen species. See text for details.

recruitment of the Fas-associated death domain (FADD) and procaspases 8 and 10 (Benn and Woolf, 2004). The FADD–caspase-8/10 complex forms the death-inducing signaling complex that cleaves and activates caspase-3. As with the intrinsic pathway, active caspase-3 inactivates PARP and allows DNA fragmentation. In addition, active caspase-8 cleaves the Bcl family protein, Bid. Truncated Bid translocates to the mitochondria where it can activate the intrinsic pathway by promoting insertion of Bax-Bax homodimers into the mitochondrial membrane.

Like the intrinsic pathway, the caspase-independent pathway is mitochondria-dependent. Following release of apoptosis inducing factor (AIF) from the mitochondrial intermembrane space, it can either directly up-regulate DNase activity or cleave and inactivate PARP, thus repressing DNA repair and promoting cell degeneration.

EFFECT OF ETHANOL ON APOPTOSIS

Intrinsic Pathways

Bcl Family Proteins

Exposure to ethanol alters the in vivo expression of members of the Bcl protein family. This is apparent in changes of the mRNAs and the proteins. Changes may be rapid, as in the case of the mRNA (Moore et al., 1999; Inoue et al., 2002), or occur later, as detected in protein expression (Mooney and Miller, 2001). Cortical expression of Bcl-2, a prosurvival member of the family, is lower in the cortices of rats exposed to ethanol prenatally, most notably in the period around postnatal day (P) 6. This finding is particularly interesting in light of the lack of change in the expression of bax in cerebral cortex, the net result being a reduction in the ratio of Bcl-2 to Bax on gestational day (G) 16, P6, and P12. These times, prenatal and postnatal week, coincide with the periods of both naturally occurring and ethanol-induced cell death in the proliferative zones and in the immature cortex (Kuhn and Miller, 1998; see Chapter 5). It is noteworthy that another immunoblotting study of the cortices of rats prenatally exposed to ethanol showed an increase in Bcl-2 expression on P1 and no change between P7 and P35 (Climent et al., 2002). The differences in reported Bcl-2 expression in the two studies may reflect the feeding paradigms. Although fetuses were exposed to ethanol in both studies, in the study by Climent and colleagues ethanol exposure continued into the postnatal period.

The change in cortex contrasts with the lack of a change in the relative amounts of bcl-2 and bax in the thalamus. The thalamus is a structure that exhibits no neuronal death following prenatal exposure to ethanol (Mooney and Miller, 1999; Livy et al., 2001). Thus, these data indicate that the change in the balance of bcl-2 and bax is a key determinant of neuronal death and survival.

The expression of Bcl proteins is altered in the murine cerebellum following early postnatal exposure to ethanol (Heaton et al., 2002a, 2003a). Expression of the anti-apoptotic protein Bcl-2 decreases and of pro-apoptotic Bax and Bcl-xs increases in concomitant temporal manners that correlate with the period of Purkinje cell vulnerability (Heaton et al., 2003a). That is, during the period of vulnerability, on P4, expression of Bax and Bcl-xs increases within 2 hr of exposure to ethanol. In contrast, ethanol exposure on P7, a time of relative invulnerability, causes an early up-regulation of the survival-promoting proteins, Bcl-2 and Bcl-xl, and a down-regulation of the pro-apoptotic Bcl-xs.

The changes in protein expression apparently follow earlier changes in transcript expression. For example, exposure to ethanol induces an immediate change in the expression of bcl family transcripts in the cerebral cortex and cerebellum (Moore et al., 1999; Inoue et al., 2002). Ethanol up-regulates the expression of pro-apoptotic genes, bax and bcl-xs, in the cerebellum. Interestingly, however, the up-regulation of bax in the cerebellum occurs in the absence of an effect on cell survival. This finding concurs with data from a strain of bax knockout animals in which there was no increase in cell death following exposure to ethanol (Young et al., 2003). Overexpression of bcl-2, by contrast, confers invulnerability to ethanol-induced death of cerebellar Purkinje cells (Heaton et al., 1999).

Cytochrome C

Release of cytochrome C from mitochondria is a central event in the intrinsic apoptotic pathway (Polster and Fiskum, 2004). This release, combined with that of other proapoptotic proteins, elicits activation of initiator caspases that ultimately produces effector caspase activation. Thus, mitochondrial release of Cytochrome C is an early, feed-forward step in the apoptotic process, and combined with subsequent activation of effector caspases, is compelling evidence that apoptotic death is a work in progress.

Several laboratories have used Cytochrome C release to address ethanol-mediated apoptotic brain cell death following in vivo ethanol exposure. Appropriately, these observations have been linked to activation of caspase-3. Mitochondria isolated from fetal brains, that have been exposed to ethanol in utero (on G17 and G18), exhibit enhanced release of both cytochrome C and AIF (Ramachandran et al., 2001). This result parallels the activation of caspase-3 in whole fetal brain homogenates. Similar responses have been reported following ethanol treatment of 4- to 10-day-old rat pups (Light et al., 2002; Carloni et al., 2004) or infant mice (Young et al., 2003).

The ethanol-induced in vivo release of Cytochrome C has been replicated in vitro. Exposure of cultured fetal rat cortical neurons to ethanol generates enhanced release of Cytochrome C within 2 hr of exposure (Ramachandran et al., 2003). This is followed by activation of caspase-3 within 12 hr of treatment. Thus, neurons exposed to ethanol either in vivo or in culture can elicit mitochondrial release of Cytochrome C in some, as-yet, undetermined manner.

Caspases

The research community has focused on the effects of developmental exposure to ethanol on two caspases: caspase-3 and caspase-8. These are of interest because (a) they are from two different molecular subgroups and (b) they are involved in two pathways; caspase-3 is associated with the intrinsic apoptotic pathway and caspase-8 with the extrinsic pathway (Fig. 16–1).

There is considerable *in vitro* (Saito et al., 1999; Jacobs and Miller 2001; Jang et al., 2001; Sohma et al., 2002; Vaudry et al., 2002; Ramachandran et al., 2003) and *in vivo* (Mooney and Miller, 2001; Ramachandran et al., 2001; Climent et al., 2002; Light et al., 2002; Olney et al., 2002a, 2002b; Mitchell and Snyder-Kelly, 2003; Ragjopal et al., 2003; Young et al., 2003; Carloni et al., 2004) evidence that exposure to ethanol increases the activation of caspase-3. This activation may be model-dependent. For example, Sohma and colleagues (2002) report that although both C6 rat glioma cells and A549 human adenocarcinoma cells show evidence of apoptosis following exposure to ethanol the C6 cells increase their caspase activity, whereas the A549 cells do not.

Ethanol causes apoptosis (at least in vitro) when trophic factors are in limited supply (Oberdoerster and Rabin, 1999). Cerebellar granule neurons grown in serum-containing medium supplemented with high concentrations of potassium chloride do not undergo apoptosis in response to ethanol. Removal of the serum results in increased activation of caspase-3 and apoptosis in response to ethanol.

To date, there are few data regarding the effect of ethanol on other caspases. One in vitro study shows that ethanol-induced death of cerebellar granule neurons is accompanied by an increase in activation of initiator caspases 2, 8, and 9, and effector caspases 3 and 6 (Vaudry et al., 2002). This death is abrogated by the addition of pituitary adenylate cyclase activating polypeptide (PACAP; see Chapter 15). Addition of exogenous PACAP ameliorates the activation of caspases 3 and 6, but not caspases 2, 8, or 9. This implies that activation of an initiator caspase does not oblige a cell to die.

Extrinsic Pathways

Although little is known about the effect of developmental exposure to ethanol on tumor necrosis factor α or Apo2/TRAIL systems in the brain, the FasL system has been studied in vivo and in vitro. Fas and FasL are transiently expressed in developing cortex during the time of naturally occurring neuronal death (Cheema et al., 2000). Exposure to ethanol induces Fas mRNA expression *in vitro*, but only at subapoptotic concentrations and not at concentrations that induce apoptosis. Similarly, there is an increase in Fas receptor and ligand in cultures of cerebellar granule cells taken in the postnatal period from rats exposed to ethanol prenatally (de la Monte and Wands, 2002). Other evidence showing that ethanol activates extrinsic pathways is that the ethanol-induced death of cultured cerebellar granule cells is accompanied by an increase in the activity of caspase-8 (Vaudry et al., 2002).

Caspase-Independent Pathway

In a number of neuronal cell death paradigms in which caspases are normally activated, inhibition of caspase activity delays but does not prevent cell death from occurring (Miller et al., 1997; Stefanis et al., 1999; D'Mello et al., 2000; Keramaris et al., 2000; Selznick et al., 2000). Such data imply that prenatal exposure to ethanol affects caspase-independent pathways, but few data directly address this possibility. Ethanol exposure does induce the release of Cytochrome C and AIF from mitochondria (Ramachandran et al., 2001). Consequently, AIF can initiate a feedback loop that further induces Cytochrome C release from the mitochondria (Porter, 1999). Thus, ethanol-induced initiation of caspase-independent death can be a self-perpetuating phenomenon.

EFFECTORS OF CELL DEATH

p53-Related Factors

p53 is a critical fulcrum defining the fate of cells: whether they die or survive (Miller et al., 2000; Morrison et al., 2002). The teeter-totter is pushed one way or the other by the phosphorylation of serines on p53, and particularly by the positions of the phosphorylated serines. Although an effect of ethanol on this process has been surmised (Kuhn and Miller, 1998), direct data are lacking. Nonetheless, it is known that ethanol can affect kinase activity in other systems (e.g., Resnicoff et al., 1994; Luo and Miller, 1999).

In addition to potential effects of ethanol on post-translational modification of p53, the effectiveness of p53 can be affected by an ethanol-induced change in the amount of p53 available. Indeed, p53 expression *in vivo* is affected by prenatal exposure to ethanol in a spatiotemporal manner (Kuhn and Miller, 1998). Ethanol increases p53 expression in the fetus and reduces it in the first and second postnatal weeks. Interestingly, following chronic gestational exposure to ethanol, expression of p53 is increased in the rat cerebellum during the early postnatal period (de la Monte and Wands, 2002). The increase in p53 occurs concurrent with increases in Fas ligand and receptor, implying that the increase in p53 is related to cell death. Although many ethanol-susceptible activities occur coincidentally in the developing cerebellum, two are worth noting: the reduction in the population of proliferating granule cells (Bauer-Moffett and Altman, 1977; Kornguth et al., 1979) and the death of Purkinje neurons (e.g., Light et al., 2002; see Chapter 15). Thus, the ethanol-induced increase in cell mortality among the proliferating neuronal precursors in the cortex and cerebellum may be signaled by an increase in p53 expression.

A phosphorylated form of p53 may be recognized by the antibody ALZ-50 (Kuhn and Miller, 1998). ALZ-50 immunoreactivity is associated with dying central nervous system (CNS) neurons (Al-Ghoul and Miller, 1989; Valverde et al., 1990; Miller et al., 1991). Interestingly, the expression profile of ALZ-50 in the developing cortex parallels that of p53 expression (Kuhn and Miller, 1998). Moreover, prenatal exposure to ethanol affects both proteins similarly. It reduces the amount of peak ALZ-50 and p53 expression and induces this peak to occur earlier. The implication is that ethanol alters the timing of neuronal death in the developing cortex.

Oxidative Stress

Basic Findings

Over the last four decades, studies have linked ethanol intake to oxidative stress (Di Luzio, 1963; Shaw et al., 1983). The earliest reports connecting maternal drinking to fetal oxidative damage were by Dreosti (1987; Dreosti and Patrick, 1987), who reported that maternal ethanol intake increased malondialdehyde (MDA) in fetal rat liver mitochondria. This increase has also been described in cultured fetal hepatocytes (Devi et al., 1994, 1996). Likewise, ethanol can increase both MDA and conjugated dienes in fetal brain. Chronic prenatal ethanol exposure can reduce glutathione (GSH) content of fetal brain (Reyes et al., 1993) and ethanol produces free radical damage in neural crest cells (Chen and Sulik, 1996). Thus, ethanol-mediated oxidative damage to fetal cells occurs *in vivo* and this can be reproduced in cultured fetal cells. These data sets laid the conceptual groundwork for numerous subsequent reports on ethanol-related oxidative damage to fetal cells. They are reviewed below in the context of mechanisms underlying ethanol-mediated apoptotic death of neurons.

Ethanol induces oxidative stress and activates apoptotic pathways in the developing brain and in cultured neurons (de la Monte et al., 2001; de la Monte and Wands, 2001; Ramachandran et al., 2001, 2003; Heaton et al., 2002b, 2003a, 2003b, 2003c). The parallel observations of these two ethanol-related phenomena are correlative and do not establish oxidative stress as a causative factor for neuronal death. Extensive documentation of such concomitant events, combined with the effectiveness of anti-oxidant interventions and time lines illustrating that onset of oxidative stress can precede apoptosis, is convincing evidence that oxidative damage is one mechanism underlying the ethanol-mediated loss of neurons in the developing brain.

In utero exposure to ethanol on G17 and G18 can elicit both oxidative damage to brain mitochondria, such as 4-hydroxynonenal (HNE) formation, and induction of markers of mitochondria-mediated apoptosis. The latter includes changes of mitochondrial permeability transition, activation of caspase-3, and mitochondrial release of Cytochrome C and AIF (Ramachandran et al., 2001). A mechanism underlying the ethanol-mediated leakage of pro-apoptotic proteins from mitochondria is activation of mitochondrially generated HNE. Mitochondria isolated from the brains of fetuses treated with HNE mimic the response observed in the brains of rodents exposed to ethanol. The ability of HNE to elicit apoptosis in neurons makes it an attractive mechanism, however, a clear causative link remains to be established.

Ethanol-related increases in ROS have been examined in young rats acutely exposed to ethanol presented as a binge exposure. Increased amounts of ROS were detected in the cortices of these rats on P7 and in their

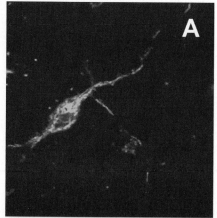

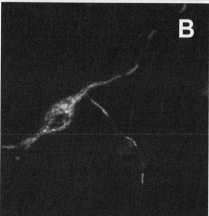

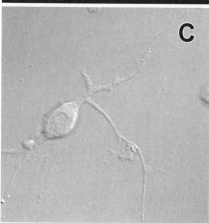

cerebella on P4, P7, or P14 (Heaton et al., 2002b, 2003c). This ethanol exposure also increased cortical Bax, pAkt, and pJNK expression. Taken together, these data strongly support the occurrence of enhanced apoptotic death concomitant with oxidative stress. Cerebella of 2-day-old rats exposed to ethanol *in utero* are hypoplastic and exhibit increased amounts of apoptosis, beyond that occurring naturally (de la Monte and Wands, 2002). In cultured granule neurons isolated from these cerebella, the previous ethanol exposure generated increased oxidative stress (dihydrorosamine fluorescence) and apoptosis (evidenced by phosphorylation of GSK-3β, Akt, and Bad), along with inhibition of insulin-stimulated viability and pro-apoptotic gene expression (e.g., increased *bad* expression). Thus, gestational ethanol exposure impairs neuronal survival systems and insulin signaling mechanisms during the early postnatal period. These ethanol effects appear to be mediated by oxidative stress.

The above reports document that ethanol can concomitantly elicit oxidative stress and enhance apoptosis in the developing brain. Using *in vitro* models, several laboratories have shown that oxidative stress can play a direct role in ethanol-mediated neuron death. One approach probed the causality of oxidative stress by determining if this phenomenon preceded or followed evidence of apoptosis and/or decreased neuron viability (Ramachandran et al., 2003). In cultured fetal rat cortical neurons, confocal microscopy of live cells preloaded with dichlorofluorescein diacetate illustrated that ethanol can stimulate ROS production within minutes of exposure. This initial ROS burst persisted for 2 hr and was followed by increased HNE in neuron mitochondria (within 2 hr; Fig. 16–2). By 2 hr, an

FIGURE 16–2 Ethanol-induced oxidative stress originating in mitochondria. Fetal cortical neurons, grown on coverslips, were exposed to ethanol (4.0 mg/ml) for 2 hr at 37°C. After 1¾ hr, hydroethidium (Het) (400 nM), which detects generation of superoxide anion radicals, and 50 nm Mitotracker Green (MG), which labels mitochondria, were added to the medium. Live cell images were acquired through confocal microscopy with an argon laser to excite MG and an He-Ne543 laser to excite Het. **A.** This image identifies enhanced generation of superoxide anion radicals in discrete areas in the cell body and in the processes. The Het fluorochrome freely crosses the plasma membrane, it is very specific for the superoxide anion radical, and, at nanomolar concentrations, it preferentially localizes in mitochondria. **B.** Mitochondria are distributed in the perinuclear region as well as in the processes. **C.** The extent of the neurites can be appreciated in a differential interference contrast image of the neuron.

increase in annexin V binding is seen, along with increased Cytochrome C release. These events were followed by caspase-3 activation. This time course of ethanol responses, with increased ROS content occurring as an upstream event, suggests causality. More convincing evidence is the mitigation of ethanol-mediated apoptosis by prevention of oxidative stress via normalization of neuron glutathione content (Ramachandran et al., 2003) and by other anti-oxidant interventions (see Anti-oxident Interventions, below).

Potential Role for Mitotoxic Effects of Ethanol

The specific mechanism(s) underlying ethanol-induced apoptosis and oxidative stress remains undetermined and are likely multifactorial and cell type–dependent. One consistent finding from numerous laboratories, however, is that ethanol is a mitotoxin, and mitochondrial damage may be an important player in both the enhanced production of ROS and apoptotic death associated with ethanol exposure (Hirano et al., 1992; Kukielka et al., 1994; Garcia-Ruiz et al., 1995; Devi et al., 1996; Chen et al., 1998, 2002; Goodlett and Horn, 2001; Mooney and Miller, 2001; Bailey and Cunningham, 2002).

With respect to the fetus, there is abundant evidence that ethanol negatively alters mitochondrial function in liver and brain. Among the earliest fetal-related studies are reports that, in cultured fetal rat hepatocytes, the ethanol-related increases in ROS (H_2O_2, superoxide anion radical) and membrane lipid peroxidation are paralleled by morphological and biochemical mitochondrial damage such as reduced complex I and IV activities and decreased synthesis of ATP (Devi et al., 1993, 1994). Since inhibition of respiratory chain components stimulates production of ROS, it has been proposed that this could be the origin of the increased ROS levels. More recently, this phenomenon has been reported in fetal brain and in cultured cerebellar and cortical neurons exposed to ethanol. Following an *in utero* binge exposure to ethanol (G17 and G18), mitochondria isolated from fetal rat brain have elevated levels of the highly pro-apoptotic product of lipid peroxidation, HNE (Ramachandran et al., 2001). This is accompanied by increased mitochondrial permeability transition and release of pro-apoptotic proteins. Likewise, cerebellar neurons isolated from ethanol-exposed 2-day-old rat

pups exhibit signs of oxidative stress and activate pathways of apoptosis along with altered mitochondria morphology and decreased cell number (de la Monte and Wands, 2002). Furthermore, *in vitro* exposure of insulin-sensitive immature human PNET2 neuronal cells to ethanol produces a variety of mitotoxic responses, including a striking reduction of complex IV/Cytochrome C oxidase (CytOx) expression. Although no measures of CytOx activities have been reported, inhibition of this complex has been shown to stimulate formation of ROS (Shigenaga et al., 1994).

Parallel to impaired mitochondrial function is evidence of apoptosis. Similarly, following 24 hr of exposure to ethanol, rat postmitotic cerebellar granular neurons show an inhibition of multiple measures of insulin-stimulated mitochondrial function, signs of apoptosis, and generation of H_2O_2 (de la Monte et al., 2001). Thus, disruption of mitochondrial function is a central event in the apoptotic death of cells, and oxidative stress, which is often a product of mitochondrial damage, is a proven initiator of apoptosis. There is compelling evidence that the mitotoxic effects of ethanol play a role in ethanol-mediated apoptotic death of neurons in the developing brain.

Anti-oxidant Interventions

Many anti-oxidant interventions aimed at ameliorating the effects of ethanol on the developing brain have used vitamin E (α-tocopherol), a lipid-soluble anti-oxidant that preferentially concentrates in lipoid compartments of the cell, where it can block membrane lipid peroxidation. It is present in mitochondrial membranes (approximately 1 molecule per 2100 molecules of phospholipid) and is a highly effective peroxyl radical trap with a one-electron oxidation product that can undergo several reactions that consume (but can also generate) radicals (Liebler and Burr 1992). As such, it is a late-stage defense against the formation of toxic lipid peroxidation products such as HNE. This capability, combined with its relative low toxicity, makes its use an alluring anti-oxidant intervention strategy.

Ethanol-induced death of cultured neonatal rat hippocampal cells can be mitigated by treatment with vitamin E or β-carotene (Mitchell et al., 1999a, 1999b). Ethanol activates caspase-3 and increases at least one marker of apoptosis (annexin V binding). Both vitamin E and the anti-oxidant Pycnogenol (a bioflavonoid mixture) block these responses

(Siler-Marsiglio et al., 2004). Likewise, vitamin E enhances the survival of ethanol-exposed cultured cerebellar granule cells. This survival occurs concomitantly with increased amounts of the anti-apoptotic proteins Bcl-2, Bcl-xl and activated Akt kinase (Heaton et al., 2004). The mechanisms underlying the protective effects of vitamin E remain to be established, but it is tempting to propose that blockade of membrane (possibly mitochondrial) lipid oxidation is an important factor. The setting is complex and vitamin E treatment can normalize cellular GSH content as well as prevent an ethanol-related reduction of neurotrophin secretion (Heaton et al., 2004). The former manipulation can, by itself, block the ethanol-mediated apoptosis of cultured cortical neurons (Ramachandran et al., 2003).

The ultimate clinical value of anti-oxidant treatment for the neurotoxic effects of ethanol in the developing brain remains to be determined. A possible insight into the future of such interventions is reflected by a study in which behavioral alterations induced by ethanol were at best only partially alleviated by vitamin E treatment (Marino et al., 2004; Tran et al., 2005). The pathogenesis of FAS behavioral deficits is complex and oxidative damage to neurons is likely only one underlying mechanism. The above reports, however, do support the concepts that ethanol can induce oxidative stress in neurons from the developing brain and that this is one means by which apoptotic death is induced.

SUMMARY AND CONCLUSIONS

Evidence is abundant that exposure to ethanol *in vivo* or *in vitro* can cause neuronal death and that it does so via multiple pathways: the caspase-dependent intrinsic and extrinsic pathways, and the caspase-independent pathway. The integration, or cross-talk, among these pathways is extensive. Nevertheless, there is compelling evidence that each of the three pathways is targeted by ethanol. Further analyses of the effects of ethanol might be best focused on key upstream players such as p53 and receptors that mediate death-related signals, as well as PARP, a player presumed to be common to all three pathways. The factors that define the effects of ethanol are the developmental state of the cells and the concentration of ethanol. These issues are addressed in the previous chapter.

Although beyond the scope of this chapter, it also must be kept in mind that ethanol-induced cell death may also occur by other mechanisms such as necrosis (Obernier et al., 2002). Awareness of the diversity of death mechanisms is important when conceptualizing possible interventions. It is nonetheless unrealistic to expect that blocking the activity of a single protein can rescue a cell from death. Indeed, it has been shown that blocking one mechanism of death may alter the time line and pathway of cell death, but not the outcome (Miller et al., 1997; Stefanis et al., 1999; D'Mello et al., 2000; Keramaris et al., 2000; Selznick et al., 2000).

Progress in establishing a causal link between oxidative stress and cell death has been made. Through documentation of relevant time lines, the upstream effectors of ethanol-mediated oxidative stress in the neuron can be pinpointed and opportunities created for reversing or preventing the related apoptosis with anti-oxidant treatments. The latter venture is an especially exciting research direction, as it may be one path to an intervention that does not have an adverse impact on normal brain development. As laboratories narrow their focus on the underlying mechanisms of ethanol-mediated death of neurons, it is hoped that more potential therapeutic interventions will evolve.

Abbreviations

AIF   apoptosis inducing factor

ATP   adenosine triphosphate

CNS   central nervous system

CytOx   cytochrome C oxidase

FADD   Fas-associated death domain

FasL   Fas ligand

G   gestational day

GSH   glutathione

HNE   4-hydroxynonenal

MDA   malondialdehyde

P   postnatal day

PACAP   pituitary adenylate cyclase activating polypeptide

PARP   poly-adenosine diphosphate ribose polymerase

ROS   reactive oxygen species

ACKNOWLEDGMENTS Work on this chapter was supported by the National Institute of Alcohol Abuse and Alcoholism and the Department of Veterans Affairs.

References

Al-Ghoul WM, Miller MW (1989) Transient expression of Alz-50-immunoreactivity in developing rat neocortex: a marker for naturally occurring neuronal death? Brain Res 481:361–367.

Bailey SM, Cunningham CC (2002) Contribution of mitochondria to oxidative stress associated with alcoholic liver disease. Free Radic Biol Med 32:11–16.

Bauer-Moffett C, Altman J (1977) The effect of ethanol chronically administered to preweanling rats on cerebellar development: a morphological study. Brain Res 119:249–268.

Benn SC, Woolf CJ (2004) Adult neuron survival strategies—slamming on the brakes. Nat Rev Neurosci 5:686–699.

Carloni S, Mazzoni E, Balduini W (2004) Caspase-3 and calpain activities after acute and repeated ethanol administration during the rat brain growth spurt. J Neurochem 89:197–203.

Cheema ZF, West JR, Miranda RC (2000) Ethanol induces Fas/Apo [apoptosis]-1 mRNA and cell suicide in the developing cerebral cortex. Alcohol Clin Exp Res 24:535–543.

Chen J, Schenker S, Frosto TA, Henderson GI (1998) Inhibition of Cytochrome C oxidase activity by 4-hydroxynonenal: role of HNE adduct formation with enzyme subunits. Biochim Biophys Acta 1380:336–344.

Chen J, Schenker S, Henderson G (2002) HNE degradation by mitochondrial glutathione S-transferase is compromised by short-term ethanol consumption. Alcohol Clin Exp Res 26:1252–1258.

Chen, SY, Sulik KK (1996) Free radicals and ethanol-induced cytotoxicity in neural crest cells. Alcohol Clin Exp Res 20:1071–1076.

Climent E, Pascual M, Renau-Piqueras J, Guerri C (2002) Ethanol exposure enhances cell death in the developing cerebral cortex: role of brain-derived neurotrophic factor and its signaling pathways. J Neurosci Res 68:213–225.

de la Monte SM, Neely TR, Cannon J, Wands JR (2001) Ethanol impairs insulin-stimulated mitochondrial function in cerebellar granule neurons. Cell Mol Life Sci 58:1950–1960.

de la Monte SM, Wands JR (2001) Mitochondrial DNA damage and impaired mitochondrial function contribute to apoptosis of insulin-stimulated ethanol-exposed neuronal cells. Alcohol Clin Exp Res 25:898–906.

—— (2002) Chronic gestational exposure to ethanol impairs insulin-stimulated survival and mitochondrial function in cerebellar neurons. Cell Mol Life Sci 59:882–893.

Devi BG, Henderson GI, Frosto TA, Schenker S (1993) Effect of ethanol on rat fetal hepatocytes: studies on cell replication, lipid peroxidation and glutathione. Hepatology 18:648–659.

—— (1994) Effect of acute ethanol exposure on cultured fetal rat hepatocytes: relation to mitochondrial function. Alcohol Clin Exp Res 18:1436–1442.

Devi BG, Schenker S, Mazloum B, Henderson GI (1996) Ethanol-induced oxidative stress and enzymatic defenses in cultured fetal rat hepatocytes. Alcohol 16:1–6.

Di Luzio NR (1963) Prevention of the acute ethanol-induced fatty liver by antioxidants. Physiologist 6:169–173.

D'Mello SR, Kuan CY, Flavell RA, Rakic P (2000) Caspase-3 is required for apoptosis-associated DNA fragmentation but not for cell death in neurons deprived of potassium. J Neurosci Res 59:24–31.

Dreosti IE (1987) Micronutrients, superoxide and the fetus. Neurotoxicology 8:445–450.

Dreosti IE, Patrick EJ (1987) Zinc, ethanol, and lipid peroxidation in adult and fetal rats. Biol Trace Element Res 14:179–191.

Garcia-Ruiz C, Morales A, Colell A, Ballesta A, Rodes J, Kaplowitz N, Fernandez-Checa JC (1995) Feeding S-adenosyl-L-methionine attenuates both ethanol-induced depletion of mitochondrial glutathione and mitochondrial dysfunction in periportal and perivenous rat hepatocytes. Hepatology 21:207–214.

Goodlett CR, Horn KH (2001) Mechanisms of alcohol-induced damage to the developing nervous system. Alcohol Res Health 25:175–184.

Heaton MB, Madorsky I, Paiva M, Mayer J (2002b) Influence of ethanol on neonatal cerebellum of BDNF gene–deleted animals: analyses of effects on Purkinje cells, apoptosis-related proteins, and endogenous antioxidants. J Neurobiol 51:160–176.

Heaton MB, Madorsky I, Paiva M, Siler-Marsiglio KI. (2004) Vitamin E amelioration of ethanol neurotoxicity involves modulation of apoptosis-related protein levels in neonatal rat cerebellar granule cells. Dev Brain Res 150:117–124.

Heaton MB, Moore DB, Paiva M, Gibbs T, Bernard O (1999) Bcl-2 overexpression protects the neonatal cerebellum from ethanol neurotoxicity. Brain Res 817:13–18.

Heaton MB, Moore DB, Paiva M, Madorsky I, Mayer J, Shaw G (2003a) The role of neurotrophic factors, apoptosis-related proteins, and endogenous antioxidants in the differential temporal vulnerability of neonatal cerebellum to ethanol. Alcohol Clin Exp Res 27:657–669.

Heaton MB, Paiva M, Madorsky I, Mayer J, Moore DB (2003b) Effects of ethanol on neurotrophic factors, apoptosis-related proteins, endogenous antioxidants, and reactive oxygen species in neonatal striatum: relationship to periods of vulnerability. Dev Brain Res 140:237–252.

Heaton MB, Paiva M, Madoesky I, Shaw G (2003c) Ethanol effects on neonatal rat cortex: comparative analysis of neurotrophic factors, apoptosis-related proteins, and oxidative processes during vulnerable and resistant periods. Dev Brain Res 145:249–262.

Heaton MB, Paiva M, Mayer J, Miller R (2002a) Ethanol-mediated generation of reactive oxygen species in developing rat cerebellum. Neurosci Lett 334:83–86.

Hirano T, Kaplowitz N, Tsukamoto H, Kamimura S, Fernandez-Checa JC (1992) Hepatic mitochondrial glutathione depletion and progression of experimental alcoholic liver disease in rats. Hepatology 16:1423–1427.

Inoue M, Nakamura K, Iwahashi K, Ameno K, Itoh M, Suwaki H (2002) Changes of bcl-2 and bax mRNA expressions in the ethanol-treated mouse brain. Nihon Arukoru Yakubutsu Igakkai Zasshi 37:120–129.

Jacobs JS, Miller MW (2001) Proliferation and death of cultured fetal neocortical neurons: effects of ethanol on the dynamics of cell growth. J Neurocytol 30: 391–401.

Jang MH, Shin MC, Kim YJ, Chung JH, Yim SV, Kim EH, Kim Y, Kim CJ (2001) Protective effects of puerariaeflos against ethanol-induced apoptosis on human neuroblastoma cell line SK-N-MC. Jpn J Pharmacol 87:338–342.

Keramaris E, Stefanis L, MacLaurin J, Harada N, Takaku K, Ishikawa T, Taketo MM, Robertson GS, Nicholson DW, Slack RS, Park DS (2000) Involvement of caspase 3 in apoptotic death of cortical neurons evoked by DNA damage. Mol Cell Neurosci 15:368–379.

Kim YY, Park BJ, Kim DJ, Kim WH, Kim S, Oh KS, Lim JY, Kim J, Park C, Park SI (2004) Modification of serine 392 is a critical event in the regulation of p53 nuclear export and stability. FEBS Lett 572:92–98.

Kornguth SE, Rutledge JJ, Sunderland E, Siegel F, Carlson I, Smollens J, Juhl U, Young B (1979) Impeded cerebellar development and reduced serum thyroxine levels associated with fetal alcohol intoxication. Brain Res 177:347–360.

Kuhn PE, Miller MW (1998) Expression of p53 and ALZ-50 immunoreactivity in rat cortex: effect of prenatal exposure to ethanol. Exp Neurol 154: 418–429.

Kukielka E, Dicher E, Cederbaum AI (1994) Increased production of reactive oxygen species by rat liver mitochondria after chronic ethanol treatment. Arch Biochem Biophys 309:377–386.

Liebler DC, Burr JA (1992) Oxidation of vitamin E during iron-catalyzed lipid peroxidation: evidence for electron-transfer reactions of the tocoperoxyl radical. Biochemistry 31:8278–8284.

Light KE, Belcher SM, Pierce DR (2002) Time course and manner of Purkinje neuron death following a single ethanol exposure on postnatal day 4 in the developing rat. Neuroscience 114:327–337.

Livy DJ, Maier SE, West JR (2001) Fetal alcohol exposure and temporal vulnerability: effects of binge-like alcohol exposure on the ventrolateral nucleus of the thalamus. Alcohol Clin Exp Res 25:774–780.

Luo J, Miller MW (1999) Platelet-derived growth factor-mediated signal transduction underlying astrocyte proliferation: site of ethanol action. J Neurosci 19:10014–10025.

Marino MD, Aksenov MY, Kelly SJ (2004) Vitamin E protects against alcohol-induced cell loss and oxidative stress in the neonatal rat hippocampus. Int J Dev Neurosci 22: 363–377.

Miller FD, Pozniak CD, Walsh GS (2000) Neuronal life and death: an essential role for the p53 family. Cell Death Differ 7:880–888.

Miller MW (1999) A longitudinal study of the effects of prenatal ethanol exposure on neuronal acquisition and death in the principal sensory nucleus of the trigeminal nerve: interaction with changes induced by transection of the infraorbital nerve. J Neurocytol 28:999–1015.

—— (2003) Describing the balance of cell proliferation and death: a mathematical model. J Neurobiol 57:172–182.

Miller MW, Al-Ghoul WM, Murtaugh M (1991) Expression of ALZ-50-immunoreactivity in the developing principal sensory nucleus of the trigeminal nerve: effect of transecting the infraorbital nerve. Brain Res 560:132–138.

Miller MW, Kuhn PE (1997) Neonatal transection of the infraorbital nerve increases the expression of proteins related to neuronal death in the principal sensory nucleus of the trigeminal nerve. Brain Res 769:233–244.

Miller TM, Moulder KL, Knudson CM, Creedon DJ, Deshmukh M, Korsmeyer SJ, Johnson EM Jr (1997) Bax deletion further orders the cell death pathway in cerebellar granule cells and suggests a caspase-independent pathway to cell death. J Cell Biol 139:205–217.

Mitchell ES, Snyder-Keller A (2003) c-fos and cleaved caspase-3 expression after perinatal exposure to ethanol, cocaine, or the combination of both drugs. Dev Brain Res 147:107–117.

Mitchell JJ, Paiva M, Heaton MB (1999a) The antioxidants vitamin E and beta-carotene protect against ethanol-induced neurotoxicity in embryonic rat hippocampal cultures. Alcohol 17:163–168.

—— (1999b) Vitamin E and beta-carotene protect against ethanol combined with ischemia in an embryonic rat hippocampal culture model of fetal alcohol syndrome. Neurosci Lett 263:189–192.

Mooney SM, Miller MW (1999) Effects of prenatal exposure to ethanol on systems matching: the number of neurons in the ventrobasal thalamic nucleus of the mature rat thalamus. Dev Brain Res 117:121–125.

—— (2001) Effects of prenatal exposure to ethanol on the expression of bcl-2, bax and caspase 3 in the developing rat cerebral cortex and thalamus. Brain Res 911:71–81.

Moore DB, Walker DW, Heaton MB (1999) Neonatal ethanol exposure alters bcl-2 family mRNA levels in the rat cerebellar vermis. Alcohol Clin Exp Res 23:1251–1261.

Morrison RS, Kinoshita Y, Johnson MD, Ghatan S, Ho JT, Garden G (2002) Neuronal survival and cell death signaling pathways. Adv Exp Med Biol 513:41–86.

Oberdoerster J, Rabin RA (1999) Enhanced caspase activity during ethanol-induced apoptosis in rat cerebellar granule cells. Eur J Pharmacol 385:273–282.

Obernier JA, Bouldin TW, Crews FT (2002) Binge ethanol exposure in adult rats causes necrotic cell death. Alcohol Clin Exp Res 26:547–557.

Olney JW, Tenkova T, Dikranian K, Muglia LJ, Jermakowicz WJ, D'Sa C, Roth KA (2002a) Ethanol-induced caspase-3 activation in the in vivo developing mouse brain. Neurobiol Dis 9:205–219.

Olney JW, Tenkova T, Dikranian K, Qin YQ, Labruyere J, Ikonomidou C (2002b) Ethanol-induced apoptotic neurodegeneration in the developing C57BL/6 mouse brain. Dev Brain Res 133:115–126.

Polster BM, Fiskum G (2004) Mitochondrial mechanisms of neural cell apoptosis. J Neurochem 90:1281–1289.

Porter AG (1999) Protein translocation in apoptosis. Trends Cell Biol 9:394–401.

Rajgopal Y, Chetty CS, Vemuri MC (2003) Differential modulation of apoptosis-associated proteins by ethanol in rat cerebral cortex and cerebellum. Eur J Pharmacol 470:117–124.

Ramachandran V, Perez A, Chen J, Senthil D, Schenker S, Henderson GI (2001) In utero ethanol exposure causes mitochondrial dysfunction which can result in apoptotic cell death in fetal brain: a potential role for 4-hydroxynonenal. Alcohol Clin Exp Res 25:862–871.

Ramachandran V, Watts LT, Maffi SK, Chen J, Schenker S, Henderson G (2003) Ethanol-induced oxidative stress precedes mitochondrially mediated apoptotic death of cultured fetal cortical neurons. J Neurosci Res 74:577–588.

Resnicoff M, Rubini M, Baserga R, Rubin R (1994) Ethanol inhibits insulin-like growth factor-1–mediated signalling and proliferation of C6 rat glioblastoma cells. Lab Invest 71:657–662.

Reyes E, Ott S, Robinson B (1993) Effects of in utero administration of alcohol on glutathione levels in brain and liver. Alcohol Clin Exp Res 17:877–881.

Saito M, Saito M, Berg MJ, Guidotti A, Marks N (1999) Gangliosides attenuate ethanol-induced apoptosis in rat cerebellar granule neurons. Neurochem Res 24:1107–1115.

Selznick LA, Zheng TS, Flavell RA, Rakic P, Roth KA (2000) Amyloid beta-induced neuronal death is bax-dependent but caspase-independent. J Neuropathol Exp Neurol 59:271–279.

Shaw S, Rubin KP, Lieber CS (1983) Depressed hepatic glutathione and increased diene conjugates in alcoholic liver disease. Evidence of lipid peroxidation. Dig Dis Sci 28:585–589.

Shigenaga MK, Hagen TM, Ames BN (1994) Oxidative damage and mitochondrial decay in aging. Proc Natl Acad Sci USA 91:10771–10778.

Siler-Marsiglio KI, Shaw G, Heaton MB (2004) Pycnogenol® and vitamin E inhibit ethanol-induced apoptosis in rat cerebellar granule cells. Neurobiology 59:261–271.

Sohma H, Ohkawa H, Hashimoto E, Sakai R, Saito T (2002) Ethanol-induced augmentation of annexin IV expression in rat C6 glioma and human A549 adenocarcinoma cells. Alcohol Clin Exp Res 26:44S–48S.

Stefanis L, Park DS, Friedman WJ, Greene LA (1999) Caspase-dependent and -independent death of camptothecin-treated embryonic cortical neurons. J Neurosci 19:6235–6247.

Tran TD, Jackson HD, Horn KH, Goodlett CR (2005) Vitamin E does not protect against neonatal ethanol-induced cerebellar damage or deficits in eyeblink classical conditioning in rats. Alcohol Clin Exp Res 29:117–129.

Valverde F, Lopez-Mascaraque L, de Carlos JA (1990) Distribution and morphology of Alz-50-immunoreactive cells in the developing visual cortex of kittens. J Neurocytol 19:662–671.

Vaudry D, Rousselle C, Basille M, Falluel-Morel A, Pamantung TF, Fontaine M, Fournier A, Vaudry H,
Gonzalez BJ (2002) Pituitary adenylate cyclase-
activating polypeptide protects rat cerebellar granule neurons against ethanol-induced apoptotic cell
death. Proc Natl Acad Sci USA 99:6398–6403.

Young C, Klocke BJ, Tenkova T, Choi J, Labruyere J,
Qin YQ, Holtzman DM, Roth KA, Olney JW
(2003) Ethanol-induced neuronal apoptosis *in vivo*
requires BAX in the developing mouse brain. Cell
Death Differ 10:1148–1155.

17

Neural Crest and Developmental Exposure to Ethanol

Susan M. Smith

Katherine A. Debelak-Kragtorp

The realization that the developing neural crest is a target of ethanol dates to the original descriptions of the fetal alcohol syndrome (FAS; Lemoine et al., 1968; Jones et al., 1973). A key observation was the finding of a characteristic facial dysmorphology that often, but not necessarily, accompanies the neurobehavioral and neurocognitive deficits. Early evidence that ethanol targets the neural crest comes from a series of mouse model studies (Sulik et al., 1981). Yet neural crest encompasses many more structures than the face, including key components of the peripheral nervous system. The present chapter summarizes the literature on neural crest and ethanol, and highlights issues that can benefit from further research.

OVERVIEW OF NEURAL CREST DEVELOPMENT

The neural crest, sometimes known as the fourth germ layer, is a transient yet critical contributor to embryogenesis. It is of neuroectodermal origin, yet it differentiates into populations as diverse as peripheral neurons, glia, chondrocytes, melanocytes, and connective tissue. Its accessibility and migratory properties have made it attractive for study for over 100 years, especially in avian and amphibian models and more recently in mouse. Recent work has greatly expanded our understanding of neural crest development at the cellular and molecular levels. Before addressing how alcohol affects the development of this complex population, it is first helpful to understand how these originate and to appreciate where their progeny may be found in the adult. An in-depth summary of neural crest can be found in the excellent book by Le Douarin and Kachiem (1999).

Neural crest arises at the border between the presumptive neural plate and lateral ectoderm. It appears quite early in development, shortly after the onset of neurulation. Its specification and induction involve signals between ectoderm and neural plate and the underlying mesendoderm. These signals are incompletely understood and appear to include members of the Wnt, fibroblast growth factor (FGF), and bone morphogenic protein (BMP) families (Basch et al., 2004). Their induction occurs in a rostrocaudal manner commensurate with overall development along that axis. Figure 17–1 illustrates these populations as defined by the expression of the transcription factor *slug*.

The upward rolling of the neural plate during early somitogenesis places neural crest populations at the dorsal lip of the neural folds. Shortly before this, or as the neural folds fuse to form the neural tube (depending on the species), the neural crest undergoes a transformation from epithelia to mesenchyme. Subsequently, the cells delaminate and migrate into the periphery of the embryo. Their migratory routes are defined by extracellular matrix proteins such as fibronectin and specific integrins (notably α1β4) on the neural crest. Once neural crest cells reach their targets they differentiate into appropriate cell types.

Three distinctive populations of neural crest are defined: cranial (or cephalic), cardiac, and truncal. Cranial neural crest originates from the forebrain, midbrain, and selected hindbrain segments (rhombomeres 1/2, 4, 6, 7/8). Transplantation studies show that their rostrocaudal identity (for example, mandible vs. hyoid) is dictated by the level of the neuraxis from which they originate, as defined by their expression of segment polarity genes (*hox, emx, otx*). Recent evidence suggests there is some plasticity in this aspect (Trainor et al., 2002). Cranial neural crest cells have the most diverse fates, and, depending on their level of origin and time of emergence, they differentiate to form the facial bones and cartilage, melanocytes, tooth papilla, sensory components of certain cranial nerves, and other features (Table 17–1). Cells forming the connective tissues emerge first, followed by neuronal and melanocytic lineages. Thus both the positional identity and differentiation fate of cranial neural crest cells are determined

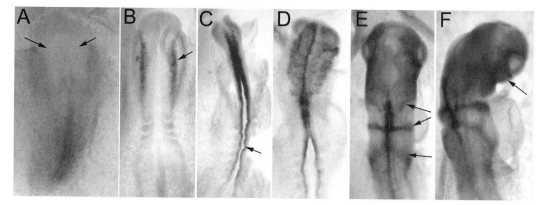

FIGURE 17–1 Morphogenetic sequence of neural crest induction and migration. Steps describing chick neural crest development are exemplified by changes in the expression of the transcription factor *slug*. **A.** Prechordal plate stage. At this time, neural crest cells are *slug* negative. Arrows indicate their location (also see Fig. 17–2A). *Slug* expression at this stage is restricted to migrating cells of the primitive streak. **B.** 3 somite stage. The first pre-migratory neural crest cells have appeared at the dorsal margin of the folding neural plate (arrow). **C.** 6 somite stage. As the neural folds fuse, neural crest cells receive their cues to begin migration. Younger populations are being induced more caudally, and these have a low *slug* expression (arrow). **D.** 10 somite stage. Neural crest migration occurs in a rostral-to-caudal sequence. Cells that are rostral to the otic vesicle have commenced migration. **E.** 15 somite stage. The segmental nature of neural crest migration is depicted. Arrows indicate the migratory waves that emerge from rhombomeres 2, 4, and 6. These cells are fated to form facial bones and cartilage. Within the hindbrain, neural crest cells that migrate slightly later will attain neuronal fates. Rostral neural crest cells have entered the mesenchyme that forms the upper facial region. **F.** 18 somite stage. Neural crest populations have reached their targets within the face. With their cessation of migration, they down-regulate *slug* (arrow) and begin to differentiate. Migration of neural crest from trunk and cardiac regions is still on-going at this stage.

TABLE 17–1 Neural crest contributions to the adult

Cranial

Bones and cartilage of the face and skull*

Cartilaginous bones: nasal capsule (ect-, mesethmoid, interorbital septum), basipresphenoid, sclerotic ossicles, ethmoid, pterygoid, Meckel's cartilage, quadratoarticular, hyoid (basihyal, entoglossum, basi-, epi-, ceratobranchial), otic capsule (pars cochlearis [partly], parotic process)

Membranous bones: nasal, vomer, maxilla, jugal, quadratojugal, palatine, mandibular

Membranous bones of skull: frontal (partly), parietal, squamosal, columella

Cranial nerves*

Sensory ganglia: portions of nerves V (posterior portion of trigeminal ganglion), VII (facial, root ganglion), IX (glossopharyngeal superior ganglion), X (vagal, jugular ganglion)

Neurons of the sympathetic and parasympathetic ganglia: superior cervical, ciliary (otic, submandibular, lingual, ethmoid, spheropalatine)

Glia and Schwann cells for all cranial ganglia and nerves

Other cranial tissues

Melanocytes of skin and internal organs (except the retinal pigmented epithelium)

Dermis of scalp

Dermis, smooth muscle, and adipose tissue of skin in face and ventral neck region

Meninges of the forebrain (pachymeninx and leptomeninx); not its blood vessels

Connective tissue of cranial glands: lacrimal, pituitary, parathyroid, salivary, thymus, thyroid

Connective tissues associated with facial muscles

Calcitonin-producing C cells

Type I chemoreceptor cells and type II supporting cells of the carotid body

Portions of the teeth: odontoblasts, cementoblasts

Eye: stromal and endothelial cells of cornea and orbit*

Ciliary muscles

*Cardiac**

Smooth muscle of the outflow tract

Mesenchymal cells of the outflow tract

Conotruncal cushions of the outflow tract

Cardiac ganglia

Truncal

Sensory neurons and glial cells of the dorsal root ganglia†

The entirety of the autonomic nervous system:

    Catecholaminergic and noncatecholaminergic neurons and satellite cells of the sympathetic ganglia and plexuses

    Cholinergic and noncholinergic neurons and satellite cells of the parasympathetic ganglia and plexuses

    Enteric ganglia

Schwann cells of the peripheral nerves

Neuroendocrine (adrenal chromaffin and small intensely fluorescent) cells of the adrenal medulla†

Parasympathetic ganglia of the pancreas

Merkel cells (mechanoreceptor cells of the mammalian whisker follicle)

Melanocytes of skin and internal organs

*Affected by ethanol, evidence based on *in vivo* work in animal models or humans.

†Affected by ethanol, evidence based on cell culture work.

Source: Adapted from Le Douarin and Kacheim (1999); this list may be incomplete.

predominantly prior to their emigration from the neural tube.

The cardiac neural crest is a relatively small, specialized subpopulation that emerges from neural tube at the level between the otic vesicle and somite 4, including rhombomeres 6–8 (Kirby 1999). Like cranial crest, they migrate into the third, fourth, and sixth pharyngeal arches, but instead contribute to the smooth muscle and connective tissue mesenchyme of the outflow tract and aortic arches. They also participate in the remodeling of these early structures into the aorta, pulmonary aorta, and affiliated vasculature. Deficits in this neural crest population lead to severe cardiac defects, such as double-outlet right ventricle, patent truncus arteriosus, and tetralogy of Fallot.

Neural crest populations caudal to somite 5 contribute to much of the peripheral nervous system (both sympathetic and parasympathetic neurons and their supporting Schwann cells), the enteric nervous system, and melanocytes. Cells that follow ventromedial migratory routes contribute to the peripheral nervous system. These cells only migrate through the rostal half of each sclerotome, and this restriction contributes to the segmentation of the sympathetic and dorsal root ganglia. Cells fated to become melanocytes follow a dorsolateral route and migrate somewhat later. Trunk neural crest cells appear to have a much greater plasticity with respect to fate and identity and hence seem to have a greater regenerative capacity than that of cranial and cardiac populations; when one region is ablated, neighboring cells migrate in and replace the missing cells. In general, fairly large losses must occur before anatomical and physiological changes are seen.

A preponderance of genetic and experimental data show that the basic rules and signals governing neural crest development are largely conserved among vertebrates. This is best shown in the numerous human neurocristopathies that are recapitulated by specific mouse null mutants. There can also be small differences in the timing or identity of regulatory molecules; for these finer details investigators are encouraged to consult the primary literature on their species of interest.

NEURAL CREST POPULATIONS AFFECTED BY ETHANOL

For obvious reasons, the best evidence that ethanol exposure disrupts neural crest development comes from animal models. As discussed below, the critical window for human neural crest development is between weeks three and eight postconception, and embryos that young are generally unavailable for study. A further limitation is the apparent lack of systemic descriptions of neural crest derivatives and their fate in humans exposed to heavy gestational alcohol exposure. Thus, this section emphasizes animal models, incorporates human observations when possible, and highlights instances where the human evidence is suggestive and would benefit from clarifying work. The reader should further note that findings in rodent and chick, the two most popular models for this work, are largely in agreement. Their concurrence enhances their applicability and relevance for human development.

Ethanol Targets Cranial Skeletal Derivatives

The facial changes observed in humans with heavy gestational alcohol exposure are similar to known neurocristopathies, prompting the first hypotheses that neural crest was targeted by ethanol exposure (Lemoine et al., 1968; Jones et al., 1973). The facial changes in humans include midfacial flattening, shortened nose with upturned nares, micrognathia, and hypoplastic maxilla (Clarren and Smith, 1978: Frias et al., 1982; Johnson et al., 1996; Mattson et al., 1997). Midfacial clefting and degrees of holoprosencephaly are sometimes seen. Anthropometric studies (Moore et al., 2001, 2002) report that facial dimensions are reduced overall in children with FAS (also known as dysmorphic fetal alcohol spectrum disorder [FASD]) and to a similar, but lesser extent, in those with alcohol-related neurodevelopmental disorder (ARND; also known as nondysmorphic FASD). Diagnostics emphasize soft tissue changes, particularly the trio of thin upper lip, reduced or absent philtrum, and small palpebral fissures in affected individuals. The great value of these changes arises from their ease of assessment and their relative uniqueness to alcohol (and toluene) exposure. Not surprisingly, they are important components of diagnostic screens for ARND and FAS (Astley and Clarren 1996). This emphasis on soft tissue may seem contradictory because facial skeletal muscle is not neural crest derived. Soft tissue shape, however, is dictated by the underlying skeletal elements (proof of this is in the forensic scientist's ability to recreate a person's likeness from the bare skull). Thus, the size and shape of the philtrum, lip, and palpebral fissures are a direct consequence of dysmorphologies in the underlying neural crest–derived skeletal elements.

Several other conclusions can be drawn from the human evidence. The facial appearance transcends racial characteristics, reinforcing the robust nature of ethanol-induced changes. Second, in no instance does ethanol exposure alter the segmental identity of the face. Effects instead are manifested in dimensional shifts in otherwise normal structures, indicating that ethanol targets aspects of neural crest cellularity and outgrowth, a finding that provides important clues to locating the molecular targets of ethanol action.

Animal studies confirm the hypotheses that alcohol targets the developing neural crest. Studies of rats prenatally exposed to ethanol have the constellation of malformations in the craniofacial skeleton that is characteristic of humans with FAS (Edwards and Dow-Edwards, 1991). Murine studies have refined the temporal window of vulnerability (Sulik et al., 1981; Webster et al., 1983). In mice on gestational day (G) 7, i.e., at the time of gastrulation, ethanol exposure (as two acute doses 4 hr apart) causes craniofacial defects consistent with human FAS. These defects include midline reductions, reduced midface, and hypoplastic primordia of the maxilla and mandible. Ethanol exposure one day later (G8, headfold stage) also affects the face, but causes a facial appearance more similar to that of DiGeorge syndrome (Sulik et al., 1986). For both treatment windows, these morphological changes are preceded by significant cell death within their respective neural crest precursors as well as in adjacent regions (Kotch and Sulik 1992a, 1992b; Dunty et al., 2001). These two critical windows for mouse correspond to weeks 3 and 4, respectively, in human pregnancy. Identical ethanol doses at G9 or G10 do not appreciably affect facial appearance (Webster et al., 1983), reinforcing the observation that ethanol targets early events in neural crest induction, expansion, and/or migration, rather than later events of differentiation.

A similar phenotype occurs in chick embryos exposed to acute ethanol. As with mouse, the precise facial changes depend on stage of treatment (Cartwright and Smith, 1995b). Gastrulation-stage (HH4) or neurulation-stage (HH6) exposure produces a wider, taller chick face with a shorter maxilla and nasal bone, whereas exposure at the onset of migration (HH10-12) produces an overall hypoplastic face (Debelak-Kragtorp, Moyers, and Smith, unpublished results). The facial appearance is preceded by significant cell death in regions including the cranial chondrogenic precursors of neural crest, and immunostaining corroborates the loss of these neural crest populations (Cartwright and Smith 1995a; Cartwright et al., 1998). Pretreatment of chick embryos with a caspase-3 antagonist prevented both the ethanol-induced cell death and the changes in beak length (Debelak-Kragtorp, Moyers, and Smith, unpublished results). This finding reinforces the concept that cell death contributes to the facial dysmorphology. Susceptibility to ethanol-induced apoptosis is greatest for premigratory neural crest; migratory and postmigratory cells are more resistant (Cartwright and Smith, 1995b). This timing suggests that unique developmental events prior to neural crest migration may

govern their sensitivity; some of these targets are discussed below.

These animal data predict that humans at weeks 3 and 4 of gestation are the most sensitive to the facial teratogenic effects. A study in pregnant macaques reinforces this prediction. Once weekly doses of alcohol (mean blood ethanol concentration [BEC] ~220 mg/dl) are associated with facial dysmorphology in the offspring only when the exposure coincide with G19 or G20 (Astley et al., 1999). These findings suggest that a sufficiently high BEC during a critical window is required to induce the characteristic facial changes of FAS. The implication is that if a pregnant woman has restricted or no access to alcohol during the critical window, her child may lack the facial dysmorphology, despite having profound nervous system deficits from later exposure. The diagnostic implications of this are obvious for professionals and affected families.

Ethanol Targets Neuronal Derivatives of Neural Crest

The literature on this point is sadly scant with respect to humans. In mice, ethanol causes significant apoptosis in the otic region and in the neural crest and placodal components of the cranial sensory ganglia (Dunty et al., 2001). Ethanol-exposed chick embryos display reductions in cranial nerve cellularity and aberrant migration of their neuronal branches (Cartwright and Smith, unpublished results). The functional consequences of such losses have not been studied. There are hints, however, that these populations also are targeted in humans. For example, an infant with FAS often has a reduced rooting reflex when nursing, a behavior partly dependent on the ability of facial cranial nerves to sense and process a tactile stimulus. This tactile loss can be so significant that some affected individuals require soft or liquid diets because they have trouble sensing food texture and when it is appropriate to swallow. There can also be significant hearing losses and persistent ear canal infections that are partly attributed to changes in the neural crest–derived bone and cartilage structures and in the acoustical nerves, which are supported by glia and Schwann cells originating from neural crest (Church et al., 1996, 1997). Further investigation into cranial and peripheral nerves, and the consequences of any such dysfunctions, should be a high priority.

The situation regarding neural crest precursors of the peripheral nervous system is even less clear. Embryos treated at G7 and G8 have increased cell death within regions populated by trunk neural crest (Sulik et al., 1988; Kotch and Sulik, 1992b). The consequences of such losses have yet to be detailed. Segmentation of the dorsal root ganglia appears normal by gross inspection, although culture studies suggest that ethanol impairs the survival and outgrowth of DRG neurons (Dow and Riopelle, 1990); reduced synthesis of and responses to trophic factors are noted (Dow and Riopelle, 1990; Heaton et al., 1992; Bradley et al., 1995). Adverse affects on the sympathetic and parasympathetic nervous system have not been reported for humans and in animal models. Impaired balance is observed, but follow-up testing implicates targets in the central nervous system rather than the neural crest–derived peripheral nervous system (Church et al., 1997; Roebuck et al., 1998). Moreover, obstructive bowel problems characteristic of impaired enteric nervous system development are not widely reported. Whereas glia and supporting cells of the brain are appreciated as a target of ethanol (Chapter 18), little attention has been paid to supporting cells of the peripheral nervous system. In summary, our best answer to this question is that these populations can be targeted by ethanol, but the functional consequences are essentially unexplored.

Ethanol Targets Cardiac Neural Crest Derivatives

Outflow tract anomalies are more frequent in children with FAS than in the general population (Abel, 1990), prompting studies into potential effects of ethanol on the cardiac neural crest. In mouse and chick models, ethanol exposure causes apoptosis of cardiac neural crest precursors (Kotch and Sulik, 1992b; Cartwright et al., 1995b). On the basis of extirpation studies (Kirby, 1999), such losses should result in aorticopulmonary defects such as persistent truncus arteriosus, double-outlet right ventricle, and tetralogy of Fallot. Indeed, ethanol causes such defects in both mouse (Daft et al., 1986) and chick (Fang et al., 1987) with an incidence of 10%–20%. These dysmorphologies are preceded by the expected malpositioning and reductions of the conal cushions (Daft et al., 1986) and hypoplasia of the proximal bulbar ridges (Fang et al., 1987; Bruyere and Stith, 1993). The critical window for these effects is during the time of cardiac crest migration, invasion, and expansion into the outflow tract and pharyngeal arches (G8.5 for mouse, Daft et al., 1986; 72–80 hr incubation in chick, Fang et al., 1987). But are these changes actually due to the neural crest losses? Our view is that the heart defects represent defects in cardiac populations other than neural crest. We exposed chick embryos to ethanol at critical times of cardiac neural crest and outflow tract development; despite significant losses of cardiac crest, inspection at later time points found normal neural crest distributions within the outflow tract, and no aorticopulmonary or septal defects (Cavieres and Smith, 2000).

Bruyere and colleagues (1994a) note inconsistencies between the heart defects commonly seen in human prenatal alcohol exposure and those caused in the laboratory by neural crest ablation. In ethanol-exposed humans, the most common cardiac defects are not aorticopulmonary. Rather, they are isolated ventricular septal defects (VSDs) and atrial septal defects (ASDs; ~75% of congenital cardiac anomalies). These two septa are not neural crest derived. VSDs and ASDs are generally secondary responses to primary changes in flow dynamics (Kirby, 1999; Firulli and Conway, 2004). Significant effects in cardiac output, heart rate, metabolism, and cardiomyocyte differentiation are documented in models of prenatal ethanol exposure (Nyquist-Battie and Freter, 1988; Ruckman et al., 1988; Adickes et al., 1993; Bruyere and Stith, 1994a; Bruyere et al., 1994b). Fang and colleagues (1987) suggest that ethanol has a biphasic effect on the developing heart, with lower BECs causing VSDs (perhaps targeting cardiomyocytes) and higher concentrations targeting aorticopulmonary events (and cardiac crest). Lower ethanol exposures, though deleting some cardiac crest, may allow the survivors to repopulate and replace their missing neighbors. Determining the extent to which neural crest losses contribute to cardiac defects in FAS will require additional research. Careful morphological studies using, for example, the lacZ-wnt1 reporter mouse (in which neural crest can be followed by merit of lacZ expression) could nicely resolve this question.

Ethanol Targets Melanocyte Derivatives

Alcohol likely has no long-term consequences on melanocyte development, although this conclusion rests on negative data. Melanocytes are the pigmented cells within the dermis, and to our knowledge there are no reports of reduced pigmentation or altered pigmental patterns in either individuals prenatally exposed to alcohol or exposed mice. Melanin is still synthesized in salamander neural crest cultured with ethanol, and its unusual perinuclear deposition may be secondary to microfilament dysarrangements (Hassler and Moran, 1986). The pigmented chicks we have hatched show no sign of altered feather coloration (Smith, Tessmer, and Debelak-Kragtorp, unpublished results). This lack of effect may reflect the lack of segmental identity within melanocytes, which facilitates their ability to expand and compensate for losses.

Other Neural Crest Populations Targeted by Ethanol

There are hints in the literature that additional neural crest subpopulations may be affected by ethanol. Carones and colleagues (1992) and Miller and Beauchamp (1988) document multiple cases of ocular defects involving the cornea endothelia, a neural crest–derived population that contributes to the anterior segment of the eye. Tooth problems are mentioned, although it was not indicated whether this involves the neural crest–based papilla. Similarly, it is not known whether problems of thymocyte maturation and thyroid hormone production are linked to aberrant stroma of their respective glands. A similar question can be raised with the altered signals of the hypothalamic-pituitary-adrenal (HPA) axis. In that light, it is worth noting that a cell line popular for studies of ethanol-mediated neuronal signaling, PC12 cells (Messing et al., 1986; Luo et al., 1999), is an adrenochromaffin tumor originating from neural crest lineage of the adrenal medulla. Again, a systematic study of neural crest derivatives in humans (Table 17–1) would provide important clues as to the effects of ethanol on nonclassic neural crest populations.

EVENTS OF NEURAL CREST DEVELOPMENT AFFECTED BY ETHANOL

Data from animal models, as discussed above, point to early events of neural crest induction, determination, and migration as the major targets for ethanol teratogenicity (Fig. 17–2). Evidence summarized below indicates that no single event is affected; rather, multiple targets likely lead to a cumulative effect on this cell population.

Neural Induction

A key, early event of embryogenesis is the anterior extension of the prechordal plate and its subsequent induction of the neural plate, including neural crest, at the midline of the overlying ectoderm. Prechordal plate size affects neuronal—and neural crest—population size. Ethanol reduces the migratory capacity of these anterior mesodermal cells in both chick (Sanders et al., 1987) and zebrafish embryos (Blader and Strahle, 1998). Unfortunately, any consequences for neural crest population size have yet to be tested. Reduced prechordal plate migration may also contribute to the holoprosencephalic aspects of acute prenatal alcohol exposure (Sulik et al., 1988; Blader and Strahle, 1998), although a major midline mediator, *sonic hedgehog* (*shh*), does not appear to be a direct target of ethanol in this model.

Neural Crest Migration

Rovasio and colleagues have detailed how ethanol impairs neural crest migration. Co-culture of chick embryos (3 somites) with 0.25% ethanol causes significant reductions in the number of cranial and truncal neural crest cells exiting the neural tube, as visualized in cross-section via immunostaining with the neural crest–specific antibody NC-1 (Rovasio and Battiato, 1995). Primary cultures of neural crest cells treated with 150 mM ethanol lose their mesenchymal appearance and become spindle shaped. They have fewer filopodia, increased surface blebbing, and pronounced rearrangements of the actin cytoskeleton that are accompanied by dramatic reductions in their migratory capacity (Rovasio and Battiato, 2002). Cranial and truncal populations are similarly affected. Lower BECs (100–200 mg/dl) do not affect migration, but they do lead to thickened actin and tubulin filaments in cultured primary neural crest (Hassler and Moran, 1986). Cell–cell contacts are disrupted. Migratory pathways in the trunk are directed by the somites; the segmental anomalies in alcohol-exposed somites (Sanders and Cheung,

A. Induction events

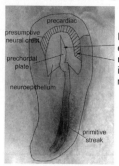

Reduced prechoral plate extension would reduce the number of neural crest cells induced at the neuroepithelial margin.

B. Apoptotic events

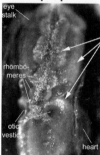

Apoptosis due to:
- oxidative stress;
- altered Ca⁺⁺ signals;
- loss of L1-mediated cell-cell interactions;
- loss of retinoid signals;
- loss of trophic signals

C. Migration and differentiation

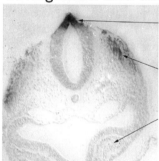

Altered identity and/or delayed emergence from neural tube.

Impaired migration and/or cellular expansion into target tissues

Delayed or arrested differentiation within target tissue regions.

FIGURE 17–2 Candidate targets of ethanol during neural crest development. **A.** Targets during the window of neural crest induction. A chick embryo at the prechordal plate stage (HH5+) was prepared to visualize *slug* transcripts by in situ hybridization. The presumptive neural crest–forming region (shaded) lies at the boundary of the neuroectoderm and ectoderm. **B.** Targets that could cause neural crest apoptosis are summarized. Shown is a chick embryo of the 17 somite stage. Apoptotic cells are visualized by the vital dye acridine orange. This embryo was exposed to ~60 mM ethanol at gastrulation, as described by Cartwright and colleagues (1998). **C.** Targets during the window of neural crest migration and differentiation. This image depicts a transverse view through the hindbrain (level of rhombomere 6) of a chick embryo at the

1990) may have deleterious effects on neural crest migration and fate.

Neural Crest Expansion

Reduced prechordal plate size and increased apoptosis could reduce the population size of neural crest. It should be noted, however, that embryos have robust repair mechanisms; autoregulatory signals and group-effect responses can restore population size in response to addition or loss. Signals that regulate the size of the neural crest population include *shh*, *bmp*, *fgf*, and *wnt*. The degree to which these are ethanol targets likely depends on the timing and dose of exposure. The homeotic selector gene, *msx2*, is expressed in premigratory and migratory neural crest and is associated with both expansion and apoptosis. One report notes near ablation of *msx2* expression in ethanol-treated mouse embryos and calvarial osteoblasts (Rifas et al., 1997), however, the BECs in this study are very high. Preparations exposed to more physiologically relevant exposures do not affect *msx2* (Cartwright et al., 1998). Ethanol may affect *shh*, a mediator of directional outgrowth, and such suppression might contribute to neural crest reductions (Ahlgren et al., 2002). *Shh* within the face is transiently reduced by ethanol exposure commensurate with reduced mesenchymal proliferation and elevated *fgf* and *msx* expression (Smith et al., 2001). These changes are proportionate to later shifts in directional outgrowth. Yet there is no evidence that any such changes are associated with neural crest apoptosis at these times (see below). Much more work is needed to understand the effects of ethanol on these morphoregulatory cues.

Apoptosis

Cell death is an important component of ethanol teratogenicity. Sandor (1968) observed a prominent cellular "necrosis" within the neuroepithelium of ethanol-exposed chick embryos, a region that includes neural crest precursors. Sulik and colleagues (1981) documented cytoplasmic and nuclear extrusions from

36 somite stage. The pharnyx lies ventral to the hindbrain. Neural crest cells are visualized by in situ hybridization for *slug*.

neural folds of mice treated with ethanol at G8. Similar foci of necrotic and degenerating cells were observed in neuronal populations of the mouse on G9 (Bannigan and Burke, 1982; Bannigan and Cottell, 1984). Sulik's work using vital dyes and high-magnification histology had established that this "necrosis" actually represents pyknosis (Sulik et al., 1986, 1988; Kotch and Sulik, 1992a, 1992b). This pyknosis is part of an ethanol-induced apoptotic death; caspase inhibitor pretreatment prevents it (Cartwright et al., 1998) and the DNA is labeled by terminal transferase (TUNEL-positive) (Cartwright et al., 1998; Dunty et al., 2001).

Apoptosis is a well-described, active, energy-dependent process that is a mechanism for the removal of unwanted cells (Reed, 2000). It is prominent in the developing embryo, for example, in removing interdigital webbing. It also is used to eliminate cells that have aberrantly activated their proliferative machinery, such as self-recognizing T cells; tumors represent cells that fail to apoptose when promitotic signals become activated. Teratogens frequently act by expanding existing domains of endogenous cell death. Under this model, the teratogen recruits susceptible populations by merit of their latent capacity for apoptosis.

This certainly is the case for acute ethanol. Sulik and colleagues (Sulik et al., 1988; Kotch and Sulik, 1992b; Dunty et al., 2001) have comprehensively mapped the cell death patterns for normal mouse embryogenesis and following ethanol treatment. This work elegantly shows that ethanol-induced apoptosis is selective. Populations are not affected uniformly and the precise target depends on the stage of treatment. Regions of cell death coincided with tissues and structures affected by ethanol treatment, including neural crest of cranial, cardiac, and trunk populations. A critical implication of this work is that there are inherent properties within certain cell populations that govern their susceptibility to ethanol. These properties are reviewed in detail below.

Our recent work with chick embryos emphasizes the mechanisms underlying ethanol-induced death of neural crest cells. Cranial neural crest apoptosis in the chick coincides with the endogenous death of neural crest precursors in rhombomeres 3 and 5. Thus, we hypothesize that ethanol exposure might activate those endogenous signals. These signals are well described and involve the *wnt*-dependent activation of *bmp4* synthesis within rhombomeres 3 and 5. *Bmp4* acts in an autocrine–paracrine manner to

stimulate *msx2* expression and the apoptosis sequence (Graham et al., 1994). Neither *bmp4* nor *msx2*, however, are elevated in the hindbrains of ethanol-exposed chick embryos (Cartwright et al., 1998). Thus the initial machinery of ethanol-induced apoptosis must lie upstream of the endogenous death signals. We recently ascertained that these signals involve the activation by ethanol of a pertussis toxin–sensitive G protein and intracellular Ca^{2+} transients (Garic-Stankovic, et al., 2005; see below).

HOW DOES ETHANOL KILL NEURAL CREST CELLS?

Four major mechanisms have received considerable scrutiny: oxidative stress, L1-mediated cell adhesions, induction of Ca^{2+} transients, and retinoid-dependent signals. It should be stressed that evidence for the first three is quite good. Ethanol has pleiotropic effects, and it is quite likely that ultimately these mechanisms will prove to be interrelated.

Oxidative Stress

Ethanol exposure leads to oxidative stress in the neural crest. Migratory and postmigratory neural crest cells lack appreciable superoxide dismutase (SOD) activity (Davis et al., 1990), and exposure of neural crest to a free-radical source (such as xanthine oxidase) is sufficient to impede their survival (Chen and Sulik, 1996). Superoxide, hydrogen peroxide, and hydroxy radical concentrations all increase after exposure to 50–100 mM ethanol, and upon supplementation with SOD those concentrations return to normal (Davis et al., 1990; Chen and Sulik 1996). In whole embryos treated with ethanol, lipid peroxidases and superoxide radicals are selectively enriched within the neural crest and neuroepithelium (Kotch et al., 1995). Co-culture of whole embryos (Kotch et al., 1995) or postmigratory neural crest (Davis et al., 1990; Chen and Sulik, 1996) with free-radical scavengers (SOD or catalase) improves cell survival and reduces ethanol-induced cytotoxicity. It should be noted, however, that these treatments provide only a partial rescue. Iron chelators such as deferoxamine and phenarthroline also offer protection against ethanol-induced cell death (Chen and Sulik, 2000). This is an interesting finding because ethanol exposure can elevate iron concentrations as in the brain stem

(Miller et al., 1995). In two separate studies, however, vitamin E is less effective at ameliorating these effects, a surprising outcome given that this free-radical scavenger preferentially acts on lipid and membrane compartments (Davis et al., 1990; Chen and Sulik, 1996).

There is little question that free radicals contribute to neural crest death, just as oxidative stress contributes to many instances of neuronal death in the fetus. Less clear is the precise role of oxidative stress in the sequence of events. Does ethanol itself directly cause this stress? Neural crest at these stages does not express Cyp2E1 (Deltour et al., 1996), but it does have an ADH4 capable of metabolizing ethanol at high concentrations (Deltour et al., 1996; Haselbeck and Duester, 1998). The resulting imbalances in NADP/NADPH ratios would invoke a metabolic stress, an effect well documented for adult heart and liver. Alternatively, these increased free-radical levels could simply reflect that the cells are dying, perhaps through changes in the mitochondrial transition pore that are part of apoptosis itself. Studies to date have emphasized time points of 12 hr and later following ethanol treatment. Additional studies looking at much earlier times would clarify this question. Our current view is that the pro-oxidant effects are likely secondary to the primary action of ethanol, because of this lack of earlier time point data and because of the effects on Ca^{2+} signaling detailed below.

Cell Adhesion and L1

Ethanol also disrupts the development of neural crest cells and promotes their apoptosis through L1, a cell adhesion molecule (CAM) of the immunoglobulin CAM superfamily. Ethanol inhibits L1-mediated cell adhesion (Charness et al., 1994; Ramanathan et al., 1996; Wilkemeyer and Charness, 1998). L1 is strongly expressed by neural crest (Chen et al., 2001), and in this context it is noteworthy that disruptions of neural crest cell–cell adhesion, at least at the level of gap junctions, results in their apoptosis (Bannerman et al., 2000). L1 deficits cause craniofacial dysgenesis in humans (CRASH syndrome) that shares aspects of that with alcohol exposure (Fransen et al., 1995). Ethanol likely acts on L1 through its ability to sit within hydrophilic pockets of membrane proteins, stabilizing protein structure and enhancing or repressing its activity (Mihic et al., 1997). In this model, ethanol would bind L1 to disrupt crucial trophic cues that the protein supplies to neural crest.

Low concentrations of n-octanol block the actions of L1; they block L1-mediated cell adhesion (Wilkemeyer et al., 2000). Furthermore, n-octanol ameliorates the toxic consequences of ethanol on cultured mouse embryos (Chen et al., 2001). Their appearance is more normal and they exhibit significantly less cell death, including neural crest–populated regions. N-octanol may act by competitively inhibiting ethanol from binding to the hydrophilic pockets of L1.

Ethanol antagonism of L1 is prevented by the peptides NAPVSIPQ (NAP) and SALLRSIPA (SAL), fragments of the larger glial-derived activity-dependent neuroprotective protein (ADNP) and activity-dependent neurotrophic factor (ADNF), respectively. These peptides confer protection against numerous neuronal insults, including ethanol (Spong et al., 2001). NAP reduces several of the adverse actions of ethanol, such as the antagonism of L1 adhesion (Wilkemeyer et al., 2002, 2003), the depletion of glutathione (Spong et al., 2001), and the growth inhibition of embryos, including craniofacial regions (Spong et al., 2001; Wilkemeyer et al., 2003). How NAP does this is unclear. Charness and colleagues speculate that disruption of L1 adhesions may trigger an oxidative death process called *anoikis* (Wilkemeyer et al., 2000, 2003). NAP may override these death signals as part of its broader neuroprotection. It may also have direct effects on L1 action. Further investigations into L1 will provide additional, important insights into the molecular mechanisms that underlie the sensitivity of neural crest to ethanol.

Ca^{2+} Signaling

The early mouse blastocyst responds to ethanol (0.10%) with immediate generation of an intracellular Ca^{2+} transient, the source of which is through PLC-mediated inositol 1,4,5-triphosphate (IP3) release (Stachecki et al., 1994; Rout et al., 1997). IP3-dependent Ca^{2+} transients occur spontaneously in neural crest, and these are essential for the neural differentiation of neural crest cells (Carey and Matsumoto 1999, 2000). Ethanol treatment of HH8 chick embryos stimulates an immediate (< 5 sec) intracellular Ca^{2+} transient. Moreover, this transient is essential to induce neural crest apoptosis, because pretreatment with an intracellular Ca^{2+} chelator (BAPTA-AM) prevents the ethanol-induced but not endogenous cell death (Debelak-Kragtorp et al., 2003). Generation of this transient requires the activity of a pertussis toxin–sensitive G protein, PLCβ, and IP3 release (Garic-Stankovic et al., 2005). Gαi2, but not Gαi1 or Gαio, is expressed in these cells. Extracellular Ca^{2+} contributes about 30% of this Ca^{2+} signal (Debelak-Kragtorp et al., 2003). We recently detected a Ca^{2+} oscillation in ethanol-treated neural crest, with a repeat every 15 to 20 sec over 1 to 2 min (Garic-Stankovic, Hernandez, and Smith, unpublished results). A potential contribution of this oscillation is under investigation. These events are sensitive to inhibition by decanol (Garic-Stankovic et al., 2006).

The source of this Ca^{2+} transient involves the Gi/oβγ stimulation of a phosphoinositidyl-PLCβ. Ethanol-mediated amplification of endogenous Giβγ and phosphoinositidyl-PLCβ signals is implicated in the dopaminergic rewarding properties of ethanol in neurons (Yao et al., 2002, 2003). Ethanol enhances the activation of Gαs, protein kinase A, and cAMP response element binding protein signals, as well as Giβγ, and synergism through these pathways permits intracellular signaling at ligand levels that normally would not transduce signal. The identity of the G-protein coupled receptor and other participants in this transient is actively being investigated. It is of interest that two different cellular targets and outcomes of ethanol, addiction/reward and apoptosis, use overlapping signaling pathways.

Retinoic Acid Signaling

One mechanism proposed for ethanol-induced craniofacial dysmorphology involves the perturbation of retinoic acid (RA) signaling. Some isoforms of alcohol dehydrogenase (ADH), notably ADH4, will metabolize both ethanol and retinol, a precursor of RA (Chou et al., 2002). Several groups have postulated that ethanol competes with retinol metabolism, and thus RA production, in the developing embryo (Duester, 1991; Grummer et al., 1993; Deltour et al., 1996). RA signaling through the nuclear retinoic acid receptors (RARs) directly regulates the expression of genes critical for the development of numerous embryonic structures including neural crest. These include the *hox* genes, which define rostral–caudal patterning of the embryo (Langston and Gudas, 1994); the loss of retinoid signaling leads to ablation of posterior hindbrain regions, including their neural crest derivatives (Maden et al., 1996). RA also sustains the identity

(Plant et al., 2000) and outgrowth (Schneider et al., 2001) of the frontonasal primordial, in part through its support of *fgf8* and *shh* pro-proliferative cues. RA deficiency at these stages leads to failure of frontonasal and forebrain outgrowth as well as apoptosis in craniofacial precursors (Zile, 2001).

Until recently, this hypothesis was challenging to investigate, because of the low circulating concentrations of RA (K_d of RA for RARs is in the 0.5 nM range) and the high retinol stores of standard rodent models. To circumvent these difficulties, Duester and colleagues generated null-mutant mice to identify ADH1 as a major ethanol dehydrogenase and ADH4 as a major retinol dehydrogenase (Deltour et al., 1999). Clinically relevant ethanol concentrations can compete for retinol oxidation for both enzymes; Molotkov and Duester (2002) cite K_i values of 0.040–3.8 mM for ADH1 and 6–12 mM for ADH4. They further show that both ethanol and *adh1* null mutation prolongs retinol half-life through suppression of RA synthesis rather than RA catabolism. One hundred mM but not 10 mM ethanol inhibits RA synthesis in G7.5 but not G8.5 mouse embryos, as measured by a lacZ-RARE reporter construct (Deltour et al., 1996). In rat whole-embryo cultures, retinol and ethanol had synergistic effects on dysmorphology, but no effect on tissue RA and retinal content (Chen et al., 1996a). Using liquid diets (36% calories as ethanol; BEC ~260 mg/dl) and *in utero* exposure, however, Zachman and colleagues report that tissues from 12-day-old mouse fetuses had two- to three-fold higher retinol and lower RA expression, as well as altered RAR and cellular retinol binding protein transcript levels (Zachman and Grummer, 1998). In the developing quail, 10 nM RA rescued the cardiac dysmorphology caused by exposure to 1.0% ethanol (Twal and Zile, 1997).

Evidence of a specific interaction between ethanol and endogenous retinoid signaling in neural crest is lacking. ADH may be expressed in premigratory neural crest cells, although this particular expression is not always observed and does not appear to correlate with RA production (Ang et al., 1996; Haselbeck and Duester, 1998). More certain is the expression of ADH4 (and the subsequent production of RA) in migratory neural crest and the developing craniofacial mesenchyme (Ang et al., 1996). It is likely, therefore, that any effects of ethanol on retinoid signaling would act on the migratory and postmigratory neural crest, rather than affecting premigratory populations with respect to their survival. Indeed, ethanol-exposed, RARE-lacZ reporter mice have reduced expression of this RA-dependent construct, an outcome most likely explained by a reduction of RA-mediated signaling (Deltour et al., 1996).

A major caveat is that endogenous RA specifically acts on frontonasal development. Once patterned, there is no apparent retinoid requirement for maxilla, mandible, and hyoid outgrowth (e.g., Wedden, 1987; Dickman et al., 1997; Schneider et al., 2001). At this time, the retinoid hypothesis does not adequately explain the sensitivity of neural crest to ethanol-induced apoptosis, nor does it wholly account for the changes in maxillary and lower jaw development. Nonetheless, this remains an attractive hypothesis and it merits additional, careful investigation.

GENETIC FACTORS

Genetic factors modulate neural crest sensitivity to ethanol, just as they modulate the risk of other congenital anomalies and neurobehavioral outcomes. We screened 11 leghorn chicken strains and found that they differed widely in their sensitivity to ethanol-induced apoptosis within neural crest and the subsequent craniofacial outcome (Debelak and Smith, 2000; Su et al., 2001). Cultured neural crest cells from inbred C57Bl/6J mice are more sensitive to ethanol-induced toxicity than those from outbred ICR mice (Chen et al., 2000). Their sensitivity correlates positively with indicators of membrane fluidity and negatively with GM1 ganglioside content. Moreover, GM1 application attenuates ethanol-induced damage to C57Bl/6J neural crest (Chen et al., 1996b). Chick strains also differ with respect to aorticopulmonary defects associated with the cardiac neural crest (Bruyere and Stith, 1993). In all three models, ethanol metabolism is not appreciably different, which suggests that factors intrinsic to the embryo and neural crest are responsible.

Maternal and fetal capacity for ethanol metabolism affects risk for ethanol-induced malformations of the fetus. The more efficient alcohol dehydrogenase allele 1B*3 confers increased protection against teratogenic effects of ethanol in a human cohort (McCarver et al., 1997), and contributions of Cytochrome P450 2E1 may be protective (Rasheed et al., 1997). These findings extend to facial dysmorphology and reinforce the notion that alcohol rather than acetaldehyde is the proximate teratogen (Das et al., 2004).

FUTURE DIRECTIONS

It is now clear that the effects of ethanol on facial appearance represent a response at a relatively narrow developmental window. Facial appearance remains a highly useful diagnostic tool, and the study of its neural crest precursors continues to provide important insights into the molecular mechanisms that underlie neurotoxic effects of ethanol. One such avenue is to investigate whether ethanol exposure ultimately affects common signaling pathways within otherwise diverse cell types.

It is disconcerting that the consequences of ethanol exposure to neural crest–derived structures other than the face remain largely unstudied, because these populations contribute to critical activities such as hearing, vision, texture sensation, chewing, the autonomic nervous system, and hormonal actions that include the adrenal medulla, pituitary, parathyroid, and thyroid glands. Studies of these less-appreciated neurochristopathies and their consequences for health is an important gap in FAS research. The addressing of this question should become a high priority in the assessment of affected individuals and in detailed investigation using animal models.

ABBREVIATIONS

ADH   alcohol dehydrogenase

ADNF   activity-dependent neurotrophic factor

ADNP   activity-dependent neuroprotective protein

ARND   alcohol-related neurodevelopmental disorder

ASDs   atrial septal defects

BEC   blood ethanol concentration

BMP   bone morphogenic protein

CAM   cell adhesion molecule

FAS   fetal alcohol syndrome

FASD   fetal alcohol spectrum disorder

FGF   fibroblast growth factor

G   gestational day

HPA   hypothalamic-pituitary-adrenal

IP3   inositol 1,4,5-triphosphate

RA   retinoic acid

RAR   retinoic acid receptor

SOD   superoxide dismutase

VSDs   ventricular septal defects

ACKNOWLEDGMENTS   This work was supported by the National Institute of Alcohol Abuse and Alcoholism and National Institute for Environmental Health Sciences, and the March of Dimes Birth Defects Foundation.

References

Able EL (1990) *Fetal Alcohol Syndrome*. Medical Economics Books, Oradell, NJ.

Adickes ED, Mollner TJ, Makoid MC (1993) Teratogenic effects of ethanol during hyperplastic growth in cardiac myocyte cultures. Alcohol Clin Exp Res 17:988–992.

Ahlgren SC, Thakur V, Bronner-Fraser M (2002) Sonic hedgehog rescues cranial neural crest from cell death induced by ethanol exposure. Proc Natl Acad Sci USA 99:10476–10481.

Ang HL, Deltour L, Hayamizo TF, Zgombic-Knight M, Duester G (1996) Retinoic acid synthesis in mouse embryos during gastrulation and craniofacial development linked to class IV alcohol dehydrogenase gene expression. J Biol Chem 271:9526–9534.

Astley SJ, Clarren SK (1996) A case definition and photographic screening tool for the facial phenotype of fetal alcohol syndrome. J Pediatr 129:33–41.

Astley SJ, Magnuson SI, Omnell LM, Clarren SK (1999) Fetal alcohol syndrome: changes in craniofacial form with age, cognition, and timing of ethanol exposure in the macaque. Teratology 59:163–72.

Bannerman P, Nichols W, Puhalla S, Oliver T, Berman M, Pleasure D (2000) Early migratory rat neural crest cells express functional gap junctions: evidence that neural crest cell survival requires gap junction function. J Neurosci Res 61:605–615.

Bannigan J, Burke P (1982) Ethanol teratogenicity in mice: a light microscopic study. Teratology 26:247–254.

Bannigan J, Cottell D (1984) Ethanol teratogenicity in mice: an electron microscopy study. Teratology 30:281–290.

Basch ML, Garcia-Castro MI, Bronner-Fraser M (2004) Molecular mechanisms of neural crest induction. Birth Defects Res Part C 72:109–123.

Blader P, Strahle U (1998) Ethanol impairs migration of the prechordal plate in the zebrafish embryo. Dev Biol 201:185–201.

Bradley DM, Paiva M, Tonjes LA, Heaton MB (1995) In vitro comparison of the effects of ethanol and acetaldehyde on dorsal root ganglion neurons. Alcohol Clin Exp Res 19:1345–1350.

Bruyere HJ, Stith CE (1993) Strain-dependent effect of ethanol on ventricular septal defect frequency in white leghorn chick embryos. Teratology 48:299–303.

Bruyere HJ, Stith CE (1994a) Ethyl alcohol reduces cardiac output, stroke volume, and end diastolic volume in the embryonic chick. Teratology 49:104–112.

Bruyere HJ, Stith CE, Thorn TA (1994b) Cardioteratogenic dose of ethanol reduces both lactic dehydrogenase and succinic dehydrogenase activity in the bulbar ridges of the embryonic chick heart. J Appl Toxicol 14:27–31.

Carey MB, Matsumoto SG (1999) Spontaneous calcium transients are required for neuronal differentiation of murine neural crest. Dev Biol 215:298–313.

Carey MB, Matsumoto SG (2000) Calcium transient activity in cultured murine neural crest cells is regulated at the IP(3) receptor. Brain Res 862:201–210.

Carones F, Brancato R, Venturi E, Bianchi S, Magni R (1992) Corneal endothelial anomalies in the fetal alcohol syndrome. Arch Ophthalmol 110:1128–1131.

Cartwright MM, Smith SM (1995a) Increased cell death and reduced neural crest cell numbers in ethanol-exposed embryos: partial basis for the fetal alcohol syndrome phenotype. Alcohol Clin Exp Res 19:378–386.

Cartwright MM, Smith SM (1995b) Stage-dependent effects of ethanol on cranial neural crest cell development: partial basis for the phenotypic variations observed in fetal alcohol syndrome. Alcohol Clin Exp Res 19:1454–1462.

Cartwright MM, Tessmer LL, Smith SM (1998) Ethanol-induced neural crest apoptosis is coincident with their endogenous death, but is mechanistically distinct. Alcohol Clin Exp Res 22:142–149.

Cavieres MF, Smith SM (2000) Genetic and developmental modulation of cardiac deficits in prenatal alcohol exposure. Alcohol Clin Exp Res 24:102–109.

Charness ME, Safran RM, Perides G (1994) Ethanol inhibits neural cell–cell adhesion. J Biol Chem 269:9304–9309.

Chen H, Yang JV, Namkung MJ, Juchau MR (1996a) Interactive dysmorphogenic effects of all-*trans*-retinol and ethanol on cultured whole rat embryos during organogenesis. Teratology 54:12–19.

Chen SY, Periasamy A, Yang B, Herman B, Jacobson K, Sulik KK (2000) Differential sensitivity of mouse neural crest cells to ethanol-induced toxicity. Alcohol 20:75–81.

Chen SY, Sulik KK (1996) Free radicals and ethanol-induced cytotoxicity in neural crest cells. Alcohol Clin Exp Res 20:1071–1076.

—— (2000) Iron-mediated free radical injury in ethanol-exposed mouse neural crest cells. J Pharmacol Exp Ther 294:134–140.

Chen SY, Wilkemeyér MF, Sulik KK, Charness ME (2001) Octanol antagonism of ethanol teratogenesis. FASEB J 15:1649–1651.

Chen SY, Yang B, Jacobson K, Sulik KK (1996b) The membrane disordering effect of ethanol on neural crest cells in vitro and the protective role of GM1 ganglioside. Alcohol 13:589–595.

Chou CF, Lai CL, Chang YC, Duester G, Yin SJ (2002) Kinetic mechanism of human class IV alcohol dehydrogenase functioning as retinol dehydrogenase. J Biol Chem 277:25209–25516.

Church MW, Abel EL, Kaltenbach JA, Overbeck GW (1996) Effects of prenatal alcohol exposure and aging on auditory function in the rat: preliminary results. Alcohol Clin Exp Res 20:172–179.

Church MW, Eldis F, Blakley BW, Bawle EV (1997) Hearing, language, speech, vestibular, and dentofacial disorders in fetal alcohol syndrome. Alcohol Clin Exp Res 21:227–237.

Clarren SK, Smith DW (1978) The fetal alcohol syndrome. N Engl J Med 298:1063–1067.

Daft PA, MC Johnston, KK Sulik (1986) Abnormal heart and great vessel development following acute ethanol exposure in mice. Teratology 33:93–104.

Das UG, Cronk CE, Martier SS, Simpson PM, McCarver DG (2004) Alcohol dehydrogenase 2*3 affects alterations in offspring facial morphological associated with maternal ethanol intake in pregnancy. Alcohol Clin Exp Res 28:1598–1606.

Davis WL, Crawford LA, Cooper OJ, Farmer GR, Thomas DL, Freeman PB (1990) Ethanol induces the generation of reactive free radicals by neural crest in vitro. J Craniofac Genet Dev Biol 10:277–293.

Debelak KA, SM Smith (2000) Avian genetic background modulates the neural crest apoptosis induced by ethanol exposure. Alcohol Clin Exp Res 24:307–314.

Debelak-Kragtorp KA, Armant DR, Smith SM (2003) Ethanol-induced cephalic apoptosis requires phopholipase C–dependent intracellular calcium signaling. Alcohol Clin Exp Res 27:515–523.

Deltour L, Ang HL, Duester G (1996) Ethanol inhibition of retinoic acid synthesis as a potential mechanism for fetal alcohol syndrome. FASEB J 10:1050–1057.

Deltour L, Foglio MH, Duester G (1999) Metabolic deficiencies in alcohol dehydrogenase Adh1, Adh3, and Adh4 null mutant mice. J Biol Chem 274:16796–16801.

Dickman ED, Thaller C, Smith SM (1997) Temporally regulated retinoic acid depletion produces specific neural crest, ocular, and nervous system defects. Development 124:3111–3121.

Dow KE, Riopelle RJ (1990) Specific effects of ethanol on neurite-promoting proteoglycans of neuronal origin. Brain Res 508:40–45.

Duester G (1991) A hypothetical mechanism for fetal alcohol syndrome involving ethanol inhibition of retinoic acid synthesis at the alcohol dehydrogenase step. Alcohol Clin Exp Res 15:568–572.

Dunty WC, Chen SY, Zucker RM, Dehart DB, Sulik KK (2001) Selective vulnerability of embryonic cell populations to ethanol-induced apoptosis: implications for alcohol-related birth defects and neurodevelopmental disorder. Alcohol Clin Exp Res 25:1523–1535.

Edwards HG, Dow-Edwards DL (1991) Craniofacial alterations in adult rats prenatally exposed to ethanol. Teratology 44:373–378.

Fang T-T, Bruyere HJ, Kargas SA, Nishikawa T, Takagi Y, Gilbert EF (1987) Ethyl alcohol–induced cardiovascular malformations in the chick embryo. Teratology 35:95–103.

Firulli AB, Conway SJ (2004) Combinatorial transcriptional interaction within the cardiac neural crest: a pair of HANDs in heart formation. Birth Defects Res Part C 72:151–161.

Fransen E, Lemmon V, Vancamp G, Vits L, Coucke P, Willems PJ (1995) CRASH syndrome—clinical spectrum of corpus callosum hypoplasia, retardation, adducted thumbs, spastic paraparesis and hydrocephalus due to mutations in one signal gene, L1. Eur J Hum Genet 3:273–284.

Frias JL, Wilson AL, King GF (1982) A cephalometric study of fetal alcohol syndrome. J Pediatr 191:870–873.

Garic-Stankovic A, Hernandez MR, Chiang PJ, Debelak-Kragtorp KA, Flentke GR, Armant DR, Smith SM (2005) Ethanol triggers neural crest apoptosis through the selective activation of a pertussis toxin-sensitive G protein and a phospholipase Cβ-dependent Ca^{2+} transient. Alcohol Clin Exp Res 29:1237–1246.

Garic-Stankovic A, Hernandez MR, Flentke GR, Smith SM (2006) Structural constraints for alcohol-stimulated Ca^{2+} release in neural crest, and dual agonist/antagonist properties on n-octanol. Alcohol Clin Exp Res in press.

Graham A, Francis-West P, Brickell P, Lumsden A (1994) The signaling molecule BMP4 mediates apoptosis in the rhombencephalic neural crest. Nature 372:684–686.

Grummer MA, Langhough RE, Zachman RD (1993) Maternal ethanol ingestion effects in fetal rat brain vitamin A as a model for fetal alcohol syndrome. Alcohol Clin Exp Res 17:592–597.

Haselbeck RJ, Duester G (1998) ADH4-lacZ transgenic mouse reveals alcohol dehydrogenase localization in embryonic midbrain/hindbrain, otic vesicles, and mesencephalic, trigeminal, facial and olfactory neural crest. Alcohol Clin Exp Res 22:1607–1613.

Hassler JA, Moran DJ (1986) Effects of ethanol on the cytoskeleton of migrating and differentiating neural crest cells: possible role in teratogenesis. J Craniofac Genet Dev Biol 2(Suppl):129–136.

Heaton MB, Swanson DJ, Paiva M, Walker DW (1992) Ethanol exposure affects trophic factor activity and responsiveness in chick embryo. Alcohol 9:161–166.

Johnson VP, Swayze VW, Sato Y, Andreasen NC (1996) Fetal alcohol syndrome: craniofacial and central nervous system manifestations. Am J Med Genet 61:329–339.

Jones KL, Smith DW, Ulleland CN, Streissguth AP (1973) Pattern of malformation in offspring of chronic alcoholic mothers. Lancet 1:1267–1271.

Kirby ML (1999) Contribution of neural crest to heart and vessel morphology. In: Harvey RP, Rosenthal N (eds). Heart Development. Academic Press, London, pp 179–193.

Kotch LE, Chen SY, Sulik KK (1995) Ethanol-induced teratogenesis: free radical damage as a possible mechanism. Teratology 52:128–136.

Kotch LE, Sulik KK (1992a) Experimental fetal alcohol syndrome: proposed pathogenic basis for a variety of associated facial and brain anomalies. Am J Med Genet 44:168–176.

Kotch LE, Sulik KK (1992b) Patterns of ethanol-induced cell death in the developing nervous system of mice: neural fold states through the time of anterior neural tube closure. Int J Dev Neurosci 10:273–279.

Langston AW, Gudas LJ (1994) Retinoic acid and homeobox gene regulation. Curr Opin Gen Dev 4:550–555.

Le Douarin NM, Kalcheim C (1999) The Neural Crest, 2nd Edition. Cambridge University Press, Cambridge, UK.

Lemoine P, Harrousseau H, Borteyru JP, Menuet JC (1968) Les enfants de parents alcooliques: anomalies observees a proposos de 127 cas. Ouest Med 21:476–482.

Luo J, West JR, Cook RT, Pantazis NJ (1999) Ethanol induces cell death and cell cycle delay in cultures of pheochromocytoma PC12 cells. Alcohol Clin Exp Res 23:644–656.

Maden M, Gale E, Kostetski I, Zile M (1996) Vitamin A deficient quail embryos have half a hindbrain and other neural defects. Curr Biol 6:417–426.

Mattson SN, Riley EP, Gramling L, Delis DC, Jones KL (1997) Heavy prenatal alcohol exposure with or without physical features of fetal alcohol syndrome leads to IQ deficits. J Pediatr 131:718–721.

McCarver DG, Thomasson HR, Martier SS, Sokol RJ, Li TK (1997) Alcohol dehydrogenase-2*3 allele protects against alcohol-related birth defects among African Americans. J Pharmacol Exp Ther 283:1095–1101.

Messing RO, Carpenter CL, Diamond I, Greenberg DA (1986) Ethanol regulates calcium channels in clonal neural cells. Proc Natl Acad Sci USA 83:6213–6215.

Mihic SJ, Ye Q, Wick MJ, Koltchine VV, Krasowski MD, Finn SE, Mascia MP, Valenzuela CF, Hanson KK, Grennblatt EP, Harris RA, Harrison NL (1997) Sites of alcohol and volatile anaesthetic action on GABAa and glycine receptors. Nature 389:385–389.

Miller MT, Beauchamp GR (1988) The role of neural crest cells in fetal alcohol syndrome children with anterior segment anomalies of the eye. Am J Med Genet 4–5(Suppl):180–181.

Miller MW, Roskams AJI, Connor JR (1995) Iron regulation in the developing rat brain: effect of in utero ethanol exposure. J Neurochem 65:373–380.

Molotkov A, Duester G (2002) Retinol/ethanol drug interaction during acute alcohol intoxication in mice involves inhibition of retinol metabolism to retinoic acid by alcohol dehydrogenase. J Biol Chem 277:22553–22557.

Moore ES, Ward RE, Jamison PL, Morris CA, Bader PI, Hall BD (2001) The subtle facial signs of prenatal exposure to alcohol: an anthropometric approach. J Pediatr 139:215–219.

Moore ES, Ward RE, Jamison PL, Morris CA, Bader PI, Hall BD (2002) New perspectives on the face in fetal alcohol syndrome: what anthropometry tells us. Am J Med Genet 109:249–260.

Nyquist-Battie C, Freter M (1988) Cardiac mitochondrial abnormalities in a mouse model of the fetal alcohol syndrome. Alcohol Clin Exp Res 12:264–267.

Plant MR, MacDonald ME, Grad LI, Ritchie SJ, Richman JM (2000) Locally released retinoic acid repatterns the first branchial arch cartilages in vivo. Dev Biol 222:12–26.

Ramanathan R, Wilkemeyer MF, Mittal B, Perides G, Charness ME (1996) Ethanol inhibits cell–cell adhesion mediated by human L1. J Cell Biol 133:381–390.

Rasheed A, Hines RN, McCarver DG (1997) Variation in induction of human placental CYP2E1: possible role in susceptibility to fetal alcohol syndrome? Toxicol Appl Pharmacol 144:396–400.

Reed JC (2000) Mechanisms of apoptosis. Am J Pathol 157:1415–1430.

Rifas L, Towler DA, Avioli LV (1997) Gestational exposure to ethanol suppresses msx2 expression in developing embryos. Proc Natl Acad Sci USA 94:7549–7554.

Roebuck TM, Simmons RW, Richardson C, Mattson SN, Riley EP (1998) Neuromuscular responses to disturbance of balance in children with prenatal exposure to alcohol. Alcohol Clin Exp Res 22: 1992–1997.

Rout UK, Krawetz SA, Armant DR (1997) Ethanol-induced intracellular calcium mobilization rapidly alters gene expression in the mouse blastocyst. Cell Calcium 22:463–474.

Rovasio RA, Battiato NL (1995) Role of early migratory neural crest cells in developmental anomalies induced by ethanol. Int J Dev Biol 39:421–422.

—— (2002) Ethanol induces morphological and dynamic changes on in vivo and in vitro neural crest cells. Alcohol Clin Exp Res 26:1286–1298.

Ruckman RN, Messersmith DJ, O'Brien SA, Getson PR, Boeckx RL, Morse DE (1988) Chronic ethanol exposure in the embryonic chick heart: effect on myocardial function and structure. Teratology 37:317–327.

Sanders EJ, Cheung E (1990) Ethanol treatment induces a delayed segmentation anomaly in the chick embryo. Teratology 41:289–297.

Sanders EJ, Cheung E, Mahmud E (1987) Ethanol treatment inhibits mesoderm cell spreading in the gastrulating chick embryo. Teratology 36:209–216.

Sandor S (1968) The influence of aethyl alcohol on the developing chick embryo. II. Rev Roum d'Embr et de Cyt Série d'Embr 5:167–171.

Schneider RA, Hu D, Rubenstein JL, Maden M, Helms JA (2001) Local retinoid signaling coordinates forebrain and facial morphogenesis by maintaining FGF8 and SHH. Development 128:2755–2767.

Smith SM, Su B, Tessmer LA, Debelak KA, Flentke GR, Hahn SH (2001) Prenatal alcohol exposure redirects sonic hedgehog signaling during craniofacial morphogenesis. Alcohol Clin Exp Res 25:35A.

Spong CY, Abebe DT, Gozes I, Brenneman DE, Hill JM (2001) Prevention of fetal demise and growth restriction in a mouse model of fetal alcohol syndrome. J Pharmacol Exp Ther 297:774–779.

Stachecki JJ, Yelian FD, Schultz JF, Leach RE, Armant DR (1994) Blastocyst cavitation is accelerated by ethanol- or ionophore-induced elevation of intracellular calcium. Biol Reprod 50:1–9.

Su B, Debelak KA, Tessmer LL, Cartwright MM, Smith SM (2001) Genetic influences on craniofacial outcome in an avian model of prenatal alcohol exposure. Alcohol Clin Exp Res 25:60–69.

Sulik KK, Cook CS, Webster WS (1988) Teratogens and craniofacial malformations: relationships to cell death. Development 103(Suppl):213–232.

Sulik KK, Johnston MC, Daft PA, Russell WE, Dehart DB (1986) Fetal alcohol syndrome and DiGeorge anomaly: critical ethanol exposure periods for craniofacial malformations as illustrated in an animal model. Am J Med Genet 2(Suppl):97–112.

Sulik KK, Johnston MC, Webb MA (1981) Fetal alcohol syndrome: embryogenesis in a mouse model. Science 214:936–938.

Trainor PA, Ariza-McNaughton L, Krumlauf R (2002) Role of the isthmus and FGFs in resolving the paradox of neural crest plasticity and prepatterning. Science 295:1288–1291.

Twal WO, Zile MH (1997) Retinoic acid reverses ethanol-induced cardiovascular abnormalities in quail embryos. Alcohol Clin Exp Res 21:1137–1143.

Webster WS, Walsh DA, McEwen SE, Lipson AH (1983) Some teratogenic properties of ethanol and acetaldehyde in C57Bl/6J mice: implications for the study of the fetal alcohol syndrome. Teratology 27:231–243.

Wedden SE (1987) Epithelial–mesenchymal interactions in the development of chick facial primordia and the target of retinoid action. Development 99:341–351.

Wilkemeyer MF, Charness ME (1998) Characterization of alcohol-sensitive and insensitive fibroblast cell lines expressing human L1. J Neurochem 71: 2382–2391.

Wilkemeyer MF, Chen SY, Menkari CE, Brenneman DE, Sulik KK, Charness ME (2003) Differential effects of ethanol antagonism and neuroprotection in peptide fragment NAPVSIPQ prevention of ethanol-induced developmental toxicity. Proc Natl Acad Sci USA 100:8543–8548.

Wilkemeyer MF, Menkari C, Spong CY, Charness ME (2002) Peptide antagonists of ethanol inhibition of L1-mediated cell–cell adhesion. J Pharmacol Exp Ther 303:110–116.

Wilkemeyer MF, Sebastian AB, Smith SA, Charness ME (2000) Antagonists of alcohol inhibition of cell adhesion. Proc Natl Acad Sci USA 97:3690–3695.

Yao L, Arolfo MP, Dohrman DP, Jiang Z, Fan P, Fuchs S, Janak PH, Gordon AS, Diamond I (2002) βγ-Dimers mediate synergy of dopamine D2 and adenosine A2 receptor-stimulated PKA signaling and regulate ethanol consumption. Cell 109:733–743.

Yao L, Fan P, Jiang Z, Mailliard WS, Gordon AS, Diamond I (2003) Addicting drugs utilize a synergistic molecular mechanism in common requiring adenosine and Gi-βγ dimers. Proc Natl Acad Sci USA 100:14379–14384.

Zachman RD, Grummer MA (1998) The interaction of ethanol and vitamin A as a potential mechanism for the pathogenesis of fetal alcohol syndrome. Alcohol Clin Exp Res 22:1544–1556.

Zile MH (2001) Function of vitamin A in vertebrate embryonic development. J Nutr 131:705–708.

18

Glial Targets of Developmental Exposure to Ethanol

Consuelo Guerri

Gemma Rubert

Maria Pascual

The word *glia* is derived from the Greek word *gliok*, meaning glue, which Virchow (Letterer, 1958) applied in the sense of nerve glue. The traditional point of view of glia as a passive component of the central nervous system (CNS) has changed drastically during the past decade. Glia are now recognized as active partners with neurons as participants in neurotransmission and they play essential roles in axonal conduction, synaptic plasticity, and information processing (Nagler et al., 2001; Ullian et al., 2001, 2004; Fields-Graham, 2002). Further, glia can respond to insults and are capable of proliferating throughout life (Chen and Swanson, 2003).

In the adult human brain, glia outnumber neurons by one order of magnitude. There are two classes of glia: microglia (which mediate inflammatory responses in the CNS) and macroglia. The latter cells are oligodendrocytes (which form the insulating myelin sheaths) and astrocytes, the most paradigmatic glia (which are abundant and ubiquitous within the CNS). The present chapter focuses on astrocytes.

ROLE OF GLIA IN THE DEVELOPING CENTRAL NERVOUS SYSTEM

Glia are present and integral throughout CNS development. Glial–neuronal interactions play critical roles in multiple developmental events. For example, radial glia (RG) provide physical and chemical guidance for the migration of young neurons from the embryonic proliferative zones into the developing cortex (Rakic, 1972; Hatten and Mason, 1990) (see Chapter 3). When the migration is completed, most RG transform into astrocytes. RG also serve as a multipotential precursor cell, as they are able to self-renew and generate neurons (Malatesta et al., 2000; Noctor et al., 2001, 2002; Götz et al., 2002; Sanai et al., 2004).

Astroglia and glial-derived factors are key to synaptogenesis, since they promote the formation of mature functional synapses (Nagler et al., 2001; Ullian et al., 2001, 2004). Disturbances of glia or of neuronal–glial communication during the well-established critical periods of brain development can cause irreversible deficits in CNS function (Hatten, 1999; Lammens, 2000; Ross and Walsh, 2001; Crespel et al., 2002). Such findings strongly support the crucial role of glia in development and the notion that their dysfunction underlies anomalies in brain development.

An increasing number of studies shows (a) that a prime target of ethanol within the developing brain is astrocytes (Guerri and Renau-Piqueras, 1997; Guerri et al., 2001) and (b) that ethanol impairs astrogliogenesis. The present chapter reviews clinical, experimental, and *in vitro* evidence about the actions of ethanol on astroglia and their functions. Special attention is paid to the effects that prenatal ethanol exposure has on neural stem cells (e.g., RG) and to the actions of ethanol on astroglial proliferation and cell survival. Since astroglia regulate synaptogenesis and synaptic transmission, the potential effects of ethanol on these processes are also discussed.

GLIAL ABNORMALITIES CAUSED BY ETHANOL

Since the first neuropathological studies on children with fetal alcohol syndrome (FAS) (Clarren et al., 1978), abnormalities in glial development have been suspected as contributing to the adverse effects of ethanol on the developing brain. Ethanol-exposed brains exhibit abnormal glial placement primarily associated with the meninges (meningeal neuroglial heterotopias) (Clarren et al., 1978; Peiffer et al., 1979; Clarren, 1986), gyral malformations, cerebral dysgenesis, and, in some cases, reactive gliosis (Peiffer et al., 1979; Wisniewski et al., 1983). White matter, a repository of glia, appears to be affected by prenatal ethanol exposure (PEE). Several studies using magnetic resonance imaging and single photon emission computed tomography have shown that children with FAS have hypoplasia of the corpus callosum and anterior commissure (the anlage of which are formed by glia) (Riley et al., 1995; Johnson et al., 1996; Swayze et al., 1997). PEE can lead to a reduction in white matter and delayed myelination (Riikonen et al., 1999; Sowell et al., 2001b).

Animals exposed to ethanol during brain development exhibit alterations in glia-related development, including aberrant neuronal migration, delayed astrogliogenesis, and a reduction of cortical astrocytes (Miller, 1986, 1988; Miller and Potempa, 1990;

Gressens et al., 1992; Miller and Robertson, 1993; Vallés et al., 1996). Moreover, studies of a primate model of FAS implicate glial involvement. Ethanol-exposed monkeys have glial heterotopias (Clarren and Bowden, 1984) and dysgenic corpora callosa (Miller et al., 1999). These alterations are consistent with the concept that one of the developmental stages most vulnerable to ethanol is the brain-growth spurt (Bonthius and West, 1991). This period is characterized by major development of glia and myelin structures.

ETHANOL AFFECTS ASTROGLIAL ONTOGENY

Radial Glia

Normal Ontogeny of Radial Glia

Among the first cells to differentiate from the neuroepithelium are RG (Misson et al., 1991), which appear before the onset of neuronogenesis (Caviness et al., 1995). RG have a bipolar morphology: each RG has a soma in the ventricular or subventricular zone and bears a long apical process that extends toward the pial surface and a shorter basal process that contacts the ventricular wall. The term *radial glia* was introduced by Rakic (1972) in his classic description of neural migration in the fetal primate neocortex.

Most RG transform into mature, stellate-appearing astrocytes after the neuronal migration is completed (Schmechel and Rakic, 1979; Pixley and DeVellis, 1984; Voigt, 1989; Cameron and Rakic, 1991; Misson et al., 1991; Miller and Robertson, 1993). Changes in the morphology of RG are linked to changes in the expression of specific proteins. Vimentin and nestin (including its immunorecognized antigenic determinants RC1 and RC2) are prenatally present in RG of rodent CNS, whereas glial fibrillary acidic protein (GFAP) appears in neonates (e.g., Hockfield and McKay, 1985; Miller and Robertson, 1993; Sancho-Tello et al., 1995; Chanas-Sacre et al., 2000).

Effects of Ethanol on Radial Glia Development

Cerebral Cortex. Ethanol exposure during embryogenesis induces irreversible alterations in the CNS (Guerri, 1998, 2002). The first suggestion that ethanol impairs migration originates from neuropathological examination at autopsy of brains from children with FAS (Clarren et al., 1978; Wisniewski et al., 1983). Most notable among the findings were neuroglial heterotopias located near the pial surface of the cerebral cortex. Alterations observed in humans have been reproduced in studies of animals exposed to ethanol in utero. Prenatal exposure to moderate amounts of ethanol (100–200 mg/dl) causes leptomeningeal heterotopias with breaches in the glia limitans and reduces the number and alters the morphology of RG (Kotkoskie and Norton, 1988; Gressens et al., 1992; Komatsu et al., 2001; Mooney et al., 2004). At least in the rat, heterotopias persist into adulthood (Komatsu et al., 2001).

Cultured RG harvested from 12-day-old fetuses are affected by pre- and postconception exposure to ethanol (Vallés et al., 1996). These RG exhibit short glial processes, reduced numbers of cells, and delays in their transformation into GFAP-positive astrocytes (Vallés et al., 1996) (Figs. 18–1 and 18–2). A developmental delay in GFAP expression has also been described in rat whole brains in vivo. During normal rat brain development, GFAP mRNA appears on gestational day (G) 14, then both GFAP transcript and protein expression increase during late fetal and early postnatal development. Prenatal ethanol exposure delays the appearance of GFAP mRNA until G19 and decreases GFAP expression (Vallés et al., 1996, 1997). A comparable delay is evident among astrocytes proximal to the dorsal and medial raphe (Tajuddin et al., 2003).

An in vivo study focusing on the RG and astrocytes in the cortical plate–derived laminae of cortex, i.e., layers II–VIa, shows that GFAP expression is ubiquitously delayed (Miller and Robertson, 1993). In control rats, nestin-positive RG are present through the period of neuronal generation (past postnatal day [P] 8). GFAP-positive astrocytes, though common in the intermediate zone (the anlage of the white matter), only appear in deep layer VIa on P3. With time, they progressively appear in more superficial positions. In contrast, in ethanol-treated rats RG begin to regress by P5 and GFAP immunoreactivity appears in cortical gray matter on P1. From the effects of ethanol on the paired changes in nestin and GFAP expression, the compelling conclusion is that ethanol causes the premature transformation of RG into astrocytes in cortex—this underlies the migration of late-generated neurons to ectopic sites (Miller, 1986, 1988, 1997). The different timing of GFAP expression in whole

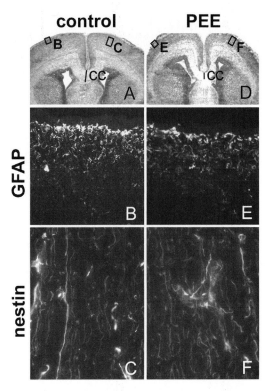

FIGURE 18–1 Effect of ethanol on nestin and glial fibrillary acidic protein (GFAP) expression. Coronal sections of 21-day-old control (**A**) and prenatal ethanol-exposed (PEE) (**D**) fetuses, stained with hematoxilin-eosin. **B, C, E, F.** Higher magnification of boxed regions to show nestin-positive glia (RG) and GFAP-positive astrocytes. Brain sections from PEE fetuses show a reduction in the corpus callosum (CC), alternations in the morphology of RG fibers, and reduction in the generation of astrocytes.

brain vs. cortex and the effect of ethanol on that timing (cf. Miller and Robertson, 1993; Vallés et al., 1996) likely reflect the effect of ethanol on astrocytes in the intermediate zone, the primary (sole) site of GFAP expression in the fetus.

Cerebellar Cortex. The cerebellum is another brain region that is sensitive to ethanol toxicity during development (Guerri, 1998). The cell bodies of Bergmann glia, the cerebellar subpopulation of RG (Sievers et al., 1994; Yuasa, 1996), initially assume a position periventricular to the Purkinje cell layer. Postnatally, their cell bodies translocate peripherally so that they can guide the inward migration of granule neurons.

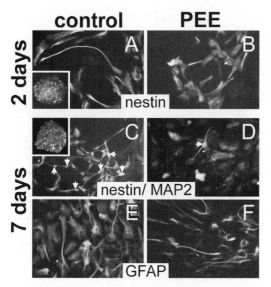

FIGURE 18–2 Radial glia at 2 and 7 days of culture. Radial glia were isolated from the brains of 12-day-old control or prenatal ethanol-exposed (PEE) fetuses. **A, B.** During the initial days of culture, control cells expressed mainly nestin (RG marker) and formed aggregates resembling neurospheres (A) composed of newly born neurons (Tuj1$^+$) and radial glia (nestin$^+$). **C–F.** The neurosphere-like aggregates increased in number and size with culture time (C), and radial glia were transformed into more mature neurons (MAP2$^+$; D, arrowheads) and into GFAP-positive astrocytes (E, F). Cultured radial glial cells isolated from PEE fetuses displayed morphological alterations and impaired neurogenic potential, as demonstrated by the decrease in number of neurons and astrocytes generated. Nuclei were stained with Hoechst (g Rubert, r Miñana, and c Guerri, unpublished results).

Ethanol, given either acutely or chronically during fetal and neonatal development, delays the maturation of Bergmann glia, decreases the number of GFAP-positive fibers, and induces the growth of abnormal glial processes (e.g., shorter, thinner, and irregular) (Shetty et al., 1994; Perez-Torrero et al., 1997). Moreover, gestational exposure to ethanol causes defects in the cerebellar glial limitans (formed by Bergmann glial end feet on the cerebellar surface) of the rat and the appearance of solitary or clustered ectopic granule cells (Sakata-Haga et al., 2001). Damage to the glial limitans may underlie the fusion of the folia V and VI of the cerebellar vermis and the disruption of the cerebellar cortical structure.

Factors Regulating Radial Glial Transformation. Our current understanding of mechanism(s) and factors that regulate the transformation of RG into astrocytes or neurons development is limited. Extrinsic cues such as ciliary neurotrophic factors, epidermal growth factors, neuregulin 1-erbB2 signaling and members of the bone morphogenetic protein family may induce cortical progenitors to differentiate into astrocytes (Hughes et al., 1988; Gross et al., 1996; Johe et al., 1996; Kuhn and Miller, 1996; Burrows et al., 1997; Schmid et al., 2003).

Critical determinants of GFAP expression and astrocyte differentiation in fetal brain are changes in DNA methylation and chromatin structure (Takizawa et al., 2001; Song and Ghosh, 2004). These changes are regulated by hormones and growth factors. The methylation of genomic DNA at CpG dinucleotides regulates cell- or tissue-specific gene expression (Razin,1998; Bird and Wolffe, 1999). During embryogenesis and differentiation, most tissue- and cell-specific genes are almost fully methylated and undergo programmed demethylation at the moment of activation and transcription (Barresi et al., 1999).

Chronic in utero ethanol exposure decreases the demethylation of GFAP gene, affecting both its transcription and expression (Vallés et al., 1997). Ethanol exposure interferes with the release and action of growth factors (Luo and Miller, 1998), which might affect the developmentally regulated epigenetic modifications, leading to the changes in both DNA methylation and GFAP expression.

Cell Adhesion Proteins. Ethanol affects glial elaboration of cell adhesion proteins and growth factors (e.g., transforming growth factor [TGF] β1) mediating neuronal–glial interactions. Among the cell adhesion proteins, neural cell adhesion molecules (nCAM and L1), integrins, and astrotactin mediate neuronal–glial attachments and communication (Edelman,1994; Hatten, 2002, Nadarajah and Parnavelas, 2002; Schmid and Anton, 2003).

Ethanol affects the expression and function of several neural cell adhesion proteins both *in vitro* (Miller and Luo, 2002; Miñana et al., 1998, 2000) and *in situ* (Siegenthaler and Miller, 2004). Ethanol also disrupts (a) L1-dependent cell adhesion and homophilic interactions among L1 molecules (Wilkemeyer et al.,

1999, 2000; Bearer, 2001) and (b) integrin expression in fetal brain organotypic cultures (Siegenthaler and Miller, 2004). Likewise, TGFβ1, which promotes neuronal migration in cortex and increases expression of adhesion proteins, is profoundly affected by ethanol (Miller and Luo, 2002; Siegenthaler and Miller, 2004).

Radial Glia as Neuronal Precursors.   The recently described role of RG as neuronal precursors (Malatesta et al., 2000; Noctor et al., 2001, 2002; Götz et al., 2002) dramatically changes our understanding of CNS development under normal and pathological conditions. Taking into account the contribution of RG as a neuronal progenitor cell, it is plausible to speculate that alteration of RG by ethanol might cause dysgeneration of both astrocytes and neurons. The number of neurons and astrocytes generated from cultured RG isolated from ethanol-exposed fetuses is reduced (Rupert, Miñana and Guerri, unpublished results) (Fig. 18–2). *In vivo* studies have shown that prenatal exposure to ethanol causes a reduction in neuronogenesis and gliogenesis (e.g., Miller, 1986, 1988; Gressens et al., 1992) (see Chapter 13). Although it has been interpreted that this reduction results from ethanol-induced changes in the output from the cortical proliferative zones, a contribution from RG must be considered.

It has been suggested that RG (a) comprise a heterogeneous population, (b) vary in growth factor expression according to their location within the CNS, and (c) differ in the types of cells they generate (Kriegstein and Götz, 2003). In contrast, other investigators argue that RG in all parts of the CNS serve as neuronal progenitors (Anthony et al., 2004). In either case, controlled studies of the potential effect of ethanol on the stem cell role of RG are required to clarify whether ethanol decreases the pool of stem cells or only induces abnormalities in the RG–astrocyte lineage.

Astroglial Proliferation

Effects of Ethanol on Cell Cycle

The most active period of glial proliferation is the brain growth spurt, a time when the brain undergoes its most rapid growth (Dobbing and Sands, 1993). In humans, this period occurs during the final trimester of gestation and early infancy, whereas in the rat it occurs during the first 2 postnatal weeks. During the brain growth spurt, neural development is particularly sensitive to the toxic effects of environmental agents such as methylmercury, lead, and ethanol (Costa et al., 2004). An implication is that glia are a target for this neurotoxicity (Aschner et al., 1999).

Ethanol exposure during gestation can impair the proliferation and differentiation of astroglia. The cortices of rats prenatally exposed to ethanol have one-third fewer glia (and also of neurons) than controls (Miller and Potempa, 1990). Prenatal exposure to ethanol reduces the expression of the astrocyte marker GFAP during postnatal brain development (Vallés et al., 1996; Tajuddin et al., 2003). Cultured astrocytes from the pups of ethanol-fed rats exhibit reduced [³H]thymidine and [³H]leucine incorporation and GFAP-positive cells (Guerri et al., 1990; Guerri and Renau-Piqueras, 1997). These data are consistent with an ethanol-induced decrease in glial proliferation and differentiation.

Direct demonstration that ethanol affects the proliferation of astroglial cells comes from experiments using primary cultures of astrocytes prepared from the brains of neonatal rats. Ethanol (110–880 mg/dl) impairs cell proliferation, inhibits the increase in the astrocyte number, and reduces [³H]thymidine incorporation (Kennedy and Mukerji, 1986; Davies and Cox, 1991; Snyder et al., 1992; Aroor and Baker, 1997; Guizzetti et al., 1997; Luo and Miller, 1998, 1999; Miller and Luo, 2002). Ethanol affects the cycling population in multiple ways: it inhibits the cell cycle in the G0/G1 phase of the cell cycle, impedes the progression of cells into S phase, and decreases the number of mitotic cells (Guerri et al., 1990; Mikami et al., 1997; Luo and Miller, 1999). Impairment of cell proliferation through ethanol exposure has also been shown in glial tumor cells, principally C6 astrocytoma cells (Waziri et al., 1981; Isenberg et al., 1992; Luo and Miller, 1996, 1998; Guizzetti et al., 1997; Miller and Luo, 2002). This effect is concentration-dependent.

Mechanisms of Ethanol Toxicity among Proliferating Astroglial Populations

Astrocytic proliferation is regulated by mitogenic growth factors and growth inhibitory agents (Luo and Miller, 1998) (see Chapter 11). In turn, these proteins trigger signaling pathways involving tyrosine kinases, protein kinase C (PKC), and mitogen-activate protein kinase (MAPK). Ethanol inhibits the proliferative effects of several growth factors, including basic fibroblast growth factor, platelet-derived growth factor (PDGF), and insulin-like growth factor 1 (Resnicoff et al., 1994; Luo and Miller, 1996, 1999). These factors affect both MAPK and PKCs. In addition, ethanol potentiates the antiproliferative activity of TGFβ1 (Miller and Luo, 2002). Neural cells actively stimulated by growth factors are more susceptible to the antiproliferative effects of ethanol, although ethanol does not affect the action of all growth factors equivalently (Luo and Miller, 1998, 1999).

Ethanol potently inhibits mitogenic signals initiated by binding (by carbachol or acetylcholine) to astroglial muscarinic receptors, particularly M_3 subtype (Catlin et al., 2000; Costa and Guizzetti, 2002). Binding of M_3 receptors increases DNA synthesis by glia (Costa et al., 2001). Ethanol (46–460 mg/dl) prevents these mitogenic effects in the human 1321N1 astrocytoma cells, fetal human astrocytes, and rat cortical astrocytes (Guizzetti et al., 1998, 2003; Costa et al., 2001). Ethanol affects at least two pathways triggered by activation of M_3 receptors. First, ethanol targets the activation of phospholipase D (PLD), which hydrolyzes phosphatidylcholine to choline and PA. Thus ethanol decreases phosphatidic acid (PA) concentration. PA stimulates downstream targets such as protein kinases, including PKC, and is a mitogenic signaling cascade in astrocytes (Schatter et al., 2003). When ethanol is present, PLD can catalyze a trans-phosphatidylation reaction generating phosphatidyl ethanol (PEt) rather than PA (Kötter and Klein, 1999). This diversion essentially blocks the signal transduction cascade because PEt does not activate the downstream targets of PA (Schatter et al., 2003). The second pathway affected by ethanol is the inhibition of atypical PKCζ, Subsequently, this down-regulates the activation of both the p70s6 kinase and the nuclear factor κB (Costa and Guizzetti, 2002).

A prime metabolite of ethanol, acetaldehyde, can inhibit cell growth (Holownia et al., 1996). Astrocytes exposed to ethanol can produce acetaldehyde (Eysseric et al., 1997). Ethanol can be metabolized into acetaldehyde via alcohol dehydrogenase (ADH), catalase, and cytochrome P450 2E1 (CYP2E1). The effects of ethanol may not be transduced through ADH, as ethanol-induced cell growth inhibition is observed in glia treated with the ADH inhibitor 4-methylpyrazole (Isenberg et al., 1992). On the other hand, catalase and CYP2E1 are present in astrocytes (Montoliu et al., 1995; Eysseric et al., 2000). These enzymes may be key players in the toxic effects of ethanol on the developing CNS.

Astrocytic Death

Cell death is a normal feature of CNS development (e.g., Oppenheim, 1991; Raff et al., 1993). It is regulated by growth factors, cytokines, neurotransmitters, and cell–cell signaling, including glial–neuronal interactions (Johnson and Deckwerth, 1993; Raff et al., 1993). Although mainly ascribed to neurons, death among developing astrocytes is also common (Soriano et al., 1993).

Developmental ethanol exposure affects most normal regulatory factors, exacerbating the processes associated with naturally occurring neural death in the rat developing cortex (Mooney and Miller, 2001; Climent et al., 2002; see Chapters 15 and 16). This ethanol exposure increases the number of neurons and astroglial cells that die by necrosis and by apoptosis (Climent et al., 2002). Ethanol can also induce necrotic (Holownia et al., 1997) or apoptotic (Pascual et al., 2003) death in cultured astrocytes. These effects are concentration-dependent.

Astrocytes die as a result of ethanol-induced activation of sphingomyelinase (SMase) (Pascual et al., 2003), leading to the hydrolysis of sphingomyelin to ceramide (Ohanian and Ohanian, 2001). Treatment with low or moderate ethanol concentrations (46–230 mg/dl) either in vitro or *in vivo* increases astrocyte susceptibility to cell death via tumor necrosis factor (TNF)-α (De Vito et al., 2000). Conceivably, ethanol shifts the balance of the sphingolipid metabolism by decreasing the mitogenic signals in favor of a pathway (SMase/ceramide) that increases astrocyte susceptibility to the cytotoxic effect of TNFα.

Sphingomyelins are cell membrane phospholipids that contains ceramide and phosphorylcholine. Ceramide is an important regulator of cell proliferation, differentiation, and apoptosis. It has trophic effects at low concentrations and triggers apoptosis at high concentrations (Hannum and Luberto, 2000). Increased ceramide production participates in the cell death occurring during early neural differentiation (Herget et al., 2000) and in neuronal apoptosis induced by nutrient deprivation (Toman et al., 2002).

A variety of stimuli and stressors (e.g., oxidants and cytokines) stimulate SMase (Andriu-Abadie and

Levade, 2002), leading to ceramide generation. Ethanol induces a stress response (e.g., oxidative stress) by astrocytes (Montoliu et al., 1995). Stimulation of SMase activity and ceramide generation appears to be a key event in the subsequent ethanol-induced cell death (Pascual et al., 2003). Further investigation is required to evaluate the quantitative participation of this mechanism in ethanol-induced astroglial cell death during *in vivo* brain development (Climent et al., 2002) and to clarify if other mechanisms are involved.

GLIA AND NEURONAL SYNAPSIS

Pivotal Role of Glia in Synaptogenesis

It has been suggested that glia play a role in synapse formation because astrocytes and synaptic terminals are intimately related (Ventura and Harris, 1999; Schikorski and Stevens, 1999; Grosche et al., 2002) and glial development and synaptogenesis are spatiotemporally related (Aghajanian and Bloom, 1967; Miller and Peters, 1981; Parnavelas et al., 1983). For example, in rat cortex, neurons form most of their synapses during the third postnatal week after the differentiation of astrocytes is largely complete. Furthermore, cultured retinal ganglion cells, hippocampal neurons, and spinal motor neurons form several-fold more functional synapses when astrocytes are present (Ullian et al., 2001, 2004; Song et al., 2002). Thus, astrocytes appear to promote synapse formation. Indeed, astrocytes are considered active partners that participate with the pre- and postsynaptic terminals in tripartite synaptic structures (Araque et al., 1999, 2001; Haydon, 2001).

Various glial-derived factors mediate synaptogenesis. One such factor is cholesterol, which is produced by astrocytes and secreted in apolipoprotein E–containing lipoproteins (Mauch et al., 2001). Another glial factor, activity-dependent neurotrophic factor (ADNF), is released by astrocytes in response to vasoactive intestinal polypeptide. ADNF may play a role in synaptic development and neuronal differentiation (Blondel et al., 2000) and is also a neuroprotector (Gozes and Brenneman, 2000).

Not only are glia important for synapse formation, they are also key players in synaptic function. They enhance postsynaptic responsiveness and help to maintain efficient synaptic connectivity. In the presence of glia, retinal ganglion cells have larger glutamate-induced miniature postsynaptic currents (Ullian et al., 2001, 2004). Experiments conducted on both cultured and intact-tissue preparations have demonstrated that transmitters released from neurons can stimulate and cause the glia to release glutamate, ATP, and other neuroactive substances (Bezzi and Volterra, 2001; Fields and Stevens-Graham, 2002). These neuroactive substances can feed back onto the presynaptic terminals, enhancing or depressing further release of neurotransmitters. Moreover, astrocytes can respond to electrical neuronal activity, elevating their intracellular Ca^{2+} concentration and hence triggering glutamate release (Araque et al., 1998; Innocenti et al., 2000; Pascual et al., 2001; Pasti et al., 2001) through a Ca^{2+}-dependent exocytotic process (Araque et al., 2001; Bezzi et al., 2004). Confirmation that this release occurs through such a process is provided by the abolition of glutamate release by tetanus toxin (e.g., Pascual et al., 2001). Glutamate release from nerve terminals and astrocytes can be triggered by potassium chloride (KCl) and brain-derived neurotrophic factor (BDNF) (Fig. 18–3).

Glia can indirectly modulate synaptic transmission by regulating the ionic extracellular environment, clearing neurotransmitters from the synaptic cleft (Bergles and Jahr, 1998; Anderson and Swanson, 2000), and responding to the metabolic demands of synaptic transmission (Shulman et al., 2001). Glia can also affect glutamatergic neurotransmission by releasing co-factors. Glia (astrocytes in the brain and Müller cells in the retina) are the only source of D-serine in the CNS. D-serine, rather than glycine, appears to be the endogenous agonist that activates the glycine-binding site at the N-methyl-D-aspartate (NMDA) receptors (Wolosker et al., 1999; Steven et al., 2003).

Effects of Ethanol

Ethanol exposure during brain ontogeny alters brain synaptology, decreases synaptic formation, and impairs development and maturation of synapses in both the hippocampal formation and neocortex (Guerri, 1987; Al-Rabiai and Miller, 1989; Tanaka et al., 1991; Kuge et al., 1993; Sutherland et al., 1997). Although specific studies have not yet broached the role of glia in these ethanol-induced synaptogenesis, various data compel us to consider glial-mediated synaptic formation as a target of ethanol.

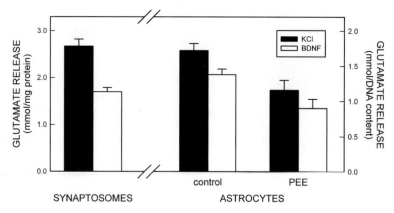

FIGURE 18–3 Induced glutamate release from synaptosomes and cortical astrocytes. A spectrofluorimetric assay was used to determine the Ca^{2+}-dependent release of glutamate evoked by potassium chloride (KCl; 30 mM) or brain-derived neurotrophic factor (BDNF; 100 ng/ml) from nerve terminals and from control or prenatal ethanol-exposed (PEE) astrocytes (4-day-old cultures). Data are means ± standard deviations ($n = 3$). An asterisk signifies a significant ($p < 0.01$) difference between PEE and control astrocytes treated with KCl or BDNF.

Astrocytes from prenatally ethanol-exposed fetuses release less glutamate after being stimulated with KCl (Fig. 18–3). This finding indicates that PEE compromises the KCl-stimulated elevation of intracellular Ca^{2+}. Thus prenatal ethanol exposure likely affects the glial response to neuronal activity and causes abnormalities in both synaptic function and synaptic stabilization. Several studies have shown that fetal and/or neonatal ethanol exposure not only alters ligand binding to the NMDA receptors but also affects NMDA receptor function (Savage et al., 1991; Vallés et al., 1995; Spuhler-Phillips et al., 1997; Gruol et al., 1998). The compelling inference is that ethanol-induced alterations in glia affect D-serine release, thereby altering the function of the NMDA receptors during brain development.

GLIAL DEVELOPMENT IN THE
CORPUS CALLOSUM

The *corpus callosum* (CC) is a large fiber tract formed fetally that interconnects neurons in the right and left cerebral hemispheres. In humans, the CC appears during the sixth prenatal week and grows in a rostral-to-caudal direction. Midline glial populations as well as axonal guidance molecules play critical roles in CC development (Richards, 2002). Agenesis, dysgenesis, and changes in the shape of the CC are observed in 7% of children prenatally exposed to alcohol (Riley et al., 1995; Bookstein et al., 2001, 2002; Sowell et al., 2001a) which is more than 20-fold that for the general population. Since the midline glia are involved in the development of the CC, ethanol targeting of these cells may initiate CC dysmorphology.

Glia positioned at the midline produce a number of different molecules that regulate axonal pathfinding at the midline and determine which axons project ipsilaterally and which project contralaterally (Fig. 18–4). These glia are hypothesized to participate in the adhesion and closure of the interhemispheric fissure (Silver et al., 1993). Concurrently, they secrete repellent and growth-suppressive molecules that cause callosal axons to turn away from the midline. The importance of the midline glial populations in the development of the CC is further supported by experiments showing that when these glial structures are excised and replaced by cortical grafts that do not contain midline glia, the callosal axons actually fail to turn and cross the midline (Shu and Richards, 2001; Richards, 2002).

Hypothetically, ethanol alters glial production and secretion of chemoattractive and chemorepellent

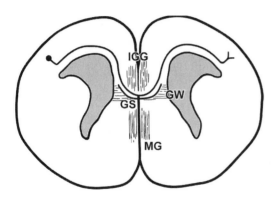

FIGURE 18–4 Midline glial populations. This schematic view of a coronal section represents the various populations of glia at the level of the septal nuclei. GS, glial sling; GW, glial wedge; IGG, glia within indusium griseum, MG, midline zipper glia. *Source:* Adapted from Richards, 2002.

molecules that affect the guidance of midline callosal axons that leads to disrupted CC formation. These molecules are secreted in the glial wedge and indusium griseum and mediate pre- and postcrossing axonal guidance; their depletion has been found to cause axons to defasciculate or to enter the septum aberrantly (Shu et al., 2003). We have recently found abnormalities in the glial wedge and in indusium griseum glial cell populations, along with hypoplasia of the CC, in the brain of 21-day-old fetuses from ethanol-fed mothers (Rubert et al., 2003). Alterations in the CC were accompanied by cortical atrophy and microcephaly (Fig. 18–1).

In contrast with these findings, studies of rats and nonhuman primates show that the number of axons in the CC is increased following ethanol exposure between G11 and G21 (Qiang et al., 2002) or 1 day per week throughout gestation (Miller et al., 1999), respectively. Results from these studies contrast with the agenesis and dysgenesis noted in children with FAS. This discrepancy likely reflects the peak blood ethanol concentration in the children (estimated at >300 mg/dl) vs. that obtained in the animals (100–300 mg/dl). In fact, a dose–response relationship in the amount of hypertrophy has been described for monkeys (Miller et al., 1999). Differences in the amount of ethanol exposure and/or nutritional deficiencies occurring during critical stages of CC development (e.g., embryogenesis) may also contribute to the variability of effects (e.g., agenesis, dysgenesis,

and changes in shape) reported in children prenatally exposed to alcohol.

GLIAL-DERIVED FACTORS AND THE NEURON: THE POTENTIAL EFFECTS OF ETHANOL

Astrocytes synthesize and release a large variety of compounds, including growth factors (Lafon-Cazal et al., 2003). These substances have myriad effects on neurons and CNS function. Proliferating astrocytes release more growth factors than do differentiating glia (e.g., Vallés et al., 1994), perhaps because of the considerably higher (two-fold higher) number of genes expressed by neonatal than by adult astrocytes (Nakagawa and Schwartz, 2004). A particularly interesting factor released by glia is the activity-dependent neuroprotective protein (ADNP) (Bassan et al.,1999). This protein, its active fragment NAP (asn-ala-pro-val-ser-ile-pro-gln), and the active fragments of ADNF are strongly protective against neural insults (Brenneman et al., 1998; Gozes et al., 2000; Beni-Adani et al., 2001), including ethanol-induced insults (Spong et al., 2001; Wilkemeyer et al., 2003).

Given the actions of ethanol on glia and the number and importance of the trophic and signaling functions of glia, it is reasonable to propose that at least some of the detrimental developmental effects of ethanol are mediated by defects in the production of glial factors, such as S100B (Eriksen et al., 2002) and ADNP (Pascual et al., 2004). S100B is a glial trophic factor that is essential for the development of serotonergic neurons (Liu and Lauder, 1992), and ADNP has potent growth-promoting and neuroprotective actions (Bassan et al., 1999; Gozes et al., 2003).

Astrocytes raised in a medium conditioned by ethanol-treated astrocytes stunt process outgrowth by neurons and reduce the survival of serotoninergic neurons (Kim and Druse, 1996; Eriksen and Druse, 2001). Moreover, astrocytes treated with ethanol can increase or reduce the secretion of soluble factors that influence dendritic growth (Yanni et al., 2002).

Secretion of growth factors is reduced in astrocytes isolated from fetuses of ethanol-fed female rats (PEE) and cultured in the absence of ethanol. Ethanol alters the intracellular vesicular transport in astrocytes (Guerri et al., 2001), leading to impairment of both the expression of neurotrophic factors

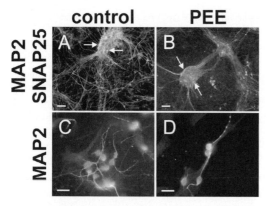

FIGURE 18-5 Co-culture of cortical neurons with control or prenatal ethanol exposed (PEE) astrocytes. Neurons grown on control (A, C) or PEE (B, D) astrocytes were stained the neuronal marker MAP2 and with the synaptic vesicle protein marker SNAP25 (arrows, A, B). Neurons co-cultured with PEE astrocytes (B, D) showed a marked reduction in neuronal differentiation and synaptic connections compared to co-cultures with control astrocytes (A, C). Scale bars = 50 μm (A, B) and 10 μm (C, D).

receptors and the production and release of growth factors such as nerve growth factor (NGF) (Vallés et al., 1994; Climent et al., 2000). PEE astrocytes also exhibit a remarkable reduction in cellular NGF (Vallés et al., 1994) and ADNP (Pascual et al., 2004) mRNA. Co-culture of PEE astrocytes with cortical neurons from control rats leads to a reduction in neuronal differentiation and synaptic connections (Fig.18-5). Interestingly, these effects are blocked by NAP (Pascual et al., 2004). ADNP and its active peptide NAP antagonize ethanol-induced inhibition of L1 adhesion and protect against ethanol embryotoxicity (Spong et al., 2001; Wilkemeyer et al., 2003). These findings may form the basis for future therapeutic approaches to to protect neurons from the toxic effects of ethanol by means of glial-derived factors.

SUMMARY AND CONCLUSIONS

Clinical and experimental studies provide compelling evidence that fetal and/or neonatal exposure to ethanol profoundly affects astroglia. Among the critical periods of brain development in which glial

cells are particularly susceptible to ethanol is embryogenesis. Ethanol exposure during embryogenesis, a stage during which RG are generated, not only impairs neuronal migration but also can affect the generation and maturation of astrocytes. Importantly, the novel role of RG as neural stem cells (Noctor et al., 2001; Götz et al., 2002; Anthony et al., 2004) raises questions as to whether the effects of ethanol on RG underlie the reduction in numbers of neurons and astrocytes generated.

The second critical period during which ethanol can affect glia is the brain growth spurt. Ethanol antagonizes the proliferative effects of astroglial mitogens, interfering with signaling transduction pathways associated with the activation of growth factors and neurotransmitters important for glial proliferation. Exposure to ethanol during this period can also enhance neuronal and astrocytic apoptotic death. The ability of ethanol to interfere with astroglial mitogens and the increase in cell death may contribute to ethanol-induced microencephaly. Exposure to high concentrations of ethanol during the brain growth spurt can induce reactive astrogliosis (Goodlett et al., 1993), thereby activating glia to release toxic compounds that damage neurons (Luo et al., 2001; Blanco et al., 2004). Ethanol-induced astroglial damage can affect many developmental process, such as guidance and availability of trophic support molecules; modulation of the formation, maturation, and maintenance of synapses; and regulation of synaptic transmission (Fields and Stevens-Graham, 2002; Nedergaard et al., 2003).

We are just starting to understand the role of glia in many processes of the adult and developing brain (Ransom et al., 2003). The importance of glia is illustrated by the severity of the more common form of Alexander disease, a rare disorder that results from mutations in the gene for GFAP (Brenner et al., 2001). The genetic modification of *Drosophila melanogaster* resulting in glial ablation causes dramatic defects in neuronal proliferation and differentiation, axonal growth, and neuronal death (Jones et al., 1995; Booth et al., 2000). This finding stresses the importance of glia for neuronal ontogeny. More studies are needed to confirm the roles of astrocytes and to identify molecular targets of ethanol on astroglia. Recent advances in these topics have relied on studies performed in cell culture, where glial network organization may not exactly mirror that in the intact brain.

Abbreviations

ADNF   activity-dependent neurotrophic factor

ADNP   activity-dependent neuroprotective protein

ADH   alcohol dehydrogenase

BDNF   brain-derived neurotrophic factor

CC   corpus callosum

CNS   central nervous system

CYP2E1   cytochrome P450 2E1

FAS   fetal alcohol syndrome

G   gestational day

GFAP   glial fibrillary acidic protein

KCl   potassium chloride

MAPK   mitogen-activated protein kinase

NAP   asn-ala-pro-val-ser-ile-pro-gln

nCAM   neural cell adhesion molecule

NGF   nerve growth factor

NMDA   N-methyl-D-aspartate

P   postnatal day

PA   phosphatidic acid

PDGF   platelet-derived growth factor

PEE   prenatal ethanol exposure

PEt   phosphatidyl ethanol

PKC   protein kinase C

PLD   phospholipase

RG   radial glia

SMase   sphingomyelinase

TGF   transforming growth factor

TNF   tumor necrosis factor

ACKNOWLEDGMENTS The authors thank Dr. Vicente Rubio for his valuable help in the critical reading of this manuscript. Research was supported by Spanish MCYT (projects BFI 2001-0123-01) and SAF (2003-06217) and by Conselleria Sanidad (Direc. Gen. Atencion a la Dependencia).

References

Aghajanian GK, Bloom FE (1967) The formation of synaptic junctions in developing rat brain: a quantitative electron microscopic study. Brain Res 6: 716–727.

Al-Rabiai S, Miller MW (1989) Effects of prenatal exposure to ethanol on the ultrastructure of layer V in somatosensory cortex of mature rats. J Neurocytol 18:711–729.

Anderson CM, Swanson RA (2000) Astrocyte glutamate transport: review of properties, regulation, and physiological functions. Glia 32:1–14.

Andriu-Abadie N, Levade T (2002) Sphingomyelin hydrolysis during apoptosis. Biochim Biophys Acta 1585:126–134.

Anthony TE, Klein C, Fishell G, Heintz N (2004) Radial glia serve as neuronal progenitors in all regions of the central nervous system. Neuron 41:881–890.

Araque A, Carmignoto G, Haydon PG (2001) Dynamic signaling between astrocytes and neurons. Annu Rev Physiol 63:795–813.

Araque A, Parpura V, Sanzgiri RP, Haydon PG (1998) Glutamate-dependent astrocyte modulation of synaptic transmission between cultured hippocampal neurons. Eur J Neurosci 10:2129–2142.

——— (1999) Tripartite synapses: glia, the unacknowledged partner. Trends Neurosci 22:208–215.

Aroor AR, Baker RC (1997) Negative and positive regulation of astrocyte DNA synthesis by ethanol. J Neurosci Res 50:1010–1017.

Aschner M, Allen JW, Kimelberg HK, LoPachin RM, Streit WJ (1999) Glial cells in neurotoxicity development. Ann Rev Pharmacol Toxicol 39:151–173.

Barresi V, Condorelli DF, Gluffrida Stella AM (1999) GFAP gene methylation in different neural cell types from rat brain. Int J Dev Neurosci 17: 821–828.

Bassan M, Zamostiano R, Davidson A, Pinhasov A, Giladi E, Perl O, Bassan H, Blat C, Gibney G, Glazner G, Brenneman DE, Gozes I (1999) Complete sequence of a novel protein containing a femtomolar-activity-dependent neuroprotective peptide. J Neurochem 72:1283–1293.

Bearer CF (2001) L1 cell adhesion molecule signal cascades: targets for ethanol developmental neurotoxicity. Neurotoxicology 22:625–633.

Beni-Adani L, Gozes I, Cohen Y, Steingart RA, Brenneman DE, Eizenberg O, Trembolver A, Shohami E (2001) A peptide derived from activity-dependent neuroprotectiva protein (ADNP) ameliorates injury response in close head injury mice. J Pharmacol Exp Ther 296:57–63.

Bergles DE, Jahr CE (1998) Glial contribution to glutamate uptake at Schaffer collateral–commissural synapses in the hippocampus. J Neurosci 18: 7709–7716.

Bezzi P, Gundersen V, Galbete JL, Seifert G, Steinhäuser Ch, Pilati E, Volterra A (2004) Astrocytes contain a vesicular compartment that is competent for regulated exocytosis of glutamate. Nat Neurosci 7:613–620.

Bezzi P, Voltera A (2001) A neuron–glia signaling network in the active brain. Curr Opin Neurobiol 11: 387–394.

Bird AP, Wolffe AP (1999) Methylation-induced repression—belts, braces, and chromatin. Cell 99: 451–454.

Blanco AM, Pascual M, Vallés LS, Guerri C (2004) Ethanol-induced iNOS and COX-2 expression in cultured astrocytes via NF-kB. Neuroreport 15: 681–685.

Blondel O, Collin C, McCarran WJ, Zhu S, Zamostiano R, Gozes I, Brenneman DE, McKay RD (2000) A glia-derived signal regulating neuronal differentiation. J Neurosci 20:8012–8020.

Bonthius DJ, West JR (1991) Permanent neuronal deficits in rats exposed to alcohol during the brain growth spurt. Teratology 44:147–163.

Bookstein FL, Sampson PD, Streissguth AP, Connor PD (2001) Geometric morphometrics of corpus callosum and subcortical structures in the fetal-alcohol-affected brain. Teratology 64:4–32.

Bookstein FL, Streissguth AP, Sampson PD, Connor PD, Barr HM (2002) Corpus callosum shape and neuropsychological deficits in adult males with heavy fetal alcohol exposure. Neuroimage 15: 233–251.

Booth GE, Kinrade EF, Hidalgo A (2000) Glia maintain follower neuron survival during Drosophila CNS development. Development 127:237–244.

Brenneman DE, Hauser J, Neale E, Rubinraut S, Fridkin M, Davidson A, Gozes I (1998) Activity-dependent neurotrophic factor: structure–activity relationships of femtomolar-acting peptides. J Pharmacol Exp Ther 285:619–627.

Brenner M, Johnson AB, Boespflug-Tanguy O, Rodriguez D, Goldman JE, Messing A (2001) Mutations in GFAP, encoding glial fibrillary acidic protein, are associated with Alexander disease. Nat Genet 27:117–120.

Burrows RC, Wancio D, Levitt P, Lillien L (1997) Response diversity and the timing of progenitor cell maturation are regulated by developmental changes in EGFr expression in the cortex. Neuron 19:251–267.

Cameron RS, Rakic P (1991) Glial cell lineage in the cerebral cortex: a review and synthesis. Glia 4:124–137.

Catlin MC, Guizzetti M, Costa LG (2000) Effect of ethanol on muscarinic receptor–induced calcium responses in astroglia. J Neurosci Res 60:345–355.

Caviness VS Jr, Takahashi T, Nowakowski RS (1995) Numbers, time and neocortical neurogenesis: a general developmental and evolutionary model. Trends Neurosci 18:379–383.

Chanas-Sacre G, Rogister B, Moonen G, Leprince P (2000) Radial glia phenotype: origin, regulation and transdifferentiation. J Neusoci Res 61:357–363.

Chen Y, Swanson RA (2003) Astrocytes and brain injury. J Cereb Blood Flow Metab 23:137–149.

Clarren SK (1986) Neuropathology in fetal alcohol syndrome. In: West JR (ed). Alcohol and Brain Development. Oxford University Press, New York, pp 158–166.

Clarren SK, Alvord EC, Sumi SM, Streissguth AP, Smith DW (1978) Brain malformations related to prenatal exposure to ethanol. J Pediatr 92:64–67.

Clarren SK, Bowden DM (1984) Measures of alcohol damage in utero in the pigtailed macaque (Macaca nemestrina). In: O'Connor M (ed). Mechanisms of Alcohol Damage in Utero. Pitman, London, pp 157–175.

Climent E, Pascual M, Renau-Piqueras J, Guerri C (2002) Ethanol exposure enhances cell death in the developing cerebral cortex: role of brain-derived neurotrophic factor and its signaling pathways. J Neurochem Res 68:213–225.

Climent E, Sancho-Tello M, Miñana R, Barettino D, Guerri C (2000) Astrocytes in culture express the full-length Trk-B receptor and respond to brain derived neurotrophic factor by changing intracellular calcium levels: effect of ethanol exposure in rats. Neurosci Lett 288:53–56.

Costa LG, Aschner M, Vitalone A, Syversen T, Soldin OP (2004) Developmental neuropathology of environmental agents. Annu Rev Pharmacol Toxicol 44: 87–110.

Costa LG, Guizzette M (2002) Inhibition of muscarinic receptor–induced proliferation of astroglial cells by ethanol: mechanisms and implications for the fetal alcohol syndrome. Neurotoxicology 23:685–691.

Costa LG, Guizzetti M, Oberdoerster J, Yagle K, Costa-Mallen P, Tita B, Bordi F, Vitalone A, Palmery M, Valeri P (2001) Modulation of DNA synthesis by muscarinic cholinergic receptors. Growth Factors 18:227–236.

Crespel A, Coubes P, Rousset MC, Alonso G, Bockaert J, Baldy-Moulinier M, Lerner-Natoli M (2002) Immature-like astrocytes are associated with dendate granule cell migration in human temporal lobe epilepsy. Neurosci Lett 330:114–118.

Davies DL, Cox WE (1991) Delayed growth and maturation of astrocytic cultures following exposure to ethanol: electron microscopic observation. Brain Res 547:53–61.

De Vito WJ, Stone S, Shamgochian M (2000) Ethanol increases the neurotoxic effect of tumor necrosis factor-α in cultured rat astrocytes. Alcohol Clin Exp Res 24:82–92.

Dobbing J, Sands J (1993) The quantitative growth and development of the human brain. Arch Dis Child 48:757–767.

Edelman GM (1994) Adhesion and counter adhesion morphogenetic functions of the cell surface. Prog Brain Res 101:1–14.

Eriksen JL, Druse MJ (2001) Potential involvement of S100B in the protective effects of a serotonin-1a agonist on ethanol-treated astrocytes. Dev Brain Res 128:157–164.

Eriksen JL, Gillespie R, Druse MJ (2002) Effects of ethanol and 5-HT$_{1A}$ agonists on astroglial S100B. Dev Brain Res 139:97–105.

Eysseric H, Gonthier B, Soubeyran A, Bessard G, Saxod R, Barret L (1997) Characterization of the production of acetaldehyde by astrocytes in culture after ethanol exposure. Alcohol Clin Exp Res 21:1018–1023.

Eysseric H, Gonthier B, Soubeyran A, Richard MJ, Daveloose D, Barret L (2000) Effects of chronic ethanol exposure on acetaldehyde and free radical production by astrocytes in culture. Alcohol 21:117–125.

Fields RD, Stevens-Graham B (2002) New insights into neuron–glia communication. Science 298:556–562.

Goodlett CR, Leo JT, O'Callaghan JP, Mahoney JC, West JR (1993) Transient cortical astrogliosis induced by alcohol exposure during the neonatal brain growth spurt in rats. Brain Res Dev Brain Res 72:85–97.

Götz M, Hartfuss E, Malatesta P (2002) Radial glial cells as neuronal precursors: a new perspectives on the correlation of morphology and linage restriction in the developing cerebral cortex of mice. Brain Res Bull 57:777–788.

Gozes I, Brenneman DE (2000) A new concept in the pharmacology of neuroprotection. J Mol Neurosci 14:61–68.

Gozes I, Divinsky I, Pilzer I, Fridkin M, Brenneman DE, Spier AD (2003). From vasoactive intestinal peptide (VIP) through activity-dependent neuroprotective protein (ADNP) to NAP: a view of neuroprotection and cell division. J Mol Neurosci 20:315–322.

Gozes I, Giladi E, Pinhasov A, Brenneman DE (2000) Activity-dependent neurotrophic factor intranasal administration of femtomolar-acting peptides improve performance in a water maze. J Pharmacol Exp Ther 293:1091–1098.

Gressens P, Lammens M, Picard JJ, Evrard P (1992) Ethanol-induced disturbances of gliogenesis and neurogenesis in the developing murine brain: an in vitro and in vivo immunohistochemical and ultrastructural study. Alcohol Alcohol 27:219–226.

Grosche J, Kettenmann H, Reichenbach A (2002) Bergmann glial cells form distinct morphological structures to interact with cerebellar neurons. J Neurosci Res 68:138–149.

Gross RE, Mehler MF, Mabie PC, Zang Z, Santschi L, Kessler JA (1996) Bone morphogenetic proteins promote astroglial lineage commitment by mammalian subventricular zone progenitor cells. Neuron 17:595–606.

Gruol DL, Ryabinin AE, Parsons KL, Cole M, Wilson MC, Qiu Z (1998) Neonatal alcohol exposure reduces NMDA induced Ca^{2+} signaling in developing cerebellar granule neurons. Brain Res 793:12–20.

Guerri C (1987) Synaptic membrane alterations in rats exposed to alcohol. Alcohol Alcohol Suppl 1:467–472.

—— (1998) Neuroanatomical and neurophysiological mechanisms involved in central nervous system dysfunctions induced by prenatal alcohol exposure. Alcohol Clin Exp Res 22:304–312.

—— (2002) Mechanisms involved in central nervous system dysfunctions induced by prenatal ethanol exposure. Neurotoxicol Res 4:327–335.

Guerri C, Pascual M, Renau-Piqueras J (2001) Glia and fetal alcohol syndrome. Neurotoxicology 22:593–599.

Guerri C, Renau-Piqueras J (1997) Alcohol, astroglia, and brain development. Mol Neurol 15:65–81.

Guerri C, Sáez R, Sancho-Tello M, Martin de Aguilera M, Renau-Piqueras J (1990) Ethanol alters astrocyte development: a study of critical periods using primary cultures. Neurochem Res 15:559–565.

Guizzetti M, Catlin M, Costa LG (1997) Effects of ethanol on glial cell proliferation: relevance to the fetal alcohol syndrome. Front Biosci 2:e93–98.

Guizzetti M, Moller T, Costa LG (2003) Ethanol inhibits muscarinic receptor–mediated DNA synthesis and signal transduction in human fetal astrocytes. Neurosci Lett 344:68–70.

Guizzetti M, Wei M, Costa LG (1998) The role of protein kinase C alpha and epsilon isozymes in DNA synthesis induced by muscarinic receptors in a glial cell line. Eur J Pharmacol 359:223–233.

Hannun YA, Luberto Ch (2000) Ceramide in the eukaryotic stress response. Trends Cell Biol 10:73–80.

Hatten ME (1999) Central nervous system neuronal migration. Annu Rev Neurosci 22:511–539.

—— (2002) New directions in neuronal migration. Science 297:1660–1663.

Hatten ME, Mason CA (1990) Mechanisms of glial-guided neuronal migration in vitro and in vivo. Experientia 46:907–916.

Haydon PG (2001) Glia: listening and talking to the synapse. Nat Rev Neurosci 2:185–193.

Herget T, Esdar Ch, Oehrlein SA, Heinrich M, Schütze S, Maelicke A, Van Echten-Deckert G (2000) Production of ceramides causes apoptosis during early neural differentiation in vitro. J Biol Chem 275: 30344–30354.

Hockfield S, McKay RD (1985) Identification of major cell classes in the developing mammalian nervous system. J Neurosci 5:3310–3328.

Holownia A, Ledig M, Mapoles J, Menez JF (1996) Acetaldehyde-induced growth inhibition in cultured rat astroglial cells. Alcohol 13:93–97.

Holownia A, Ledig M, Menez JF (1997) Ethanol-induced cell death in cultured rat astroglia. Neurotoxicol Teratol 19:141–146.

Innocenti B, Parpura V, Haydon PG (2000) Imaging extracellular waves of glutamate during calcium signaling in cultured astrocytes. J Neurosci 20:1800–1808.

Isenberg K, Zhou X, Moore BW (1992) Ethanol inhibits C6 cell growth: fetal alcohol syndrome model. Alcohol Clin Exp Res 16:695–699.

Johe KK, Hazel TG, Muller T, Dugich-Djordjevic MM, McKay RD (1996) Single factors direct the differentiation of stem cells from the fetal and adult central nervous system. Genes Dev 10:3129–3140.

Johnson EM, Deckwerth TL (1993) Molecular mechanisms of developmental neuronal death. Ann Rev Neurosci 16:31–46.

Johnson VP, Swayze VW II, Sato Y, Andreasen NC (1996) Fetal alcohol syndrome: craniofacial and central nervous system manifestations. Am J Med Genet 6:329–339.

Jones BW, Fetter RD, Tear G, Goodman CS (1995) Glial cells missing: a genetic switch that controls glial versus neuronal fate. Cell 82:1013–1023.

Kennedy LA, Mukerji S (1986) Ethanol neurotoxicity. I. Direct effects on replicating astrocytes. Neurobehav Toxicol Teratol 8:11–21.

Kim JA, Druse MJ (1996) Deficiency of essential neurotrophic factors in conditioned media produced by ethanol-exposed cortical astrocytes. Dev Brain Res 96:1–10.

Komatsu S, Sakata-Haga H, Sawada K, Hisano S, Fukui Y (2001) Prenatal exposure to ethanol induces leptomeningeal heterotopia in the cerebral cortex of the rat fetus. Acta Neuropathol 101:22–26.

Kotkoskie LA, Norton S (1988) Prenatal brain malformations following acute ethanol exposure in the rat. Alcohol Clin Exp Res 12:831–836.

Kötter K, Klein J (1999) Ethanol inhibits astroglial cell proliferation by disruption of phospholipase D–mediated signaling. J Neurochem 73:2517–2523.

Kriegstein AR, Götz M (2003) Radial glia diversity: a matter of cell fate. Glia 43:37–43.

Kuge R, Asayama T, Kakuta S, Murakami K, Ishikawea Y, Kuroda M, Imai T, Seki K, Omoto M, Kishi K (1993) Effect of ethanol on the development and maturation of synapses in the rat hippocampus: a quantitative electron-microscopic study. Environ Res 62:99–105.

Kuhn PE, Miller MW (1996) Developmental expression of c-neu proteins in cerebral cortex: relationship to epidermal growth factor receptor. J Comp Neurol 372:189–203.

Lafon-Cazal M, Adjali O, Galeotti N, Poncet J, Jouin P, Homburger V, Bockaert J, Marin P (2003) Proteomic analysis of astrocytic secretion in the mouse. Comparison with the cerebrospinal fluid proteome. J Biol Chem 278:24438–24448.

Lammens M (2000) Neuronal migration disorders in man. Eur J Morphol 38:327–333.

Letterer E (1958) Virchows contribution to modern pathology; on the 100th anniversary of cellular pathology, August 20, 1858. Hippokrates 29:505–511.

Liu JP, Lauder JM (1992) S-100 and insulin-like growth factor-II differentially regulate growth of developing serotonin and dopamine neurons in vitro. J Neurosci Res 33:248–256.

Luo J, Lindström CLB, Donahue A, Miller MW (2001) Differential effects of ethanol on the expression of cyclooxygenase in cultured cortical astrocytes and neurons. J Neurochem 76:1354–1363.

Luo J, Miller MW (1996) Ethanol inhibits bFGF-mediated proliferation of C6 glioma cells. J Neurochem 67:1448–1456.

—— (1998) Growth factor-mediated neural proliferation:target of ethanol toxicity. Brain Res Rev 27:157–167.

—— (1999) Platelet-derived growth factor–mediated signal transduction underlying astrocyte proliferation: site of ethanol action. J Neurosci 19:10014–10025.

Malatesta P, Hartfuss E, Götz M (2000) Isolation of radial glial cells by fluorescent-activated cell sorting shows a neuronal lineage. Development 127:5253–5263.

Mauch DH, Nägler K, Schumacher S, Göritz C, Müller EC, Otto A, Pfrieger FW (2001) CNS synaptogenesis promoted by glia-derived cholesterol. Science 294:1354–1357.

Mikami K, Haseba T, Ohno Y (1997) Ethanol induces transient arrest of cell division (G2 + M block) followed by G0/G1 block: dose effect of short- and longer-term ethanol exposure on cell cycle and cell functions. Alcohol Alcohol 32:145–152.

Miller MW (1986) Fetal alcohol effects on the generation and migration of cerebral cortical neurons. Science 233:1308–1311.

—— (1988) Effect of prenatal exposure to ethanol on the development of cerebral cortex: I. Neuronal generation. Alcohol Clin Exp Res 12:440–449.

—— (1997) Effects of prenatal exposure to ethanol on callosal projection neurons in rat somatosensory cortex. Brain Res 766:121–128.

Miller MW, Astley SJ, Clarren SK (1999) Number of axons in the corpus callosum of the mature Macaca *nemestrina*: increases caused by prenatal exposure to ethanol. J Comp Neurol 412:123–131.

Miller MW, Luo J (2002) Effects of ethanol and basic fibroblast growth factor on the transforming growth factor 1 regulated proliferation of cortical astrocytes and C6 astrocytoma cells. Alcohol Clin Exp Res 26:671–676.

Miller M, Peters A (1981) Maturation of the rat visual cortex. II. A combined Golgi-electron microscope study of the pyramidal neuron. J Comp Neurol 203:555–573.

Miller MW, Potempa G (1990) Numbers of neurons and glia in mature rat somatosensory cortex: effects of prenatal exposure to ethanol. J Comp Neurol 293: 92–102.

Miller MW, Robertson S (1993) Prenatal exposure to ethanol alters the postnatal development and transformation of radial glia to astrocytes in the cortex. J Comp Neurol 337:253–266.

Miñana R, Climent E, Barettino D, Segui JM, Renau-Piqueras J, Guerri C (2000) Alcohol exposure alters the expression pattern of neural cell adhesion molecules during brain development. J Neurochem 75: 954–964.

Miñana R, Sancho-Tello M, Climent E, Segui JM, Renau-Piqueras J, Guerri C (1998) Intracellular location, temporal expression, and polysialylation of neural cell adhesion molecule in astrocytes in primary culture. Glia 24:415–427.

Misson JP, Takahashi T, Caviness VS Jr (1991) Ontogeny of radial and other astroglial cells in murine cerebral cortex. Glia 4:138–148.

Montoliu C, Sancho-Tello M, Azorin I, Burgal M, Vallés S, Renau-Piqueras J, Guerri C (1995) Ethanol increases cytochromo P4502E1 and induces oxidative stress in astrocytes. J Neurochem 65:2561–2570.

Mooney SM, Miller MW (2001) Effects of prenatal exposure to ethanol on the expression of bcl-2, bax and caspase 3 in the developing rat cerebral cortex and thalamus. Dev Brain Res 911:71–81.

Mooney SM, Siegenthaler JA, Miller MW (2004) Ethanol induces heterotopias in organotypic cultures of rat cerebral cortex. Cereb Cortex 14:1071–1080.

Nadarajah B, Parnavelas JG (2002) Modes of neuronal migration in the developing cerebral cortex. Nat Rev Neurosci 3:423–432.

Nagler K, Mauch DH, Pfrieger PW (2001) Glial-derived signals induce synapse formation in neurons of the rat central nervous system. J Physiol 533:665–679.

Nakagawa T, Schwartz JP (2004) Gene expression patterns in *in vivo* normal adult astrocytes compared with cultured neonatal and normal adult astrocytes. Neurochem Intl 45:203–242.

Nedergaard M, Ransom B, Goldman SA (2003) New roles for astrocytes: redefining the functional architecture of the brain. Trends Neurosci 26:523–530.

Noctor SC, Flint AC, Weissman TA, Dammerman RS, Kriegstein AR (2001) Neuron-derived radial glia cells establish radial units in neocortex. Nature 409:714–720.

Noctor SC, Flint AC, Weissman TA, Wong WS, Clinton BK, Kriegstein AR (2002) Dividing precursor cells of the embryonic cortical ventricular zone have morphological and molecular characteristics of radial glia. J Neurosci 22:3161–3173.

Ohanian J, Ohanian V (2001) Sphingolipids in mammalian cell signalling. Cell Mol Life Sci 58: 2053–2068.

Oppenheim RW (1991) Cell death during development of the nervous system. Ann Res Neurosci 14: 453–501.

Parnavelas JG, Luder R, Pollard SG, Sullivan K, Liberman AR (1983) A qualitative and quantitative ultrastructural study of glial cells in the developing visual cortex of the rat. Phil Trans R Soc Lond B Biol Sci 301:55–84.

Pascual M, Climent E, Guerri C (2001) BDNF induces glutamate release in cerebrocortical nerve terminals and in cortical astrocytes. Neuroreport 12: 2673–2677.

Pascual M, Vallés S, Renau-Piqueras J, Guerri C (2003) Ceramide pathways modulate ethanol-induced cell death in astrocytes. J Neurochem 87:1535–1545.

Pascual M, Garcia-Minguillan MC, Guerri C (2004) Antioxidants prevent ethanol-induced cell death in developing brain and in cultured cells. Alcohol Clin Exp Res 28 (Suppl 8):61A.

Pasti L, Zonta M, Pozan T, Vicini S, Carmignoto G (2001) Cytosolic calcium oscillation in astrocytes may regulate exocytotic release of glutamate. J Neurosci 21:477–484.

Peiffer J, Majewski F, Fischbach H, Bierich JR, Volk B (1979) Alcohol embryo- and fetopathy. J Neurol Sci 41:125–137.

Perez-Torrero E, Duran P, Granados L, Gutierrez-Ospina G, Cintra L, Diaz-Cintra S (1997) Effects of acute prenatal ethanol exposure on Bergmann glia cells early postnatal development. Brain Res 746:305–308.

Pixley SKR, DeVellis J (1984) Transition between immature radial glia and mature astrocytes studies with a monoclonal antibody to vimentin. Dev Brain Res 15:201–209.

Qiang M, Wang MW, Elberger AJ (2002) Second trimester prenatal alcohol exposure alters development of rat corpus callosum. Neurotoxicol Teratol 24:719–732.

Raff MC, Barres BA, Burne JF, Coles HS, Ishizaki Y, Jacobson MD (1993) Programmed cell death and the control of cell survival: lessons from the nervous system. Science 262:695–700.

Rakic P (1972) Mode of cell migration to the superficial layers of fetal monkey neocortex. J Comp Neurol 145:61–84.

Ransom B, Behar T, Nedergaard M (2003) New roles for astrocytes (stars at last). Trends Neurosci 26:520–522.

Razin A (1998) CpG methylation, chromatin structure and gene silencing a three-way connection. EMBO J 17:4905–4908.

Resnicoff M, Rubini M, Baserga R, Rubin R (1994) Ethanol inhibits insulin-like growth factor I–mediated signalling and proliferation of C6 rat glioblastoma cells. Lab Invest 71:657–662.

Richards LJ (2002) Axonal pathfinding mechanisms at the cortical midline and in the development of the corpus callosum. Braz J Med Biol Res 35:1431–1439.

Riikonen R, Salonen I, Partanen K, Verho S (1999) Brain perfusion SPECT and MRI in foetal alcohol syndrome. Dev Med Child Neurol 41:652–659.

Riley EP, Mattson SN, Sowell ER, Jernigan TL, Sobel DF, Jones KL (1995) Abnormalities of the corpus callosum in children prenatally exposed to alcohol. Alcohol Clin Exp Res 19:1198–1202.

Ross ME, Walsh CA (2001) Human brain malformations and their lessons for neuronal migration. Annu Rev Neurosci 24: 1041–1070.

Rubert G, Vallés S, Guerri C (2003) Fetal alcohol exposure alters radial glia and may affect corpus callosum formation. Alcohol Alcohol 38:462.

Sakata-Haga H, Sawada K, Hisano S, Fukui Y (2001) Abnormalities of cerebellar foliation in rats prenatally exposed to ethanol. Acta Neuropathol 102:36–40.

Sanai N, Tramontin AD, Quiñones-Hinojosa A, Barbaro NM, Gupta N, Kunwar S, Lawton MT, McDermott MW, Parsa AT, Garcia-Verdugo JM, Berger MS, Alvarez-Buylla A (2004) Unique astrocyte ribbon in adult human brain contains neural stem cells but lacks chain migration. Nature 427:740–744.

Sancho-Tello M, Vallés S, Montoliu C, Renau-Piqueras J, Guerri C (1995) Developmental pattern of GFAP and vimentin gene expression in rat brain and in radial glial cultures. Glia 15:157–166.

Savage DD, Montano CY, Otero MA, Paxton LL (1991) Prenatal ethanol exposure decreases hippocampal NMDA-sensitive (^{3}H)-glutamate binding site density in 45-day-old rats. Alcohol 8:193–201.

Schatter B, Walev I, Klein J (2003) Mitogenic effects of phospholipase D and phosphatidic acid in transiently permeabilized astrocytes: effects of ethanol. J Neurochem 87:95–100.

Schikorski T, Stevens CF (1999) Quantitative fine-structural analysis of alfatory cortical synapses. Proc Natl Acad Sci USA 96:4107–4112.

Schmechel DE, Rakic P (1979) A Golgi study of radial glial cells in developing monkey telencephalon: morphogenesis and transformation into astrocytes. Anat Embryol 156:115–152.

Schmid RS, Anton ES (2003) Role of integrins in the developing of the cerebral cortex. Cereb Cortex 13:219–224.

Schmid RS, McGrath B, Berechid BE, Boyles B, Marchionni M, Sestan N, Anton ES (2003) Neuregulin 1-erbB2 signaling is required for the establishment of radial glia and their transformation into astrocytes in cerebral cortex. Proc Natl Acad Sci USA 100:4251–4256.

Shetty AK, Burrows RC, Wall KA, Phillips DE (1994) Combined pre- and postnatal ethanol exposure alters the development of Bermann glia in rat cerebellum. Int J Dev Neurosci 12:641–649.

Shu T, Li Y, Keller A, Richards LJ (2003) The glial sling is a migratory population of developing neurons. Development 130:2929–2937.

Shu T, Richards LJ (2001) Cortical axon guidance by the glial wedge during the development of the corpus callosum. J Neurochem 21:2749–2758.

Shulman EG, Hyder F, Rothman DL (2001) Cerebral energetics and the glycogen shunt: neurochemical basis of functional imaging. Proc Natl Acad Sci USA 98:6417–6422.

Siegenthaler JA, Miller MW (2004) Transforming growth factor β1 modulates cell migration in rat cortex: effects of ethanol. Cereb Cortex 14:791–802.

Sievers J, Pehlemann FW, Gude S, Hartmann D, Berry M (1994) The development of the radial glial scaffold of the cerebellar cortex from GFAP-positive cells in the external granular layer. J Neurocytol 23:97–115.

Silver J, Edwards MA, Levitt P (1993) Immunocytochemical demonstration of early appearing astroglial structures that form boundaries and pathways along axon tracts in the fetal brain. J Comp Neurol 328:415–436.

Snyder AK, Singh SP, Ehmann S (1992) Effects of ethanol on DNA, RNA and protein synthesis in rat astrocyte cultures. Alcohol Clin Exp Res 16:295–300.

Song H, Stevens CF, Gage FH (2002) Astroglia induce neurogenesis from adult neural stem cells. Nature 417:29–32.

Song M-R, Ghosh A (2004) FGF2-induced chromatin remodeling regulates CNTF-mediated gene expression and astrocyte differentiation. Nat Neurosci 7:229–235.

Soriano E, Del Rio JA, Auladell C (1993) Characterization of the phenotype and birthdates of pyknotic dead cells in the nervous system by a combination of DNA staining and immunohistochemistry for 5'-bromodeoxyuridine and neural antigens. J Histochem Cytochem 41:819–827.

Sowell ER, Mattson SN, Thompson PM, Jernigan TL, Riley EP, Toga AW (2001a) Mapping callosal morphology and cognitive correlates. Effects of heavy prenatal alcohol exposure. Neurology 57: 235–244.

Sowell ER, Thompson PM, Mattson SN, Tessner KD, Jernigan TL, Riley EP, Toga AW (2001b) Voxel-based morphometric analyses of the brain in children and adolescents prenatally exposed to alcohol. Neuroreport 12:515–523.

Spong CY, Abebe DT, Gozes I, Brenneman DE, Hill JM (2001) Prevention of fetal demise and growth restriction in a mouse model of fetal alcohol syndrome. J Pharmacol Exp Ther 297:774–779.

Spuhler-Phillips K, Lee YH, Hughes P, Randoll L, Leslie SW (1997) Effects of prenatal ethanol exposure on brain region NMDA-mediated increase in intracellular calcium and the NMDAR1 subunit in forebrain. Alcohol Clin Exp Res 21:68–75.

Steven ER, Esguerra M, Kim PM, Newman EA, Snyder SH, Zahs KR, Miller RF (2003) D-serine and serine racemase are present in the vertebrate retina and contribute to the physiological activation of NMDA receptors. Proc Natl Acad Sci USA 100: 6789–6794.

Sutherland RJ, McDonald RJ, Savage DD (1997) Prenatal exposure to moderate levels of ethanol can have long-lasting effects on hippocampal synaptic plasticity in adult offspring. Hippocampus 7:232–238.

Swayze VW, Johnson VP, Hanson JW, Piven J, Sato Y, Giedd JN, Mosnik D, Andreasen NC (1997) Magnetic resonance imaging of brain anomalies in fetal alcohol syndrome. Pediatrics 99:232–240.

Tajuddin NF, Orrico LA, Eriksen JL, Druse MJ (2003) Effects of ethanol and ipsapirone on the development of midline raphe glial cells and astrocytes. Alcohol 29:157–164.

Takizawa T, Nakashima K, Namihira M, Ochiai W, Uemura A, Yanagisawa M, Fujita N, Nakao M, Taga T (2001) DNA methylation is a critical cell-intrinsic determinant of astrocyte differentiation in the fetal brain. Dev Cell 1:749–758.

Tanaka H, Nasu F, Inomata K (1991) Fetal alcohol effects: decreased synaptic formations in the field CA3 of fetal hippocampus. Intl J Dev Neurosci 9: 509–517.

Toman RE, Movsesyan V, Murthy SK, Milstien S, Spiegel S, Faden AI (2002) Ceramide-induced cell death in primary neuronal cultures:upregulation of ceramide levels during neuronal apoptosis. J Neurosci Res 68:323–330.

Ullian EM, Harris BT, Wu A, Chan JR, Barres BA (2004) Schwann cells and astrocytes induce synapse formation by spinal motor neurons in culture. Mol Cell Neurosci 25:241–251.

Ullian EM, Sapperstein SK, Christopherson KS, Barres BA (2001) Control of synapse number by glia. Science 291:657–661.

Vallés S, Felipo V, Montoliu C, Guerri C (1995) Alcohol exposure during brain development reduces ^{3}H-MK 801 binding and enhances metabotropic-glutamate receptor–stimulated phosphoinositide hydrolysis in rat hippocampus. Life Sci 56:1373–1383.

Vallés S, Lindo L, Montoliu C, Renau-Piqueras J, Guerri C (1994) Prenatal exposure to ethanol induces changes in the nerve growth factor and its receptor in proliferating astrocytes in primary culture. Brain Res 656:281–286.

Vallés S, Pitarch J, Renau-Piqueras J, Guerri C (1997) Ethanol exposure affects glial fibrillary acidic protein gene expression and transcription during rat brain development. J Neurochem 69:2484–2493.

Vallés S, Sancho-Tello M, Miñana R, Climent E, Renau-Piqueras J, Guerri C (1996) Glial fibrillary acidic protein expression in rat brain and in radial glia culture is delayed by prenatal ethanol exposure. J Neurochem 67:2425–2433.

Ventura R, Harris KM (1999) Three-dimensional relationships between hippocampal synapses and astrocytes. J Neurosci 19:6897–6906.

Voigt T (1989) Development of glial cells in the cerebral wall of ferrets: direct tracing of their transformation from radial glia into astrocytes. J Comp Neurol 289: 74–88.

Waziri R, Kamath SH, Sahu S (1981) Alcohol inhibits morphological and biochemical differentiation of C6 glial cells in culture. Differentiation 18:55–59.

Wilkemeyer MF, Chen S-Y, Menkari CE, Brenneman DE, Sulik KK, Charness ME (2003) Differential effects of ethanol antagonism and neuroprotection in peptide fragment NAPVSIPQ prevention of ethanol-induced developmental toxicity. Proc Natl Acad Sci USA 100:8543–8548.

Wilkemeyer MF, Pajerski M, Charness ME (1999) Alcohol inhibition of cell adhesion in BMP-treated NG108-15 cells. Alcohol Clin Exp Res 23:1711–1720.

Wilkemeyer MF, Sebastian AB, Smith SA, Charness ME (2000) Antagonists of alcohol inhibition of cell adhesion. Proc Natl Acad Sci USA 97: 3690–3695.

Wisniewski K, Dambska M, Sher JH, Qazi Q (1983) A clinical neuropathological study of the fetal alcohol syndrome. Neuropedia 14:195–201.

Wolosker H, Blackshaw S, Snyder SH (1999) Serine racemase: a glial enzyme synthesizing D-serine to regulate glutamate-*n*-methyl-D-aspartate neurotransmission. Proc Natl Acad Sci USA 96:13409–13414.

Yanni PA, Rising LJ, Ingraham CA, Lindsley TA (2002) Astrocyte-derived factors modulate the inhibitory effect of ethanol on dendritic development. Glia 38:292–302.

Yuasa S (1996) Bergmann glial development in the mouse cerebellum as revealed by tenascin expression. Anat Embryol 194:223–234.

III

NICOTINE-AFFECTED DEVELOPMENT

19

Tobacco Use During Pregnancy: Epidemiology and Effects on Offspring

Jennifer A. Willford

Nancy L. Day

Marie D. Cornelius

Tobacco use during pregnancy affects fetal development on multiple levels. Nicotine readily crosses the placenta, concentrating in fetal tissue, and results in fetal concentrations of nicotine that can be 15% higher than those in the pregnant woman (Luck et al., 1985). The direct actions of nicotine on the fetus affect growth and neural development during the intrauterine period and have long-term effects on brain function, cognition, and behavior (Abreu-Villaca et al., 2004a, 2004b).

Tobacco use during pregnancy has indirect effects on fetal development. Prenatal tobacco use affects the nutritional status of the mother, leading to an increased risk of having an infant with low birth weight (LBW) (Haste et al., 1990), and causes increased vascular resistance in the placenta, resulting in reduced oxygen flow to the fetus (Lambers and Clark, 1996). Intermittent fetal hypoxia, secondary to exposure to carbon monoxide and the metabolite carboxyhemoglobin, may also affect oxygen flow to the fetus.

The present chapter reviews the epidemiology of tobacco use during pregnancy and then focuses on the effects of prenatal tobacco exposure (PTE).

SCOPE OF THE PROBLEM

Epidemiology of Tobacco Use During Pregnancy

In general populations surveys, 10% to 20% of women report that they smoked during pregnancy (National Institute on Drug Abuse [NIDA], 1996; LeClere and Wilson, 1997; Centers for Disease Control and Prevention [CDC], 2002, 2003). Data collected on the U.S. Standard Certificates of Live Births show that the proportion of women who smoked during pregnancy declined from 19.5% to 11.4% between 1989 and 2002 (Martin et al., 2003). This decrease mirrors a general decrease in smoking among women of reproductive age, although one group, young women aged 18–20, increased their use slightly from 1987 to 1996 (Ebrahim et al., 2000). This overall decline in smoking during pregnancy results from low rates of smoking initiation in women, rather than changes in smoking before or during pregnancy (Wisborg et al., 1996; Cnattingius and Haglund, 1997; Department of Health and Human Services [DHHS], 2001).

Smoking during pregnancy is more prevalent among Caucasian women than among African-American or Hispanic women (NIDA, 1996; CDC, 2002). The rates vary by age (Cornelius et al., 1999b; Kahn et al., 2002), with younger women smoking more cigarettes. Use also varies by trimester of pregnancy. A Maternal Health Practices and Child Development (MHPCD) study of teenage mothers reports that the rate of smoking during pregnancy is 47% in the first trimester and 58% in the third trimester (Cornelius et al., 2004). In general, women who smoke during pregnancy are younger and less likely to be married, have less education and lower incomes, and attend fewer prenatal visits compared with women who do not smoke during pregnancy (Day et al., 1992; Cornelius et al., 1994; DHHS, 2001; CDC, 2003). Women who smoke during pregnancy also have higher rates of antisocial behavior, mates that have more antisocial behaviors, higher rates of depression, and lower socioeconomic status (SES) (Maughan et al., 2004).

Women are less likely to decrease their tobacco use during pregnancy than they are to decrease other substance use, including alcohol, marijuana, and other illicit drugs (Cornelius et al., 1995; Day et al., 2000), and are more likely to continue to smoke in the postpartum period (Cornelius et al., 1999a; Leech et al., 1999). In a National Pregnancy and Health Study (NIDA, 1996), approximately two-thirds of the women who smoke prior to their pregnancy continue smoking through the last trimester. By contrast, only one-quarter of the women who use alcohol prior to conception continue to drink in the third trimester. Women who continue to smoke during pregnancy are more likely to have had previous pregnancies, to have a younger age at smoking onset, to be heavy smokers, and to have less education (Cnattingius, 2004).

Women who smoke during pregnancy also continue to smoke in the postpartum period. This means that the offspring of a woman who uses tobacco during pregnancy are exposed continuously to tobacco smoke in the household. This environmental, or passive, exposure also affects child development. In the MHPCD cohort of adult mothers, for example, the correlation between prenatal tobacco use and tobacco use 10 years later was 0.63 (Cornelius et al., 2000). In addition, as many as 60% of women who quit smoking during pregnancy began again within 6 months of delivery (Mullen et al., 1997; Hajek et al., 2001). Significant predictors of relapse after pregnancy include living with another smoker, less education, and lower income (Kahn et al., 2002).

Women who smoke during pregnancy have higher rates of other substance use as well. Among women in the MHPCD project, 76% of the women over the age of 18 who smoked during the first trimester of pregnancy drank alcohol during this period (Day et al., 1992). Among pregnant teenagers, 61% of those who smoked in the first trimester drank alcohol (Cornelius et al., 1995). Tobacco use is also highly associated with the use of illicit drugs during pregnancy. In the National Pregnancy and Health Survey (NIDA, 1996), women who smoked cigarettes during pregnancy reported using illicit drugs (26%), drinking (16%), or both (32%). Therefore, it is important to control for the covariates of PTE and other prenatal substance exposures, as well as current maternal tobacco and other substance use. In the absence of considering these other risk factors, it is not possible to identify accurately the unique effects of prenatal tobacco exposure.

Mortality and Morbidity

A meta-analysis estimates that PTE was responsible for up to 4800 infant deaths, 61,000 infants with LBW, and 26,000 neonatal intensive care admissions per year (DiFranza and Lew, 1995). An earlier report estimates that maternal smoking was responsible for approximately 10% of fetal and infant deaths (Kleinman et al., 1988). This report, along with another (Singleton et al., 1986), find that the impact of PTE is greater among African Americans than for Caucasians and is greater among the offspring of older mothers (Cnattingius et al., 1988).

PTE is a significant risk factor for sudden infant death syndrome (SIDS) (National Cancer Institute [NCI], 1999). SIDS results from the PTE-related chronic hypoxia (Bulterys et al., 1990). Postnatal passive exposure of the infant also significantly increases the risk of SIDS (Klonoff-Cohen et al., 1995; Dwyer et al., 1999).

GROWTH AND MATURATION

Human Studies

PTE has long been identified as a significant risk factor for intrauterine growth restriction (DHHS, 1980, 2001; Stillman et al., 1986; Floyd et al., 1993; NCI, 1999; CDC, 2003). Birth weight decreases in direct proportion to the number of cigarettes smoked (Yerushalmy, 1971; Persson et al., 1978), and offspring of smokers are 150 to 250 g lighter than the offspring of non-smokers (DHHS, 1980). The effects of PTE can be seen even at lower levels of exposure: in one report, 11.5% of infants born to light smokers (≤six cigarettes/day) have LBW, compared to 7.5% of those born to non-smokers (Martin et al., 2003). The reduction in infant weight is not due to earlier gestation, as infants of smokers exhibit growth retardation at all gestational ages (NCI, 1999).

Birth length and head and chest circumferences are reduced in infants who are prenatally exposed to tobacco (Kline et al., 1987; Day et al., 1992; Cornelius et al., 1995). In a cohort of 1513 Caucasian women, infants of smokers are shorter and have lower ponderal indices and smaller mean upper arm circumferences than do the offspring of non-smokers (Haste et al., 1991). In a study of neonatal body composition, PTE is significantly related to reduced fat-free mass (Lindsay et al., 1997), and the authors conclude that the lower birth weight of infants exposed to prenatal smoking is primarily due to reduced fat-free mass or lean tissue.

In a MHPCD study of pregnant teenagers (Cornelius et al., 1995, 1999b), PTE is significantly related to reduced birth weight, length, and head and chest circumference. These reductions are more pronounced than the effects of PTE in a similar cohort of pregnant adult women and their offspring at birth (Day et al., 1992). The increased problems associated with younger maternal age and poorer fetal outcomes (Ketterlinus et al., 1990; Fraser et al., 1995), coupled with the high prevalence of smoking among pregnant teenagers (Cornelius et al., 1994), magnify the risks to offspring of pregnant teenagers who smoke.

The duration and timing of tobacco exposure during pregnancy are important in determining growth outcomes. Smoking only during the first trimester produces an average 55 g reduction in birth weight, whereas continuous smoking throughout pregnancy leads to a reduction in birth weight of 189 g (Cliver

et al., 1995). One study reports no relation between PTE and LBW among the offspring of women who stopped smoking early in pregnancy (MacArthur and Knox, 1988). Fox and colleagues (1990) studied the height and weight of 714 three-year-old children. The children of women who quit smoking during pregnancy are heavier and taller than those of women who do not quit. Adjustment for postpartum exposure to tobacco smoke reduces the difference in the children's weight, but has little effect on the differences in height. Another study describes no differences in head circumference among children whose mothers stopped smoking before 32 weeks of gestation compared to children whose mothers did not smoke (Vik et al., 1996).

The National Health Interview Survey describes an increased relative risk (1.6 times) of having a LBW infant among women with high levels of exposure to passive smoke (Mainous and Hueston, 1994) as have other researchers (Haddow et al., 1986; Rubin et al., 1986; Mathai et al., 1990). Martin and Bracken (1986) find that passive exposure correlates with LBW among offspring of nonsmoking women, resulting in newborns who are, on average, 24 g lighter.

The effects of PTE on growth over the longer term are less clear. At 8 years of age, there is an association between PTE and growth in exposed children (Jones et al., 1999). Children with PTE have lower bone mass at the lumbar spine and femoral neck, although not in the total body. Naeye (1981) detects a small difference in height and head circumference in exposed 7-year-old offspring, using data from the Collaborative Perinatal Project. Rantakallio (1983) shows that exposed offspring are shorter at age 14, and Fogelman and Manor (1988) report decreased height at 7, 11, and 23 years of age that is mediated by birth weight. These studies do not control for the offsprings' passive exposure to tobacco smoke or for other prenatal exposures.

In a MHPCD study of adult mothers and their offspring (Day et al., 1992) which controls for prenatal alcohol and other drug exposures and current maternal tobacco and other substance use, there is a significant inverse relation between PTE and weight, length, and head circumference at birth. At 8 months of age, only length continues to be associated with PTE. By 18 months of age, there are no associations between PTE and size of the offspring after controlling for the appropriate covariates (Day et al., 1992). Other studies also have not found growth retardation over the long term (Hardy and Mellitus, 1972; Fried and O'Connell, 1987; Vik et al., 1996). More recently, it has been argued that the association between PTE and reduced height at 6.5 and 13 months postpartum is attributable to prenatal exposure to alcohol (Jacobson et al., 1994), highlighting the importance of controlling for the effects of other drugs.

Recent reports demonstrate that PTE leads to an increase in weight at older ages. Power and Jefferis (2002) note that although PTE is associated with lower birth weight, this relation reversed by adolescence, and by age 33, exposed offspring have 1.5 greater odds of being obese. In a MHPCD cohort of teenage mothers and their offspring, a positive association is evident between PTE and increased skinfold thickness, and higher body mass index an indication that the children are overweight for their height (Cornelius et al., 2002). Similar findings have been reported by other authors (Vik et al., 1996; Fried et al., 1999; Toschke et al., 2003). Thus, the preponderance of evidence from longitudinal studies that have controlled for passive tobacco exposure and other covariates of pre- and postnatal tobacco exposure is that the growth deficits that are evident at birth are not maintained, and over the long term there appears to be an increase in weight.

The mean age at menarche is approximately 6 months earlier among the female offspring exposed to a pack or more of cigarettes per day during gestation than that of girls unexposed during pregnancy (Windham et al., 2004). Girls with both high prenatal and childhood passive exposure to tobacco have onset of menarche 4 months earlier than the girls who are not exposed at either time. Early onset of menarche is present after adjusting for alcohol, coffee, and tea exposure, mothers' age at menarche, parity, race, education, and income.

The complexity of relations between prenatal nicotine exposure and growth are demonstrated in animal models. Navarro and colleagues (1989) report effects of PTE on viability, growth, and nervous system development of the offspring at high doses of nicotine (>6 mg/kg/day). At lower doses (2 mg/kg/day), which are approximately equivalent to ≤one pack of cigarettes per day, there are changes in cell development (Navarro et al., 1989), but the overall growth of the offspring is not affected (Sobrian et al., 1995; Romero and Chen, 2004).

An animal study examined the effects of early exposure to nicotine on growth (Slotkin et al., 1993).

Using osmotic minipumps, nicotine was administered to pregnant rats three times during the pregnancy: on gestational day (G) 8 to G13, G8 to G21, and G8 to postnatal day (P) 17. Nicotine exposure early in gestation does not affect maternal weight gain or offspring growth outcomes. Continuous exposure through much of the pregnancy and into the early postnatal period (G4 to P17) causes significant growth deficits. Thus, the effects of prenatal nicotine exposure on growth occur later in gestation.

The effects of prenatal nicotine exposure occur in parallel with an increase in ornithine decarboxylase (ODC) activity in the fetus (Slotkin et al., 1986, 1993). ODC is a sensitive marker of the initial steps in polyamine formation, which regulates cellular development (Heby, 1981; Slotkin and Bartalome, 1986). Thus, the effects on growth of prenatal nicotine parallel the development of the nicotinic receptor system and at a time of increased cellular development, as reflected in ODC activity.

Central Nervous System

PTE produces neonatal central nervous system (CNS) defects, including poorer auditory orientation (Picone et al., 1982), autonomic regulation (Picone et al., 1982; Franco et al., 2000), and increased tremors and startles (Fried and Makin, 1987). Using data from the Neonatal Intensive Care Unit Network Neurobehavioral Scale, one study demonstrates dose–response relations between PTE and stress/abstinence signs and higher excitability scores in infants (Law et al., 2003). PTE is also significantly related to muscle tone abnormalities after controlling for prenatal cocaine and alcohol exposures, head circumference, and the quality of prenatal care (Dempsey et al., 2000).

In a sample of predominantly young, unmarried, and lower-SES mothers, PTE is associated with a four-point decrease on the Stanford-Binet Intelligence Scale at 3 and 4 years of age (Olds et al., 1994). Another study shows that cognitive functioning at age 3 is higher among children whose mothers quit smoking during pregnancy than in children whose mothers smoke throughout pregnancy (Sexton et al., 1990). The Ottawa Prospective Prenatal Study (OPPS) reports that lower cognitive scores are associated with PTE among 2-, 3- and 4-year-old children (Fried and Watkinson, 1988). This association between PTE and

IQ is also evident at ages 9 to 12 years (Fried, 2002) and 13 to 16 years (Fried et al., 2003) for the OPPS cohort. Another prospective study (Streissguth et al., 1989), however, shows no effect of PTE on IQ in 4-year-olds.

PTE produces deficits in visual memory and verbal learning on the Wide Range Assessment of Memory and Learning (Sheslow and Adams, 1990) among the 10-year-old offspring of adult mothers in a study from the MHPCD (Cornelius et al., 2001). These findings are significant after controlling for SES, maternal psychological status, home environment, other prenatal substance exposures, and current maternal substance use. In the OPPS cohort, when the offspring are 9 to 12 years old, PTE produces visual perceptual deficits (Fried and Watkinson, 2000). A later report on this cohort at ages 13 to 16 years shows that PTE produces poorer auditory functioning (Fried et al., 2003).

Poor language development is reported in 2- (Fried and Watkinson, 1988), 3-, and 4-year-olds with PTE (Fried and Watkinson, 1990). Among 9- to 12-year-old children in this study, PTE is negatively associated with language and reading abilities (Fried et al., 1997). Smoking during pregnancy is also significantly related to poorer performance on spelling, reading, and arithmetic assessments among 5- to 11-year-olds in another study (Batstra et al., 2003).

In animals, learning and memory deficits are seen on a number of complex cognitive behavioral tasks, including decreased performance on a two-way avoidance task (Vaglenova et al., 2004), deficits in spatial learning and memory (Sorenson et al., 1991; Yanai et al., 1992; Levin et al., 1993, 1996), operant learning (Martin and Becker, 1971), and discrimination learning (Johns et al., 1982). These impairments in cognitive function are consistent with the learning and memory deficits observed in children with PTE.

Behavior

Associations between PTE and errors of omission and commission, measures of inattention and impulsivity, respectively, are detectable in 4-year-olds (Streissguth et al., 1984). There is a significant relation between PTE and impulsivity among 6-year-olds in the OPPS cohort (Fried et al., 1992). In a MHPCD study of offspring of adult mothers, PTE significantly predicted increased errors of commission, or inattention, on a continuous performance test in 6-year-olds (Leech et al., 1999). In the MHPCD, however, the mother's current tobacco use is so highly correlated with the prenatal exposure that the effects of the prenatal and current exposures could not be separated. Kristjansson and colleagues (1989) show that PTE produces impulsivity and increases overall activity among 4- to 7-year-olds. A prospective study of 9000 children in Finland (Kotimaa et al., 2003) found a 30% higher rate in hyperactivity among 8-year-olds who had PTE than in those who did not, after controlling for gender, family structure, SES, maternal age, and prenatal alcohol exposure. In the OPPS cohort of 9- to 12-year-olds, there was a dose-dependent association between PTE and impulse control (Fried, 2002). Eskenazi and Trupin (1995), however, report that there is no association between PTE and activity levels at 5 years of age in their study.

In a case–control study of children with and without attention deficit hyperactivity disorder (ADHD), Mick and colleagues (2002) report that 6- to 7-year-old children with ADHD are 2.1 times more likely to have been exposed to tobacco during gestation, even after controlling for prenatal alcohol and drug exposures. There is a positive association between maternal smoking during pregnancy and the risk of ADHD in study children between the ages of 6 and 17 (Milberger et al., 1996). Maternal smoking during pregnancy is significantly associated with ADHD symptoms in twins, controlling for the heritability of ADHD (Thapar et al., 2003).

The effects of prenatal nicotine exposure on motor activity in laboratory animals are equivocal. Some studies show increased activity (Johns et al., 1982; Fung and Lau, 1988; Richardson and Tizabi, 1994; Tizabi et al., 1997; Ajarem and Ahmad, 1998; Thomas et al., 2000), whereas others show no effect (Martin and Becker, 1970). On the other hand, prenatal nicotine exposure is linked to abnormal development of spontaneous alternation, a behavior that is associated with cholinergic neurotransmitter function and hyperactivity (Fung, 1989; Shacka et al., 1997; Tizabi et al., 2000). Studies also show that prenatal nicotine exposure changes cellular communication (Maggi et al., 2003), electrophysiology (Ehlers et al., 1997; Slawecki et al., 2000), and neurotransmitter function (Tizabi et al., 2000) in the hippocampus, changes that could affect activity levels.

There is consistent evidence that children exposed to tobacco during pregnancy are at an increased risk for behavioral problems, specifically externalizing behaviors. In an MHPCD cohort of adult mothers, 3-year-old offspring exposed prenatally to tobacco have significantly more oppositional and aggressive behaviors and are more immature (Day et al., 2000). These effects persist after controlling for SES, factors in the current home environment, maternal psychological status, and other prenatal and current drug exposures. In another study of 3-year-olds (Orlebeke et al., 1997), there is a significant effect of PTE on externalizing behaviors, primarily higher aggression, in both genders. In a prospective study of 5-year-olds, Williams and colleagues (1998) describe a relative risk of 2.6 for externalizing behavior in children with PTE compared to unexposed children. Another study reports a significant positive association between PTE and externalizing behaviors in 5- to 11-year-olds (Batstra et al., 2003). By contrast, Weitzman and colleagues (1992) do not find significant effects of PTE on children who are exposed only during gestation. They show that children whose mothers smoked both during and after pregnancy have more behavior problems. In the latter group, the rate of behavior problems is increased by 1.17 times among those exposed to less than one pack of cigarettes per day and 2.04 times among those exposed to one pack or more per day.

These behavioral effects persist into the adolescent and adult years. Among children whose mothers smoked at least 10 cigarettes per day during pregnancy, there is a fourfold increase in the rate of prepubertal onset of conduct disorder among boys (<13 years old), a twofold increase in the rate of ADHD in girls (<13 years old), and a fivefold increase in the risk of drug dependence in girls ages 13–17 (Weissman et al., 1999). This association is significant after controlling for the other covariates of maternal smoking however, the study does not control for other prenatal substance exposures or postnatal environmental tobacco exposures. Fergusson and colleagues (1993) report that PTE is related to childhood behavior problems at 12 years of age, whereas current maternal smoking is not. PTE is predictive of higher rates of conduct disorder among 16- to 18-year-olds in this cohort (Fergusson et al., 1998). Wakschlag and colleagues (1997) also show a significant relationship between PTE and conduct disorder at ages 13–18 years. Maternal smoking during pregnancy predicts persistent criminal outcomes in adult male offspring in a Danish prospective study (Brennan et al., 1999),

and in a prospective study in Finland, maternal smoking during pregnancy is significantly associated with an increase in violent offenses among adult male offspring (Rasanen et al., 1999).

A significant relation between maternal smoking during pregnancy and conduct disorder is found in boys 12 to 17 years old (Silberg et al., 2003). When maternal conduct symptoms are considered, however, that association is no longer significant. Similar conclusions are reached by Maughan and colleagues (2004), who show that the associations between PTE and childhood conduct problems are confounded by other risks for the development of behavior problems, including parental antisocial behavior, maternal depression, SES, and genetic influences. The higher rates of antisocial behavior in children could also result from the genetic transmission of anti-social traits and/or the effects of parental traits on the pre- and postnatal environment (Wakschlag et al., 2003). In a recent twin study, although nearly half of the association between PTE and conduct problems is explained by genetic heritability, PTE has a direct effect on conduct problems even after the genetic contribution to antisocial behavior is controlled (Maughan et al., 2004).

TOBACCO USE

Direct Exposure

In an MHPCD cohort of adult women, the 10-year-old offspring exposed to half a pack or more per day during gestation have a 5.5-fold increased risk of early tobacco experimentation, controlling for other prenatal substance exposures, mothers' current smoking, and other covariates (Cornelius et al., 2000). A retrospective study reports a comparable four-fold increased risk of tobacco use among girls 9 to 17 years old prenatally exposed to tobacco (Kandel et al., 1994). In follow-up to the latter study, Griesler and colleagues (1998) confirm the link between PTE and offspring behavior problems and demonstrate that these behavior problems mediate the increased rate of smoking among the adolescent girls with PTE. In a study of young adults, those with PTE are significantly more likely to meet DSM-IV criteria for lifetime tobacco dependence, although this analysis does not control for other prenatal substance exposure or environmental exposures (Buka et al., 2003).

Abnormalities in cell development and responsivity associated with prenatal nicotine exposure may lead to permanent functional deficits when brain regions and the related circuitry mature in adolescence and adulthood (Ernst et al., 2001). An up-regulation of nicotinic acetylcholine receptors is evident among adult rats exposed to nicotine in the immediate neonatal period, a time comparable to the third trimester in humans (Slotkin et al., 1991). A recent study (Klein et al., 2003) shows that peri-adolescent male mice exposed to gestational nicotine have increased nicotine preference. Prenatal nicotine exposure leads to cholinergic hypoactivity, decreased cell numbers in the midbrain, and increased cell size in the hippocampus in adolescent animals (Abreu-Villaca et al., 2004a, 2004b). Kane and colleagues (2004) show decreased responsivity to dopamine in the nucleus accumbens, a brain region associated with reward and the reinforcing effects of drugs, in adolescent rats. Thus, there are direct biological associations that parallel the smoking behavior outcomes in human studies.

Psychological Status

There are few reports of effects of PTE on psychological symptoms. Mothers who smoked during pregnancy are significantly more likely to have toddlers who display negativity than mothers who only smoked after delivery (Brook et al., 2000). Among 16- to 18-year-olds in another cohort, PTE predicts higher rates of depression (Fergusson et al., 1998).

Recent animal studies identify links between prenatal nicotine exposure and anxiety. The open-field and elevated plus-maze tests have been used to evaluate activity, anxiety, and emotionality in animals. Prenatal nicotine is associated with poor adaptation and anxiety in a novel environment (Vaglenova et al., 2004). Female offspring with prenatal nicotine exposure do not show a normal increase in activity in an open-field test across multiple days of testing (Romero and Chen, 2004). This suggests an inability to adapt to a novel environment, learn contextual cues, or retrieve learned information on the familiarity of the testing environment. In an open-field test, male mice exposed in utero to nicotine show increased locomotor hyperactivity, whereas females have an attenuated behavioral response (Pauly et al., 2004). These animal studies demonstrate a link between prenatal nicotine exposure and anxiety, or the inability to adapt to

new environments, and they may provide an explanation for some of the mechanisms underlying the behavioral outcomes in humans.

Exposure to Environmental Tobacco Smoke

Pregnant women who live with or spend time with smokers expose their children to environmental tobacco smoke (ETS). The levels of newborn exposure correlate significantly with the levels of nicotine and cotinine in the mothers (Eliopoulos et al., 1994; Ostrea et al., 1994).

As with PTE, there are growth, cognitive, and behavioral effects from exposure to ETS during pregnancy. ETS exposure in early pregnancy (20–24 weeks) leads to a decrease in biparietal diameter, a measure useful in predicting fetal weight (Hanke et al., 2004). Kharrazi and colleagues (2004) demonstrate a dose–response relation between ETS exposure and birth weight; increasing levels of maternal cotinine are associated with declining birth weight. Other studies have also found that birth weight is negatively associated with ETS exposure (Martin and Bracken, 1986; Rebagliato et al., 1995). The relative risk for LBW is 2.17-fold higher among the offspring of nonsmoking mothers who are exposed to ETS, and the exposed infants, on average, are 24 g lighter than nonexposed infants (Martin and Bracken, 1986). Another study, however, describes effects of ETS on birth weight and preterm delivery only in infants of older mothers (Ahluwalia et al., 1997).

Makin and colleagues (1991) examined the long-term effects of ETS during gestation on 6- to 9-year-olds. They show that on tests of speech and language skills, intelligence, visual/spatial abilities and on the mother's ratings of offspring behavior, the performance of offspring of passive smokers is intermediate to that of the children of active smokers and nonsmokers.

Exposure to ETS is prevalent in the postnatal period and can negatively affect child outcomes. In one study, 71% of inner-city children of low SES lived in households with smokers (Cornelius et al., 2003). Postnatal exposure to ETS increases the risk of SIDS, asthma, respiratory problems, and otitis media (DHHS, 1999). Postnatal ETS is associated with a reduction in IQ scores in 3-year-olds (Johnson et al., 1999) and developmental language impairments in kindergartners (Tomblin et al., 1997). Note, however, that neither of these analyses controlled for the effects of PTE. ETS is also associated with decreased performance on measures of receptive vocabulary and reasoning ability in a study of 10-year-olds (Bauman et al., 1991). Among 6- to 11-year-old children of non-smoking mothers, postnatal exposure to ETS results in deficits on central auditory processing tasks (McCartney et al., 1994).

Two studies evaluate the relations between exposure to ETS and child outcomes controlling for PTE. In the MHPCD cohort of adolescent mothers and their 6-year-old children, the children's current urine cotinine levels inversely correlate with scores on a measure of receptive language controlling for PTE (Cornelius et al., 2000). Five-year-olds with postnatal ETS have significantly lower scores on the Raven Test and Peabody Picture Vocabulary Test, measures of cognitive development, and are rated as more active by their mothers, compared to children who are not exposed to ETS (Eskenazi and Trupin, 1995).

SUMMARY AND CONCLUSIONS

There are significant effects of PTE on the growth, cognitive development, and behavior of exposed children. Children with PTE are smaller at birth, and recent research reports suggest that these children have a greater risk of obesity as they reach adolescence. Cognitive deficits in reasoning and memory have been described and the exposed children do less well on tests of language, reading, and vocabulary than nonexposed children. PTE predicts higher rates of activity, inattention, and impulsivity. Increases in oppositional and aggressive behavior and higher rates of delinquency and criminality in adolescence and adulthood have been found in a number of studies. In general, these outcomes are consistent whether the mother is a smoker or the exposure to the mother is through ETS. In addition, there appear to be differential effects that depend on duration and pattern of exposure and on whether the offspring are exposed only during gestation, during gestation and after birth, or only after birth. For most of the identified outcomes of PTE, there are parallel data from laboratory studies on animals that lend credence to the human data.

Women who use tobacco during pregnancy are often different from women who do not in many ways, including in their SES, race/ethnicity, use of other substances, and psychiatric disorders. In addition, even women who do not smoke tobacco can be exposed to ETS, resulting in exposure to the fetus. Many of the studies currently in the literature fail to control for these significant covariates of tobacco use or for ETS, making definitive conclusions about the effects of exposure more difficult. There are several studies, however, that can assess the competing effects of other substance use during pregnancy as well as the role of the other covariates and ETS. The general conclusions are validated by the results of these studies.

Characteristics of the rearing environment are also significantly associated with both PTE and ETS, as well as with the outcomes in the offspring. Women who smoke during pregnancy are highly likely to smoke after delivery. This means that children who are prenatally exposed to tobacco are at higher risk for continued exposure due to ETS exposure from the mother and/or other household smokers. Heredity is another important factor to consider in the interpretation of these findings. As the mother and child share genetic components, they share factors that might predict their response to exposure or could increase vulnerability for specific outcomes. Studies that have controlled for role of heredity, nonetheless, find independent effects of PTE.

For all of the above reasons, it is difficult to enumerate definitively the effects of PTE whether it be from a smoking mother or from exposure to ETS. Nevertheless, it is imperative that the short- and long-term effects of both prenatal and postnatal exposure to tobacco on the growth and neurobehavioral development of children be identified. Although many of the effects of PTE are subtle, they have important effects on the long-term functioning of the exposed offspring.

Future studies must evaluate the separate and combined effects of exposure to tobacco and other substance exposures during gestation. It is also critical to measure the other factors that coexist with tobacco use, as well as to evaluate the co-occurrence of PTE and ETS both during pregnancy and in the postpartum period. Studies that measure all of these factors across time allows a more specific definition of the effects of prenatal and postnatal tobacco exposure on the offspring.

Abbreviations

ADHD   Attention Deficit Hyperactivity Disorder

CNS   central nervous system

ETS   environmental tobacco smoke

G   gestational day

LBW   low birth weight

MHPCD   Maternal Health Practices and Child Development

ODC   ornithine decarboxylase

OPPS   Ottawa Prospective Prenatal Study

P   postnatal day

PTE   prenatal tobacco exposure

SES   socioeconomic status

SIDS   sudden infant death syndrome

ACKNOWLEDGMENTS This work was supported by the National Institute of Alcohol Abuse and Alcoholism (JAW, NLD), the National Institute of Drug Abuse (NLD, MDC), and the National Institute of Child Health and Human Development (NLD).

References

Abreu-Villaca Y, Seidler F, Slotkin T (2004a) Does prenatal nicotine exposure sensitize the brain to nicotine-induced neurotoxicity in adolescence? Neuropsychopharmacology 29:1440–1450.

Abreu-Villaca Y, Seidler FJ, Tate CA, Cousins MM, Slotkin TA (2004b) Prenatal nicotine exposure alters the response to nicotine administration in adolescence: effects on cholinergic systems during exposure and withdrawal. Neuropsychopharmacology 29:879–890.

Ahluwalia IB, Grummer-Strawn L, Scanlon SK (1997) Exposure to environmental tobacco smoke and birth outcome: Increased effects on pregnant women aged 30 years of older. Am J Epidemiol 146:42–47.

Ajarem JS, Ahmad M (1998) Prenatal nicotine exposure modifies behavior of mice through early development. Pharmacol Biochem Behav 59:313–318.

Batstra L, Neeleman J, Haddars-Algra M (2003) Can breast feeding modify the adverse effects of smoking during pregnancy on the child's cognitive development? J Epidemiol Commun Health 57: 403–404.

Bauman K, Flewelling R, LaPrelle J (1991) Parental cigarette smoking and cognitive performance of children. Health Psychol 10:282–288.

Brennan P, Grekin E, Mednick S (1999) Maternal smoking during pregnancy and adult male criminal outcomes. Arch Gen Psychiatry 56:215–219.

Brook J, Brook D, Whiteman M (2000) The influence of maternal smoking during pregnancy on the toddler's negativity. Arch Pediatr Adolesc Med 154: 381–385.

Buka S, Shenassa E, Niaura R (2003) Elevated risk of tobacco dependence among offspring of mothers who smoked ruing pregnancy: a 30-year prospective study. Am J Psychiatry 160:1978–1984.

Bulterys MG, Greenland S, Kraus JF (1990) Chronic fetal hypoxia and sudden infant death syndrome: interaction between maternal smoking and low hematocrit during pregnancy. Pediatrics 86:535–540.

Centers for Disease Control and Prevention (CDC) (2002) Prevalence of selected maternal behaviors and experiences, pregnancy risk assessment monitoring system. MMWR Morb Mortal Wkly Rep 51(SS-2).

Cliver SP, Goldenberg RL, Cutter GR, Hoffman HJ, Davis RO, Nelson KG (1995) The effect of cigarette smoking on neonatal anthropometric measurements. Obstet Gynecol 85:625–630.

Cnattingius S (2004) The epidemiology of smoking during pregnancy: smoking prevalence, maternal characteristics, and pregnancy outcomes. Nicotine Tob Res 6:125–140.

Cnattingius S, Haglund B (1997) Decreasing smoking prevalence during pregnancy in Sweden: the effect on small-for-gestational-age births. Am J Public Health 87:410–413.

Cnattingius S, Haglund B, Meirik L (1988) Cigarette smoking as risk factor for late fetal and early neonatal death. BMJ 297:258–261.

Cornelius M, Day N, Richardson G, Taylor P (1999a) Epidemiology of substance abuse during pregnancy. In: Ott P, Tarter R, Ammerman R (eds). *Sourcebook on Substance Abuse: Etiology, Epidemiology, Assessment and Treatment.* Allyn and Bacon, Needham Heights, MA, pp 1–13.

Cornelius M, Geva D, Day N (1994) Patterns and covariates of tobacco use in a recent sample of pregnant teenagers. J Adolesc Health 15:528–535.

Cornelius M, Goldschmidt L, Day N, Larkby C (2002) Prenatal substance use among pregnant teenagers: a six-year follow-up of effects on offspring growth. Neurotoxicol Teratol 24:703–710.

Cornelius M, Goldschmidt L, Dempsey D (2003) Environmental tobacco smoke exposure in low income six-year-olds: parent-report and urine cotinine measures. Nicotine Tob Res 5:147–154.

Cornelius M, Goldschmidt L, Taylor P, Day N (1999b) Prenatal alcohol use among teenagers: effects on neonatal outcomes. Alcohol Clin Exp Res 23: 1238 –1244.

Cornelius M, Leech S, Goldschmidt L (2004) Characteristics of persistent smoking among pregnant teenagers followed to young adulthood. Nicotine Tob Res 6:1–11.

Cornelius M, Leech S, Goldschmidt L, Lebow H, Day N (2000) Prenatal tobacco exposure: is it a risk factor in preadolescent tobacco experimentation? Nicotine Tob Res 2:45–52.

Cornelius M, Ryan C, Day N, Goldschmidt L, Willford J (2001) Prenatal tobacco effects on neuropsychological outcomes among preadolescents. Dev Behav Pediatr 22:217–225.

Cornelius M, Taylor P, Geva D (1995) Prenatal tobacco and marijuana use among adolescents: effects on offspring gestational age, growth and morphology. Pediatrics 95:438–443.

Day N, Cornelius M, Goldschmidt L (1992) The effects of prenatal tobacco and marijuana use on offspring growth from birth through age 3 years. Neurotoxicol Teratol 14:407–414.

Day N, Richardson G, Goldschmidt L, Cornelius M (2000) Prenatal tobacco exposure and preschooler behavior. J Behav Dev Pediatr 21:180–188.

Dempsey D, Hajnal B, Jacobson S, Jones R, Ferriero D (2000) Tone abnormalities are associated with maternal cigarette smoking during pregnancy in in utero cocaine-exposed infants. Pediatrics 106: 79–85.

Department of Health and Human Services (USDHHS) (1980) The Health Consequences of Smoking for Women: A Report of the Surgeon General. HHS 396. Public Health Service. Office of the Surgeon General, Rockville, MD.

Department of Health and Human Services (USDHHS) (1999) Health Effects of Exposure to Environmental Tobacco Smoke: The Report of the California Environmental Protection Agency. Smoking and Control Monograph No. 10, NIH #99-4645. National Cancer Institute, Bethesda, MD.

Department of Health and Human Services (USDHHS) (2001) Women and Smoking: A Report of the Surgeon General. Office of the Surgeon General, Washingon, DC.

DiFranza J, Lew R (1995) Effect of maternal cigarette smoking on pregnancy complications and sudden infant death syndrome. J Family Pract 40: 385–394.

Dwyer T, Ponsonby AL, Couper D (1999) Tobacco smoke exposure at one month of age and subset risk of SIDS—a prospective study. Am J Epidemiol 149: 603–606.

Ebrahim SF, Floyd R, Merritt RK, Decoufle P, Holtzman D (2000) Trends in pregnancy-related smoking rates in the United States, 1987–1996. JAMA 283:361–366.

Ehlers CL, Somes C, Thomas J, Riley EP (1997) Effects of neonatal exposure to nicotine on electrophysiological parameters in adult rats. Pharmacol Biochem Behav 58:713–720.

Eliopoulos C, Klein J, Phan MK, Knie B, Greewald M, Chitayat D, Koren G (1994) Hair concentrations of

nicotine and cotinine in women and their newborn infants. JAMA 271:621–623.

Ernst M, Moolchan E, Robinson M (2001) Behavioral and neural consequences of prenatal exposure to nicotine. J Am Acad Child Adolesc Psychiatry 40: 630–641.

Eskenazi B, Trupin L (1995) Passive and active maternal smoking during pregnancy as measured by serum cotinine and postnatal smoke exposure. II. Effect on neurodevelopment at age 5 years. Am J Epidemiol 142:S19–S29.

Fergusson D, Horwood L, Lynskey M (1993) Maternal smoking before and after pregnancy: effects on behavioral outcomes in middle childhood. Pediatrics 92:815–822.

Fergusson D, Woodward L, Horwood L (1998) Maternal smoking during pregnancy and psychiatric adjustment in late adolescence. Arch Gen Psychiatry 55: 721–727.

Floyd R, Rimer B, Giovino G, Mullen P, Sullivan S (1993) A review of smoking in pregnancy: effects on pregnancy outcomes and cessation efforts. Annu Rev Public Health 14:379–411.

Fogelman K, Manor O (1988) Smoking in pregnancy and development into early adulthood. BMJ 297: 1233–1236.

Fox N, Sexton M, Hebel J (1990) Prenatal exposure to tobacco: I. Effects on physical growth at age three. Int J Epidemiol 19:66–71.

Franco P, Chabanski S, Szliwowksi H, Dramaix M, Kahn A (2000) Influence of maternal smoking on autonomic nervous system in healthy infants. Pediatric Res 47:215–220.

Fraser A, Brockert J, Ward R (1995) Association of young maternal age with adverse reproductive outcomes. N Engl J Med 332:1113–1117.

Fried PA (2002) Adolescents prenatally exposed to marijuana: examination facets of complex behaviors and comparisons with the influence of in utero cigarettes. J Clin Pharmacol 42:97S–102S.

Fried P, Makin J (1987) Neonatal behavioural correlates of prenatal exposure to marihuana, cigarettes and alcohol in a low risk population. Neurotoxicol Teratol 9:1–7.

Fried PA, O'Connell CM (1987) A comparison of the effects of prenatal exposure to tobacco, alcohol, annabis and caffeine on birth size and subsequent growth. Neurotoxicol Teratol 9:79–85.

Fried P, Watkinson B (1998) 2- and 24-month neurobehavioral follow-up of children prenatally exposed to marihuana, cigarettes and alcohol. Neurotoxicol Teratol 10:305–313.

Fried PA, Watkinson B (1990) 36- and 48-month neurobehavioral follow-up of children prenatally exposed to marijuana, cigarettes and alcohol. J Dev Behav Pediatr 11:49–58.

Fried PA, Watkinson B (2000) Visuoperceptual functioning differs in 9- to 12-year olds prenatally exposed to cigarettes and marihuana. Neurotoxicol Teratol 22:11–20.

Fried P, Watkinson B, Gray R (1992) A follow-up study of attentional behavior in 6-year-old children exposed prenatally to marihuana, cigarettes, and alcohol. Neurotoxicol Teratol 14:299–311.

Fried PA, Watkinson B, Gray R (1999) Growth from birth to early adolescence in offspring prenatally exposed to cigarettes and marijuana. Neurotoxicol Teratol 21:513–525.

Fried PA, Watkinson B, Gray R (2003) Differential effects on cognitive functioning in 13- to 16-year-olds prenatally exposed to cigarettes and marijuana. Neurotoxicol Teratol 25:427–436.

Fried P, Watkinson B, Siegel L (1997) Reading and language in 9- to 12-year olds prenatally exposed to cigarettes and marijuana. Neurotoxicol Teratol 19:171–183.

Fung YK (1989) Postnatal effects of maternal nicotine exposure on the striatal dopaminergic system in rats. J Pharm Pharmacol 41:576–578.

Fung YK, Lau YS (1988) Receptor mechanisms of nicotine-induced locomotor hyperactivity in chronic nicotine-treated rats. Eur J Pharmacol 152:263–271.

Griesler P, Kandel D, Davies M (1998) Maternal smoking in pregnancy, child behavior problems and adolescent smoking. J Res Adolesc 8:159–185.

Haddow J, Palmaki G, Knight G (1986) Use of cotinine to assess the accuracy of self-reported non-smoking. BMJ 293:1306–1309.

Hajek P, West R, Lee A, Foulds J, Owen L, Eiser J R, Main N (2001) Randomized controlled trial of a midwife-delivered brief smoking cessation intervention in pregnancy. Addiction 96:485–494.

Hanke W, Sobala W, Kalinka J (2004) Environmental tobacco smoke exposure among pregnant women: impact on fetal biometry at 20–24 weeks of gestation and newborn child's birth weight. Int Arch Occup Environ Health 77:47–52.

Hardy J, Mellitus E (1972) Does maternal smoking during pregnancy have a long-term effect on the child? Lancet 2:1332–1336.

Haste F, Brooke O, Anderson H, Bland J, Shaw A, Griffin J, Peacock J (1990) Nutrient intakes during pregnancy: observations on the influence of smoking and social class. Am J Clin Nutrition 51:29–36.

Haste FM, Anderson HR, Brooke OG, Bland JM, Peacock JL (1991) The effects of smoking and drinking on the anthropometric measurements of neonates. Paediatr Perinat Epidemiol 5:83–92.

Heby O (1981) Role of polyamines in the control of cell proliferation and differentiation. Differentiation 19:1–20.

Jacobson J, Jacobson S, Sokol R (1994) Effects of prenatal exposure to alcohol, smoking and illicit drugs on postpartum somatic growth. Alcohol Clin Exp Res 18:317–323.

Johns JM, Louis TM, Becker RF, Means LW (1982) Behavioral effects of prenatal exposure to nicotine in guinea pigs. Neurotoxicol Teratol 4:365–369.

Johnson DL, Swank PR, Baldwin CD, McCormick D (1999) Adult smoking in the home environment and children's IQ. Psychol Rep 84:149–154.

Jones G, Riley M, Dwyer T (1999) Maternal smoking during pregnancy, growth, and bone mass in prepubertal children. J Bone Mineral Res 14:146–151.

Kahn R, Certain L, Whitaker R (2002) A reexamination of smoking before, during, and after pregnancy. Am J Public Health 92:1801–1808.

Kandel D, Wu P, Davies M (1994) Maternal smoking during pregnancy and smoking by adolescent daughters. Am J Public Health 84:1407–1413.

Kane V, Fu Y, Matta S, Sharp B (2004) Gestational nicotine exposure attenuates nicotine-stimulated dopamine release in the nucleus accumbens shell of adolescent Lewis rats. J Pharmacol Exp Ther 308:521–528.

Ketterlinus R, Henderson S, Lamb M (1990) Maternal age, sociodemographics, prenatal health and behavior: influences on neonatal risk status. J Adolesc Health Care 11:423–331.

Kharrazi M, DeLorenze GN, Kaufman FL, Eskenazi B, Bernert JT, Graham S, Pearl M, Pirkle J (2004) Environmental tobacco smoke and pregnancy outcomes. Epidemiology 15:660–670.

Klein LC, Stine MM, Pfaff DW, Vandenbergh DJ (2003) Maternal nicotine exposure increases nicotine preference in periadolescent male but not female C57B1/6J mice. Nicotine Tob Res 5:117–124.

Kleinman JC, Pierre MB, Madans JH, Land GH, Schramm WF (1988) The effects of maternal smoking on fetal and infant mortality. Am J Epidemiol 127:274–282.

Kline J, Stein Z, Hutzler M (1987) Cigarettes, alcohol and marijuana: varying associations in birthweight. Int J Epidemiol 16:44–51.

Klonoff-Cohen H, Edelstein S, Sefkowitz I, Srinivasan I, Kaegi D, Chang J, Wiley K (1995) The effect of passive smoking and tobacco exposure through breast milk on sudden infant death syndrome. JAMA 273:795–798.

Kotimaa A, Moilanen I, Taanila A, Ebeling H, Smalley S, McGough J, Hartikainen A, Jarvelin M (2003) Maternal smoking and hyperactivity in 8-year-old children. J Am Acad Child Adolesc Psychiatry 42: 826–833.

Kristjansson E, Fried P, Watkinson B (1989) Maternal smoking during pregnancy affects children's vigilance performance. Drug Alcohol Depend 24: 11–19.

Lambers D, Clark K (1996) The maternal and fetal physiologic effects of nicotine. Semin Perinatol 290: 115–126.

Law KL, Stroud LR, LaGasse LL, Niaura R, Liu J, Lester BM (2003) Smoking during pregnancy and newborn neurobehavior. Pediatrics 111:1318–1323.

LeClere FB, Wilson JB (1997) Smoking behavior of recent mothers, 18–44 years of age, before and after pregnancy: United States 1990. Ad Data Vital Health Stat #288. National Center for Health Statistics, Hyattsville, MD.

Leech S, Richardson G, Goldschmidt L, Day N (1999) Prenatal substance exposure: effects on attention and impulsivity of 6-year-olds. Neurotoxicol Teratol 21:109–118.

Levin ED, Briggs SJ, Christopher NC, Rose JE (1993) Prenatal nicotine exposure and cognitive performance in rats. Neurotoxicol Teratol 15: 251–260.

Levin ED, Wilkerson A, Jones JP, Christopher NC, Briggs SJ (1996) Prenatal nicotine effects on memory in rats: pharmacological and behavioral challenges. Dev Brain Res 97:207–215.

Lindsay C, Thomas A, Catalano P (1997) The effect of smoking tobacco on neonatal body composition. Am J Obstet Gynecol 177:1124–1128.

Luck W, Nau H, Hansen R, Steldinger R (1985) Extent of nicotine and cotinine transfer to the human fetus, placenta and amniotic fluid of smoking mothers. Dev Pharmacol Ther 8:384–395.

MacArthur C, Knox EG (1988) Smoking in pregnancy: effects of stopping at different stages. Br J Obstet Gynecol 95:551–555.

Maggi L, Le Magueresse C, Changeux JP, Cherubini E (2003) Nicotine activates immature "silent" connections in the developing hippocampus. Proc Natl Acad Sci USA 100:2059–2064.

Mainous A, Hueston W (1994) Passive smoke and low birth weight. Evidence of a threshold effect. Arch Family Med 3:875–878.

Makin J, Fried P, Watkinson B (1991) A comparison of active and passive smoking during pregnancy: long-term effects. Neurotoxicol Teratol 13:5–12.

Martin JA, Hamilton BE, Sutton PD, Ventura SJ, Menacker F, Munson ML (2003) Births: final data for 2002. Natl Vital Stat Rept 52:1–116.

Martin JC, Becker RF (1970) The effects of nicotine administration *in utero* upon activity in the rat. Psychol Sci 19:59–60.

Martin JC, Becker RF (1971) The effects of maternal nicotine absorption or hypoxic episodes upon appetitive behavior of rat offspring. Dev Psychobiol 4:133–147.

Martin T, Bracken M (1986) Association of low birthweight with passive smoke exposure in pregnancy. Am J Epidemiol 124:633–642.

Matthai M, Skinner A, Lawton K, Weindling A (1990) Maternal smoking, urinary cotinine levels and birthweight. Aust NZJ Obstet Gynecol 30:33–36.

Maughan B, Taylor A, Caspi A, Moffitt T (2004) Prenatal smoking and early childhood conduct problems. Arch Gen Psychiatry 61:836–843.

McCartney J, Fried P, Watkinson B (1994) Central auditory processing in school-age children prenatally exposed to cigarette smoke. Neurotoxicol Teratol 16:269–276.

Mick E, Biederman J, Faraone SV, Sayer J, Kleinman, S (2002) Case–control study of attention-deficit hyperactivity disorder and maternal smoking, alcohol use, and drug use during pregnancy. J Am Acad Child Adolesc Psychiatry 41:378–385.

Milberger S, Biederman J, Faraone S, Chen L, Jones J (1996) Is maternal smoking during pregnancy a risk factor for attention deficit hyperactivity disorder in children? Am J Psychiatry 153:1138–1142.

Mullen PD, Richardson MA, Quinn VP, Ershoff DH (1997) Postpartum return to smoking: who is at risk and when. Am J Health Promot 11:323–330.

Naeye R (1981) Influence of maternal cigarette smoking during pregnancy on fetal and childhood growth. Obstet Gynecol 57:18–21.

National Cancer Institute (NCI) (1999) Health effects of exposure to environmental tobacco smoke: the report of the California Environmental Protection Agency. Smoking and Tobacco Control Monograph no. 10. NIH Pub # 9904645. National Cancer Institute, Bethesda, MD.

National Institute on Drug Abuse (NIDA) (1996) National pregnancy and health survey. NIH Pub #96-3819. National Institute of Drug Abuse, Rockville, MD.

Navarro HA, Seidler FJ, Schwartz RD, Baker FE, Dobbins SS, Slotkin TA (1989) Prenatal exposure to nicotine impairs nervous system development at a dose which does not affect viability or growth. Brain Res Bull 23:187–192.

Nordstrom ML, Cnattingius S (1994) Smoking habits and birthweights in two successive births in Sweden. Early Hum Dev 37:195–204.

Olds D, Henderson C, Tatelbaum R (1994) Intellectual impairment in children of women who smoke cigarettes during pregnancy. Pediatrics 93:221–227.

Orlebeke J, Knol D, Verhulst F (1997) Increase in child behavior problems resulting from maternal smoking during pregnancy. Arch Environ Health 52:317–321.

Ostrea EM, Knapp DK, Romero A, Montes M, Ostrea AR (1994) Meconium analysis to assess fetal exposure to nicotine by active and passive manternal smoking. J Pediatr 124:471–476.

Pauly JR, Sparks JA, Hauser KF, Pauly TH (2004) *In utero* nicotine exposure causes persistent, gender-dependent changes in locomotor activity and sensitivity to nicotine in C57Bl/6 mice. Int J Dev Neurosci 22:329–337.

Persson P, Grennert L, Gennser G (1978) A study of smoking and pregnancy with special reference to fetal growth. Acta Obstet Gynecol Scand 78:33–39.

Picone T, Allen L, Olsen P (1982) Pregnancy outcome in North American women. II. Effects of diet, cigarette smoking, stress, and weight gain on placentas, and on neonatal physical and behavioral characteristics. Am J Clin Nutrition 36:1214–1224.

Power C, Jefferis B (2002) Fetal environment and subsequent obesity: a study of maternal smoking. Int J Epidemiol 31:413–419.

Rantakallio P (1983) Family background to and personal characteristics underlying teenage smoking. Scand J Social Med 11:17–22.

Rasanen P, Hakko H, Isohanni M, Hodgins S, Jarvelin M, Tihonen J (1999) Maternal smoking during pregnancy and risk of criminal behavior among adult male offspring in Northern Finland 1966 birth cohort. Am J Psychiatry 156:857–862.

Rebagliato M, Florey C, du V, Bolumar F (1995) Exposure to environmental tobacco smoke in nonsmoking pregnant women in relation to birth weight. Am J Epidemiol 142:531–537.

Richardson SA, Tizabi Y (1994) Hyperactivity in the offspring of nicotine-treated rats: role of the mesolimbic and nigrostriatal dopaminergic pathways. Pharmacol Biochem Behav 47:331–337.

Romero R, Chen WJ (2004) Gender-related response in open-field activity following developmental nicotine exposure in rats. Pharmacol Biochem Behav 78:675–681.

Rubin D, Krasilnikoff P, Leventhal J, Weile B, Berget A (1986) Effects of passive smoking on birth weight. Lancet 2:415–417.

Schacka J, Fennell O, Robinson S (1997) Prenatal nicotine sex-dependently alters agonist-induced locomotion and stereotypy. Neurotoxicol Teratol 19:467–476.

Sexton M, Fox N, Hebel J (1990) Prenatal exposure to tobacco: II. Effects on cognitive function at age three. Int J Epidemiol 19:72–77.

Sheslow D, Adams W (1990) *Manual for the Wide Range Assessment of Memory and Learning.* Jastak Associates, Wilmington, DE.

Silberg J, Parr T, Neale M, Rutter M, Angold A, Eaves L (2003) Maternal smoking during prgnancy and risk to boys' conduct disturbance: an examination of the causal hypothesis. Biol Psychol 53:130–135.

Singleton EG, Harrell JP, Kelly LM (1986) Racial differentials in the impact of maternal cigarette smoking during pregnancy on fetal development and mortality: concerns for black psychologists. J Black Psychol 12:71–83.

Slawecki CJ, Thomas JD, Riley EP, Ehlers CL (2000) Neonatal nicotine exposure alters hippocampal EEG and event-related potentials (ERPs) in rats. Pharmacol Biochem Behav 65:711–718.

Slotkin TA, Bartolome J (1986) Role of ornithine decarboxylase and the polyamines in nervous system development: a review. Brain Res Bull 17:307–320.

Slotkin TA, Greer N, Faust J, Cho H, Seidler F (1986) Effects of maternal nicotine injections on brain development in the rat: ornithine decarboxylase activity, nucleic acids and proteins in discrete brain regions. Brain Res Bull 17:41–50.

Slotkin TA, Lappi S, Seidler F (1993) Impact of nicotine exposure on development of rat brain regions: critical sensitive periods or effects of withdrawal? Brain Res Bull 31:319–328.

Slotkin TA, Lappi SE, Tayyeb MI, Seidler FJ (1991) Chronic prenatal nicotine exposure sensitizes rat brain to acute postnatal nicotine challenge as assessed with ornithine decarboxylase. Life Sci 49:665–670.

Sobrian SK, Ali SF, Slikker W, Holson RR (1995) Interactive effects of prenatal cocaine and nicotine exposure on maternal toxicity, postnatal development and behavior in the rat. Mol Neurobiol 11:121–143.

Sorenson CA, Raskin LA, Suh Y (1991) The effects of prenatal nicotine on radial-arm maze performance in rats. Pharmacol Biochem Behav 40:991–993.

Stillman R, Rosenberg M, Sach B (1986) Smoking and reproduction. Fertil Steril 46:545–566.

Streissguth A, Martin D, Barr H (1984) Intrauterine alcohol and nicotine exposure: attention and reaction time in 4-year-old children. Dev Psychol 20:533–541.

Streissguth AP, Sampson PD, Barr HM (1989) Neurobehavioral dose–response effects of prenatal alcohol exposure in humans from infancy to adulthood. Ann NY Acad Sci 562:145–158.

Thapar A, Fowler T, Rice F, Scourfield J, Van den Bree M, Thomas H, Harold G, Hay D (2003) Maternal smoking during pregnancy and attention deficit hyperactivity disorder symptoms in offspring. Am J Psychiatry 160:1985–1989.

Thomas J, Garrison M, Slawecki C, Ehlers C, Riley E (2000) Nicotine exposure during the neonatal brain growth spurt produces hyperactivity in preweanling rats. Neurotoxicol Teratol 22:695–701.

Tizabi Y, Popke E, Rahman M, Nespor S, Grunberg N (1997) Hyperactivity induced by prenatal nicotine exposure is associated with an increase in cortical nicotinic receptors. Pharmacol Biochem Behav 58: 141–146.

Tizabi Y, Russel L, Nspor S, Perry D, Grunberg N (2000) Prenatal nicotine exposure: effects on locomotor activity and central binding in rats. Pharmacol Biochem Behav 66:495–500.

Tomblin J, Smith E, Zhang X (1997) Epidemiology of specific language impairment: prenatal and perinatal risk factors. J Commun Disord 30:325–344.

Toschke AM, Montgomery SM, Pfeiffer U, von Kries R (2003) Early intrauterine exposure to tobacco-inhaled products and obesity. Am J Epidemiol 158: 1068–1074.

Vaglenova J, Birru S, Pandiella N, Breese C (2004) An assessment of the long-term developmental and behavioral teratogenicity of prenatal nicotine exposure. Behav Brain Res 150:159–170.

Vik T, Jacobsen G, Vatten L, Bakketeig L (1996) Pre- and post-natal growth in children of women who smoked in pregnancy. Early Hum Dev 45: 245–255.

Wakschlag L, Lahey B, Loeber, R, Green S, Gordon R, Leventhal B (1997) Maternal smoking during pregnancy and the risk of conduct disorder in young boys. Arch Gen Psychiatry 54:670–676.

Wakschlag LS, Pickett KE, Middlecamp MK, Walton LL, Tenzer P, Leventhal BL (2003) Pregnant smokers who quit, pregnant smokers who don't: does history of problem behavior make a difference? Social Sci Med 56:2449–2460.

Weissman M, Warner V, Wickramaratne P, Kandel D (1999) Maternal smoking during pregnancy and psychopathology in offspring followed to adulthood. J Am Acad Child Adolesc Psychiatry 38: 892–899.

Weitzman M, Gortmaker S, Sobol A (1992) Maternal smoking and behavior problems of children. Pediatrics 90:342–349.

Williams GM, O'Callaghan M, Najman JM, Bor W, Andersen MJ, Richards D, Chunley U (1998) Maternal cigarette smoking and child psychiatric morbidity: a longitudinal study. Pediatrics 102:e11.

Windham GC, Bottomley C, Birner C, Fenster L (2004) Age at menarche in relation to maternal use of tobacco, alcohol, coffee, and tea during pregnancy. Am J Epidemiol 159:862–871.

Wisborg K, Henriksen TB, Hedegaard M, Secher NJ (1996) Smoking among pregnant women and the significance of socio-demographic factors on smoking cessation. Ugeskrift Laeger 158: 3784–3788.

Yanai J, Pick CG, Rogel-Fuchs Y, Zahalka EA (1992) Alterations in hippocampal cholinergic receptors and hippocampal behaviors after early exposure to nicotine. Brain Res Bull 29:363–368.

Yerushalmy J (1971) The relationship of parent's cigarette smoking to outcome of pregnancy complications as to the problem of inferring causation from observed associations. Am J Epidemiol 93:443–456.

20

Prenatal Nicotine Exposure and Animal Behavior

Brenda M. Elliott
Neil E. Grunberg

Cigarette smoking affects prenatal brain development and subsequent behavior. Mothers who smoke cigarettes during pregnancy are more likely than nonsmoking mothers to bear children who are hyperactive, impulsive, and have impairments in learning, memory, and attention (Naeye, 1992; DiFranza and Lew, 1995; Eskenazi and Trupin, 1995; Ernst et al., 2001; Thapar et al., 2003). Children exposed to tobacco smoke during pregnancy are also more likely to smoke cigarettes later in life (Kandel et al., 1994; Abreu-Villaca et al., 2004a; 2004b). These effects are in addition to the retarded fetal growth, premature births, stillbirths, and increased neonatal mortality associated with cigarette smoking during pregnancy (Butler and Goldstein, 1973; Denson et al., 1975; Kristjansson et al., 1989; Buka et al., 2003).

Although cigarettes contain roughly 400 chemicals and cigarette smoke contains >4000 chemicals, nicotine is the most widely studied chemical. Various properties of nicotine make it a neurotoxin. Nicotine crosses the blood–brain barrier, binds to specific receptors in the brain, and affects many behaviors, including addiction, appetite, stress responses, and attention (Grunberg, 1982, 1985; Luck and Nau, 1985; Levin, 1992; Scheufele et al., 2000; Trauth et al., 2000; Slawecki and Ehlers, 2002; Slotkin, 2002; Slawecki et al, 2003; Faraday et al, 2003). Animal models of nicotine and tobacco exposure provide valuable information on the behavioral effects of prenatal smoking.

The present chapter discusses knowledge gained from studies of the effects of prenatal nicotine and tobacco exposure on the behavior and development of the offspring. It focuses on rodents because most of the research on the effects of prenatal nicotine exposure has been done in these animals and the findings parallel research on humans.

VALUE OF ANIMAL MODELS TO ASSESS THE EFFECTS OF PRENATAL SMOKING

Animals have been studied for centuries to learn about anatomy and physiology. In ancient Greece, Galen dissected goats, pigs, and monkeys to explore the structure of the body and to test specific hypotheses about how the body worked (Nutton, 2002). During the eighteenth and nineteenth centuries, animal experimentation contributed to our knowledge of physiology, pharmacology, bacteriology, and immunology (Nutton, 2002).

Darwin's landmark *Origin of the Species* (1859) included several concepts that further expanded the study of animals: (1) the continuity of species, (2) natural selection, and (3) spontaneous mutation. Darwin argued that the senses and intuitions, various emotions, and aspects of cognition such as memory, attention, curiosity, and reason (attributes once thought to be unique to humans) might be found in a well-developed form in lower animals. Darwin's compelling arguments led to the study of animal biology and behavior to learn more about humans. Animals were used to study attention, learning, emotions, and social interaction.

Darwin's argument that there is a continuity of species in the animal kingdom provides the rationale for studying infrahuman species to learn about human behavior. Ethologists, including Lorenz and Tinbergen, observed the behavior of animals in their natural habitats and provided compelling evidence that supported Darwin's ideas (Dewsbury, 2003). Pavlov, Thorndike, and Skinner separately examined animal behavior in controlled laboratory settings in an attempt to understand human learning and provided empirical evidence that the study of animal behavior is relevant to the human condition.

Pavlov (1927) developed the concept of classical conditioning on the basis of his study of gastric reflexes in dogs (Kimble and Schlesinger, 1985). He observed that dogs respond to cues other than food, cues that had been previously associated with food. He labeled these new responses *conditioned* (or conditional) responses, to distinguish them from the naturally occurring responses, that occur without prior training. Classical conditioning is a pillar of learning principles and applies to humans as well as to animals.

Around the same time that Pavlov was experimenting with dogs, Thorndike (1911) was studying cats to explore how animals learn tricks. As part of his investigation, Thorndike constructed the puzzle box, a box containing several levers and handles from which a cat must learn how to escape. From careful observations of the cats' behaviors, Thorndike proposed the Law of Effect. This behavioral law states that an animal will repeat an action that brings desirable consequences, but it will not repeat an action that brings undesirable consequences. This law also holds for humans.

Skinner studied the behavior of rats and pigeons and expanded Thorndike's findings (Skinner, 1935). Building on the concept that animals operate on their environment to obtain desirable consequences or to avoid negative consequences, Skinner proposed the concept of operant conditioning. Specifically, Skinner found that the frequency of a given behavior could be increased by following the occurrence of the behavior with positive consequences (reinforcement) or decreased by following the behavior with negative consequences (punishment). Together, the studies by Pavlov, Thorndike, and Skinner laid the groundwork for modern-day theories of learning and provide convincing evidence that animal models are a useful representation of human behavioral and psychological processes.

Animal studies are valuable for assessing drug effects, including the effects of nicotine on development and behavior. Animal models allow investigators to evaluate and manipulate separately the components of tobacco smoking (e.g., nicotine) that might affect prenatal development. Investigators can control aspects of drug delivery (e.g., dosage, timing of exposure, duration of exposure, route of administration, and environmental context). In addition, they can isolate variables to focus on nicotine and avoid variables, such as prenatal care, socioeconomic status, nutrition, or use of other substances, that confound human studies. Animal models offer unique advantages for studying drug effects, including those of nicotine, on behavior.

ANIMAL MODELS OF NICOTINE AND TOBACCO ADMINISTRATION

It is well established that tobacco smoking has deleterious effects on health. A single cigarette, an object smaller than a standard pencil, delivers more than 4000 chemicals that separately or together may contribute to these effects (Dube and Green, 1982; Department of Health and Human Services [DHHS], 1989). Nicotine has been identified as the addictive component in tobacco smoking and is the central drug contributing to the maintenance of tobacco use (DHHS, 1988; Fielding et al., 1998; Center for Disease Control and Prevention, 2002). Nicotine acts in the brain and results in many behavioral and psychological actions including enhancement of reward, decreased appetite, focused attention, and changes in activity. Further, nicotine and its metabolites readily cross the placental membrane, penetrate the preimplantation blastocyst, and cross the blood–brain barrier (Fabro and Sieber, 1969; Shiverick and Salafia, 1999).

In rodents, tobacco can be administered in many different ways: through tobacco-extract administration, tobacco-smoke exposure, and topical application of tobacco tars. *Tobacco-extract administration* refers to daily subcutaneous injections (SC) of nicotine-free tobacco. Some studies using this method have reported significant degenerative changes in various organs, including the thyroid, pituitary gland, and pancreas (Suematsu, 1931), or gangrene in the toes of male rats (Friedlander et al., 1936; Harkavy, 1937). *The tobacco-smoke exposure model* involves exposing rats to cigarette smoke for days or years and has been used to simulate the human smoking experience. Kulche and colleagues (1952) report that rats exposed to tobacco smoke exhibit increased tear secretion, salivation, and copious bowel movements. Other studies show that rodents exposed to tobacco smoke either lose weight or grow less than control animals (Pechstein and Reynolds, 1937; Passey, 1957). Tobacco tar, when applied topically to rats, retards growth, slows weight gain, and causes gastric lesions (McNally, 1932; Roffo, 1942).

Although tobacco-smoke exposure is meant to simulate the human smoking experience, nicotine is the actual substance in tobacco smoke that exerts the addictive and psychobiological effects and maintains self-administration (DHHS, 1988; Stolerman and Jarvis, 1995). Therefore, nicotine administration paradigms have been the focus of animal studies in recent decades. Nicotine can be administered by oral nicotine administration (e.g., nicotine in drinking water), single or repeated nicotine injections (SC or intraperitoneal [IP]), intravenous self-administration, or sustained nicotine administration (e.g., an osmotic pump). The effects of nicotine vary with dosage,

timing, duration of exposure, route of administration, and chemical form of nicotine (Levin et al., 1996; Slotkin, 1998; Phillips et al., 2004).

Oral Nicotine Administration

Nicotine is ingested by animals via drinking fluids or forced oral administration. Some studies report that consumption of nicotine retards the growth of mice and rats (Nice, 1913; Wilson and De Eds, 1936) or reduces litter size of pregnant mice (Wilson, 1942), but other studies report no such effects (Nice, 1912). The utility of oral-administration method is limited by the difficulty in getting rats and mice to drink nicotine-containing solutions (Murrin et al., 1987; Le Houezec et al., 1989). Another disadvantage of using this method is that nicotine is poorly absorbed through the gastrointestinal tract, leading to lower concentrations of nicotine in the blood. Therefore, more nicotine may be needed to obtain desirable amounts of nicotine to serve as a model of human consumption. SC injections and delivery via a subcutaneously implanted pump are more commonly used than oral-administration paradigms because the amount of nicotine administered can be better controlled and the absorption of the drug is not limited by passage through the gastrointestinal tract.

Repeated Nicotine Injections

Most studies examining the effects of chronic exposure to nicotine on behavior have used one of two methods: (1) repeated daily injections or (2) sustained nicotine release. Repeated daily injections involve parenteral injections—SC or IP a few times a day or once a day for several days (Pietila and Ahtee, 2000). This approach has been widely used to examine the effect of nicotine on behavior (e.g., locomotion, acoustic startle response (ASR), prepulse inhibition [PPI] of the ASR, social interaction, elevated plus maze, and nociception) and generates reliable and reproducible results (Levin et al., 1997; Hahn and Stolerman, 2002; Faraday et al., 2003; Elliott et al., 2004; Olausson et al., 2004). When nicotine is injected repeatedly into pregnant dams, similar behavioral disruptions in offspring are observed (Slotkin, 2004). It is possible that these behavioral changes reflect the consequences of uteroplacental vasoconstriction and fetal hypoxia associated with the high peak plasma concentrations of nicotine that occur with repeated injections (Jonsson and Hall-man, 1980; Seidler and Slotkin, 1990; Carlos et al., 1991; Slotkin, 2004). That is, nicotine injections may result in high peak plasma concentrations of nicotine accompanied by brief hypoxic episodes associated with each dose (McFarland et al., 1991; Slotkin, 1992). These episodic hypoxic events can alter brain development (Jonsson and Hallman, 1980; Slotkin, 1986; Seidler and Slotkin, 1990). Consequently, any observed effects cannot be fully attributed to nicotine per se. The osmotic pump provides an alternate and preferable way of administering nicotine prenatally.

Osmotic Pump

Osmotic pumps are miniature, subcutaneously implantable pumps used to continuously deliver drugs or other agents at controlled rates up to 4 weeks. The pump is a small object, resembling a pill capsule in shape but larger in size. The pump has two compartments: an inner capsule and an outer chamber. The inner capsule is filled with the drug or control liquid to be delivered. The outer chamber, which surrounds the capsule, contains a salt and is referred to as the *salt sleeve*. When placed underneath the skin or in an aqueous medium, an osmotic pressure difference develops between this outer salt filled chamber and the tissue environment, pulling water from the tissue into the pump through a semipermeable membrane that forms the surface of the pump. The pressure of the water in this outside chamber puts pressure on the impermeable capsule, displacing the drug from the inner core into the body at a controlled and steady rate much like the slow squeezing of a toothpaste tube. This method produces a constant administration of nicotine and a steady-state level of plasma nicotine (Carr et al., 1989; Pauly et al., 1992; Slotkin, 1998), therefore, avoiding the stress associated with and the hypoxia induced by repeated nicotine injections (Levin et al., 1996; Slotkin, 1998).

Grunberg (1982) was the first to use an osmotic minipump to subcutaneously administer nicotine continuously to rats for a week and to examine their body weight and food consumption. The findings from this experiment parallel results from a study of cigarette smoking in humans. Such parallels between data generated from osmotic pump-delivered nicotine models and findings from research on human cigarette smoking have been described in various other studies as well (Bowen et al., 1986; Grunberg et al.,

1986; Murrin et al., 1987; Richardson and Tizabi, 1994; Levin et al., 1996; Faraday et al., 2001; Irvine et al., 2001; Malin, 2001). The osmotic pump is now widely used to examine long-term effects of nicotine in rodents.

Prenatal Nicotine Models

Studies examining prenatal effects of nicotine have used most of the methods described above. The two most common approaches to evaluating prenatal smoking effects are repeated injections of nicotine into the pregnant dam and SC administration of nicotine in the pregnant dam via an osmotic pump. Administration of nicotine to pregnant dams by repeated injections has provided consistent evidence that prenatal nicotine exposure causes cellular damage in the fetal brain that may explain subsequent behavioral and cognitive deficits (Slotkin et al., 1986). Repeated nicotine injections, however, also cause peak plasma concentrations of drug that are associated with ischemia, an effect that has the potential to disrupt fetal brain development (McFarland et al., 1991; Slotkin, 1992).

The osmotic pump has become the standard choice for examining prenatal effects of nicotine (Murrin et al., 1987; Ulrich et al., 1997). It delivers drugs or other agents at controlled rates for up to 4 weeks, avoids peak plasma concentrations associated with repeated injections, allows for better control over nicotine delivery, and eliminates the risk of hypoxic episodes. The continuous infusion of nicotine via osmotic minipump is analogous to nicotine patch delivery but differs markedly from nicotine self-administration through smoking tobacco.

Overview of Behavioral Assessment in Animals

The study of animal behavior has become common practice and behavioral models are frequently included in studies of psychology, pharmacology, and behavioral and cognitive neuroscience. Animal models provide information about normal behavior and responses to drugs, disease, or adverse environmental conditions. The behavioral patterns observed range from studies of basic sensory (e.g., olfactory, taste, auditory, and tactile), motor (e.g., balance), and neurological (e.g., eye blink, righting reflex, and ear twitch) functions to unconditioned behaviors (e.g., food consumption, locomotor activity, and sexual behavior), to more complex assessments of attention, learning, and memory (e.g., Morris water maze, T-maze, radial arm maze, and PPI). The following section discusses key findings from prenatal nicotine studies in which some of these behavioral paradigms were used and offers suggestions for future studies.

EFFECTS OF PRENATAL EXPOSURE TO NICOTINE IN ANIMAL MODELS

Outcome measures of prenatal effects include birth weight and fetal liability, locomotor activity, and cognition. The effect of nicotine on these variables is a function of the amount of nicotine administered, route of administration, timing of administration, and animal species (Ernst et al., 2001). Prenatal nicotine exposure compromises the health of the newborn and can have long-lasting deleterious effects on offspring behavior.

Studies of prenatal nicotine effects date back to the early 1900s (Nakasawa, 1931; Sodano, 1934; Grumbecht and Loeser, 1941). Most of these early studies were conducted in rabbits and dogs. Generally, these studies focused on effects of nicotine on pregnancy duration and the size and viability of the young. Early studies in the rabbit repeatedly show that daily injections of tobacco-smoke solutions, chronic nicotine infusions, or nicotine administration caused spontaneous abortions or premature deliveries (Guillain and Gy, 1907; Benigni, 1911; Perazzi, 1912). Tissues from fetuses of rabbits that received daily SC injections of nicotine for up to 12 weeks are damaged (Vara and Kinnunen, 1951). Hofstatter (1923) notes that pregnancies occurring during nicotine administration frequently abort.

Body Weight

Animals exposed to nicotine prenatally consistently weigh less than animals not exposed to nicotine prenatally (Bassi et al., 1984; Paulson et al., 1993; Ajarem and Ahman, 1998; Vaglenova et al., 2004). Animals receiving 4.0 mg/kg/day of nicotine prenatally (oral administration) weigh less than controls, and these effects persist until postnatal day (P) 29 (Paulson et al., 1993). Ajarem and Ahmed (1998) administered nicotine (0.50 mg/kg) or saline to pregnant mice via SC injections for 9–10 days and assessed offspring development. The nicotine-exposed animals

gained weight at a slower rate than that of controls. Such findings are interesting because they parallel reports from humans and suggest that prenatal smoking affects prenatal and postnatal development. Specifically, women who smoke during pregnancy have a greater number of spontaneous abortions, premature births, and infants with low-birth weights (Eskenazi et al., 1995; Hofhuis et al., 2003). In addition, nicotine-induced reduction in postnatal weight gain also has been reported in human offspring (Martin et al., 1977).

Hyperactivity

Several studies have reported hyperactivity in the offspring of nicotine-treated animals (Martin et al., 1976; Lichtensteiger et al., 1988; Ajarem and Ahmad, 1998; Fung and Lau, 1998; Newman et al., 1999; Tizabi and Perry, 2000). In rats, hyperactivity is indexed by measuring open-field activity or activity in other novel environments such as the elevated plus maze.

Open-field activity refers to the behavior of an animal when it is placed in a novel environment. Initially, activity levels are high when an animal explores its new environment. As the environment becomes familiar, ambient activity decreases. Persistent heightened activity is interpreted as evidence of hyperactivity, a behavior frequently observed in the offspring of mothers who smoked during pregnancy.

Rats exposed to nicotine (1.5 mg/kg/day via SC injections) throughout gestation have increased spontaneous locomotor activity compared to that of saline-exposed controls (Fung and Lau, 1988). Similarly, Tizabi and colleagues (1997), who administered nicotine (9.0 mg/kg/day) via osmotic minipumps to pregnant dams throughout gestation, show that 20–24-day-old offspring prenatally exposed to nicotine exhibit more locomotor activity than that of saline controls.

The elevated plus maze is used to test anxiety and to measure activity and impulsivity. Accordingly, an animal is placed in the center of an elevated four-arm maze that includes two open and two closed arms. The total number of times an animal enters any of the four arms provides an index of activity and impulsivity. Ajarem and Ahmad (1998) administered nicotine (0.50 mg/kg) or saline to pregnant mice for 9–10 days and measured activity on the elevated plus maze of weaned offspring. Nicotine-exposed offspring made more entries in the arms of the maze than did saline controls. This finding suggests that prenatal exposure to nicotine promotes hyperactivity and impulsivity. Sobrian and colleagues (2003) report similar effects of prenatal nicotine exposure on activity in an elevated plus maze. They administered nicotine (2.5 or 5.0 mg/kg) or saline via an osmotic pump to pregnant dams throughout gestation. Adult rats exposed to high doses of nicotine prenatally are less timid and more impulsive than controls. These findings are consistent with reports from human studies, that prenatal smoking to nicotine results in hyperactivity in offspring (Milberger et al., 1996; Mick et al., 2002; Thapar et al., 2003).

Attention

Prenatal smoking disrupts attention in exposed offspring (Kristjansson et al., 1998). In rats, attention can be measured using the PPI of the ASR. PPI refers to the reduction of a startle response when the startling stimulus is preceded by a nonstartling stimulus. Control animals exhibit a reduced startle response to a sudden, loud noise if the noise is preceded by a softer sound. Disorders that disrupt attention, such as schizophrenia and attention deficit hyperactivity disorder (ADHD), disrupt PPI (Swerdlow et al., 2000; Geyer et al., 2001).

Reports of prenatal nicotine on attention in rats are limited, but data that are available show that rats respond to prenatal nicotine exposure. Prenatal nicotine exposure (6 mg/kg/day via osmotic minipump) throughout gestation reduces the PPI of the ASR to a 98 dB stimulus in female offspring (Popke et al., 1997). These findings are consistent with the observed attentional deficits reported in humans exposed to nicotine prenatally. Future studies using other attentional paradigms (e.g., five-choice serial reaction time test) will further help to characterize the attentional domains affected by prenatal nicotine exposure.

Learning and Memory

Prenatal nicotine exposure alters learning and memory (Cornelius et al., 2000). In rats, the effects of prenatal exposure to nicotine on learning and memory have been evaluated primarily by use of a radial arm maze, which presents a challenge that assesses the ability of an animal to learn and remember multiple spatial locations. The animal is placed in the center of a maze containing eight or more radiating arms. Food is placed at the end of four arms. The animal must enter an arm to retrieve the food. The numbers of repeat entries by a rat into the arms already entered are recorded as working memory errors (Olton, 1987; Hodges, 1996). The numbers of reentries into arms never having contained food are recorded as reference memory errors.

Several studies report impairments on the radial arm maze following prenatal nicotine exposure. Following administration of nicotine (6.0 mg/kg) to pregnant dams in their drinking water throughout gestation, offspring exhibit impaired performance in the radial arm maze (Sorenson et al., 1991). Several other studies describe similar findings (Yanai et al., 1992; Levin et al., 1996). Levin and colleagues used a radial arm maze to assess the effects of prenatal nicotine exposure (2.0 mg/kg/day via osmotic minipump) on learning and memory. They report that nicotine-exposed animals do not differ from controls in the acquisition of the task, but these rats make more errors when spatial cues are changed, hence adding to the demands of the task.

Prenatal effects of nicotine have been evaluated using the two-way active avoidance (shuttle box) task. In this task, classical conditioning procedures are used to assess learning and long-term memory. The apparatus consists of two equally divided compartments connected by a center opening. During the training the animal is presented with a combined light and tone (conditioned stimuli), followed by the presentation of shock on a grid floor (unconditioned stimulus [UCS]). Following presentation of the conditioned stimulus, the animal can avoid the UCS by passing from one compartment to another. This avoidance behavior is evidence of learning, whereas failure to avoid the UCS is evidence of no learning. Memory is assessed by re-exposing the animal to the apparatus several days later and measuring avoidance activity. Greater avoidance behavior is evidence of long-term memory.

Two-month-old male offspring of dams injected with nicotine (0.50 mg/kg/day) during pregnancy exhibit deficits in learning the avoidance response (Genedani et al., 1983). More recently, Vaglenova and colleagues (2004) administered nicotine (6.0 mg/kg/day) via osmotic minipump to pregnant dams and measured active avoidance behavior of offspring on P45. Animals of both sexes prenatally exposed to nicotine have a significantly lower number of avoidance behaviors during all days of training and during the retention test. These data are indicative of impaired learning and memory. The results of these animal studies parallel reports of memory and learning problems in humans and provide further support for the value of animals for investigating prenatal smoking effects on memory and learning in offspring (Naeye and Peters, 1983; Rantakallio and Koiranen, 1987; DiFranza and Lew, 1995; Slotkin, 1998).

Addiction Liability

Prenatal tobacco smoking increases the likelihood of smoking among exposed offspring (Kandel et al., 1994; Niaura et al., 2001; Chassin et al., 2002; Abreu-Villaca et al., 2004a, 2004b). In humans, prenatal exposure to nicotine is an important predictor of smoking in adolescents. (Cornelius et al., 2000; Niaura et al., 2001). Interestingly, this vulnerability exists, regardless of whether parents continue to smoke.

Recent animal studies examining the effects of prenatal nicotine on later biological responses to nicotine parallel the findings of human studies and provide underlying mechanisms for these observed effects (Abreu-Villaca et al., 2004a, 2004b). It has been suggested that the increased likelihood of smoking among exposed offspring reflects long-lasting changes in neural cell number, neural cell size, and cell surface area. These changes are evident in the neonate and become exaggerated when nicotine is re-administered during adolescence. Another proposed mechanism for the relationship between prenatal nicotine exposure and adolescent smoking is that prenatal nicotine exposure disrupts the programming of cholinergic function (Abreu-Villaca et al., 2004b).

After prenatal nicotine exposure, there is impairment of nicotine acetylcholine receptor (nAChR) up-regulation and receptor desensitization when nicotine is administered during adolescence. These factors may contribute to increased cigarette smoking by adolescents (Abreu-Villaca et al., 2004b). A relationship between gestational nicotine exposure and nicotine preference in peri-adolescent offspring has also been examined in mice (Klein et al., 2003). Pregnant females were administered saccharin-flavored water containing 50 μg/ml nicotine or saccharin-flavored water without nicotine from the ninth day of

gestation through P21. The nicotine preference of adolescent male offspring exposed to nicotine prenatally is increased compared to that in age-matched controls. The mechanism for this effect has not been established.

CONCLUSIONS AND FUTURE IMPLICATIONS

Animal models of nicotine administration and animal studies of behavior provide investigators with valuable ways to examine the relationship between prenatal smoking (especially prenatal nicotine) and cognitive and behavioral outcomes in affected offspring. The fact that findings from prenatal nicotine studies in animals parallel and predict findings from humans support the validity of these studies. These models are well established and have provided reliable results that help expand our understanding of the effects of tobacco. Despite this knowledge, many questions remain unanswered. For example, although we now have a better understanding of specific brain regions affected by prenatal nicotine exposure, the mechanisms by which these effects occur are poorly understood. Little research has been conducted on higher-animal species; most studies examining the effects of prenatal exposure to nicotine have been conducted in rodents. Studies conducted in animal species that more closely parallel humans (i.e., monkeys) may provide additional information about relevant mechanisms. Our understanding may offer opportunities for the development of interventions that reverse damaging effects of nicotine on the fetus.

Future studies should include other behavioral measures. In humans, prenatal nicotine exposure results in attention deficits in offspring, however, modeling animal studies that examine attention are limited. Complex measures of attention do exist and should be included in future studies of the effects of prenatal exposure to nicotine.

Examination of sensory and motor functions would be instructive, but few animal studies have included such behavioral measures (Ajarem and Ahmand, 1998). Human offspring prenatally exposed to nicotine exhibit impairments in sensory processing and basic motor functions that persist even a year postdelivery. Saxton (1978), for example, examined babies born to mothers who smoked with the Brazelton

Neonatal Behavioral Assessment Scale. These infants have reduced auditory acuity compared to that of infants of nonsmoking mothers. Further, Gusella and Fried (1984) report a decrease in motor scores, as measured by the Bayley Mental and Motor Scales, among 13-month-old offspring whose mothers smoked in during pregnancy. These findings are important because they suggest that prenatal smoking affects not only complex behaviors such as learning and memory, but also fundamental sensory and motor processes. Further studies examining these relationships are important, as disruptions in sensory and motor processing can explain learning problems, behavioral problems such as hyperactivity, and perhaps even sensitivity to drug exposure in adolescence or adulthood.

Abbreviations

ADHD   attention deficit hyperactivity disorder

ASR   acoustic startle response

IP   intraperitoneal

nAChR   nicotine acetylcholine receptor

P   postnatal day

PPI   prepulse inhibition

SC   subcutaneous

UCS   unconditioned stimulus

ACKNOWLEDGMENTS   This work was supported by the Robert Wood Johnson Foundation and the U.S. Department of Defense.

References

Abreu-Villaca Y, Seidler FJ, Slotkin TA (2004a) Does prenatal nicotine exposure sensitize the brain to nicotine-induced neurotoxicity in adolescence? Neuropsychopharmacology, 29:1440–1450.

Abreu-Villaca Y, Seidler FJ, Tate CA, Cousins MM, Slotkin TA (2004b) Prenatal nicotine exposure alters the response to nicotine administration in adolescence: effects on cholinergic systems during exposure and withdrawal. Neuropsychopharmacology, 29:879–890.

Ajarem JS, Ahmad M (1998) Prenatal nicotine exposure modifies behavior of mice through early development. Pharmacol Biochem Behav 59:313–318.

Bassi JA, Rosso P, Moessinger AC, Blanc WA, James LS (1984) Fetal growth retardation due to maternal tobacco smoke exposure in the rat. Pediatr Res 18:127–130.

Benigni PF (1911) Sulle alterazioni anatomiche indotte dall'intossicazione cronica sperimentale da tabacco. Riv Pat Nerv 16:80–100.

Bowen DJ, Eury SE, Grunberg NE (1986) Nicotine's effects on female rats' body weight: caloric intake and physical activity. Pharmacol Biochem Behav 25:1131–1136.

Buka SL, Shenassa ED, Niaura R (2003) Elevated risk of tobacco dependence among offspring of mothers who smoked during pregnancy: a 30-year prospective study. Am J Psychiatry 160:1978–1984.

Butler NR, Goldstein H (1973) Smoking in pregnancy and subsequent child development. BMJ 4:573–575.

Carlos RQ, Seidler FJ, Lappi SE, Slotkin TA (1991) Fetal dexamethasone exposure affects basal onrrithine decarboxylase activity in developing rat brain regions and alters responses to hypoxia and maternal separation. Biol Neonate, 59:69–77.

Carr LA, Rowell PP, Pierce WM (1989) Effects of subchronic nicotine administration on central dopaminergic mechanisms in the rat. Neurochem Res 14:511–515.

Center for Disease Control (CDC) (2002) Annual smoking-attributable mortality, years of potential life lost, and economic costs—United States, 1995–1999. Morbid Mortal Wkly Rpt (MMWR) 51:300–303.

Chassin L, Presson C, Rose J, Sherman SJ, Prost J (2002) Parental smoking cessation and adolescent smoking. J Pediatr Psychol 27:485–496.

Cornelius MD, Ryan CM, Day, NL, Goldschmidt, L, Willford, JA (2000). Prenatal tobacco exposure: is it a risk factor for early tobacco experimentation? Nicotine Tob Res 2:45–52.

Darwin C (1859) Origin of the Species, 2nd edition. John Murray, London.

Denson R, Nanson JL, McWatters MA (1975) Hyperkinesis and maternal smoking. Can Psychiatric Assoc J 20:183–187.

Department of Health and Human Services (DHHS) (1988) The Health Consequences of Smoking: Nicotine addiction: A Report of the Surgeon General. DHHS Publ. # 88-8406. CDC Publications, Rockville, MD.

Department of Health and Human Services (DHHS) (1989) Reducing the health consequences of smoking: 25 years of progress. A report of the Surgeon General. DHHS Publ. #89-8411. CDC Publications, Washington, DC, 11:125–133.

Dewsbury DA (2003) The 1973 Nobel prize for physiology or medicine: recognition for behavioral science? Am Psychol 58:747–752.

DiFranza JR, Lew RA (1995) Effect of maternal cigarette smoking on pregnancy complications and
sudden infant death syndrome. J Fam Pract 40:
385–394.

Dube M, Green GR (1982) Methods of collection or
smoke for analytical purposes. Rec Adv Tobacco Sci
8:42–102.

Elliott BM, Faraday MM, Phillips JM, Grunberg NE
(2004) Effects of nicotine on elevated plus maze and
locomotor activity in male and female adolescent
and adult rats. Pharmacol Biochem Behav 77:21–28.

Ernst M, Moolchan ET, Robinson ML (2001) Behavioral and neural consequences of prenatal exposure
to nicotine. J Am Acad Child Adolesc Psychiatry
40:630–641.

Eskenazi B, Trupin LS (1995) Passive and active maternal smoking during pregnancy, as measured by
serum cotinine, and postnatal smoke exposure II:
effects on neurodevelopment at age 5 years. Am J
Epidemiol 142:S19–S29.

Fabro S, Sieber SM (1969) Caffeine and nicotine penetrate the pre-implantation blastocyst. Nature 223:
410–411.

Faraday MM, Elliott BM, Grunberg NE (2001) Adult vs.
adolescent rats differ in biobehavioral responses to
chronic nicotine. Pharmacol Biochem Behav 70:
475–489.

Faraday MM, Elliott BM, Phillips JM, Grunberg NE
(2003) Adolescent and adult male rats differ in sensitivity to nicotine's activity effects. Pharmacol Biochem Behav 74:917–931.

Fielding JE, Husten CG, Eriksen MP (1998) Tobacco:
health effects and control. In Maxcy KF, Rosenau
MJ, Last JM, Wallace RB, Doebbling BN (eds).
Public Health and Preventive Medicine. McGraw-
Hill, New York, pp 817–845.

Friedlander M, Silbert S, Laskey N (1936) Toe lesions
following tobacco injections in rats. Proc Soc Exp
Biol 34:156–157.

Fung YK, Lau YS (1988) Receptor mechanisms of
nicotine-induced locomotor hyperactivity in chronic
nicotine-treated rats. Eur J Pharmacol 152:263–271.

Genedani S, Bernardi M, Bertolini A (1983) Sex-linked
differences in avoidance learning in the offspring of
rats treated with nicotine during pregnancy. Psychopharmacology 80:93–95.

Geyer MA, Krebs-Thomson K, Braff DL, Swerdlow NR
(2001) Pharmacological studies of prepulse inhibition models of sensorimtor gating deficits in schizophrenia: a decade in review. Psychopharmacoly
156:117–154.

Grumbrecht P, Loeser A (1941) Nicotin und innere
Sekretion. II. Arbeitsschaden der Frau in Tabakfab-
riken? Arch Exp Pathol 195:143–151.

Grunberg NE (1982) The effects of nicotine and cigarette smoking on food consumption and taste preferences. Addict Behav 7:317–331.

—— (1985) Nicotine, cigarette smoking, and body
weight. Br J Addict 80:369–377.

Grunberg NE, Bowen DJ, Winders SE (1986) Effects of
nicotine on body weight and food consumption in
female rats. Psychopharmacology 90:101–105.

Gulillan G, Gy A (1907) Recherches experimentales sur
l'influence de l'intoxification tabagique sur la gestation. C Rend Soc Biol 63:583–584.

Gusella JL, Fried PA (1984) Effects of maternal social
drinking and smoking on offspring at 13 months.
Neurobehav Toxicol Teratol 6:13–17.

Hahn B, Stolerman IP (2002) Nicotine-induced attentional enhancement in rats: effects of chronic exposure to nicotine. Neuropsychopharmacology 27:712–
722.

Harkavy J (1937) Tobacco sensitization in rats. J Allergy
9:275–277.

Hodges H (1996) Maze procedures: the radial-arm and
water maze compared. Cognit Brain Res 3:167–181.

Hofhuis W, Jongste JC, Merkus PJ (2003) Adverse health
effects of prenatal and postnatal tobacco smoke
exposure on children. Arch Dis Child 88:1086–
1090.

Hofstatter R (1923) Experimentelle Studie uber die Ein-
wirkung des Nicotins auf die Keimdrusen und auf
der Frotpflanzung. Virchows Arch 244:183–213.

Irvine EE, Cheeta S, Marshall M, File SE (2001) Different treatment regimens and the development of tolerance to nicotine's anxiogenic effects. Pharmacol
Biochem Behav 68:769–776.

Jonsson G, Hallman H (1980) Effects of neonatal nicotine administration on the postnatal development
of central noradrenaline neurons. Acta Physiol
Scand Suppl 479:25–26.

Kandel DB, Wu P, Davies M (1994) Maternal smoking
during pregnancy and smoking by adolescent
daughters. Am J Public Health 84:1407–1413.

Kimble GA, Schlesinger K (1985) Topics in the History
of Psychology, Vol 2. Hillsdale NJ, Erlbaum.

Klein LC, Stine MM, Pfaff DW, Vandenbergh DJ
(2003) Maternal nicotine exposure increases nicotine preference in periadolescent male but not
female C57B1/6J mice. Nicotine Tob Res 5:117–
124.

Kristjansson EA, Fried PA, Watkison B (1989) Maternal
smoking during pregnancy affects children's vigilance performance. Drug Alcohol Depend 24:11–19.

Kulche H, Loesser A, Meyer G, Schmidt C, Sturmer E
(1952) Tabakarauch. Ein Beitrag zur Wirkung von
Tabakfeuchthaltemitteln. Zeitschr Gest Exp Med
18:554–572.

Le Houezec J, Martin C, Cohen C, Molimard R (1989) Failure of behavioral dependence induction and oral bioavailablity in rats. Physiol Behav 45:103–108.

Levin E (1992) Nicotinic systems and cognitive function. Psycopharmacology 108:417–431.

Levin E, Wilkerson A, Jones JP, Christopher NC, Briggs SJ (1996) Prenatal nicotine effects on memory in rats: pharmacological and behavioral challenges. Dev Brain Res 97:207–215.

Levin ED, Kaplan S, Boardman A (1997) Acute nicotine interactions with nicotinic and muscarinic antagonists: working and reference memory effects in the 16-arm radial arm. Behav Pharmacol 8:236–242.

Luck W, Nau H (1985) Nicotine and cotinine concentrations in serum and urine of infants exposed via passive smoking or milk from smoking mothers. J Pediatr 107:816–820.

Lichtensteiger W, Ribary U, Schlumpf M, Odermatt B, Widmer HR (1988) Prenatal adverse effects of nicotine on the developing brain. Prog Brain Res 73: 137–157.

Malin DH (2001) Nicotine dependence: studies with a laboratory model. Pharmacol Biochem Behav 70: 551–559.

Martin JC, Martin DC, Radow B, Sigman G (1976) Growth, development, and activity in rat offspring following maternal drug exposure. Exp Aging Res 2:235–251.

Martin J, Martin DC, Lund CA, Streissguth AP (1977) Maternal alcohol ingestion and cigarette smoking and their effects on newborn conditioning. Alcohol Clin Exp Res 3:243–247.

McFarland BJ, Seidler FJ, Slotkin TA (1991) Inhibition of DNA synthesis in neonatal rat brain regions caused by acute nicotine administration. Dev Brain Res 58:223–229.

McNally WD (1932). The tar in cigarette smoke and its possible effects. Am J Cancer, 16:1502–1514.

Mick E, Biderman J, Faranone SV, Sayer J, Kleimans S (2002) Case-control study of attention-deficit hyperactivity disorder and maternal smoking, alcohol use, and drug use during pregnancy. J Am Ac Child Adolesc Psychiatry 41:378–385.

Milberger S, Biederman J, Faranone SV, Chen L, Jones J (1996) Is maternal smoking during pregnancy a risk factor for attention deficit hyperactivity disorder in children? American Journal of Psychiatry, 153: 1138–1142.

Murrin LC, Ferrer JR, Zeng WY, Haley NJ (1987) Nicotine administration to rats: methodological considerations. Life Sci 40:1699–1708.

Nakasawa R (1931) Der Einfluss der chronischen Nicotinvergiftung auf die funktion der geschlechtsfunktion der weiblichen ratten. Jpn J Sci Phar 5:109–111.

Naeye RL (1992) Cognitive and behavioral abnormalities in children whose mothers smoke Cigarettes during pregnancy. J Dev Behav Pediatr 13:425–428.

Naeye RL, Peters EC (1984) Maternal development of children whose mothers smoked during Pregnancy. Obstet Gynecol 64:601–607.

Newman MB, Shytle RD, Sandberg PR (1999) Locomotor behavioral effects of prenatal and postnatal nicotine exposure in rat offspring. Behav Pharmacol 10: 699–706.

Niaura R, Bock B, Lloyd EE, Brown R, Lipsitt LP, Buka S (2001) Maternal transmission of nicotine dependence: psychiatric, neurocognitive and prenatal factors. Am J Addict Dis 10:16–29.

Nice LB (1912) Comparative studies on the effects of alcohol, nicotine, tobacco smoke and caffeine on white mice. I. Effects on reproduction and growth. J Exp Zool 12:135–152.

—— (1913) Studies on the effects of alcohol, nicotine, tobacco smoke, and caffeine on white mice. II. Effects on activity. J Exp Zool 14:123–151.

Nutton V (2002) Logic, learning and experimental medicine. Science 295:800–801.

Olausson P, Jentsch JD, Taylor JR (2004) Repeated nicotine exposure enhances responding with condition reinforcement. Psychopharmcology 173:98–104.

Olton DS (1987) The radial arm maze as a tool in behavioral pharmacology. Physiol Behav 40:793–797.

Passey RD (1957) Carcinogenicity of cigarette tars. Br Empire Cancer Camp Annu Rpt 35:65–66.

Paulson RB, Shanfeld J, Vorhees CV, Sweazy A, Gagni S, Smith AR, Paulson JO (1993) Behavioral effects of prenatally administered smokeless tobacco on rat offspring. Neurotoxicol Teratol 15:183–192.

Pauly JR, Grun EU, Collins AC (1992) Tolerance to nicotine following chronic treatment by injections: a potential role for corticosterone. Psychopharmacology 108:33–39.

Pavlov, I. P. (1927) Conditioned Reflexes. London, Routledge and Kegan Paul.

Pechstein LA, Reynolds WR (1937) The effect of tobacco smoke on the growth and learning behavior of the albino rat and its progeny. J Comp Psychol 24: 459–469.

Perazzi P (1912) Studio sperimentale sui rapporti fra tabagismo e gravidanza. Folgynsec 7:295–334.

Pietila K, Ahtee L (1999) Chronic nicotine administration in the drinking water affects the striatal dopamine in mice. Pharmacol Biochem Behav 66:95–103.

Phillips JM, Schechter LE, Grunberg NE (2004) Nicotine abstinence syndrome in rats depends on form of nicotine. Presented at the Society on Research Nicotine and Tobacco, Scottsdale, AZ.

Popke EJ, Tizabi Y, Rahman MA, Nespor SM, Grunberg NE (1997) Prenatal exposure to nicotine: effects on prepulse inhibition and central nicotinic receptors. Pharmacol Biochem Behav 58:843–849.

Rantakallio P, Koiranen M (1987) Neurological handicaps among children whose mothers smoked during pregnancy. Prev Med 16:597–606

Richardson SA, Tizabi Y (1994) Hyperactivity in the offspring of nicotine-treated rats: role of mesolimbic and nigrostriatal dopaminergic pathways. Pharmacol Biochem Behav 47:331–337.

Roffo AH (1942) Cancerización gástrica por ingestiónde alquitrán tabáquico. Prensa Med Argent 29:18–35.

Saxton DW (1978) The behavior of infants whose mothers smoke in pregnancy. Early Hum Dev 2:363–369.

Scheufele PM, Faraday MM, Grunberg NE (2000) Nicotine administration interacts with housing conditions to alter social and non-social behaviors in male and female Long-Evans rats. Nicotine Tob Res 2:169–178.

Seidler FJ, Slotkin TA (1990) Effects of acute hypoxia on neonatal rat brain: regionally selective long-term alterations in catecholamine levels and turnover. Brain Res Bull 24:157–161.

Shiverick KT, Salafia C (1999) Cigarette smoking and pregnancy. I: Ovarian, uterine and placental effects. Placenta 20:265–272.

Skinner BF (1935) Two types of conditioned reflex and a pseudo type. J Gen Psychol 12:66–77.

Slawecki CJ, Ehlers CL (2002) Lasting effects of adolescent nicotine exposure on the electroencephalogram, event related potentials, and the locomotor activity in the rat. Dev Brain Res 138:15–25.

Slawecki CJ, Gilder A, Roth J, Ehlers CL (2003) Increased anxiety-like behavior in adult rats exposed to nicotine as adolescents. Pharmacol Biochem Behav 75:355–361.

Slotkin TA (1986) Endocrine control of synaptic development in the sympathetic nervous system: the cardiac-sympathetic axis. In: Gootman PM (ed). Developmental Neurobiology of the Autonomic Nervous System. Humana Press, Clifton, NJ, pp 97–133.

Slotkin TA (1992) Prenatal exposure to nicotine: what can we learn from animal models? In: Zagon IS, Slotkin TA (eds). Maternal Substance Abuse and the Developing Nervous System. Academic Press, San Diego, pp 97–124.

—— (1998) Fetal nicotine or cocaine exposure: which one is worse? J Pharmacol Exp Ther 285:931–945.

—— (2002) Nicotine and the adolescent brain: insights from an animal model. Neurotoxicol Teratol 24: 369–384.

—— (2004) Cholinergic systems in brain development and disruption by neurotoxicants: nicotine, environmental tobacco smoke, organophosphates. Toxicol Appl Pharmacol 198:132–151.

Slotkin, TA, Greer, N, Faust, J., Cho, H. and Seidler, FJ (1986) Effects of maternal nicotine injections on brain developments in the rat: ornithine decarboxylase activity, nucleic acids and proteins in discrete brain regions. Brain Res Bull 17: 41–50.

Sobrian SK, Marr L, Ressman K (2003) Prenatal cocaine and/or nicotine exposure produces depression and anxiety in aging rats. Prog Neuropsychopharmacol Biol Psychiatry 27:501–518.

Sodano A (1934) Ricerche sperimentali sull' influenca della nicotina sulla funzione genital della donna. Arch Oste Gin 41:559–569.

Sorenson CA, Raskin LA, Suh Y (1991) The effects of prenatal nicotine on radial-arm maze performance in rats. Pharmacol Biochem Behav 40:991–993.

Stolerman IP, Jarvis MJ (1995) The scientific case that nicotine is addictive. Psychopharmacology 117: 2–10.

Swerdlow NR, Braff DL, Geyer MA (2000) Animal models of deficient sensorimotor gating: what we know, what we think we know, and what we hope to know soon. Behav Pharmacol 11:185–204.

Thapar A, Fowler T, Rice F, Scourfield J, Van den Bree M, Thomas H, Harold G, Hay D (2003) Maternal smoking during pregnancy and attention deficit hyperactivity disorder symptoms in offspring. Am J Psychiatry 160:1985–1989.

Thorndike EL (1911) Animal Intelligence. Macmillan, New York.

Tizabi Y, Perry DC (2000) Prenatal nicotine exposure is associated with an increase in 125 epibatidine binding in discrete cortical regions in rats. Pharmacol Biochem Behav 67:319–323.

Tizabi Y, Popke EJ, Rahman MA, Nespor SM, Grunberg NE (1997) Hyperactivity induced by prenatal nicotine exposure is associated with an increase in cortical nicotinic receptors. Pharmacol Biochem Behav 58:141–146.

Trauth JA, Seidler FJ, Slotkin TA (2000) Persistent and delayed behavioral changes after nicotine treatment in adolescent rats. Brain Res 880:167–172.

Ulrich YA, Hargreaves, KM, Flores, CM (1997). A comparison of multiple injections versus continuous infusion of nicotine for producing up-regulation of neuronal [3H]-epibatidine binding sites. Neuropharmacology, 36, 1119–1125.

Vaglenova J, Birru S, Pandiella NM, Breese CR (2004) An assessment of the long-term developmental and behavioral teratogenicity of prenatal nicotine exposure. Behav Brain Res 150:159–170.

Vara P, Kinnunen O (1951) The effect of nicotine on the female rabbit and developing fetus. An experimental study. Ann Med Exp Biol Fenn 29:202–213.

Wilson RH, De Eds F (1936) Chronic nicotine toxicity: I. Feeding of nicotine sulfate, tannate, and bentonite. J Industr Hyg Toxicol 18:553–564.

Wilson JR (1942) The effect of nicotine on lactation in white mice. Am J Obstet Gynecol 43:839–844.

Yanai J, Pick CG, Rogel-Fuchs Y, Zahalka EA (1992) Alternations in hippocampal cholinergic receptors and hippocampal behaviors after early exposure to nicotine. Brain Res Bull 29:363–368.

21

Neuronal Receptors for Nicotine: Functional Diversity and Developmental Changes

Huibert D. Mansvelder

Lorna W. Role

The nicotinic acetylcholine receptor (nAChR) is the principal target–mediator of nicotine from smoking and chewing of tobacco (Hogg et al., 2003; Picciotto, 2003; Gotti and Clementi, 2004; Wonnacott et al., 2005). The effects of nicotine on offspring of pregnant smokers are widespread, ranging from altered neural development to increased susceptibility to addiction in adolescence (Kandel et al., 1992; Broide and Leslie, 1999; Everitt et al., 2001; Frank et al., 2001; Walsh et al., 2001; Slotkin, 2002, 2004; Abreu-Villaca et al., 2004a, 2004b; Cohen et al., 2005; Slotkin et al., 2005). These facts, coupled with epidemiological findings that >20% of pregnant women smoke, underscore the importance of understanding nAChR functions in the prenatal mammalian brain (Chassin et al., 1996; Ebrahim et al., 2000; Walsh et al., 2001; Cohen et al., 2005).

Intrinsic cholinergic signaling participates in behaviors as fundamental as memory, motivation, and movement (Picciotto and Corrigall, 2002; Picciotto, 2003; Gotti and Clementi, 2004; Laviolette and van der Kooy, 2004; Wonnacott et al., 2005). Alterations in nAChR numbers and profiles are associated with numerous disorders, including Alzheimer dementia, schizophrenia, and, not surprisingly, addiction (Cordero-Erausquin et al., 2000; Marubio and Changeux, 2000; Changeux and Edelstein, 2001; Sabbagh et al., 2002; Freedman et al., 2003; Hogg et al., 2003; Gotti and Clementi, 2004; Newhouse et al., 2004b; Sacco et al., 2004). In view of the central role of nAChRs in such diverse conditions, it may seem surprising that more is not known of the precise composition, localization, and overall role of nAChRs in synaptic signaling in the central nervous system (CNS).

A major obstacle to advancing the field is that CNS cholinergic synapses, in contrast to their cousins in the peripheral nervous system (PNS), have largely eluded direct electrophysiological scrutiny. In defense of efforts to date, several difficulties should be noted. First, central cholinergic neurons are few in number and their projections are

341

diffuse (Woolf, 1991). Second, there are multiple subunit-combination variants of nAChRs. This structural medley is reflected in a comparable functional diversity that includes differences in nAChR sensitivity to both endogenous agonists and exogenously administered nicotine (Le Novere et al., 2002a, 2002b; Hogg et al., 2003; Gotti and Clementi, 2004). The cellular targeting of nAChRs is also diverse. Some nAChRs are shipped to presynaptic or preterminal sites, others to postsynaptic and perisynaptic locales, and all nAChR subtypes are expressed at strikingly low amounts compared with ionotropic receptors for glutamate or γ-aminobutyric acid (GABA) (Colquhoun and Patrick, 1997; Temburni et al., 2000; Le Novere et al., 2002a, 2002b; Hogg et al., 2003). Perhaps most discouraging is how quickly nAChRs transit into closed (desensitized) states in response to even minute concentrations of agonist. This trait, too, varies among neurons and among nAChR subtypes (Lu et al., 1999; Quick and Lester, 2002; Wooltorton et al., 2003; Alkondon and Albuquerque, 2004, 2005).

Although such features present serious obstacles to investigators, these same characteristics underlie the important contribution of nAChRs to the computational flexibility of circuits where signaling is subject to modulation, rather than just "on/off" control. Recent molecular biological, biochemical, and pharmacological studies have generated a powerful armamentarium of new probes and approaches for analyzing nAChR subunit compositions and subtypes (Gotti and Clementi, 2004; Laviolette and van der Kooy, 2004; Nicke et al., 2004; Wonnacott et al., 2005). The challenge now is to advance the current understanding of how cholinergic synapses, in general and pre- and postsynaptic nAChRs in particular, contribute to the functions and dysfunctions of the developing nervous system.

The last decade has witnessed considerable advances in basic knowledge of the function, development, and plasticity of nAChRs. Several recent reviews have presented novel perspectives on nAChR signaling mechanisms and on emergent views on nAChR involvement in neuropsychiatric disorders (Jones et al., 1999; Picciotto et al., 2001; Hogg et al., 2003; Picciotto, 2003; Dajas-Bailador and Wonnacott, 2004; Fucile, 2004; Gotti and Clementi, 2004; Laviolette and van der Kooy, 2004; Lester et al., 2004; Newhouse et al., 2004a, 2004b; Sacco et al., 2004; Wonnacott et al., 2005). The present chapter focuses on fundamental aspects of the acetylcholine (ACh)

receptors with which nicotine interacts in the context of potential effects on neural development and plasticity.

STRUCTURAL DIVERSITY OF NEURONAL NICOTINIC ACETYLCHOLINE RECEPTORS

Twelve separate genes encoding distinct neuronal nicotinic receptor subunit proteins have been identified and iteratively labeled as α2, α3, α4, α5, α6, α7, α8, α9, and α10, or β2, β3, and β4 (Le Novere and Changeux, 1995; Le Novere et al., 2002b; Hogg et al., 2003; Gotti and Clementi, 2004). Each of the five subunits that comprise the assembled oligomeric complex is a four-transmembrane domain protein with considerable homology among the membrane spanning regions (Fig. 21–1A, B). All nicotinic receptor subunits are characterized by a two C-loop containing N-terminal domain, the signature of their membership in the broader family of ligand-gated ion channels, along with $GABA_A$, glycine, and muscle nicotinic receptor subunits (Le Novere and Changeux, 1995; Le Novere et al., 2002a; Hogg et al., 2003; Gotti and Clementi, 2004; Lester et al., 2004). Similar to the muscle nicotinic α1 receptor subunit, neuronal α subunits are identified by the presence of vicinal cysteine residues within the N-terminal domain, a unique tag of the ligand-binding region (Brejc et al., 2001; Karlin, 2002; Le Novere et al., 2002a, 2002b). The assembled receptor protein is a pentamer with a hydrophilic core lined primarily by the second transmembrane domain of each subunit (Fig. 21–1B, C). The contribution of specific subunits to assembled receptors and key features of the ligand-binding domains and ion channel pore are being scrutinized with "knock-down," single- and double-nAChR subunit gene knockout mice (Le Novere et al., 2002b; Champtiaux et al., 2003; Hogg et al., 2003; Lester et al., 2003). The ligand-binding domain in neuronal nAChRs, like muscle-type nAChRs, is formed by the N-terminal domains of α subunits and at the interface of adjacent subunits in the assembled pentamer. The identification of sequences involved in the ionic "gate" of nAChRs has emerged from studies using ingenious combinations of mutagensis to incorporate cysteine residues at key sites, and subsequent biochemical and biophysical probing with special cysteine-reactive reagents (Karlin, 2002; Jensen et al., 2005).

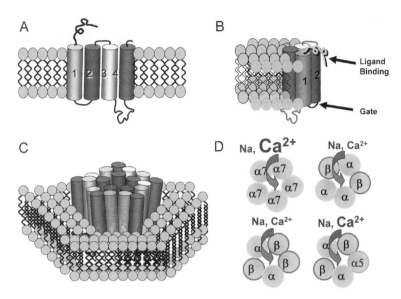

FIGURE 21–1 Current models of neuronal nicotinic receptor (nAChR) subunit complexes. Panels A and B illustrate single α- or β-type nicotinic receptor subunit protein in the membrane bilayer. **A.** Each of the neuronal nicotinic receptor subunit genes encodes a protein that traverses the membrane four times (labeled 1–4). The N-terminal domain is on the external face of the membrane, the first and second transmembrane domains (TM) are linked by short amino acid sequences on the internal face, and the second and third TM are connected by a short external linker. The cytoplasmic loop between TM 3 and 4 is the most variable portion of the subunit sequences. It has been implicated in both the modulation and membrane targeting of assembled nAChR complexes. The C terminae are short extracellular domains. **B.** Disposition of the TM within a single α subunit relative to each other and to the hydrophobic surrounds. The linker between TM1 and TM2 and the intracellular side TM2 amino acids comprise the ion channel gate (see text and Karlin, 2002). Panels C and D show models of the arrangement of five nAChR subunits (e.g., α7 alone or α and β subunits) assembled as neuronal nAChR complexes. **C.** This simplified structural model of a neuronal-type nAChR pentamer is largely inferred from studies of the muscle and torpedo electroplax nAChR. Key features include the "staves of a barrel" arrangement of each subunit around the hydrophilic pore, and the contribution of the TM2 to the lining of the channel. **D.** Examples of proposed subunit compositions of neuronal nAChRs and experimentally derived differences in Ca^{2+}:Na permeability of the illustrated subtypes.

The multiplicity of nAChR-subunit types begs the question, "why so many ?". This issue received a considerable research effort over the last decade resulting in the conclusion that different subunit combinations are functionally and pharmacologically distinct from one another (Fig. 21–1D; see Diversity of Nicotinic Acetylcholine Receptors, below). The physiological justification for the subunit diversity, however, raises the difficult question of how to identify the combinations and stoichiometries of subunits that comprise *native* nAChRs (Colquhoun and Patrick, 1997; Champtiaux et al., 2003; Nai et al., 2003; Alkondon and Albuquerque, 2005). Despite a concerted effort, this issue remains largely unresolved. Nevertheless, several generalizations about nAChR composition have held up to scrutiny: there is reasonable agreement that the α4, β2, and α7 subunits are the major players in nAChRs expressed in the CNS, whereas α3, β4, and α7 subunits are more typical components of PNS nAChRs (Cordero-Erausquin et al., 2000; Picciotto et al., 2001; Le Novere et al., 2002b; Hogg et al., 2003; Gotti and Clementi, 2004). Likewise, it is generally agreed that (1) α2, α3, and α4 require co-assembly with a β subunit to make functional channels; (2) β2 and β4 require co-assembly with an α subunit to make functional channels; (3) α5, α6, and β3 require co-assembly with both another α and β subunit to make functional channels; and (4) only α7, α8, α9, and α10 can form functional homopentamers (Wang et al., 1996; Cordero-Erausquin et al., 2000; Changeux and Edelstein, 2001; Berg and Conroy, 2002; Le Novere et al., 2002b; Hogg et al., 2003; Gotti and Clementi, 2004; Nicke, 2004).

This is what nAChR subunits can do in terms of co-assembly. What happens in vivo is less clear, although a clearer picture is emerging as native nAChRs become better defined through combined molecular, pharmacological, and biophysical approaches (Sivilotti et al., 1997; Yu and Role, 1998a, 1998b; Cuevas et al., 2000; Champtiaux et al., 2003; Nai et al., 2003; Fucile, 2004; Fischer et al., 2005). In recognition of compositional uncertainty, a consortium of "nicotinologists" have adapted a nomenclature in which the inclusion of a subunit in an nAChR complex is indicated by an asterisk (Lukas et al., 1999) For example, the designation α4β2* is used for nAChR complexes that include α4 and β2 subunits, regardless of stoichiometry, i.e., $(α4)_2 (β2)_3$ or $(α4)_3 (β2)_2$, and allows for the possibility that other subunits may participate in the native complex. So far, reports on native nAChR composition include everything from the simplest configuration (i.e., homopentameric, such as $(α7)_5$ to the most complicated versions (i.e., different α and β subunits) of nAChRs (Le Novere et al., 2002b). Mercifully, studies of the overlaps in nAChR-subunit gene expression patterns suggest that the subunit composition of native nAChRs is not as horrific as the simple mathematical calculation with 12 subunits in groups of five would predict ($>10^5$ possible outcomes!). In addition, the expression patterns for several subunits are relatively restricted (e.g., α5, α6, and β3) (Le Novere et al., 1996; Klink et al., 2001; Le Novere et al., 2002b; Zoli et al., 2002); α8 has not been identified in mammalian systems and α9 and α10 appear to be largely restricted to innervated sensory epithelia (Elgoyhen et al., 2001; Keiger et al., 2003). In sum, the subunit composition and

stoichiometry of native neuronal nAChRs is more complicated than can be resolved with any one of the current analytic techniques, but is probably less baroque than straight combinatorial analyses might suggest.

DIVERSITY OF NEURONAL NICOTINIC ACETYLCHOLINE RECEPTORS

Functional Groups

The functional distinctions among nAChRs of different composition are not trivial. Each is an important determinant of how the gating of a particular nicotinic receptor could contribute to synaptic excitability and/or be affected by exogenously delivered nicotine. In the beginning of the 1990s, biochemical and biophysical analyses combined to rescue α5, α6, and β3 from their orphan status (Le Novere et al., 1996; Ramirez-Latorre et al., 1996; Wang et al., 1996; Groot-Kormelink et al., 1998; Lena et al., 1999; Kuryatov et al., 2000). More recent work has honed these techniques to better define the functional properties that distinguish one nAChR subtype from another (Nai et al., 2003). It is now clear that the inclusion of each of these subunits in nAChR complexes can change the kinetics, unitary conductance, and calcium permeability of the resultant channels (Ramirez-Latorre et al., 1996; Wang et al., 1996; Yu and Role, 1998a, 1998b; Nai et al., 2003). For example, biophysical studies show that α3β4* and a3α5β4* nAChRs, which are present at many peripheral sites and involved in the cardiovascular effects of nicotine pass more picoamps per millisecond than α4β2* nAChRs (Gerzanich et al., 1998). The activation profiles and desensitization rates of these nAChRs are also dissimilar from one another and are very different from α7 homomeric nAChRs (Berg and Conroy, 2002; Quick and Lester, 2002; Khiroug et al., 2004).

Rectification properties of the various channel subtypes as well as agonist and antagonist binding properties are distinct, but perhaps the most functionally important difference among nAChR subtypes is in their relative Ca^{2+} permeability (e.g., Fig. 21–1D). The subject of Ca^{2+} conductance and nAChRs requires an extra comment on α7* nAChRs, the poster-child equivalent for decades of "grind and bind" and autoradiographic assays of CNS α-bungarotoxin

(αBgTx) sites. The dogged efforts of several investigators brought the beguiling finding that the archetypal muscle αBgTx-binding site was peppered all over the CNS, to the ultimate resolution of a unique set of nicotine-gated ion channels (Wonnacott et al., 1982; Clarke et al., 1985; Dajas-Bailador and Wonnacott, 2004; Fucile, 2004; Nicke et al., 2004). The calcium permeability of $\alpha7^*$ nAChRs is greater than that of other neuronal nAChRs and much larger than that of the muscle nAChR. In fact, the fractional current through $\alpha7^*$ nAChRs that is attributable to Ca^{2+} is comparable to N-methyl-D-aspartate (NMDA)–type glutamate receptors, but without the extra control afforded by the voltage and Mg-dependent gating that constrains NMDA receptors (Dajas-Bailador and Wonnacott, 2004). In other words, $\alpha7^*$ nAChRs are essentially Ca^{2+} flood gates just waiting for ligand to happen! Judicious targeting of such receptors to presynaptic domains can (and apparently does) provide a local trigger for Ca^{2+}-dependent transmitter release. More subtle to an electrophysiologist, but not to the nAChR-bearing neurons, are the many downstream molecular targets of calcium influx (Dajas-Bailador and Wonnacott, 2004). These sorts of Ca^{2+}-dependent tuning, by both $\alpha7$ and non-$\alpha7$ nAChRs, appear to be important loci of nicotine's effects on the developing nervous system (see Nicotinic Acetylcholine Receptors, Synaptic Plasticity, and Brain Development, below).

The essential contribution of $\alpha2\beta4^*$ nAChRs at synapses and circuits related to nicotine-elicited responses has been repeatedly and compellingly demonstrated (Picciotto and Corrigall, 2002; Lester et al., 2003; Picciotto, 2003; Gotti and Clementi, 2004; Laviolette and van der Kooy, 2004; Wonnacott et al., 2005). Since Changeux and colleagues (Picciotto et al., 1995) first reported the altered avoidance learning in knockout mice of the high-affinity $\beta2^*$ nAChRs, the chorus has mounted on the key role of these nAChRs in CNS function, culminating with the recent identification of a single site deemed essential to $\alpha2\beta4^*$-mediated addiction (Tapper et al., 2004). The role of changes in the number of nAChRs (not confined to, but exemplified by, $\alpha2\beta4^*$ nAChRs) in the effects of long-term nicotine exposure is still under debate (Gentry and Lukas, 2002; Wonnacott et al., 2005).

In addition to compositional diversity in nAChRs, other factors and conditions that may differ from cell to cell and from synapse to synapse regulate the functional efficacy of nAChRs. Thus, marked differences in the physiological profile of native nAChRs vs. their recombinant versions expressed in heterologous systems underscore the potential role of local or cell-specific regulatory molecules in determining nAChR function in vivo. Extracellular modulators of nAChRs abound, including endotoxins, endocannabionoids, and neuropeptides (Miwa et al., 1999; Di Angelantonio et al., 2003; Le Foll and Goldberg, 2004; Oz et al., 2004).

A striking example of native receptors being more functionally complex than their heterologous equivalents has emerged from studies of $\alpha7$-containing nAChRs (Yu and Role, 1998b; Berg and Conroy, 2002; Khiroug et al., 2002; Drisdel et al., 2004). Comparison of many in vitro expression studies with neuronal studies has led to the conclusion that most native $\alpha7^*$ nAChRs are homopentameric complexes with very rapid desensitization, low agonist affinity, and long-lasting αBgTx binding. Other work indicates that a subset of native $\alpha7^*$ nAChRs may include other subunits, or $\alpha7$ subunits that have been subjected to post-translational modifications, yielding nAChRs with very different agonist-induced activation and desensitization from $(\alpha7)_5$ (Yu and Role, 1998a; Cuevas et al., 2000; Khiroug et al., 2002; Drisdel et al., 2004).

Diversity in Targeting of Nicotinic Acetylcholine Receptors in the Central Nervous System

The development of better pharmacological tools and new molecular probes to nAChRs have unveiled impressive intricacies in the cellular trafficking of nAChRs (Williams et al., 1998; Temburni et al., 2000, 2004; Berg and Conroy, 2002; Brumwell et al., 2002; Blank et al., 2004; Liu et al., 2005). Depending on subunit composition (and in the case of $\alpha3$, on identified subunit sequences) an nAChR complex can be selectively targeted to somatic-dendritic vs. axonal domains, as well as to synaptic, pre-, or perisynaptic subdomains within a neuron.

As ACh and nicotine can influence synaptic transmission via pre- and postsynaptic nAChRs, and since "extrasynaptic" nAChRs may exert important regulatory effects on neuronal activity, the trafficking to all loci is likely important (Fig. 21–2) (Hogg et al., 2003; Dajas-Bailador and Wonnacott, 2004; Gotti and

A. POSTSYNAPTIC NICOTINIC AChRs

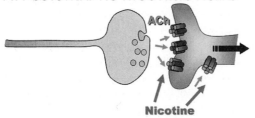

B. PRE-SYNAPTIC NICOTINIC AChRs

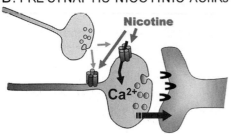

FIGURE 21–2   Proposed disposition and physiological effects of pre-, post- and perisynaptic nicotinic receptors. **A.** This image depicts neuron–neuron connections where postsynaptic nAChRs participate in direct transmission. Acetylcholine (ACh) acts as a primary synaptic transmitter in peripheral autonomic ganglia and at some CNS sites. ACh is released from closely apposed presynaptic elements, leading to the direct activation of postsynaptic nAChRs. Note that despite their perisynaptic location on ciliary ganglion neurons, $\alpha 7^*$ nAChRs participate in direct synaptic responses. Administration of nicotine could activate and/or desensitize receptors at both peri- and directly postsynaptic locales. **B.** Presynaptic (and/or preterminal) nAChRs contribute to the modulation of synaptic transmission. ACh may be released from nearby cholinergic projections, leading to the activation of nAChRs localized at or near presynaptic terminals. Depending on the position and subtype of nAChR, as well as the ambient vs. stimulated concentration of ACh, the spontaneous and/or evoked release of transmitter is facilitated or depressed by added nicotine. The ambiguity of these statements, and those in the text, as well as the fanciful nature of the diagram reflect the very real difficulties in assessing the actions of nicotine in vivo.

Clementi, 2004). Many groups have advanced the proposal that, despite the relatively low concentrations of nAChRs in the CNS, nAChRs do play an important role in fine-tuning CNS synaptic transmission because of their strategic localization to presynaptic sites (Dani, 2001; Fucile, 2004; Sher et al., 2004).

Early demonstrations of presynaptic effects of nicotine receptor activation came from studies of synaptosome preparations by Wonnacott, Collins, and colleagues (Rapier et al., 1988; Wonnacott et al., 1989; Grady et al., 1992) and from electrophysiological studies of Changeux and colleagues (Vidal and Changeux, 1993; Gioanni et al., 1999). The presynaptic modulation of central glutamatergic transmission by nAChRs at several sites was initially distinguished by its αBgTx sensitivity and its ablation following knock-down of $\alpha 7$ subunits (McGehee et al., 1995; Gray et al., 1996). The high Ca^{2+} permeability of the $\alpha 7^*$ nAChRs serves to escort Ca^{2+} into axon terminals, thus facilitating spontaneous and stimulus-evoked transmission at numerous sites of glutamate release. Non-$\alpha 7$–containing presynaptic nAChRs has been implicated in the regulation of glutamate and GABA release (Vidal and Changeux, 1993). The cumulative literature suggests that the receptor pharmacology and presumed composition of presynaptic nAChRs appear to be just as elaborate as those of peri- and postsynaptic nAChRs (Mulle et al., 1991; Jones et al., 2001; Jones and Wonnacott, 2004; Fischer et al., 2005).

Despite evidence that nAChRs can participate in the modulation of transmitter release in the CNS, one should not get too carried away. There is increasing evidence for direct synaptic transmission (i.e., mediated by ACh release and postsynaptic nAChR activation) in several CNS regions, including the hippocampus, nigrostriatal system, and in sensory cortex (Jones and Yakel, 1997; Alkondon and Albuquerque, 2004; Matsubayashi et al., 2004). The variety of nAChR subtypes that have been accused of mediating postsynaptic transmission in the CNS is also very broad, including both $\alpha 7^*$ and non-$\alpha 7^*$ nAChRs. Last, but not least, regardless of whether the nAChR population density is sufficient to support a synaptic current, activation of pre- and/or postsynaptic nAChRs may be sufficient to elicit important downstream signaling and metabolic responses (Berg and Conroy, 2002; Dajas-Bailador and Wonnacott, 2004).

The mechanisms underlying the release, and the ambient vs. stimulated concentrations, of ACh in the CNS remain a bit of a mystery. Both published and unpublished reports hint at less than classical mechanisms of ACh release (de Rover et al., 2002; Lester, Jo, and Role, personal communication). Electron microscopy studies examining the localization of cholinergic synaptic terminals have revealed considerable distance from cholinoceptive terminals, consistent with a volume mode of cholinergic transmission (Descarries et al., 1997; Zoli et al., 1999; Jones and Wonnacott, 2004). Such vagaries in the local concentrations of ACh at pre- or postsynaptic cholinocepetive sites in the CNS must be addressed before the contribution of nAChR activation (and inactivation) to the developing nervous system can be understood.

DEVELOPMENTAL EXPRESSION OF NICOTINIC ACETYLCHOLINE RECEPTORS

Prenatal Expression of Neuronal Nicotinic Acetylcholine Receptors

Constituents of the Cholinergic System

Acetylcholine and nAChRs play critical roles in virtually all phases of brain maturation, during embryogenesis as well as postnatal development. Choline acetyltransferase (ChAT), the synthetic enzyme for ACh, appears very early during embryogenesis (Smith et al., 1979), and ACh influences development as early as gastrulation (Fig. 21–3). Initially, ACh promotes cell division at a stage when ACh synthesis occurs in preneural undifferentiated cells. During gastrulation and postgastrulation, ACh regulates cell movements that are blocked by ACh antagonists in sea urchin embryos (Falugi, 1993; Lauder and Schambra, 1999), and sea urchin oocytes and early embryos contain nAChRs (Ivonnet and Chambers, 1997; Buznikov and Rakich, 2000). This finding suggests that in addition to ChAT, other proteins involved in cholinergic signaling are expressed by embryonic cells during these stages. Indeed, acetylcholinesterase (AChE), the enzyme that breaks down ACh, is present during sea urchin gastrulation (Falugi, 1993). Messenger RNA coding for nAChR subunits is detected in cultures of premigratory neural crest cells (Howard et al., 1995), which in the fetus will give rise to most neurons in the PNS. Thus, even before neuronal differentiation, cholinergic signaling through nAChRs occurs and may even contribute to development of non-neuronal cells.

In prenatal neural tissue, both muscarinic acetylcholine receptors (mAChRs) and nAChRs are detected, but nAChRs are expressed earlier than mAChRs (Lauder and Schambra, 1999). nAChR expression as well as ChAT immunoreactivity and AChE activity show a caudorostral gradient of appearance in the fetal brain (Zoli et al., 1995; Lauder and Schambra, 1999). Functional nAChR expression has been detected in stem and progenitor cells of the rat cerebral cortex at gestational day (G) 10 (Atluri et al., 2001) and in mesencephalon of developing brain at G11 (Zoli et al., 1995). Early expression of subunit mRNAs seems characteristic of nAChR, since other ligand-gated ion channels become expressed somewhat later. GABA and NMDA receptor mRNAs are not detected in rat brain until G14–G15 (Laurie et al., 1992; Monyer et al., 1994). During this stage, ACh promotes the switch from cell division to neuronal differentiation (Slotkin, 1998), and guidance of nerve growth cones appears to be one of the roles of cholinergic signaling through nAChRs (Hume et al., 1983; Zheng et al., 1994). At the onset of neuronal nAChR-subunit expression, innervation-independent factors are responsible for neuronal differentiation before cholinergic projections arrive (Zoli et al., 1995). Indeed, although cholinergic neurons are among the first neurons to differentiate in the CNS, in rat fetuses, cholinergic neurons are not generated before G11 and are generated first in the spinal cord, brain stem, and basal ganglia. In most other brain regions, cholinergic neurons are not detected until G12 to G16 (Lauder and Schambra, 1999).

ChAT-immunoreactive nerve terminals are detectable during the first postnatal weeks, especially in the forebrain. The major cholinergic innervation originating from the nucleus basalis of Meynert enters the cerebral cortex at about postnatal day (P) 0 (Hohmann and Berger-Sweeney, 1998), but is initially confined to the subplate, a transient, synapse-rich layer of neurons located directly under the cortical plate. Thus, the initial profile of nAChR expression may be induced by local endogenous differentiation signals rather than by cholinergic inputs per se. This contrasts with findings on cholinergic synapses in the developing autonomic nervous system (Devay et al., 1999). Here, nAChR-subunit expression in neuronal cholinergic synapses is regulated by signals from the autonomic target tissue that is innervated. Depending on the innervated tissue type, different types of nAChRs are expressed that have different kinetic properties (Devay et al., 1999).

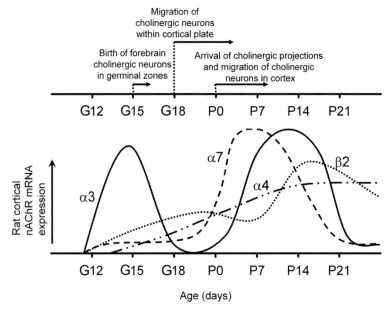

FIGURE 21–3   Developmental expression of nicotinic acetylcholine receptors (nAChRs) in rat forebrain and cortex. nAChR subunits are expressed in rat forebrain and cortex at different sites and at different times during development. Interestingly, the expression of nAChRs precedes the birth of cholinergic cells with a neuronal phenotype, suggesting that cholinergic signaling through nAChRs may be involved in the differentiation of neurons. During early postnatal development, when cholinergic projections arrive in the cortex, different nAChR subtypes show different expression dynamics, indicating that cholinergic signaling through nAChRs is involved in synaptic refinement of the neuronal circuitry.

Spatiotemporal Patterns

Expression of nAChRs is not constant during fetal development; it varies among regions and subunit. At G10, when the mouse cortex consists of dividing stem and progenitor cells, these cortical cells express α3, α4, and α7 receptor subunits that give rise to ACh-evoked inward currents (Atluri et al., 2001). Although these nAChR subunits can be detected from G10 until birth, the incidence of these subunits declines with increasing gestational age. In fetal rat brain, α3, α4, β2, and β4 nAChR subunit mRNA expression is detectable in the hindbrain and midbrain, but not forebrain, at G11 (Zoli et al., 1995). In forebrain, mRNA for α3, α4, and β2 subunits becomes detectable at G12. β2 mRNA seems to be the most widely expressed and at relatively stable levels throughout the remaining prenatal development. α4-subunit mRNA is at lower levels than β2 mRNA throughout gestation,

but shows a similarly wide distribution. In contrast, α3 and β4 mRNA are less abundantly distributed and expression can be transient in some brain regions. For instance, α3 mRNA is present in the rat forebrain on G12, G13, and G15, but is not detected there anymore at G17, G19, and P0 (Zoli et al., 1995). β4 mRNA is absent from forebrain during embryogenesis, but shows transient expression in other brain areas. It is detected in midbrain on G12 and G15, but is not detected in midbrain nuclei at G19 and P0 (Zoli et al., 1995). In developing chick brain, similar regional specificity and transient expression occur throughout gestational stages (Torrao et al., 2000). α2, α3, α5, and β2 mRNAs are expressed very early on in ganglia at embryonic day 4, and are expressed throughout the chick brain at G18. α7 mRNA was detected in Purkinje neurons of chick cerebellum at G12, but expression decreased after G18 (Kaneko et al., 1998). Taken together, the early onset, regional specificity, and transient nature of nAChR expression suggest that they may play important roles during embryonic development of rodent and chick brain. This theory is underscored by findings in transgenic mice with inducible expression of α2 subunits. Restoration of β2 subunit expression during development in thalamocortical projections of β2 knockout mice normalizes passive-avoidance learning in these animals, suggesting that β2 expression in these projections during development is critical for normal development of this behavior (King et al., 2003).

In fetal human brain, nAChR gene transcripts and proteins are also detected at very early gestational stages. nAChR protein and gene transcripts are readily detected by 4 to 5 weeks of gestation (Hellstrom-Lindahl et al., 1998). Messenger RNAs of α3, α4, α5, α7, β2, β3, and β4 are found widely distributed over the fetal brain between 4 and 12 weeks of gestation. In most brain areas, radio-ligand binding of nAChRs by [³H] epibatidine and [³H] cysteine increased from weeks 4 to 12. The highest specific binding of these ligands was detected in spinal cord, pons, and medulla oblongata, whereas binding by the α7 subunit–specific probe [¹²⁵I]αBgTx was found to be strongest in pons, medulla oblongata, and midbrain (Hellstrom-Lindahl and Court, 2000). Periods of transient high nAChR density were found in frontal cortex, hippocampus, cerebellum, and brainstem of humans during mid-gestation and neonatal periods (Kinney et al., 1993; Court et al., 1997). A significant positive correlation between gestational age and the expression of α7 mRNA was observed in all brain regions except cortex (Falk et al., 2002). From the late fetal stage, human brain nAChR expression has been shown to fall with increasing age (Hellstrom-Lindahl et al., 1998; Hellstrom-Lindahl and Court, 2000; Falk et al., 2003). Thus, nAChRs also appear to play an important role in human development, neurogenesis, and synaptogenesis.

Response to Prenatal Nicotine Exposure

Depending on the developmental phase, ACh promotes or prevents neuronal apoptosis: when cells are poorly differentiated, the effect is primarily pro-apoptotic, whereas in differentiated cells, it is anti-apoptotic (Hohmann and Berger-Sweeney, 1998). The early expression of nAChRs during fetal development gives rise to a vulnerability of the human fetus to exogenous nicotine exposure. A substantial percentage of pregnant woman continue smoking during pregnancy. In the United States, nearly half of all women smokers continue to smoke during their pregnancies (Ebrahim et al., 2000), or about 12% of all women who give birth (Mathews, 2001). More than 500,000 infants each year are exposed to cigarette smoke in utero.

Fetal exposure to nicotine damages the developing brain, interfering with cell replication and differentiation. It also evokes apoptosis, culminating in reduced cell number and aberrant cell proportions (Slotkin, 2002; Abreu-Villaca et al., 2004a). In rat fetus, during neurulation in the neural tube stage at G9.5, nicotine exposure causes cytotoxicity in all brain areas and incidences of apoptosis sharply increase (Roy et al., 1998). Prenatal exposure to nicotine increases cortical mRNA expression of α4, β2, and α7 nAChR subunits in rats (Shacka and Robinson, 1998a; Frank et al., 2001). Also, when pregnant primates are exposed to nicotine at concentrations experienced by smokers, fetal brain damage is induced (Slotkin et al., 2005). Nicotine exposure during 30 to 160 days of gestation induced α4β2 and α7 nAChR upregulation in several brain areas, including cortex. In addition, cell loss, reduction in cell size and reduced neuritic outgrowth was observed. In humans, these prenatal nicotine effects lead to behavioral deficits during later life (Slotkin, 2004). Nicotine treatment of primary neuronal cultures of human prenatal brain increases expression of α3 and α7 nAChR subunits (Hellstrom-Lindahl et al., 2001). In longitudinal studies of prenatally exposed infants, fetal tobacco exposure affects attention and impulsivity behavior (Leech et al., 1999), and can lead to lower intelligence quotient and conduct disorder in later life (Ernst et al., 2001; Wakschlag et al., 2002).

Postnatal Expression of Neuronal Nicotinic Acetylcholine Receptors

Expression Patterns and Integration with Other Neurotransmitter Systems

In humans as well as in rodents and other mammals, brain development is far from complete at birth, and many neuronal systems need to mature in response to ongoing interaction with the ex utero environment. Indeed, neuroproliferation, apoptosis, and synaptic rearrangement persist into adolescence. Cholinergic signaling continues to play an important role in postnatal brain development, which is emphasized by brain region–specific and transient expression profiles of nAChR subunits (Fuchs, 1989; Broide et al., 1995, 1996; Zhang et al., 1998). Disruption of cholinergic innervation during early postnatal development results in delayed cortical neuronal development and permanent changes in cortical cytoarchitecture and cognitve behaviors (Hohmann and Berger-Sweeney, 1998). $\alpha3$, $\alpha7$, and $\beta4$ subunit mRNA expression is low during mid-gestation and increases during late gestation and early postnatal life (Winzer-Serhan and Leslie, 1997). During the first few postnatal weeks, various subunits are transiently expressed in select sites in the brain: $\alpha2$ in the hippocampus and in brain stem; $\alpha3$ in the striatum, cerebellum, and cortex; $\alpha4$ in hippocampus, striatum, and cerebellum; $\alpha7$ in the cerebellum and cortex; and $\beta2$ in the striatum (Broide et al., 1995, 1996; Zhang et al., 1998). In rat cortex, $\alpha4$ mRNA is maximal by P14 after which its expression remains high. $\beta2$ mRNA is low on P7 but peaks at P14. $\alpha7$ mRNA expression reaches a maximum on P7 (Shacka and Robinson, 1998b). These expression patterns suggest that nAChR subunits play specific roles during postnatal development. Genetic silencing of $\alpha4$, $\beta2$, and $\beta3$ nAChR subunits shows that each subunit is involved in particular neuronal and behavioral phenotypes, hinting at their unique roles in brain development (Cordero-Erausquin et al., 2000). Only the $\alpha3$-subunit knockout mice have a high fraction of mortality during the first postnatal week (Xu et al., 1999), most likely because this subunit is an essential component of nAChRs that mediate fast synaptic transmission in the autonomic nervous system, and, as such, is essential for perinatal survival. To illustrate the contributions of cholinergic signaling to postnatal brain development, developmental changes in nAChR expression and function in primary sensory cortex are described below.

Cholinergic transmission is present in the early developing rat parietal cortex at birth (Descarries et al., 1997; Mechawar and Descarries, 2001). In the first 2 weeks after birth, the cholinergic innervation increases greatly in number of varicosities and number of branches per axon. The association of these new cholinergic terminals with postsynaptic densities is low (<15%), by contrast, and remains constant

throughout adulthood (Mechawar et al., 2002). Ultrastructural analyses of some monoaminergic nerve terminals in the cortex (Audet et al., 1988, 1989) and hippocampus (Vizi and Kiss, 1998) show that most of these nerve terminals do not make contact with structurally identifiable postsynaptic elements. These terminals are equipped for vesicle release despite not making direct synaptic contacts (Seguela et al., 1989, 1990; Descarries and Mechawar, 2000). This phenomenon suggests that they communicate with postsynaptic targets through volume transmission (Zoli et al., 1999). By comparison, the percentage of GABAergic and glutamatergic axons that terminate on a postsynaptic site approaches 100% (Seguela et al., 1990; Umbriaco et al., 1994, 1995). Cholinergic innervation is almost exclusively extrasynaptic in several areas of the rat brain, including the parietal cortex (Umbriaco et al., 1994; Mechawar et al., 2002), hippocampus (Umbriaco et al., 1995), neostriatum (Contant et al., 1996), and visual, sensory, and parietal cortices (Avendano et al., 1996; Turrini et al., 2001). Cholinergic communication through volume transmission has wideranging implications for nAChR impact on neuronal function, especially when one takes differences in activation and desensitization properties of nAChRs into account (Mansvelder et al., 2002; Quick and Lester, 2002).

Functionality of the Cholinergic Receptors

During postnatal development of sensory cortices there is a dramatic, transient increase in the expression of AChE (Robertson et al., 1991). Concurrently, nAChR $\alpha7$ subunit gene expression also transiently increases in sensory cortices. Binding of $[^{125}I]\alpha BgTx$ in rat sensory cortex starts at P0, peaks at P10, and then declines to adult concentration by P20 (Fuchs, 1989). Expression of $\alpha7$ subunit mRNA follows a similar time course (Broide et al., 1995). During fetal development, $\alpha7$ mRNA is expressed in low amounts on G13 in the ventricular zone of the neocortex, and on G15 in the thalamic neuroepithelium. A marked increase in $\alpha7$ mRNA concentrations is observed during the late prenatal period in both sensory and nonsensory regions of the cortex and thalamus. Moderate to high levels of messenger RNA are maintained into the first postnatal week, followed by a decline into adulthood (Broide et al., 1995). The increase in cortical α7 mRNA follows the arrival of AChE-labeled thalamocortical afferents. Preventing these afferents from reaching the cortex strongly reduces the α7 subunit mRNA and [^{125}I]αBgTx binding in layers IV and VI (Broide et al., 1996). These data suggest that the expression of α7 subunit–containing nAChRs is regulated by thalamic inputs. These α7 subunit–containing nAChRs could be located postsynaptically as well as presynaptically on thalamic afferents. It has been hypothesized that presynaptic α7 nAChRs in primary auditory cortex are involved in the maturation of glutamate synapses by facilitating the conversion of "silent synapses" (defined as those containing only NMDA receptors) into mature α-amino-3-hydroxy-5-methyl-4-isoxazole-propionic acid (AMPA) and NMDA receptor–containing synapses (Metherate and Hsieh, 2003; Metherate, 2004). The authors of this hypothesis suggest that through this mechanism of nAChR-induced maturation of glutamate synapses, the expression of α7 subunits in the auditory cortex could define a critical period of sensory cortex development in which synaptic refinement of cortical circuitry and tuning to sensory inputs takes place. nAChR activation has been shown to alter synaptic strength of glutamatergic synaptic transmission in other brain areas as well, as described below.

In developing hippocampus, nAChRs containing α7 subunits can also activate silent synapses that show a low probability of being active and turn them into high-probability synapses (Maggi et al., 2003). Schaffer collateral to CA1 synapses that have a high probability of being active during development can be down-regulated by α7 and β2 subunit–containing nAChRs (Maggi et al., 2004). These findings suggest that nicotinic receptors also can play a role during postnatal development of excitatory glutamatergic connections and can contribute to shaping of the hippocampal neuronal circuitry.

To understand the physiological effect of the activation of nAChRs by neuronal activity during postnatal development, it is important to consider their cellular and subcellular distribution. As mentioned above, nAChRs modulate presynaptic glutamate release (McGehee et al., 1995; Gray et al., 1996; McGehee and Role, 1996; MacDermott et al., 1999). In addition, nAChRs can modulate GABAergic transmission in multiple brain areas, such as the ventral tegmental area (VTA), thalamus, neocortex,

and hippocampus (Lena et al., 1993; Alkondon et al., 1997, 2000; Lena and Changeux, 1997; Fisher et al., 1998; Radcliffe et al., 1999; Mansvelder and McGehee, 2002). Modulation of GABAergic neurons by nAChRs has been most extensively studied in the hippocampus, where GABAergic local circuit neurons (LCNs; also known as interneurons) express multiple nAChR subtypes (Alkondon et al., 1997, 1999; Jones and Yakel, 1997; Frazier et al., 1998; McQuiston and Madison, 1999; Ji and Dani, 2000; Alkondon and Albuquerque, 2004). There is evidence for nAChR expression at two sites: (1) at presynaptic terminals (where they directly modulate GABA release, independent of action potential firing) (Fisher et al., 1998; Lu et al., 1999; Radcliffe et al., 1999) and (2) away from synaptic terminals (where modulation of GABA release is dependent on action potential firing) (Alkondon et al., 1997, 1999; Frazier et al., 1998). The expression of nAChRs depends on the type of LCN (McQuiston and Madison, 1999; Alkondon and Albuquerque, 2004; see below).

Activation of nAChRs on cortical and hippocampal LCNs results in either inhibition or disinhibition of projection neurons (PNs) (Alkondon et al., 2000; Ji and Dani, 2000; Ji et al., 2001). Inhibition is likely to be induced via nAChR-mediated increase in the GABAergic transmission directly onto PNs. Disinhibition of PNs results from an increase of inhibitory GABAergic transmission to GABAergic LCNs by activation of nAChRs. Consequently, PNs may receive less GABAergic input and are disinhibited.

Effect on Neuronal Subpopulations

There are few data on nicotinic modulation of different types of neurons in the prefrontal cortex (PFC). As in other parts of the neocortex, the PFC has a layered structure in which most of the neurons are PNs. PNs and LCNs can be distinguished on the basis of distinctive physiological, morphologically, and immunocytochemical criteria (Peters and Jones, 1984; Kawaguchi, 1993, 1995; Gabbott et al., 1997; Connors and Telfeian, 2000; Kawaguchi and Kondo, 2002; Gabbott et al., 2003). In rat, among the targets of thalamocortical afferents are PNs with somata in layers III, IV, or V of the PFC. These inputs are modulated by α4β2-containing nAChRs (Vidal and

Changeux, 1993; Gil et al., 1997; Gioanni et al., 1999; Lambe et al., 2003). Nicotinic modulation of thalamocortical projections by α4β2-containing nAChRs appears to be a general phenomenon throughout the cortex (Metherate, 2004).

An elegant study in the rat motor cortex identified distinct LCN subtypes that both express nAChR mRNA for α4, α5, and β2 subunits and show somatic nicotinic currents (Porter et al., 1999). PNs, as well as LCNs expressing either parvalbumin or somatostatin, showed no effect of agonist application in this study. LCNs expressing vasoactive intestinal peptide (VIP) and cholecystokinin (CCK), by contrast, did show nicotinic currents, and pharmacological analysis implicated non-α7 nAChRs. In human cerebral cortical slices, bipolar and multipolar LCNs exhibited either α7 or α4β2 nAChR-mediated currents (Alkondon et al., 2000).

An interesting but seldom addressed aspect of cholinergic signaling in the cortex is the role of cholinergic LCNs in cortical microcircuit function. Cholinergic LCNs in the nucleus accumbens (NAc) can affect GABAergic transmission within the NAc itself via nAChR activation (de Rover et al., 2002). In addition, these cholinergic LCNs could be important in the production of lasting changes in microcircuitries that affect animal behavior, since their intrinsic firing properties are altered during behavioral sensitization to amphetamine (de Rover et al., 2004). Furthermore, immunohistochemical data show that a small fraction of bipolar LCNs in layer II/III of the rodent sensory and motor cortices are cholinergic (Houser et al., 1985). A more recent study using single-cell reverse-transcriptase polymerase chain reaction found a subgroup of cortical LCNs that are immunopositive for VIP and calretinin and also express ChAT transcripts (Cauli et al., 1997). These same VIP-positive cells are the main LCN subtype expressing nicotinic currents and nAChR mRNA (Porter et al., 1999). The National Institute of Neurological Disorders and Stroke (NINDS) GENSAT BAC Transgenics Project shows that ChAT-positive staining is evident in almost every part of the cortex, including the PFC (http://www.gensat.org/makeconnection.jsp). The putative presence of cholinergic LCNs in the cortex introduces the possibility of cortical nAChR activation independent of cholinergic terminals that originate from lower brain areas. Since the PFC is implicated in behavioral sensitization (see below), intrinsic properties of cholinergic LCNs and ACh release in the PFC could also be modified during behavioral sensitization following the intake of drugs of abuse, as described in the NAc (de Rover et al., 2004).

NICOTINIC ACETYLCHOLINE RECEPTORS, SYNAPTIC PLASTICITY, AND BRAIN DEVELOPMENT

Activation of α7 nAChRs in primary sensory cortex during postnatal development may alter synaptic strength of glutamatergic synapses (Metherate, 2004). In recent years, several studies in different brain areas have revealed lasting effects of nicotine or ACh on synaptic connections (Mansvelder and McGehee, 2000; Dani et al., 2001; Girod and Role, 2001; Ji et al., 2001; Mansvelder et al., 2002). Long-term modulation of glutamatergic and GABAergic synaptic connections by nAChRs can alter functioning of neuronal circuits for many days and possibly induce lasting changes that could be important for postnatal development of these brain areas. These properties of cholinergic signaling through nAChRs are discussed in the context of findings on nicotinic modulation of the mesolimbic DAergic system.

In rat, the DA reward system shows considerable plasticity during postnatal life and does not complete maturation until late adolescence or early adulthood (Benes et al., 2000). Since this system exhibits a similar make-up in the human brain, adolescence might well represent a time window prone to aberrations by exposure to drugs of abuse. The mammalian brain is particularly sensitive to developing addictions during adolescence. The unique behavioral features of adolescence are driven largely by maturational changes in the CNS, a process prone to environmental influences such as drug exposure. Epidemiological studies show that exposure to addictive drugs during adolescence increases the risk of becoming a drug addict later in life (Kandel et al., 1992; Grant and Dawson, 1997). Adolescent smoking is clearly correlated with smoking in later life. Moreover, adolescent smoking is a strong predictor of the occurrence of adult depression (Chassin et al., 1996).

In the VTA, nAChRs are expressed on DAergic neurons, GABAergic neurons, and glutamatergic terminals (Fig. 21-4) (Pidoplichko et al., 1997;

Charpantier et al., 1998; Mansvelder and McGehee, 2000; Klink et al., 2001; Champtiaux et al., 2002; Mansvelder et al., 2002; Pidoplichko et al., 2004). VTA DAergic neurons express three pharmacologically identifiable nAChRs—one that is likely a homomeric α7 nAChR and two that do not contain the α7 subunit. Most DAergic neurons express nAChR that can be blocked by mecamylamine, whereas less than half of the DAergic neurons express α7 nAChRs (Pidoplichko et al., 1997; Klink et al., 2001; Wooltorton et al., 2003; Pidoplichko et al., 2004). GABAergic neurons in the VTA express a similar variety of

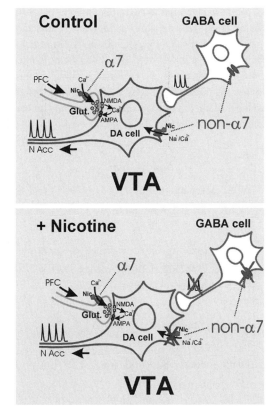

FIGURE 21–4 Nicotinic modulation of synaptic communication in rat ventral tegmental area (VTA). In the VTA, nAChRs are present on dopamine (DA)ergic neurons, GABAergic neurons, and glutamatergic terminals. Arrival of low concentrations of nicotine, as experienced by smokers, rapidly activates and desensitizes non-α7 nAChRs, whereas α7 nAChRs on glutamatergic terminals are activated but suffer much less from desensitization. (*Source:* Modified from Mansvelder and McGehee, 2002)

nAChR subunits. As with DA neurons, only a minority of GABAergic neurons express α7 nAChRs (Wooltorton et al., 2003). The majority of the VTA GABAergic neurons express nAChRs that most likely contain α4 and β2 subunits, which are blocked by dihydro-β-erythroidine (DHβE) (Mansvelder et al., 2002).

Glutamatergic transmission onto DAergic neurons is enhanced by activation of presynaptic nAChRs (Mansvelder and McGehee, 2000; Jones and Wonnacott, 2004). Interestingly, cholinergic synaptic terminals are not found in close vicinity to glutamatergic terminals expressing α7-containing nAChR, consistent with a "volume" mode of cholinergic signaling (Descarries et al., 1997; Zoli et al., 1999; Jones and Wonnacott, 2004). When nicotine arrives in the VTA, it stimulates glutamatergic terminals as well as dopamine neurons, thereby favoring conditions of pre- and postsynaptic paired activation and a Hebbian type of synaptic plasticity. Nicotine-induced pairing resulted in long-term potentiation (LTP) of glutamatergic inputs (Mansvelder and McGehee, 2000). Nicotine also induced LTP *in vivo*, measured as an increase in AMPA/NMDA receptor ratio (Saal et al., 2003). Taken together, these findings suggest that synaptic plasticity in the VTA may be induced after smoking a single cigarette and most likely underlies the persistent effects of the drug on DA release in the NAc and PFC.

The α7-containing nAChRs involved in this mechanism are not desensitized by low nicotine concentrations associated with tobacco smoking (Mansvelder et al., 2002; Wooltorton et al., 2003). However, the non-α7 nAChRs on GABAergic neurons undergo rapid desensitization within minutes after the start of nicotine exposure and, as a consequence, reduce the inhibitory input to the DA neurons (Mansvelder et al., 2002; Wooltorton et al., 2003). Desensitization of the nAChRs on GABAergic neurons not only prevents further activation by nicotine but also precludes the contribution of these receptors to endogenous cholinergic transmission (Mansvelder et al., 2002). VTA dopamine neurons are thus disinhibited by desensitization of non-α7-type nAChRs (Mansvelder et al., 2002). Despite rapid desensitization properties, genetically engineered mice lacking β2 subunits (Picciotto et al., 1998) or expressing α4 subunits hypersensitive to nicotine (Tapper et al., 2004) have been used to show that these subunits are key in nicotine addiction.

NICOTINIC ACETYLCHOLINE RECEPTORS AND SYNAPTIC PLASTICITY IN OTHER BRAIN AREAS

Currently, it is unknown whether long-term modulation of synaptic connections by nicotine occurs within the PFC. Data on long-term modulation of synaptic contacts by nicotine anywhere in the neocortex are lacking. On the other hand, nicotine does modulate synaptic plasticity in brain areas other than the VTA. In rat spinal cord, the α7 subunit containing nAChR affects the induction of synaptic plasticity (Genzen and McGehee, 2003). In the absence of nicotine, pairing of pre- and postsynaptic activity in dorsal horn neurons induces LTP in some of the neurons. With nicotine, the prevalence of LTP induction is enhanced. In the hippocampus, in a minority of the glutamatergic synapses nicotine induces LTP by itself, but in most of glutamatergic synapses nicotine modulates the induction of synaptic plasticity (Fujii et al., 1999; Ji et al., 2001; Mann and Greenfield, 2003). Activation of postsynaptic nAChRs on CA1 PNs can boost short-term plasticity into LTP in Schaffer collateral synapses (Ji et al., 2001). Activation of nAChRs on LCNs that synapse on PNs can prevent LTP in glutamatergic synapses (Ji et al., 2001). Thus, timing and localization of nAChR activity in the hippocampus can determine whether LTP will occur or not. These types of nicotinic mechanisms on LTP induction may contribute to the well-known effects of nicotine on learning and memory.

SUMMARY AND CONCLUSIONS

Over the past 30 years, research on cholinergic signaling in the developing nervous system has shown that nAChR play an important role in shaping neuronal circuits. The subunit composition of nAChRs expressed in different brain regions changes during pre- and postnatal development; the subunit mRNA profiles are highly dynamic during this time. Given the variety of biophysical and pharmacological properties conferred by differences in nAChR composition, the types of signals mediated by nAChRs are most likely subject to important changes throughout normal development. In this regard, cholinergic signaling during gestation and postnatal development changes from facilitating cell division, cell differentiation, and axon guidance to fine-tuning neuronal circuits, activating silent synapses, and modulating synaptic strength. The same holds true for nicotine exposure during development: depending on the developmental stage, the magnitude of damage induced and the specific targets affected by smoking during pregnancy will vary.

The findings reviewed in this chapter describe part of what is surely a much bigger picture of the role of nAChR-signaling in development; many gaps in this picture remain. Molecular and electrophysiological techniques, despite their great sensitivity, still lack the flexibility to precisely define which combinations of nAChR subunits combine to determine the full spectrum of responses to ACh. Cholinergic signaling during development is the culmination of the integrated action of different nAChRs, acting in somato-dendritic vs. axonal domains, transducing either electrical information or calcium signaling. Future studies will need to address these questions before sketches of cholinergic signaling in development can emerge in more vibrant detail.

Abbreviations

ACh   acetylcholine

AChE   acetylcholinesterase

αBgTx   α-bungarotoxin

AMPA   α-amino-3-hydroxy-5-methyl-4-isoxazole-propionic acid

CCK   cholecystokinin

ChAT   choline acetyltransferase

CNS   central nervous system

DA   dopamine

DHβE   dihidro-β-erythroidine

G   gestational day

GABA   γ-aminobutyric acid

LCN   local circuit neuron

LTP   long-term potentiation

mAChR   muscarinic acetylcholine receptor

NAc   nucleus accumbens

nAChR   nicotinic acetylcholine receptor

NMDA   N-methyl-D-aspartate

P   postnatal day

PFC   prefrontal cortex

PN   projection neuron

PNS   peripheral nervous system

VIP   vasoactive intestinal peptide

VTA   ventral tegmental area

ACKNOWLEDGMENTS   This work was supported by grants from the Netherlands Royal Academy of Arts and Sciences (KNAW) and the Netherlands Council for Medical Research (Zon-MW) to H.D.M. and from the National Institute of Neurological Disorders and Stroke to L.W.R.

References

Abreu-Villaca Y, Seidler FJ, Slotkin TA (2004a) Does prenatal nicotine exposure sensitize the brain to nicotine-induced neurotoxicity in adolescence? Neuropsychopharmacology 29:1440–1450.

Abreu-Villaca Y, Seidler FJ, Tate CA, Cousins MM, Slotkin TA (2004b) Prenatal nicotine exposure alters the response to nicotine administration in adolescence: effects on cholinergic systems during exposure and withdrawal. Neuropsychopharmacology 29:879–890.

Alkondon M, Albuquerque EX (2004) The nicotinic acetylcholine receptor subtypes and their function in the hippocampus and cerebral cortex. Prog Brain Res 145:109–120.

—— (2005) Nicotinic receptor subtypes in rat hippocampal slices are differentially sensitive to desensitization and early in vivo functional upregulation by nicotine and to block by bupropion. J Pharmacol Exp Ther 313:740–750.

Alkondon M, Pereira EF, Barbosa CT, Albuquerque EX (1997) Neuronal nicotinic acetylcholine receptor activation modulates γ-aminobutyric acid release from CA1 neurons of rat hippocampal slices. J Pharmacol Exp Ther 283:1396–1411.

Alkondon M, Pereira EF, Eisenberg HM, Albuquerque EX (1999) Choline and selective antagonists identify two subtypes of nicotinic acetylcholine receptors that modulate GABA release from CA1 interneurons in rat hippocampal slices. J Neurosci 19:2693–2705.

—— (2000) Nicotinic receptor activation in human cerebral cortical interneurons: a mechanism for inhibition and disinhibition of neuronal networks. J Neurosci 20:66–75.

Atluri P, Fleck MW, Shen Q, Mah SJ, Stadfelt D, Barnes W, Goderie SK, Temple S, Schneider AS (2001) Functional nicotinic acetylcholine receptor expression in stem and progenitor cells of the early embryonic mouse cerebral cortex. Dev Biol 240:143–156.

Audet MA, Descarries L, Doucet G (1989) Quantified regional and laminar distribution of the serotonin innervation in the anterior half of adult rat cerebral cortex. J Chem Neuroanat 2:29–44.

Audet MA, Doucet G, Oleskevich S, Descarries L (1988) Quantified regional and laminar distribution of the noradrenaline innervation in the anterior half of the adult rat cerebral cortex. J Comp Neurol 274:307–318.

Avendano C, Umbriaco D, Dykes RW, Descarries L (1996) Acetylcholine innervation of sensory and motor neocortical areas in adult cat: a choline acetyltransferase immunohistochemical study. J Chem Neuroanat 11:113–130.

Benes FM, Taylor JB, Cunningham MC (2000) Convergence and plasticity of monoaminergic systems in the medial prefrontal cortex during the postnatal period: implications for the development of psychopathology. Cereb Cortex 10:1014–1027.

Berg DK, Conroy WG (2002) Nicotinic α7 receptors: synaptic options and downstream signaling in neurons. J Neurobiol 53:512–523.

Blank M, Triana-Baltzer GB, Richards CS, Berg DK (2004) A-protocadherins are pre-synaptic and axonal in nicotinic pathways. Mol Cell Neurosci 26:530–543.

Brejc K, van Dijk WJ, Klaassen RV, Schuurmans M, van Der OJ, Smit AB, Sixma TK (2001) Crystal structure of an ACh-binding protein reveals the ligand-binding domain of nicotinic receptors. Nature 411:269–276.

Broide RS, Leslie FM (1999) The α7 nicotinic acetylcholine receptor in neuronal plasticity. Mol Neurobiol 20:1–16.

Broide RS, Robertson RT, Leslie FM (1996) Regulation of α7 nicotinic acetylcholine receptors in the developing rat somatosensory cortex by thalamocortical afferents. J Neurosci 16:2956–2971.

Broide RS, O'Connor LT, Smith MA, Smith JA, Leslie FM (1995) Developmental expression of α7 neuronal nicotinic receptor messenger RNA in rat sensory cortex and thalamus. Neuroscience 67:83–94.

Brumwell CL, Johnson JL, Jacob MH (2002) Extrasynaptic α7-nicotinic acetylcholine receptor expression in developing neurons is regulated by inputs, targets, and activity. J Neurosci 22:8101–8109.

Buznikov GA, Rakich L (2000) Cholinoreceptors of early (preneural) sea urchin embryos. Neurosci Behav Physiol 30:53–62.

Cauli B, Audinat E, Lambolez B, Angulo MC, Ropert N, Tsuzuki K, Hestrin S, Rossier J (1997) Molecular and physiological diversity of cortical nonpyramidal cells. J Neurosci 17:3894–3906.

Champtiaux N, Gotti C, Cordero-Erausquin M, David DJ, Przybylski C, Lena C, Clementi F, Moretti M, Rossi FM, Le Novere N, McIntosh JM, Gardier AM, Changeux JP (2003) Subunit composition of functional nicotinic receptors in dopaminergic neurons investigated with knock-out mice. J Neurosci 23:7820–7829.

Champtiaux N, Han ZY, Bessis A, Rossi FM, Zoli M, Marubio L, McIntosh JM, Changeux JP (2002) Distribution and pharmacology of α6-containing nicotinic acetylcholine receptors analyzed with mutant mice. J Neurosci 22:1208–1217.

Changeux J, Edelstein SJ (2001) Allosteric mechanisms in normal and pathological nicotinic acetylcholine receptors. Curr Opin Neurobiol 11:369–377.

Charpantier E, Barneoud P, Moser P, Besnard F, Sgard F (1998) Nicotinic acetylcholine subunit mRNA expression in dopaminergic neurons of the rat substantia nigra and ventral tegmental area. Neuroreport 9:3097–3101.

Chassin L, Presson CC, Rose JS, Sherman SJ (1996) The natural history of cigarette smoking from adolescence to adulthood: demographic predictors of continuity and change. Health Psychol 15: 478–484.

Clarke PB, Schwartz RD, Paul SM, Pert CB, Pert A (1985) Nicotinic binding in rat brain: autoradiographic comparison of [^{3}H]acetylcholine, [^{3}H]nicotine, and [^{125}I]-α-bungarotoxin. J Neurosci 5:1307–1315.

Cohen G, Roux JC, Grailhe R, Malcolm G, Changeux JP, Lagercrantz H (2005) Perinatal exposure to nicotine causes deficits associated with a loss of nicotinic receptor function. Proc Natl Acad Sci USA 102:3817–3821.

Colquhoun LM, Patrick JW (1997) Pharmacology of neuronal nicotinic acetylcholine receptor subtypes. Adv Pharmacol 39:191–220.

Connors BW, Telfeian AE (2000) Dynamic properties of cells, synapses, circuits, and seizures in neocortex. Adv Neurol 84:141–152.

Contant C, Umbriaco D, Garcia S, Watkins KC, Descarries L (1996) Ultrastructural characterization of the acetylcholine innervation in adult rat neostriatum. Neuroscience 71:937–947.

Cordero-Erausquin M, Marubio LM, Klink R, Changeux JP (2000) Nicotinic receptor function: new perspectives from knockout mice. Trends Pharmacol Sci 21:211–217.

Court JA, Lloyd S, Johnson M, Griffiths M, Birdsall NJ, Piggott MA, Oakley AE, Ince PG, Perry EK, Perry RH (1997) Nicotinic and muscarinic cholinergic receptor binding in the human hippocampal formation during development and aging. Brain Res Dev Brain Res 101:93–105.

Cuevas J, Roth AL, Berg DK (2000) Two distinct classes of functional 7-containing nicotinic receptor on rat superior cervical ganglion neurons. J Physiol 525(Pt 3):735–746.

Dajas-Bailador F, Wonnacott S (2004) Nicotinic acetylcholine receptors and the regulation of neuronal signalling. Trends Pharmacol Sci 25:317–324.

Dani JA (2001) Overview of nicotinic receptors and their roles in the central nervous system. Biol Psychiatry 49:166–174.

Dani JA, Ji D, Zhou FM (2001) Synaptic plasticity and nicotine addiction. Neuron 31:349–352.

de Rover M, Lodder JC, Kits KS, Schoffelmeer AN, Brussaard AB (2002) Cholinergic modulation of nucleus accumbens medium spiny neurons. Eur J Neurosci 16:2279–2290.

de Rover M, Mansvelder HD, Lodder JC, Wardeh G, Schoffelmeer AN, Brussaard AB (2004) Long-lasting nicotinic modulation of GABAergic synaptic transmission in the rat nucleus accumbens associated with behavioural sensitization to amphetamine. Eur J Neurosci 19:2859–2870.

Descarries L, Gisiger V, Steriade M (1997) Diffuse transmission by acetylcholine in the CNS. Prog Neurobiol 53:603–625.

Descarries L, Mechawar N (2000) Ultrastructural evidence for diffuse transmission by monoamine and acetylcholine neurons of the central nervous system. Prog Brain Res 125:27–47.

Devay P, McGehee DS, Yu CR, Role LW (1999) Target-specific control of nicotinic receptor expression at developing interneuronal synapses in chick. Nat Neurosci 2:528–534.

Di Angelantonio S, Giniatullin R, Costa V, Sokolova E, Nistri A (2003) Modulation of neuronal nicotinic receptor function by the neuropeptides CGRP and substance P on autonomic nerve cells. Br J Pharmacol 139:1061–1073.

Drisdel RC, Manzana E, Green WN (2004) The role of palmitoylation in functional expression of nicotinic α7 receptors. J Neurosci 24:10502–10510.

Ebrahim SH, Floyd RL, Merritt RK 2nd, Decoufle P, Holtzman D (2000) Trends in pregnancy-related smoking rates in the United States, 1987–1996. JAMA 283:361–366.

Elgoyhen AB, Vetter DE, Katz E, Rothlin CV, Heinemann SF, Boulter J (2001) α10: a determinant of nicotinic cholinergic receptor function in mammalian vestibular and cochlear mechanosensory hair cells. Proc Natl Acad Sci USA 98:3501–3506.

Ernst M, Moolchan ET, Robinson ML (2001) Behavioral and neural consequences of prenatal exposure to nicotine. J Am Acad Child Adolesc Psychiatry 40: 630–641.

Everitt BJ, Dickinson A, Robbins TW (2001) The neuropsychological basis of addictive behaviour. Brain Res Brain Res Rev 36:129–138.

Falk L, Nordberg A, Seiger A, Kjaeldgaard A, Hellstrom-Lindahl E (2002) The α7 nicotinic receptors in human fetal brain and spinal cord. J Neurochem 80: 457–465.

—— (2003) Higher expression of α7 nicotinic acetylcholine receptors in human fetal compared to adult brain. Brain Res Dev Brain Res 142:151–160.

Falugi C (1993) Localization and possible role of molecules associated with the cholinergic system during "non-nervous" developmental events. Eur J Histochem 37:287–294.

Fischer H, Orr-Urtreger A, Role LW, Huck S (2005) Selective deletion of the α5 subunit differentially affects somatic-dendritic versus axonally targeted nicotinic ACh receptors in mouse. J Physiol 563: 119–137.

Fisher JL, Pidoplichko VI, Dani JA (1998) Nicotine modifies the activity of ventral tegmental area dopaminergic neurons and hippocampal GABAergic neurons. J Physiol Paris 92:209–213.

Frank MG, Srere H, Ledezma C, O'Hara B, Heller HC (2001) Prenatal nicotine alters vigilance states and AchR gene expression in the neonatal rat: implications for SIDS. Am J Physiol (Regul Integr Comp Physiol) 280:R1134–1140.

Frazier CJ, Rollins YD, Breese CR, Leonard S, Freedman R, Dunwiddie TV (1998) Acetylcholine activates an α-bungarotoxin-sensitive nicotinic current in rat hippocampal interneurons, but not pyramidal cells. J Neurosci 18:1187–1195.

Freedman R, Olincy A, Ross RG, Waldo MC, Stevens KE, Adler LE, Leonard S (2003) The genetics of sensory gating deficits in schizophrenia. Curr Psychiatry Rep 5:155–161.

Fuchs JL (1989) [^{125}I]α-bungarotoxin binding marks primary sensory area developing rat neocortex. Brain Res 501:223–234.

Fucile S (2004) Ca^{2+} permeability of nicotinic acetylcholine receptors. Cell Calcium 35:1–8.

Fujii S, Ji Z, Morita N, Sumikawa K (1999) Acute and chronic nicotine exposure differentially facilitate the induction of LTP. Brain Res 846:137–143.

Gabbott PL, Dickie BG, Vaid RR, Headlam AJ, Bacon SJ (1997) Local-circuit neurones in the medial prefrontal cortex (areas 25, 32 and 24b) in the rat: morphology and quantitative distribution. J Comp Neurol 377:465–499.

Gabbott PL, Warner TA, Jays PR, Bacon SJ (2003) Areal and synaptic interconnectivity of prelimbic (area 32), infralimbic (area 25) and insular cortices in the rat. Brain Res 993:59–71.

Gentry CL, Lukas RJ (2002) Regulation of nicotinic acetylcholine receptor numbers and function by chronic nicotine exposure. Curr Drug Targets CNS Neurol Disord 1:359–385.

Genzen JR, McGehee DS (2003) Short- and long-term enhancement of excitatory transmission in the spinal cord dorsal horn by nicotinic acetylcholine receptors. Proc Natl Acad Sci USA 100:6807–6812.

Gerzanich V, Wang F, Kuryatov A, Lindstrom J (1998) α5 subunit alters desensitization, pharmacology, Ca^{++} permeability and Ca^{++} modulation of human neuronal α3 nicotinic receptors. J Pharmacol Exp Ther 286:311–320.

Gil Z, Connors BW, Amitai Y (1997) Differential regulation of neocortical synapses by neuromodulators and activity. Neuron 19:679–686.

Gioanni Y, Rougeot C, Clarke PB, Lepouse C, Thierry AM, Vidal C (1999) Nicotinic receptors in the rat prefrontal cortex: increase in glutamate release and facilitation of mediodorsal thalamo-cortical transmission. Eur J Neurosci 11:18–30.

Girod R, Role LW (2001) Long-lasting enhancement of glutamatergic synaptic transmission by acetylcholine contrasts with response adaptation after exposure to low-level nicotine. J Neurosci 21: 5182–5190.

Gotti C, Clementi F (2004) Neuronal nicotinic receptors: from structure to pathology. Prog Neurobiol 74: 363–396.

Grady S, Marks MJ, Wonnacott S, Collins AC (1992) Characterization of nicotinic receptor–mediated [^{3}H]dopamine release from synaptosomes prepared from mouse striatum. J Neurochem 59:848–856.

Grant BF, Dawson DA (1997) Age at onset of alcohol use and its association with DSM-IV alcohol abuse and dependence: results from the National Longitudinal Alcohol Epidemiologic Survey. J Subst Abuse 9:103–110.

Gray R, Rajan AS, Radcliffe KA, Yakehiro M, Dani JA (1996) Hippocampal synaptic transmission enhanced by low concentrations of nicotine. Nature 383:713–716.

Groot-Kormelink PJ, Luyten WH, Colquhoun D, Sivilotti LG (1998) A reporter mutation approach shows incorporation of the "orphan" subunit β3 into a functional nicotinic receptor. J Biol Chem 273:15317–15320.

Hellstrom-Lindahl E, Court JA (2000) Nicotinic acetylcholine receptors during prenatal development and brain pathology in human aging. Behav Brain Res 113:159–168.

Hellstrom-Lindahl E, Gorbounova O, Seiger A, Mousavi M, Nordberg A (1998) Regional distribution of nicotinic receptors during prenatal development of human brain and spinal cord. Dev Brain Res 108: 147–160.

Hellstrom-Lindahl E, Seiger A, Kjaeldgaard A, Nordberg A (2001) Nicotine-induced alterations in the expression of nicotinic receptors in primary cultures from human prenatal brain. Neuroscience 105: 527–534.

Hogg RC, Raggenbass M, Bertrand D (2003) Nicotinic acetylcholine receptors: from structure to brain function. Rev Physiol Biochem Pharmacol 147: 1–46.

Hohmann CF, Berger-Sweeney J (1998) Cholinergic regulation of cortical development and plasticity. New twists to an old story. Perspect Dev Neurobiol 5:401–425.

Houser CR, Crawford GD, Salvaterra PM, Vaughn JE (1985) Immunocytochemical localization of choline acetyltransferase in rat cerebral cortex: a study of cholinergic neurons and synapses. J Comp Neurol 234:17–34.

Howard MJ, Gershon MD, Margiotta JF (1995) Expression of nicotinic acetylcholine receptors and subunit mRNA transcripts in cultures of neural crest cells. Dev Biol 170:479–495.

Hume RI, Role LW, Fischbach GD (1983) Acetylcholine release from growth cones detected with patches of acetylcholine receptor–rich membranes. Nature 305:632 634.

Ivonnet PI, Chambers EL (1997) Nicotinic acetylcholine receptors of the neuronal type occur in the plasma membrane of sea urchin eggs. Zygote 5:277–287.

Jensen ML, Schousboe A, Ahring PK (2005) Charge selectivity of the Cys-loop family of ligand-gated ion channels. J Neurochem 92:217–225.

Ji D, Dani JA (2000) Inhibition and disinhibition of pyramidal neurons by activation of nicotinic receptors on hippocampal interneurons. J Neurophysiol 83: 2682–2690.

Ji D, Lape R, Dani JA (2001) Timing and location of nicotinic activity enhances or depresses hippocampal synaptic plasticity. Neuron 31:131–141.

Jones IW, Bolam JP, Wonnacott S (2001) Pre-synaptic localisation of the nicotinic acetylcholine receptor β2 subunit immunoreactivity in rat nigrostriatal dopaminergic neurones. J Comp Neurol 439:235–247.

Jones IW, Wonnacott S (2004) Precise localization of α7 nicotinic acetylcholine receptors on glutamatergic axon terminals in the rat ventral tegmental area. J Neurosci 24:11244–11252.

Jones S, Sudweeks S, Yakel JL (1999) Nicotinic receptors in the brain: correlating physiology with function. Trends Neurosci 22:555–561.

Jones S, Yakel JL (1997) Functional nicotinic ACh receptors on interneurones in the rat hippocampus. J Physiol 504:603–610.

Kandel DB, Yamaguchi K, Chen K (1992) Stages of progression in drug involvement from adolescence to adulthood—further evidence for the gateway theory. J Stud Alcohol 53:447–457.

Kaneko WM, Britto LR, Lindstrom JM, Karten HJ (1998) Distribution of the α7 nicotinic acetylcholine receptor subunit in the developing chick cerebellum. Dev Brain Res 105:141–145.

Karlin A (2002) Emerging structure of the nicotinic acetylcholine receptors. Nat Rev Neurosci 3:102–114.

Kawaguchi Y (1993) Groupings of nonpyramidal and pyramidal cells with specific physiological and morphological characteristics in rat frontal cortex. J Neurophysiol 69:416–431.

—— (1995) Physiological subgroups of nonpyramidal cells with specific morphological characteristics in layer II/III of rat frontal cortex. J Neurosci 15: 2638–2655.

Kawaguchi Y, Kondo S (2002) Parvalbumin, somatostatin and cholecystokinin as chemical markers for specific GABAergic interneuron types in the rat frontal cortex. J Neurocytol 31:277–287.

Keiger CJ, Prevette D, Conroy WG, Oppenheim RW (2003) Developmental expression of nicotinic receptors in the chick and human spinal cord. J Comp Neurol 455:86–99.

Khiroug SS, Harkness PC, Lamb PW, Sudweeks SN, Khiroug L, Millar NS, Yakel JL (2002) Rat nicotinic ACh receptor α7 and β2 subunits co-assemble to form functional heteromeric nicotinic receptor channels. J Physiol 540:425–434.

Khiroug SS, Khiroug L, Yakel JL (2004) Rat nicotinic acetylcholine receptor α2β2 channels: comparison of functional properties with α4β2 channels in Xenopus oocytes. Neuroscience 124:817–822.

King SL, Marks MJ, Grady SR, Caldarone BJ, Koren AO, Mukhin AG, Collins AC, Picciotto MR (2003) Conditional expression in corticothalamic efferents reveals a developmental role for nicotinic acetylcholine receptors in modulation of passive avoidance behavior. J Neurosci 23:3837–3843.

Kinney HC, O'Donnell TJ, Kriger P, White WF (1993) Early developmental changes in [³H]nicotine binding in the human brainstem. Neuroscience 55:1127–1138.

Klink R, de Kerchove dEA, Zoli M, Changeux JP (2001) Molecular and physiological diversity of nicotinic acetylcholine receptors in the midbrain dopaminergic nuclei. J Neurosci 21:1452–1463.

Kuryatov A, Olale F, Cooper J, Choi C, Lindstrom J (2000) Human $\alpha 6$ AChR subtypes: subunit composition, assembly, and pharmacological responses. Neuropharmacology 39:2570–2590.

Lambe EK, Picciotto MR, Aghajanian GK (2003) Nicotine induces glutamate release from thalamocortical terminals in prefrontal cortex. Neuropsychopharmacology 28:216–225.

Lauder JM, Schambra UB (1999) Morphogenetic roles of acetylcholine. Environ Health Persp 107(Suppl 1):65–69.

Laurie DJ, Wisden W, Seeburg PH (1992) The distribution of thirteen $GABA_A$ receptor subunit mRNAs in the rat brain. III. Embryonic and postnatal development. J Neurosci 12:4151–4172.

Laviolette SR, van der Kooy D (2004) The neurobiology of nicotine addiction: bridging the gap from molecules to behaviour. Nat Rev Neurosci 5:55–65.

Leech SL, Richardson GA, Goldschmidt L, Day NL (1999) Prenatal substance exposure: effects on attention and impulsivity of 6-year-olds. Neurotoxicol Teratol 21:109–118.

Le Foll B, Goldberg SR (2004) Rimonabant, a CB1 antagonist, blocks nicotine-conditioned place preferences. Neuroreport 15:2139–2143.

Lena C, Changeux JP (1997) Role of Ca^{2+} ions in nicotinic facilitation of GABA release in mouse thalamus. J Neurosci 17:576–585.

Lena C, Changeux JP, Mulle C (1993) Evidence for "preterminal" nicotinic receptors on GABAergic axons in the rat interpeduncular nucleus. J Neurosci 13:2680–2688.

Lena C, de Kerchove D'Exaerde A, Cordero-Erausquin M, Le Novere N, del Mar Arroyo-Jimenez M, Changeux JP (1999) Diversity and distribution of nicotinic acetylcholine receptors in the locus ceruleus neurons. Proc Natl Acad Sci USA 96:12126–12131.

Le Novere N, Changeux JP (1995) Molecular evolution of the nicotinic acetylcholine receptor: an example of multigene family in excitable cells. J Mol Evol 40:155–172.

Le Novere N, Corringer PJ, Changeux JP (2002a) The diversity of subunit composition in nAChRs: evolutionary origins, physiologic and pharmacologic consequences. J Neurobiol 53:447–456.

Le Novere N, Grutter T, Changeux JP (2002b) Models of the extracellular domain of the nicotinic receptors and of agonist- and Ca^{2+}-binding sites. Proc Natl Acad Sci USA 99:3210–3215.

Le Novere N, Zoli M, Changeux JP (1996) Neuronal nicotinic receptor $\alpha 6$ subunit mRNA is selectively concentrated in catecholaminergic nuclei of the rat brain. Eur J Neurosci 8:2428–2439.

Lester HA, Dibas MI, Dahan DS, Leite JF, Dougherty DA (2004) Cys-loop receptors: new twists and turns. Trends Neurosci 27:329–336.

Lester HA, Fonck C, Tapper AR, McKinney S, Damaj MI, Balogh S, Owens J, Wehner JM, Collins AC, Labarca C (2003) Hypersensitive knockin mouse strains identify receptors and pathways for nicotine action. Curr Opin Drug Disc Dev 6:633–639.

Liu Z, Tearle AW, Nai Q, Berg DK (2005) Rapid activity-driven SNARE-dependent trafficking of nicotinic receptors on somatic spines. J Neurosci 25:1159–1168.

Lu Y, Marks MJ, Collins AC (1999) Desensitization of nicotinic agonist-induced [^{3}H]γ-aminobutyric acid release from mouse brain synaptosomes is produced by subactivating concentrations of agonists. J Pharmacol Exp Ther 291:1127–1134.

Lukas RJ, Changeux JP, Le Novere N, Albuquerque EX, Balfour DJ, Berg DK, Bertrand D, Chiappinelli VA, Clarke PB, Collins AC, Dani JA, Grady SR, Kellar KJ, Lindstrom JM, Marks MJ, Quik M, Taylor PW, Wonnacott S (1999) International Union of Pharmacology. XX. Current status of the nomenclature for nicotinic acetylcholine receptors and their subunits. Pharmacol Rev 51:397–401.

MacDermott AB, Role LW, Siegelbaum SA (1999) Presynaptic ionotropic receptors and the control of transmitter release. Annu Rev Neurosci 22:443–485.

Maggi L, Le Magueresse C, Changeux JP, Cherubini E (2003) Nicotine activates immature "silent" connections in the developing hippocampus. Proc Natl Acad Sci USA 100:2059–2064.

Maggi L, Sola E, Minneci F, Le Magueresse C, Changeux JP, Cherubini E (2004) Persistent decrease in synaptic efficacy induced by nicotine at Schaffer collateral-CA1 synapses in the immature rat hippocampus. J Physiol 559:863–874.

Mann EO, Greenfield SA (2003) Novel modulatory mechanisms revealed by the sustained application of nicotine in the guinea-pig hippocampus in vitro. J Physiol 551:539–550.

Mansvelder HD, Keath JR, McGehee DS (2002) Synaptic mechanisms underlie nicotine-induced excitability of brain reward areas. Neuron 33:905–919.

Mansvelder HD, McGehee DS (2000) Long-term potentiation of excitatory inputs to brain reward areas by nicotine. Neuron 27:349–357.

—— (2002) Cellular and synaptic mechanisms of nicotine addiction. J Neurobiol 53:606–617.

Marubio LM, Changeux J (2000) Nicotinic acetylcholine receptor knockout mice as animal models for studying receptor function. Eur J Pharmacol 393:113–121.

Mathews TJ (2001) Smoking during pregnancy in the 1990s. Natl Vital Stat Rep 49:1–14.

Matsubayashi H, Amano T, Seki T, Sasa M, Sakai N (2004) Post-synaptic $\alpha 4$ $\beta 2$ and $\alpha 7$ type nicotinic acetylcholine receptors contribute to the local and endogenous acetylcholine-mediated synaptic transmissions in nigral dopaminergic neurons. Brain Res 1005:1–8.

McGehee DS, Heath MJ, Gelber S, Devay P, Role LW (1995) Nicotine enhancement of fast excitatory synaptic transmission in CNS by pre-synaptic receptors. Science 269:1692–1696.

McGehee DS, Role LW (1996) Pre-synaptic ionotropic receptors. Curr Opin Neurobiol 6:342–349.

McQuiston AR, Madison DV (1999) Nicotinic receptor activation excites distinct subtypes of interneurons in the rat hippocampus. J Neurosci 19:2887–2896.

Mechawar N, Descarries L (2001) The cholinergic innervation develops early and rapidly in the rat cerebral cortex: a quantitative immunocytochemical study. Neuroscience 108:555–567.

Mechawar N, Watkins KC, Descarries L (2002) Ultrastructural features of the acetylcholine innervation in the developing parietal cortex of rat. J Comp Neurol 443:250–258.

Metherate R (2004) Nicotinic acetylcholine receptors in sensory cortex. Learn Mem 11:50–59.

Metherate R, Hsich CY (2003) Regulation of glutamate synapses by nicotinic acetylcholine receptors in auditory cortex. Neurobiol Learn Mem 80:285–290.

Miwa JM, Ibanez-Tallon I, Crabtree GW, Sanchez R, Sali A, Role LW, Heintz N (1999) lynx1, an endogenous toxin-like modulator of nicotinic acetylcholine receptors in the mammalian CNS. Neuron 23:105–114.

Monyer H, Burnashev N, Laurie DJ, Sakmann B, Seeburg PH (1994) Developmental and regional expression in the rat brain and functional properties of four NMDA receptors. Neuron 12:529–540.

Mulle C, Vidal C, Benoit P, Changeux JP (1991) Existence of different subtypes of nicotinic acetylcholine receptors in the rat habenulo-interpeduncular system. J Neurosci 11:2588–2597.

Nai Q, McIntosh JM, Margiotta JF (2003) Relating neuronal nicotinic acetylcholine receptor subtypes defined by subunit composition and channel function. Mol Pharmacol 63:311–324.

Newhouse PA, Potter A, Singh A (2004a) Effects of nicotinic stimulation on cognitive performance. Curr Opin Pharmacol 4:36–46.

Newhouse P, Singh A, Potter A (2004b) Nicotine and nicotinic receptor involvement in neuropsychiatric disorders. Curr Top Med Chem 4:267–282.

Nicke A (2004) Learning about structure and function of neuronal nicotinic acetylcholine receptors. Lessons from snails. Eur J Biochem 271:2293.

Nicke A, Wonnacott S, Lewis RJ (2004) A-conotoxins as tools for the elucidation of structure and function of neuronal nicotinic acetylcholine receptor subtypes. Eur J Biochem 271:2305–2319.

Oz M, Zhang L, Ravindran A, Morales M, Lupica CR (2004) Differential effects of endogenous and synthetic cannabinoids on $\alpha 7$-nicotinic acetylcholine receptor-mediated responses in Xenopus oocytes. J Pharmacol Exp Ther 310:1152–1160.

Peters A, Jones EG (1984) Cerebral Cortex. Vol. 1. Cellular Components of the Cerebral Cortex. Wiley-Liss, New York.

Picciotto MR (2003) Nicotine as a modulator of behavior: beyond the inverted U. Trends Pharmacol Sci 24:493–499.

Picciotto MR, Caldarone BJ, Brunzell DH, Zachariou V, Stevens TR, King SL (2001) Neuronal nicotinic acetylcholine receptor subunit knockout mice: physiological and behavioral phenotypes and possible clinical implications. Pharmacol Ther 92:89–108.

Picciotto MR, Corrigall WA (2002) Neuronal systems underlying behaviors related to nicotine addiction: neural circuits and molecular genetics. J Neurosci 22:3338–3341.

Picciotto MR, Zoli M, Lena C, Bessis A, Lallemand Y, Le Novere N, Vincent P, Pich EM, Brulet P, Changeux JP (1995) Abnormal avoidance learning in mice lacking functional high-affinity nicotine receptor in the brain. Nature 374:65–67.

Picciotto MR, Zoli M, Rimondini R, Lena C, Marubio LM, Pich EM, Fuxe K, Changeux JP (1998) Acetylcholine receptors containing the $\beta 2$ subunit are involved in the reinforcing properties of nicotine. Nature 391:173–177.

Pidoplichko VI, DeBiasi M, Williams JT, Dani JA (1997) Nicotine activates and desensitizes midbrain dopamine neurons. Nature 390:401–404.

Pidoplichko VI, Noguchi J, Areola OO, Liang Y, Peterson J, Zhang T, Dani JA (2004) Nicotinic cholinergic synaptic mechanisms in the ventral tegmental area contribute to nicotine addiction. Learn Mem 11:60–69.

Porter JT, Cauli B, Tsuzuki K, Lambolez B, Rossier J, Audinat E (1999) Selective excitation of subtypes of neocortical interneurons by nicotinic receptors. J Neurosci 19:5228–5235.

Quick MW, Lester RA (2002) Desensitization of neuronal nicotinic receptors. J Neurobiol 53:457–478.

Radcliffe KA, Fisher JL, Gray R, Dani JA (1999) Nicotinic modulation of glutamate and GABA synaptic transmission of hippocampal neurons. Ann NY Acad Sci 868:591–610.

Ramirez-Latorre J, Yu CR, Qu X, Perin F, Karlin A, Role L (1996) Functional contributions of α5 subunit to neuronal acetylcholine receptor channels. Nature 380:347–351.

Rapier C, Lunt GG, Wonnacott S (1988) Stereoselective nicotine-induced release of dopamine from striatal synaptosomes: concentration dependence and repetitive stimulation. J Neurochem 50:1123–1130.

Robertson RT, Mostamand F, Kageyama GH, Gallardo KA, Yu J (1991) Primary auditory cortex in the rat: transient expression of acetylcholinesterase activity in developing geniculocortical projections. Dev Brain Res 58:81–95.

Roy TS, Andrews JE, Seidler FJ, Slotkin TA (1998) Nicotine evokes cell death in embryonic rat brain during neurulation. J Pharmacol Exp Ther 287:1136–1144.

Saal D, Dong Y, Bonci A, Malenka RC (2003) Drugs of abuse and stress trigger a common synaptic adaptation in dopamine neurons. Neuron 37:577–582.

Sabbagh MN, Lukas RJ, Sparks DL, Reid RT (2002) The nicotinic acetylcholine receptor, smoking, and Alzheimer's disease. J Alzheimers Dis 4:317–325.

Sacco KA, Bannon KL, George TP (2004) Nicotinic receptor mechanisms and cognition in normal states and neuropsychiatric disorders. J Psychopharmacol 18:457–474.

Seguela P, Watkins KC, Descarries L (1989) Ultrastructural relationships of serotonin axon terminals in the cerebral cortex of the adult rat. J Comp Neurol 289:129–142.

Seguela P, Watkins KC, Geffard M, Descarries L (1990) Noradrenaline axon terminals in adult rat neocortex: an immunocytochemical analysis in serial thin sections. Neuroscience 35:249–264.

Shacka JJ, Robinson SE (1998a) Exposure to prenatal nicotine transiently increases neuronal nicotinic receptor subunit α7, α4 and β2 messenger RNAs in the postnatal rat brain. Neuroscience 84:1151–1161.

—— (1998b) Postnatal developmental regulation of neuronal nicotinic receptor subunit α7 and multiple α4 and β2 mRNA species in the rat. Dev Brain Res 109:67–75.

Sher E, Chen Y, Sharples TJ, Broad LM, Benedetti G, Zwart R, McPhie GI, Pearson KH, Baldwinson T, De Filippi G (2004) Physiological roles of neuronal nicotinic receptor subtypes: new insights on the nicotinic modulation of neurotransmitter release, synaptic transmission and plasticity. Curr Top Med Chem 4:283–297.

Sivilotti LG, McNeil DK, Lewis TM, Nassar MA, Schoepfer R, Colquhoun D (1997) Recombinant nicotinic receptors, expressed in Xenopus oocytes, do not resemble native rat sympathetic ganglion receptors in single-channel behaviour. J Physiol 500:123–138.

Slotkin TA (1998) Fetal nicotine or cocaine exposure: which one is worse? J Pharmacol Exp Ther 285:931–945.

—— (2002) Nicotine and the adolescent brain: insights from an animal model. Neurotoxicol Teratol 24:369–384.

—— (2004) Cholinergic systems in brain development and disruption by neurotoxicants: nicotine, environmental tobacco smoke, organophosphates. Toxicol Appl Pharmacol 198:132–151.

Slotkin TA, Seidler FJ, Qiao D, Aldridge JE, Tate CA, Cousins MM, Proskocil BJ, Sekhon HS, Clark JA, Lupo SL, Spindel ER (2005) Effects of prenatal nicotine exposure on primate brain development and attempted amelioration with supplemental choline or vitamin C: neurotransmitter receptors, cell signaling and cell development biomarkers in fetal brain regions of rhesus monkeys. Neuropsychopharmacology 30:129–144.

Smith J, Fauquet M, Ziller C, Le Douarin NM (1979) Acetylcholine synthesis by mesencephalic neural crest cells in the process of migration in vivo. Nature 282:853–855.

Tapper AR, McKinney SL, Nashmi R, Schwarz J, Deshpande P, Labarca C, Whiteaker P, Marks MJ, Collins AC, Lester HA (2004) Nicotine activation of α4* receptors: sufficient for reward, tolerance, and sensitization. Science 306:1029–1032.

Temburni MK, Blitzblau RC, Jacob MH (2000) Receptor targeting and heterogeneity at interneuronal nicotinic cholinergic synapses in vivo. J Physiol 525(Pt 1):21–29.

Temburni MK, Rosenberg MM, Pathak N, McConnell R, Jacob MH (2004) Neuronal nicotinic synapse assembly requires the adenomatous polyposis coli tumor suppressor protein. J Neurosci 24:6776–6784.

Torrao AS, Carmona FM, Lindstrom J, Britto LR (2000) Expression of cholinergic system molecules during development of the chick nervous system. Dev Brain Res 124:81–92.

Turrini P, Casu MA, Wong TP, De Koninck Y, Ribeiro-da-Silva A, Cuello AC (2001) Cholinergic nerve terminals establish classical synapses in the rat cerebral cortex: synaptic pattern and age-related atrophy. Neuroscience 105:277–285.

Umbriaco D, Garcia S, Beaulieu C, Descarries L (1995) Relational features of acetylcholine, noradrenaline, serotonin and GABA axon terminals in the stratum radiatum of adult rat hippocampus (CA1). Hippocampus 5:605–620.

Umbriaco D, Watkins KC, Descarries L, Cozzari C, Hartman BK (1994) Ultrastructural and morphometric features of the acetylcholine innervation in adult rat parietal cortex: an electron microscopic study in serial sections. J Comp Neurol 348:351–373.

Vidal C, Changeux JP (1993) Nicotinic and muscarinic modulations of excitatory synaptic transmission in the rat prefrontal cortex in vitro. Neuroscience 56:23–32.

Vizi ES, Kiss JP (1998) Neurochemistry and pharmacology of the major hippocampal transmitter systems: synaptic and nonsynaptic interactions. Hippocampus 8:566–607.

Wakschlag LS, Pickett KE, Cook E Jr, Benowitz NL, Leventhal BL (2002) Maternal smoking during pregnancy and severe antisocial behavior in offspring: a review. Am J Public Health 92:966–974.

Walsh RA, Lowe JB, Hopkins PJ (2001) Quitting smoking in pregnancy. Med J Aust 175:320–323.

Wang F, Gerzanich V, Wells GB, Anand R, Peng X, Keyser K, Lindstrom J (1996) Assembly of human neuronal nicotinic receptor α5 subunits with α3, β2, and β4 subunits. J Biol Chem 271:17656–17665.

Williams BM, Temburni MK, Levey MS, Bertrand S, Bertrand D, Jacob MH (1998) The long internal loop of the α3 subunit targets nAChRs to subdomains within individual synapses on neurons in vivo. Nat Neurosci 1:557–562.

Winzer-Serhan UH, Leslie FM (1997) Codistribution of nicotinic acetylcholine receptor subunit α3 and β4 mRNAs during rat brain development. J Comp Neurol 386:540–554.

Wonnacott S, Harrison R, Lunt G (1982) Immunological cross-reactivity between the α-bungarotoxin-binding component from rat brain and nicotinic acetylcholine receptor. J Neuroimmunol 3:1–13.

Wonnacott S, Irons J, Rapier C, Thorne B, Lunt GG (1989) Pre-synaptic modulation of transmitter release by nicotinic receptors. Prog Brain Res 79:157–163.

Wonnacott S, Sidhpura N, Balfour DJ (2005) Nicotine: from molecular mechanisms to behaviour. Curr Opin Pharmacol 5:53–59.

Woolf NJ (1991) Cholinergic systems in mammalian brain and spinal cord. Prog Neurobiol 37:475–524.

Wooltorton JR, Pidoplichko VI, Broide RS, Dani JA (2003) Differential desensitization and distribution of nicotinic acetylcholine receptor subtypes in midbrain dopamine areas. J Neurosci 23:3176–3185.

Xu W, Gelber S, Orr-Urtreger A, Armstrong D, Lewis RA, Ou CN, Patrick J, Role L, De Biasi M, Beaudet AL (1999) Megacystis, mydriasis, and ion channel defect in mice lacking the α3 neuronal nicotinic acetylcholine receptor. Proc Natl Acad Sci USA 96:5746–5751.

Yu CR, Role LW (1998a) Functional contribution of the α7 subunit to multiple subtypes of nicotinic receptors in embryonic chick sympathetic neurones. J Physiol 509:651–665.

—— (1998b) Functional contribution of the α5 subunit to neuronal nicotinic channels expressed by chick sympathetic ganglion neurones. J Physiol 509:667–681.

Zhang X, Liu C, Miao H, Gong ZH, Nordberg A (1998) Postnatal changes of nicotinic acetylcholine receptor α2, α3, α4, α7 and β2 subunits genes expression in rat brain. Int J Dev Neurosci 16:507–518.

Zheng JQ, Felder M, Connor JA, Poo MM (1994) Turning of nerve growth cones induced by neurotransmitters. Nature 368:140–144.

Zoli M, Jansson A, Sykova E, Agnati LF, Fuxe K (1999) Volume transmission in the CNS and its relevance for neuropsychopharmacology. Trends Pharmacol Sci 20:142–150.

Zoli M, Le Novere N, Hill JA Jr, Changeux JP (1995) Developmental regulation of nicotinic ACh receptor subunit mRNAs in the rat central and peripheral nervous systems. J Neurosci 15:1912–1939.

Zoli M, Moretti M, Zanardi A, McIntosh JM, Clementi F, Gotti C (2002) Identification of the nicotinic receptor subtypes expressed on dopaminergic terminals in the rat striatum. J Neurosci 22:8785–8789.

22

Neural Precursors as Preferential Targets for Drug Abuse: Long-Term Consequences and Latent Susceptibility to Central Nervous System Disorders

Kurt F. Hauser

Nazira El-Hage

Shreya Buch

Gregory N. Barnes

Henrietta S. Bada

James R. Pauly

The production of new neurons and glia occurs throughout life and is exceedingly sensitive to disruption by drug abuse. New neural cells originate within specialized regions of the central nervous system (CNS) that maintain an environmental milieu necessary for cell proliferation, and they appear to be essential for the maintenance of stem cells (Fig. 22–1). The germinal zones also provide spatial cues that establish cell polarity and organization. The appearance of germinal zones is highly ordered and follows precise spatiotemporal guidelines that arise in the ventricular zone (VZ) and are sustained in the subventricular zone (SZ), cerebellar external granular (or germinal) layer (EGL), and intrahilar zone (IHZ) of the dentate gyrus (Ramón y Cajal, 1960; Boulder Committee, 1970; Goldman, 1998; Alvarez-Buylla and Garcia-Verdugo, 2002; Taupin and Gage, 2002).

Considerable evidence indicates that drugs with abuse liability disrupt development by affecting the production of new neurons and glia. Moreover, the effects of drug abuse are not limited to a particular cell type, germinal zone, or stage of development, but rather they uniquely affect individual neuronal and glial precursor types within various germinal zones. Germinal zones are targeted to varying degrees by most substances with abuse liability (Lauder et al., 1998; Luo and Miller, 1998; Hildebrandt et al., 1999; Teuchert-Noodt et al., 2000; Buznikov et al., 2001; Duman et al., 2001; Radley and Jacobs, 2002; Crews and Nixon, 2003; Lin and Rosenthal, 2003; Gordon and Hen, 2004; see Chapters 11 and 12). Like their progeny, neural precursors express an inexplicably rich variety of receptor and neurotransmitter types, which seemingly contributes to their pronounced sensitivity to multiple neurotransmitters and drugs of abuse that mimic the endogenous neurochemical systems. Drugs of abuse that effect the genesis of new neural cells likely include cocaine, methamphetamine, opiates, nicotine, alcohol, and perhaps ecstasy (via serotonergic actions) (Hauser and Mangoura, 1998; Lauder et al., 1998; Hildebrandt et al., 1999; Teuchert-Noodt et al., 2000; Buznikov et al., 2001;

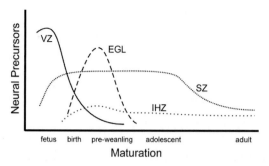

FIGURE 22-1 Schematic diagram showing sites of neural precursor production throughout rodent ontogeny. Neural cells are initially produced in the ventricular zone (VZ) and then in the subventricular zone (SZ). The cerebellar external granular (or germinal) layer (EGL) is a secondary proliferative zone that arises from the brain stem and exclusively generates neurons (Hauser et al., 2003). The SZ becomes a major source of supragranular neurons and macroglia relatively early during maturation (approximately at birth in rodents and during the third trimester in humans), whereas the intrahilar zone (IHZ) of the dentate gyrus is a major site of adult neuronogenesis. There is compelling evidence that opiates and nicotine affect germinal cells in all four of the zones.

Duman et al., 2001; Radley and Jacobs, 2002; Hauser et al., 2003; Lin and Rosenthal, 2003; Gordon and Hen, 2004). Although we will focus on the effects of opiates and nicotine on the genesis of neural cells, most other drugs with abuse potential also seem to affect neural development to varying degrees through direct actions on the CNS.

As noted earlier, it is assumed that drugs of abuse disrupt the genesis of neurons and glia by disrupting the endogenous neurochemical systems that normally regulate maturation (Hauser et al., 2003). It is also important to consider that, besides mimicry, the unique pharmacological actions of drugs of abuse may activate novel signaling events and genes, resulting in qualitatively different responses from those seen with normal neurotransmitter systems.

OPIATES

Opiates, which we will define as being derived from the opium poppy (e.g., heroin and morphine), act by mimicking endogenous "opioid" peptides and preferentially activating μ-opioid receptors (MOR). Opiate

exposure can modulate the production of neural cells in the VZ and SZ (Dodge Miller et al., 1982; Reznikov et al., 1999; Stiene-Martin et al., 2001) and the EGL (Zagon and McLaughlin, 1983, 1987) during maturation in experimental animal models. More recently, opiates have been additionally implicated in affecting neurogenesis in the adult IHZ (Eisch et al., 2000; Mandyam et al., 2004), which suggests that the ability of opiates to disrupt the genesis of neural precursors is lifelong. The extent to which cellular changes in the germinative zones translates into neurocognitive defects in opiate-exposed children is uncertain. Exposure to opiates in utero, however, is highly correlated with low infant birth weight and length, reduced head circumference, as well as alterations in cognitive, motor, and/or behavioral milestones during the first 3 years (Messinger et al., 2004; Shankaran et al., 2004).

Although providing essential evidence that opiates effect CNS development irrespective of a variety of psychosocial factors, whole-animal studies present some limitations in approaching certain mechanistic questions. For example, the endogenous opioid system—i.e., endogenous peptides and MOR, δ- (DOR) and κ-opioid receptors (KOR)—regulates a variety of physiological functions that may secondarily effect development (Hauser and Mangoura, 1998). Besides direct effects on opioid-receptor expressing neural progenitors, opioid exposure can induce changes in, for example, respiration, nutrition, and endocrine function (Martin, 1983; Akil et al., 1984; Simon, 1991; Simon and Hiller, 1994; Rogers and Peterson, 2003), which may in turn affect neural development. Dissociating the direct from indirect effects of opiates *in vivo* can be quite challenging (Hammer, 1993). For this reason, tissue culture has been proven an invaluable tool in isolating different neural cell types and studying the role of opioids in the regulation of the proliferation, differentiation, or death of neural cells (Hauser and Stiene-Martin, 1993; Hauser and Mangoura, 1998).

Endogenous opioids and opiate drugs have marked effects on cell neuronal differentiation (Zagon and McLaughlin, 1986a, 1986b; Vernadakis et al., 1990; Mangoura and Dawson, 1993). In particular, Hammer has shown that morphine, the major bioactive form of heroin in the brain, inhibits pyramidal cell differentiation in the cerebral cortical pyramidal neurons (Hammer et al., 1989; Ricalde and Hammer, 1991). Although the effects on differentiation during development are significant, many aspects of the effects of opioid on CNS maturation has been extensively reviewed in the past (Zagon, 1987; Hammer and Hauser, 1992; Hammer, 1993; Hauser and Stiene-Martin, 1993; Hauser et al., 2003; Eisch and Mandyam, 2004; Slotkin, 2004). For this reason, the present chapter focuses on the effects of opiates as related to the genesis of neurons and glia in the CNS.

Neuronogenesis

Alterations in the endogenous opioid system, either by manipulating the endogenous opioids themselves or through opiate drug treatment, cause profound changes in the developing nervous system. Opioids affect multiple regions, including the cerebellum (Zagon and McLaughlin, 1986a, 1987; Hauser et al., 1989; Lorber et al., 1990; Hauser and Stiene-Martin, 1991) and forebrain regions such as the cerebral cortex and hippocampus (Zagon and McLaughlin, 1986b; Hauser et al., 1989; Hauser and Stiene-Martin, 1991). In excess, opiates reportedly inhibit the proliferation of neuroblasts and/or glia (Steele and Johannesson, 1975; Vértes et al., 1982; Zagon and McLaughlin, 1986a, 1986b, 1987; Kornblum et al., 1987b; Hammer et al., 1989; Schmahl et al., 1989; Lorber et al., 1990; Seatriz and Hammer, 1993), although these initial studies relied on labeling indices with thymidine analogs to assess cell proliferation, which may only yield a partial understanding of cell cycle changes (Mandyam et al., 2004). By contrast, continuous treatment with opioid receptor antagonists during development generally has the opposite effects of continuous agonist treatment. Continuous opioid receptor blockade increases (1) the rate of thymidine incorporation into DNA, (2) the area and volume of cortical cell layers, (3) neuronal and glial numbers/unit area, (4) dendritic size and the number of spines/unit length, and (5) increased differentiation and synaptogenesis (Zagon and McLaughlin, 1986a, 1986b, 1987; Hauser et al., 1987, 1989).

Many of the above developmental studies suggested that opiate drugs could modulate the genesis of neurons and glia in the VZ or SZ. Initial studies showed that opiate exposure (morphine or methadone) markedly reduced cell numbers in the forebrain when the genesis of the cells originates from the VZ/SZ (Steele and Johannesson, 1975; Zagon and McLaughlin, 1977b, 1982b). Initially, it was uncertain whether neural progenitors expressed opioid receptors or whether the effects of opioids were direct. Later studies used radioligand binding (Kornblum et al., 1987a; Leslie and Loughlin, 1993), in situ hybridization (Leslie et al., 1998; Zhu et al., 1998), and immunocytochemistry (Reznikov et al., 1999; Stiene-Martin et al., 2001) to identify MOR, DOR, and KOR on germinal cells in the VZ/SZ. Conversely, it was later shown that chronic opioid receptor blockade increased thymidine incorporation and cell numbers (Zagon and McLaughlin, 1983, 1986b, 1987), which was generally the opposite effect of opiate drug treatment. Importantly, the findings from opioid antagonist studies additionally provided circumstantial evidence that the endogenous opioid system is tonically active and inhibits development.

Opioid peptides and receptors are highly expressed by immature EGL cells, which consist of neuroblasts and immature post-mitotic neurons, but are not expressed by more mature granule neurons derived from this germinative layer (Zagon et al., 1985; Kinney and White, 1991; Osborne et al., 1993). This finding suggests that the expression of the opioid system by EGL cells is unrelated to the onset of expression of adult neurochemical systems and therefore likely to be involved in maturational processes (Hauser et al., 2003). In the cerebellum, manipulation of the opioid system alters the proliferation of cerebellar EGL neuroblasts and/or their granule neuron progeny (Zagon and McLaughlin, 1983, 1986a, 1987; Hauser et al., 1987, 1989; Lorber et al., 1990), as well as their differentiation (Zagon and McLaughlin, 1986a; Hauser et al., 1989, 2000) and survival (Hauser et al., 2000). Similarly, exposure to preferential MOR-acting opiates such as morphine or methadone causes decreased thymidine incorporation and/or reductions in cell numbers (Zagon and McLaughlin, 1977a, 1977c, 1982a). In cells isolated from the murine EGL, morphine exposure significantly reduces neuroblast numbers and DNA synthesis and the effects of morphine can be prevented by the selective MOR antagonist β-funaltrexamine, findings suggesting that MOR regulates cell proliferation. By contrast, DOR agonists selectively reduce neurite outgrowth from granule neurons as they differentiate from EGL precursors, while morphine has no effect on this measure (Hauser et al., 2000). This action suggests that individual opioid receptor types may regulate different aspects of development in the same cell.

The death of neuronal precursors is an occasionally reported consequence of exposure to opiates alone (Meriney et al., 1985). Opioids can modulate the effects of existing apoptotic signals (especially in immune cells [Singhal et al., 2001, 2002]), and opiates may be co-factors in regulating neural cell death (Gurwell et al., 2001; Khurdayan et al., 2004). Cell death is evident in cultured Purkinje cells with more chronic exposure (Hauser et al., 1994). Purkinje cell losses have been reported in chronic heroin abusers who are HIV seronegative (Oehmichen et al., 1996). Although the mechanisms underlying opiate-induced cell death are incompletely understood and likely differ among cell types, opiate-induced modulation of cell death has been proposed to involve phosphoinositol 3-phosphokinase and extracellular signal regulated kinase (ERK) (Polakiewicz et al., 1998). Singhal and coworkers report that p38 mitogen-activated protein kinase (MAPK), p53, and caspases 3 and 8 mediate morphine-induced death in macrophages (Singhal et al., 2002), whereas morphine-induced T cell losses involve c-jun-N-terminal kinase activation and reductions in ERK phosphorylation (Singhal et al., 2001). By contrast, cell death is not seen with concentrations of morphine exceeding 1 μm in cultured mouse EGL cells (Hauser et al., 2000) or in astrocytes (Gurwell and Hauser, 1993). Thus, in some instances, opiates may affect cell survival in addition to their effects on proliferation, although this is not a consistent observation.

Gliogenesis

There are considerable indications that glial-restricted precursors (GRPs), as well as their astroglial and oligodendroglial progeny, are a direct target of opiates during maturation. Most glial types in the forebrain arise from the SZ and gliogenesis typically follows the production of neurons in a particular brain region (Fig. 22–2).

Many have proposed that astroglia are targets for drugs with abuse liability (Eriksson et al., 1991; Stiene-Martin and Hauser, 1991; Beitner-Johnson et al., 1993; Hauser and Mangoura, 1998; Fattore et al., 2002; Belcheva et al., 2003). Astroglial growth is inhibited by opioids in cell culture and in vivo (Schmahl et al., 1989; Stiene-Martin and Hauser, 1990, 1991; Hauser and Stiene-Martin, 1991; Stiene-Martin et al., 1991, 2001; Zagon and McLaughlin, 1991; Hauser et al., 1996; Hauser and Mangoura, 1998). Astroglia can express MOR, DOR, and/or

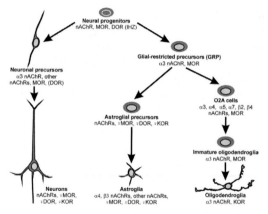

FIGURE 22–2 Presence of opioid and nicotinic acetylcholine receptors (nAChRs) on neuronal and glial precursors. μ-, δ-, and κ-opioid receptors (MOR, DOR, and KOR, respectively) are variably expressed (±) on neuronal and astroglial precursors, and nAChRs are variably expressed by neuronal precursors (±). IHZ, intrahilar zone; O2A, oligodendrocyte-type 2 astrocyte progenitor; SZ, subventricular zone.

KOR (Eriksson et al., 1990, 1991; Stiene-Martin and Hauser, 1990, 1991; Ruzicka et al., 1995; Gurwell et al., 1996; Hauser et al., 1996; Stiene-Martin et al., 1998, 2001; Thorlin et al., 1998), and opioid receptor expression is developmentally regulated and/or differs among brain regions (Hauser and Stiene-Martin, 1991; Eriksson et al., 1992; Ruzicka et al., 1994, 1995; Gurwell et al., 1996; Stiene-Martin et al., 1998; Thorlin et al., 1999). Activation of MOR, KOR, or DOR causes reductions in cell proliferation and increased cellular hypertrophy (Stiene-Martin and Hauser, 1991; Gurwell et al., 1996; Hauser et al., 1996). The inhibition of cell proliferation and astroglial hypertrophy are mediated by opioid-induced increases in intracellular concentration of Ca^{2+} ($[Ca^{2+}]_i$) (Gurwell et al., 1996; Hauser et al., 1996). The "reactive" cellular hypertrophy is accompanied by increased glial fibrillary acidic protein (GFAP) immunoreactivity and aspects may mimic reactive gliosis in vivo (Hauser et al., 1996, 1998).

Unlike in neurons and astroglia, where MOR activation inhibits cell replication, in immature oligodendroglia, MOR activation is mitogenic (Knapp et al., 1998). By contrast to MOR, KOR is expressed in more mature, nondividing oligodendroglia. KOR blockade increases the death of cultured oligodendrocytes, inferring that KOR couples to enhanced survival in this cell type (Knapp et al., 2001). Similar to granule neurons, different aspects of oligodendroglial development appear to be independently regulated by MOR and KOR. As mentioned, unlike granule neurons and their EGL precursors, which do not express KOR in vitro (Hauser et al., 2000), MOR activation is mitogenic in oligodendroglia (Knapp et al., 1998). Collectively, the findings in neurons and glia suggest that opioid effects are highly complex—affecting the maturation of each cell type differently.

Adult hippocampal progenitors (AHPs) from the rat IHZ express β-endorphin (a post-translational product of the proopiomelanocortin gene) (Persson et al., 2003a). β-endorphin stimulates the maturation and perhaps cell fate decisions of IHZ cells through autocrine/paracrine mechanisms of action (Persson et al., 2003a). Interestingly, AHPs express MOR and DOR, and blockade of these receptors by naloxone increases the AHPs, resulting in increases in neuroblast replication with apparent compensatory reductions in the genesis of astroglia and oligodendroglia (Persson et al., 2003a, 2003b). These findings suggest that, in addition to modulating the proliferation and death of neuronal and glial precursors, opioids may influence cell fate decisions of bi- or multipotential neural cell precursors.

Importantly, opioids can modulate basic fibroblast growth factor (bFGF) and/or epidermal growth factor (EGF) activation of ERK in C6 glioma cells or in primary astrocytes (Bohn et al., 2000; Belcheva et al., 2002, 2003). The proliferative effects of β-endorphin in adult hippocampal progenitors was mediated through a signaling pathway involving PI3-kinase, $[Ca^{2+}]_i$, and MAPK activation (Persson et al., 2003a), which overlaps with events associated with MOR-mediated cell death in Chinese hamster ovary cells (Polakiewicz et al., 1998).

NICOTINE

In adults, acetylcholine is a significant neurotransmitter in several neural pathways (Rand, 1989; Luetje et al., 1990; Heinemann et al., 1991a; Albuquerque et al., 1995). During development, acetylcholine (and perhaps related substances) additionally provides trophic support to guide the maturation and survival of incipient cholinergic neurons (Zahalka et al.,

1992; Role and Berg, 1996). Nicotine is known to alter adult neural function. In the maturing nervous system, there is considerable evidence that nicotine exposure (as a component of cigarette smoke) disrupts the normal interactions between acetylcholine and the cellular targets that express subtypes of nicotinic acetylcholine receptors (nAChRs).

Cigarette smoking during pregnancy can have multiple direct and indirect effects on fetal development and is strongly associated with developmental and behavioral abnormalities in newborns (Economides and Braithwaite, 1994; McIntosh et al., 1995; Shu et al., 1995; Lambers and Clark, 1996). Epidemiological studies suggest that low infant birth weight, delayed fetal development, and premature births are closely correlated with smoking (Opanashuk et al., 2001). Neurobehavioral development is also altered. In addition, children born to smoking mothers have an increased incidence of attention deficit hyperactivity disorder (McIntosh et al., 1995). Smoke exposure may also increase the incidence of sudden infant death syndrome (Slotkin et al., 1995). Although cigarette smoke contains over 4000 chemical compounds, many studies have shown that nicotine is the principal insulting agent in development.

In animal models, prenatal exposure to tobacco or nicotine disrupts somatic (Paulson et al., 1991) and CNS development and causes defects in morphological, neurochemical, and behavioral indices (Slotkin et al., 1987, 1993; Fuxe et al., 1989; Paulson et al., 1994a, 1994b; Pennington et al., 1994; Witschi et al., 1994; Court et al., 1995, 1997; Roy et al., 1998; Pauly et al., 2004). Interestingly, nicotine can affect brain development in the absence of overt changes in body weight, which suggests that effect of nicotine on the brain is direct (Zahalka et al., 1992). Additional evidence suggests that the effects of nicotine are gender-specific (Pauly et al., 2004). Although assessing the effect of in utero exposure to cigarette smoke is potentially confounded by reduced maternal–placental–fetal circulation (Birnbaum et al., 1994) or amino acid uptake (Sastry, 1991), studies in chick embryos suggest that nicotine retards neurobehavioral development (Pennington et al., 1994); studies in vitro similarly suggest that nicotine can directly affect developing neural cells (Opanashuk et al., 2001). Perinatal exposure to nicotine causes lasting changes evident in adult brains (Nordberg et al., 1991; Miao et al., 1998; Eriksson et al., 2000).

Epidemiological and/or experimental studies of Parkinson and Alzheimer diseases have shown that nicotine alone (or from cigarette smoking, chewing gum, and/or dermal patches) may have neuroprotective properties (Baron, 1986; Sershen et al., 1987; van Duijn and Hofman, 1991; Jones et al., 1992; Ishikawa and Miyatake, 1993). Some interest originates from studies showing that there is a selective reduction in neuronal nAChRs, in comparison to age-matched controls, in several neurodegenerative diseases (Perry et al., 2002). Acute exposure to nAChR agonists enhances some measures of cognitive function, and chronic exposure to nicotine agonists paradoxically increases the number of neuronal nAChRs (Jones et al., 1992; Wilson et al., 1995). Nicotine can protect against β-amyloid toxicity in vitro (Kihara et al., 1997), prompting an interest in attempting to understand interactions between nAChRs and the pathophysiology of these neurodegenerative diseases. In the aging nervous system, nicotine appears to be trophic in neurons that express nAChRs and perhaps secondarily in other non–nAChR-expressing cells. Although the trophic effects of nicotine in aging may be neuroprotective, the developmental trophic actions of nicotine may be detrimental to the fetus, and it is important to note that an inappropriate blockade of normal programmed cell death or an abnormally high rate of cell proliferation is also likely to be detrimental (Opanashuk et al., 2001).

Nicotine has long been proposed to modulate neural development by influencing the proliferation and/or survival of neural precursors (Slotkin et al., 1987, 1993; Slotkin, 2004). Recent findings that perinatal exposure to nicotine has long-lasting consequences on behavior in rats, combined with clinical observations of low infant birth weight, the potential for psychiatric problems, and predilection toward substance abuse (Lambers and Clark, 1996; Ernst et al., 2001), underscore the importance of examining effects of nicotine in development. Targeted deletion of specific nAChR subunit genes, including α3, β2, and β4 subunits, can be lethal early during development, whereas deletion of many other nAChR subunits significantly modifies adult behaviors (Cordero-Erausquin et al., 2000). Finally, nicotine decreases neurogenesis in the IHZ of adult male rats (Abrous et al., 2002), a finding suggesting that nicotine's ability to influence the production of new neural cells is lifelong.

Neuronogenesis

The appearance of cholinergic synthetic enzymes and multiple nAChR subtypes in the germinal zones of the developing CNS suggests that acetylcholine might potentially influence CNS maturation in the VZ/SZ and EGL (Gould and Butcher, 1987; Clos et al., 1989; Perry et al., 1993; Court et al., 1995; Atluri et al., 2001; Opanashuk et al., 2001; Hauser et al., 2003; Cai et al., 2004). For example, the maturation of cholinergic systems in the cerebellum (Brooksbank et al., 1989; Perry et al., 1993; Court et al., 1995; Jaarsma et al., 1997) coincides with critical periods of neurogenesis in this brain region in rodents (Miale and Sidman, 1961; Altman, 1972a, 1972b). The mechanisms by which nicotine modulates maturation are likely to be complex and differ among cell types. nAChRs are members of the ligand-gated ion channel receptor superfamily. Binding to nAChRs induces a conformational change in an intrinsic ion channel, which increases Na^+ influx (Heinemann et al., 1991b; Dani and Heinemann, 1996). Although nicotine may acutely activate cells, desensitization and/or possibly permanent inactivation follows the activation of the receptor (Collins and Marks, 1996). It has been shown that individual neurons can express multiple nAChR subtypes (i.e., differing subunit composition), with each serving unique functions (Conroy and Berg, 1995). It has long been known that nicotine induces inward Ca^{2+} currents, especially through α7 nAChR subunit–containing complexes, as well as through some other nAChR subtypes (Dajas-Bailador and Wonnacott, 2004). $[Ca^{2+}]_i$ has well-documented effects on cell proliferation, differentiation, and survival. Interestingly, the expression of some nicotinic receptor types may be linked to key regulators with neural cell development. Sox10, an important transcription regulator of neural maturation and cell fate decisions, activates β4 and α3 subunits in a cell type–specific manner, and Sox10 directly affects regulatory region of the β4 nAChR subunit promoter (Liu et al., 1999).

Nicotine increases the rate of proliferation of neuroblasts in the EGL (Opanashuk et al., 2001), which are predecessors of granule neurons. When isolated EGL precursors are continuously exposed for 7 days to selective α3/α4 (epibatidine) or α4 (cytisine) nAChR agonists or to partial agonists, epibatidine, but not cytisine, concentration-dependent increases in DNA synthesis and content are produced (Opanashuk et al., 2001). This result indicates that $\alpha 3$ nAChR stimulation is mitogenic to cerebellar granule neuroblasts. Moreover, significant effects were significantly attenuated by concurrent administration of the nAChR antagonist dihydro-β-erythroidine (DHβE), suggesting the involvement of specific nAChRs. In summary, these data provide novel evidence that nAChRs directly affect the development of granule cell precursors and further suggest that the effects are mediated through specific $\alpha 3$ nAChR subtypes (Opanashuk et al., 2001). Importantly, $\alpha 7$ nAChR subunits are expressed by differentiating granule neurons, thus other nAChR subtypes may regulate alternative aspects of development such as differentiation, including synaptogenesis and/or survival (Didier et al., 1995; Fucile et al., 2004). The role of nicotine in the EGL of the developing cerebellum has been reviewed in detail elsewhere (Hauser et al., 2003).

Importantly, besides regulating cell proliferation, nicotine can modulate programmed cell death (Renshaw et al., 1993; Roy et al., 1998; Opanashuk et al., 2001; Prendergast et al., 2001; Abrous et al., 2002). Chronic nicotine exposure is neuroprotective in organotypic cultures of the rat hippocampus by up-regulating calbindin expression, which buffers toxic increases in intracellular Ca^{2+} (Prendergast et al., 2001) and modulates nAChR-specific membrane currents in neural stem cells (Cai et al., 2004). Similarly, in cultured cerebellar EGL neuroblasts (Opanashuk et al., 2001) or their progeny (Fucile et al., 2004), chronic activation of $\alpha 3$ nAChRs prevents cell death and the activation of $\alpha 7$ nAChR subunits protects spinal cord neurons against arachidonic acid–induced death (Garrido et al., 2003). By contrast, the activation of $\alpha 7$ nAChR subtypes permits Ca^{2+} influx and causes cell death in dissociated hippocampal neurons (Delbono et al., 1997; Berger et al., 1998; Ferchmin et al., 2003), fetal rat neural cells (Roy et al., 1998), and vascular cells (Villablanca, 1998). Taken together, these findings suggest that nicotine can modulate the proliferation and death of neurons and their precursors, and these effects may differ markedly among different cell types and subtypes. Like opioids, nicotine can elicit highly individualized and diverse intracellular responses. The varied responses are likely determined by varying

nAChR subunit compositions and by nAChR coupling to particular intracellular effectors.

Gliogenesis

There is emerging evidence that the maturation of astroglia, oligodendroglia, and potentially GRPs is directly affected by nicotine. As noted earlier, most glia arise from the SZ. Importantly, glial precursors isolated largely from the SZ express nicotinic receptors, and suggesting immature glia are important targets for nicotine in neural development (Layer, 1991). Despite recent findings that astroglia can express nicotinic receptors (Hosli et al., 2000; Mesulam et al., 2002; Lim and Kim, 2003; Gahring et al., 2004), few studies have assessed the role of nicotine in astroglial function and especially during development. Astroglia express $\alpha 4$ and $\beta 4$ nAChRs, and likely express other nAChR subunit types (Hosli et al., 2000). Isolated astrocytes treated with nicotine in culture show disruptions in glutamate uptake that was influenced by the duration of nicotine exposure, and preconditioned astrocytes displayed sensitization to nicotine. Glutamine synthetase activity was also disrupted in astroglia, as was sodium/potassium-dependent ATPase activity, which tended to respond inversely to glutamine synthetase activity (Lim and Kim, 2003). Butyrylcholinesterase, which may pay play an important ancillary role to acetylcholinesterase in nicotine degradation, is predominantly expressed by astroglia (Mesulam et al., 2002). Collectively, these results suggest that astrocytes, in addition to neurons, may be direct targets for the actions of nicotine. This targeting may have important consequences during CNS development.

Oligodendrocyte precursors (O2A progenitors) can express $\alpha 3$, $\alpha 4$, $\alpha 5$, $\alpha 7$, $\beta 2$, and $\beta 4$ nicotinic receptors subunits (Rogers et al., 2001). Activation of nAChRs causes long-lasting oscillatory increases in intercellular calcium, although it is not entirely certain which subunit(s) mediated this effect. As noted elsewhere, $\alpha 7$ nAChRs permit sustained inward Ca^{2+} currents following exposure to nicotine. Many of the Ca^{2+} currents in these cells could be reversed by DHβE and are not mimicked by the activation of L-type calcium channels or carbachol. Interestingly, acetylcholine receptor–inducing protein (ARIA), a member of the neuregulin family (Falls, 2003; Corfas et al., 2004), is widely expressed by oligodendroglial progenitors in the SZ and triggers nAChR expression in skeletal muscle and neural cells (Vartanian et al., 1994). ARIA exposure causes O2A progenitors to develop along an oligodendroglial fate in vitro, although the maturational changes result from neuregulin signaling and it is unclear whether ARIA drives nAChR expression in oligodendroglia. Taken together, these findings suggest that nicotine may have a profound influence on the maturation of GRPs and direct them to an oligodendroglial fate. Importantly, untimely exposure to nicotine may disrupt gliogenesis and, in particular, the production of oligodendroglia.

DRUG INTERACTIONS WITH DISEASE OR TRAUMA

Considerable evidence here and elsewhere suggests that drug abuse can influence neurogenesis and gliogenesis and affect long-term organizational changes in the brain. On the basis of this insight, we question whether the maladaptive, organizational changes might predispose the CNS to failure when confronted with non–drug-related insults. A remarkable aspect of the CNS is that despite significant insults during critical developmental periods, opposing neuroadaptive processes are capable of considerable recovery. The neuroplastic response to perinatal drug exposure may itself be maladaptive when the CNS is challenged with other insults unrelated to drug abuse. For example, does exposure to nicotine or opiates before disease onset or concurrently increase the risk and/or severity of diseases not typically attributed to deficits in the genesis of new cells, such as Alzheimer or Parkinson disease, neurological acquired immunodeficiency syndrome (AIDS), or neurotrauma? As with drug abuse, disruptions in adult neurogenesis have been implicated in Alzheimer disease (Haughey et al., 2002), traumatic brain injury (Braun et al., 2002; Chirumamilla et al., 2002), neuropsychiatric disorders (Jacobs, 2002; Kempermann, 2002; McEwen, 2002), and use of psychotropic drugs (Duman et al., 2001), as well as in schizophrenia (Corfas et al., 2004; Stefansson et al., 2004), depression (Jacobs et al., 2000), and seizure disorders (Parent and Lowenstein, 2002; Ribak and Dashtipour, 2002). Moreover, although neural progenitors may be vulnerable to a single insult, when multiple insults are combined, such as drug abuse and disease, this combination may exacerbate losses in neural progenitors.

Assuming drug abuse modulates CNS organization and plasticity, might the developmental effects of opiates and/or nicotine exposure on CNS organization be revealed or exaggerated by aging, disease, or environmental stressors? Although this is an important issue, it is difficult to address because of challenges in modeling drug abuse and CNS diseases in the laboratory.

HIV–Drug Interactions

To address whether drug exposure might exacerbate CNS disorders, we have been exploring opiate–HIV interactions in several murine and human models of HIV. There are several key reasons for choosing HIV as a disease to explore drug abuse–disease interactions. First, drug abuse and HIV are interlinked epidemics. In the United States, AIDS is now largely spread through injection drug use or through the exchange of sex for drugs (Nath et al., 2000, 2002). Second, opiate drugs exacerbate the pathogenesis and neurological complications of HIV (Bell et al., 1998; Nath et al., 2002). Opiates likely exacerbate the neuropathogenesis of HIV indirectly by modulating immune function (Peterson et al., 1998; Rogers and Peterson, 2003; Donahoe, 2004) and directly by modulating the intrinsic response of neurons and glia to HIV and/or viral products (Gurwell et al., 2001; Khurdayan et al., 2004; El-Hage et al., 2005).

The HIV gene regulatory protein Tat has been implicated as a mediator of HIV-induced neurotoxicity. Tat is a transactivating, nonstructural viral nuclear regulatory protein composed of 101 amino acids encoded by two exons (Atwood et al., 1993). Tat is released by infected lymphoid cells (Ensoli et al., 1993) and glia (Tardieu et al., 1992). Tat is intrinsically cytotoxic to neurons (Sabatier et al., 1991; Magnuson et al., 1995; Weeks et al., 1995; Maragos et al., 2002; Singh et al., 2004). Extracellular Tat is neurotoxic, in part through interactions with excitatory amino acid receptors (Magnuson et al., 1995; Nath et al., 1996; Haughey and Mattson, 2002), which are accompanied by increases in $[Ca^{2+}]_i$ and reactive oxygen species (Nath et al., 1996; Kruman et al., 1998; Bonavia et al., 2001).

Neuronogenesis

Although HIV-1 infection results in neurodegeneration, the neurons themselves are not directly infected.

Instead, HIV-1 affects microglia and astroglia, subsequently contributing to neurodegeneration through inflammatory signaling and the release of toxic viral products by glia (Brack-Werner, 1999; Nath, 1999; Kaul et al., 2001; Garden, 2002). A novel finding is that multipotential neural progenitors can become infected and serve as a reservoir for HIV-1 (Lawrence et al., 2004). Interestingly, if the infected neural progenitors are allowed to differentiate toward an astroglial phenotype, there are marked increases in viral production. This result suggests that neuronal progenitors can become infected, but commitment to a neuronal fate is incompatible with viral expression. Besides being a site for viral infection, neural precursors express several key chemokine receptors that are co-factors involved in HIV binding, fusion, and infection (Lazarini et al., 2000; Kao and Price, 2004; Peng et al., 2004), including CXCR4 and CCR5 (Peng et al., 2004). In addition, immature neurons express major histocompatibility complex (MHC) class I and other key immune signaling molecules that blur distinctions between neuroplasticity and neuropathology (Boulanger and Shatz, 2004). Interestingly, both monotropic and T-tropic strains of HIV, respectively, inhibit the proliferation of neural progenitors through CCR5- or CXCR4-mediated activation of ERK (Krathwohl and Kaiser, 2004). Although there is evidence that neuroblasts are a target for HIV, no studies have examined the combined effects of opiates and HIV on neurogenesis.

Gliogenesis

Unlike neuronal precursors, preliminary *in vitro* evidence suggests that opiates can exacerbate the cytotoxic effects of HIV in glial precursors (Khurdayan et al., 2004). On the basis of findings that neural progenitors are targets of HIV, we have been assessing whether drug abuse might further disrupt the actions of HIV in neural progenitors. Interestingly, glial progenitors appear to be especially vulnerable to the combined effect of opiates and HIV, resulting in increases in activated caspase-3 and increased cell death as assessed by a failure of cells to exclude ethidium monoazide (Khurdayan et al., 2004). Most of the dying cells are glial precursors having characteristics of O2A glial progenitors (Raff et al., 1983; Fulton et al., 1992), whereas there is a tendency for some immature oligodendrocytes and immature astrocytes to be preferentially lost. A vast majority of cultured O2A

progenitors would have developed into oligodendroglia with further maturation, thus, it appears that cells committed to an oligodendroglial fate may be preferentially vulnerable to combined opiate–HIV-1 toxicity (Khurdayan et al., 2004). Interestingly, there tended to be greater numbers of dying oligodendrocytes with combined morphine-Tat exposure, although this trend was not statistically significant at 96 hr. Since morphine and Tat in combination preferentially kill O2A cells, significant oligodendrocyte losses might become apparent with exposure that is more prolonged. It can be predicted that gliogenesis is affected and that oligodendroglial progenitors are especially vulnerable in HIV-infected individuals who abuse opiates.

The consequences of losing glial precursors are uncertain. Fated glial precursors may have lifespans lasting years, so that deficits in gliogenesis would only become evident with time. A tentative notion is that a sustained destruction of glial precursors with chronic opiate abuse in HIV-infected individuals and subsequent loss in total glial numbers might contribute to accelerated neurocognitive defects. Thus, chronic opiate abuse may have debilitating effects on the long-term stability of glial populations and CNS function in HIV-infected individuals.

SUMMARY AND CONCLUSIONS

Collectively, the above findings suggest that glial precursors are novel targets for HIV and opiate abuse, and disruptions in the genesis and fate of new neural cells may contribute to the pathogenesis of neuro-AIDS. The extent to which findings in opiate and HIV Tat-treated glia can be generalized to other drugs of abuse or diseases is uncertain, however, considering the apparent susceptibility of neural progenitors to substances with abuse liability and pathologic insults, it is likely that precursors will be affected. Furthermore, assuming the loss of precursors inevitably contributes to the pathology of the disease, the prognosis for slow, progressive cognitive decline may be assured.

Abbreviations

AHP   adult hippocampal progenitor

AIDS   acquired immunodeficiency syndrome

ARIA   acetylcholine receptor–inducing protein

bFGF   basic fibroblast growth factor

$[Ca^{2+}]_i$ intracellular concentration of Ca^{2+}

CNS   central nervous system

DHβE   dihydro-β-erythroidine

EGF   epidermal growth factor

DOR   δ-opioid receptors

EGL   external granular layer of the cerebellum

ERK   extracellular signal regulated kinase

GFAP   glial fibrillary acidic protein

GRP   glial-restricted precursor

IHZ   intrahilar zone

KOR   κ-opioid receptors

MAPK   mitogen-activated protein kinase

MHC   major histocompatibity complex

MOR   μ-opioid receptors

nAChR   nicotinic acetylcholine receptor

SZ   subventricular zone

VZ   ventricular zone

ACKNOWLEDGMENTS This work was supported by the National Institute of Drug Abuse (KFH), the National Institute of Child Health and Human Development (HSB), and the National Institute of Neurological Disorders and Stroke (JRP).

References

Abrous DN, Adriani W, Montaron MF, Aurousseau C, Rougon G, Le MM, Piazza PV (2002) Nicotine self-administration impairs hippocampal plasticity. J Neurosci 22:3656–3662.

Akil H, Watson SJ, Young E, Lewis ME, Khachaturian H, Walker JM (1984) Endogenous opioids: biology and function. Annu Rev Neurosci 7:223–255.

Albuquerque EX, Pereira EF, Castro NG, Alkondon M, Reinhardt S, Schroder H, Maelicke A (1995) Nicotinic receptor function in the mammalian central nervous system. Ann NY Acad Sci 757:48–72.

Altman J (1972a) Postnatal development of the cerebellar cortex in the rat. III. Maturation of the components of the granular layer. J Comp Neurol 145:465–514.

—— (1972b) Postnatal development of the cerebellar cortex in the rat. I. The external germinal layer and the transitional molecular layer. J Comp Neurol 145:353–398.

Alvarez-Buylla A, Garcia-Verdugo JM (2002) Neurogenesis in adult subventricular zone. J Neurosci 22:629–634.

Atluri P, Fleck MW, Shen Q, Mah SJ, Stadfelt D, Barnes W, Goderie SK, Temple S, Schneider AS (2001) Functional nicotinic acetylcholine receptor expression in stem and progenitor cells of the early embryonic mouse cerebral cortex. Dev Biol 240:143–156.

Atwood WJ, Tornatore CS, Meyers K, Major EO (1993) HIV-1 mRNA transcripts from persistently infected human fetal astrocytes. Ann NY Acad Sci 693: 324–325.

Baron JA (1986) Cigarette smoking and Parkinson's disease. Neurology 36:1490–1496.

Beitner-Johnson D, Guitart X, Nestler EJ (1993) Glial fibrillary acidic protein and the mesolimbic dopamine system: regulation by chronic morphine and Lewis-Fischer strain differences in the rat ventral tegmental area. J Neurochem 61:1766–1773.

Belcheva MM, Haas PD, Tan Y, Heaton VM, Coscia CJ (2002) The fibroblast growth factor receptor is at the site of convergence between μ-opioid receptor and growth factor signaling pathways in rat C6 glioma cells. J Pharmacol Exp Ther 303:909–918.

Belcheva MM, Tan Y, Heaton VM, Clark AL, Coscia CJ (2003) μ opioid transactivation and down-regulation of the epidermal growth factor receptor in astrocytes: implications for mitogen-activated protein kinase signaling. Mol Pharmacol 64:1391–1401.

Bell JE, Brettle RP, Chiswick A, Simmonds P (1998) HIV encephalitis, proviral load and dementia in drug users and homosexuals with AIDS. Effect of neocortical involvement. Brain 121:2043–2052.

Berger F, Gage FH, Vijayaraghavan S (1998) Nicotinic receptor–induced apoptotic cell death of hippocampal progenitor cells. J Neurosci 18:6871–6881.

Birnbaum SC, Kien N, Martucci RW, Gelzleichter TR, Witschi H, Hendrickx AG, Last JA (1994) Nicotine- or epinephrine-induced uteroplacental vasoconstriction and fetal growth in the rat. Toxicology 94:69–80.

Bohn LM, Belcheva MM, Coscia CJ (2000) μ-opioid agonist inhibition of κ-opioid receptor–stimulated extracellular signal–regulated kinase phosphorylation is dynamin-dependent in C6 glioma cells. J Neurochem 74:574–581.

Bonavia R, Bajetto A, Barbero S, Albini A, Noonan DM, Schettini G (2001) HIV-1 Tat causes apoptotic death and calcium homeostasis alterations in rat neurons. Biochem Biophys Res Commun 288:301–308.

Boulanger LM, Shatz CJ (2004) Immune signalling in neural development, synaptic plasticity and disease. Nat Rev Neurosci 5:521–531.

Boulder Committee (1970) Embryonic vertebrate central nervous system: revised terminology. Anat Rec 166:257–261.

Brack-Werner R (1999) Astrocytes: HIV cellular reservoirs and important participants in neuropathogenesis. AIDS 13:1–22.

Braun H, Schafer K, Höllt V (2002) βIII tubulin–expressing neurons reveal enhanced neurogenesis in hippocampal and cortical structures after a contusion trauma in rats. J Neurotrauma 19:975–983.

Brooksbank BW, Walker D, Balazs R, Jorgensen OS (1989) Neuronal maturation in the foetal brain in Down's syndrome. Early Hum Dev 18:237–246.

Buznikov GA, Lambert HW, Lauder JM (2001) Serotonin and serotonin-like substances as regulators of early embryogenesis and morphogenesis. Cell Tissue Res 305:177–186.

Cai J, Cheng A, Luo Y, Lu C, Mattson MP, Rao MS, Furukawa K (2004) Membrane properties of rat embryonic multipotent neural stem cells. J Neurochem 88:212–226.

Chirumamilla S, Sun D, Bullock MR, Colello RJ (2002) Traumatic brain injury–induced cell proliferation in the adult mammalian central nervous system. J Neurotrauma 19:693–703.

Clos J, Ghandour S, Eberhart R, Vincendon G, Gombos G (1989) The cholinergic system in developing cerebellum: comparative study of normal, hypothyroid and underfed rats. Dev Neurosci 11:188–204.

Collins AC, Marks MJ (1996) Are nicotinic receptors activated or inhibited following chronic nicotine treatment? Drug Dev Res 38:231–242.

Conroy WG, Berg DK (1995) Neurons can maintain multiple classes of nicotinic acetylcholine receptors distinguished by different subunit compositions. J Biol Chem 270:4424–4431.

Cordero-Erausquin M, Marubio LM, Klink R, Changeux JP (2000) Nicotinic receptor function: new perspectives from knockout mice. Trends Pharmacol Sci 21:211–217.

Corfas G, Roy K, Buxbaum JD (2004) Neuregulin 1-erbB signaling and the molecular/cellular basis of schizophrenia. Nat Neurosci 7:575–580.

Court JA, Lloyd S, Johnson M, Griffiths M, Birdsall NJ, Piggott MA, Oakley AE, Ince PG, Perry EK, Perry RH (1997) Nicotinic and muscarinic cholinergic receptor binding in the human hippocampal formation during development and aging. Dev Brain Res 101:93–105.

Court JA, Perry EK, Spurden D, Griffiths M, Kerwin JM, Morris CM, Johnson M, Oakley AE, Birdsall NJ, Clementi F (1995) The role of the cholinergic system in the development of the human cerebellum. Dev Brain Res 90:159–167.

Crews FT, Nixon K (2003) Alcohol, neural stem cells, and adult neurogenesis. Alcohol Res Health 27:197–204.

Dajas-Bailador F, Wonnacott S (2004) Nicotinic acetylcholine receptors and the regulation of neuronal signalling. Trends Pharmacol Sci 25:317–324.

Dani JA, Heinemann S (1996) Molecular and cellular aspects of nicotine abuse. Neuron 16:905–908.

Delbono O, Gopalakrishnan M, Renganathan M, Monteggia LM, Messi ML, Sullivan JP (1997) Activation of the recombinant human α7 nicotinic acetylcholine receptor significantly raises intracellular free calcium. J Pharmacol Exp Ther 280:428–438.

Didier M, Berman SA, Lindstrom J, Bursztajn S (1995) Characterization of nicotinic acetylcholine receptors expressed in primary cultures of cerebellar granule cells. Mol Brain Res 30:17–28.

Dodge Miller CR, O'Steen WK, Deadwyler SA (1982) Effect of morphine on ^{3}H-thymidine incorporation in the subependyma of the rat: an autoradiographic study. J Comp Neurol 208:209–214.

Donahoe RM (2004) Multiple ways that drug abuse might influence AIDS progression: clues from a monkey model. J Neuroimmunol 147:28–32.

Duman RS, Malberg J, Nakagawa S (2001) Regulation of adult neurogenesis by psychotropic drugs and stress. J Pharmacol Exp Ther 299:401–407.

Economides D, Braithwaite J (1994) Smoking, pregnancy and the fetus. J R Soc Health 114:198–201.

Eisch AJ, Barrot M, Schad CA, Self DW, Nestler EJ (2000) Opiates inhibit neurogenesis in the adult rat hippocampus. Proc Natl Acad Sci USA 97:7579–7584.

Eisch AJ, Mandyam CD (2004) Drug dependence and addiction, II: Adult neurogenesis and drug abuse. Am J Psychiatry 161:426.

El-Hage N, Gurwell JA, Singh IN, Sullivan PG, Nath A, Hauser KF (2005) Synergistic increases in intracellular Ca^{2+}, and the release of MCP-1, RANTES, and IL-6 by astrocytes treated with opiates and HIV-1 Tat. Glia 50:91–106.

Ensoli B, Buonaguro L, Barillari G, Fiorelli V, Gendelman R, Morgan R, Wingfield P, Gallo R (1993) Release, uptake, and effects of extracellular human immunodeficiency virus type-1 Tat protein on cell growth and viral replication. J Virol 67:277–287.

Eriksson P, Ankarberg E, Fredriksson A (2000) Exposure to nicotine during a defined period in neonatal life induces permanent changes in brain nicotinic receptors and in behaviour of adult mice Brain Res 853:41–48.

Eriksson PS, Hansson E, Rönnbäck L (1990) δ and κ opiate receptors in primary astroglial cultures from rat cerebral cortex. Neurochem Res 15:1123–1126.

—— (1992) δ and κ opiate receptors in primary astroglial cultures. Part II: Receptor sets in cultures from various brain regions and interactions with β-receptor activated cyclic AMP. Neurochem Res 17:545–551.

—— (1991) μ and δ opiate receptors in neuronal and astroglial primary cultures from various regions of the brain-coupling with adenylate cyclase, localisation on the same neurones and association with dopamine (D_1) receptor adenylate cyclase. Neuropharmacology 30:1233–1239.

Ernst M, Moolchan ET, Robinson ML (2001) Behavioral and neural consequences of prenatal exposure to nicotine. J Am Acad Child Adolesc Psychiatry 40:630–641.

Falls DL (2003) Neuregulins and the neuromuscular system: 10 years of answers and questions. J Neurocytol 32:619–647.

Fattore L, Puddu MC, Picciau S, Cappai A, Fratta W, Serra GP, Spiga S (2002) Astroglial in vivo response to cocaine in mouse dentate gyrus: a quantitative and qualitative analysis by confocal microscopy. Neuroscience 110:1–6.

Ferchmin PA, Perez D, Eterovic VA, de Vellis J (2003) Nicotinic receptors differentially regulate N-methyl-D-aspartate damage in acute hippocampal slices. J Pharmacol Exp Ther 305:1071–1078.

Fucile S, Renzi M, Lauro C, Limatola C, Ciotti T, Eusebi F (2004) Nicotinic cholinergic stimulation promotes survival and reduces motility of cultured rat cerebellar granule cells. Neuroscience 127:53–61.

Fulton BP, Burne JF, Raff MC (1992) Visualization of O-2A progenitor cells in developing and adult rat optic nerve by quisqualate-stimulated cobalt uptake. J Neurosci 12:4816–4833.

Fuxe K, Andersson K, Eneroth P, Jansson A, von EG, Tinner B, Bjelke B, Agnati LF (1989) Neurochemical mechanisms underlying the neuroendocrine actions of nicotine: focus on the plasticity of central cholinergic nicotinic receptors. Prog Brain Res 79:197–207.

Gahring LC, Persiyanov K, Rogers SW (2004) Neuronal and astrocyte expression of nicotinic receptor subunit β4 in the adult mouse brain. J Comp Neurol 468:322–333.

Garden GA (2002) Microglia in human immunodeficiency virus–associated neurodegeneration. Glia 40:240–251.

Garrido R, Springer JE, Hennig B, Toborek M (2003) Apoptosis of spinal cord neurons by preventing depletion nicotine attenuates arachidonic acid–induced of neurotrophic factors. J Neurotrauma 20:1201–1213.

Goldman SA (1998) Adult neurogenesis: from canaries to the clinic. J Neurobiol 36:267–286.

Gordon JA, Hen R (2004) The serotonergic system and anxiety. Neuromol Med 5:27–40.

Gould E, Butcher LL (1987) Transient expression of choline acetyltransferase–like immunoreactivity in Purkinje cells of the developing rat cerebellum. Brain Res 431:303–306.

Gurwell JA, Duncan MJ, Maderspach K, Stiene-Martin A, Elde RP, Hauser KF (1996) κ-Opioid receptor expression defines a phenotypically distinct subpopulation of astroglia: relationship to Ca^{2+} mobilization, development, and the antiproliferative effect of opioids. Brain Res 737:175–187.

Gurwell JA, Hauser KF (1993) Morphine does not affect astrocyte survival in developing primary mixed-glial cultures. Dev Brain Res 76:293–298.

Gurwell JA, Nath A, Sun Q, Zhang J, Martin KM, Chen Y, Hauser KF (2001) Synergistic neurotoxicity of opioids and human immunodeficiency virus-1 Tat protein in striatal neurons in vitro. Neuroscience 102:555–563.

Hammer RP Jr (1993) Effects of opioids on the developing brain. In: Hammer RP Jr (ed). The Neurobiology of Opiates. CRC Press, Boca Raton FL, pp 1–21.

Hammer RP Jr, Hauser KF (1992) Consequences of early exposure to opioids on cell proliferation and neuronal morphogenesis. In: Miller MW (ed). Development of the Central Nervous System: Effects of Alcohol and Opiates. Wiley-Liss, New York, pp 319–339.

Hammer RP Jr, Ricalde AA, Seatriz JV (1989) Effects of opiates on brain development. Neurotoxicology 10:475–484.

Haughey NJ, Liu D, Nath A, Borchard AC, Mattson MP (2002) Disruption of neurogenesis in the subventricular zone of adult mice, and in human cortical neuronal precursor cells in culture, by amyloid β-peptide: implications for the pathogenesis of Alzheimer's disease. Neuromol Med 1:125–135.

Haughey NJ, Mattson MP (2002) Calcium dysregulation and neuronal apoptosis by the HIV-1 proteins Tat and gp120. J Acquir Immune Defic Syndr 31 (Suppl 2):S55–S61.

Hauser KF, Gurwell JA, Turbek CS (1994) Morphine inhibits Purkinje cell survival and dendritic differentiation in organotypic cultures of the mouse cerebellum. Exp Neurol 130:95–105.

Hauser KF, Harris-White ME, Jackson JA, Opanashuk LA, Carney JM (1998) Opioids disrupt Ca^{2+} homeostasis and induce carbonyl oxyradical production in mouse astrocytes in vitro: transient increases and adaptation to sustained exposure. Exp Neurol 151:70–76.

Hauser KF, Houdi AA, Turbek CS, Elde RP, Maxson W III (2000) Opioids intrinsically inhibit the genesis of mouse cerebellar granule cell precursors in vitro: differential impact of μ and δ receptor activation on proliferation and neurite elongation. Eur J Neurosci 12:1281–1293.

Hauser KF, Khurdayan VK, Goody RJ, Nath A, Pauly JR, Saria A (2003) Selective vulnerability of cerebellar granule neuroblasts and their progeny to drugs with abuse liability. Cerebellum 2:184–195.

Hauser KF, Mangoura D (1998) Diversity of the endogenous opioid system in development: novel signal transduction translates multiple extracellular signals into neural cell growth and differentiation. Perspect Dev Neurobiol 5:437–449.

Hauser KF, McLaughlin PJ, Zagon IS (1987) Endogenous opioids regulate dendritic growth and spine formation in developing rat brain. Brain Res 416: 157–161.

—— (1989) Endogenous opioid systems and the regulation of dendritic growth and spine formation. J Comp Neurol 281:13–22.

Hauser KF, Stiene-Martin A (1991) Characterization of opioid-dependent glial development in dissociated and organotypic cultures of mouse central nervous system: critical periods and target specificity. Dev Brain Res 62:245–255.

—— (1993) Opiates and the regulation of nervous system development: evidence from in vitro studies. In: Hammer RP Jr (ed). *Neurobiology of Opiates*. CRC Press, Boca Raton FL, pp 23–61.

Hauser KF, Stiene-Martin A, Mattson MP, Elde RP, Ryan SE, Godleske CC (1996) μ-Opioid receptor-induced Ca^{2+} mobilization and astroglial development: morphine inhibits DNA synthesis and stimulates cellular hypertrophy through a Ca^{2+}-dependent mechanism. Brain Res 720:191–203.

Heinemann SF, Boulter J, Connolly J, Deneris E, Duvoisin R, Hartley M, Hermans-Borgmeyer I, Hollmann M, O'Shea-Greenfield A, Papke R (1991a) Brain nicotinic receptor genes. NIDA Res Monogr 111:3–23.

Heinemann S, Boulter J, Connolly J, Deneris E, Duvoisin R, Hartley M, Hermans-Borgmeyer I, Hollmann M, O'Shea-Greenfield A, Papke R (1991b) The nicotinic receptor genes. Clin Neuropharmacol 14(Suppl 1):S45–S61.

Hildebrandt K, Teuchert-Noodt G, Dawirs RR (1999) A single neonatal dose of methamphetamine suppresses dentate granule cell proliferation in adult gerbils which is restored to control values by acute doses of haloperidol. J Neural Transm 106:549–558.

Hosli E, Ruhl W, Hosli L (2000) Histochemical and electrophysiological evidence for estrogen receptors on cultured astrocytes: colocalization with cholinergic receptors. Int J Dev Neurosci 18:101–111.

Ishikawa A, Miyatake T (1993) Effects of smoking in patients with early-onset Parkinson's disease. J Neurol Sci 117:28–32.

Jaarsma D, Ruigrok TJ, Caffe R, Cozzari C, Levey AI, Mugnaini E, Voogd J (1997) Cholinergic innervation and receptors in the cerebellum. Prog Brain Res 114:67–96.

Jacobs BL (2002) Adult brain neurogenesis and depression. Brain Behav Immun 16:602–609.

Jacobs BL, Praag H, Gage FH (2000) Adult brain neurogenesis and psychiatry: a novel theory of depression. Mol Psychiatry 5:262–269.

Jones GM, Sahakian BJ, Levy R, Warburton DM, Gray JA (1992) Effects of acute subcutaneous nicotine on attention, information processing and short-term memory in Alzheimer's disease. Psychopharmacology 108:485–494.

Kao AW, Price RW (2004) Chemokine receptors, neural progenitor cells, and the AIDS dementia complex. J Infect Dis 190:211–215.

Kaul M, Garden GA, Lipton SA (2001) Pathways to neuronal injury and apoptosis in HIV-associated dementia. Nature 410:988–994.

Kempermann G (2002) Regulation of adult hippocampal neurogenesis—implications for novel theories of major depression. Bipolar Disord 4:17–33.

Khurdayan VK, Buch S, El-Hage N, Lutz SE, Goebel SM, Singh IN, Knapp PE, Turchan-Cholewo J, Nath A, Hauser KF (2004) Preferential vulnerability of astroglia and glial precursors to combined opioid and HIV-1 Tat exposure in vitro. Eur J Neurosci 19:3171–3182.

Kihara T, Shimohama S, Sawada H, Kimura J, Kume T, Kochiyama H, Maeda T, Akaike A (1997) Nicotinic receptor stimulation protects neurons against β-amyloid toxicity. Ann Neurol 42:159–163.

Kinney HC, White WF (1991) Opioid receptors localize to the external granular cell layer of the developing human cerebellum. Neuroscience 45:13–21.

Knapp PE, Itkis OS, Zhang L, Spruce BA, Bakalkin G, Hauser KF (2001) Endogenous opioids and oligodendroglial function: possible autocrine/paracrine effects on cell survival and development. Glia 35:156–165.

Knapp PE, Maderspach K, Hauser KF (1998) Endogenous opioid system in developing normal and jimpy oligodendrocytes: μ and κ opioid receptors mediate differential mitogenic and growth responses. Glia 22:189–201.

Kornblum HI, Hurlbut DE, Leslie FM (1987a) Postnatal development of multiple opioid receptors in rat brain. Dev Brain Res 37:21.

Kornblum HI, Loughlin SE, Leslie FM (1987b) Effects of morphine on DNA synthesis in neonatal rat brain. Dev Brain Res 31:45–52.

Krathwohl MD, Kaiser JL (2004) HIV-1 promotes quiescence in human neural progenitor cells. J Infect Dis 190:216–226.

Kruman II, Nath A, Mattson MP (1998) HIV-1 protein Tat induces apoptosis of hippocampal neurons by a mechanism involving caspase activation, calcium overload, and oxidative stress. Exp Neurol 154: 276–288.

Lambers DS, Clark KE (1996) The maternal and fetal physiologic effects of nicotine. Semin Perinatol 20:115–126.

Lauder JM, Liu J, Devaud L, Morrow AL (1998) GABA as a trophic factor for developing monoamine neurons. Perspect Dev Neurobiol 5:247–259.

Lawrence DM, Durham LC, Schwartz L, Seth P, Maric D, Major EO (2004) Human immunodeficiency virus type 1 infection of human brain–derived progenitor cells. J Virol 78:7319–7328.

Layer PG (1991) Cholinesterases during development of the avian nervous system. Cell Mol Neurobiol 11:7–33.

Lazarini F, Casanova P, Tham TN, De CE, Renzana-Seisdedos F, Baleux F, Dubois-Dalcq M (2000) Differential signalling of the chemokine receptor CXCR4 by stromal cell–derived factor 1 and the HIV glycoprotein in rat neurons and astrocytes. Eur J Neurosci 12:117–125.

Leslie FM, Chen Y, Winzer-Serhan UH (1998) Opioid receptor and peptide mRNA expression in proliferative zones of fetal rat central nervous system. Can J Physiol Pharmacol 76:284–293.

Leslie FM, Loughlin SE (1993) Ontogeny and plasticity of opioid systems. In: Hammer RP Jr (ed). The Neurobiology of Opiates. CRC Press, Boca Raton FL, pp 85–123.

Lim DK, Kim HS (2003) Opposite modulation of glutamate uptake by nicotine in cultured astrocytes with/without cAMP treatment. Eur J Pharmacol 476:179–184.

Lin JC, Rosenthal A (2003) Molecular mechanisms controlling the development of dopaminergic neurons. Semin Cell Dev Biol 14:175–180.

Liu Q, Melnikova IN, Hu M, Gardner PD (1999) Cell type–specific activation of neuronal nicotinic acetylcholine receptor subunit genes by Sox10. J Neurosci 19:9747–9755.

Lorber BA, Freitag SK, Bartolome JV (1990) Effects of β-endorphin on DNA synthesis in brain regions of preweanling rats. Brain Res 531:329–332.

Luetje CW, Patrick J, Seguela P (1990) Nicotine receptors in the mammalian brain. FASEB J 4:2753–2760.

Luo J, Miller MW (1998) Growth factor–mediated neural proliferation: target of ethanol toxicity. Brain Res Rev 27:157–167.

Magnuson DS, Knudsen BE, Geiger JD, Brownstone RM, Nath A (1995) Human immunodeficiency

virus type 1 tat activates non-N-methyl-D-aspartate excitatory amino acid receptors and causes neurotoxicity. Ann Neurol 37:373–380.

Mandyam CD, Norris RD, Eisch AJ (2004) Chronic morphine induces premature mitosis of proliferating cells in the adult mouse subgranular zone. J Neurosci Res 76:783–794.

Mangoura D, Dawson G (1993) Opioid peptides activate phospholipase D and protein kinase C-ε in chicken embryo neuron cultures. Proc Natl Acad Sci USA 90:2915–2919.

Maragos WF, Young KL, Turchan JT, Guseva M, Pauly JR, Nath A, Cass WA (2002) Human immunodeficiency virus-1 Tat protein and methamphetamine interact synergistically to impair striatal dopaminergic function. J Neurochem 83:955–963.

Martin WR (1983) Pharmacology of opioids. Pharmacol Rev 35:283–323.

McEwen BS (2002) Sex, stress and the hippocampus: allostasis, allostatic load and the aging process. Neurobiol Aging 23:921.

McIntosh DE, Mulkins RS, Dean RS (1995) Utilization of maternal perinatal risk indicators in the differential diagnosis of ADHD and UADD children. Int J Neurosci 81:35–46.

Meriney SD, Gray DB, Pilar G (1985) Morphine-induced delay of normal cell death in the avian ciliary ganglion. Science 228:1451–1453.

Messinger DS, Bauer CR, Das A, Seifer R, Lester BM, Lagasse LL, Wright LL, Shankaran S, Bada HS, Smeriglio VL, Langer JC, Beeghly M, Poole WK (2004) The Maternal Lifestyle Study: cognitive, motor, and behavioral outcomes of cocaine-exposed and opiate-exposed infants through three years of age. Pediatrics 113:1677–1685.

Mesulam MM, Guillozet A, Shaw P, Levey A, Duysen EG, Lockridge O (2002) Acetylcholinesterase knockouts establish central cholinergic pathways and can use butyrylcholinesterase to hydrolyze acetylcholine. Neuroscience 110:627–639.

Miale IL, Sidman RL (1961) An autoradiographic analysis of histogenesis in the mouse cerebellum. Exp Neurol 4:277–296.

Miao H, Liu C, Bishop K, Gong ZH, Nordberg A, Zhang X (1998) Nicotine exposure during a critical period of development leads to persistent changes in nicotinic acetylcholine receptors of adult rat brain. J Neurochem 70:752–762.

Nath A (1999) Pathobiology of human immunodeficiency virus dementia. Semin Neurol 19:113–127.

Nath A, Hauser KF, Wojna V, Booze RM, Maragos W, Prendergast M, Cass W, Turchan JT (2002) Molecular basis for interactions of HIV and drugs of abuse. J Acquir Immune Defic Syndr 31(Suppl 2):S62–S69.

Nath A, Jones M, Maragos W, Booze R, Mactutus C, Bell J, Hauser KF, Mattson M (2000) Neurotoxicity and dysfunction of dopamine systems associated with AIDS dementia. Psychopharmacology 14: 222–227.

Nath A, Psooy K, Martin C, Knudsen B, Magnuson DS, Haughey N, Geiger JD (1996) Identification of a human immunodeficiency virus type 1 Tat epitope that is neuroexcitatory and neurotoxic. J Virol 70: 1475–1480.

Nordberg A, Zhang XA, Fredriksson A, Eriksson P (1991) Neonatal nicotine exposure induces permanent changes in brain nicotinic receptors and behaviour in adult mice. Dev Brain Res 63: 201–207.

Oehmichen M, Meissner C, Reiter A, Birkholz M (1996) Neuropathology in non-human immunodeficiency virus–infected drug addicts: hypoxic brain damage after chronic intravenous drug abuse. Acta Neuropathol 91:642–646.

Opanashuk LA, Pauly JR, Hauser KF (2001) Effect of nicotine on cerebellar granule neuron development. Eur J Neurosci 13:48–56.

Osborne JG, Kindy MS, Spruce BA, Hauser KF (1993) Ontogeny of proenkephalin mRNA and enkephalin peptide expression in the cerebellar cortex of the rat: spatial and temporal patterns of expression follow maturational gradients in the external granular layer and in Purkinje cells. Dev Brain Res 76:1–12.

Parent JM, Lowenstein DH (2002) Seizure-induced neurogenesis: are more new neurons good for an adult brain? Prog Brain Res 135:121–131.

Paulson RB, Shanfeld J, Mullet D, Cole J, Paulson JO (1994a) Prenatal smokeless tobacco effects on the rat fetus. J Craniofac Genet Dev Biol 14:16–25.

Paulson RB, Shanfeld J, Prause L, Iranpour S, Paulson JO (1991) Pre- and post-conceptional tobacco effects on the CD-1 mouse fetus. J Craniofac Genet Dev Biol 11:48–58.

Paulson RB, Shanfeld J, Vorhees CV, Cole J, Sweazy A, Paulson JO (1994b) Behavioral effects of smokeless tobacco on the neonate and young Sprague Dawley rat. Teratology 49:293–305.

Pauly JR, Sparks JA, Hauser KF, Pauly TH (2004) In utero nicotine exposure causes persistent, gender-dependant changes in locomotor activity and sensitivity to nicotine in C57Bl/6 mice. Int J Dev Neurosci 22:329–337.

Peng H, Huang Y, Rose J, Erichsen D, Herek S, Fujii N, Tamamura H, Zheng J (2004) Stromal cell–derived factor 1-mediated CXCR4 signaling in rat and human cortical neural progenitor cells. J Neurosci Res 76:35–50.

Pennington SN, Sandstrom LP, Shibley IAJ, Long SD, Beeker KR, Smith CPJ, Lee K, Jones TA, Cummings KM, Means LW (1994) Biochemical changes, early brain growth suppression and impaired detour learning in nicotine-treated chicks. Dev Brain Res 83:181–189.

Perry DC, Xiao Y, Nguyen HN, Musachio JL, Davila-Garcia MI, Kellar KJ (2002) Measuring nicotinic receptors with characteristics of $\alpha4\beta2$, $\alpha3\beta2$ and $\alpha3\beta4$ subtypes in rat tissues by autoradiography. J Neurochem 82:468–481.

Perry EK, Court JA, Johnson M, Smith CJ, James V, Cheng AV, Kerwin JM, Morris CM, Piggott MA, Edwardson JA (1993) Autoradiographic comparison of cholinergic and other transmitter receptors in the normal human hippocampus. Hippocampus 3: 307–315.

Persson AI, Thorlin T, Bull C, Eriksson PS (2003a) Opioid-induced proliferation through the MAPK pathway in cultures of adult hippocampal progenitors. Mol Cell Neurosci 23:360–372.

Persson AI, Thorlin T, Bull C, Zarnegar P, Ekman R, Terenius L, Eriksson PS (2003b) μ- and δ-opioid receptor antagonists decrease proliferation and increase neurogenesis in cultures of rat adult hippocampal progenitors. Eur J Neurosci 17:1159–1172.

Peterson PK, Molitor TW, Chao CC (1998) The opioid–cytokine connection. J Neuroimmunol 83: 63–69.

Polakiewicz RD, Schieferl SM, Gingras AC, Sonenberg N, Comb MJ (1998) μ-Opioid receptor activates signaling pathways implicated in cell survival and translational control. J Biol Chem 273:23534–23541.

Prendergast MA, Harris BR, Mayer S, Holley RC, Hauser KF, Littleton JM (2001) Chronic nicotine exposure reduces N-methyl-D-aspartate receptor–mediated damage in the hippocampus without altering calcium accumulation or extrusion: evidence for calbindin-D28K overexpression. Neuroscience 102: 75–85.

Radley JJ, Jacobs BL (2002) 5-HT1A receptor antagonist administration decreases cell proliferation in the dentate gyrus. Brain Res 955:264–267.

Raff MC, Miller RH, Noble M (1983) A glial progenitor cell that develops in vitro into an astrocyte or an oligodendrocyte depending on culture medium. Nature 303:390–396.

Ramón y Cajal S (1960) *Studies on Vertebrate Neurogenesis* (translated by L Guth). Charles C. Thomas, Springfield, IL, p 448.

Rand MJ (1989) Neuropharmacological effects of nicotine in relation to cholinergic mechanisms. Prog Brain Res 79:3–11.

Renshaw G, Rigby P, Self G, Lamb A, Goldie R (1993) Exogenously administered α-bungarotoxin binds to embryonic chick spinal cord: implications for the toxin-induced arrest of naturally occurring motoneuron death. Neuroscience 53:1163–1172.

Reznikov K, Hauser KF, Nazarevskaja G, Trunova Y, Derjabin V, Bakalkin G (1999) Opioids modulate cell division in the germinal zone of the late embryonic neocortex. Eur J Neurosci 11:2711–2719.

Ribak CE, Dashtipour K (2002) Neuroplasticity in the damaged dentate gyrus of the epileptic brain. Prog Brain Res 136:319–328.

Ricalde AA, Hammer RP Jr (1991) Perinatal opiate treatment delays growth of cortical dendrites. Neurosci Lett 115:137–143.

Rogers SW, Gregori NZ, Carlson N, Gahring LC, Noble M (2001) Neuronal nicotinic acetylcholine receptor expression by O2A/oligodendrocyte progenitor cells. Glia 33:306–313.

Rogers TJ, Peterson PK (2003) Opioid G protein–coupled receptors: signals at the crossroads of inflammation. Trends Immunol 24:116–121.

Role LW, Berg DK (1996) Nicotinic receptors in the development and modulation of CNS synapses. Neuron 16:1077–1085.

Roy TS, Andrews JE, Seidler FJ, Slotkin TA (1998) Nicotine evokes cell death in embryonic rat brain during neurulation. J Pharmacol Exp Ther 287:1136–1144.

Ruzicka BB, Fox CA, Thompson RC, Akil H, Watson SJ (1994) Opioid receptor mRNA expression in primary cultures of glial cells derived from different rat brain regions. Regul Pept 54:251–252.

Ruzicka BB, Fox CA, Thompson RC, Meng F, Watson SJ, Akil H (1995) Primary astroglial cultures derived from several rat brain regions differentially express μ, δ and κ opioid receptor mRNA. Mol Brain Res 34:209–220.

Sabatier JM, Vives E, Mabrouk K, Benjouad A, Rochat H, Duval A, Hue B, Bahraoui E (1991) Evidence for neurotoxicity of tat from HIV. J Virol 65:961–967.

Sastry BV (1991) Placental toxicology: tobacco smoke, abused drugs, multiple chemical interactions, and placental function. Reprod Fertil Dev 3: 355–372.

Schmahl W, Funk R, Miaskowski U, Plendl J (1989) Long-lasting effects of naltrexone, an opioid receptor antagonist, on cell proliferation in developing rat forebrain. Brain Res 486:297–300.

Seatriz JV, Hammer RP Jr (1993) Effects of opiates on neuronal development in the rat cerebral cortex. Brain Res Bull 30:523–527.

Sershen H, Hashim A, Lajtha A (1987) Behavioral and biochemical effects of nicotine in an MPTP-induced mouse model of Parkinson's disease. Pharmacol Biochem Behav 28:299–303.

Shankaran S, Das A, Bauer CR, Bada HS, Lester B, Wright LL, Smeriglio V (2004) Association between patterns of maternal substance use and infant birth weight, length, and head circumference. Pediatrics 114:e226–e234.

Shu XO, Hatch MC, Mills J, Clemens J, Susser M (1995) Maternal smoking, alcohol drinking, caffeine consumption, and fetal growth: results from a prospective study. Epidemiology 6:115–120.

Simon EJ (1991) Opioid receptors and endogenous opioid peptides. Med Res Rev 11:357–374.

Simon EJ, Hiller JM (1994) Opioid peptides and opioid receptors. In: Siegel GJ, Agranoff BW, Albers RW, Molinoff PB (eds). Basic Neurochemistry. Raven Press, New York, pp 321–339.

Singh IN, Goody RJ, Dean C, Ahmad NM, Lutz SE, Knapp PE, Nath A, Hauser KF (2004) Apoptotic death of striatal neurons induced by HIV-1 Tat and gp120: differential involvement of caspase-3 and endonuclease G. J Neurovirol 10:141–151.

Singhal P, Kapasi A, Reddy K, Franki N (2001) Opiates promote T cell apoptosis through JNK and caspase pathway. Adv Exp Med Biol 493:127–135.

Singhal PC, Bhaskaran M, Patel J, Patel K, Kasinath BS, Duraisamy S, Franki N, Reddy K, Kapasi AA (2002) Role of p38 mitogen-activated protein kinase phosphorylation and Fas–Fas ligand interaction in morphine-induced macrophage apoptosis. J Immunol 168:4025–4033.

Slotkin TA (2004) Cholinergic systems in brain development and disruption by neurotoxicants: nicotine, environmental tobacco smoke, organophosphates. Toxicol Appl Pharmacol 198:132–151.

Slotkin TA, Lappi SE, McCook EC, Lorber BA, Seidler FJ (1995) Loss of neonatal hypoxia tolerance after prenatal nicotine exposure: implications for sudden infant death syndrome. Brain Res Bull 38: 69–75.

Slotkin TA, Lappi SE, Seidler FJ (1993) Impact of fetal nicotine exposure on development of rat brain regions: critical sensitive periods or effects of withdrawal? Brain Res Bull 31:319–328.

Slotkin TA, Orband-Miller L, Queen KL, Whitmore WL, Seidler FJ (1987) Effects of prenatal nicotine exposure on biochemical development of rat brain regions: maternal drug infusions via osmotic minipumps. J Pharmacol Exp Ther 240:602–611.

Steele WJ, Johannesson T (1975) Effects of prenatally administered morphine on brain development and resultant tolerance to the analgesic effect of morphine in offspring of morphine-treated rats. Acta Pharmacol Toxicol 36:243–256.

Stefansson H, Steinthorsdottir V, Thorgeirsson TE, Gulcher JR, Stefansson K (2004) Neuregulin 1 and schizophrenia. Ann Med 36:62–71.

Stiene-Martin A, Gurwell JA, Hauser KF (1991) Morphine alters astrocyte growth in primary cultures of mouse glial cells: evidence for a direct effect of opiates on neural maturation. Dev Brain Res 60:1–7.

Stiene-Martin A, Hauser KF (1990) Opioid-dependent growth of glial cultures: suppression of astrocyte DNA synthesis by Met-enkephalin. Life Sci 46:91–98.

—— (1991) Glial growth is regulated by agonists selective for multiple opioid receptor types in vitro. J Neurosci Res 29:538–548.

Stiene-Martin A, Knapp PE, Martin KM, Gurwell JA, Ryan S, Thornton SR, Smith FL, Hauser KF (2001) Opioid system diversity in developing neurons, astroglia, and oligodendroglia in the subventricular zone and striatum: impact on gliogenesis in vivo. Glia 36:78–88.

Stiene-Martin A, Zhou R, Hauser KF (1998) Regional, developmental, and cell cycle–dependent differences in μ, δ, and κ-opioid receptor expression among cultured mouse astrocytes. Glia 22:249–259.

Tardieu M, Hery C, Peudenier S, Boespflug O, Montagnier L (1992) Human immunodeficiency virus type 1–infected monocytic cells can destroy human neural cells after cell-to-cell adhesion. Ann Neurol 32:11–17.

Taupin P, Gage FH (2002) Adult neurogenesis and neural stem cells of the central nervous system in mammals. J Neurosci Res 69:745–749.

Teuchert-Noodt G, Dawirs RR, Hildebrandt K (2000) Adult treatment with methamphetamine transiently decreases dentate granule cell proliferation in the gerbil hippocampus. J Neural Trans 107:133–143.

Thorlin T, Eriksson PS, Persson PA, Aberg ND, Hansson E, Rönnbäck L (1998) δ-opioid receptors on astroglial cells in primary culture: mobilization of intracellular free calcium via a pertussis sensitive G protein. Neuropharmacology 37:299–311.

Thorlin T, Persson PA, Eriksson PS, Hansson E, Rönnbäck L (1999) δ-opioid receptor immunoreactivity on astrocytes is upregulated during mitosis. Glia 25:370–378.

van Duijn CM, Hofman A (1991) Relation between nicotine intake and Alzheimer's disease. BMJ 302:1491–1494.

Vartanian T, Corfas G, Li Y, Fischbach GD, Stefansson K (1994) A role for the acetylcholine receptor–inducing protein ARIA in oligodendrocyte development. Proc Natl Acad Sci USA 91:11626–11630.

Vernadakis A, Sakellaridis N, Geladopoulos T, Mangoura D (1990) Function of opioids early in embryogenesis. Ann NY Acad Sci 579:109–122.

Vértes Z, Melegh G, Vértes M, Kovács S (1982) Effect of naloxone and D-Met²-Pro⁵-enkephalinamide treatment on the DNA synthesis in the developing rat brain. Life Sci 31:119–126.

Villablanca AC (1998) Nicotine stimulates DNA synthesis and proliferation in vascular endothelial cells in vitro. J Appl Physiol 84:2089–2098.

Weeks BS, Lieberman DM, Johnson B, Roque E, Green M, Lowenstein P, Oldfield EH, Kleinman HK (1995) Neurotoxicity of the human immunodeficiency virus type 1 Tat transactivator to PC12 cells requires the Tat amino acid 49–58 basic domain. J Neurosci Res 42:34–40.

Wilson AL, Langley LK, Monley J, Bauer T, Rottunda S, McFalls E, Kovera C, McCarten JR (1995) Nicotine patches in Alzheimer's disease: pilot study on learning, memory, and safety. Pharmacol Biochem Behav 51:509–514.

Witschi H, Lundgaard SM, Rajini P, Hendrickx AG, Last JA (1994) Effects of exposure to nicotine and to sidestream smoke on pregnancy outcome in rats. Toxicol Lett 71:279–286.

Zagon IS (1987) Endogenous opioids, opioid receptors, and neuronal development. NIDA Res Monogr 78:61–71.

Zagon IS, McLaughlin PJ (1977a) Effect of chronic maternal methadone exposure on perinatal development. Biol Neonate 31:271–282.

—— (1977b) Methadone and brain development. Experientia 33:1486.

—— (1977c) Morphine and brain growth retardation in the rat. Pharmacology 15:276–282.

—— (1982a) Comparative effects of postnatal undernutrition and methadone exposure on protein and nucleic acid contents of the brain and cerebellum in rats. Dev Neurosci 5:385–393.

—— (1982b) Neuronal cell deficits following maternal exposure to methadone in rats. Experientia 38:1214–1216.

—— (1983) Increased brain size and cellular content in infant rats treated with an opioid antagonist. Science 221:1179–1180.

—— (1986a) Opioid antagonist (naltrexone) modulation of cerebellar development: histological and morphometric studies. J Neurosci 6:1424–1432.

—— (1986b) Opioid antagonist–induced modulation of cerebral and hippocampal development: histological and morphometric studies. Dev Brain Res 28:233–246.

—— (1987) Endogenous opioid systems regulate cell proliferation in the developing rat brain. Brain Res 412:68–72.

—— (1991) Identification of opioid peptides regulating proliferation of neurons and glia in the developing nervous system. Brain Res 542:318–323.

Zagon IS, Rhodes RE, McLaughlin PJ (1985) Distribution of enkephalin immunoreactivity in germinative cells of developing rat cerebellum. Science 227:1049–1051.

Zahalka EA, Seidler FJ, Lappi SE, McCook EC, Yanai J, Slotkin TA (1992) Deficits in development of central cholinergic pathways caused by fetal nicotine exposure: differential effects on choline acetyltransferase activity and [^{3}H]hemicholinium-3 binding. Neurotoxicol Teratol 14:375–382.

Zhu Y, Hsu MS, Pintar JE (1998) Developmental expression of the μ, κ, and δ opioid receptor mRNAs in mouse. J Neurosci 18:2538–2549.

23

Nicotinic Receptor Regulation of Developing Catecholamine Systems

Frances M. Leslie

Layla Azam

Kathy Gallardo

Kathryn O'Leary

Ryan Franke

Shahrdad Lotfipour

Central catecholamine systems, consisting of dopaminergic, noradrenergic, and adrenergic cell groups, serve numerous integrative neural functions and critically regulate action, emotion, motivation, and cognition (Berridge and Robinson, 1998; Berridge and Waterhouse, 2003; Nieoullon and Coquerel, 2003). These neural pathways are functional at an early stage of brain development and have important roles in neuronal maturation and behaviors that are critical for neonatal survival (Levitt et al., 1997; Sullivan, 2003). Dysregulation of these systems has been implicated in numerous disease states, particularly those in which there are cognitive, emotional, and/or motor deficits (Aston-Jones et al., 2000; Nieoullon and Coquerel, 2003).

Numerous clinical studies have shown that smoking during pregnancy can lead to long-standing neurobehavioral deficits in the offspring that may result from catecholaminergic dysfunction, including attention deficit hyperactivity disorder (ADHD), conduct disorder, cognitive deficits, and substance abuse (Ernst et al., 2001; Fried and Watkinson, 2001; Buka et al., 2003; Kahn et al., 2003; Thapar et al., 2003). Whereas tobacco smoke contains over 4000 constituents, many of which may be harmful to the developing fetus, animal studies have focused on and confirmed a neuroteratogenic role for nicotine (Slotkin, 1998). Gestational nicotine exposure in rodents results in cognitive impairments (Levin et al., 1996), enhanced spontaneous locomotor activity (Fung, 1988; Newman et al., 1999; Pauly et al., 2004), and increased nicotine-induced locomotion (Shacka et al., 1997). Neurochemical studies provide further evidence of an adverse effect of prenatal nicotine exposure on central catecholamine development (Ribary and Lichtensteiger, 1989; Slotkin, 1998; Muneoka et al., 1999), with norepinephrine (NE) more highly affected than dopamine (DA). Route of administration is a critical variable in such studies, however, with continuous administration producing results opposite to those of intermittent injection (Navarro et al., 1988). Such findings have led Slotkin and colleagues to propose that nicotine-induced hypoxia may produce many of the observed deficits in catecholamine development (Slotkin, 1998).

Nicotine binds to specfic cholinergic receptors. A nicotinic acetylcholine receptor (nAChR) is a ligand-gated cation channel. Each receptor consists of five subunit proteins surrounding a channel pore that mediate many of the biological effects of acetylcholine (ACh) (Leonard and Bertrand, 2001; Picciotto et al., 2001). Radioligand binding and mRNA expression studies have shown substantial expression of nAChRs in fetal human and rodent brain (Naeff et al., 1992; Zoli et al., 1995; Ospina et al., 1998; Hellstrom-Lindahl and Court, 2000). Therefore, these receptors may play a critical physiological role in regulating brain development (Role and Berg, 1996; Broide and Leslie, 1999; Metherate and Hsieh, 2004) and may also serve as a target for the neurotoxic actions of nicotine on developing brain. As outlined in the present chapter, a combination of biochemical, anatomical, and behavioral approaches have been used to evaluate the hypothesis that functional nAChRs are expressed on catecholamine neurons during critical phases of brain development.

DOPAMINE NEURONS

Adult

The forebrain dopaminergic system arises from two main cell groups located in the midbrain, the substantial nigra (SN) and ventral tegmental area (VTA). The nigrostriatal system, arising from the SN, controls sensorimotor integration and motor output. Mesolimbic and mesocortical projections, arising from the VTA, regulate reward and motivated behavior. A wide variety of nAChR subunits, $\alpha3$–$\alpha7$ and $\beta2$–$\beta4$, are expressed on DAergic neurons both in the SN and VTA of adult rodents (Klink et al., 2001; Azam et al., 2002), giving rise to a rich pharmacological complexity. At least two classes of nAChR are expressed on DAergic terminals within the striatum, which are discriminated on the basis of their affinity for the antagonist α-CtxMII (Kulak et al., 1997; Kaiser et al., 1998; Cui et al., 2003; Marubio et al., 2003). α-CtxMII-sensitive nAChRs consist of $\alpha6\beta2\beta3$ and $\alpha4\alpha6\beta2\beta3$ subunits. Those not blocked by α-CtxMII contain $\alpha4\beta2$ and $\alpha4\alpha5\beta2$ subunits (Salminen et al., 2004). A separate population of $\alpha7$

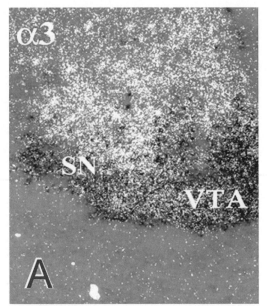

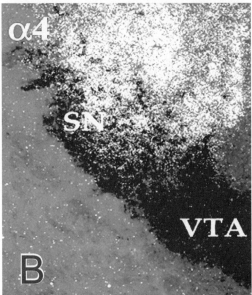

FIGURE 23–1 Expression of nicotinic receptor subunits in dopaminergic (DAergic) neurons. The photomicrographs show expression of $\alpha3$ (**A**) and $\alpha4$ (**B**) nAChR subunit mRNA within substantial nigra (SN) and ventral tegmental area (VTA) at G15. mRNAs for nAChR subunits (silver grains) are expressed in both DAergic cells expressing tyrosine hydroxylase (TH) mRNA (dark cells) and non-DAergic neurons. Note the differential distribution of $\alpha4$ mRNA within SN and VTA at this age.

nAChRs has also been identified on DAergic cell bodies (Pidoplichko et al., 1997; Klink et al., 2001).

Perinatal Period

DA-containing neurons of the SN and VTA are born between gestational day (G) 12 and G14 (Voorn et al., 1988), with nAChR binding appearing in the anlage shortly thereafter (Naeff et al., 1992; Zoli et al., 1995). By G15, several nAChR subunit mRNAs are expressed by DAergic neurons including $\alpha3$, $\alpha4$, $\alpha5$, $\alpha7$, $\beta2$, and $\beta4$ (Fig. 23–1, Table 23–1). At this age, both high-affinity [^{3}H]nicotine binding and $\alpha4$ mRNA expression are higher in the SN than in the VTA. At later stages of fetal and postnatal development, however, no differences are detectable between nAChR expression in DAergic neurons of these two nuclei (Azam et al., 2002). The postnatal decline in [^{3}H]nicotine binding to lower adult concentrations in the SN and VTA parallels a decrease in the expression of mRNAs for $\alpha3$, $\alpha4$, and $\beta2$ subunits. In contrast, $\alpha6$ and $\beta3$ mRNAs are expressed at low amounts in fetal DAergic neurons, with transcript levels increasing during the postnatal period. Such findings suggest that the types of nAChRs expressed on DAergic neurons change with age. Functional studies support this view (Azam et al., 2005).

By examining in vitro neurotransmitter release from striatal slices, the presence of functional nAChRs on rat striatal DA terminals as early as G17 has been shown (Azam et al., 2005) (Table 23–2).

Maximal nicotine-stimulated [^{3}H]DA release declines by 50% at birth, then gradually increases during the postnatal period to reach adult levels by postnatal day (P) 21. There is a concomitant increase in nicotine potency, as indicated by the concentration inducing a half maximum response (EC_{50}) at P21 being almost an order of magnitude lower than that observed in fetal brain. Thus, during the first postnatal month there is a switch in the type of nAChR(s) expressed on striatal DAergic terminals from those with low affinity for nicotine to those with high affinity.

Data on the functional influence of $\alpha4$-containing nAChRs on developing DAergic neurons are consistent with those from studies on a mutant mouse model in which the $\alpha4$ subunit was modified to be hypersensitive to nicotine and endogenous ligands (Labarca et al., 2001). Whereas fetuses of these transgenic mice have the same number of midbrain DAergic neurons as wild-type controls on G14, they exhibit a dramatic decline in DA cell number by G16 and G18. Thus, fetal DAergic neurons in these transgenic lines degenerate following hyperactivation of the mutant $\alpha4^*$ nAChRs by endogenous ACh or choline.

Adolescence

Adolescence, defined as P28 to P42 in rodents, is a time at which youths start to execute higher-level cognitive functions and establish independence (Spear, 2000). Novelty seeking and impulsivity are hallmarks of this developmental period, as is

TABLE 23–1 Nicotinic acetylcholine receptor subunit mRNAs and binding sites in the developing substantial nigra and ventral tegmental area

	Prenatal	Early Postnatal	Late Postnatal	Adolescence	Adult
$\alpha3$	++++	+++	++	+	+
$\alpha4$	+++/++++*	++	++	+	+
$\alpha5$	++	+	++	+/++	+
$\alpha6$	–/+	+	++	+/++	+
$\alpha7$	+	+	++	+	+
$\beta2$	+++	++	++	+	+
$\beta3$	+	+/++	+	+	+
[^{3}H]NIC	++/++++*	+++	++	+	+
[^{125}I]α-BgTX	–	+	+	+	+

α-BgTX, α-bungarotoxin; NIC, nicotine; +++, concentrations at least threefold over those in adults; ++, concentrations about twofold over adult; +, concentrations similar to adult; –/+, concentrations below adult; –, concentrations at background.

*Higher in substantia nigra than in ventral tegmental area on G15.

TABLE 23–2 Nicotine-induced [³H] dopamine release from striatal slices during the first 3 postnatal weeks

Age	EC_{50} (mM)	Maximum Release (%)
G17–G18	9.2*** (5.7–15)	4.84 ± 0.55
P1	4.0 (0.4–42)	2.50 ± 0.58**
P4	3.09 (1.5–6.6)	2.59 ± 0.30**
P7	5.78** (2.0–17)	3.15 ± 0.56**
P14	2.48 (1.3–4.8)	3.76 ± 0.48*
P21	1.65 (0.8–3.3)	6.19 ± 0.86

EC_{50} values (95% confidence intervals) and maximum release (mean ± SEM) are from three to four independent experiments. G, gestational day; P, postnatal day.

*$p < 0.05$, **$p < 0.01$, ***$p < 0.001$ values significantly different on P21.

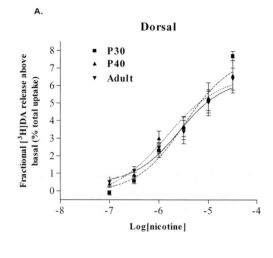

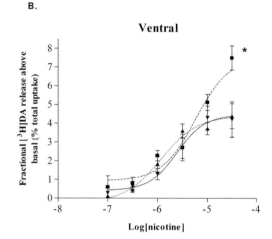

FIGURE 23–2 Release of dopamine (DA) from striatal slices. These dose–response curves depict nicotine-stimulated [³H]DA release from dorsal (**A**) and ventral (**B**) striatal slices from adolescent male rats on P30 and P40 and from adults. Maximal release is significantly higher from ventral striatum at P30 than at P40 or in adults. *$p < 0.05$, Dunnett's post-hoc analysis with adult as control.

initiation of addictive behaviors. There is increasing evidence from both rodent and primate studies that DAergic systems continue to mature throughout this developmental period. DAergic innervation of prefrontal cortex increases until young adulthood (Benes et al., 2000; Lambe et al., 2000), with some evidence of an "overshoot" at puberty and subsequent pruning of nonspecific innervation (Lewis, 1997). Both D1 and D2 receptor levels in prefrontal cortex reach peak concentrations in young male adult rats, then decline substantially (Andersen et al., 2000; Tarazi and Baldessarini, 2000). Overproduction of D1 and D2 receptors also occurs in the caudate nucleus and putamen, with peak content reached at puberty followed by substantial declines. A gender difference has been noted in this effect, with striatal receptor pruning occurring only in males and not in females (Andersen and Teicher, 2000).

Whereas the majority of nAChR mRNAs in the SN and VTA reach mature expression prior to adolescence, transcript amounts for α5, α6, and β4 subunits continue to decrease toward lower adult concentrations (Table 23–1). Nicotine-stimulated DA release in the ventral striatum, which includes the nucleus accumbens, is also higher during early adolescence (P30) than during late adolescence (P40) or adulthood (Fig. 23–2). This transient increase in nicotine efficacy is not observed in the caudoputamen. Such findings suggest an enhanced sensitivity of motivational circuitry to the activating effects of nicotine during early adolescence. Although a recent microdialysis study suggests that a similar enhanced effect of nicotine on the release of DA from the nucleus accumbens is not detectable in vivo (Badanich and Kirstein, 2004), other neurochemical findings are consistent with evidence that early adolescence is a period of unique sensitivity to the rewarding effects of nicotine (Vastola et al., 2002; Laviola et al., 2003; Belluzzi et al., 2004, 2005; Rezvani and Levin, 2004).

NOREPINEPHRINE NEURONS

Adult

The noradrenergic system projects extensively throughout the central nervous system (CNS) and modulates a variety of cognitive and visceral functions. NE projections stem from nuclei in the pons and medulla, each with a role in regulating responses to sensory input and to environmental and visceral stressors. Nicotinic receptors are widely expressed throughout these catecholamine nuclei.

Locus Coeruleus

A dorsal pontine tegmental nucleus, the locus coeruleus (LC), is the CNS structure with the most widespread projections (Loughlin et al., 1986). It gives rise to a network of fibers that extend throughout the neuraxis. The LC provides the exclusive NE input to the majority of brain structures, including the neocortex, hippocampus, and cerebellum, and plays a critical role in attention and arousal.

A wealth of nAChR subunits are expressed in the adult LC (Lena et al., 1999). In situ hybridization studies show high expression of several nAChR subunit mRNAs, including α6, β2, and β3, with lower levels of expression of α4, α5, and α7 (Gallardo et al., 2005). Consistent with the low expression of α4 and α7 subunits, very low amounts of [³H]nicotine and [¹²⁵I]α-bungarotoxin binding, respectively, are present in the adult LC. Both α3 and β4 mRNAs are topographically distributed, with much higher expression in dorsal than in ventral cells. These findings are consistent with a single-cell reverse transcriptase–polymerase chain reaction study in which α3 and β4 mRNAs were found to be expressed in less than half of all LC cells tested (Lena et al., 1999).

LC efferent projections are organized topographically, with dorsal cells projecting to more rostral brain regions (Loughlin et al., 1986). The topographic distribution of nAChR mRNAs in LC cells suggests that different terminal fields express nAChRs with differ-

TABLE 23.3 Nicotine EC_{50} values for stimulation of [³H] norephinephrine release from brain slices in the neonate and adult

Brain region	Nicotine EC_{50} (μM)	
	neonate	adult
Cortex	1.4	14.1
Cerebellum	9.1	10.3
Hippocampal formation	26	39
Hypothalamus	20	75

ing pharmacological properties. This issue has not been examined systematically. A preliminary comparison of nicotine potency to stimulate [³H]NE release in slice preparations from four brain regions suggests that there may be pharmacological differences in nAChR regulation (Table 23–3). Immunoreactivity for α6 and β3 subunits has been shown in the hippocampal formation, leading to the suggestion that the nAChR on LC terminals in this structure consist of an α6β2β3 subunit combination (Lena et al., 1999). On the other hand, nAChRs regulate hippocampal [³H]NE release by both direct and indirect mechanisms, with nicotine-stimulated GABA release leading to an anomalous excitation of LC terminals (Leslie et al., 2002). In organotypic slice cultures of parietal cortex, in contrast, nicotine-stimulated [³H]NE release is mediated entirely by nAChRs located on LC terminals (data not shown).

Medullary Nuclei

Medullary catecholamine neurons cells are found within the nucleus tractus solitarius (NTS) and the ventrolateral medulla (VLM) and consist of both NE- and epinephrine-containing cells. The NTS is the initial site of integration for central and peripheral autonomic systems, with afferents projecting from multiple visceral modalities (Andresen and Kunze, 1994). The NTS sends reciprocal projections to numerous brain stem nuclei that mediate peripheral autonomic outflow and to the hypothalamus, where it serves a critical role in regulating plasma glucose via activation of the hypothalamic-pituitary-adrenal (HPA) axis and food intake (Ritter et al., 2001, 2003). The caudal and rostral VLM generally have opposing effects on autonomic output, such as central fluid and cardiovascular homeostasis (Heslop et al., 2004). The NEergic neurons of the rostral VLM also provide the major inhibitory input to the LC, thus providing coordinate regulation of cognitive and autonomic responses to external stimuli (Aston-Jones et al., 1992).

Data from in situ hybridization studies provide evidence for expression of nAChRs on adult medullary catecholamine neurons (Gallardo et al., 2005). Unlike the LC, where most neurons exhibit a rich complexity of subunit mRNAs, fewer nAChR subunits are expressed within these neurons (data not shown). In contrast to the LC, there is no expression of α6 and β3 subunits in the NTS. The predominant subunits expressed in catecholaminergic neurons of this nucleus

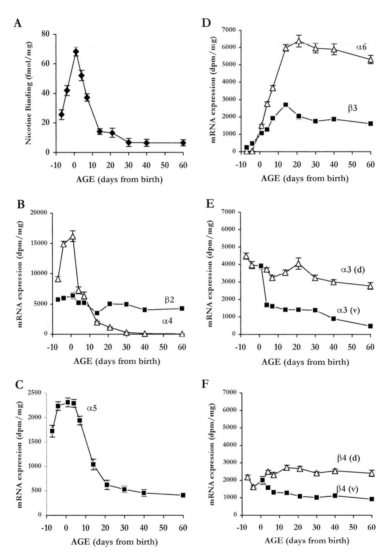

FIGURE 23–3 Quantitative analysis of nicotine binding site and nAChR subunit mRNA expression in the locus coeruleus as a function of age. **A.** Specific [³H]nicotine binding (fmol/mg tissue). **B.** α4 (triangles) and β2 (squares) mRNA expression. **C.** α5 mRNA expression. **D.** α6 (triangles) and β3 (squares) mRNA expression. **E.** α3 mRNA expression, dorsal (d; triangles) and ventral (v; squares) subdivisions. **F.** β4 in dorsal (d; triangles) and ventral (v; squares) subdivisions. The day of birth was G22.

are α3, α5, and β2/4. In the VLM, there is expression of β3 mRNA in scattered cells, with a more widespread expression of α6 mRNA in ~50% of catecholamine neurons. In contrast to both LC and NTS, almost all cells of the VLM express both α7 and β2 subunit mRNAs, with 30%–50% also expressing α3–α5. Such findings are consistent with functional studies in which nicotine microinjections into brain stem nuclei have been reported to increase NE release in the hypothalamus (Fu et al., 1997) and to regulate both HPA axis (Fu et al., 1997) and cardiovascular functions (Ferreira et al., 2000).

Ontogeny

Locus Coeruleus

Neurons of the LC are born between G10 and G13 in rat, and first exhibit the biosynthetic enzyme tyrosine hydroxylase (TH) on G12 (e.g., Lauder and Bloom, 1974; Specht et al., 1981; Konig et al., 1988). These neurons rapidly extend axons into immature brain structures, where they are believed to serve an

important morphogenetic role (Ruiz et al., 1997; Naqui et al., 1999). LC cells are also highly sensitive to early sensory input (Nakamura et al., 1987; Marshall et al., 1991) and regulate functions critical to the survival of the neonate such as olfactory imprinting (Sullivan, 2003). A number of studies show that the hyper-reactivity of the LC to innocuous sensory stimuli decreases after birth, and that these changes are accompanied by alterations in the properties of adrenoceptors expressed by LC neurons (Kimura and Nakamura, 1987; Williams and Marshall, 1987; Nakamura et al., 1988). Interestingly, little attention has been given to date to possible changes in the expression of other receptor types.

Anatomical and functional studies demonstrate major changes in the expression of nAChR subunits in the LC over the course of development (Gallardo et al., 2005). Fetal LC neurons exhibit high-affinity [³H]nicotine binding that decreases to low adult amounts during the early postnatal period (Figs. 23–3, 23–4, and 23–5). Consistent with earlier findings that high-affinity [³H]nicotine binding sites are comprised of α4 and β2 subunits (Zoli et al., 1998),

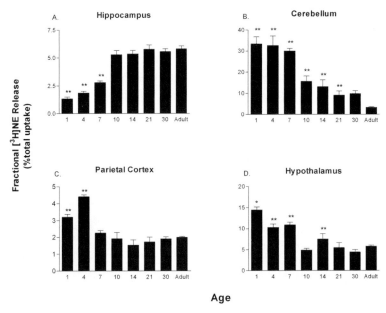

FIGURE 23–4 Stimulation of norepinephrine (NE) in developing forebrain. Developmental changes in nicotine-stimulated [³H]NE from slices of hippocampus (**A**), cerebellum (**B**), parietal cortex (**C**), and hypothalamus (**D**). Significant differences ($p < 0.01$, Dunnett's test) relative to the adult are signified by asterisks.

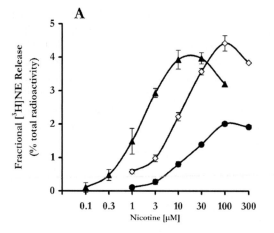

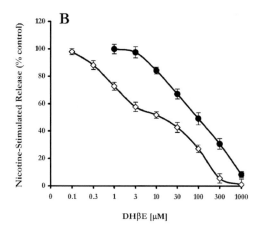

FIGURE 23–5 Properties of nAChRs that stimulate [³H]norepinephrine (NE) release from locus coeruleus terminals in developing parietal cortex. **A.** Nicotine concentration–response curves on P1(triangles), P4 (diamonds), and P60 (adult; circles). Nicotine potency and maximal release values differ with age. **B.** DHβE inhibition of nicotine-induced [³H]NE release from cortical slices on P4 (diamonds) and P60 (adult; squares). Antagonist inhibition on P4 is biphasic, indicating that nicotine acts at two different types of nAChR. In contrast, the antagonist inhibition curve is monophasic in adults.

high amounts of expression of α4 and β2 mRNAs occurs in the LC during the perinatal period, along with α3, α5, and β4 mRNAs (Fig. 23–3) (Gallardo et al., 2005). Expression of α4 and α5 mRNAs declines during the first postnatal week, in parallel with the loss of high-affinity [³H]nicotine binding. Whereas perinatal expression of α3 and β4 subunit mRNAs is

homogeneously distributed throughout the entire nucleus, there is an emergence of a topographic expression during the early postnatal period, with higher levels of expression in the dorsal LC. At the same time, the phenotype of the mature LC nAChR emerges, with increasing postnatal expression of α6 and β3 mRNAs.

Fetal LC cells dissected from dorsal rhombencephalon on G14 and cultured for 4 days have been shown to take up and release [³H]NE in response to appropriate physiological stimuli (Raymon and Leslie, 1994). Nicotine stimulates [³H]NE release from fetal cultured LC cells via activation of a receptor with high affinity for nicotine and properties consistent with that of an α4β2* nAChR (Gallardo and Leslie, 1998). The EC_{50} value for nicotine stimulation of this nAChR was found to be <1 μM, which is within the range of blood nicotine levels found in moderate to heavy smokers (Benowitz, 1990).

In order to evaluate possible postnatal changes in the properties of nAChRs that regulate NE release, similar studies with slices taken from LC terminal fields were conducted (Fig. 23–4) (Leslie et al., 2002). Using this approach, a remarkable regional heterogeneity in nAChR regulation of transmitter release from LC terminals during the postnatal period was shown. In the hippocampus, a late-maturing structure, there is no major developmental switch in nAChR regulation of NE release (Leslie et al., 2002). There is a monotonic increase in nicotine-stimulated NE release from hippocampal slices during the first postnatal week to reach adult concentrations by P10. There is also no change in the pharmacological profile of hippocampal nAChRs, with major contributions of both direct and indirect pathways at each postnatal stage (Leslie et al., 2002). In contrast, another structure that matures largely during the postnatal period in rat, the cerebellum, exhibits substantial postnatal changes in nAChR regulation of NE release (O'Leary and Leslie, 2003). During the first postnatal week, nicotine is highly efficacious, releasing almost 40% of cerebellar NE stores at a maximal effective concentration. There is a gradual decline in nAChR efficacy during the next month to reach low adult levels. Pharmacological analysis has shown that neonatal and adult nAChRs on cerebellar LC terminals have different subunit compositions, with decreasing involvement of β2 subunits in the adult receptor (O'Leary and Leslie, 2003).

In parietal cortex, there is increased maximal nicotine-induced release in the neonatal period with a subsequent decline to lower adult concentrations by P7 (Fig. 23–4C) (Gallardo et al., 2005). More detailed pharmacological analysis has shown that there is a switch in the properties of nAChRs on cortical LC terminals during the first postnatal week (Fig. 23–5) (Gallardo et al., 2005). Whereas at birth nicotine stimulates cortical NE release with high affinity, there is an order of magnitude decrease in potency by P4. At this age, nAChRs on cortical LC terminals are in a period of transition between the neonatal receptor that has high affinity for the $\alpha4\beta2$-selective antagonist, DHβE, and the adult low-affinity form.

Hypothalamus was examined because, unlike the other brain regions studied, it has substantial input from the medullary catecholamine nuclei as well as the LC. This region also shows enhanced efficacy of nicotine to release [^{3}H]NE during the first postnatal week (Fig. 3–4D). Subsequently, there are complex changes in nicotine-induced transmitter release, with adult profiles not reached until adolescence (P30). Pharmacological comparisons of nAChR properties at P7 and adult have shown that, similar to the cerebellum and neocortex, the neonatal receptor in hypothalamus has distinct properties from that of adult. The neonatal form of the receptor in all three terminal fields appears to have a predominance of β2 subunits compared to adult amounts, however, the neonatal receptor is not identical across regions. In the hypothalamus and cerebellum, unlike neocortex, the neonatal receptor does not have high affinity for nicotine (Table 23–3). Although hypothalamus receives mixed inputs from NEergic neurons of both the pons and medulla, lesion studies in adult show that hypothalamic nAChRs selectively regulate NE release from LC terminals (Sperlagh et al., 1998). Similarly, nAChRs are exclusively localized on hypothalamic LC terminals in the neonate, since nicotine-stimulated [^{3}H]NE release is abolished by the LC-selective neurotoxin DSP-4 (O'Leary and Leslie, 2005).

These findings are consistent with an important and changing role of nAChRs in regulating release of NE from LC terminals throughout development. Unique patterns of nicotinic regulation of individual LC terminal fields indicate that the specific role of nAChRs may vary by brain region. Despite these individual differences, there is a consistent trend in most brain regions for enhanced nAChR efficacy during the perinatal period when LC is hyperreactive to external stimuli. Thus cholinergic inputs may provide an important mechanism for regulating LC responsiveness during this critical neonatal period.

Medullary Nuclei

The VLM, which provides the major inhibitory input to the LC (Aston-Jones et al., 1992), exhibits coordinated developmental regulation of nAChR subunit expression. There is high perinatal expression of α4 and α5 mRNAs, with a slow decline to adult concentrations after birth. There is also a parallel increase in α6 and β3 mRNA expression during the postnatal period, indicating that some cells of the VLM may switch their nAChR phenotype. In contrast to the LC and VLM, the NTS exhibits less dynamic alterations in nAChR subunit expression throughout development. Other than a brief up-regulation of α4 mRNA in fetal NTS, no transient nAChR expression has been observed. Rather, there is a slow maturation during the postnatal period to adult concentrations.

The absence of nAChRs on medullary hypothalamic terminals precludes the type of functional analysis of developmental changes in the properties of nAChRs described for the LC (Gallardo et al., 2005). More complex in vivo studies are required to evaluate this issue. Whereas nicotine administration in vivo activates the HPA axis via stimulation of nAChRs within the medulla (Fu et al., 1997), no such stimulation is evident during early adolescence (data not shown). Such findings suggest that there is a late postnatal maturation of nAChR regulation of HPA function, consistent with the late developmental maturation of nAChR expression within the NTS.

DEVELOPMENTAL EXPOSURE

Gestation

Although there are functionally active nAChRs on fetal DA terminals, they have relatively low affinity for nicotine (~10 μM) (Azam et al., 2005). Thus, given the low concentration of nicotine in blood (~500 nM), one would expect there to be minimal occupancy of these sites. In contrast, nAChRs on fetal LC neurons and neonatal cortical terminals express nAChRs with high affinity for nicotine that would be activated by blood concentrations of nicotine in pregnant female smokers. Such findings predict that prenatal exposure to nicotine has a more harmful effect on developing NEergic systems than on DAergic systems. Although a number of studies suggest that gestational nicotine treatment does affect the development of the striatal DAergic pathway (Oliff and Gallardo, 1999), chronic prenatal infusion of nicotine in moderate doses more profoundly affects postnatal ontogeny of NEergic systems (Slotkin, 1998).

Gestational treatment with nicotine infusion (3 mg/kg/day) induces a long-term change in the efficacy of nAChRs on cortical LC terminals (Fig. 23–6) (Gallardo et al., 2005). Maximal nicotine-stimulated [³H]NE release is greatly increased during the first postnatal month and, although reduced, is still significant in the adult. This does not result from an overall increase in the excitability of LC terminals, since potassium-stimulated transmitter release is unchanged by gestational nicotine. Nor does it result from a delayed transition in the properties of terminal nAChRs; both anatomical and functional studies have demonstrated that there is a normal postnatal switch in nAChR phenotype on LC cells and cortical terminals in gestationally treated animals. One change in nAChR properties, however, is a much greater acute nicotine-induced receptor desensitization, that is most evident at low drug concentrations (data not shown). This finding may explain an apparent discrepancy between in vitro data (Gallardo et al., 2005) and those of an earlier in vivo study (Seidler et al., 1992) of NE turnover, which found prenatal nicotine treatment to induce hypoactivity in the response of NE systems to acute postnatal nicotine treatment.

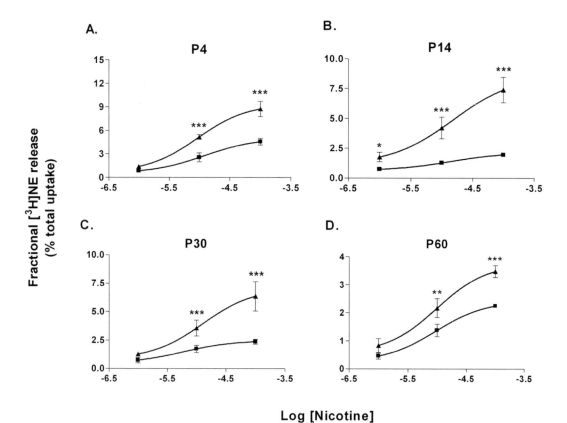

FIGURE 23–6 Effect of gestational treatment with nicotine (3.0 mg/kg/day) on subsequent nicotine-induced [³H]norepinephrine (NE) release from locus coeruleus terminals in parietal cortex. Nicotine concentration–response curves are from pups of nicotine- (triangles) or saline- (squares) treated dams on P4 (A), P14 (B), P30 (C), or P60 (adult) (D). Significant differences relative to the saline-treated group are identified by **($p < 0.01$) and *** ($p < 0.001$).

Adolescence

It is well established that catecholamine systems, particularly DA, are not fully matured by adolescence (Spear, 2000; Chambers et al., 2003). Functional studies show that nAChR regulation of mesolimbic DAergic and medullary NEergic systems has not yet fully matured in adolescent rats (Azam et al., 2005). Such findings suggest that brain catecholamine systems are vulnerable to nicotine exposure during adolescence. A growing body of evidence supports this view. Exposure to drug for relatively short periods during adolescence in rodent induces permanent changes in behaviors mediated by forebrain DA systems, including locomotion and reward (Slotkin, 2002; Adriani et al., 2003; Faraday et al., 2003; Belluzzi et al., 2004). Similar changes are not observed following equivalent exposure in adult. Neurochemical studies confirm that chronic nicotine treatment during adolescence produces permanent alterations in DA and NE systems in rat brain (Trauth et al., 2001). Thus, catecholamine systems within adolescent brain may be particularly vulnerable to the neuroteratogenic effects of nicotine.

PHYSIOLOGICAL AND CLINICAL IMPLICATIONS

Methodological Issues

Whereas early in vivo studies have shown lasting changes induced by gestational nicotine treatment (Slotkin, 1998; Ernst et al., 2001), the underlying mechanisms are unclear. A systematic in vitro analysis was performed to clarify mechanisms underlying nAChR regulation of developing catecholaminergic neurons. Accordingly, it was demonstrated that nAChR are key regulators of developing catecholaminergic neurons. Interpretation of these data must be qualified because nAChR pharmacology is extremely complex, and subunit composition of native receptors is difficult to assess (Cordero-Erausquin et al., 2000; Whiteaker et al., 2000). Furthermore, several types of nAChR may be expressed within a single cell, with differential localization of receptor subtypes in terminal and somatodendritic regions (Champtiaux et al., 2003). Given these caveats, it is difficult to draw conclusions about the nature of nAChR regulation of somatodendritic areas that have been shown to have critical functional roles.

Physiological Implications

nAChRs are expressed on immature DA and NE neurons and function to regulate transmitter release in fetal brain. Such findings suggest a critical interaction of cholinergic and catecholamine brain systems during the earliest phase of brain development. There is a late postnatal maturation of most cholinergic systems (Hohmann and Ebner, 1985; Dinopoulos et al., 1989; Kiss and Patel, 1992), however, a brief perinatal phase of cholinergic neuronal expression has been described in several brain regions, including neocortex and cerebellum (Gould and Butcher, 1987; Dori and Parnavelas, 1989). Thus, transient cholinergic innervation may provide critical regulation of developing catecholamine systems via activation of nAChRs.

Although there are regional differences in the properties of nAChRs that regulate terminal catecholamine release during the perinatal period, there are some commonalities. Most fetal catecholaminergic cells, both DAergic and NEergic, express high amounts of [^{3}H]nicotine binding and $\alpha4/\beta2$ mRNAs. Many cells also express the $\alpha5$ structural subunit, which combines with other subunits to alter agonist affinity, calcium permeability, and agonist desensitization (Wang et al., 1996; Gerzanich et al., 1998). Although quite rare in adult brain, nAChRs comprised of $\alpha4\alpha5\beta2$ subunits are highly expressed during the perinatal period and may serve unique functional roles (Conroy and Berg, 1998). After birth, there is a decline in $\alpha4$ and $\alpha5$ subunit expression and of [^{3}H]nicotine binding. During this period, there is increased expression of $\alpha6$ and $\beta3$ subunits. These subunits do not appear to contribute to fetal nAChRs but are important constituents of nAChRs in adult catecholamine terminal fields (Lena et al., 1999). Concomitant changes in the pharmacological properties of nAChRs that regulate terminal catecholamine release are observed. Thus, in both NE and DA neurons there is a postnatal switch in the properties of terminal nAChRs to the mature phenotype. These findings suggest that nAChRs serve critical regulatory roles for catecholamine pathways at all stages of ontogeny but that the nature of the functional interaction changes with age.

Clinical Implications

Fetal LC neurons and their cortical terminals have nAChRs with sufficiently high affinity for nicotine to be activated by maternal smoking. Chronic gestational exposure to nicotine, at concentrations approximating blood concentrations in smokers, induces long-term changes in the properties of nAChRs on cortical LC terminals such that their efficacy is increased, but they are more readily desensitized by agonist exposure. Given the critical role of central NE in modulating cognitive and visceral functions and the apparent functional importance of nAChRs in regulating NEergic systems throughout development, such findings have substantial implications for understanding the etiology of many of the adverse effects of maternal smoking. In particular, altered sensitivity of central NEergic systems to nAChR stimulation and to perinatal hypoxia has been implicated in the etiology of sudden infant death syndrome (Slotkin et al., 1995). Given the critical role of the LC in cognition and attention at all stages of development (Aston-Jones et al., 1999; Moriceau and Sullivan, 2004), it is likely that disrupted development of forebrain NEergic systems may also contribute to the cognitive dysfunction and ADHD that are associated with maternal smoking.

DA systems are less severely disrupted by gestational nicotine exposure, however, there is evidence for long-term alterations in forebrain DAergic function (Slotkin, 1998; Muneoka et al., 1999). Striatal DAergic terminals express a lower-affinity nAChR during the fetal period, which would not be activated by blood-borne nicotine in the pregnant female (Azam et al., 2005). Some types of nAChR, however, are desensitized by nicotine at far lower concentrations than those required to activate the receptor (Lu et al., 1999; Wooltorton et al., 2003). Furthermore, somatodendritic nAChRs, which are critically implicated in the effects of systemic nicotine on DA release (Champtiaux et al., 2003), have not been evaluated. Thus, gestational nicotine exposure may directly influence the ontogeny of DAergic systems via modulation of nAChR function.

Adolescence is also a critical time for maturation of forebrain limbic systems and their afferent catecholamine inputs (Spear, 2000; Chambers et al., 2003). DAergic systems, in particular, are still quite immature and terminal nAChRs in ventral striatum are more highly activated by nicotine at this age than in the adult. Biochemical and behavioral studies indicate that both acute and chronic nicotine have unique effects on catecholamine systems during adolescence that are not observed in adult (Slotkin,

2002). Thus, early smoking in adolescence may reinforce subsequent addiction, as has been suggested by epidemiological studies (Kandel and Logan, 1984; Kandel et al., 1992), by modifying forebrain catecholamine development.

Tobacco smoke contains thousands of chemicals, many of which disrupt development. This has led to the recommendation that nicotine replacement therapy (NRT) be used extensively as an alternative to smoking by pregnant women (Dempsey and Benowitz, 2001). Some studies, however, have questioned the efficacy of NRT as a smoking cessation aid for pregnant women and adolescents (Hurt et al., 2000; Wisborg et al., 2000). Furthermore, a growing body of evidence shows (a) that nAChRs play a critical role in modulating neural development and (b) that exposure of immature brain to nicotine can disrupt normal cholinergic regulation of ontogenetic processes. Thus, the safety of NRT as a therapeutic regimen during pregnancy and adolescence needs to be evaluated more thoroughly.

Abbreviations

ACh acetylcholine

ADHD attention deficit hyperactivity disorder

CNS central nervous system

DA dopamine

EC_{50} concentration effecting a half maximal response

G gestational day

HPA hypothalamic-adrenal-pituitary

LC locus coeruleus

nAChR nicotinic acetylcholine receptor

NE norepinephrine

NRT nicotine replacement therapy

NTS nucleus tractus solitarius

P postnatal day

SN substantial nigra

TH tyrosine hydroxylase

VLM ventrolateral medulla

VTA ventral tegmental area

ACKNOWLEDGMENTS This work was supported by a grant from the National Institute of Drug Abuse and by graduate fellowships from the California Tobacco-Related Disease Research Program. We would like to thank Drs. Yiling Chen, Ursula Winzer-Serhan, and Sandra Loughlin for their helpful contributions.

References

Adriani W, Spijker S, Deroche-Gamonet V, Laviola G, Le Moal M, Smit AB, Piazza PV (2003) Evidence for enhanced neurobehavioral vulnerability to nicotine during periadolescence in rats. J Neurosci 23:4712–4716.

Andersen SL, Teicher MH (2000) Sex differences in dopamine receptors and their relevance to ADHD. Neurosci Biobehav Rev 24:137–141.

Andersen SL, Thompson AT, Rutstein M, Hostetter JC, Teicher MH (2000) Dopamine receptor pruning in prefrontal cortex during the periadolescent period in rats. Synapse 37:167–169.

Andresen MC, Kunze DL (1994) Nucleus tractus solitarius- gateway to neural circulatory control. Annu Rev Physiol 56:93–116.

Aston-Jones G, Astier B, Ennis M (1992) Inhibition of noradrenergic locus coeruleus neurons by C1 adrenergic cells in the rostral ventral medulla. Neuroscience 48:371–381.

Aston-Jones G, Rajkowski J, Cohen J (1999) Role of locus coeruleus in attention and behavioral flexibility. Biol Psychiatry 46:1309–1320.

——— (2000) Locus coeruleus and regulation of behavioral flexibility and attention. Prog Brain Res 126: 165–182.

Azam L, Chen Y, Leslie FM (2005) Developmental regulation of nicotinic acetylcholine receptors on midbrain dopamine neurons. Submitted.

Azam L, Winzer-Serhan UH, Chen Y, Leslie FM (2002) Expression of neuronal nicotinic acetylcholine receptor subunit mRNAs within midbrain dopamine neurons. J Comp Neurol 444:260–274.

Badanich KA, Kirstein CL (2004) Nicotine administration significantly alters accumbal dopamine in the adult but not in the adolescent rat. Ann NY Acad Sci 1021:410–417.

Belluzzi JD, Lee AG, Oliff HS, Leslie FM (2004) Age-dependent effects of nicotine on locomotor activity and conditioned place preference in rats. Psychopharmacology 174:389–395.

Belluzzi JD, Wang R, Leslie FM (2005) Acetaldehyde enhances acquisition of nicotine self-administration in adolescent rats. Neuropsychopharmacology 30: 705–712.

Benes FM, Taylor JB, Cunningham MC (2000) Convergence and plasticity of monoaminergic systems in the medial prefrontal cortex during the postnatal period: implications for the development of psychopathology. Cereb Cortex 10:1014–1027.

Benowitz NL (1990) Pharmacokinetic considerations in understanding nicotine dependence. Ciba Found Symp 152:186–200.

Berridge CW, Waterhouse BD (2003) The locus coeruleus–noradrenergic system: modulation of behavioral state and state-dependent cognitive processes. Brain Res Rev 42:33–84.

Berridge KC, Robinson TE (1998) What is the role of dopamine in reward: hedonic impact, reward learning, or incentive salience? Brain Res Rev 28:309–369.

Broide RS, Leslie FM (1999) The $\alpha7$ nicotinic acetylcholine receptor in neuronal plasticity. Mol Neurobiol 20:1–16.

Buka SL, Shenassa ED, Niaura R (2003) Elevated risk of tobacco dependence among offspring of mothers who smoked during pregnancy: a 30-year prospective study. Am J Psychiatry 160:1978–1984.

Chambers RA, Taylor JR, Potenza MN (2003) Developmental neurocircuitry of motivation in adolescence: a critical period of addiction vulnerability. Am J Psychiatry 160:1041–1052.

Champtiaux N, Gotti C, Cordero-Erausquin M, David DJ, Przybylski C, Lena C, Clementi F, Moretti M, Rossi FM, Le Novere N, McIntosh JM, Gardier AM, Changeux JP (2003) Subunit composition of functional nicotinic receptors in dopaminergic neurons investigated with knock-out mice. J Neurosci 23:7820–7829.

Conroy WG, Berg DK (1998) Nicotinic receptor subtypes in the developing chick brain: appearance of a species containing the $\alpha4$, $\beta2$, and $\alpha5$ gene products. Mol Pharmacol 53:392–401.

Cordero-Erausquin M, Marubio LM, Klink R, Changeux JP (2000) Nicotinic receptor function: new perspectives from knockout mice. Trends Pharmacol Sci 21:211–217.

Cui C, Booker TK, Allen RS, Grady SR, Whiteaker P, Marks MJ, Salminen O, Tritto T, Butt CM, Allen WR, Stitzel JA, McIntosh JM, Boulter J, Collins AC, Heinemann SF (2003) The $\beta3$ nicotinic receptor subunit: a component of α-conotoxin MII-binding nicotinic acetylcholine receptors that modulate dopamine release and related behaviors. J Neurosci 23:11045–11053.

Dempsey DA, Benowitz NL (2001) Risks and benefits of nicotine to aid smoking cessation in pregnancy. Drug Safety 24:277–322.

Dinopoulos A, Eadie LA, Dori I, Parnavelas JG (1989) The development of basal forebrain projections to the rat visual cortex. Exp Brain Res 76: 563–571.

Dori I, Parnavelas JG (1989) The cholinergic innervation of the rat cerebral cortex shows two distinct phases in development. Exp Brain Res 76:417–423.

Ernst M, Moolchan ET, Robinson ML (2001) Behavioral and neural consequences of prenatal exposure to nicotine. J Am Acad Child Adolesc Psychiatry 40:630–641.

Faraday MM, Elliott BM, Phillips JM, Grunberg NE (2003) Adolescent and adult male rats differ in sensitivity to nicotine's activity effects. Pharmacol Biochem Behav 74:917–931.

Ferreira M, Singh A, Dretchen KL, Kellar KJ, Gillis RA (2000) Brainstem nicotinic receptor subtypes that influence intragastric and arterial blood pressures. J Pharmacol Exp Ther 294:230–238.

Fried PA, Watkinson B (2001) Differential effects on facets of attention in adolescents prenatally exposed to cigarettes and marihuana. Neurotoxicol Teratol 23:421–430.

Fu Y, Matta SG, Valentine JD, Sharp BM (1997) Adrenocorticotropin response and nicotine-induced norepinephrine secretion in the rat paraventricular nucleus are mediated through brainstem receptors. Endocrinology 138:1935–1943.

Fung YK (1988) Postnatal behavioural effects of maternal nicotine exposure in rats. J Pharm Pharmacol 40:870–872.

Gallardo KA, Chen Y, Leslie, FM (2005) Developmental switch in nicotinic receptors that regulate cortical norepinephrine release. Submitted.

Gallardo KA, Leslie FM (1998) Nicotine-stimulated release of [^{3}H]norepinephrine from fetal rat locus coeruleus cells in culture. J Neurochem 70: 663–670.

Gerzanich V, Wang F, Kuryatov A, Lindstrom J (1998) α5 Subunit alters desensitization, pharmacology, Ca^{++} permeability and Ca^{++} modulation of human neuronal α3 nicotinic receptors. J Pharmacol Exp Ther 286:311–320.

Gould E, Butcher LL (1987) Transient expression of choline acetyltransferase–like immunoreactivity in Purkinje cells of the developing rat cerebellum. Brain Res 431:303–306.

Hellstrom-Lindahl E, Court JA (2000) Nicotinic acetylcholine receptors during prenatal development and brain pathology in human aging. Behav Brain Res 113:159–168.

Heslop DJ, Bandler R, Keay KA (2004) Haemorrhage-evoked decompensation and recompensation mediated by distinct projections from rostral and caudal midline medulla in the rat. Eur J Neurosci 20:2096–2110.

Hohmann CF, Ebner FF (1985) Development of cholinergic markers in mouse forebrain. I. Choline acetyltransferase enzyme activity and acetylcholinesterase histochemistry. Brain Res 355: 225–241.

Hurt RD, Croghan GA, Beede SD, Wolter TD, Croghan IT, Patten CA (2000) Nicotine patch therapy in 101 adolescent smokers: efficacy, withdrawal symptom relief, and carbon monoxide and plasma cotinine levels. Arch Pediatr Adolesc Med 154:31–37.

Kahn RS, Khoury J, Nichols WC, Lanphear BP (2003) Role of dopamine transporter genotype and maternal prenatal smoking in childhood hyperactive-impulsive, inattentive, and oppositional behaviors. J Pediatr 143:104–110.

Kaiser SA, Soliakov L, Harvey SC, Luetje CW, Wonnacott S (1998) Differential inhibition by α-conotoxin-MII of the nicotinic stimulation of [^{3}H]dopamine release from rat striatal synaptosomes and slices. J Neurochem 70:1069–1076.

Kandel DB, Logan JA (1984) Patterns of drug use from adolescence to young adulthood: I. Periods of risk for initiation, continued use, and discontinuation. Am J Public Health 74:660–666.

Kandel DB, Yamaguchi K, Chen K (1992) Stages of progression in drug involvement from adolescence to adulthood: further evidence for the gateway theory. J Stud Alcohol 53:447–457.

Kimura F, Nakamura S (1987) Postnatal development of α-adrenoceptor–mediated autoinhibition in the locus coeruleus. Brain Res 432:21–26.

Kiss J, Patel AJ (1992) Development of the cholinergic fibres innervating the cerebral cortex of the rat. Int J Dev Neurosci 10:153–170.

Klink R, de Kerchove d'Exaerde A, Zoli M, Changeux JP (2001) Molecular and physiological diversity of nicotinic acetylcholine receptors in the midbrain dopaminergic nuclei. J Neurosci 21:1452–1463.

Konig N, Wilkie MB, Lauder JM (1988) Tyrosine hydroxylase and serotonin containing cells in embryonic rat rhombencephalon: a whole-mount immunocytochemical study. J Neurosci Res 20:212–223.

Kulak JM, Nguyen TA, Olivera BM, McIntosh JM (1997) α-Conotoxin MII blocks nicotine-stimulated dopamine release in rat striatal synaptosomes. J Neurosci 17:5263–5270.

Labarca C, Schwarz J, Deshpande P, Schwarz S, Nowak MW, Fonck C, Nashmi R, Kofuji P, Dang H, Shi W, Fidan M, Khakh BS, Chen Z, Bowers BJ, Boulter J, Wehner JM, Lester HA (2001) Point mutant mice with hypersensitive α4 nicotinic receptors show dopaminergic deficits and increased anxiety. Proc Natl Acad Sci USA 98:2786–2791.

Lambe EK, Krimer LS, Goldman-Rakic PS (2000) Differential postnatal development of catecholamine and serotonin inputs to identified neurons in pre-frontal cortex of rhesus monkey. J Neurosci 20: 8780–8787.

Lauder JM, Bloom FE (1974) Ontogeny of monoamine neurons in the locus coeruleus, raphe nuclei and substantia nigra of the rat. I. Cell differentiation. J Comp Neurol 163:251–264.

Laviola G, Macri S, Morley-Fletcher S, Adriani W (2003) Risk-taking behavior in adolescent mice: psychobiological determinants and early epigenetic influence. Neurosci Biobehav Rev 27:19–31.

Lena C, de Kerchove D'Exaerde A, Cordero-Erausquin M, Le Novere N, del Mar Arroyo-Jimenez M, Changeux JP (1999) Diversity and distribution of nicotinic acetylcholine receptors in the locus ceruleus neurons. Proc Natl Acad Sci USA 96: 12126–12131.

Leonard S, Bertrand D (2001) Neuronal nicotinic receptors: from structure to function. Nicotine Tob Res 3:203–223.

Leslie FM, Gallardo KA, Park MK (2002) Nicotinic acetylcholine receptor–mediated release of [3H]nor-epinephrine from developing and adult rat hippocampus: direct and indirect mechanisms. Neuropharmacology 42:653–661.

Levin ED, Wilkerson A, Jones JP, Christopher NC, Briggs SJ (1996) Prenatal nicotine effects on memory in rats: pharmacological and behavioral challenges. Dev Brain Res 97:207–215.

Levitt P, Harvey JA, Friedman E, Simansky K, Murphy EH (1997) New evidence for neurotransmitter influences on brain development. Trends Neurosci 20:269–274.

Lewis DA (1997) Development of the prefrontal cortex during adolescence: insights into vulnerable neural circuits in schizophrenia. Neuropsychopharmacology 16:385–398.

Loughlin SE, Foote SL, Bloom FE (1986) Efferent projections of nucleus locus coeruleus: topographic organization of cells of origin demonstrated by three-dimensional reconstruction. Neuroscience 18: 291–306.

Lu Y, Marks MJ, Collins AC (1999) Desensitization of nicotinic agonist–induced [3H]γ-aminobutyric acid release from mouse brain synaptosomes is produced by subactivating concentrations of agonists. J Pharmacol Exp Ther 291:1127–1134.

Marshall KC, Christie MJ, Finlayson PG, Williams JT (1991) Developmental aspects of the locus coeruleus–noradrenaline system. Prog Brain Res 88:173–185.

Marubio LM, Gardier AM, Durier S, David D, Klink R, Arroyo-Jimenez MM, McIntosh JM, Rossi F, Champtiaux N, Zoli M, Changeux JP (2003) Effects of nicotine in the dopaminergic system of mice lacking the α4 subunit of neuronal nicotinic acetylcholine receptors. Eur J Neurosci 17:1329–1337.

Metherate R, Hsieh CY (2004) Synaptic mechanisms and cholinergic regulation in auditory cortex. Prog Brain Res 145:143–156.

Moriceau S, Sullivan RM (2004) Unique neural circuitry for neonatal olfactory learning. J Neurosci 24:1182–1189.

Muneoka K, Nakatsu T, Fuji J, Ogawa T, Takigawa M (1999) Prenatal administration of nicotine results in dopaminergic alterations in the neocortex. Neurotoxicol Teratol 21:603–609.

Naeff B, Schlumpf M, Lichtensteiger W (1992) Pre- and postnatal development of high-affinity [3H]nicotine binding sites in rat brain regions: an autoradiographic study. Dev Brain Res 68:163–174.

Nakamura S, Kimura F, Sakaguchi T (1987) Postnatal development of electrical activity in the locus ceruleus. J Neurophysiol 58:510–524.

Nakamura S, Sakaguchi T, Kimura F, Aoki F (1988) The role of α1-adrenoceptor-mediated collateral excitation in the regulation of the electrical activity of locus coeruleus neurons. Neuroscience 27:921–929.

Naqui SZ, Harris BS, Thomaidou D, Parnavelas JG (1999) The noradrenergic system influences the fate of Cajal-Retzius cells in the developing cerebral cortex. Dev Brain Res 113:75–82.

Navarro HA, Seidler FJ, Whitmore WL, Slotkin TA (1988) Prenatal exposure to nicotine via maternal infusions: effects on development of catecholamine systems. J Pharmacol Exp Ther 244:940–944.

Newman MB, Shytle RD, Sanberg PR (1999) Locomotor behavioral effects of prenatal and postnatal nicotine exposure in rat offspring. Behav Pharmacol 10: 699–706.

Nieoullon A, Coquerel A (2003) Dopamine: a key regulator to adapt action, emotion, motivation and cognition. Curr Opin Neurol 16 (Suppl 2):S3–9.

O'Leary KT, Leslie FM (2003) Developmental regulation of nicotinic acetylcholine receptor–mediated [3H]norepinephrine release from rat cerebellum. J Neurochem 84:952–959.

—— (2005) Enhanced nicotinic acetylcholine receptor–mediated [3H]norepinephrine release from neonatal rat hypothalamus. Submitted.

Oliff HS, Gallardo KA (1999) The effect of nicotine on developing brain catecholamine systems. Front Biosci 4:D883–897.

Ospina JA, Broide RS, Acevedo D, Robertson RT, Leslie FM (1998) Calcium regulation of agonist binding to α7-type nicotinic acetylcholine receptors in adult and fetal rat hippocampus. J Neurochem 70: 1061–1068.

Pauly JR, Sparks JA, Hauser KF, Pauly TH (2004) In utero nicotine exposure causes persistent, gender-dependant changes in locomotor activity and sensitivity to nicotine in C57Bl/6 mice. Int J Dev Neurosci 22:329–337.

Picciotto MR, Caldarone BJ, Brunzell DH, Zachariou V, Stevens TR, King SL (2001) Neuronal nicotinic acetylcholine receptor subunit knockout mice: physiological and behavioral phenotypes and possible clinical implications. Pharmacol Ther 92:89–108.

Pidoplichko VI, DeBiasi M, Williams JT, Dani JA (1997) Nicotine activates and desensitizes midbrain dopamine neurons. Nature 390:401–404.

Raymon HK, Leslie FM (1994) Opioid effects on [^{3}H]norepinephrine release from dissociated embryonic locus coeruleus cultures. J Neurochem 62:1015–1024.

Rezvani AH, Levin ED (2004) Adolescent and adult rats respond differently to nicotine and alcohol: motor activity and body temperature. Int J Dev Neurosci 22:349–354.

Ribary U, Lichtensteiger W (1989) Effects of acute and chronic prenatal nicotine treatment on central catecholamine systems of male and female rat fetuses and offspring. J Pharmacol Exp Ther 248:786–792.

Ritter S, Bugarith K, Dinh TT (2001) Immunotoxic destruction of distinct catecholamine subgroups produces selective impairment of glucoregulatory responses and neuronal activation. J Comp Neurol 432:197–216.

Ritter S, Watts AG, Dinh TT, Sanchez-Watts G, Pedrow C (2003) Immunotoxin lesion of hypothalamically projecting norepinephrine and epinephrine neurons differentially affects circadian and stressor-stimulated corticosterone secretion. Endocrinology 144:1357–1367.

Role LW, Berg DK (1996) Nicotinic receptors in the development and modulation of CNS synapses. Neuron 16:1077–1085.

Ruiz S, Fernandez V, Belmar J, Hernandez A, Perez H, Sanhueza-Tsutsumi M, Alarcon S, Soto-Moyano R (1997) Enhancement of central noradrenaline release during development alters the packing density of neurons in the rat occipital cortex. Biol Neonate 71:119–125.

Salminen O, Murphy KL, McIntosh JM, Drago J, Marks MJ, Collins AC, Grady SR (2004) Subunit composition and pharmacology of two classes of striatal presynaptic nicotinic acetylcholine receptors mediating dopamine release in mice. Mol Pharmacol 65:1526–1535.

Seidler FJ, Levin ED, Lappi SE, Slotkin TA (1992) Fetal nicotine exposure ablates the ability of postnatal nicotine challenge to release norepinephrine from rat brain regions. Dev Brain Res 69:288–291.

Shacka JJ, Fennell OB, Robinson SE (1997) Prenatal nicotine sex-dependently alters agonist-induced locomotion and stereotypy. Neurotoxicol Teratol 19:467–476.

Slotkin TA (1998) Fetal nicotine or cocaine exposure: which one is worse? J Pharmacol Exp Ther 285:931–945.

Slotkin TA (2002) Nicotine and the adolescent brain: insights from an animal model. Neurotoxicol Teratol 24:369–384.

Slotkin TA, Lappi SE, McCook EC, Lorber BA, Seidler FJ (1995) Loss of neonatal hypoxia tolerance after prenatal nicotine exposure: implications for sudden infant death syndrome. Brain Res Bull 38:69–75.

Spear LP (2000) The adolescent brain and age-related behavioral manifestations. Neurosci Biobehav Rev 24:417–463.

Specht LA, Pickel VM, Joh TH, Reis DJ (1981) Light-microscopic immunocytochemical localization of tyrosine hydroxylase in prenatal rat brain. I. Early ontogeny. J Comp Neurol 199:233–253.

Sperlagh B, Sershen H, Lajtha A, Vizi ES (1998) Co-release of endogenous ATP and [^{3}H]noradrenaline from rat hypothalamic slices: origin and modulation by α2-adrenoceptors. Neuroscience 82:511–520.

Sullivan RM (2003) Developing a sense of safety: the neurobiology of neonatal attachment. Ann NY Acad Sci 1008:122–131.

Tarazi FI, Baldessarini RJ (2000) Comparative postnatal development of dopamine D(1), D(2) and D(4) receptors in rat forebrain. Int J Dev Neurosci 18:29–37.

Thapar A, Fowler T, Rice F, Scourfield J, van den Bree M, Thomas H, Harold G, Hay D (2003) Maternal smoking during pregnancy and attention deficit hyperactivity disorder symptoms in offspring. Am J Psychiatry 160:1985–1989.

Trauth JA, Seidler FJ, Ali SF, Slotkin TA (2001) Adolescent nicotine exposure produces immediate and long-term changes in CNS noradrenergic and dopaminergic function. Brain Res 892:269–280.

Vastola BJ, Douglas LA, Varlinskaya EI, Spear LP (2002) Nicotine-induced conditioned place preference in adolescent and adult rats. Physiol Behav 77:107–114.

Voorn P, Kalsbeek A, Jorritsma-Byham B, Groenewegen HJ (1988) The pre- and postnatal development of the dopaminergic cell groups in the ventral mesencephalon and the dopaminergic innervation of the striatum of the rat. Neuroscience 25:857–887.

Wang F, Gerzanich V, Wells GB, Anand R, Peng X, Keyser K, Lindstrom J (1996) Assembly of human neuronal nicotinic receptor α5 subunits with α3, β2, and β4 subunits. J Biol Chem 271:17656–17665.

Whiteaker P, Marks MJ, Grady SR, Lu Y, Picciotto MR, Changeux JP, Collins AC (2000) Pharmacological and null mutation approaches reveal nicotinic receptor diversity. Eur J Pharmacol 393:123–135.

Williams JT, Marshall KC (1987) Membrane properties and adrenergic responses in locus coeruleus neurons of young rats. J Neurosci 7:3687–3694.

Wisborg K, Henriksen TB, Jespersen LB, Secher NJ (2000) Nicotine patches for pregnant smokers: a randomized controlled study. Obstet Gynecol 96: 967–971.

Wooltorton JR, Pidoplichko VI, Broide RS, Dani JA (2003) Differential desensitization and distribution of nicotinic acetylcholine receptor subtypes in midbrain dopamine areas. J Neurosci 23:3176–3185.

Zoli M, Lena C, Picciotto MR, Changeux JP (1998) Identification of four classes of brain nicotinic receptors using β2 mutant mice. J Neurosci 18: 4461–4472.

Zoli M, Le Novere N, Hill JA Jr, Changeux JP (1995) Developmental regulation of nicotinic ACh receptor subunit mRNAs in the rat central and peripheral nervous systems. J Neurosci 15:1912–1939.

Index